*In still
and stormy
waters*

REAY TANNAHILL

In still and stormy waters

St. Martin's Press
New York

Library of Congress Cataloging-in-Publication Data

Tannahill, Reay.
In still and stormy waters / Reay Tannahill.
p.   cm.
ISBN 0-312-11411-7
1. Inheritance and succession—Scotland—
History—19th century—Fiction.   2. Man-woman
relationships—Scotland—Fiction.   3. Cousins—
Scotland—Fiction.   4. Women—Scotland—Fiction.
I. Title.
PR6070.A543I5   1994
823'.914—dc20   94-13080   CIP

First published in Great Britain by Orion

First U.S. Edition: November 1994
10 9 8 7 6 5 4 3 2 1

CONTENTS

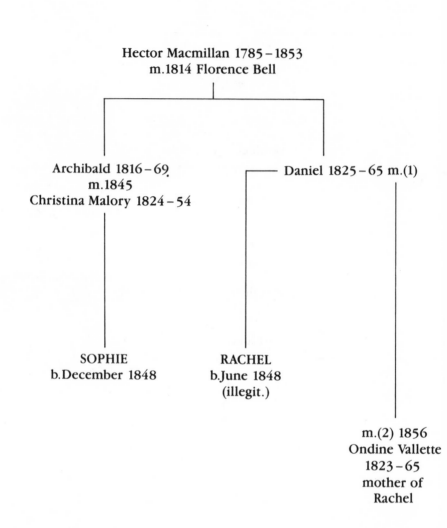

Hector Macmillan 1785–1853
m.1814 Florence Bell

Archibald 1816–69
m.1845
Christina Malory 1824–54

Daniel 1825–65 m.(1)

SOPHIE
b.December 1848

RACHEL
b.June 1848
(illegit.)

m.(2) 1856
Ondine Vallette
1823–65
mother of
Rachel

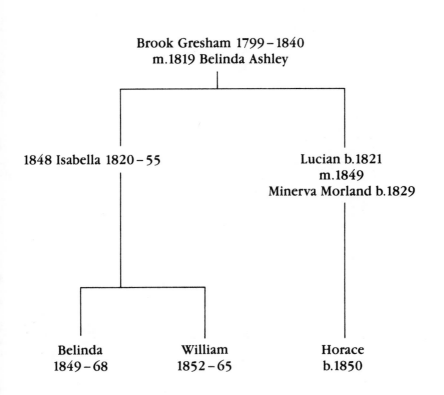

Brook Gresham 1799 – 1840
m.1819 Belinda Ashley

1848 Isabella 1820 – 55

Lucian b.1821
m.1849
Minerva Morland b.1829

Belinda
1849 – 68

William
1852 – 65

Horace
b.1850

PROLOGUE

June
1879

PROLOGUE

1

PEACE was not something Sophie Macmillan had ever known, or a sun that did not burn, or the cool, salt freshness of a northern sea.

Strange to her, too, were mosses soft and springing as velvet and green as emeralds, skies where blue coexisted with white and grey and faintest amethyst, trees planted by the random hand of nature, mountains that changed colour and contour with every hour that passed, and the sound of small birds singing.

She was coming home, though not from choice, to a home she had never seen in a country she had never known in all the thirty years of her life. It was a country that her husband, for his own good reasons, had told her was cold, wet and windy; her father had said the same, when he was sober. But every sweet and scented breath she drew denied them.

In a critical corner of her brain she recognised that it could not always be like this, might rarely be like this, but it troubled her not at all. Beauty, although she had once thought otherwise, was incomplete without change. But what would not, could not, change was the one thing that above all she desired from this magical Highland landscape; the one constant that had little to do with physical perceptions, everything to do with the heart and mind and soul.

Freedom.

2

She had never been without servants, or guards when she needed them, but as she rode through the mountains of Argyll towards the western sea she was escorted only by a pair of amiable young stable lads she had hired in Inveraray. They had thought it highly comical when she had said she expected them to be armed.

'Och, aye, mistress,' the elder of them had assured her. 'Wee

Wullie'll bring his peashooter. That should see us right.'

Sophie wasn't used to having her orders questioned, far less ridiculed, and had said so with a crispness that caused the young men to look slightly chastened, though not for long. But as they rode quietly through the empty hills she had come to appreciate that the idea of a band of cutthroats leaping out from behind some rock was preposterous.

Even so, as they came in sight of the sea, she asked, 'Are there pirates in this part of the world?'

'Och, I dunno,' Wullie muttered dubiously. 'What would ye say, Jamie?'

'Weel, there's the gamekeepers . . .'

'. . . an' the excisemen . . .'

'. . . an' the shopkeepers in Glasgow . . .'

They were an engaging pair. Sophie laughed and said, 'Well, there are real pirates where I come from. Is that the Atlantic?'

The vista was magnificent, the sea deep, blue and horizonless, the sky limitless and the mountains like raw silk woven with indigo and purple shadows.

As they descended from the heights – Wullie and Jamie explaining everything with proprietorial pride – they came on red deer grazing by the banks of rivers and streams. Further down, under the fresh new green of the trees, wide patches of turf began to open out, cropping grounds for a few quiet sheep, dancing floors for their white-fleeced, irresistible lambs.

Sophie said, 'I've never seen a sheep before except as cutlets.'

Reaching sea level at last, they found their track running along the line of the beach, on one side tall banks of whin, blazing gold, and on the other great sheets of sea pinks and bluebells that grew half in grass, half in silvery shell sand, rippling delicately in the slight onshore breeze.

Sophie said, 'Is it far? It will soon be dark.'

But the end of their journey was near and, in any case, Jamie told her, in June in these parts the light never went completely.

Sophie fell silent. They were beginning to see one or two people now, the women beachcombing on the edge of the tide, the men with scythes over their shoulders, people who gazed openmouthed at the strangers, and especially at the dark-haired, fashionable young woman who had a foreign look despite her deep blue Highland eyes, and who smiled remotely at them as if her mind was elsewhere.

'It's just around the next bend,' Jamie said.

3

And so at last, Juran lay before them.

Sophie reined in her horse. She hadn't known what to expect of this place that, for better or for worse, had shaped her father's life, and so her own; had formed the object and the force behind so many dreams; had for so many years been a focus not of reality but of imagination, built not of stone but of mists and mystery.

What she saw was a castle, low and square and white, with battlements and a round tower at each corner and, rising from the centre, a taller tower whose arched windows glowed with rose-gold fire reflected from the sinking sun. It was not a very large castle, but it was beautifully cared for, lying calm and sheltered within the embrace of the darkening hills. A wide, grassy drive led between banks of rhododendrons, flowering purple, gold, pink and scarlet, to a large, gothic-arched entrance porch.

Taking a deep breath, Sophie said, 'I will go on alone.'

4

Her horse's hooves were soundless on the grass as she rode up the drive.

No one came running to help her, so she dismounted and looped the reins through an iron staple in the wall, and climbed the few steps to the porch and tugged decisively at the stirrup-shaped bellpull.

A servant answered, though not at once, a country girl who bobbed a curtsey and looked nervous and enquiring.

Sophie said, 'Good evening. I am Sophie Macmillan . . .'

That was as far as she got. The girl, murmuring something she didn't understand, curtseyed again and then vanished.

In the world she had always lived in, Sophie would have been impatient, but here it didn't seem to matter. Turning, she looked outward again at the sea. The whole horizon was a blush of salmon and peach and rose, touched with whispers of slate blue, and there was a wide, gold, gleaming path lying across the water from setting sun to silver shore. Never in her life had Sophie felt such a powerful sense of calm, a calm that seemed to her kindly, complete, and immutable.

Her reverie was broken by an awareness of someone behind her, someone who had been watching her, perhaps, for longer than she knew. So she turned, slowly and collectedly, and saw a slight woman of about her own age half hidden in the shadows of the doorway.

It wasn't hard to guess who she was. Sophie, who had travelled all the way across the world for this moment, said with a faint smile, 'You must be Rachel?'

There was no answering smile.

Rachel Macmillan looked at her for a long, long moment and when she spoke it was quietly and unemotionally. 'Yes, I am Rachel Macmillan. And you, I understand, are my cousin Sophie?'

Then she stepped back and said, 'You had better come in.'

PART ONE
*1856–
1864*

CHAPTER ONE

❧❧❧

I

'Dearly beloved, we are gathered together . . .'

Ellie Vallette was eight years old, a harmless-looking child with cloudy brown curls and artless blue eyes, when on a wet and windy December morning her parents entered at last – though not without reluctance – into the state of holy matrimony. There had been times when Ellie had thought she was never going to get them to the altar.

'. . . an honourable estate . . . a remedy against sin, and to avoid fornication . . .'

Standing behind her mother with eyes primly lowered, silver-frilled posy clutched in hot little fists and heart pounding under the pink taffeta plaid of her bodice, Ellie silently willed the old gabble-grinder to stop preachifying and get to the bit that mattered. Because, until he did, her pa still had time to change his mind.

It was something that didn't bear thinking about, but she thought about it just the same, teasing at it like a cat with a mouse between its paws, so absorbed that she almost missed the vital moment when it came.

'Wilt thou, Daniel Alexander Macmillan . . .'

Please God, make him say yes. Make him say yes and cross-my-heart I'll be good, for ever and ever, amen. Please God, I'll be good . . .

And then her father's 'I will!' rang out with a heartiness that caused the lustres of the chandelier to tinkle and one or two of the guests to twitch nervously. Daniel Macmillan often had that effect on people. Even the minister blinked and took a moment to pull himself together again before he went on, 'Wilt thou, Ondine Marie Vallette . . .'

The bride's 'I will!' sounded calm and a little husky. If there was a trace of exasperation in her voice no one noticed it – certainly not her daughter, who was much too busy fighting down an urge to burst out laughing and skipping and swaggering about, crowing, 'They're

9

married, they're married! *My ma and pa are married.* They're married, and I'm not a bastard any more!'

2

Prevented by the vast circumference of her mother's crinolines from giving her the biggest and most enthusiastic hug ever, Ellie – whose proper name was Rachel – caught her father's eye and, obedient to its message, removed herself from among the crowd of guests thronging round the happy couple.

Looking for some place where she wouldn't be in anybody's way, she found it behind a small, fat, marble statue of either St George in a loincloth or Cupid in a helmet – she wasn't sure which – and was able, for the first time, to take a proper look round the warm, snug, stuffy drawing room of the house Daniel Macmillan had borrowed for the occasion. Churches in winter, he had said, were too dashed chilly for anything jollier than a funeral. And so, in place of stained glass windows and walls of cold Calvinist stone, there were velvet draperies and Persian rugs and red flock paper. Stout, squashy chairs, deeply padded and buttoned, deputised for stern wooden pews. And the nearest thing to an odour of sanctity was the scents of pot pourri and beeswax doing their unavailing best to combat the reek of gas mantles and coal fires.

The guests, Ellie noted with a giggle, looked exactly as if they had been chosen to match the furnishings, being comfortably cushioned, solidly built and quietly expensive, even if the gentlemen smelled more of damp serge than pot pourri. All were strangers to her, but all – her father had told her – were members of the landed gentry. They had a tremendous air about them; their ancestors had been having forelocks tugged to them for centuries, and it showed.

Even so, Ellie was surprised. If they were so special, she would have expected the ladies, at least, to be well dressed, but they were shockingly dull and dowdy, and it was obvious from the way they walked that, under their wide skirts, they were carrying around the weight of half a dozen petticoats of horsehair, quilted satin and starched muslin instead of the single, lightweight crinoline frame which was all that supported her mother's eighteen billowing yards of flounced lavender silk, with its trimming of ruby velvet ribbons.

The new Mrs Macmillan – plump, pretty and stylish – made all the other ladies look like frumps, but Ellie, wrinkling her nose, wondered with sudden uneasiness whether her ma's crinoline mightn't be a bit too dashing for the provinces. Every time she moved, her skirts swayed and tilted like an insecurely anchored bell tent in a breeze. Up at the front, down at the back. Down at the front, up at the back. From the expressions on their faces, Ellie could tell that the guests were being afforded a view of far more laced-edged pantaloons than they were used to.

The gentlemen didn't seem to mind, but she saw one of the ladies, herself clad in a grey poplin that was drab to the point of invisibility, carefully avert her eyes from the second Mrs Macmillan's ankles and whisper something in her neighbour's ear. It wasn't hard to guess that it was something impolite.

Ellie, who loved her mother dearly, glowered at the lady's oblivious back.

3

But she was much too full of bounce to worry about disagreeable things, on this of all days, and the point soon came when she couldn't bear to stand about fidgeting for a moment longer. So, unobtrusively, she abandoned her statue and set out on a tiptoed tour of Mr Raikes' big double drawing room, trying – in case anyone happened to be watching – to look as if she found nothing worthy of remark in its serried ranks of statues and family portraits, its noble vistas of patterned Axminster and crimson plush. Her parents had both told her, with much frequency and even more emphasis, that on no account was she to let anyone guess that she had never even been inside a proper gentleman's residence before, far less lived in one.

She had seen them from outside, of course, with the gas lamps lit and one liveried footman putting coals on the fire, another bringing in a tray of decanters, and a neat little maid scurrying round plumping up cushions and straightening ornaments. There were always dozens of ornaments, and Ellie had thought they must take a lot of dusting. Luckily, there had never been much dusting to do in the leaky, garlic-smelling, sparsely furnished Soho garret that had been her home until a few days before.

Mr Raikes' taste in ornaments was something of a disappointment to her, running mainly to painted china elephants two feet tall, stuffed birds in glass domes and huge vases full of dried grasses. But, just as Ellie was deciding she didn't like them much, she reached the big double doors separating the front from the rear part of the room and saw the harp.

Huge, golden and radiant, it stopped her as sharply as if she had walked into a sheet of glass and she stood staring at it for a long, long time, speechless and saucer-eyed as some embryo saint having her first vision of the divine.

She had always had a lively imagination. Like many children without brothers or sisters, she had learned to read quite early – long before she went to charity school – and, as a result, had never had any trouble in finding building blocks for her dreams. Sometimes she would pretend that she was one of the royal princesses; sometimes a beautiful maiden wooed by a knight in shining armour; sometimes (in more elevated mood) Joan of Arc or Boadicea. But she hadn't succeeded in conjuring up any believable picture of the life that was soon to be hers.

She knew that her parents' wedding would transform her from what she had been into what she would be, from inglorious little Ellie Vallette, the illegitimate daughter sired by her father in the days before his first marriage, into genteel little Rachel Macmillan, respectable 'stepdaughter' of his second. And she would go with her parents to her pa's beautiful home in the wild, majestic Highlands of Scotland, where she would be demure and docile and virtuous, and live happily ever after. Everything was going to be *wonderful*.

So she had told herself, but she hadn't really believed any of it until she saw the harp.

It was queer, the effect it had on her, because she wasn't in the least musical; she had a struggle to keep in tune even with the street ballads that were all she knew, though she supposed that the harp wouldn't, in any case, be the right instrument for 'Cat's Meat Nell' or 'Red Nosed Jemmy and Bandy Bet'. But, somehow or other, it presented itself to her awestruck sight as a single, magical symbol of the new world of riches and refinement she was about to enter.

If she hadn't promised to behave like a model child, she would have done a jig of excitement, but model children weren't supposed to do jigs; they weren't supposed to do anything except be seen and not heard.

There would be a harp at her new home, too, she realised. Because Juran was a castle. Her father had said so. A really, truly castle.

Ellie admired her father, a big, jovial John Bull of a man with curly brown hair and side whiskers, but there was no denying that he had a habit of saying whatever happened to suit him at the time, which meant you couldn't always rely on it being the unvarnished truth. In this case, though, she thought it was probably safe to believe him. After all, it would be silly to say Juran was a castle if it wasn't.

So there *would* be a harp, and already she could see herself playing it. In no time at all her imagination had swept her forward through the years – via a somewhat accelerated adolescence – to the mature age of sixteen and ever such a romantic scene (set in Juran's huge and sumptuous baronial hall) in which the musical, beautiful and much sought-after Miss Rachel Macmillan, absolutely dripping with pearls and diamonds and wearing a blue silk gown that exactly matched her eyes, was listening graciously to a declaration of undying love from a besotted prince of the blood royal. He was a foreigner, but his English was awfully good.

4

He had just reached the bit about worshipping the ground she trod on when she was brought back to the unsympathetic present by the sound of a high, childish, affected voice behind her saying, *'There* she is! That's her.'

Slowly, Ellie turned.

There were two of them and she had seen them earlier, though only for a moment and from a distance.

The girl was a few months younger than she was, the boy about four, and the resemblance between them was striking. Identically clad in cinnamon-coloured dresses with little white pantaloons showing beneath their skirts, they were plump and pale-skinned, with round, unblinking brown eyes that looked as if they might shine but never sparkle, and a mass of ringlets several degrees redder than Ellie's own chestnut ones – more like the colour of autumn leaves. If it hadn't been for the furious expressions on their faces, they could easily have served as models for The Good Little Boy and Girl in some improving tale.

Ellie didn't need to be told who they were – her new sister and brother, Belinda and William. Her father's children by his previous marriage. Who didn't know that their father was *her* father, too.

They weren't going to know for years and years, either. It was a point on which Daniel Macmillan had refused to budge.

'Yes, yes,' he had said testily. 'I *know* you're my real daughter, but

I've taken dashed good care all these years that no one should find out. When your mother and I are married, it will make you legitimate according to the laws of Scotland, but it doesn't change anything, except for the lawyer johnnies, of course! Dashed if I'm going to be embarrassed by having my sins shouted from the house tops. When I'm dead, you can tell anyone you like, but not before.'

Since he was only thirty-one, Ellie was going to have a long wait, and although she knew that good things improved with keeping, she wasn't sure it applied in this case.

'But, pa . . .'

'*No*. Most fellows sow a few wild oats before they marry and settle down. Sheer bad luck that one of mine germinated. Just be quiet and think yourself lucky everything's worked out as it has. I don't want to hear another word about it.'

It was Daniel Macmillan's answer to every inconvenient problem. If he didn't hear about it, it would go away. And since he was big and overpowering, it quite often did.

Ellie was annoyed. She didn't think it was fair that she should be the one to suffer just because her parents hadn't had enough sense to get married when they should, even if they *were* making up for it now. Being a so-called stepdaughter was miles better than being a bastard, of course, but it wasn't nearly as good as being a real daughter.

When she was older, she was going to have to do something about it.

5

Politely, she smiled at Belinda and William, but they didn't smile back.

She hadn't a notion how she was going to deal with them. Until today, she had done her best to ignore even the fact of their existence, but she couldn't ignore them any more or put off thinking about them, because here before her were the two flesh-and-blood children with whom she was doomed to share her life. She had known she wasn't going to like them, and she didn't.

Cripes! she thought, eyeing their expressions. If they were as cross as that about having a new stepsister thrust upon them, what would they be like if they knew the truth!

Belinda, her unflickering gaze fixed on Ellie, said scoldingly to her brother, 'I don't know why I always have to tell you everything. Even if you couldn't see her face from where we were sitting, you must have been able to see That Dress.'

Ellie opened her mouth and closed it again. The dress in question, chosen to complement her mother's, was a blinding affair in huge checks of light and dark rose, with a crossover bodice and three extravagant flounces on the calf-length crinoline skirt. It was the newest fashion, the kind of dress you could scarcely help noticing (especially when worn by someone who wasn't very big), and Ellie had loathed it on sight. She didn't like drawing attention to herself, not because it was ungenteel but because it was inconvenient. You couldn't get away with *anything* when people had their eye on you.

'Is she coming to live with us?' William whined. 'Don't want her.'

Briefly, Ellie yearned to be back in the streets of Soho, where she could have given the brat a clip over the ear and told him to stow his jabber or she'd sell him to the flue faker for a chummy. As it was, all she could do was take a deep breath and say, 'Er . . . 'ullo, Willyum. 'ullo, Berlinda. I'm Ellie – I mean Rachel.'

There was a moment's stunned silence. Then, 'My goodness, aren't you *common*!' exclaimed Belinda.

Ellie could feel the hot colour flooding to her cheeks. She had been practising her aitches for weeks, because she didn't want her pa to be ashamed of her, but learning to talk proper wasn't easy when, for most of the time, you were surrounded by people who didn't talk proper and didn't see any reason why they should. Even her ma dropped her aitches all over the place – though nobody minded because she was French and the French were hopeless with their aitches. Ellie could have kicked herself for not having had enough sense to pretend that she, too, had a foreign accent.

And then Belinda rushed on, 'We don't want you. You don't belong. You'll spoil everything. We don't want your horrid mama, either. Why don't you go back where you came from? We don't like you and we never will. Never, ever. So there!'

The bossy voice stopped abruptly, leaving Ellie gasping and deeply frustrated that she couldn't be rude right back. But her father had said he wouldn't take her to Juran at all if she didn't behave herself.

She was still trying to think of something mollifying to say that wouldn't actually choke her when a general drift towards the dining room began and a stout and flustered servant appeared beside them.

'Ye're to come in to yer meal now. I don't know why ye're not all sitting together, but ye're not. C'mon. I'll show ye.'

15

Belinda tossed her head. 'You don't need to,' she said, and flounced off dragging William by the hand. Ellie might as well not have existed.

The servant, frilly white cap askew over a round, red, heated face, muttered, 'Tch! Some folks haven't got any manners. Never you mind, my wee lamb! Just you come wi' me.'

Ellie took the proffered hand and dutifully followed where the motherly woman led. She didn't know what she was going to do about Beastly Belinda and Wailing Willy. She supposed she'd just have to try and think of Juran as the silver lining and them as the cloud.

6

There were thirty places set round the white damasked dining table, which was arrayed with a profusion of glass, silver, candelabra and arrangements of dried flowers and berries, as well as four gleaming soup tureens and sixteen silver-domed dishes of entrées lined up along the sides with regimental precision. Ellie, who had spent a goodly part of her eight years getting under people's feet in restaurant kitchens, wasn't impressed. What mattered was how everything tasted and the shoals of salt cellars among the silver didn't strike her as a very good sign. Her mother said that if there was salt in the kitchen it shouldn't be needed on the table, too. Maybe there wasn't any salt in Mr Raikes' kitchen.

She was pleased to find that she wasn't sitting near Belinda and William – already settled one on either side of an elderly, governessy-looking female with a long-suffering expression and a bosom of awe-inspiring proportions – but her pleasure took a tumble when she discovered that her own place was next to the grey poplin lady who had been making remarks about her mother.

The lady was deep in conversation with her neighbour and didn't notice as, with a darkling look, Ellie slipped into her seat. Nor did she notice when Ellie had to get up again because she had sat on one of her crinoline hoops, causing the front of her skirt to swing up and hit the underside of the table a resounding whack. Carefully, she hitched the hoops up and sat down again on the edge of her chair, so that they settled into a kind of concertina at the back. Something squeaked, and she had to slap it lightly to make it stop.

Devoutly, she hoped the lady would go on not noticing her. The only things grownups seemed able to talk about when they deigned to take notice of a little girl were her progress in the three Rs, and her catechism, and whether she could sew a fine seam. Ellie didn't want to have to smile dutifully and say yes and no in all the right places, because, if the worst came to the worst, that was all she was going to say. She wasn't going to risk dropping any more aitches if she could help it and, anyway, her parents had told her not to talk to anyone in case she gave something away by mistake.

Addressing herself to her plate of leek soup – from which she deduced that they did have salt in the kitchen, and rather too much of it – she tried to pretend she wasn't there, and was doing very well until William spoiled things, his chubby fists drumming on the table and his voice exploding into the genteel murmur of conversation, the faint clatter of silver and clink of glasses, with an earsplitting howl of, 'Ny-a-err! Don't take it 'way. More! Want more!'

All the guests pretended not to notice.

'William, behave yourself,' said the governessy-looking female.

'Hush!' squawked Belinda.

And 'Dear little William,' said a voice on Ellie's right as a servant hastened to refill William's bowl. 'Such a passionate child, and so fond of his food.'

7

'I am Mrs Gresham,' the lady went on in tones of such calm authority that, if she had said, 'I am Queen Victoria,' Ellie would have believed her. 'And you must be dear little Rachel. We are going to be great friends.'

'Ha!' Ellie thought. In her experience, grownups were never charming to children unless they wanted them to run an errand and didn't mean to fork out the dibs.

Mrs Gresham, she judged, was about the same age as her mother, though nowhere near as pretty; indeed, her forehead was rather low and her nose snub, while her fine mousy hair ended in two fat ringlets that Ellie – daughter of a connoisseur – instantly identified as false. Her eyes, however, were remarkable, large, luminous and of a very clear hazel.

'You will soon become accustomed to William's high spirits,' the lady went on, the beguiling eyes so full of warmth and interest that Ellie was momentarily unnerved, feeling as if she were having melted butter sauce poured all over her. 'Though how odd it must be for you, suddenly to find yourself with both a new papa and a whole new family thrust upon you. You poor little thing!'

Ellie, who was very good at being a poor little thing when it suited her, thoroughly objected to being called one when she wasn't even trying. 'Oh, no! I like it!' she lied earnestly.

'Do you remember your own papa?'

Given the circumstances, it was a natural enough question but it pulled Ellie up sharply, even though her mother had told her exactly what she was to say if the subject should arise. Frowning inside, she shook her head and did her best to look like a fatherless orphan.

'Did he die in an accident?'

Ellie nodded.

'How sad! And was that in France?'

She nodded again.

'So your mama must have brought you to London when you were still quite a baby?'

One of the disadvantages of answering only with a nod, a yes or a no, was that you couldn't change the subject. 'Yes,' Ellie said, and shut her mouth with such a snap that her loose front tooth wiggled.

Mrs Gresham smiled. 'Then that explains why you are so unmistakably English, when your mother is so – er – delightfully French.'

They could both hear Ellie's mother being delightfully French at the gentleman sitting next to her, though only Ellie knew that Ondine donned and discarded her Frenchness as readily as a shawl on an April day. She had lived in London since she was a child, and her English could be perfectly all right when she wanted it to be, but she said gentlemen liked her better when she was being foreign.

She didn't look or sound even remotely like the genteel widow she was supposed to be.

The servants having taken away the soup tureens and replaced them with the remove, chairs were pushed back as a number of gentlemen rose preparatory to serving the ladies. Ellie wished they'd hurry up; at least Mrs Gresham couldn't eat and talk at the same time. Glancing up, she saw that her pa was frowning at her slightly from the head of the table, though she didn't know what he thought she could do about silencing her inquisitive neighbour.

And then Mrs Gresham, smoothing her napkin carefully over her grey poplin lap, resumed, 'Tell me, now, my dear, how did your mama and your new step papa first chance to meet? Because it is quite unusual, you know, for people from different circles to become acquainted.'

18

The question was accompanied by a smile of extraordinary splendour, blinding and beautiful, sparkling and overflowing with stars.

Ellie's mouth opened in a silent *Oh!*

To most children, the question might have sounded harmless enough, but Ellie's charity school had not been very richly endowed, so that she had learned her reading from the Bible, her writing from copying out a book of etiquette, and her arithmetic from an accountancy primer. As a result, she was extremely well versed in everything to do with morals and manners, even if she still had a slight, temporary difficulty with her sums. And she knew that people in the best circles *never* asked personal questions.

Especially not bleeding 'orrible ones like that.

Her inner self gave her a nudge. 'G'arn, shock the smile orf 'er face,' it said impishly. 'Tell 'er.'

8

Ellie was too young to know all the details, of course, but she knew quite enough to bring a scandalised blush to the noseyparkering lady's cheek – if she had been allowed to.

The story had begun when a merry, well set up, roving-eyed youth by the name of Daniel Macmillan had struck up a casual acquaintance with the *patron* of Chez Vallette, one of the first French restaurants in London, and had proved highly susceptible to the charms of the *patron*'s daughter, Ondine, who was the cook, and a good one, too. They had fallen in love. Some months later, however – and Ellie, having been vouchsafed only an edited version, was still hazy about what exactly had happened in the interval – the roving-eyed young man had pressed a few spare sovereigns into Ondine's hand, uttered a bracing farewell, and gone off and married someone else. Someone more suitable.

The *patron* had been exceedingly cross with his daughter and, pausing only to reckon up the cost of finding, training and paying a replacement cook, had told her never to darken his smart, gold-lettered door again. As a result, Ellie had been born a few months later in the kitchen of a common chophouse. Her ma had been grilling kidneys for a customer at the time – a man without taste, Ondine said, who had insisted on having them well done.

Her mother's misadventures had been the first bedtime story Ellie could remember, an oft-repeated tale that nearly always ended with Ondine telling her daughter she must learn that there was no one in the world one could trust except oneself. Quite often, seeing the tears in her mother's eyes, Ellie had flung her arms round her neck and assured her passionately, 'You can trust me! You can trust *me!*'

Not until Ellie went to charity school and heard the ladies tut-tutting about it had she begun to worry about not having a father – bastards, after all, were ten a penny in the streets of Soho – but afterwards she had worried about it constantly. As a result, when Daniel Macmillan had reappeared on the horizon, complaining that his suitable wife didn't understand him, he had received a very much warmer welcome from Ellie than he did from Ondine, whose rose-coloured vision had vanished with her virtue.

It was a shocking story, deliciously so, and Ellie regretted very much that she had been forbidden to impart it to anyone.

All she could do was sigh a little, open her eyes wide, and say, 'I don't know'.

9

And then a new voice spoke from on high.

'Halibut?' it drawled.

Thus, ludicrously, Lucian Gresham entered Ellie's life, and no one could have foretold how very far from ludicrous the consequences were destined to be. Certainly not Ellie herself, looking up to see a man in his middle thirties whose air of worldweary superiority said, as clearly as coronet and ermine, 'blue blood'.

Startled, she wondered how it was possible for a man to be at once so aristocratic and so ugly. It wasn't that he was misshapen, or anything like that. Even his features might have been all right, one at a time. It was the combined effect that was disagreeable – the nose like the Duke of Wellington's and the neck like a tree trunk; the unemphatic brown eyes, shallowly set, and the rather lank fair hair; the sulkily drooping mouth that, together with the harsh lines bracketing his cheeks, gave him an expression permanently poised between smirk and sneer; above all, the impression that his face was carved out of wax. His skin didn't seem to have any pores in it, and Ellie had the horrid feeling that in warm weather he might begin to melt.

But his manner was godlike.

She watched him, fascinated, as he disdainfully spooned halibut on to an ornate pink and gold plate and passed it across to Mrs Gresham, whose husband, it seemed, he was. Ellie herself was beneath his notice. Carelessly dishing some more fish and a splash or two of sauce on to another ornate pink and gold plate, he dumped it in front of her without asking, without smiling, without even looking. Then he served himself, sank back into his chair, and took no further interest in the proceedings.

Although Ellie was possessed of a sturdy independence that had manifested itself in the cradle and rarely faltered since, she suddenly felt in need of a reassuring smile from her mother. But when she sneaked a glance up the table, Ondine was putting her knife and fork down after tasting the halibut and then, with an exaggeratedly French pout on her pretty, tinted lips, pushing her plate away and turning to resume her conversation with the gentleman beside her.

Ondine's standards were her daughter's standards, too. With deep misgivings, Ellie raised her fork to her lips. The fish was dry and limp, and the sauce tasted of nothing but flour and milk. It was *awful*.

'Delicious,' said Mrs Gresham with every evidence of sincerity. 'Eat it up, Rachel. Waste not, want not.'

10

Little girls weren't allowed to push their plates away, and Ellie had to swallow every last sickening mouthful. She thought afterwards that it might have been that that caused her mood to change so abruptly, so that, from being all bright-eyed and bushy-tailed inside, she began to feel jumpy and unsure of herself.

She didn't like Mr and Mrs Gresham in the very least. In fact, she didn't like anybody. She felt like crying. What was she doing here among all these unknown people, in this unknown house, in this unknown city? Desperately, she wanted to go home, back to the garret in Soho, back to the restaurant kitchen and charity school, back to her friends and the dirty, noisy, teeming London to which she belonged.

She didn't belong here – and neither did her bright, pretty, stylish mother.

Not for years was she to be capable of analysing the perceptions that went to make up the sense of exclusion that took brief possession of her eight-year-old soul on that cold, sleety December morning. She hadn't foreseen that all the guests, even William and Belinda, would be so unmistakably cast from the same mould. She hadn't guessed what sublime assurance they would draw from the security of knowing their place in the world. It hadn't occurred to her that theirs was a club that didn't admit new members, because you couldn't be a member unless you observed the rules and the rules were secret except to people born in the knowledge of them.

Most of this was beyond her at the time. All she felt was out of place, miserable and crosspatchy, with the result that when she was reminded by a faint scraping noise that one of the chief architects of her discomfort was sitting right next to her, she directed a fizzing glare at Mrs Gresham which would have startled that lady a good deal had she not been engaged with the last forkful of her halibut.

And then Ellie had a brainwave that cheered her right back up again.

II

When Minerva Gresham turned to resume her inquisition a moment or two later, it was to find that little Rachel had almost vanished from sight, rummaging on the floor for the napkin that appeared to have slipped from her lap. When she sat up again, flushed and sparkling of eye, Minerva began to feel more hopeful of inducing her to talk. So far, the child had been sadly negative, not saying enough even to reveal whether her accent was respectable. Minerva doubted it.

The last two hours had made it abundantly clear why, prior to the wedding, Daniel Macmillan had been so secretive about his bride. One look had been sufficient to tell Minerva – and everyone else – that the new Mrs Macmillan was an outsider. It wasn't only that she lacked that indefinable 'something' that went with an acceptable pedigree. She was also much too strikingly turned out to be well bred; a true lady never drew attention to herself. Indeed, the faint hum of conversation that had accompanied the bride to the altar had consisted largely of ladies remarking to their husbands on the extravagance of her attire and diagnosing (in the most dulcet of undertones) henna in her hair and rouge on her cheeks.

Minerva was determined to find out everything she could about her and the likeliest source of information was the woman's small and inoffensive-looking daughter. With, therefore, a lavish expenditure of The Smile, she said, 'So, Rachel! You must be quite thrilled by the thought of your new home. Because, however delightful the place you have lived in until now, no ordinary house can be held to compare with a castle.'

It had exactly the desired effect. Because the child sat up with a jerk and spoke unguardedly for the first time. 'Yer mean . . . Yer *know* what Juran's like? 'ave – have – yer been there?'

Minerva felt quite faint for a moment. She had no personal experience of how slum children talked, of course, but . . . Daniel Macmillan must have taken leave of his senses!

After a moment, puzzlement overcoming shock, she repeated, 'Have I been there? Yes, of course. Frequently. Were you not aware that the first Mrs Macmillan – your mother's late, lamented predecessor – was my husband's only sister? Mr Gresham and I are dear little Belinda and William's uncle and aunt.'

12

Ellie, who had been consoling herself that she'd never see the grey poplin lady and her ugly husband ever again, was reminded of the snake swallower in Dean Street who'd told her about an awful occasion when he'd suddenly remembered – just as he was congratulating himself on how smoothly the snake was gliding down his throat – that he'd forgotten to cut the venom out of its tongue.

She knew *just* how he'd felt.

Fortunately, at that moment a peculiar expression appeared on Mrs Gresham's face, a faint wrinkling of her nose and forehead and a slackening of her mouth. Her beautiful eyes went narrow and blank.

Interestedly, Ellie watched. The next thing was that the lady moved sharply in her chair, and then reached down with her hand as if she wanted to scratch an itchy spot, and then sat up again holding her breath and looking as rigid as if she had been stuffed.

It lasted for only a few seconds. Then her eyes flew wide open and, with a penetrating screech, she pushed her chair back, leapt to her feet and, screeching still, scrambled up on to the seat of it with a speed and agility that were amazing considering the weight and volume of her skirts.

Ellie was pleased to see that she had been right. Mrs Gresham *was* wearing half a dozen petticoats, everything from muslin to horsehair. She was showing a shocking amount of ankle, too, and it was nowhere near as shapely as Ellie's mother's.

Mrs Gresham's sudden, inexplicable activity had no effect at all on her husband, who merely raised a bored eyebrow, but several of the other guests began rising to their feet, their anxious voices braving the counterpoint of Mrs Gresham's screams.

'My dear lady, are you all right?'

'What is the matter?'

'Do you need assistance?'

'Take care! You might fall!'

Mrs Gresham scarcely seemed to hear them but went on shrieking and flapping her skirts even more wildly, as if she were doing an Irish jig.

And then, just when everyone was wondering whether she had gone mad, there was a tiny flurry of extra movement and a small white mouse dropped to the floor.

'There it is! *There it is!*' screeched Mrs Gresham.

13

That was the point at which all the other ladies also began screaming and scrambling on to their chairs.

In the succeeding rumpus, two servants bringing in the roasts were bumped into and a haunch of venison and a rump of beef went flying. The venison collided with a flower vase, and the beef caught a gentleman behind the knees with such force that he sat down on it with a resounding and gloriously squelchy thud.

Ellie, who had retreated innocently to the corner between sideboard and wall, hadn't enjoyed herself so much for ages.

The pandemonium lasted for a good ten minutes, and the only lady who retained her dignity was Ellie's mother. But in the end two gentlemen came in from the hall brandishing heavy walking sticks and Ellie, with regret, decided it was time to beat the retreat.

After a moment, in response to the gentle, rhythmical taps of her foot, she felt her pet's neat little paws pattering up the leg of her pantaloons, heading for refuge in the special pocket sewn inside her skirt. His name was Señor Fonseca, after the animal trainer who had taught him his tricks, but she called him Fonsy for short.

Allowing herself, at last, to meet her mother's not-quite-reproving eye, she smiled angelically.

She hoped there would be mice at Juran for Fonsy to make friends with. She couldn't wait to get there.

CHAPTER TWO

1

On the evening of that same December day, on the other side of the world, the muddy surface of the Pearl River was gaudy with scarlet and saffron, crimson and copper. Sunset run wild.

But it wasn't the sun that coloured river, earth and heavens. It was flames – flames that ran, jumped, skipped and galloped along the buildings and gardens lining the river bank, flames quite unlike those of the domestic hearth, flames full of malice – huge, devouring, red as blood.

Down by the water's edge, Rachel Macmillan's unknown and unknowing cousin Sophie, whose eighth birthday had fallen just a few days before, wrenched her arm free from her Chinese nursemaid's grip and ran, not away from the flames but towards them.

2

Along the crowded waterfront of the European settlement at Canton, the walls of the stately white offices, residences and storerooms of the Western merchants swelled and cracked. Fire leapt from the rooftops, sprang vermilion from classically proportioned windows now glass-less and empty as eyeholes in a carnival mask. The flagstaffs that, only a few hours before, had towered above the shady gardens, arrogantly proclaiming the presence of Britain, America, France and Holland on China's unwelcoming soil, had been reduced to charred poles touched with flickering lights small and blue as marsh gas.

None of it was accidental. The Chinese had put the settlement to the torch.

The heat was intense and the noise like a physical pain – the roaring of flames, the crash of collapsing masonry, the spitting of bamboo, the furious hiss of steam from the defenders' hosepipes, the shouting and screaming, the rattling of shots and clanking of steel. The stench was breathstopping; cordite and sweat and excitement, burning wood, scorching broadcloth and scalding sewage.

But although Sophie Macmillan was terrified of the flames and the fury, the smoke and the smells, in her heart there was a terror far greater – the terror of losing her father, the only person she loved in the world.

An hour before, he had left her with her amah at the water's edge, saying cheerfully, 'Wait here for me! Back soon!' But he hadn't come back. And hadn't come back. With every moment that passed, Sophie had become more certain that something awful had happened.

If he had been hurt she knew that there would be no one to help him, even though there were people dashing about everywhere, clerks struggling to save valuable papers, merchants laden with chests of silver, servants staggering along under mountains of household goods, bookkeepers with abaci and ledgers, valuers with baskets and trays, interpreters with letter books and manifests. Most of the men wore anxious, harried looks, and some were slackmouthed with fear; only the griffins, the European clerks new to the China coast, were laughing and shouting at one another as if it was all a great lark.

None of them had a thought for anyone or anything other than themselves and their own affairs.

Sophie had felt as if she were going to burst with the worry of it, because her father wasn't just the only person she loved in the world, he was the only person she had. And she was all *he* had, the sole surviving child of the five her mother had borne him before dying two years earlier with her last, stillborn son in her arms and an apology on her lips.

She tried and tried to tell herself that everything was all right, really, but anxiety won in the end. She couldn't just go on standing there when he might need her. And so she tore away from her amah and dived into the mêlée in search of him, a small girl in a sailor suit with a straw hat on her head and, forgotten in her hand, the covered bamboo cage containing her beloved little linnet, Mr Happy Song.

3

As she fought her way against the tide of hurrying humanity, stinging eyes scanning every passerby and seeing not a face she recognised, she learned for the first time the harsh lesson of how insignificant her own little world was in the greater world of the settlement. She learned, too, that fear wasn't just nasty thoughts that would go away if she ignored them. Within seconds her stomach was churning, her heart pounding, her head aching, and she was hot all over – or thought she was, until she brushed a curl back from her forehead and discovered that the tips of her fingers were as cold as ice.

Jostled and buffeted in the crush of people, all of them so much bigger than she was, she began to lose any sense of why she was there at all, and it was only when the tide eased that she realised how silly she was being and slowed down, hesitating, trying to think sensibly about where her father might have gone. There wasn't much doubt about it. He must have gone back to the offices of Macmillan and Venturi for something his clerks had forgotten – offices that were right at the other end of the settlement.

She was just telling herself stoutly that it wasn't *really* far – less than a quarter of a mile when the sun was shining and the air fresh and the world friendly – when a rough English voice from one of the gun emplacements detached itself from the uproar.

'Hey! Oi! You there, nipperkin! What are you doing! Get down to the shore! *Pronto! Vite! Jildi!*'

Like a startled rabbit, Sophie bolted into the walled shrubbery of the English Garden and stood waiting, gasping with panic and ready to take to her heels again instantly if the man followed. But he didn't, though he would have, she knew, if he hadn't mistaken her for a boy – an easy mistake to make when boys wore skirts and long hair until they were six or seven. Sophie's father never allowed her to wear frilly, little-girl clothes outdoors because there was something in the Eight Regulations forbidding females to live in the European settlement, and he said only the Lord knew what he was going to do about her when she was a few years older and there was no more possibility of error.

After a while, cautiously, she ventured out again on the far side of the eerily quiet, blackened, litter-strewn shrubbery and found herself in front of the Jardine Matheson building, by now scarcely recognisable. Its balustrades had gone, and so had its columns and bamboo blinds. Even as Sophie looked, coughing and spluttering from the thick, roiling smoke, a section of the pediment swayed and sagged, and she barely had time to skip back before it collapsed with an earsplitting crash. A plume of dust and rubble rose, half blinding her and starting her off on a succession of shattering sneezes.

But her sneezes stopped dead when the dust eddied and swirled, opening a brief tunnel to her view and closing it again on the sight of three huge, long-moustached Chinamen, flatbacked against the wall of a neighbouring building, waiting to pounce on anyone who came by. They had pikes in their hands, which meant they were pirates. Horrified, Sophie realised that every pirate junk on the Pearl River had probably homed in on the settlement, hoping to make profit out of chaos.

And then, just as she was about to bolt back into the sanctuary of the shrubbery, she heard a burst of shouting and the fast, disciplined tramp of British soldiers moving at the double. There were a few shots, and the clash of metal, and when the dust cleared again both pirates and soldiers had vanished.

Sophie didn't – couldn't – move for several minutes. It wasn't that she was frightened, she assured herself. Not really. She just needed time to get her breath back. So she lifted the cloth covering the birdcage and peered in. Mr Happy Song raised his head from some urgent preening and eyed her reproachfully.

Sniffling a little, Sophie whispered, 'I'm sorry, Mr Happy. But it's all right, really, I promise. It'll be a bit bumpy now, because I'm going to run, but I'll give you grasshoppers and honey water to make up for it. Don't fret. Please don't fret.'

4

Now that she was sure of her bearings, all she had to do was follow a straight line along the front of the buildings. It was important to look as if she knew where she was going. The man in the gun emplacement would probably never have noticed her if she hadn't been standing hesitating.

Mr Happy's cage bouncing awkwardly in her hand, she flitted past the consulate where sailors from the *Calcutta*'s pinnace were trying to make a fire break; past the godowns – the warehouses – of Holliday Wise; and then those of Gibb Livingstone. After that it wasn't so easy keeping up an even pace as, looking about her all the time for a sight of her father, she wove her way under trees with leaves sere and limp from the heat; stumbled over fallen timbers and abandoned baggage; ducked out of sight, the breath knotting in her chest, when two Chinese soldiers rushed past with bluejackets in pursuit.

One of the Chinamen fell, blood gushing from a shot in his neck, and the British midshipmen, with shouts of glee, cut off his pigtail as a trophy.

She wasn't going to be sick, Sophie told herself. She *wasn't*.

Wiping the back of a trembling, smutty hand under her nose, she gave a resounding sniff and suddenly, miraculously, instead of burning wood and frizzling cloth, her head became full of the fragrance of Manila cigar smoke from one of the burning warehouses. It made her feel better. Her father always smelled of cigars.

Hugging the cage to her chest and gripping her lips tightly between her teeth, she set out on the last lap. The flames were no less fierce but there were fewer people about and none of them with a glance to spare for an anxious, filthy child wearing a sailor hat and carrying a birdcage.

Just as she drew level with the ashy column of the French flagstaff a gust of hot wind stirred it into glowing life again and she shied nervously. There was a doll lying sprawled at its foot, a doll with a china head and arms and soft body, its pretty pink frock tawdry with smoke and sparks. It looked so unhappy, so lost, so deserted, that she bent down to pick it up, wondering who it could belong to. There weren't any other little girls in the settlement. Perhaps some gentleman had bought it as a present for his own daughter at Macao, where the Chinese insisted that all the ladies stay with their children while their husbands worked here at Canton. Sophie had lived at Macao with her mother until she was six, and although her father should really have left her there after her mother died, he'd said he couldn't bear to abandon her to the care of strangers.

She was almost within sight of the Macmillan and Venturi building now, the place that had been her home for the last two years, and suddenly she was frightened to go on. If her father wasn't there, she didn't know what she would do.

On her right, the colonnades of the Russell building shuddered and slowly, slowly, begin to subside.

Wrapped up in her fears, Sophie recoiled too late. She felt a heavy blow on her shoulder and another on the side of her head and a third on her leg. The walls were raining on her, peppering her with stone.

But although she could feel blood running down her temple, although her face crumpled with the shock of it, although the heat blasted at her with such force that she cried out, swayed and sank to her knees, none of it was important. Because now she could see the narrow building beyond, the building where her father must surely be. It was furiously ablaze and utterly deserted.

She gave in then and, child that she was, wept in misery and despair,

29

still on her knees, smoke-stinging eyes open and fixed on the building that leered at her like a Hallowe'en pumpkin, a core of all-consuming fire encased within a grinning shell.

She had no idea how long it was before her stomach turned over violently inside her and she saw a tall, lithe, black-haired demon materialise from among the flames.

5

The tall, lithe, black-haired demon, whose name happened to be Rainer Blake, was feeling thoroughly annoyed with everything and everybody as he paused for a last moment in the doorway, listening for any small sound beneath the roaring of the fire that would betray a human presence. He didn't expect to hear anything. He had been as thorough as it was humanly possible to be.

Being thorough was one of Blake's talents, and one which had, in the past, brought about the discomfiture of several persons who had allowed themselves to be deceived by the carefree rakishness of his looks and manner. Even in influential circles, which should have known better, he was generally thought of as a young man who went out of his way to court danger and excitement. How else could he have made a nabob's fortune by the age of twenty-three?

But although Blake did, indeed, have a strong – and, in his own view, perfectly natural – distaste for boredom and inactivity, he also had an excellent brain and a genius for assessing risks, so that, while perfectly prepared to embark on the most hair-raising exploits when his intellect approved, he had no patience at all with dangers arising out of stupidity or lack of foresight.

And the burning of Canton, in his view, was just that – a typical example of British colonial bungling. The British, as usual, had chosen to stand on their sainted dignity at quite the wrong time, with the result that he, Rainer Blake – in whose veins ran an eccentric mixture of American, Scottish and Dutch blood – had spent the last, overheated two hours searching through tomorrow's ruins for anyone who might have been trapped by the flames. Blake was not one of Nature's philanthropists, but the search was something that needed to be done and no one else seemed to be doing it.

So far, he had salvaged one snapping pi-dog, a small litter of kittens, and a drunken British sailor who had consented to be rescued only under the most violent and vociferous protest.

It was the last straw when he turned away from the Macmillan and Venturi building and found himself confronted by a woeful small girl who didn't think she needed rescuing, either.

6

Gulping and sniffling, Sophie struggled to her feet, one hand burdened with Mr Happy Song's cage, the other still clutching the forlorn and dirty doll. The tall, menacing figure looming over her was scorched and blackened with soot and smoke, but he wasn't Satan after all.

He was an American and he wasn't in a very good temper.

He snapped, 'What are you doing here?'

'Looking for my papa.' Her chin was trembling so much that the words came out as a strangulated wail.

'What a tiresome brat! And you could do with a handkerchief, couldn't you? I guess I'd better take you down to the shore, though God knows I have more important things to attend to.'

There wasn't a trace of sympathy in his voice or manner.

She didn't want a handkerchief. She didn't want to be taken down to the shore. She had more important things to do, too. She had to go on looking for her father.

It hurt when the man took an iron grip on her bruised shoulder, and she let out a scream equally compounded of pain and rage. 'Let me go! Let me go! I don't want you to take me anywhere!'

'That, young lady, is your misfortune. Here, give me that damned birdcage.'

Removing the cage without gentleness from her grasp, he took her by the hand and – oblivious of her tripping and stumbling as she tried to dig her toes into the churned-up earth – began dragging her briskly along behind him. 'I have spent the last two hours,' he informed her exasperatedly, 'checking that no one is injured or trapped in any of these buildings, and I am not about to leave you wandering around on your own to force me to check again.'

'Let me go, let me go! I'm looking for my papa. I don't want to go with you. I *won't* go!'

'Like that, is it?' Scarcely pausing in his stride, he picked her up, one-handed and with mortifying ease, and tucked her under his arm, face down, legs kicking, arms flailing.

'Put me down! Put me down!' she screamed, lashing out wildly. 'I

31

don't like you! I don't even know you! Who *are* you?'

'Ouch!' Blake, smacked in the eye by the scruffy doll, found his sense of humour unexpectedly reawakened. Although he was perfectly accustomed to being assaulted, it was usually by larger people armed with deadlier weapons. As a general rule, he had only a limited interest in children – mealymouthed little milksops, most of them – but this one, tiresome though she was, didn't lack personality. Blake guessed that she must be Archie Macmillan's daughter; despite Macmillan's fond belief that his breach of the Eight Regulations was a well-kept secret, everyone in Canton knew about her. Blake wondered how such an amiable fellow had contrived to father such a little firebrand.

'Naughty temper,' he said reprovingly. 'That was my eye. My name is Blake. Rainer Blake. And what is yours?'

'Sophia Mary Macmillan.' She tried to sound lofty, but it was difficult considering the indignity of her position. 'My papa is the senior partner of Macmillan and Venturi, so there!'

'I thought so. You don't look much like him, do you?'

'Who *are* you?' she screamed again.

'I've told you. And you won't find your father here. He went to his office to collect something and I saw him leave again a while back. Unless I miss my guess, he is presently scouring the river bank for his little shrew of a daughter. *Now* will you behave yourself?'

Sophie didn't know whether to believe him or not, but he was right.

A few minutes later, dumping his burden unceremoniously before a worried Archie Macmillan, her disagreeable rescuer said, 'Yours, I believe?' and departed with a blackened grin and not another word.

Archie Macmillan engulfed her in a bear hug. 'What am I going to do with you! But I had to go back, you know. We'd forgotten The Bowl.'

The Bowl. The piece of blue-and-white Chinese porcelain with the specially painted picture of the castle of Juran on it.

CHAPTER THREE

❦

I

Ellie's knowledge of castles had been gleaned largely from two sources, Mrs Howitt's *Wonderful Stories for Children* and a tattered old picture book about *The Eglinton Tournament*. As a result, she had a very clear idea in her mind of what Juran ought to look like – a 'Rapunzel, Rapunzel, let down your hair' kind of place, with bright, airy pinnacles, banners flying, a wondrous array of gaily striped tents on the sunny greensward, and knights in armour jousting for the honour of their ladies fair. Remembering an engraving of the 'Monarch of the Glen' that she had seen in a picture dealer's window in London, she had introduced a touch of Scottishness by adding a small mountain in the background with a stag on top.

It was an enchanted vision and it sustained her all the way from Glasgow to the Highlands, despite the rain, mist, sleet, and snow that successively assailed the carriage on the first stages of the journey, and the gales that battered the hired yacht on the second.

'Have to get used to the sea,' Daniel Macmillan announced bracingly at Inveraray, leading his new wife towards a windswept landing stage. 'It's that or ponyback. No carriage roads in our part of the world. We'd have sailed all the way from Glasgow – usually do, as a matter of fact – except that it can be rough in December, and you might not have liked it, not being used to it.'

He smiled in a self-congratulatory way, but it didn't cut any ice with his bride, who demanded to know why he hadn't told her before. Her tone was shrill and Ellie knew why, having learned very early in life that the state of her mother's temper was always directly related to the state of her appearance. It wasn't that she was vain; not really. It was just that twenty years of battling to stay pretty against the odds of hot stoves, steamy cooking pots, dirty vegetables, bleeding meats and cold, greasy washing-up water had made her a bit obsessive.

What was worrying her now wasn't the probable effect of rough weather on her insides, but its undoubted effect on her outsides; already, even in the short walk from carriage to landing stage, the wind had caught and ruthlessly teased out the careful ringlets that had started the day nestling artistically under the brim of her bonnet. Ellie hoped it wasn't going to give her a permanent dislike of the Highlands.

To Ellie, it seemed the most romantic thing imaginable that Juran should be reachable only by sea and the sight of the wide green waters aroused no qualms in her, even though her sole previous experience of sailing had been a steamer trip to Margate. She didn't say so, of course. She wasn't going to give Belinda the chance to sneer. It had taken just one day of Belinda's acquaintance for her to discover that her new sister was waiting with spiteful eagerness to pounce on even the smallest error, the merest hint of ignorance or inexperience which would serve to emphasise that Ellie was 'not one of *us*'.

The scenery, as they sailed down Loch Fyne, through the Crinan Canal and up the coast towards Juran, was amazingly impressive but overpoweringly different from anything Ellie had ever seen before. She wasn't at all sure that she liked it. Sturdily, she told herself that it was probably an acquired taste, like snails or caviar.

But whatever else it was, it wasn't friendly – especially when the rollers built up to a great ice-green swell and darkness began falling behind thick, gunmetal grey clouds. The little ship was hugging the shore so tightly that the mountains seemed to be toppling over it, fierce, forbidding and much too close for comfort. This, Ellie supposed shiveringly, was what the poetically inclined mistress at her charity school had meant when she talked of 'the wild, savage grandeur of Nature'.

She knew it was weak of her but, just at the moment – cold, wet, tired and queasy – she would have preferred to see a few signs of light and warmth and human comfort.

She would have preferred to see Juran.

And then her father shouted against the howling of the wind, 'Almost home. Juran's over there. You'll see it when we land.'

They had to land from a rowing boat, and the ten minutes between disembarking from the yacht and reaching the shore felt longer to Ellie than the whole of the day that had preceded it. The little boat swooped down into the huge troughs between the waves as if it was never going to come up again, and it was some time before she was able to pull herself together sufficiently to observe that her father still looked perfectly cheerful and that William was amusing himself by trying to spit holes in the green, translucent wall of water looming over them. Belinda – brown hood crammed down over her shapeless, muffling cloak so that she looked like a large, wet cottage loaf – didn't take her eyes off her new stepsister for a moment, avid for even the faintest sign of weakness.

Imminent death by drowning, it seemed, was a perfectly run-of-the-mill affair to the Macmillans, so Ellie sat up straight and, through the rain and the spray and the wind, surveyed the heaving turmoil of the waters calmly and interestedly, just to show that she wasn't disturbed in the least, thank you very much.

2

Reaching the shore at last, the sailors at the oars manoeuvred the boat in among some half submerged rocks, and then held it steady by backwatering while Daniel Macmillan and his bride engaged in a shouting match about what happened next.

The waves were battering against the rocks, and the wind was howling, and the rain was coming down in torrents. Everyone was drenched, and Ellie's mother – bonnet whisked away and coiffure in ruins – had long ago come to the end of her tether and jettisoned every last ounce of self-restraint.

'Deuce take it!' Daniel yelled. 'I know these rocks. There's flat, safe sand in between them and only a foot of water on top. Pick up your skirts and paddle, you fool woman!'

Even her partisan daughter thought her ma was overdoing things when she screeched back, 'Never! I will not get out. I do not believe you. I do not know how to paddle. I do not wish to be swept away and drowned. *Mon dieu*, if it is so very safe and you are a gentleman, you will carry me ashore!'

'Not on your life! I know what you weigh, my girl.'

The boat rocked violently as a rogue wave struck sideways and Ondine, her mouth already open for a furious reply, received several gallons of sea full in the face.

She was still gasping and choking – and William still shrieking with laughter – when the other occupants of the boat became aware of two heavily muffled figures, heads down to the wind, approaching them from the top of the beach.

It was so dark by then that Ellie couldn't believe what she thought

35

she was seeing through her dripping eyelashes. But she was. Each of the figures was carrying a dining chair.

'Sensible fellows!' her father bellowed. 'Put them down and we can get ashore.'

With the chairs wedged between the rocks, their seats made excellent stepping stones. Ellie, her little tartan carpet bag clutched in one hand and, in the other, the anonymous-looking box that was Fonsy's private conveyance, made her way safely across them to land, and then, waved on by her father, trudged up the beach to some rough grass that proved to be the edge of the castle lawn.

There, looking up, she saw Juran at last.

3

There were no bright, airy pinnacles, no gaily striped tents, no lush and lovely greensward. Even allowing for the fact that it was late on a stormy December day, the castle of Juran was the most unwelcoming place Ellie could ever have imagined.

It looked as if someone had painted the Tower of London grey all over, then dumped it in the grimmest and most isolated spot they could find – at the foot of a craggy, snowcapped mountain covered with scrub the colour of used tea leaves and streaked with black, shiny gullies that looked as if they had been hewn out of coal.

There wasn't a light to be seen, nor any sign of life at all.

4

Only when the little party was halfway across the lawn did someone begin lighting candles in a downstairs room, and the small, dim points of light didn't improve things at all. Indeed, Juran began to look more like the Fleet prison than the Tower of London. Ellie's heart plummeted even further down into her sopping little brown buttoned boots.

But then the moon broke through the clouds to bathe the castle's ancient stones in a green, unearthly glow and, instantly and without a trace of regret, she abandoned her fairytale vision of knights and ladies and replaced it with a saga bursting at the seams with dark secrets, family feuds, and splendid, spine-chilling tales of doom and disaster. Juran wasn't what she had expected; it was much, *much* better.

The Great Hall, when they entered, was spine-chilling enough by anyone's standards, despite the better part of a tree trunk smouldering in the massive fireplace and the thin, wavering light cast by two newly lit and still smoking oil lamps. On the walls were enough family portraits to fuel a dozen feuds. And by the time Ellie had followed the housekeeper – who, in true gothic style, didn't seem to understand English – up four flights of steep stairs, the candle flame guttering wildly all the way, to the small, unheated stone chamber that was to be hers, she was utterly entranced.

Being a practical child, however, she lost no time in unpacking her carpet bag and putting on all three of her chemises, three of her six pairs of drawers and two pairs of cotton stockings. Then she took a shivering Fonsy out of his box and made a cosy little nest for him under the bed, and fed him, and sat and looked around her at the bare walls and the battered old furniture, and waited for someone to take her on a tour of the castle and tell her all the things about it that her imagination craved.

No one did. Miss Irving, the governess, shooed Belinda and William straight up to the schoolroom for their supper and Ellie had to go trailing along behind, no longer a person in her own right but just 'one of the children'.

5

'Here at Juran,' Miss Irving told her, as if imparting information for which Ellie ought to be grateful, 'all that is expected of you children is that you learn your lessons, do as you are told, and stay out of everyone's way.' Ellie thought at first it was just the kind of thing grownups always said to children, a statement of general principles rather than a law handed down from Sinai, but after three weeks of schoolroom routine she began to realise that it was the literal truth.

Nothing in her eight years of almost unfettered days had prepared her for the realities of Juran under the rule of Miss Irving, rigidly disciplined in everything, even the corsetry that embraced her massive bosom, the pince-nez clipped vice-like to her nose, and the greying brown locks wound into a knot so tight that her hair strained at the roots. Ellie was to learn that the governess didn't really like children and lived for the day when she could afford to retire and share her sister's house in Cheltenham.

In the meantime, Ellie, Belinda and William were roused every morning at six-thirty, in the dark, with no candle, no fire, no warm water, and the cold water often frozen in the ewer. Then they were sent downstairs to the huge, stonevaulted, russet-curtained Red Drawing Room where, still without light or warmth, they practised icy-fingered scales on a variety of musical instruments – including a harp, which didn't look nearly as golden and glorious at that hour of the day – until the schoolroom fire was lit at half past seven and they had a breakfast of porridge and milk. After that lessons began – arithmetic, astrology, poetry, geography, French, drawing – ending at midday with nature study which consisted, Miss Irving being town bred and, it seemed, less than enthusiastic about the outdoors, of a five-minute scuttle round the shrubbery in the rain, wind, sleet or snow.

Dinner, of either brown stew or boiled beef – invariably accompanied by carrots and potatoes and followed by pudding once a week – was succeeded by more lessons, which ended at five, after which Ellie or Belinda, according to the governess's whim, read aloud from such instructive works as Peter Parley's *Annual* and Felix Summerly's *Home Treasury*, while the other sorted the household sheeting and shirting and towelling, or practised hemming and mending. A cup of milk and a bannock at seven, and they were in bed by eight.

The only day that differed was Sunday, when lessons were replaced by Bible study and there was nothing but cold food, because cooking wasn't permitted on the Sabbath.

6

Ellie soon found that, where Belinda and William were concerned, she laid herself open to attack every time she opened her mouth, either for what she said or how she said it, often for both. Innocently asking about her 'step papa' one day after not having seen him for a week, she was told repressively by Miss Irving that the laird was a very busy man.

'And even if he wasn't,' Belinda added, 'I don't suppose he'd waste time on *you*! He doesn't like vulgar little girls who can't even speak the Queen's English.'

It wasn't fair. Ellie had always been a perfectly presentable child, neat, clean and civil, at least when she was under her mother's eye. And at charity school, she had learned not just the three Rs but deportment and correct behaviour – qualities that hadn't exactly been at a premium in the eyes of her playmates in Soho but were coming in very handy now. She could see that Miss Irving was taken aback to discover what a model child she was, though this was largely because, better acquainted with the theory than the practice, Ellie didn't at first realise that she was overdoing things. What worried her most was her diction, but she reassured herself that once she became used to hearing 'proper' English spoken every day, it would improve by leaps and bounds. In the meantime, she helped her aitches along by repeating to herself regularly – every night before she went to sleep and every morning as she scrambled into her freezing clothes – 'Heaven helps her who helps herself'.

She wondered sometimes if it was worth it, if anyone would even notice. But she had to try, because she was *not* going to go on being treated as a vulgar poor relation, with Belinda twisting whatever she said into an opportunity to criticise.

There wasn't a single subject that was safe, not even the weather. One evening, as they sat in the schoolroom sorting the sheets for mending and listening to the rain clattering like gravel against the windows, she said without thinking, 'I'n'it ever going ter get better?'

She had been quite unprepared for the way the weather dominated life in the Highlands; in London, rain had been merely a routine inconvenience, snow a rare, thrilling excuse for a frost fair on the Thames. But in winter at Juran it was dark for seventeen hours out of the twenty-four and, for most of the time, a freezing rain came lashing down and the waterfalls in the hills roared as loudly as the wind and waves. Sometimes, spray from the Atlantic rollers reached up over beach and dunes and grass to shower the castle itself, and the lawn was transformed into a vast series of puddles that never drained away.

Nowhere was it possible to get away from the weather. From every window in the castle there was a view of lowering sky, raging sea and rainswept headlands. There was no colour anywhere. Only grey, grey and more grey.

No one had thought to tell Ellie that this was the wettest and most dismal winter in living memory.

'I don't know what you mean, "better",' Belinda replied with the now familiar toss of her thick red hair. 'Rain's awfully good for the complexion, and cold weather never hurt anyone. But I don't expect you'll ever get used to it. You'd rather be back in London with all those filthy, smelly coal fires instead of good healthy logs, wouldn't you? Well, wouldn't you?'

There was nothing Ellie could say. All she had against Juran's good healthy logs was their miserly number, which made no impression at all on the chill given off by bare walls and flagged floors or the draughts that howled through ill-fitting windows and doors. She shook her head slightly.

'You would, of course you would. You've no idea what's good for you. Why are you putting those linen sheets on the same pile as the cotton ones? Goodness, aren't you ignorant? I don't expect you'll ever learn. Why don't you and your horrid mama go back where you came from!'

William, sprawled on the floor in front of the fire and blocking such heat as there was, added his mite. 'Go away! We don't want you!'

7

It was unmitigated torture, made even worse by the fact that Ellie couldn't sleep at night, no matter how tired she was. Her inner clock had been set in babyhood to synchronise with her mother's working pattern of late to bed, late to rise, and all her instincts rebelled against putting her head down on the pillow before midnight.

With a room of her own for the first time in her life, she felt strange and lonely and lost, missing her mother desperately. Never before had they been apart for more than a few hours. But although only two flights of stair separated the children's quarters from those of the grownups, it might as well have been two hundred. Ellie even had to ask Miss Irving's permission to visit her mother and permission was not always forthcoming, since the governess did not hold with children pestering their parents.

Ellie knew her parents better than Miss Irving did. The new Mrs Macmillan never exerted herself if she could help it, which meant that, if anything was to get done, it was absolutely *essential* to pester her. Ellie set to work at the earliest opportunity.

Her mother's boudoir, following a spectacular confrontation between bride and groom, had been hurriedly converted into the prettiest room in the castle. It wasn't saying much, because the frilly curtains, embroidered screens and flowery cushions seemed to emphasise rather than soften the prevailing starkness, but at least there were enough logs on the fire to raise the room temperature to lukewarm and the trivet was even hot enough for the curling tongs.

Picking them up, Ellie tested them with a licked forefinger and applied them to her mother's golden locks, holding them steady until her mother said, 'Enough!' and then carefully inserting a finger and drawing the curl out into a flawless ringlet.

'But you *must* be able to tell Miss Irving wot's wot!' she said for the second time. 'You can *make* 'er let me come and see yer.'

For the second time, her mother failed to respond. 'She tells me you are being a very good girl, which worries me. Are you all right?'

'Yes, thanks. Belinda's still being 'orrible, though, and I'm getting proper fed up with 'er. And she can play the pianoforte and William can sort-of play the flute, and I can't play anyfing yet. But Miss Irving's teaching me the 'arp and when I'm good enough she says we can 'ave family concerts before supper on Saturdays.'

'Family concerts?' With a delicate shudder, Ondine wondered what had possessed her to bring herself and her daughter to this terrible place, miles from anywhere. 'How delightful. Do you know that I sent a footman to Oban last week and he tells me they have never heard of cherry lip salve, or geranium petals to colour the cheeks, or lemons to make a rinse for the hair?'

Ellie, familiar with her mother's reluctance to stick to the point, said, 'Really?' And then, for the third time, 'But you can *make* Miss Irving let me come and see yer whenever I want!'

Carefully, she drew out another ringlet.

Ondine sighed. 'Perhaps. But not yet. Life here is as strange to me as it is to you. I am not sure what is permitted and what is not. And if we do not behave exactly *comme il faut*, everything will become unbearable.'

It hadn't occurred to Ellie – though it should have done – that her mother, too, might be feeling like a stranger in a strange land.

So she threw her arms round Ondine's neck and said earnestly, 'All right, ma – I mean, mama – I'll be good. I won't make a fuss. It's sure to get better when we're used to things.'

8

Everything had seemed quite easy from faraway London. One of the mistresses at Ellie's charity school had said kindly that, since she was quick in the uptake and had excellent powers of concentration, she should have little difficulty in adapting to her new life.

But there was so much to learn and no one to explain. Neither Belinda nor William would tell her as much as the time of day unless they thought she didn't want to know, and they certainly weren't going to tell her how a laird's stepdaughter ought to behave. After two months of being a virtual prisoner in the schoolroom, learning nothing at all about what went on in the great wide world below the nursery floor, Ellie decided that she was going to have to take the law into her own hands.

By peering through the banisters at every opportunity and indulging in some unashamed eavesdropping, she soon learned that there was a constant coming and going of lairds visiting from neighbouring estates, of blackclad men of business with huge bundles of papers under their arms, and grave-looking persons with mournful moustaches and tweed hats for whom managing Juran's ten thousand acres was a fulltime occupation. In the castle itself there was also the steward, Mr Nielson, a Jehovah-like figure who moved along the corridors with the solid, undeviating majesty of a steam roller. Ellie had the feeling that anyone who made the mistake of getting in his way was likely to finish up ironed as flat as a gingerbread man. But although Mr Nielson was a very intimidating person, he was not the god of Juran.

The god of Juran was her father, who was not the same person as she had been acquainted with in London. He didn't look or behave any differently, but here his word was law. When he said do something, people did it – just like that. Ellie, busy though she was with her own affairs, gave the matter some thought and decided that it couldn't be good for him.

Gaining in confidence, she began slipping downstairs when she was supposed to be in bed – exploring, like a small and self-effacing shadow, all the rooms she had never entered, whose functions she didn't even know. There was an alarming profusion of them, all fully furnished but most of them chill with disuse. The oldest part of the castle turned out to be deeply disappointing, a wilderness of grey stone with worn squares of carpet on the floors and mouldy tapestries on the walls. Ellie didn't see a sign of any mournful spectres, nor hear floorboards creaking when there was no one there – though, as she told herself prosaically, that was probably because the floors were of stone and spectres didn't start serious prowling until dead of night.

It was different in the inhabited part of the castle. Although she knew nothing about formal decoration, Ellie was still perfectly capable, as she flitted from room to room with nothing but the dim haze from outdoors to light her way, of recognising than Juran was the queerest hotchpotch of styles. It was to be years before she learned that

42

no one had ever decorated more than one or two rooms at a time because the money had always run out, with the result that outposts of Elizabethan oak still survived amid the Queen Anne walnut, and William and Mary japanning amid the Georgian mahogany.

The Blue Drawing Room, the one that was most used – and which she was able to admire by the light of logs and candles, her parents having abandoned it temporarily for the dining room – owed its inspiration to Belinda and William's mother, who had been determined to have at least one room decorated in the style to which she had been accustomed in Somersetshire, regardless of how inappropriate it might be in the more austere surroundings of Juran.

By her decree, its walls had been covered with a pale turquoise paper, damasked with shiny roses on a matt ground, and most of the furniture turned into a rhapsody in blue and gilt. The pale carpet was patterned with blue and pink fans; the fireplace, an Adam design, was white with gilt relief; there were Classical bronze urns on torchères in the corners of the room; and on the walls huge mirrors in ornate gilt frames. There was a splendid chandelier, too, whose thousand lustres (when properly washed and polished) were capable of reflecting enough light from thirty candles to make the room appear bright as day.

It was all frighteningly magnificent, as if it were just waiting for the Queen and Prince Albert to come and take tea with their crowns on.

But the room that interested Ellie most was her father's book room, where she was lucky enough to find a fire still burning one evening. It wasn't the simple oak cupboards, or the endless shelves of dusty volumes, or the piles of ribboned papers that drew her eye, but the yellowed drawings and watercolours on the walls recording changes to the castle at various stages in its history. Under each picture was a caption written in an old, spiky hand, explaining all about it.

9

Like so many castles along the wild western coast of the Scottish Highlands, Juran had originated as a simple watchtower in the early 1200s. Built by one William Macmillan, who was to meet his end in battle against Norse raiders a few years later, it had been extended over the next four hundred years with an assortment of rickety-looking barns and sheds until, in the days of Cavaliers and Roundheads, John Macmillan had decided to have them demolished and replaced with a rectangle of low stone buildings surrounding the tower.

Cavalier John's fate had been no happier than William's. In fact, he had died on the scaffold for being a supporter of King Charles I. His portrait, in all the splendour of plumed hat and lace-frilled, high-heeled boots, still hung in the place of honour in the Great Hall.

Another hundred years had passed before the more prudent James took a hand in things. Having averted the same fate as John by changing both his religion and his allegiance within twenty-four hours of hearing that King Charles' no less calamitous descendant, Bonnie Prince Charlie, had set foot on Scotland's shores, he had devoted himself to adding, in fits and starts, the turrets and battlements, porches and Gothick windows that – in the eyes of its critics – made Juran's antiquity look more fake than real.

Unfortunately, James's additions had been in such direct imitation of the Duke of Argyll's improvements at Inveraray that the Duke had threatened to sue him. But James had at least succeeded in dying in his bed.

No one since then, as far as Ellie could discover, had added or subtracted anything at all.

10

It took her some time to absorb all this information, but by the beginning of April she was beginning to feel thoroughly smug in the belief that she knew very nearly everything about her new home that she needed to know. No longer could Belinda or William sneer at her for her ignorance; she knew as much as they did. It was all *most* satisfactory.

She was even sleeping well, the history of the castle having provided her with materials for a lovely new dream about being a great lady in Days of Yore, with a neat little gold coronet holding a tablecloth in place over her head as she took her turn standing lookout on the roofwalk and keeping watch for the dreaded Viking longships. Once or twice she even dreamed of being captured and carried off by a specially handsome Viking raider wearing a big helmet with horns on it. In these new dreams, her hair was fair instead of brown and even the weather was lovely.

The influence of the weather, unfortunately, was the one thing she had left out of her calculations. During the Highland winter, no one took a step out of doors if they didn't have to, which had made it easy for Ellie to brush the estate's ten thousand acres of loch, moor and mountain under a kind of mental carpet and forget that getting to know all about Juran meant more, much more, than merely learning about the castle itself and the life within it.

She was to find out that she had been congratulating herself too soon when the rain and the wind died at last – from exhaustion, she suspected – and she asked permission to venture out into the wide, wet, empty hills to see what it was like up there.

Muffled in a heavy cloak, its drawstringed hood pulled tight over her neat poke bonnet, she went marching off, a brave and lonely little figure, into the unknown. Miss Irving had provided her with a pair of Belinda's castoff boots and had even suggested that Belinda and William accompany her, but Belinda said they had more important things to do than plod up that boring old hill for the thousandth time, and in exchange for the boots Rachel would have to mend the sheets for her this evening. Belinda always referred to her as 'Rachel' or 'she', never as Ellie.

The first part of the climb was all right, because Ellie could still turn her head and see the grey, reassuring bulk of the castle. But after that it was eerie, as if she were all alone in the universe.

She had been out for almost an hour when she finally came to a halt, biting her lip, her skin crawling with the overpowering remoteness of it, its inhumanity. It wasn't a place for people. It made her feel small, and though she was small in physical truth – indeed, it was a source of the greatest frustration to her that Belinda, though six months younger, was an inch taller – she wasn't used to feeling small *inside*.

In the end, stubbornly, and to prove she wasn't afraid, she decided to go as far as the next dip before turning back.

Climbing with care so as to avoid the boggy patches and the clumps of dead, tangled heather that lay in wait to trip up the unwary, she reached the top of the slope and raised her eyes to see what lay beyond, expecting it to be yet another stretch of wet black peat and grey rock, browned bracken and ochre-yellow scrub, empty as the world at the beginning of time.

But it wasn't.

The wide hollow before her was full to the brim of big, heavy-bodied, dirty-looking sheep with black faces and threatening expressions. Every single one of them was staring at her, motionless and unblinking, and every single one of them had huge, curling horns.

Her heart stopped beating and then started again, unevenly. She didn't dare move and soon began to wonder if she even could. Her legs felt weighted down and clumsy and unrelated to her, as if they were swelling and thickening, taking root in the ground like tree trunks. The silence and the tension began to close in on her, filling her mouth and her nostrils so that she couldn't breathe.

It was the first time in her life that she had known the meaning of fear.

The animal nearest to her was only two or three yards away and, after a while, it gave a small sideways jerk of its head and a single stamp of each of its front feet. Then she saw a ripple run through the massive body as if it was preparing to charge.

The spell broke. Letting out a full-throated screech, Ellie turned and ran, the breath tearing in her lungs and her heart lurching inside her. A dozen times, she caught her foot in a clump of heather roots and took a wild toss, but picked herself up at once, dashing the tears from her eyes with a scratched and peat-blackened hand, and ran on, slipping and floundering, cloak and skirt bunching between her knees, with a stitch in her side and her legs numbing from weariness, but never daring to look back.

It seemed a very long way home and not until she was in sight of the castle did she slow down, and only a little.

She didn't know much about the country but she did know that rams could be every bit as dangerous as bulls. People ought to be warned!

There wasn't a soul in sight except Belinda and William, engaged on Belinda's important business of setting out croquet hoops on the sodden lawn in preparation for the good weather two or three months hence.

Even they were better than no one.

Trying to control her breathing, Ellie gasped, 'Up on the hill . . . A flock of rams! They . . .'

That was as far as she got before Belinda's rosebud mouth opened and she let out a whoop of mirth.

Ellie stopped so abruptly that she bit her tongue.

Brown eyes shining, Belinda squealed, 'You were scared!' and then she and William laughed, and Ellie had to stand there, seething, until their mirth began to sound artificial even to them.

When they had finished, Belinda said in her sneering little voice, 'I can't imagine how it's *possible* for anyone to be so ignorant about the countryside! Goodness me. One would think you had been dragged up in a slum. You don't know *anything* about the things that really matter.'

Ellie took a deep breath. She had been behaving well for months and months, and she wasn't going to stop now. In her most reasonable tones, she said, 'How can I learn if you won't tell me?'

'Pooh. *I've* got better things to do than explain things to *you*! Come along, William. That's the croquet hoops done. Now we can go and make a list of how many of your socks have holes in them so that Bessie Laundry can darn them.'

Given the excuse, Belinda would have made a list of the slates on the roof, the leaves on the trees, the pebbles on the beach. Organising things was her passion. Another one was counting pennies.

She was *mean* all through, Ellie thought venomously as she went in search of Jeannie, the most comprehensible of the maids, to have the flock of rams explained to her.

'Och, it was chust sheep you was seeing,' Jeannie said. 'It is a kind that has horns, that is all. They would neffer be hurting you. Juran has only the one ram, and he is kept tied up except at the tupping – when he is set to the ewes, so that they can haff lambs, do you see? The lambs is due later this month. You will like them.'

'Shan't!' muttered little Ellie Vallette to herself. 'Who bleeding well cares about their bleeding 'orrible old sheep and lambs! Who cares about their bleeding 'orrible old countryside!'

II

In bed that night, Ellie faced up for the first time to the truth of what Belinda was always telling her, and which she herself had glimpsed at the wedding breakfast. She didn't belong, and never would. She didn't like being Rachel Macmillan of Juran; she wanted to go back to being Ellie Vallette of Soho.

As she lay in the wavering light of her single candle, staring at the black darkness outside her window, hearing the sea roar and the wind howl, she yearned to see instead the acid glow of gaslit streets, hear the old, familiar sounds of dogs snarling, tramps scrabbling in dustbins, judies soliciting from doorways, knives clashing when rival gangs met, roisterers singing their way home through the alleys and backyards.

She missed it all bitterly. She missed her freedom. She missed her disreputable friends. She missed Pierre at the restaurant, who was always kind and jolly. She missed the feeling of being a tiny cog in the great and exciting wheel of a place where things *happened*, the simmering undercurrent of hope that went with the thought that some day, perhaps today, chance would bring her into contact with the one person in the whole wide world who would turn out to be her kindred spirit, the other half of herself.

Juran was giving her nothing in return for what she missed. She knew, now, not to expect anyone other than her mother to pay attention to her, or her needs, or her feelings. Everything was as cold and cheerless indoors as out, emotionally as physically, and although she couldn't believe that life just went on like this, for ever and ever, no one had even hinted that it didn't.

Nor did there seem to be a chance in a million of meeting a kindred spirit. She hadn't seen a single new face at Juran since the day she arrived, except for the servants, of whom there were dozens in the castle, odd creatures, strange and ignorant, running about getting in everyone's way. She had worried herself stiff for the first few days, uncertain how the laird's stepdaughter ought to address them, only to discover that, with one or two exceptions like Jeannie, most of them didn't speak English, anyway, and appeared to be in mortal terror of anyone who did.

Sniffling miserably, she burrowed under the blankets and hugged the stone hot water bottle to her thin, flannelled chest. If this was what it meant to be part of a proper family, she thought, she'd rather be part of an improper one any day. Life had been *much* happier when there had been just her and her ma.

And then something tickled the sole of one cold foot and she squeaked, 'Ootch!' and sat up abruptly, oblivious of the freezing air. 'Come out of there!'

After a moment Fonsy emerged from under the blankets looking, if it were possible for a mouse so to look, faintly sheepish. Scooping him up in her hands, Ellie told him sternly, 'You know you're not supposed to be in my bed. If I turned over in my sleep, you'd get squashed. And you're the only friend I've got.'

He twitched his whiskers at her.

'Oh, all right,' she said. 'Just this once.'

It was comforting to snuggle down again with Fonsy half burrowed under the pillow beside her and, gradually, she began to feel more positive again, ashamed of herself, even. It was silly to brood. If there was more to learn about Juran than she had thought, then there was more to learn. That was all! And when she had learned it, everyone would have to start being more polite to her. It was quite simple, really – though she wished she could persuade her mother to look at things the same way as she did.

'What are we going to do about her?' she murmured to Fonsy as she drifted off to sleep. 'She just won't make the effort.'

12

And then, almost as if God had decided to give Ellie a helping hand, the sun came out and the sky stopped being grey and turned to a clear blue that made her think of hair ribbons. Until then, 'sky blue' had been nothing but the name of a colour to her, like 'Japanese rose' or 'Bosphorus green' and just as meaningless. In London, the sky never *was* blue. It was yellowish grey from the coal smoke that lay over the city like a sheet of marzipan on a cake, though all you could ever see of it was the slices between the buildings. It didn't matter much, because most people never bothered to look up, anyway.

At Juran it was different. Ever since Ellie had arrived, the world had been veiled in melancholy, the sky a leaden blanket, the land a shrouded vista of hills beyond hills, dim, grey and remote, the sea a stretch of roughness shading into mist. She had had no impression of space at all. But now, with the mists rolled back, her senses reeled as she tried to take in the extent of a sky that stretched as far as the eye could see in every direction, merging so smoothly with the newly blue sea that there appeared to be no horizon.

Ellie, brought up in a place where even elbow room was a luxury, found it almost impossible to grasp the idea that, from where she was sitting, the vastness of sky and sea stretched all the way to Canada, with nothing in between except the two small islands of Meall and Corran, a mile offshore. Meall was a round hump of a hill, Corran long, low and sickle-shaped, and they lay on the satin surface of the sea looking like an enormous question mark.

Like most people born and bred in cities, Ellie had always thought of the countryside as a place of green fields and plump cattle, but at Juran there were no fields, no cattle nor even the promised lambs, and in early April no trace of green – nothing but blue, russet and violet, with a tinge of pale yellow in a few sheltered crannies where primroses were beginning to show. The shell sand beach was blindingly white, the trunks of the leafless birches a pearly silver, and thick snow still capped the mountains to the north.

Ellie sat with her mouth open, and discovered that it was all

49

amazingly beautiful in a sackcloth-and-ashes kind of way, as if it had been designed with holy penitents in mind, people who had sworn off all human comforts. There was something else, too, that made her feel vaguely ill at ease. In years to come, she was to learn that, even in April, life was stirring; that she could expect to hear newborn ravens squawking, see otters playing in green water, catch a glimpse of herons fishing. But in her first Highland spring, her eyes and ears were not attuned. She couldn't see a sign of life anywhere.

13

Two days later, there was life in abundance. One of the many things no one had told Ellie was that, although Juran from late October until Easter might be as unvisited as a desert island, in the other half of the year the opposite was true.

Easter that year was in the middle of April, and between one day and the next Juran was transformed. Instead of neighbours and factors and lawyers, the castle and grounds filled up with large rubicund gentlemen in hodden grey tweeds, strapped trousers and earflapped hats, striding around with fishing rods in their hands and purposeful looks on their faces.

Queen Victoria's obsession with the Highlands, culminating in the building of Balmoral, had in recent years had a profound effect on life in the area, bringing the moors and mountains bang into fashion. It was already almost obligatory for rising politicians and other distinguished persons to make a regular pilgrimage there, quartering themselves – in the absence of any civilised alternative – on the owners of the larger estates. Ellie was to discover that a good proportion of these people simply turned up out of the blue, bearing letters of introduction from distant acquaintances, while others were forwarded, like misdirected parcels, by nearby lairds who kept open house throughout the sporting season and sometimes found themselves with more guests than rooms.

Belinda, peering through the banisters, said in a very superior way, 'My goodness, we do seem to be short of company this spring. What a dull set of people – nothing but manufacturers and Members of Parliament! It's always more exciting in the autumn, the shooting season, of course, but I don't suppose you'll still be here then.'

Ellie didn't care whether they were dull. They were *people*, even if she wasn't allowed to talk to them, or even let them catch a glimpse of her.

'I should not need to remind you,' said Miss Irving, with a minatory glare, 'that, while your papa's guests are here, we must remain in the schoolroom at all times, except when I have ascertained that the gentlemen have departed outdoors to engage in their sporting pursuits. Then, and only then, may we leave the schoolroom, and only to go outdoors ourselves. We must all be as invisible as mice.'

William, a wooden Mr Noah in one hand and Mrs Noah in the other, banged their heads together, shrieking, 'We *know*, we *know*, we *know*!'

He raised his arm and threw Mrs Noah, hard, at Ellie.

'William!' said Miss Irving, but he paid no more attention to her than he ever did. Ellie, on the other hand, was always obedient and well behaved, and the governess favoured her with something not unlike a smile as she went on to announce that Easter Saturday would be the day on which schoolroom routine became more flexible. With winter over and the flora and fauna, like humans, emerging from hiding, it was time for the children to devote more attention to nature study and the life of the estate. Once the Easter influx of fishing guests had departed, she would even allow them to go off on their own, as long as they produced drawings or notes as proof that they had not been wasting their time.

Ellie hadn't known that the schoolroom routine she hated wasn't an all-the-year-round affair, and she was almost speechless with delight. Knowledge was belonging, which meant that until winter came again, she was going to have to make use of every single minute.

14

So hard did she work, observing, reading, asking questions, that the months went flying past. By August, when the shooting guests began turning up in droves, she was able to saunter into the schoolroom saying, as easily as if she had been born with the words on her lips, 'The gentlemen seem to have had excellent sport today. They are gathering on the lawn to be photographised with their bag. Two hundred brace of partridge, ptarmigan and woodcock. Not at all bad!'

No one congratulated her on this knowledgeable pronouncement. Miss Irving, in fact, made a rather sour remark about little pitchers with big ears.

The one problem that continued to fret Ellie was stalking, because the children were forbidden on the hills during the season. 'It is dangerous,' Miss Irving said, 'and stalking is, moreover, a serious matter. You would not wish to disturb the deer just when the gentlemen have gone to a great deal of trouble to get within range.'

Ellie shook her head virtuously.

She hadn't yet discovered what people actually did when they went stalking, which was annoying, because she was most anxious to pick up a few tips on how they managed to get to within three or four hundred yards of the deer – the range of the guns – when she couldn't get within half a mile of them herself. And *she* didn't even want to shoot them, just look at them.

Two days later, therefore, she set off in forbidden pursuit of a small party of guests, skipping along unobserved at a safe distance behind as they strode along the peat track towards the jumble of hills north of the castle where deer were most often to be found. Though red deer liked to be high, they weren't mountaineers.

Even Ellie, who had been far too busy during the last few months to have much time for the scenery, recognised what a miraculous day it was. There was a light wind from the south-east, and the Juran river in its lower reaches was a chain of clear, lovely pools fed by burns that, brown and glittering after a night of rain, seemed to chuckle as they danced their way down from the high tops. The landscape had begun to change into its autumn livery and patches of dying bracken were showing like spills of ginger amid the green, while here and there a rowan tree flamed out like a sentinel in scarlet. The heather was richly purple, and the deer grass a haze of copper. There was a pair of buzzards wheeling and mewing high up in the heavens, and the pipits were calling, and the sun was coaxing the scent of bog myrtle into the air.

When the stalkers reached the corrie that seemed to be their objective, Ellie diverged to a little hollow, high on the ridge, which gave her a godlike view of the wide green and purple amphitheatre below. There, for almost two hours, she sat entranced by the comedy being played out below her.

And comedy it was, to watch the large and important-looking gentlemen who had been marching portentously around the castle and its policies for days – looking as if the great world was having a hard time getting on without them – all flat on their stomachs like hatted and booted snakes, struggling through matted blaeberries, cracking their shins against outcrops of rock, inching through bogs, getting blackened with peat, slithering up the sides of burns, and being eaten alive by midges. Midges loved people when they were hot and sweaty.

It was very peaceful up in Ellie's little hollow, with the sun shining and the bees droning among the heather, and after a time she began to drowse. She was nearly asleep when one of the bees went whizzing over her shoulder with a queer, whistling sound. A few seconds later it happened again, though this time it sounded more like a twanged fiddle string and she felt the wind of its passing on her cheek before it flattened itself against a boulder.

It wasn't a bee.

Without even pausing to think, she leapt to her feet shrieking, 'No! Stop it! Stop it! You're shooting the wrong way. I'm not a deer! I'm a *person*. Stop it, stop it!'

15

It took no more than a moment for her to realise what she had done.

The deer were already streaming away over the brow of the hill. One of the gentlemen, with a crashing oath, jumped up out of a patch of myrtle, took a snap shot at them, and missed. Then, one by one, the other gentlemen rose from their various hiding places and stood staring grimly up at the lonely little figure on the hilltop.

Ellie, knowing she had committed a terrible crime, decided it wasn't the best time for lingering to discover who had let off the shots that might easily have put an end to her brief life.

Scuttling off as fast as her legs would carry her, she reached the gully by which she had ascended, shaking like a leaf, to discover that it was no longer empty but tenanted by a boy of about fourteen, standing legs astride and arms akimbo, with a full-sized rifle in his hand and a huge grin on his good-looking face.

A few months earlier, the aftermath of fright would have caused her to suffer a serious social relapse, but little Ellie Vallette was, by now, reasonably under control and so were her aitches. It was therefore a perfectly refined small girl who said, in a surprisingly steady voice, 'How do you do? Who are you, please? I'm Rachel Macmillan. Did you just shoot at me?'

The boy had a square jaw, a complexion deeply tanned by sun and wind, and hair that was dark red, wiry and exuberantly curly. Under very straight brows, his eyes glowed like those of a marmalade cat. In his grey shirt and grey tweed kilt he looked sturdy, muscular and competent, and his feet were planted on the hill with as much assurance as if he owned it. He had a fine leg for a kilt and knew it.

'Philip Roy,' he said in a firm, faintly Scots voice, his grin fading. It was clear that he thought he shouldn't have needed to tell her, and when he saw that his name didn't mean anything to her, either, the grin vanished completely. He was offended. 'I am Philip Roy of Altsigh.'

'I don't care if you're the King of the Cannibal Isles! Did you just shoot at me?'

'Yes.'

'Did you *mean* to shoot at me?'

'Of course.'

She was even more outraged. 'Of course? But you can't just go around shooting at people!'

Philip wasn't accustomed to being taken to task, and certainly not by small girls about whose mothers he had heard nothing good. The Roys, being of royal descent – albeit a good few hundred years before, and on the wrong side of the blanket – were selective about their acquaintance, and Philip's own mama had been quite shocked when she had ridden over with his father to pay a call on the new Mrs Macmillan. 'Not our kind of person at all,' she had said with finality. 'I do not propose to call on her again.'

Seeing the little girl on the hill, Philip had guessed that she must be the second Mrs Macmillan's daughter; sporting guests didn't bring their children with them and, since she wasn't Belinda, he couldn't think of anyone else she might be. Assuming, therefore – perfectly naturally, he thought – that she would be a vulgar brat whose good fortune had made her cocky, he had decided she would be none the worse for being taken down a peg or two. If he had suspected otherwise, he would not have dreamed of shooting at her. He knew better than to frighten a *lady*.

When he saw her close up and discovered that she was quite presentable-looking in a rather shy way – even if her manner wasn't as shy as the rest of her – he was momentarily taken aback. Her father, he supposed, must have been a respectable class of person who had married beneath him. But since it was entirely the fault of the girl's mother that Philip had been mistaken about her, he would have felt no need to apologise even if he had been an apologising kind of person.

Loftily, he said, 'I wasn't going around "shooting *at* people"! I was shooting *past* you, to make you jump. You'd no right to be lying there spying on your stepfather's guests. And I can tell you, if I'd been shooting *at* you, you wouldn't be here now.'

She sat down with a thud on the turf. 'Well, I think it's shocking. What if your aim had been bad?'

'My aim is never bad.'

'Isn't it?' He sounded so sure of himself that she was forced to believe him. 'Well,' she went on feebly, 'it's your fault the gentlemen's stalking was spoiled, but it'll be me that gets the blame. It's not fair.'

The grin returned to his face. 'You fairly leapt out of your skin, though, didn't you! Besides, the gentlemen deserved to have their stalking spoiled. They were after those young stags. Quite wrong. You should never shoot the young ones. It's not sporting.'

'Isn't it?' she said automatically and then added – as she felt sure a laird's daughter ought to – 'Anyway, what are you doing on my stepfather's land? Don't you have any deer of your own to stalk?'

'Hundreds. But I'm home on vacation from school and Mr Macmillan invited my pater and me over here for the day.' Philip was a little too old to add, 'So there!' but it was implied. 'And since I don't care for stalking in parties,' he concluded airily, 'I branched off by myself. I prefer to be my own ghillie.'

She didn't know what a pater was so she ignored it. 'Do you?' she said worshipfully. 'Ooooh, I wish you'd tell me about it. You must be awfully clever.'

It was the right thing to say.

For the next two hours, Philip scarcely stopped talking, even when masticating the crumbling game pie he produced from one of his pockets and graciously shared with Ellie.

'. . . and sometimes, to get near the more experienced beasts, you have to put as much effort into covering a few hundred yards of hill as you would climbing the Matterhorn.' His golden eyes glowed. 'It's the finest sport in the world.'

'Oh, I'm sure it is,' Ellie breathed.

No boy could have asked for a more appreciative audience. Philip said, 'You know, you're quite a nice little thing.'

'Thank you.' She meant it. He was a gift from heaven, not only because she yearned for a friend – though she would rather he hadn't been such a self-satisfied one – but because he seemed to be master of all the country lore she still needed to know about. With luck, she might persuade him to teach her.

As she went back to the castle, she was walking on air.

16

She was returned briskly to earth when she met her father in the grounds and he followed up his usual rhetorical question – 'All right, are we?' – with the information that the Greshams were coming to stay and she was to take care what she said. 'You remember the Greshams? You were sitting between them at the wedding. They're a pair of dashed noseyparkers, so watch your Ps and Qs when they're here.'

Ever since the previous December, Daniel Macmillan had been waiting gloomily for his former inlaws to descend on Juran to inspect the wife he had chosen to succeed Lucian Gresham's idolised sister, Isabella. He had made sure at the wedding that they didn't have a chance to say more to Ondine than a how-de-do, but he'd known that wouldn't be the last of it.

Daniel disliked Gresham, an ugly autocratic fellow whose normal human instincts – if he had ever had any – had been ruined by the fact that the excellence of his ancestors' lineage hadn't been matched by the excellence of their investments. Although he had inherited, when still a boy, a respectable estate at Priors Mead in Somersetshire and a sufficient fortune to maintain it, he had never been able to treat money with the careless contempt he would have wished. On reaching years of discretion, therefore, he had chosen to compensate for his physical and financial disadvantages by cultivating a manner that was lofty, drawling and totally uninterested, deliberately calculated to reduce his inferiors to a state of gabbling servility. The effects had been so gratifying – to Gresham, if to no one else – that, in the end, the manner had become the man. Lucian Gresham now viewed the rest of humanity, including his wife and son, with a detachment little short of Olympian.

Only Isabella had been exempt, and Daniel had no doubt at all that Gresham had interpreted his own choice of second bride as a calculated insult to the memory of his first.

Daniel didn't regret 'poor, dear Isabella' in the least. As a wife she had been a disaster, plain, patrician, and so languid by temperament and upbringing that going to bed with her had been a penance. How

56

he had managed to beget two children on her remained one of the great mysteries of his life.

A few days later, however, when his inlaws arrived and he was forced to watch Ondine trying to charm Gresham into unbending – and overplaying her hand, as usual – he found himself thinking, not for the first time, that it had been a mistake to go to the other extreme. Plump, pretty and coquettish as Ondine was, it was sadly obvious that she wasn't out of the top social drawer.

He had always known it, of course, but he'd found himself in a cleft stick. Marrying his mistress had never ranked high – or indeed anywhere – on his list of priorities until the suggestion had been put to him in terms that he still preferred not to dwell on; it had been blackmail, pure and simple. At the time, he had succeeded in reconciling himself to the situation by fixing his mind firmly on the pleasures in store, but as the months passed it had become steadily clearer that the pleasures weren't great enough to compensate for the social disadvantages. He'd taken care to impress on Ondine that she mustn't expect to entertain or be entertained by Juran's neighbours, and had told her that it would be quite improper for her to preside over his sporting house parties, but he couldn't keep her entirely hidden away. And although he was perfectly ready to admit that her manners couldn't be faulted, he knew very well that no one would ever mistake her for a lady.

Even so, once he had taken all the precautions he could think of – which amounted to threatening both Ondine and Ellie with the direst retribution if they said one word out of place – Daniel had felt able to look forward to the Greshams' visit with reasonable confidence. They were bound to recognise that Ondine was a *bourgeoise* and had probably already guessed that she had formerly been his mistress, but at least they weren't going to find out that she had ever been anything as shockingly low as a cook in a restaurant.

17

If Daniel's optimism on that score had not turned out to be misplaced, Lucian Gresham's loathing and scorn might not have reached the proportions they did and Ellie's life would have taken a very different course.

As it was, Ondine, Ellie and the Greshams' seven-year-old son, Horace, were to be jointly responsible for letting the fatal cat out of the bag.

A few weeks earlier, Ellie had begun pestering her mother about the food in the schoolroom. 'It's awful, ma. Mrs Lauder can't cook. When are you going to do something about it?'

From Ellie's point of view, it was a perfectly reasonable question, but from her mother's it was not. As the laird's wife and thus a lady, if only by adoption, she was expected to be genteelly ignorant and never to interfere in the affairs of the kitchen; the first Mrs Macmillan, she knew, had never done so.

'There is nothing I can do,' she said.

Ellie had expected it. 'Well,' she persevered, 'I'm going to be sick if I see any more brown stew.'

'Is that what you have in the schoolroom?' her mother enquired with absent interest, studying her reflection in the glass, pleased to see that the thread veins were disappearing at last. 'Downstairs, it is congealing mutton chops and underhung game. But I fear Mrs Lauder is not just being slovenly. She knows no better.'

Ellie wasn't convinced. Mrs Lauder was the fattest woman she had ever seen, and not with the muscle that went with heaving haunches of beef around or smashing twenty-eight-pound blocks of salt to smithereens. Peering through the kitchen window one day, Ellie had come to the conclusion that she was fat because she was bone lazy.

However, cooking was the one subject other than aids to beauty on which Ellie knew her mother was never, ever, wrong, so she said, 'Well, she'll just have to learn, won't she?'

Ondine shrugged. 'Who is to teach her?'

'Really, ma! You, of course!'

'Certainly not! Your papa would not like it. It would not be at all *comme il faut* for an English lady to show that she knew about such things.'

It was an argument Ellie wasn't going to let her get away with. If you brought up your daughter to be accustomed to fine French cooking, it wasn't reasonable to expect her to make do with dust and ashes just because you couldn't be bothered making an effort.

'Yes, but he doesn't *have* to know,' she pointed out to the image in the glass, envying her mother's prettiness, as she always did. 'Anyway, you're not English. And everyone knows that French *gentlemen* are very interested in food. You could make it sound as if French *ladies* are, too.'

She held her breath expectantly.

Her mother had been silent for a long moment. Then, 'I suppose that might be possible,' she had conceded. 'Though not at once. I will have to handle the Lauder woman with tact. And there is nothing in the world more tedious than being tactful to females!'

Then, catching her daughter's eye, she had twinkled for the first time for months and months. 'Come here and let me hug you. You are a most abominable child, but you are clever also and I love you very much.'

18

After a few days of being ignored by her honorary Uncle Gresham – whom it would have been *lèse majesté* to address as Uncle Lucian – and ruthlessly catechised by her honorary Aunt Minerva, Ellie, who hadn't mislaid an aitch for months, was worn out from feverishly reviewing every reply before she opened her mouth to utter it.

But at least the grownups were an affliction only at suppertime. Horace Charles Gresham was a trial for every hour of the day.

Thin, mouse-haired and bespectacled, at seven he already had opinions on everything under the sun and no hesitation about airing them, even if, being a generally amiable and good-mannered child, he did so with a deceptive air of diffidence. His mama, in whose eyes he could do no wrong, considered him a budding genius, and he was inclined to agree with her, although he had yet to decide in which field that genius was to be exercised.

His current interest was in nature study, mainly the smaller fauna. He had a habit that distressed Belinda deeply – and consequently endeared him to Ellie – of allowing frogs to inhabit his pockets, carrying worms around knotted up in his handkerchiefs, and trapping wasps in insecurely stoppered glass jars which he then presented, with pride, for his cousins' closer inspection.

'Take them away, *take them away*,' Belinda screeched at last, 'or I won't like you any more!'

As threats went, it wouldn't have buttered many parsnips with Ellie, but Horace said obligingly, 'Oh, all right. I'm sorry. I didn't mean to upset you.'

Horace never meant to upset anybody, not intentionally, but he had a fine natural talent for doing so unintentionally – and on the afternoon before he left, he excelled himself.

Stealthily pursuing an unusually fine specimen of cockroach, he tiptoed down the stairs to the lower ground floor of the castle, which was virgin territory to him. Two hundred years before, a great wedge of rocky soil had been dug out of the mountainside to make space for Cavalier John's ambitious rebuilding project, and a twenty-foot-high retaining wall had been built to hold back the excavated face. Since the rear ground floor rooms stared across a flagged terrace straight into this wall, they were unsuitable for living accommodation and had therefore been allocated to storerooms, laundry rooms and – Horace sniffed appreciatively – the kitchens. The cockroach, no less apprecia-tive, seemed to know where it was going, and Horace followed.

Ellie, entering the front hall as he left it, was just in time to catch a glimpse of him and, with a squeak of horror, picked up her skirts and raced after him, while Aunt Minerva, observing these manoeuvres from the main staircase, unhesitatingly joined the procession.

A few moments later, Ellie's mother – sleeves rolled up, a large apron over her pink crinolines, and her hair tied back under a napkin – paused in her expert peeling of some calves' sweetbreads to discover that she was being observed by a weedy small boy, her own dismayed daughter, and Minerva Gresham, her worst suspicions confirmed.

'Ha!' said Minerva.

Ondine, professional pride taking precedence over social catas-trophe, ignored her. To the cook she said, 'Bring me the cloth and the weights, woman! *Vite, vite!*' and to the figure by the kitchen range, still more imperiously, 'Stir, man! Stir!'

Minerva was diverted. 'Who is that man?' she demanded, staring at him with revulsion.

It had to be admitted that, small, middle-aged and unprepossessing, the man in question looked very much out of place in the kitchen, being clad in a venerable black serge jacket and waistcoat, trousers whose loud and dandyish checks failed to disguise their decrepitude, a shirt with neither neckcloth nor collar, and a stovepipe hat that was literally green with age.

The only surroundings in which he would have looked *in* place, Ellie had decided when she first saw him, were in the seedier parts of some large city. Well acquainted, in her own youthful way, with the seamy side of life, she thought she had a fairly good idea of what his occupation might have been before he arrived in the Highlands and persuaded the local lairds to club together and employ him (though not as a *commis-chef*) in the glens. He was exactly the kind of man, wearing exactly the kind of clothes, whom she had often seen emerging, dogs at heel, from badger baiting dens and ratting pits in the back streets of London, and she supposed there must be the same kind of places in Glasgow, where he came from. The owner of successful fighting dogs could make quite a bit of money from the betting. Maybe this man's hadn't been successful enough.

In no way disconcerted, the small man grinned at Minerva and addressed her in accents you could have cut with a knife. 'Och, I just came in for a wee cuppy tea, and see what happens! She puts me tae work before you c'n say "S'help me, Bob". That was two hours bye, and my tongue's still hanging out. She's French, and they're fair ignorant about tea, the French, so they are.'

Understanding not one word, Minerva continued to stare. 'Who is that man?' she repeated. 'What is he doing?'

Weakly, Ellie said, 'He's called Hogg. He's the glen foxhunter. He's stirring the béchamel sauce for the fish course at dinner.'

'*Foxhunter?*'

'He is more sensible than the maids,' Ondine declared, 'and he understands what I say, even if I do not understand what *he* says. But perhaps you would prefer to stir the sauce yourself? Or there are quenelles still to be made, and a leg of mutton to be stuffed. The cook is not competent, which is why I am here. I grudge no effort on behalf of Juran's guests. If you do not wish to be of help, then be so good as to leave the kitchen.'

They left.

The immediate results of this regrettable contretemps – the collective responsibility of Ellie, Ondine, Horace and the cockroach – were that Daniel Macmillan snapped Lucian and Minerva Gresham's joint nose off for hinting that his wife was socially inferior to them, and then, privately, nearly came to blows with Ondine for allowing them to find out.

The following day, Mrs Lauder gave in her notice, on the grounds that never before had she been so insulted in her own kitchen and in front of The Quality, too. And a week after that, a replacement arrived who was, if anything, an even worse cook than Mrs Lauder had been.

Ondine said it was a judgement, and never in her life would she enter a kitchen again.

Ellie giggled to herself off and on for days at the memory of Aunt Minerva's face.

19

And then, suddenly, it was November, and the world stopped turning.

It was back to the six long months of the Juran winter, with no comforts, no pleasures and no people. It was back to being up at six-thirty in the dark, to harp practice and brown stew and mending sheets. It was back to an emptiness of learning by rote, sitting by the tiny fire, going to bed early.

But Ellie wasn't depressed any more – or only a little and only when the mist rolled in from the sea to cocoon the castle in a soft, suffocating nothingness. Then, her nostrils would fill with the dear, familiar, sulphurous smell of a bustling London fog, and she would bury her face in her arms and weep.

Luckily, it didn't happen very often and by the time another two winters had passed, and she had discovered that winter was a far better season than summer for watching the wild creatures of the glens, all that the mist aroused in her was impatience. So eager was she to learn everything there was to learn that Miss Irving finally released her from her unproductive drawing lessons to slip outdoors, well wrapped up, and watch the eagles and red deer that had moved down from the high tops; the buzzards and kestrels perched watchfully on fencing posts; the bushy-tailed wildcats and big hill foxes; the playful stoats in ermine and mountain hares in their winter white; the hungry badgers foraging and the pine martens swinging in the trees, their orange cravats bright as bunting as they leapt on the unwary tits and wrens that were their prey.

It was wonderful beyond Ellie's imagining on crisp, cold days when the sun shone, and she yearned for each day of shining to go on for ever. But, gradually, she began to see that there was beauty in other kinds of weather, too, even in the brutal, battering wind and rain that had greeted her on her first arrival at Juran and given her so distorted a view of castle and landscape. She knew, now, that the castle itself was grim and forbidding only when the lime harling that coated its outer walls had been soaked through to the stone beneath; in good weather it was an entirely different place, trim and bright and white. And although the hill behind might sometimes look as if it were clothed in used tea leaves and sodden coal dust, more often it was a tapestry of colours that changed magically with the seasons. In the fullness of spring every conceivable shade of green was there, fading upwards through a peaty darkness to the last of the snows. In the flat noon light of summer the greens submerged themselves into a soft amethyst haze. And in autumn, as the sun dropped lower in the sky, the whole face of the mountain became a vast cameo of sculpture and shadow, purple and flame, amber and gold.

Ellie was puzzled that no one else, not even Philip Roy, ever remarked on the beauty of the landscape – they were too used to it, she supposed – but there wasn't much else, she had discovered, that escaped Philip's notice.

Their first encounter on the hill above Corrie Eileirg had been followed by others, although no one else knew about them since they took care to meet privately in a little dell where the boundary of Altsigh ran with that of Juran. Ellie had said nothing to anyone at the castle because she badly wanted a friend of her own and was almost sure that their meetings would be forbidden, while Philip, aware of how his mother felt about the second Mrs Macmillan, considerately refrained from troubling her with the knowledge that he had constituted himself guide and mentor to that lady's daughter.

Although he was away at school for much of the time, as the weeks and months slipped by and the seasons came and went Ellie learned a great deal from him, especially about the theory and practice of stalking, his particular passion; about human scent and air currents, tiny wrong notes in the music of wind and water, minute inconsistencies in the movement of heather and bracken – all the things that made deer vaguely or actively suspicious and kept them on the move.

'And every time they move, of course,' Philip explained, enjoying himself hugely in the unfamiliar rôle of dominie, 'they're liable to bring themselves down wind of you, and you have to calculate the odds and survey the terrain all over again.'

Tagging along at Philip's heels, Ellie encouraged him to lecture her on Nature and wildlife, instruct her in land management – which, as his father's heir, he claimed to know all about – and impress her with his opinions on world affairs, which he stated as if they had been handed down to him, personally, from Olympus. Provided she spread a thick layer of honey on everything she said, she had discovered she could handle him quite well.

And, in fact, although he lorded it over her and was by no means a kindred spirit, he was really quite kind and lent her a wonderful assortment of things to read – respectable things like *Tom Brown's Schooldays* and *Eric, or Little by Little* and less respectable ones like penny dreadfuls and spine-chilling tales about Varney the Vampire and Sweeney Todd. She had to read them under the bedclothes, in case Miss Irving found out.

They were a great comfort to her when she lost Fonsy, who went exploring one day and never returned. Ellie hoped he had found a lady friend but feared it more likely that a buzzard had found him.

20

By the time her twelfth birthday approached, Ellie knew far more about Juran than either Belinda or William, though in general she tried not to let it show. Their carping had become routine rather than actively spiteful over the years and she had learned that life was more comfortable when she avoided offering them provocation.

But then, one day, she did.

It was the day before her birthday and Belinda was building a sandcastle on the beach while William blew soap bubbles through a little clay pipe. Ellie sat above them on the hill thinking that it was high time she Made Her Presence Felt. She was tired of still being treated as just one of the children, of still being made to feel that she didn't belong, and although she knew she couldn't expect William to pay attention to her – after all, he was a boy, which made him superior by definition – Belinda was younger than she was and ought to be showing her some respect. The trouble was that Ellie couldn't think how to bring that happy situation about.

After a while, shading her eyes against the sun, she realised that something interesting was happening down below. What she had taken to be a fishing smack out at sea had changed course and was sailing into the northern end of the bay. Closer in, it proved not to be a fishing smack after all.

Leaping to her feet, she went scampering down the hill, white smocked pinafore and pink cotton skirts flying above her neat white pantaloons, one hand outstretched to preserve her balance and the other clamping her widebrimmed straw hat to her head.

As she pranced across the grassy dunes of the machair and out on to the smooth, silver sands fringing Juran's bay, William drew some sudsy water into his pipe and blew what was clearly meant to be a raspberry at her – though it came out as a feeble gurgling noise followed by a misshapen soap bubble which emerged reluctantly from the bowl, clung to it for a wavering moment, and then toppled over and collapsed like a deflated balloon. Ellie smiled at him.

'The builders have come,' Belinda announced, showing off as always. She tossed some more sand on to her sandcastle and whacked it with the flat of her spade to make it stay. 'To build the jetty. They're from Glasgow. My papa says he won't have somebody local making a botched job of it.' She whacked the sandcastle again.

'A jetty?' Ellie repeated airily. 'Oh, good. My mama *will* be pleased. She very much dislikes having to land from fishy-smelling rowing boats, even though less fastidious persons are not troubled by it.'

Then, nose in the air, she stalked off before Belinda had time to work out what 'fastidious' meant.

21

The builder's smack was already tied up about two hundred yards along the beach, and its crew were sitting on top of the cargo as if unloading was a matter of no urgency. One of them, mopping the back of his neck with a huge, filthy red kerchief, was eyeing – in a considering kind of way – two local men who were stretched out taking their ease on the edge of the sand.

If he was expecting them to jump to their feet and volunteer, Ellie could have told him he was going to be out of luck. The one in the old tweed trousers, homespun blue shirt and pompommed tam-o'-shanter was Jamie McLeod, the village piper who, for fear of spoiling the delicacy of his touch on the chanter, unfailingly declined any labour harder than raising a glass of whisky to his lips.

The other man was small, middle-aged, and seedy, clad in ancient check trousers and an even more ancient stovepipe hat, and there was a pack of mangy terriers sprawled asleep on the grass behind him.

'Aye, aye,' said the builder at last, inclining his head slightly to the two idlers.

'Aye, aye,' responded Jamie McLeod.

'Aye, aye,' said the little foxhunter.

The courtesies having been exchanged, all three men relapsed into silence.

Ellie decided she might as well sit down. It didn't look as if anything was going to happen for a while.

Minutes passed, and it was the builder who weakened first. Giving a thoughtful sniff, he transferred his gaze from the waiting planks and joists to the castle nestling in the shelter of the hill.

65

'Bonny place,' he said. 'Decent folk, are they? Wud they give us a wee dram, d'ye think? Thirsty work, unloading.'

The smell of whisky that already surrounded him would have felled an ox at a hundred paces and unloading appeared to be the last thing on his mind.

Hogg shook his head. 'Maybe offer you a drink o' water.'

The builder sniffed again. There was another silence, then, 'Must be awful well off tae own a place like yon,' he surmised.

'Maybe aye, maybe no,' said Hogg.

Ellie glared at him. There wasn't any maybe about it. Of course her pa was well off!

Absently, the builder tipped up a plank and leaned on it. 'The harling could do wi' attention, mind you. Can see the cracks from here. And I'd bet ye a sovereign tae a sausage yon roof needs work on it. I could make a special rate for that. My prices is aye fair. Anyone'll tell ye.'

Ellie didn't think it was right for her father to have to pay this man just for standing around finding fault, and since she was the only member of the family present, it seemed to be up to her to do something about it.

'Do you know where the jetty's supposed to go?' she intervened in her most grownup voice. 'There's no use unloading if you're in the wrong place.'

A pair of bloodshot eyes under sandy brows swivelled towards her, summed her up, and decided to ignore her.

'Queer thing,' the man said, his gaze once more on the castle. 'I've never been here before, but it looks awful familiar – all they towers and fancy windows and jaggy what-ye-ma-collums.'

Hogg nodded his stovepipe hat. 'Battlements,' he said helpfully. 'And ye're thinking of Inveraray.'

'The Duke of Argyll's place? Jings, aye! Ye're right!'

'Copied,' Hogg said. 'Anything the Duke could do, old Jamie Macmillan tried to do better. Daft bugger.'

Ellie glared at him again, offended not by his language but because she didn't think it was right that a shifty little Glasgow foxhunter should be talking like that about her great-great-grandfather, especially to a set of perfect strangers. It was to be years before she discovered that criticising the Macmillans was a cottage industry in the glens, and that everyone for miles around knew more about what went on in the castle than the people who lived there.

'Mind you,' Hogg went on, virtuously seeing both sides of the question, 'It'd give him an interest, something to occupy him. There's not much else to do hereabouts. In fact, it can be gey boring.' His yellowish eyes shifting to Ellie, he gave a gaptoothed grin and added, 'Wee Ellie can vouch for that!'

It was too much. Wee Ellie hopped on her high horse and said crossly, 'I don't think you should talk to the laird's daughter like that!'

22

A voice behind her shrieked, 'You're *not* the laird's daughter!'

Ellie had been too absorbed to hear Belinda approaching over the sand, pattering along between her father and one of the mournful men in tweed hats whom Ellie now knew to be the grieve, or estate overseer, John McBride.

'The laird's only got *one* daughter, and it's *me*!' Belinda shrieked.

Ellie hesitated but then, rebuking herself for cowardice, squared her shoulders and embarked on Making Her Presence Felt. 'I'm his daughter, too.'

'No, you're not. You're only a stepdaughter. You don't count!' Belinda's voice was piercing, her round white face livid with spite under the poke of her bonnet.

Hogg's pack of terriers, rudely awakened from their sleep in the marram grass, rose and stretched and began squabbling among themselves, rolling over, yapping and snapping. Hogg fetched the nearest one a clout with his fist and yelled, 'Hold your wheesht, will you?'

It didn't reduce the rumpus in the least, and the dog at Daniel Macmillan's heels – his favourite pointer, Bess, who hated the terriers – added to the commotion by setting up a vigorous barking.

Then the builder's crew joined in. Galvanised by the arrival of the ruling classes, they began tossing planks and timbers overboard at amazing speed and to resounding effect.

Ellie knew she was at a disadvantage and she could see that her father wasn't going to give her any help. He was much too busy shouting at the builders to stop because they were in the wrong place. The jetty was supposed to go at the other end of the bay.

Bitterly, Ellie reflected that he would stop ignoring her, soon enough, if she came out there and then with, 'No, I'm not his stepdaughter. I'm his proper daughter, and I've been bleeding well legitimated – and if you don't like it you can bleeding well stow your gab, or hook off.'

But she didn't. Staring straight in Belinda's eyes, she said quietly but with total conviction, 'I *do* count. And I'm older than you are, too, and from now on you're going to have to start being nicer to me and doing what I say.'

Even as she wondered what on earth had possessed her, Belinda's lips vanished between her teeth, her eyes dilated until the whites were visible all round, and she let out a strange, squeaky growl. Then, clawing hands outstretched, she launched herself across the yard of sand that lay between them.

She was two inches taller and almost a stone heavier than Ellie, and before Ellie knew what was happening she was flat on her back with Belinda on top of her, pulling her hair, pummelling her in the face, screaming all the while, 'You're *not* the laird's daughter, you're not, you're not, you're not . . .'

Ellie couldn't shift her, and because of the way Belinda was kneeling on her couldn't even get her hands free to push or scratch or do any of the things that might have protected her from the assault. All she could do was wriggle furiously, and wonder when one of the grownups was going to come and haul Belinda off. None of them did.

It soon became clear that no one was going to, either, and Ellie had to give up hope of turning the attack to her own advantage. It was a clear waste of time persevering with the rôle of demure and docile little thing helplessly suffering under the fists of a great big bully of a stepsister.

When Belinda landed her an uninhibited clout in the eye, it was the last straw. Ellie kicked out violently, but not at Belinda. Her foot, swiftly extended and even more swiftly retracted, caught one of Hogg's terriers hard on its behind, and the terrier, justifiably incensed, whipped round with a yelp and sank its teeth into Belinda's button-booted ankle. Belinda let out an ear-splitting squawk and, distracted, gave Ellie the opportunity she had been waiting for. Weaned on juvenile wars in the back streets of Soho, she did what she had to do briskly and efficiently. Reaching up, she clamped her fingers round Belinda's nose, and began twisting it as hard as if she were going to screw it right off.

Belinda flapped her arms wildly, like a hen fleeing the axe, and screeched for all she was worth.

It gave Ellie much satisfaction, but she knew when to stop, and by the time Belinda's howls began to fade, Ellie was standing over her looking down with an expression that – wild hair, marked face and scratched arms notwithstanding – conveyed nothing but a mild, reproachful concern.

The builder was saying, '. . . and if ye put the jetty here, it'd be handy for the village as well as the castle.'

'Dash it all,' said the laird. 'Will you stop arguing! I want it at . . .'

Belinda tugged at his buff linen coat tails, moaning, 'Papa! Papa! She hit me.'

'Don't do that,' he said testily. 'Anyway, you hit her first.'

'But only because she's not the laird's daughter. That's me, isn't it? It is, it *is*!'

'I said, don't *do* that! Dashed silly question, anyway.'

'But papa . . .'

'That's enough!' He gave a gusty, long-suffering sigh. 'Now, be quiet. I don't want to hear any more about it.' Then he turned back to the builder and started arguing again.

Ellie was annoyed that she hadn't won. But she hadn't lost, either. And she *had* made her presence felt – a little bit.

She wished Hogg wouldn't just sit there with that knowing yellow grin on his face. Why didn't he go and hunt some foxes?

Hogg, as it happened, was grinning because he had noted her battle tactics and been pleased to have his suspicions confirmed. He had observed Ellie more closely than she knew during the years of her sojourn at Juran, and had come to the conclusion that she was a spunky wee thing under her prim and proper façade. He'd wondered where she'd got her early upbringing, and today had given him his answer. Screwing the other lassie's nose had been a real gutter trick.

He winked at her.

<h1 style="text-align:center">23</h1>

Next day, her birthday, Ellie was sitting with Philip on the heights of Carn Beg looking out to sea, though with only one eye. The other, a symphony in red, black and purple, was three-quarters closed, and the silken blue sea was the only thing she could look at with any comfort.

Philip, whose father's estate lay wholly inland, had said he wouldn't mind resting his eyes, too, and it was understandable because the West Highlands in early summer were among the most garish places on earth. Even here, on the coast, it was blinding the minute you took your eyes away from the water. The brilliant white of the beach was striped with ordered ranks of seaweeds in orange and rose and ochre. Flag irises sheeted the foreshore and the edges of the burns with brilliant yellow, clashing nastily with the furious magenta of the foxgloves. The vivid yellows of tormentil and buttercup argued with the brightness of the bluebells and the intense pink of wild roses.

But it was the greens that really hurt, varied and virulent and tropically lush. Looking at them was like wearing emerald spectacles.

'I envy this place,' Philip Roy said with his usual candour. 'Not just being able to see the sea, but smell it. Juran's got its own smell, quite different from Altsigh's.'

'Salt and seaweed, pines and bog myrtle, peat and heather.' Ellie reeled the words off fluently but without enthusiasm.

'No need to sound like that about it. You ought to be grateful to live here. Juran's a nice little estate. Wouldn't mind having it myself.'

He might as well, Ellie thought grumpily. He couldn't make a worse job of it than Wailing Willy when he inherited. It wasn't fair that boys should always be preferred to girls. *She* would know exactly how to manage Juran – how to improve it, even.

Philip was still talking. '. . . could do a lot to smarten the place up and make it more productive. Your stepfather should be raising oats and barley down on those meadows by the river.'

'Mr McBride says he'd have to fence them. It would cost a lot.'

'Nonsense. Get the tenants from the village to do it,' Philip told her robustly. 'They're an idle bunch. I doubt they even pay your stepfather his rents, do they?'

'I don't know.'

They could just see the heather-thatched roofs of the village over the headland whose rocks, crusted with palest green lichens and rosy with sea pinks, formed the northern boundary of Juran's bay, cutting it off from the wide, sleek waters of the Firth of Lorn and the hills of Mull and Morven that lay beyond; hills that rolled on and on, higher and higher, paler and paler in the featureless noon light. It was as if some giant hand had pushed on the edge of a great sheet of purple gauze, forcing it into creases that, shallow at first, became steeper and steeper until at last they turned into mountains.

'. . . important to ensure the rents are collected on quarter day,' Philip was saying.

Ellie could feel her foot going to sleep and stretched out a leg to wake it up. As she moved, her aching gaze came to rest on something she didn't understand, something further over on the hillside that her single eye couldn't decipher, a rusty patch in the prevailing green.

Out of habit, she said, 'What's that?'

'What? Where?'

Philip screwed up his marmalade eyes against the sun and, after a moment, murmured, 'Oh-ho!' Then, with extreme care, he began to rise. 'Come on. Quietly, now, and keep your mouth shut.'

It was a red deer fawn, only a few hours old, curled up in a hollow no larger than itself. The first Ellie had ever seen.

She couldn't suppress a gasp of delight, but the little animal seemed quite unafraid. It was the daintiest thing imaginable, a soft reddish-brown colour above and golden-beige below, with rows of white dapples on its back. Its graceful, creamy muzzle didn't even quiver as she bent over it, nor was there so much as a flicker of the gentle brown eyes, set in sockets as slender and curved as willow leaves.

'It's pretending,' Philip whispered. 'Pretending it isn't there. It's the deer calf's only defence when its mother's away. She's probably grazing in the next corrie.'

It was the *loveliest* thing. Ellie yearned to stroke it but she didn't need Philip to tell her that she shouldn't, because its mother wouldn't like it. Instead, she watched it for a while and then very slowly and reluctantly backed away.

24

In those few, brief minutes everything had changed for her.

Quite without warning, and certainly without understanding it, she not only saw beauty in what lay around her, but *felt* it – as if, by some strange alchemy and independently of will and thought, her brains and her flesh and her bones had become soaked in it.

Mouth half open in astonishment, she looked round at the amethyst hills and the blue, blue sea, at the silver sands and the vivid, violent new greens of bracken, moss and heather. A few minutes earlier, she had been no more than an observer, surveying a spectacularly beautiful place on a spectacularly beautiful day as if it were an unusually fine painting which she was very happy to admire but had no thought of owning. Someone who had spent three long years learning everything it was humanly possible to learn – except how to feel.

Now – all sense and reason submerged in an ecstatic flooding of primeval instinct – she was able to believe for the very first time, really believe, that here were her roots, here was her home. This was where her father and grandfather and great-grandfather belonged and had always belonged. And since she was her father's really, truly daughter, she belonged here, too. She belonged to Juran, and Juran to her.

Whatever anyone said to the contrary.

Philip Roy, watching her, couldn't think what had got into the girl. Here he was, all ready to explain everything he might previously have omitted to tell her about deer calves, and she looked as if she had forgotten he was there.

'Had a brainstorm?' he enquired huffily.

But she didn't hear him. She was too busy discovering what it was to be completely and irrevocably in love.

CHAPTER FOUR

I

Lazily, Gino Venturi wondered where young Sophie had got to. Archie Macmillan had said, 'Keep an eye on her – if you can,' which in Gino's view pretty well absolved him from responsibility. In any case, trying to stop Sophie from getting into trouble was like trying to stop a firecracker from jumping, and Gino Venturi was not a man to waste energy on unproductive enterprises.

Archie Macmillan's junior partner was quite unlike most people's idea of an Italian, being a comfortably fleshed six feet tall, with ice blue eyes, honey-coloured hair, and almost no trace of an accent. One of his better-educated mistresses had said he made her think of a Roman emperor with dimples, and he cherished the description.

He also looked quite unlike the majority of Hong Kong traders, for whom it was a matter of pride to ignore the heat and humidity of the South China seas and behave, dress and dine as if they were still at home in northern Europe. Fearing the slur of having gone native – or 'gone fanty' as old India hands put it – they were in the habit of turning out in all the suffocating formality of beard and whiskers, top hats, starched collars and four-in-hand ties, with lapelled waistcoats and dark serge jackets buttoned all the way from collarbone to mid-thigh. Nor were their manners less rigid than their dress.

Gino, in contrast, favoured linen suits and minimum starch, which, with his easy smile and relaxed manner, gave him a friendly, vaguely rumpled air that he cultivated assiduously. His fellow traders read this as indicating, at best, commercial innocence and, at worst, a reprehensible lack of self-discipline, with the result that they did not take him very seriously or waste their valuable time trying to stab him in the back. Which suited him admirably. As the third of the eleven children of a Milanese pasta merchant – a background he never revealed – he had an exceedingly shrewd head for figures and knew better than anyone in Hong Kong the profits to be made out of cents, rather than the dollars that dominated the ledgers of Macmillan and Venturi's rivals.

The truth was that Archie Macmillan was the figurehead of the partnership and Gino Venturi the brains. It was his talent alone that had kept the firm afloat ever since Archie Macmillan had made him a partner at the age of nineteen – he was still only twenty-seven – and more particularly since they had abandoned Canton seven years earlier, after the fire, for the infinitely more competitive conditions of Hong Kong.

Now, absently scanning the bustling green oasis of the Happy Valley racecourse, Gino wished it were he rather than his partner who was down at the bank in Pedder Street trying to squeeze a loan out of Rainer Blake, the cleverest fellow Gino knew (other than himself). Archie Macmillan would be no match for Blake if he chose to put him through the hoop.

This, the last day of the Chinese New Year meeting, had been the only time Blake could spare to see him, and when the most astute financier in Hong Kong took that line the petitioner didn't have much choice in the matter.

Even Archie, easygoing soul that he was, had been mildly annoyed. 'Damn it all! Why can't Blake take a holiday like everyone else? We'll be the only fellows in the place to miss the last day of the races.'

He hadn't been far wrong.

For two decades, the British had been perched on their tiny island of inhospitable rock off the Chinese coast, unable to expand until just over three years earlier, when they had bullied the Imperial Court into ceding them the additional lands of Stonecutters' Island and mainland Kowloon. Now, the boundaries of the colony of Hong Kong encompassed thirty-six square miles of sovereign British territory, housing a population of two thousand Westerners and sixty times that number of Chinese immigrants – and all of them mad about racing.

Everyone from despised coolies to lordly taipans seemed to be crammed into Happy Valley today, most of them armed with umbrellas against the noon heat. To Gino Venturi, from his position on the hill above the Parsee burying ground, the place looked as if it were populated by animated mushrooms.

The Chinese New Year meeting was the high spot of the racing year and the little valley, in the embrace of its green hills, was at its liveliest and most picturesque. It was a perfect February morning, warm, cloudless and blue. Service uniforms glittered, plumes waved,

Chinese silks gleamed. Off course, small boys played shuttlecock with their feet and older ones gambled on coins sliding off a sieve.

Gino, shading his eyes against the sun, was mildly surprised not to see Sophie among them. Neither – though less surprisingly – was she visible among the ladies who, in their prettiest dresses and most fetching bonnets, were picking their way daintily down from the grandstand, with its ornately carved verandahs and sun blinds, to the refreshment booths set up by the taipans of the great merchant houses.

On the course itself, ponies from the plains of Central Asia – unsightly nags that were less ponies than long, low, short-legged horses – went charging round at a great rate, noses down like bloodhounds on the scent, the feet of their tall, gentlemen-amateur jockeys almost touching the ground. Those jockeys who survived the experience were prone to describe it as 'a most interesting ride', while those who did not limped off the course alternately laughing and cursing about treacherous natures and iron mouths.

Gino Venturi rode fifteen stone, otherwise he'd have been down there with them. As it was, he had leisure to admire the sparkling vista of the harbour beyond, the open stretch of water between Hong Kong and Kowloon that was full, as always, of shipping of every description, from sampans and junks by the hundred to old-fashioned windjammers, clippers, barques, schooners, steam frigates and dis-masted storage hulks. Anchored in the lee of East Point he noticed the *Meall* and the *Corran*, two of Macmillan and Venturi's steam traders whose captains, the brothers Lao and Li Chang, were down there somewhere among the mushrooms.

Across the channel, on the Chinese mainland, the clouds had melted away from the hills of the Nine Dragons, the hills that still – symbolically if no longer in political reality – acted as a barricade protecting the four hundred million subjects of the Celestial Emperor from the contaminating influence of the two thousand fidgety foreign devils on their little footholds of rock.

Gino sometimes wondered how the Celestial Emperor would feel if he knew that the great majority of the foreign devils had no desire to contaminate his subjects with Western habits or Christian morality. All they wanted was to make money out of them.

He stirred and stretched himself, like the large and amiable cat he so much resembled. It was hot out in the open, even for an Italian, and besides he was hungry and thought he could fancy a morsel of Jardine Matheson's excellent pigeon pie and a few glasses of Dent's champagne. The taipans were always lavish with their hospitality on occasions like these.

2

'So the prospects are first rate,' Archie Macmillan said. He had a pleasant voice, warm and dark brown, faintly Scots; a voice that, whatever the words it uttered, reeked of its owner's desire to be on good terms with everybody.

In the relative coolness of Blake's office near the new Clock Tower – which, with its balconied rotunda, looked as if it had been transplanted straight from Tuscany – the banker sat back in his chair and tapped the ivory pen holder lightly against his lips.

'You're wasting my time and your breath, Macmillan. Unless you tell me a whole hell of a lot more than you've done so far, I'm unlikely to see my way to helping you.'

Despite his words, Blake was smiling inside, well aware that his crisp way of doing business always disconcerted Archie Macmillan, and that the unnatural silence in the office was disconcerting him even more. On a normal working day, the long, narrow upstairs room at the bank would have been deafening with the staccato chatter of Chinese voices and the shouts of Europeans; with the jingle of Mexican silver dollars being filtered through the fingers of the shroffs, the coin valuers, and the fast, rhythmic thud as the assayed coins were chopmarked; with the rattle and clunk of strings of copper cash being weighed; above all, with the flick-flick of the abacus at every highstooled high desk along the considerable length of the accounting office of the Hong Kong and South China Branch of the Clyde River Bank of Glasgow, Scotland.

No more than his visitor did Blake relish being tied to the office on a brilliant cold-weather day such as this, but it was the penalty he paid for commitment to his chosen work. Whatever he encouraged his clients to think, banking wasn't just a matter of sitting behind a desk adding up figures.

Banking ran in Blake's blood, although he had deliberately distanced himself from it in the first few years of his adult life, fearful of committing himself. The Clyde River Bank had been something unique when it was set up in 1788, the first internationally connected banking house in Britain, with two Scots partners (the Campbell brothers), one Italian (Lorenzo Landi) and one renegade American of

76

Dutch origins (Reiner Zwart). Now, almost seventy years later, the Campbells were still Campbells and the Landis, Landis, but when the partners had decided to convert from merchant to joint stock banking, Reiner Zwart the Second had thought it wise to translate himself into English. 'Rainer Black or Blake', he had said with his slanting smile, sounded less exotic, more reliable.

Reliability had never been the family's strong suit, or not in the eyes of the orthodox. Although the Zwarts had been New Yorkers since the days when it had been New Amsterdam, Blake's grandfather had chosen the wrong side – the royal side – in the American War of Independence and finished up having to flee to Canada. Half a dozen years there had led to him taking ship for Europe and ending up, logically enough, in Scotland, which had strong ties with Canada. Reiner Zwart the First had had a clever financial brain, but it had been left to his son, who was not only clever but farsighted, to re-establish relations with America.

The third of the dynasty had been a Blake since birth, a late-born child raised mainly in Boston, to which his father had retired. There Rainer Blake the Third had learned everything there was to know about the China trade, although it had been in India that, by the age of twenty-three, he had made his own, nabob's fortune. In the process, he had learned that making money was easy if you had the right kind of mind, and boring if you had the wrong kind.

Qualifying on both counts, he had been driven in the end to fall in with Colin Campbell's suggestion that he might amuse himself for a while by supervising the Clyde River Bank's expanding operations in the Orient. The suggestion had been made casually enough, but Blake knew Colin Campbell too well to take what he said at face value. Unemphatic he might be, but he was possessed of one of the most acute banking brains of his generation.

It had worked well, and it wasn't Colin Campbell's fault that, for Blake, it didn't work quite well enough. Initiating projects, developing them and seeing them through was satisfying in its way, but would have been more satisfying if everything hadn't always gone so smoothly; it was a disadvantage to be the kind of man whom people rarely argued with. The bank's operations in the East were undoubtedly flourishing under Blake's direction, but what he himself lacked, and badly wanted, was other people to pit his wits against.

Archie Macmillan wasn't a candidate.

3

Archie, hoping that Gino Venturi had remembered to lay a bet on the second race for him, said a little querulously, 'But I *have* told you.'

'You've told me nothing worth telling, not even what your mysterious collateral is. And if you don't tell me that, how can I even judge whether you're entitled to mortgage it?'

'You have my word!'

Blake was thirty years old, lean, dark and ironic, with a nasty cutting edge, and it always came as a surprise to Archie when he did anything as human as laugh. He did so now. 'Well, I guess that's something.'

Not for the first time, Archie found himself wondering why the Clyde River Bank of Glasgow, Scotland, should be represented in Hong Kong by an American. It made as much sense as Sweden and Norway naming Francis Blackwell Forbes, another Bostonian, as their consul in Shanghai, or Russia appointing Mr Heard to Hong Kong, or the Austrians choosing what-was-the-fellow's-name to represent them in Canton.

No one had ever offered Archie a sinecure and there were times when he felt discriminated against. He had felt especially discriminated against during these last months when no one would put up the fresh injection of capital Macmillan and Venturi needed unless the firm was able to offer substantial collateral. Which it didn't have. In Archie's view, if he and Venturi had had the collateral, they wouldn't have needed the loan, and not all Gino Venturi's patient explanations had been able to persuade him otherwise.

But just recently a solution had occurred to him. There was one thing he had never borrowed against.

Blake's long mouth curled. 'Come on, man! Out with it. Bankers are close kin to priests. Absolute confidentiality. And today, there's not even a soul here to eavesdrop, supposing they felt inclined.'

Archie had known he wasn't going to get away with talking airy nothings to Blake, but it had been worth a try.

'Oh, well, all right,' he said with his most disarming grin. 'It's like this, you see. I happen to be the black sheep of the family . . .'

4

When he was little more than a boy, Archie had sown one handful of wild oats too many. There had been nothing vicious about it, nothing unnatural, only a precocious fondness for girls, but it wasn't the kind of sin that his father had been prepared to countenance. Although Archie knew that the old man had himself broken most of the Ten Commandments in his day, and might have forgiven – even commended – his firstborn son for gaming, or coveting his neighbour's goods, or even bearing false witness, he had been about as sympathetic as an Old Testament prophet in the matter of sexual indulgence.

'And it wasn't even my fault,' Archie said. 'Females just seemed to gravitate naturally towards me. Still do, as a matter of fact.'

Everything had come to a head when he was seventeen. There had been the threat of a shotgun wedding, and his father had bought him a passage to India, given him a draft for a hundred pounds, and said, 'Don't come back until you have mended your ways.'

'Well, I tell you, Blake,' Archie said, 'I dashed well resented it. That's no way to treat a high-spirited lad. So I decided I was going to make myself a fortune and then – *then*, mark you, not before – go back home in style and show them all how they had misjudged me.'

'Very understandable,' Blake said drily. 'And who is, or are, "them all"?'

'Just my father and younger brother, really. My mother died when he was born.'

'I see. And you were exiled in. . . ?'

'The year of the Charter Act, 1833.'

'So you haven't been home for thirty years?'

This unsubtle reminder that he hadn't yet succeeded in making the requisite fortune escaped Archie completely. 'No. Haven't even been in touch.'

'Go on.'

'Well, I had a couple of apprentice years in India but I kept hearing about the wealth that lay waiting in Canton, now that the Charter Act had opened up the China trade to independent enterprise. So I thought, "Let's try it!" and I did. All in all, things didn't go too badly but, after the fire in '56 – well, you remember! you were there – it seemed a good idea to make the move to Hong Kong.'

Blake remembered the fire at Canton very well, and especially he remembered salvaging Macmillan's brat of a daughter, Sophie. Who, by all accounts, was as much of a handful now as she had been then.

'Anyway, you know the firm's record here well enough,' Archie went on. 'I don't need to explain all the ins and outs of it to you.' Neither did he see any need to explain that it was the fuel of his resentment alone that had carried him through, the only deep emotion other than love for his daughter that had ever possessed him. Whatever the reason, he was now senior partner and two thirds owner of what even a steely-eyed, Scots-American banker was bound to recognise as a moderately successful business in exports and imports, with a small fleet of junks and steamships operating in the coastal trade. Macmillan and Venturi might not carry as much weight as Jardine Matheson, but . . .

'So,' he concluded, 'if you do decide to let us have a loan you won't lose by it. With the telegraph probably coming soon, even middle-sized firms like ours will have access to the kind of information that only the great hongs had before. The whole pattern of trade is changing, opening up, and we want to be able to take advantage of it.'

Smiling his most clubbable smile, Archie straightened his back and tugged the waistcoat down over his stomach, which wasn't as flat as once it had been. He would soon be fifty, and wasn't looking forward to it. 'You see what I'm after, don't you?'

Rainer Blake studied him thoughtfully.

'Oh, yes,' he said. 'It's clear enough. What you're after is a private and unpublicised mortgage on this ancestral home of yours at – Juran, did you say?'

5

Gino Venturi wasn't altogether surprised that Archie Macmillan still hadn't put in an appearance at Happy Valley by the time the last race began, though it was the most entertaining of all and easily the best for a flutter. Even the colony's energetic governor, Sir Hercules Robinson, newly returned from England and itching to be back at his desk, kept his scarlet-curtained sedan and eight bearers waiting until it should be over.

It was a race for Chinese stable lads, and the spectators entered wholeheartedly into the spirit of the thing, placing bets not only on which would come in first but which would come in at all. Foiled, by and large, in their attempts to unseat the gentlemen amateurs, the ponies were raring to test the mettle of less gentlemanly and more genuinely amateur prey.

Year after year, they succeeded in grounding several of the stable lads before the race even began, and this year was no exception. Thirteen ponies started and five riders immediately fell off, pluckily remounting – to howls of encouragement from the spectators – and thundering off in pursuit of the field. As it happened, the field was not very far ahead, there being a holdup in the traffic caused by two of the ponies beginning to buck furiously, while a third, having perfected the art of rearing at the wrong end, had chosen to rid himself of his jockey by shooting him smartly forward over withers and head. The boy landed on terra firma with a hearty bump and an expression of such comical astonishment on his face that the spectators were convulsed.

And so it went on. By the time the ponies had covered a third of the mile-long course with their peculiar daisycutting stride, five of them were riderless. By halfway round, the number had increased to eight. Coming up to the finish, only four riders remained, hanging on gamely, slight figures in blue tunics and trousers, buttoned hats blown away and long black pigtails flying out behind in the wind of their passing.

Gino Venturi was standing by the finishing post, cheering with the rest, when he found himself being addressed by the governor.

'I fancy the one on the near side, don't you, Venturi?' said Sir Hercules, who had the born diplomat's memory for names and faces. 'Number Six. He's really putting his mind to it, and that's what you need with these brutes. Otherwise they take charge.'

'Yes, indeed, Your Excellency,' Gino agreed, flattered. 'Doesn't do to let your attention wander.'

The words were barely out of his mouth when Number Six, raising his head to see how far it was to the finishing post, let both of his admirers down sadly by removing one hand from the reins and clapping it over his mouth as if overcome by some powerful emotion.

'Oh, dear,' said Sir Hercules, amused. 'Swallowed a fly, do you think?'

Gino swore under his breath.

The China pony stopped dead in its tracks. If it could have laughed, it would.

Gino and the governor winced in sympathy as the rider was decanted at their feet in a flurry of legs and arms and unravelling pigtail. Kindly, Sir Hercules leaned over to help the lad up.

Unfortunately, it turned out not to be a lad at all. It turned out to be a fifteen-year-old young lady, unmistakably European under the coating of dust and yellow paint, her eyes wide with horrified embarrassment.

A scandalised female voice close by exclaimed, 'Sophie Macmillan! *Just* as one might have expected!'

6

Having dropped in at the pillared and porticoed Club on the corner of Wyndham Street for a reviver after his discussions with Rainer Blake, Archie Macmillan arrived home at Caine Road late but in excellent spirits to find his daughter waiting for him in the hall, a picture of scrubbed and shining innocence.

Approvingly, he surveyed the long, smooth dark hair tied back with blue ribbon, the pink cheeks, the gentian eyes bright above the slender, matching dress with its puffed shoulders and long tight sleeves. His daughter was an exceedingly pretty girl, and in another year or so would be a ravishing young woman. It surprised him vaguely, because she took after her mother who, while formally beautiful, had been subdued and rather colourless. He himself – though a handsome fellow, as a succession of charming ladies had assured him – had contributed little to his daughter's looks other than the colour of his eyes and his air of style.

'You look nice,' he said as, waving the servants away, she relieved him of top hat, gloves and stick and then rose on tiptoe to kiss his cheek. 'And what have you been up to, eh?'

The question was rhetorical, since he already knew that she had been going with her amah to Happy Valley, so he didn't bother to wait for an answer. 'I've had a first-rate day, myself. I think I can safely say that our worries are over.'

Being a confirmed optimist, it had taken Archie no more than an hour to translate Blake's whimsical but provisionally favourable decision into an expression of unqualified approval, even of congratulation on his, Archie Macmillan's, acumen in proposing such an admirable solution to his business difficulties. The provisos – the inspection and valuation that could not, for practical reasons, be carried out for some time – didn't trouble him at all because in the meantime, under conditions, Blake had agreed to give Macmillan and Venturi a substantial advance.

Sophie had no idea what her father's worries were, of course, or only in general terms, but she threw her arms laughingly round his neck. Archie liked to be appreciated and, since they both had a strong sense of fun, Sophie always hugged him extravagantly whenever it was clear that he deserved it, and often when he didn't.

Tucking her hand in his arm, she began walking him towards the drawing room. 'Of *course* everything's going to be all right! We've just entered the Year of the Rat, and that means fortunate *shan*. I asked Ah Foon and she says business will see an upswing and it will be easy to accumulate capital.'

It was one of those occasions when Archie felt a twinge of guilt over not having remarried, because it had meant that his daughter's upbringing had been left largely to her amah, from whom she had absorbed far too much Chinese superstition.

Ah Foon, who had joined the household as Sophie's 'baby amah' and remained as her companion and personal maid, had been reared on a silk farm in the Pearl River delta, an area where women had more independence than anywhere else in China, and Archie had discovered rather too late that she was a force to be reckoned with, quiet and retiring though she chose to appear in the master's presence. He would have liked to find a respectable European woman to keep Sophie company, but Sophie threw a tantrum every time he suggested the idea, maintaining that she needed no one but her dearest Foon *cheh*. If only, he thought, the dratted female hadn't taken a ceremonial vow of celibacy, he could have got rid of her by providing her with a dowry and having her married off to some respectable compatriot.

As it was, even the house they lived in had been taken at Ah Foon's suggestion and Sophie's urging, because the geomancer – whose task it was to assess the relationships of wind and water and pronounce on whether they supplied the correct balance between the eight elements of Nature and the forces of *yin* and *yang* – had declared its *fung shui* to be favourable. The walls, windows and doors had all been in the right places, and the house not only looked out over the waters of the harbour – which was auspicious – but didn't block any of the traditional paths used by dragons to get there when they wanted a bath.

Sophie had danced up and down, crying, 'It's perfect, it's perfect! You must take it, papa.'

And so Archie had taken it, the rooms being of the right number and size and the location desirable for reasons that had nothing to do with *fung shui*.

'Fortunate *shan*, indeed! You and your horoscopes!' He shook his head at her. 'I'd rather rely on Rainer Blake any day, thank you.'

'Oh, *him*!'

It was Sophie's unvarying reaction, and her father grinned. She had never forgiven Blake for riding roughshod over her on the night of the fire at Canton.

She had been used to getting her own way then, and she still was, the little monkey. Archie should have blamed himself, he supposed, for spoiling her. But he didn't. She had always been able to disarm him utterly, not only because she was his daughter but because there was something else about her that unfailingly twisted his heart strings. He had never been able to put a finger on what it was until one day when he had come across Ah Foon dragging her away from some Chinese children, with whom – like all Western children in the colony – she was forbidden to play. He had seen, then, that despite her half-Scots, half-English ancestry, Sophie had something of the look he always found deeply moving in Asian and, more particularly, Indian children – shy, wide-eyed, aware and yet innocent. Even in rags, even in the most deplorable slums and most criminal localities, Indian children were still beautiful with the beauty of perfect trust. Archie knew it had nothing to do with personality or character, and suspected that it was because they were so sheltered by love.

Now, Sophie sat him down in his favourite chair and, perching on the smaller one opposite, demanded, 'Well, tell me about it! What did Mr Blake say?'

If it hadn't been for his recent train of thought, Archie probably wouldn't have heard the wrong note.

He stared at her for a moment, the furrows on his brow deepening. It was so easy to forget that children grew up on the inside as well as the outside. All her life his daughter had coaxed and teased him, openly, mischievously, as if they were conspiring together to reach a mutually satisfactory conclusion. But now, it seemed, the sharing was ended. On this occasion, she was being coaxing for purposes that were entirely her own.

7

Accusingly, he said, 'You've been up to something!'

'Me?' She looked as if butter wouldn't melt in her mouth. 'Why should you think that? Oh, come on, papa. Tell me what happened with Mr Blake.'

'Out with it. You know I'll hear soon enough.'

She gave a choke of laughter. 'You will, too! In fact, you'll probably have to give audience to a full ladies' deputation tomorrow, with Mrs Moore at their head. She said I was setting a shocking example to the other gels, and letting us all down in the sight of the natives.'

'What the devil brought that on?'

Sophie told him.

Her father groaned. 'Right at the governor's feet? What possessed you?'

'Well, I didn't mean to fall off, and I wouldn't have except that I saw Mr Venturi at the winning post and guessed he was bound to recognise me. So I rather lost control of the pony, I'm afraid.'

'You should be ashamed of yourself.'

'Yes, I am, but I did stay on all the way round and it was the greatest fun. It's not fair that girls aren't allowed to race.'

'That's not what I meant.'

Sophie could see perfectly well that he was trying not to laugh. She smiled at him mischievously. In her view, her idolised father was the handsomest man in the colony, with his waving brown hair, side whiskers and smiling blue eyes. He was the nicest, too, even when he was pretending to be annoyed with her. In fact, he didn't have a single fault that she could think of.

The only thing that sometimes worried her was that, although he had been born – just – in the Year of the Rat, in many ways he was more of a Boar person. This made him bad with money and a natural target for swindlers. People born in the Year of the Snake were especially dangerous.

'When was Mr Blake born?' she asked with seeming irrelevance.

'What? How the devil should I know? He's about thirty, I suppose. But go on. What did the governor say?'

That meant he *could* be a Snake. Bother the man! But at least it helped to explain why he always made Sophie uneasy. Snakes were tricky creatures.

'Sir Hercules? Well, you know what he's like. He just said, "Good afternoon, young lady," and half smiled at me with those pale eyes of his. He's awfully good looking, isn't he? I don't think he was shocked. Actually, if he hadn't been there, I might still have got away with it, but all the old tabbies were purring round him – you know the way they do – and Mrs Moore spotted me at once. She disapproves of me because I'm such friends with Frank – her son, you remember? – and girls aren't supposed to be friends with boys.'

'Odious woman.' Archie disliked Euphemia Moore, the self-appointed moral magistrate of the colony, intensely. It was a pity that her husband, Isaac Moore, was among the richest and most influential merchants in Hong Kong.

He sighed. 'Oh, Sophie, my pet! What am I going to do about you?'

8

He had to do something about her for her own sake, because he knew, none better, that unconventionality was an invitation to disaster in the world they inhabited – a world where the façade of respectability was all that made the unrespectable reality tolerable.

The problem wasn't that Sophie did not know how to be ladylike. The problem was that being ladylike wasn't any fun. Even three years as a day scholar at the new Canossian College under the stabilising influence of Miss Emily Bowring – or Sister Aloysia, as she had recently become – hadn't been able to quench Sophie's abounding vitality or her sense of mischief. And, of course, Archie didn't want them quenched, didn't want his daughter changed in the slightest degree. She had been perfect in his eyes since the day she was born.

Most families in Hong Kong, as in India, sent their children 'Home' to aunts or grandparents in Britain when they were small, to be brought up safe from the hazards that made European cemeteries in the East the saddest places on earth, filled with infant sacrifices to the god of colonial ambition. But Sophie had been amazingly healthy and resilient, and Archie couldn't have borne to be parted from her. He still couldn't, even though it was still, in theory at least, not too late for her to go to his brother Daniel's wife – assuming he had one – to be finished, polished, and turned into a fully-fledged lady in a society that knew what ladies were. The ladies of Hong Kong, in Archie's view, were mere *arrivistes*, the wives of jumped-up merchants with all the most dislikeable qualities of middle-class pretension.

But it was impossible.

It was thirty years since Archie had departed from Juran and, if it hadn't been for the painted bowl he had commissioned from Lam Qua in Canton, he would barely remember what the place looked like. He didn't even think of it much any more except to wonder occasionally whether his brother Daniel, ten years younger, had fallen heir to their father. The old man must have passed on years ago. Queer to imagine that cocky little eight-year-old as laird – or acting laird – of Juran.

Although Archie was inclined, when the level in the bottle sank low, to become maudlin about his ancestral home, the truth was that, sober, he was in no great hurry to see it again. It had rained a lot, he remembered. And there was still time enough to make the kind of fortune that would purge his resentment. Time enough to return to Juran when he had made it; when, rich and successful, he would show them that the black sheep of the family hadn't done so badly after all. He didn't have to stay, if he didn't like it.

He would surprise them, by God he would!

It occurred to him that they probably thought he was dead by now, which would make it even better.

Anyway, he damned well wasn't going to give the game away by sending Sophie there. He'd just have to wait and see how things turned out.

It was what Archie Macmillan was best at.

PART TWO

1865–
1869

CHAPTER FIVE

I

'There is a happy land, Far far away,' carolled William at the pitch of his voice. 'Where we'll have ham and eggs, Three times a day . . .'

'For goodness' sake, be quiet!' Belinda scolded, digging her shepherd's crook into the slope and pulling herself up after it. 'Don't you ever think of anything but food? And I don't know why you always have to make such a noise about things, either.'

'I want to frighten the eagle off her nest, that's why! Besides, I like making a noise. I'll make a noise on my own hills any time I want, so there!'

A diffident voice spoke from behind him. 'Uncle Daniel wouldn't like to hear you say that. They're not your hills yet, you know.'

'Phoo! They'll be mine *some* day. There is a happy land, Far far . . .'

Horace had got only as far as, 'Yes, but . . .' when Rachel interrupted him. 'Horace, could you help me, please? This grass is so slippery.'

She had become good at managing him. Every spring for almost seven years, Aunt Minerva and Horace had arrived at Juran, prompt as the first new lambs, to stay for two weeks and brighten the lives of Horace's dear cousins – this from Aunt Minerva – after the long, lonely winter. And every autumn, simultaneously with the migrating fieldfares, they came again, accompanied this time by Horace's papa.

Rachel still felt a strong frisson of distaste every time Lucian Gresham looked at her, which fortunately wasn't often. Seven years had wrought no visible change either in him or his wife, while the only change they had made in Horace was two feet in height and a nasty outbreak of spots. He was still mouse-haired, still bespectacled, still had opinions on everything under the sun and no hesitation about airing them. He was still tiresomely moralistic and regarded right and wrong as absolutes from which there could be no deviation.

Despite his faults, however, he was still also unvaryingly polite, which made him unique among Rachel's acquaintance. And even more to the point, he was on her side, she didn't know why – perhaps because, unlike Belinda and William, she wasn't too self-centred to be polite back to him. She found his courtesy restful.

There was nothing else restful about today's outing. Twelve-year-old William, hearing that a pair of white-tailed sea eagles had built their eyrie on the island in Loch na Caorann, had grizzled on endlessly about wanting to see it. No, he didn't want to wait until the weather was better. It was already well into April and he wanted to see it *now*.

Rachel knew that he didn't want to 'see' it at all. He wanted to get there before the eggs were hatched so that he could steal them for his collection. Bird's-nesting was a craze that possessed every small boy in the Highlands.

Eilean Caorann was a small green islet, with a grassy upward slope at its westward end that gave way to a steep, ragged, rocky cliff, much as if the island had once been a promontory that had snapped off from the mainland to drift away into the loch. It was possible, with reasonable care, to work round the side of the slope to a narrow grassy platform halfway up the rock face, and when the little party from Juran reached it they were able to see, on a ledge seven or eight feet above them, the great spread of sticks, straw and moss that formed the nest. It was surprisingly accessible. Rachel supposed that the eagles must have been given a false sense of security by the fact that boats rarely disturbed the peace of the loch, an isolated stretch of water too far from the castle to be much fished.

'Phoo! It's too high,' William complained. 'I want to see in, and there's no proper footholds in the rock. Horace'll have to give me a leg up.'

Horace was tall in his own weedy way. While the girls watched, he obligingly plastered the side of his body against the rock face so that William could clamber up. Rachel knew that, although she ought to tell William to be careful, the only effect it would have would be to encourage him to do something stupid. He and Belinda always, automatically, did the exact opposite of what she said.

One foot resting on Horace's shoulder and the toe of his other foot implanted in a crack in the cliff, he leaned over at a precarious angle and began scrabbling about in the nest. It wasn't long before he gave a whoop of glee.

'Hold your hand out, Horace.'

Horace did so, suspicion furrowing his brow. It would have been just like William to present him with something disagreeable like a half-eaten hare carcase or a pile of droppings.

It was, however, a large white egg.

William yelled, 'Just a minute. There's more!'

Horace, the egg nervously clutched in one hand, pushed the wire-framed spectacles back on his nose with the side of his wrist. It was a pointless gesture. There was a soft rain falling and, since he always sported a brimless Glengarry bonnet in the fond belief that it was correct wear for the Highlands, his lenses might as well have been made of frosted glass.

'Put it back,' he said.

'What? Don't be silly.' William brandished another egg triumphantly. 'I'll be the only boy for miles with a clutch of sea eagle's eggs in my collection. They're as rare as rare, not like a golden eagle's. Here, take this one, too, in case I drop it when I'm getting down.'

'Shan't,' said Horace. His voice, which hadn't finished breaking, wavered all the way up and down the scale. 'Put them back. You mustn't take them. Put them back.'

'Not on your life. I want them. Besides, eagles are vermin. They kill our game. Mr McBride says they take grouse, and fawns and lambs and things. It's my *duty*,' William's tone became revoltingly virtuous, 'to prevent them from multiplying. If you don't take this one from me, I promise I'll just drop it. I will!'

'I'll drop *you*,' said Horace, his eyes blinking furiously.

Everyone stared at him – mild-mannered, myopic, considerate Horace, who had never made a joke in his life, and usually didn't understand when someone else made one.

'I mean it,' he said.

All he needed to do was take a step away from the rock face and William would tumble down. Rachel, glancing over her shoulder, saw that he might go on tumbling for quite a long way, right down the cliff and into the loch at its foot. And he couldn't swim; none of them could. Girls didn't, and her father said boys had to be bigger and stronger than William before they could safely learn.

'Put them back,' Horace repeated.

Belinda, blood mantling her cheeks, turned on him. At sixteen, she took umbrage with everyone. She was a big girl, five inches taller than Rachel now, instead of just two, but Rachel, who had never suffered any problems with figure or skin, found some compensation in sympathising with her about her puppy fat and poor complexion.

'Don't you tell William what to do, you silly boy,' Belinda snapped. 'Anyway, you don't mean it. You're just trying to be provoking. And William's quite right. Eagles are vermin and there are far too many of them. They have to be destroyed. My father says so.'

It was a mistake to use the word 'silly' to Horace, who was sensitive to any slur on his intellectual abilities; who felt – or so Rachel was beginning to suspect – that Juran ought to consider itself honoured by his visits. He had his reasons, of course, which had nothing to do with his attachment to his dear cousins and everything to do with what he described as a mature decision to dedicate himself to Nature. This he always pronounced with a capital N, as if it were a concept on a par with the Creation or the Resurrection and infinitely more worthy of study.

No longer did he have even a passing interest in wasps and cockroaches, or any desire to learn how to distinguish between peregrine and kestrel, field-mouse and vole. His ambition increasing with his inches, he had become besotted by the lofty concept of what he called Nature's Grand Design, and had decided that this could best be studied in the remote fastnesses of the Highlands. He didn't in the least approve of human beings upsetting the balance of it by stealing eggs or catching fish or shooting deer.

This spring, he was off on a new tack. There was a place in America he had just read about – it was called Yoze Might, he said – where a special park had recently been dedicated to the preservation of Nature (with a capital N). It seemed to Horace that it would be a splendid notion to transform Juran into the same kind of thing.

William and Belinda had found this quite uproarious. No fishing, no bird's-nesting, no stalking *at Juran*! It was the most hen-witted idea they had ever heard.

And now Horace was getting his own back.

Preparatory to annihilating Belinda, he poked his head and shoulders forward, the better to peer over his spectacles.

William yelped, 'Don't do that! I nearly fell.'

Horace ignored him.

'My dear Belinda,' he said with all the authority of fourteen complacent years, 'Uncle Daniel is simply not up to date with the latest opinion. I am reliably assured that eagles do not take lambs or fawns.'

'Yes, they do!'

'No, they don't.'

Rachel wasn't sure about Horace's facts, but the sight of an eagle floating in the heavens always set her heart singing, so she said firmly – too firmly – 'William, do put the eggs back in the nest. I'm sure Horace knows what's right.'

William, his full pink mouth tightening, stared at her for no more than a fraction of a second. Then he raised his arm and threw the egg as hard as he could against the rock face where, smashing into a hundred pieces, it spilled a half-formed, naked chick out onto the grassy platform where the others were standing.

With a 'tut!' of annoyance, Horace took a stride towards it.

2

William fell, letting out a wail of terror, hands and feet scrabbling helplessly for a hold, sixty feet of cliff face below him and beyond that the deep, icy waters of the loch.

Fortunately, it happened so quickly that the danger was over before anyone recognised it. And William was lucky. He tumbled not onto the bare, slippery grass with the sheer drop beyond, but into a clump of bracken that stopped him as decisively as a policeman's embrace.

After a paralysed moment, it became clear from the hiccuping quality of his howls that he hadn't suffered more than a fright, so Rachel spared time to administer a hearty slap to Belinda, whose mouth had opened on a hysterical, 'Oh, ohh, ohhh . . .' before she went and dragged him to his feet, making sure that no real harm had been done.

Horace was oblivious.

Bending to pick up the limp little eagle embryo, 'Look what you're done!' he said reproachfully. 'Oh, well. I'd better put the other egg back before any harm comes to it.'

The egg replaced, he wiped his hands on his knickerbockers, tipped the Glengarry over one eye, and said, 'Well, that's that. Has William seen everything he wanted to see? I'm getting awfully wet. Can we go back to the castle now?'

3

A few hours later, still undecided as to whether the whole episode had been shocking or merely funny, Rachel, washed and changed, sat before the glass in her room doing her hair preparatory to going to sit with her mother, as she always did, for the hour before supper.

She was vain of her hair, of its chestnut gloss, its length and its heaviness. Having abandoned her ringlets with childhood, she now wore it parted in the centre and swept smoothly down over her ears and back into a coil at the nape of her neck. It emphasised the almost perfect heart shape of her face and made her look older than she was, though nothing was ever going to make her look classically pretty. Her mouth was too wide, her nose too positive, and the blue of her eyes insufficiently soft. And if, as Aunt Minerva maintained, facial expression was the key to true beauty, Rachel still didn't score. She had tried once or twice, in a half-hearted way, to cultivate the sweet submissiveness expected of young ladies in the 1860s, but had come to the conclusion that her face hadn't been designed for it. Or her personality.

Even so, she had learned by now to control her emotions, to avoid argument, above all to refrain from provoking Belinda, whose spitefulness could still make her feel sick inside. It wasn't cowardice but a matter of priorities. She had more interesting things to do.

She sighed faintly. Everything would have been so different if her father had only been prepared to admit that she was his real daughter, the eldest of his children. All she wanted was recognition.

Moving to draw her hair over her shoulder and begin twisting it into a loose cable, she caught the reflection of her bed coverlet in the glass, and laughed. If ever anything had been an expression of her desire for recognition, it had been the coverlet and window curtains she had worked during her second and third winters at Juran, stitching them out of a double thickness of old linen sheets, and then secretly stencilling them with a giant version of the Dress Macmillan tartan, a warm and cheerful, if rather loud combination of scarlet and saffron. Belinda had been furious.

Her bedroom now was different in other ways, too, from the stone cell it had once been, though the alterations had taken her years to accomplish. Not until a few months ago had she finally succeeded in persuading the crusty old castle handyman to limewash the walls and help her repair the furniture – the armoire and chest of drawers, the washing table and dressing table, all of them long discarded from the grownups' bedrooms as being too plain and simple for modern taste. They were at least a hundred years old, Rachel had thought as she buffed away at them, trying to restore their polish, but however much she would have liked something more ornate and fashionable, at least the wood and the workmanship were lovely.

She still didn't regret the curtains and coverlet, although she had drawn the line when it came to new bed hangings, her most recent enterprise. Adult enough by now to admit that Macmillandom could go too far, she had abjured tartan in favour of unbleached linen woven from flax grown on the estate, edging the hangings with a deep berlin woolwork border of geometrical scarlet tulips and saffron crocuses massed together against a background of purple pansies.

She had traced the pattern from *The Ladies Companion* and stitched it with great care, but it hadn't stopped Belinda from sneering. 'Tulips? *Roses* are the correct flower for that kind of design!'

Rachel knew it perfectly well, but roses were harder to do and, besides, she didn't want any reminders of Belinda, who doted on roses, in her own private sanctum. Belinda's mother had planted a rose bed along the top of the retaining wall behind the castle terrace, and her daughter made as much fuss about looking after it as if it had been bequeathed to her as a holy charge.

Her next project was to be a new rag rug to replace the one she had made in her first winter under Miss Irving's guidance, using, of necessity, such a random assortment of household and dressmaking scraps that the final effect suggested nothing so much as the sweepings from the floor of a boiled sweets factory. The new one was going to be rather more restrained.

The thought of restraint brought her reluctantly back to Horace. She suspected that he had deliberately set out to teach William a lesson, and because he was Horace hadn't thought beyond that. Hadn't thought that William might have died as a result. No explanation other than thoughtlessness was acceptable, because – really – Horace was harmless. He might bore you to death, but even then it most certainly wouldn't be intentional.

Aunt Minerva's response to the story had been gloriously predict-able. She knew, she had said, exactly how dear little William felt about his thrilling adventure but wondered whether he was not, perhaps, exaggerating the danger just a tiny bit. Indeed, although it pained her to say so, it had really been sadly inconsiderate of dear little William to smash the egg when he must have known how much it would upset Horace.

Aunt Minerva, Rachel now knew, was a terrible fraud, though she had only become certain of it in the last year or two, when she had been considered sufficiently adult to meet the guests who came to stay at Juran in the sporting season, even if not to converse with them; youthful females were not held to be capable of rational conversation. Some of the guests, mainly the overflow from well-connected Altsigh, were quite distinguished – among them recently had been two intellectual giants, Mr Delane of *The Times* and Mr Browning, the poet – and Rachel, with a mind frustratingly underemployed and nothing to do but listen and observe, had amused herself by trying to read them as people. She flattered herself that she had become quite perceptive.

Having outsiders as a yardstick helped her to read people much closer to her, and it hadn't taken her long to confirm that Aunt Minerva's lovely, sparkling smile was a weapon, no more and no less, which came into play only when she had something to gain – information, usually, because she was inquisitive to the point of obsession, but sometimes admiration and sometimes cooperation. Rachel had even succeeded in isolating each stage in the preliminaries; first, she concentrated her mind, then she fixed her gaze on her victim, paused, drew in an audible breath, and then, and only then, brought into play the intimately focussed and dazzling smile that said, 'I am interested in no one in the world but you.' After that came the questions.

Rachel hadn't been repelled by the discovery. Indeed, she rather admired Aunt Minerva for getting away with it and, always ready to learn, had added a warm and sparkling smile to her own repertoire. She hadn't had much occasion to use it so far, but thought it might come in useful some day.

Arranging the chenille net snood – a soft willow green to match her dress – over her chignon, she patted everything into place and then, standing up, smoothed the seamed bodice over her trim waist. All that remained was to add a touch of colour to her cheeks from the little bottle of Damask Rose Drops, and then she was ready.

She wouldn't tell her mother what had happened, even though she could have made it sound quite amusing. Not because it wouldn't interest her, but because she wouldn't take it in.

4

After more than eight years at Juran, Ondine was no longer plump and pretty but fat and forgetful – perfectly groomed still, but mentally absent, as if her whole inner self had drained away.

Every evening Rachel went to see her and sit with her, weeping inside.

The withdrawal from people, from activity, from life, had been almost imperceptible at first. Hating the rain and wind which spelled ruin to the grooming on which she frittered away so much of her time, hating the emptiness of sea and country, Ondine had from the beginning been reluctant to venture outdoors. Rachel, understanding her reasons, had thought it perfectly natural; she hadn't even been worried when her mother refused, despite her daughter's conscientious pestering, to go out on days when the weather was fine and calm. It was just laziness, Rachel had thought. After all, her ma was lazy indoors, too.

And then Ondine had bestirred herself and made the foray into the kitchen that had ended in disaster. That was when she had refused to have anything more to do with the housekeeping. She had had quite enough of kitchens, she said. Her parents had set her slaving in the restaurant when she was six years old and she had still been slaving eighteen years later when Daniel Macmillan had appeared on the scene – Daniel Macmillan, who had offered her, she thought, her first and probably last chance of escaping the tyranny of having to prepare food and cook it and serve it, from dawn until midnight, day after day, week after week, year after year, all her life long. And although he had let her down – as she should have known he would – he had come back in the end. Now that they were married, she was entitled to be idle if she wished. He owed it to her.

The next stage – although Rachel, still tied to the schoolroom, had been slow to find out about it – had been that Ondine had gradually ceased, at her husband's suggestion, to put in an appearance when there were visitors in the castle. Her husband had also discouraged her, after the first two or three occasions, from accompanying him on visits to acquaintances, and she had agreed willingly enough because she had been made to feel less than welcome.

Soon, Juran had become her prison, where in the pretty cell of her boudoir or sometimes in the Blue Drawing Room, she whiled away the martyred hours leafing through *The Queen* or *The Englishwoman's Domestic Magazine* and being beguiled into ordering pretty, silly things from the advertisements that she most certainly did not need. She had always been thriftless and scatterbrained; if personality traits were doled out at birth in set quantities, Rachel had sometimes thought that her mother had been allocated only enough common sense to cook with. Even in their early days in Soho, Rachel had known that it was up to her, child that she was, to protect and look after her ma, whom she loved.

There was nothing, now, that she could do. It seemed as if Ondine's head had been emptied entirely, as if there was nothing going on inside it at all. Rachel had been coming, lately, to wonder whether it wasn't her mother's fault; whether perhaps she was ill.

5

She would have spoken of it to her father, except that he wouldn't have believed her. Because there was one thing still guaranteed to stir Ondine out of her lethargy – a visit from her husband.

Sitting with her mother and striving to sound natural, Rachel was saying, 'Do look at this Greek key border I'm embroidering on my new Figaro jacket, mama,' when the door of the boudoir crashed back and Daniel Macmillan burst in, brandishing a fistful of bills and almost incoherent with rage.

'. . . extravagance . . . frills and furbelows . . . new silver-backed brushes. And what's this bill from Nicoll's, *if* I may ask?'

'Which bill from Nicoll's?' Ondine replied after a moment, her blank eyes beginning to come into focus and her brain with them.

'What do you mean, *which* bill? Are there more? This is for a "burr walnut compendium, brass bound, with silver fittings". And what the devil is a compendium, anyway?'

'It is a kind of dressing case, with sewing tools and jars for toilet articles, and a jewellery tray. It is for travelling.'

Ondine's nonchalant tone might have been deliberately calculated to enrage her husband still further. It was as if, Rachel suddenly realised, even a shouting match made a welcome change from the killing inertia of slow days and sleepless nights.

'And you do so much travelling!' There was withering sarcasm in Daniel's voice.

Rachel, too far from the door to make her escape as a dutiful daughter should have done, stayed where she was, hands shaking as she industriously pretended to ply her needle and listened to the two people she loved tearing each other apart.

'I *wish* to do some travelling. I *wish* to be prepared in case, some day, you choose to take me with you instead of leaving me here in this drear and dreadful place while you go jaunting off all over the country.'

'*Jaunting!*' Daniel's tone was so thickly encrusted with injured innocence that no one would have given a moment's credence to what followed. 'When I am away from here, it is because I have matters of business to attend to! Raising money to maintain the estate, madam, not for you to squander!'

Ondine tilted her head and her smile was almost as flirtatious as of old. 'Business? No, you do not deceive *me*! You employ people for that. I know very well that you have no other business than hunting and gaming and drinking. And', she added in the same coquettish tone, 'whoring.'

Rachel gasped, stabbing her finger with the needle and then, blindly, staring at the drop of blood that welled out.

Daniel Macmillan didn't trouble to deny it. 'Whoring? Well, you know all about *that*, don't you!'

In London, Rachel and her mother had always shared a room and if there had been anything like that, Rachel would have known. She leapt to her mother's defence. 'Papa! That's not true!'

But her father only growled, 'Be quiet, miss.'

And then there was a rustle as Ondine levered herself to her feet and a spindly rattle as her swinging skirts knocked over a little occasional table. With disbelief, Rachel saw that she wasn't upset in the least. She was enjoying herself.

As if to confirm it, her voice soared to a full soprano. '*You!*' she shrieked. '*You* are the kind of man who thinks every woman who is not a wife must be a whore. Well, not I, my fine, honourable gentleman! Not I! When you abandoned me, I supported myself and your child with perfect respectability for five years until you came looking for me again. Your grand wife did not understand you, you said!' She laughed, and it was an unpleasantly febrile sound. 'How well I remember what kind of "understanding" you wanted. But did I ask you to pay for it? I did not. I asked only for a little money to help me clothe and educate little Ellie as she deserved.'

'And I gave it to you!'

'Bah! A few guineas, only. And not as if it were my due. You gave it to me as if you were paying off a woman of the streets!'

'Rubbish!'

But it wasn't rubbish. Rachel, remembering how she had always rushed home to see her pa before he left, could still hear the jingling sound as he tossed some coins carelessly down on the table; could see, too, the flush on her mother's face as she accepted them.

Her father's voice, she suddenly noticed, was slurred, which meant that he must be full of whisky, though it was only ten in the morning. He, too, had changed much in these last years. Once, he had been big, buoyant, gusty and magnetic, even though his bite – which was rare – had been no less fierce than his bark. But nowadays, even when he was in a cheerful mood, there was a cantankerous quality about him. The indeterminate blue of his eyes was never friendly, and the stubborn mouth, almost lost in the curly thicket of beard and whiskers which so many gentlemen had recently begun to affect, seemed to be permanently turned down at the corners.

'Rubbish, rubbish, rubbish!' he repeated on a crescendo. 'In any case, you've proved my point for me, haven't you? Money. That's all you've ever been interested in. You were a spendthrift then, and you're a spendthrift now. God knows why I ever took up with you again! And God knows I ought to be certified for having married you! Blackmail, that's what it was! Plain, common blackmail!'

And that *was* true.

Ondine smiled seraphically.

Rachel felt as if she were going to be sick. Where would it all end? she wondered, still too inexperienced to know that there was no such thing as an 'end', that the consequences of every human deed flowed on and on for ever, lapping the shores of eternity.

'. . . made me sign that paper,' her mother was suddenly screaming, 'and if that was not blackmail also then I do not know what is.'

'What's sauce for the goose is sauce for the gander!'

But then, as if aware of having descended to the level of the nursery, Daniel Macmillan put an end to the scene by saying with crushing formality, 'All that, however, is past mending. Your extravagance is not. So I shall be obliged, madam, if you will return your – umm – compendium to the makers. Because I have no intention of paying for it.'

The door slammed. There was no other sound at first except for one brief crash of breaking china, as Ondine threw an ornament after him.

A moment later, Rachel dropped everything and ran, terrified, to catch her mother as she fainted.

6

Five months later, Juran's whole world fell apart.

The social part of the shooting season had ended and the guests had gone, but the Greshams, last to leave, had dropped some remark about family feeling that caught Daniel Macmillan on the raw, making it sound, he complained, as if he didn't know his duty as a father. And who was Lucian Gresham to talk!

'Catch my sainted brother-in-law condescending to put himself out by taking Minerva and the boy on some dashed picnic or other!'

But, Daniel being Daniel, after brooding for the better part of the day he arrived at a decision. Tomorrow, he announced, the Macmillans would have a family outing. He would arrange for Tom Tanner to take them on a sea fishing trip. Just what they all needed. They would enjoy themselves. How well he remembered the fun such expeditions had been when he was a youngster himself!

That no one wanted to go was irrelevant. That the equinoctial gales were building up was immaterial. That Ondine actively hated the sea and hadn't set foot out of doors for years was a positive bonus. The family – the *whole* family – was going fishing and that was an end of it.

7

It was a disaster from the start. Even the *Catrine*'s owner was doubtful when he and his crew of one, Jamie McDougall, brought the twenty-four-foot smack in to the jetty.

'You are still wanting to go, are you, sirr?' he enquired politely. 'I am not sure that it iss the best day for the fishing.'

But Daniel Macmillan's mind was made up. 'Nonsense, Tanner. We've been out in worse than this! Belinda, will you stop looking like a wet Friday and get yourself on board!'

Tom Tanner accepted the decision courteously. He was a tall, quiet, strikingly handsome young man from the village, with hazel eyes, a brown fringe of beard framing jaw and chin, and the smoothly weather-tanned complexion with a touch of colour high on the cheekbones that was so typically West Highland. Like most of the local men, he could turn his hand to anything. Sometimes he fished, sometimes he acted as ghillie or beater, sometimes he would do a bit of log cutting. Otherwise, he worked his croft, raising potatoes and oats for food, keeping a few hens for their eggs and a goat for her milk. He had been walking out with Fiona McDougall for four years – and more than walking out, everyone knew – but still wasn't making any move to name the day.

Rachel, as he handed her on board, smiled her thanks at him, which was more than anyone else in the family troubled to do, and received his open, unshadowed smile in return. A nice man, she thought, seating herself on the starboard side towards the stern, where she would be out of the path of the boom. In this weather, it was going to be swinging hard.

She knew the moods of the sea so well by now, had become so accustomed to its living presence, that it always surprised her when Juran's guests betrayed their city-dwellers' ignorance of its power. Seeing it glassy calm, or opalescent with mist, or blue and shiny as enamel, they would remark, 'Beautiful day!' When it wore a sheen like pale grey satin, dimpled with a gentle rain, they murmured, 'Good, no wind. Just the weather for stalking.' And when the rollers came piling in, with three thousand miles of North Atlantic fury behind them, to break over Ruadh Rinn in a towering, tumbling frenzy of foam that left the rocks streaming with waterfalls white as pouring milk, it would be, 'Sea's a bit rough, what? Dashed impressive, though.'

Today, it was leaden grey, the wave crests short and breaking white, while the clouds, hustled along by a wind from the south-west, were sullen and heavy with rain. The gulls – banking and wheeling, drifting and diving as the air currents tossed them about – called hoarsely and ceaselessly, the sound grating on everyone's ears.

Since it had been obvious from the start that line fishing would be out of the question, they had brought an 'otter', a wooden contraption looking rather like a kite laden with weights and barbs, to be trailed under water behind the boat. William, the only member of the party enthusiastic about this kind of high-speed mass slaughter, was put in charge of it and caught twenty-seven whiting and mackerel in the first hour.

But after that it was useless. By then everyone on board, water-proofed cloaks clutched tight to the neck and coalheaver's hats pulled down as far as they would go, was sitting with gritted teeth wishing the trip was over but pretending they didn't. Rachel opened her mouth to shout, 'Papa, shouldn't we go back?' and then thought better of it. He was in such a contrary mood that it would probably provoke the opposite reaction. Easy to see whom William and Belinda had inherited their perversity from.

The little *Catrine* was pitching and plunging violently by this time, staggering up the face of each mountainous roller, lurching drunkenly at the top, then swooping down the other side, stern heaving as the crest passed under her. The dinghy she had in tow chased her down each wave-back and lay wallowing in the trough while the ship mounted the next crest, the rope snapping taut again with such force that it seemed as if it must either break or tear the ship itself apart.

The wind was gusting wildly, the motion dizzying, the noise inconceivable. No one in their senses, thought a shivering Rachel, could be other than terrified. Often enough, in her dreams, she had imagined herself going nobly to her death at the guillotine or the stake, head held high, but this was just silly.

Why didn't Tom Tanner do something? He was the captain. He didn't have to wait for the laird to give him instructions.

Another great gout of water slammed into the boat. By now, there was as much sea inside as there was out. The wind shrieked and howled and lashed as if its only purpose was to tear the sail from the mast. Tom Tanner and Jamie McDougall were fighting the wheel every inch of the way and Rachel had lost all sense of direction so that she had no idea where the land lay or from what quarter the wind was blowing.

Dimly, she remembered something from Shakespeare – or perhaps it was the Bible – about the raging of the elements. And they did rage, with a rage so fierce, so awesome that it paralysed heart and ears and mind and tongue. Even the idea of resisting was impossible – like resisting destiny itself.

Rachel, who knelt beside her bed every night and prayed, dutifully but without conviction, found herself for the first time in her life gabbling out real prayers to a real God. Prayers for salvation, for pity, for rescue. Please, God! Don't let us drown. Please, God, help us! Please, God, make the wind drop, and the waves, and bring us safe to shore.

I don't want to die!

Her head was still bent when she opened her eyes again, otherwise she probably wouldn't have noticed the herring swimming around at her feet.

And that was carrying things altogether too far.

'Blast and bugger!' yelped little Ellie Vallette, and dived to rummage under the thwarts.

'Bale!' she screamed at Belinda, thrusting a bucket at her. 'Bale!'

Rachel's arm was aching so much that she didn't know whether she could lift the baler one more time. Dashing the water out of her eyes, she looked over at Belinda and saw that she was crying, her shoulders heaving and shuddering with sobs. She was baling still, like an automaton, but scooping out no more than a spoonful with each toss of the round-bottomed bucket.

It was time someone else took a turn. William was sitting blind-eyed, chewing on his knuckles. Rachel gesticulated furiously at him to take Belinda's bucket, but he didn't show any sign of understanding.

Her poor, unhappy mother wasn't going to be of much use, either. Still and silent, she was clinging to the gunwale, her face green. Even before they set out, she had been feeling sick from the smell of rubberised cloth that wafted up in nauseating waves from her new mackintosh cloak, but her husband had said she was just trying to make excuses and wouldn't listen.

And Daniel Macmillan, who should have been exercising his authority, playing an active role in getting them out of the mess he had got them into, was standing balanced in the stern looking strong and fearless – and *stupid*. Rachel, who despite everything had always admired and loved him, recognised with a sharp pang of sorrow that he was a hollow man.

With a sudden, savage impatience, she leaned over and tugged at his sleeve.

It brought him back to reality. After a moment or two, he relieved Belinda of her baler and set to work, and at the same time Tom Tanner began putting the *Catrine* about.

Rachel, disoriented, hadn't guessed that the wind must be foul and that he had been waiting and hoping for it to veer a point or two so that he could change course and make a run for the shore. And now it seemed that it had.

He was a good seaman. His concentration almost palpable, he completed the difficult manoeuvre of bringing the *Catrine* round safely, and then they were racing before the wind, the waves with them rather than against them, swooping and plunging along at dizzying speed, barely outrunning the crests that followed them, curling over them, threatening to engulf them. Sooner than Rachel would have believed possible, they were approaching the familiar channel between the two little offshore islands of Meall and Corran, and it was all horribly exhilarating, so that even William stopped chewing his knuckles and reverted to his usual objectionable, obstreperous self.

Scrambling along to the stern, he stood hanging on with one hand and, with the other, thumbing his nose at the pursuing waves. 'Yah! Boo! Can't catch me!'

'William, be careful!' Rachel screamed at him, but all he did was break into a war dance.

How was it possible for a child to be so perverse? She should have known; should have had enough sense to hold her tongue.

And then a furious sideways gust hit them and the sail gibed with a fearsome cracking sound and the boom snapped loose from the mast. The big, brown sail, held only by its ropes, flapped free and wild with the boom still attached, snaking like a whip.

Rachel sensed a flurry of something heavier than water going past her even as, without hesitating, without even thinking, she threw herself at the boom, but she couldn't hold it and, as she looked up desperately for help, she saw that something else was wrong. Her father and Belinda were hanging over the stern, and Rachel didn't at first realise that the thin, high sound cutting through the roar of the elements was the sound of Belinda screaming.

William was nowhere to be seen. Nor was Ondine.

But there was no time for anything, because a new combination of wind and water laid the boat over on her port side until the deck was near vertical. A huge wave burst against the exposed bottom and came cascading down over them, and the boom was slipping into the sea, dragging the sail with it, and she knew that the extra pull on the mast would be enough to finish the job that wind and wave had begun.

They were going to capsize. Raging within, she threw her weight on the sail and pulled at it with all the strength of her slight being.

And then Tom Tanner was there with his knife, slicing and slashing, cutting lines, ripping at the sodden fabric and hauling the bulk of it inboard. She helped hold it while he struggled to bunch and tie it round the mast, like a badly rolled umbrella, so that the wind didn't have purchase.

Beyond him, she saw her father poise himself and dive into the sea even as the boat, with a heart-stopping succession of shudders, began to right itself.

And then there was a wail from Jamie McDougall, and a splintering crash, and the *Catrine* struck the rocks.

No one lived on Corran except sheep and wild goats and, in winter, huge colonies of barnacle geese, but Jamie McDougall said that if the young ladies could scramble ashore, there was an old shepherd's bothy that would give them some shelter.

Tom Tanner stayed with the *Catrine* while Jamie led the two exhausted, drenched and shaking girls through an endless wilderness of wet heather, slippery bracken and sodden peat, with the wind flaying their faces, tearing at their skirts, whirling them round, forcing them one step back for every two steps forward.

But when they arrived at the bothy there was smoke coming from the tumbledown chimney and the scarred door creaked open to allow a pack of yapping terriers to erupt round their feet. The hand on the latch belonged to a small weaselly-looking man wearing a lum hat, collarless shirt and ancient breeks.

Hogg the foxhunter was a keen student of human nature, and when he had heard Jamie's tale he was no longer surprised to see the two lassies weeping and clinging to each other for comfort, though he'd have been prepared to wager it was for the first time in their lives. And probably the last.

Kindly, he said, 'Come away in! Come away in, lassies. I've got some broth on the fire that'll put a bit of warmth into you.'

10

So extreme was Rachel's physical misery that her brain retreated into limbo, refusing to confront what had happened. When they got back to Juran, she thought dazedly, she would find that it had all been a hideous nightmare, no more. Her mother and father and William would be there, waiting for them.

But when the unseen sun went down and the wind and waves began to drop, when Hogg took them ashore in his leaky old rowing boat over a sea that, although still rainswept, was no more than ordinarily rough, when they trailed up over the machair to the castle, she found that it had all been real.

Belinda, gasping hysterically, was led away and put to bed by the housekeeper, but Rachel, throwing off her sodden cloak, just stood in front of the fire in the Great Hall, shivering, until one of the maids appeared with a pot of tea as black and tarry as if it had been brewed in

Satan's kitchen. Only after she had gulped down a whole cup, grateful for its warmth even while her stomach revolted against its strength, did it begin to dawn on her that there was not one single soul in the castle who would know what to do, not one single soul with the authority – or the gumption – to do anything even if they *had* known.

Miss Irving had resigned her post when Belinda reached the age of sixteen, and William's tutor, his charge soon to leave for public school, had gone too. Mr Nielson, the steward, whose physical resemblance to a tower of strength now proved to be a complete sham, did no more than look grave at the news, say in his magisterial way that he would inform the staff of the tragedy, and disappear at unprecedented speed.

There was no one. No one for Rachel to turn to, no one whose advice she could ask.

Whatever had to be done, she would have to do it herself and she didn't have the remotest idea where to start. She drew in her breath on a sob of barely controlled panic.

It was only then that she became aware of another presence and realised that Hogg had followed her indoors. He had helped himself to some tea and was watching her expressionlessly over the rim of the cup, holding it with his little finger genteelly crooked.

There was almost as big a puddle round his feet as round hers.

It was either laugh or cry. With Hogg's yellow eyes on her, she wasn't going to let herself down. So, with an unsteady laugh, she remarked, 'A pair of drowned rats.' It was the first metaphor that sprang to her mind but scarcely the most felicitous, and she hurried on, 'I'll have to send down to the village and ask some of the men to go out and search.'

She didn't phrase it as a question, but he took it as one and nodded, a few lingering drops of rain splashing from the brim of his disgraceful hat.

'Aye,' he said. 'Mind you, after Jamie left you wi' me on Corran, he was away to search the rest o' the island. And as soon as the wind dropped Tom Tanner would be taking the dinghy round Meall.'

One of the logs settled in a shower of sparks and Rachel, without thinking, moved a step back, although it would have taken a Guy Fawkes bonfire to make any impression on a skirt as wet as hers.

'What are you saying?' She had to make three attempts before she could force the words out.

There was no sympathy in his voice, only realism. 'Ye'll not see your folks again until the sea gives up its dead.'

The silence settled like a winding sheet on the huge, echoing stone hall, with its cold, flagged floor, its darkly varnished staircase, brooding portraits and formalised rings of rusty old swords on the walls. The thin, wavering light of the oil lamps didn't even begin to penetrate the shadows. Rachel swallowed a hiccup of overwrought mirth, remembering the night of her first arrival at Juran, when, in her innocence, she had seen it as a perfect setting for spine-chilling tales of doom and disaster. Imaginary ones.

After a long moment, she discovered that it was a relief to have the truth put into words.

'I know, but we still have to try. I'd better send for Mr Middleton. He'll know what to do.'

She couldn't think why she was talking to Hogg like this when, before today, she had scarcely exchanged more than a few dozen words with him in her life. He was only the local foxhunter and it was none of his business. She didn't trust him an inch. And now that the warmth of the fire was making his clothes steam, she was reminded that he didn't wash very often, either.

'Mr Middleton's the lawyer,' she explained.

'From Oban. Aye.'

Hogg guessed that the lassie wouldn't feel the full shock of her parents' death for several days and in the meantime, no doubt, she'd confront the most immediate hurdles and overcome them and begin to think she was capable of handling anything. At seventeen, it was easy to overrate yourself. He decided he'd better just drop her a wee hint to set her off on the right lines. Though he made it a principle never to get involved in other folks' affairs – it had caused him nothing but grief in the past – there was no doubt she needed someone on her side. If it had been the spoilt and brainless Belinda, he wouldn't have wasted his breath.

He sniffed. 'A lawyer's not going to take orders from a lassie.'

'I don't want to give him orders. I just want his help.'

'And what then?'

Giving her time to think about it, he picked up the battered silver teapot and shoogled it hopefully. It was empty, so he palmed a few biscuits and slid them into his pocket before sinking his teeth into a rather stale buttered scone. When he had finished it, he brushed the crumbs off his chin and said encouragingly, 'The laird'll likely have named a guardian for you in his Will. That's who you need.'

Rachel stared at him, her mind racing. A guardian. Uncle Gresham.

It was bound to be him, because there wasn't anyone else. And the Greshams had left only yesterday morning, on horseback for the first stage of the journey. Since Aunt Minerva never consented to exceed a gentle trot, they probably hadn't even reached Glasgow yet. She ought to send after them.

It was the last thing she wanted to do. She didn't want them back. She still recoiled at the very sight of Uncle Gresham, still obscurely feared him, knew that his contemptuous, worldweary lack of comment would be its own comment on her father's rashness. And Aunt Minerva would take up the reins of the household with an iron sweetness that would, in itself, be a condemnation of her mother's laxity. The thought of Aunt Minerva being sympathetic turned Rachel's stomach.

The whole idea was intolerable.

'Yes,' she said at last. 'You're right.'

'Aye, well. It'll not be easy. But ye'll manage.' There was a brief flash of Hogg's yellow grin. 'I'd better be away now,' he said. 'I've got the dogs to feed.'

'Thank you,' she said, and was surprised to find that she meant it.

11

Afterwards, everything seemed to fall into place and she was able to work out what needed to be done. And because, ironically, all the years of blocking Belinda and William's spite out of her mind had given her an excellent grounding, she was able, while she did it, to ignore the black dog of grief that stalked her, biding its time.

When the Greshams arrived two nights and a day later, everything was in hand. Mr Middleton, the lawyer, and Mr McBride, the grieve, had been consulted. The village carpenter had finished his work. Bessie Laundry was elbow deep in black dye. Mr Allan, the minister, had offered spiritual comfort to the bereaved and then hurried home to instruct Mrs Allan to freshen up his best frock coat (which had become sadly shiny) with coffee and turpentine, while he occupied himself with preparing the funeral oration. It was not every day that he had the felicity of presiding over the obsequies of a laird.

Even the bodies of Daniel Macmillan and his son, floated ashore separately on the same tide, had been decently laid out in the rarely used north parlour, a parlour shrouded as custom required in white linen. Daniel's body was bruised and broken after a battering against the rocks, William's unmarked. Mr Middleton, in the absence of any head of the household, had decreed it unnecessary to hold an old-fashioned wake with the local men taking turns to stand watch and professional mourning women keening over the coffins. 'Paganism,' he had muttered. 'Pure paganism.' But he couldn't stop everyone within miles from coming to view the corpses and touch them as tradition required.

There was a third trestle in the parlour with a third, empty coffin on it, although Rachel knew with a dreary, superstitious certainty that she would never see her mother again.

12

Not until after the double funeral, which females were not permitted to attend, did Rachel give in at last, weeping for her mother, her father and her dreams until she lay drained and exhausted. But still she couldn't sleep and, in the darkest hours of the night, discovered for the first time that guilt was one of the hardest lessons of death.

She had learned early in life that love didn't necessarily rule out clarity of vision. Even as a child had she seen that her mama was persuadable and not very clever, someone who needed to be looked after by her capable small daughter. But not until these last few months – when the looking after had failed, when Ondine had detached herself almost completely from what went on around her – had it occurred to Rachel to view the world from her mother's standpoint. Not until then had she begun to see how much Ondine had craved the love and approval that were denied her – denied her because she tried to attract them in the wrong way and wasn't sufficiently clever to appreciate that coquetry was not enough. Looking back to the accident, Rachel knew that her mother's struggles against the sea had been hampered not just by the volume of her skirts but by despair at life itself and the worthlessness of its gifts.

Some, at least, of Ondine's despair had been justified, because whatever her weaknesses, whatever her faults, the brutal truth was that the people she should have been able to depend on had never hesitated to make use of her for their own ends. She had always been a victim – of her father and brothers, of Daniel Macmillan, and of Rachel herself.

Filled with self-loathing, Rachel remembered how she had manipulated her mother; how, obsessed by the notion that little Ellie Valette deserved a finer future than she would ever find in Soho, she had allowed her childish ambition to take precedence over all other considerations.

Her father had spoken of being blackmailed into marriage and he had not lied. One day, soon after Rachel's eighth birthday, he had come to visit them in London and found Ondine ostensibly having trouble with the wording of a letter she was writing – a letter to Daniel's dying first wife, telling her that she, Ondine Vallette, was her husband's mistress, and that they had a daughter, and that she wished to beseech Mrs Macmillan, in Christian charity, to forgive her husband before she passed away, so that he might not have such a secret on his conscience for the rest of his life.

He had blustered and threatened, but in the end he had given in and the letter had not been sent. It wouldn't have been sent, anyway.

The bluff had been neither her mother's idea nor Rachel's; it had been suggested by old Pierre at the restaurant, who had always been a good friend to them. But Rachel's demands had been at the root of it.

'I'm tired of being a bastard!' she had complained over and over again. 'It's not respectable. I don't like it. Why can't I have a proper father like other people? Why can't you marry my pa? Please, ma. *Please!*'

And because her mother, for all her failings, had been a kindhearted and loving woman, she had put her daughter's desires before her own instincts.

Rachel had been only eight years old at the time, she told herself. She hadn't known any better.

But it wasn't an excuse.

13

That part of the story now was ended, but as the days passed, and the weeks, as Rachel slowly returned to normality, a tiny spring of excitement began to bubble up inside her. That William should have died at the same time as her parents could mean only one thing. Destiny had taken a hand in the game.

The most she had ever aspired to was being recognised as her father's daughter, his eldest child; while William lived, the idea that she might some day inherit Juran had never been more than a dream from cloud cuckoo land.

But now . . .

Everything depended on what her father had put in his Will.

CHAPTER SIX

❧❧❧

I

'Huh!' snorted Ah Foon, which was criticism enough in itself. 'Too muchee low,' she went on. 'Plopa missees no likee.'

Sophie giggled, though not at the pidgin English which, despite being likened by outsiders to the silliest of baby talk, was flexible enough to meet most of the needs of those who lived or traded on the China coast. Sophie knew exactly what Ah Foon meant, and also that she was right. The neckline was undoubtedly too low, and the 'proper' ladies were undoubtedly not going to like it. On the other hand, Sophie could think of several handsome young officers who were going to like it very much.

It was her first truly grand evening dress, white as befitted a young lady only a few weeks past her seventeenth birthday but otherwise making few, if any, concessions to maidenly modesty. All her friends were going to be green-eyed with envy. With little else to occupy their minds, the marriageable maidens of Hong Kong doted on fashion, and Sophie was no exception – or only in the sense of having an innate appreciation of style and no mother to exercise a restraining influence over her.

On this occasion, by the conscienceless expedient of purloining a copy of *The World of Fashion* (only six months out of date) from a lady who had recently arrived from England, she had been able to ensure that, instead of being merely in the height of Hong Kong fashion, she would be well ahead of it. Her dress, directly copied from the most seductive of all the seductive plates in that luscious publication, consisted of a tight silken bodice supported by whalebone, willpower and the grace of God, and skirts that foamed out over one of the swept-back crinolines that had made their first appearance in Paris only two years before. The bareness of shoulders and arms was relieved by sleeves that were no more than bracelets of artificial peach blossoms, and Sophie wore a matching spray of blossom in the intricate dark curls of her hair.

The peach blossoms were pure wickedness. Even a young lady as ambitious of cutting a dash as Sophie would scarcely have dared wear them if she had not been sure that the 'plopa missees' – wilfully and unitedly ignorant of heathen superstition – wouldn't know that, in Chinese symbolism, they promised twelve whole months of good fortune in affairs of the heart.

Sophie couldn't wait to have an affair of the heart.

Flicking open her ivory fan, she surveyed herself in the glass, trying to copy the pose and expression of the figure in the fashion plate, eyes shyly lowered, lips demurely pouting, one hand limply extended as if to ward off – though not too vigorously – an ardent lover. It didn't look like her at all.

'Look-see-pidgin!' her amah snorted. If the *lingua franca* of the Coast had run to it, she would have ticked her charge off for simpering.

Sophie chuckled. 'Why *no* look-see-pidgin?'

Why shouldn't she show off? She was going to be the belle of the ball.

2

'Oh!' said her father when she appeared downstairs, and 'Ho-ho!' said Gino Venturi.

'Shouldn't you . . .' Archie Macmillan began, surveying the expanse of bare shoulder offered to the appreciative observer's gaze, and then thought better of it. His daughter was practically incandescent with excitement and the last thing he wanted to do was spoil her fun. 'I mean, shouldn't you have some sturdier shoes with you? You're not going to be able to walk home in those satin things.'

It was the end of January and they were bound for the Chinese New Year party at Headquarters House, the office and residence of the commander of the British forces in Hong Kong. Although Sophie was to be carried there in a sedan, there was going to be no sedan home again: her father was much too soft-hearted to keep his Chinese bearers away from their own celebrations.

She knew exactly what he had intended to say and laughed at him for not saying it. 'Papa! I do have *some* sense.' Taking from Ah Foon a stringnecked shoe bag whose blue exactly matched the velvet of her *sortie de bal*, her hooded evening cloak, she handed it to him. 'And the penalty for doubting me is having to carry them.'

It was going to be a wonderful evening, she thought, even though neither the Year of the Ox, which was just ending, nor the Year of the Tiger, which was about to begin, was at all favourable for someone like herself, born in the Year of the Monkey. However, although Sophie paid close attention to the auguries when they concerned other people, she rarely worried about her own, being such a complete optimist that she found it hard to envisage a situation that couldn't be conquered by the force of *joie de vivre* alone.

Since it was January, it was cool for Hong Kong and the humidity was low, much like a spring day in England – or high summer in Scotland, remarked her father, as the small cavalcade proceeded along Caine Road. Sophie, the poles of her cane chair borne on the shoulders of two coolies, was in the centre of the group, with her father walking on one side, Gino Venturi on the other, two armed Sikhs in front and another two behind. There had been a good deal of crime recently, and New Year's Eve was an extra dangerous time because it was bad joss for a Chinese to start the new year with outstanding debts. The quickest way of getting the money to settle them was to rob somebody.

As they passed the square, ghostly, many-windowed bulk of Government House, floating above a pool of trees and darkness, Sophie could sense that, even though her father and Mr Venturi were continuing to chat quite normally, they were on the alert for trouble. It would be a fine spot for an ambush. Although light and music and the sound of many voices would normally have been spilling out from the classical white porticoes, tonight everything was silent and deserted. Sir Hercules Robinson had departed some months before to take up the governorship of Ceylon and the new governor, Sir Richard Macdonnell, had not yet arrived. Everyone in the colony knew that Mr Mercer, the Colonial Secretary, was absolutely furious that he hadn't been appointed himself, so much so that he was neglecting Government House shamefully. When Sir Richard did arrive, he was going to find it empty of even the barest domestic necessities.

Sophie hoped someone had told Lady Macdonnell that it wasn't worth shipping her pianoforte out from England because the climate would ruin it in no time.

3

Her escorts were able to relax their vigilance a few minutes later, as the little convoy turned into Cotton Tree Drive and the splendid horizon-wide panorama of Hong Kong opened out before them. Sophie had thought as a child, and still thought, that there could be no livelier or more exciting place in the world.

Especially at the New Year. Once upon a time, a terrible monster had descended on the Chinese on the last night of every lunar twelvemonth, wreaking havoc and destruction among them. It had taken many aeons before its victims had learned that there were some things of which the monster was afraid – noise and light and the colour red – and so, once a year ever since, the whole of China had given itself up to a delirious, uproarious, diabolically noisy orgy of redness and brightness.

Tonight, every sampan, junk and ship in the harbour was brilliantly illuminated, the lights doubled and trebled by their reflections in the dancing water, while the gas lighting along the Praya – which served the dual purpose of quay and waterfront promenade – had been supplemented by so many flares that it was as bright as noon. Every inch of the city – the white, elegant, vaguely Mediterranean centre as well as the native quarter – was surging with an irresistible tidal wave of gaudy banners, intricate paper lanterns, clanging gongs, cheering children, dragon dancers capering their way under intricate bamboo arches, and squibs and firecrackers jumping as if even the paving had taken on a life of its own. The light and colour were breathtaking, the noise ear-splitting and the smell sulphurous.

The colony's Chinese, their British overlords and ladies being of a nervous disposition, had for some time now been permitted to let off firecrackers only on the first two days of the New Year and it was their habit to make up for 363 days of abstinence with forty-eight hours of unremitting gluttony. Already, though the rejoicing had barely begun, the streets were scarlet with discarded paper cases, their contents – small, thick slabs of a compound of saltpetre, sulphur and other noisy and smelly delights – going off all over the place in salvoes of explosions like the rattle of musketry, each squib hopping about from one side of the street to the other, or flying ten or twelve yards in quite unpredictable directions with every bang.

'Madonna mia!' exclaimed a laughing Gino Venturi, leaping a foot into the air as one firecracker went off like a rocket behind him and a second passed sizzling by his ear. At almost the same moment, Archie's silk hat took flight and a squib exploded directly under Sophie's chair, causing her to forget that she was now a young lady and squeal with as much fearful delight as if she were a child again.

'Oh, I *wish* we had some crackers, too!' she cried.

Skipping nimbly to his right as another volley broke out, Gino Venturi said breathlessly, 'I do not think I will ever understand why a people as economical and saving as the Chinese should have so great a passion for wasting their substance on a joy so fleeting. *Mind your back,* Macmillan!'

4

The little party from Macmillan and Venturi was still bubbling with hilarity when it passed through the elegant portals of Headquarters House to find the general's less lightminded guests looking as cheerful as a Presbyterian Sunday.

'Sophie, my dear! The noise!' wailed Mrs Lieutenant Renner, fingers pressed delicately to her temples.

'Sophie, my dear! The smells!' moaned Mrs Commander Bagford, fluttering a wisp of lace under her tip-tilted nose.

'Sophie Macmillan! Your neckline!' hissed Mrs Isaac Moore, who had her own priorities. It was clear that she would not have hesitated to throw a shawl round Sophie's shoulders, had she only had the foresight to bring a spare one with her.

Sophie, more than a trifle above herself, said gaily, '*Kung hei fat choi,* Mrs Moore.'

The older woman's pale, lashless eyes glared at her. 'Really, girl, have you *no* sense of propriety? I cannot imagine what your dear mother would have said if she had lived to hear you talking in that heathen tongue.'

Smothering a remark to the effect that, since Mrs Moore had never known her mother, it was hardly surprising that she couldn't imagine what that lady would have said, Sophie explained with exaggerated innocence, 'I was only wishing you a prosperous New Year.'

Then, since there were more ways than one of paying the old cat out, she turned with delight to Mrs Moore's only son and said, '*Dearest* Frank, how lovely to see you! When did you arrive back from Europe?'

Two years of rounding off his education abroad had not cured Frank of blushing. 'Yesterday,' he stammered. 'And you can't imagine how instructive it has all been.'

The rousing strains of the military band and the dutiful words, 'Has it? How nice!' forming on Sophie's lips might not, in themselves, have been enough to persuade Archie Macmillan that his daughter didn't really need him, but a passing servant's offer of a glass of tea punch was enough to swing the balance. In no time at all, he and Gino Venturi were scuttling for cover to the Staff Officer's Room, converted for the evening into a card room, there to join the other merchants in a hand of whist, some decent brandy, and an enthralling post mortem into the deficit in the colony's balance sheet for the previous year.

Back in the ballroom, Frank took in the ravishing vision who had been his childhood's playmate and exclaimed ingenuously, 'But I say, don't you look pretty! And terribly grown up. Will you save me a dance?'

He was the first of many young gentlemen to admire Sophie's looks that evening, though the only one to express his admiration in such wishywashy terms. Lieutenant Playford threatened to call him out for it – how dared he damn those magnificent eyes with such faint praise! – while Mr Duff put in an impassioned counterclaim on behalf of her complexion, being moved to describe the roses in her cheeks as moon shadows cast by her ravishing lips. Lieutenant Grover, having studied from all angles the silken, dark brown ringlets cascading from the crown of her elegant head, made the enraptured discovery that she was one of those rare beings whose left and right profiles were equally perfect, and harped on about it all evening until his friends threatened to silence him by stuffing his cravat down his throat.

Mr Turner Berry, however, observing the belle of the ball nibbling her lips to give them colour when she thought no one was looking, came to the interested conclusion that Miss Sophie Macmillan was a minx.

6

Mr Berry was a sophisticated young gentleman who had only recently arrived in the colony and was not yet aware that in Hong Kong, nine times out of ten, appearances were deceptive. Neither did he guess that The Gup, or local gossip, had already slotted him into place as well bred, eligible, commercially untried, and much in need of being taken down a peg or two.

Sophie, standing up with him for a waltz, found him a sad disappointment. To her very correct enquiries as to when he had arrived, whether he had had an enjoyable voyage and whether he thought he was going to like Hong Kong, the only reply she received was a supercilious smile. So she settled her dimples in place and gave herself up to the pleasure of dancing. If nothing else, Mr Berry danced very well.

And then he danced her right out of the ballroom and into the garden, which wasn't on the agenda at all.

Expecting him to waltz her round a pillar or two and back into the ballroom again, she was startled when he slowed down and stopped.

'In answer to your question,' he told her, 'no, I did not think that I was going to like Hong Kong, but I am beginning to revise my opinion of it.' He took her hands in a firm grip and fixed his eyes on hers. 'I had not expected to find such a perfect jewel in such a commonplace setting.'

Sophie, aware of a light in his lazy eyes that she didn't care for at all, didn't know whether to be more annoyed with him for placing her in an embarrassingly unchaperoned situation or for daring to criticise her beloved Hong Kong.

'Mr Berry, really!' she exclaimed reprovingly, though she smiled lightly as she said it because she didn't want him to think her either missish or impolite.

'*What* a kissable young lady!' With no warning at all he bent his head and pressed his lips firmly on hers.

It hadn't occurred to Sophie, who thought that flirting was just another kind of fun, like dancing, that there might be some men who would read more into her fluttering eyelashes and teasing smiles than was actually there. The other young gentlemen of her acquaintance always entered properly into the spirit of the thing, praising her extravagantly, pretending to worship her, and never aspiring to do more than hold her hand. No one had ever kissed Sophie on the mouth before.

Mr Berry's lips were wet, and she didn't like it. Stiff with annoyance, she pulled her head away.

'No,' he said. 'You can't ask to be kissed and then refuse.'

'I *didn't* ask! Let me go this instant!'

Instead, taking her chin in his hand, he turned her head towards him with the obvious intention of kissing her again, whereupon Sophie, filled with righteous indignation, raised her hand and gave him a stinging slap. It wasn't as hard as she would have liked, but she had never slapped a gentleman's face before and didn't want to overdo it.

'Ah.' He stepped back. 'You're no more than a tease, are you?' Then, with the greatest aplomb, he waltzed her back into the ballroom again.

No one seemed to have noticed that they had been out.

It was some little time before Sophie realised, with indignation, that the reason she was still feeling disturbed wasn't annoyance but anticlimax.

7

It was another two hours before Archie Macmillan, remembering his duties as chaperon in the absence of Ah Foon, who was spending New Year at her amahs' club, decided that perhaps he'd better take a look in on the ballroom again. It was no surprise to find Sophie the toast of a large and merry group of admirers.

'That's all right then,' he said with paternal, if faintly vinous satisfaction. 'Doesn't need us, by the looks of it. Got them eating out of the palm of her hand. She's a taking little thing.'

Gino Venturi, observing Sophie's bosom friends scattered around the walls chatting vivaciously to their solitary cavaliers or even, in some cases, to each other, forebore to point out that the word 'taking' could be interpreted in more ways than one. Young Sophie, in his view, was storing up trouble for herself.

There seemed to be some good-natured wrangling going on as to which of the young men should take her in to supper, a willowy youth in civilian dress declaring that Miss Macmillan was far too intelligent to have to put up with someone who would talk only of pirate-chasing expeditions or how many bolts of cotton to a shipload. She would much prefer, he declared, to hear his own, highly original views on the present unstable climate of international finance.

'And what are they?' someone enquired derisively.

'I attribute the whole world crisis,' replied the young man, 'to the Scottish banks beginning to make their balance sheets public.'

This raised a general laugh, and someone remarked, 'You wouldn't dare say that if Rainer Blake was here!'

Gino, reminded, turned to Archie Macmillan. 'I have been intending to ask, when was Blake due to land in Scotland?'

'Eh? Oh, some time about now, I should think. Said he had business in Glasgow first, then he'd go on to Juran. Don't worry, my boy! Don't worry! Everything will be fine.'

The firm's future thus having been settled to its senior partner's satisfaction, he went on, 'Well now, wouldn't mind another glass of brandy, would you? This business of being a chaperon is giving me a thirst.' Then, his eyes still on his daughter, he sighed. 'How they grow up. She'll be wanting to marry before we know where we are. I just hope she doesn't fall in love with any of those young sparks. Take my word for it, Venturi, it's devilish hard to know what to do for the best.'

Gino, who suffered from neither indecisiveness nor daughters, said, 'Time enough to worry when it happens.' Then, catching the smiling eye of Mrs Commander Keyber, small, plump and known as 'The Partridge' to the gentlemen who enjoyed her favours, added, 'I'll join you later. I think, on the whole, I might take a turn on the floor. I could do with some exercise.'

8

The party ended at four in the morning, and Sophie didn't have to walk home after all, because Lieutenants Playford and Grover stole an unattended sedan from the Queen's Road and, aided by half a dozen boisterous comrades and under the watchful if imperfectly focussed eye of her father, bore her back to Caine Road in triumph.

Sophie had enjoyed herself enormously, despite Mr Berry. In fact, it had given her much satisfaction to respond with an extremely chilly look when he had smiled mockingly at her over the supper table.

Even if she had understood the warning implicit in what he had said, she would have forgotten it by then, anyway.

CHAPTER SEVEN

I

Although Rachel, in one part of her mind, accepted that the months following the deaths of her parents were by no means lacking in event, they still seemed to drag on for ever, each small and separate happening serving only to emphasise the suspenseful nothingness of the weeks between.

Waiting, and waiting, for the day when the contents of Daniel Macmillan's Will would be revealed, Belinda took the curious notion into her head that, by losing both father and brother, she had gained some kind of moral ascendancy over Rachel, who had lost only her mother. It enabled her to talk – and she had always been a great chatterer – of 'my' loss and 'my' family, as if she were the only one who had suffered. And every hour on the hour, or so it seemed to Rachel, she exclaimed, 'Never did I think to be mistress of Juran!'

Perhaps she was right; perhaps she would be. Perhaps Daniel Macmillan had indeed, however uncharacteristically, faced up to his responsibilities and made a choice between his two daughters, one acknowledged, one not. Perhaps he had chosen to bequeath the estate to Belinda in the event of William's death, or perhaps, as Rachel prayed every night and sometimes during the day, he had left it to her, who was his eldest child and by all the principles of justice his rightful heir. She took increasing delight in dreaming of how enraged Belinda would be when – if – that happened. And why not? For nine years Belinda had scorned, sneered at, and made use of her. Rachel had learned to be philosophical about it because there had been no other option, but being philosophical wasn't the same as liking it.

2

No one deigned to tell the girls what decisions were being taken on their behalf. Gresham said merely, and to Belinda, not Rachel, that there would be some delay before those fellows in Edinburgh – Writers to the Signet, did they call themselves? – could complete the necessary formalities in the matter of her father's Will.

He omitted to remark that the lawyers' eyes had lit up at the challenge posed by the late Daniel Macmillan's already tangled affairs, or that they had declared themselves, with a great many ahs, umms and circumlocutions, bound to inform Mr Gresham that it would be quite unprofitable to endeavour to elucidate the late Mr Macmillan's dispositions until certain associated matters had been clarified.

Mr Gresham had listened to them with little comprehension and less interest. Lawyers, in his view, were merely tradesmen whom one employed to deal with legal problems, just as one employed plumbers when the water pipes required attention, or masons when the mortar crumbled. As a gentleman and an aesthete, he had as little wish to be instructed in the intricacies of the law as in the component parts of an elbow joint.

Not for a moment did he doubt that, when the lawyers had completed their esoteric rituals, the estate would go to Belinda, Daniel Macmillan's only blood relative. There had been an elder brother once – or so Gresham remembered hearing – but he had been presumed dead many years before. Gresham felt no personal warmth for Belinda, ingratiating though she was to him, but she was his only sister's child and for that reason he would have been prepared, in the unlikely event of its proving necessary, to go to any lengths to safeguard her interests. He had been closer to Isabella than to any other human being.

In the meantime, he and his family took up residence at Juran, leaving Priors Mead in the hands of an estate manager. The isolation of the castle had a certain charm for Gresham; he had long been meditating a new translation of Juvenal and was unlikely ever to be presented with a better opportunity, freed from the need to entertain and be entertained by the Somerset squires who were his neighbours at home, their conversation an intellectual desert of fatstock prices and hunting, meat and the Meet.

It occurred to him that Daniel Macmillan's stepdaughter, who was quite literate despite her lowly origins, could pay for her keep by acting as his copyist until the Will was proved. After that, Juran could be rid of her. Depending on how she behaved herself in the meantime, he might instruct the lawyers to find a suitable post for her as a governess or something of the sort.

Since neither of the Greshams made any attempt to restrain Belinda, she was soon ordering Rachel about as if she were a paid companion.

'She had better come with us, hadn't she, Aunt Minerva? She can carry the baskets.'

It was Christmas, and Aunt Minerva, steeped in the English lady-of-the-manor tradition, had decreed that the new mistress of Juran should dispense seasonal charity to the tenants. Nothing extravagant, since the family was in mourning, but it would be an excellent opportunity to clear out the storerooms. As a result, Rachel's baskets brimmed with pots of jam showing 'only the tiniest specks of mould'; candied plums that, too sugary for an educated taste, would appear 'quite luxurious' to the ignorant crofters; knuckles of ham whose rainbow sheen was 'barely noticeable'.

'We will not, of course, enter the houses,' Aunt Minerva said. 'The homes of the poor are always full of lice. Rachel will go to each door and hand Belinda's little gifts over, and the tenants may then come out to the roadway to express their thanks.'

This the tenants dutifully did, disguising their astonishment with characteristic Highland courtesy as Rachel handed them their gifts and wished them the compliments of the season on Belinda's behalf. Some of them, she could see, were unsure of which season she was talking about. Christmas was little celebrated in Scotland, the New Year being what mattered, and Rachel wondered what Aunt Minerva was going to do about *that*, since the men of the village were accustomed to spending the entire night at the castle, drinking themselves insensible at the laird's expense.

Trying to imagine Uncle Gresham presiding over such an occasion, Rachel failed utterly, so that her gravity was already precarious when she found herself holding out a pot of ancient jam to Tom Tanner. 'Rhubarb,' she said, her voice quavering slightly. 'I hope you like rhubarb jam?'

He accepted it without a flicker. 'Indeed, yess, and especially when it iss ripe. I always say that cham, like beer, iss the better for a good, long fermentation.'

He knew. Everyone probably knew. The castle kitchen gossips must have been talking about it for days. Rachel gave a hiccup of laughter, but Tom Tanner's expression – a nice blend of respectfulness and appreciation – didn't change. Certainly, he didn't wink at her.

Did he?

'How very satisfactory it always is,' Aunt Minerva remarked on their way home, 'to be enabled to kill two birds with one stone. However' – she picked her way round a puddle – 'much though I regret having to say it, in a properly managed storeroom there should be no clearing out to be done. I fear that Rachel's lamented mama was a tiny bit lax there. I fear also that you, dear Belinda, have not received the instruction in managing a large household which, I have always held, should be part of the education of every young lady. We must see what we can do about it.'

'But we employ servants to do the housekeeping,' Belinda objected.

'Indeed, yes. Their mistress should, however, be knowledgeable enough to ensure that they carry out their duties satisfactorily.'

Belinda tossed her head. 'My mama,' she said, 'believed that consorting with menials had a coarsening effect on a lady's perceptions.'

'But your mama, my love, was a very unusual person. We lesser mortals . . .'

Oh-h-h-h! Rachel thought. Never before had Aunt Minerva given so much as a hint that she and the sainted Isabella had been anything other than perfect soulmates.

'. . . must resign ourselves to a more mundane fate. You and I, Belinda, will have a delightful chat tomorrow, and decide what is to be done.'

Rachel shuddered. Belinda, being fanatically systematic and convinced that she was always one hundred per cent right, never left a stone unturned when she set out to prove a point. If she were to begin supervising the staff, there wouldn't be a servant left in the castle after a week.

Which would serve Aunt Minerva right for criticising Ondine.

Since Belinda was still looking doubtful, Rachel said sympathetically, 'Oh, dear, all that tiresome domestic routine! You wouldn't like it at all, Belinda.'

It did the trick, as always. 'Yes, I would!' Belinda snapped.

4

It took little more than the week Rachel had foreseen for Belinda to organise Juran so thoroughly and place it under such strict budgetary controls – her passion for economy being very nearly as well developed as her aunt's – that everything was reduced to chaos and both the housekeeper and cook departed in dudgeon.

They were no great loss, if the truth were told, but Belinda was so infuriated by their defection that she refused to have any more truck with agency servants. Until she and Aunt Minerva were able to go to Glasgow and interview applicants personally, she decreed that Rachel could justify her existence by supervising the kitchen – 'where you will feel *quite* at home' – while she, Belinda, devoted herself to more refined and therapeutic tasks like counting the sheets and pruning her late mama's roses.

Taking the greatest care not to allow her satisfaction to show in case Belinda changed her mind, Rachel embarked on an intensive study of Mistress Margaret Dods' *Cook and Housewife's Manual*, which obligingly turned up in one of the larder drawers. There was another book, too, a handwritten collection of receipts dated 1712 which had been the work of some Macmillan ancestress, but Rachel put it aside. Some day, perhaps, she might feel the urge to try candying sea holly roots or experimenting with 'Mr Maine's way of dressing carp' – which entailed scalding it alive and then taking its guts out and scouring them – but not yet. Daring to remember, for the first time for years, how delicious food could be, she decided it should be her mission to elevate Juran's cuisine to the standards with which she had been familiar in her childhood.

To her exasperation, it took more than two months before her technique came within hailing distance of her taste buds, since the lady who passed as Meg Dods had not been writing for tyros like herself and didn't always take the trouble to specify quantities. Also, misled by the professional ease with which everything had been done in the kitchens of her memory, Rachel entered on her new duties in a spirit that proved to be far too sanguine. If the maids, Jeannie and Mairi, hadn't been capable of producing perfectly edible, if uninspiring, broths and stews on their own account, the household would have fared badly at first.

Once Rachel had grasped the essentials, however, things began to look up and by the beginning of spring she was producing family suppers so much improved that she was able to feel quite pleased with herself. Not that anyone complimented her on her achievements. Indeed, she sometimes suspected that no one even noticed.

Putting the finishing touches to a mutton and oyster pie one day, she wished there were someone at Juran, other than herself, with a palate sufficiently educated to appreciate it.

As it happened, just such a person was on his way.

5

Rainer Blake had landed in Scotland early in February to find himself committed by his partner, Colin Campbell, to a series of long and intricate discussions with Glasgow's leading bankers on the strategy to be pursued if the threatened worldwide economic recession developed. They were also anxious to hear from him what effect the operations of the new Hong Kong and Shanghai Banking Company Ltd were likely to have on general trade and commerce in the East.

Visiting Juran to assess Archie Macmillan's mortgage request was low on his list of priorities; indeed, he wondered, as he tried to fit the necessary week into his diary, why he hadn't simply handed the task over to someone else. And the answer, he supposed, was plain, vulgar curiosity.

The landscape through which he rode did not look hopeful. Indeed, giving it as close attention as the thrashing wind and frequent flurries of rain permitted, he began to suspect that the soil was not only un-worked but unworkable. The primroses that carpeted the banks were pretty enough, if he had been looking for beauty rather than fertility. The trees on the low ground – wild cherries, lilac, crab apple and rowan – had unfurled their leaves into a green and bronze haze that pleased his eye, but would have pleased it more if they had been timber trees. On the bare hillsides new growth was beginning to break through the old, and the green and brown blended into something halfway between mahogany and purple that was aesthetically interesting but agriculturally unpromising. Such signs of cultivation as he saw were on a small and uncommercial scale.

Only too vividly he was reminded of a letter he had received a couple of years earlier from his boyhood friend Henry Brooks Adams, grandson of the President and son of America's current Minister to England. The Highland landscape, Adams had said, was of 'a stern and melancholy savageness', and 'repulsively bare', in total contrast to his own idea of the sublime – 'the snowcapped peaks of the Italian Alps, with olive trees and vineyards at their feet.'

Blake had been amused. His New England boyhood having left him with an ineradicable dislike of being frozen stiff, he was no admirer of snowcapped peaks, but he had little fault to find with olive trees and vineyards.

Unfortunately, the castle of Juran, nestling picturesquely under its own snowcapped peak, ran to nothing so enticing – to no more, in fact, than a drowned lawn and some struggling, early-flowering rhododendrons in a depressing shade of puce.

No stable lad came running to take his horse from him, and he had to tether the animal himself before mounting the worn stone steps and hauling on the rusty bellpull. While he waited for someone to answer – half expecting an ancient and toothless crone, complete with evil eye – he had plenty of time to observe the crumbling mortar and disintegrating wrought iron of the ogee-arched porch, a piece of Strawberry Hill Gothick so hideously out of place in the rugged context of deepest Argyll that he wondered whether he shouldn't do Macmillan a favour by leaning on it, in the hope that it would fall down.

6

'My name is Blake. Rainer Blake.'

The voice was authoritative, with a faintly sardonic undertone suggesting that, while its owner was accustomed to footmen standing gaping at him, he would have been better pleased if they had ushered him in out of the rain.

'No, your master is not expecting me. But I carry a letter of introduction.'

Rachel, passing through the Great Hall, stopped, the temptation to loiter irresistible. Juran had seen no guests since the funeral more than seven months before, and she had begun to feel as if her brain was dying of slow starvation.

The visitor sounded very sure of himself, but in an accent and style that she could not decipher. There was no upper-class drawl, nor any of the bluffness affected by so many men who had made their own way in the world, men such as the manufacturers and Members of Parliament who had been among Juran's most frequent guests. Neither, she decided regretfully, could she detect a hint of the finicky tones she would have expected of one of the Writers to the Signet who were taking so long to settle her father's Will.

There was a rustle and then silence, except for the noisy bleeping of an oystercatcher somewhere on the shore. Rachel guessed that Angus was staring at the superscription of the letter, trying to look as if he knew how to read, which he didn't. As footmen went, he wasn't a success.

After a moment, Angus said, 'Yess, sir. I will chust go and ask.'

Guessing that the peremptory voice wouldn't be pleased to be left standing on the doorstep, Rachel moved forward to intervene.

'You may give that to me, Angus, and go and tell Jimsy to see to the gentleman's horse. Mr Blake – is it? – do please come in.'

Luckily, she said it before she looked at the visitor, so that she sounded quite normal and rational. Afterwards, it would have been different.

'Thank you. Is the laird at home? Perhaps you would have that letter conveyed to him.'

Glancing down at the letter Angus had handed to her, Rachel saw neither name nor address, only a reflex image of black hair and lean, sculptured features, of long firm mouth and grey Nordic eyes. The visitor's skin was so deeply bronzed that she knew he must come from a place where the sun always shone and skies were always blue. It would explain his faintly foreign, almost piratical air and the accent she couldn't quite place, though English was undoubtedly his native tongue.

There were other things strange about him, too. In an era when most men's features were falsified by beard and whiskers, he was cleanshaven. In an era when most men were instantly identifiable as either city or country dwellers, he was neither. In an era when most men had a solid, well fed look about them, Mr Blake's tall athletic figure carried not an ounce of superfluous flesh. In looks, he might have been the reincarnation of someone from the rakish early years of the century, but in every other way he seemed to Rachel utterly modern, the kind of person who would not only approve of, but actually understand things like steamships and railways and electric telegraphs.

Her heart was pounding so hard that she was unable to collect her thoughts and didn't even dare speak at first. Then, her vision clearing, she saw that the letter was addressed to Danl. Macmillan Esq. and knew she ought to tell Mr Blake that the addressee had recently passed away. But if she did, he might just turn about and depart again.

The crisp voice repeated, with a hint of impatience, 'Perhaps you would have that letter conveyed to the laird?'

'Yes,' she said hurriedly. 'Yes, of course. I will try to find my uncle, if you don't mind waiting?'

7

By the time an hour had passed, Blake was beginning to feel that it would have been easier to gain audience with the Dalai Lama.

Disappearing with his letter, the young woman failed to reappear for some considerable time, leaving him to while away the interval in speculating on her relationship with Archie Macmillan's brother, Daniel. Logic told him that she must be a niece by marriage – which seemed to tally, because she hadn't looked to Blake like a product of this damned chilly wilderness. He had always observed that natives of cold climes tended to put on a good, thick layer of flesh to insulate their bones, whereas this girl – who was about seventeen or eighteen years of age and neither plain nor pretty – was neatly, even daintily built. Even so, he reckoned she must have a constitution of iron. Estimating the inside of the castle to be about ten degrees colder than the outside, he thought that, if he had been a female, he would have been swaddled in half a dozen shawls. But she wore no extra garments over her simple black merino dress and, if the handspan waist was anything to go by, she wasn't wearing many under it, either.

Glancing round the drawing room and closing his eyes, with difficulty, to the green-figured yellow upholstery, the velvet and bobble-draped mantelshelf, the intricate net curtains and the dozen or so stags' heads mournfully regarding him from the walls, he reflected that there was probably not much wrong with the castle that couldn't be put right by stoking up the fires and laying out a few hundred pounds on repairs.

The estate was another matter. It extended, he knew, to ten thousand acres, and he could imagine it having a fair capital value if the right buyer could be found. But as a source of income . . . Mentally, he shook his head. It could not be other than a perpetual drain on Daniel Macmillan's purse, which meant that economy must always be in his mind.

Until he met the gentleman, Blake couldn't tell what form the economy would take, but hoped it would not entail neglecting the fabric of the castle. In Hong Kong, houses remained habitable only for as long as one waged unrelenting war against the effects of the sun, rain and termites; the West Highland equivalents, he guessed, would be wind, rain and salt air.

A blast of salt air swept into the room at that moment, followed in procession by the young lady with the iron constitution, a majestic butler bearing a scarcely less majestic tea tray, and a stately lady in purple who introduced herself by name only – omitting to enlighten Blake as to her rôle in the household – and proceeded to quiz him with great thoroughness and the kind of gracious condescension that always brought out the worst in him.

Although cynically giving her marks for trying, all he permitted Mrs Gresham to discover during the course of the next half hour was that he was more adept at withholding information than she was at extracting it.

In the end, she rose, saying, 'I believe I heard Mr Gresham come in. Will you excuse me? Rachel, you may tell Nièlson to remove the tray.'

8

Resigned to being kept cooling his heels by Chinese mandarins and merchants who would lose face by giving in to the foreign devils' obsession with timekeeping, Blake was much less tolerant in the context of Western society. When Mr Gresham put in his tardy appearance, therefore, he was already well on the way to disliking him.

He would have disliked him anyway. Observing the brows raised infinitesimally in the aristocratically ugly face and the limpness of the manicured hand waving him to a chair, he recognised the type only too well – impregnably secure in his own superiority and regarding his arrogance and acquisitiveness as no more than natural attributes of his right to rule. It was one of Blake's foibles, however, that – despite his own family's ill-judged adherence to the royalist side in the War of Independence – he distrusted blue blood. Experience had taught him that a gentleman's word of honour was unsatisfactory collateral for a loan, especially when the gentleman gave the impression of being at once intellectually sophisticated and commercially unworldly.

As did Mr Lucian Gresham.

It came as an irritant rather than a total surprise when Mr Gresham deigned to reveal that Danl. Macmillan Esq. was now the Late Danl. Macmillan Esq., forcing Blake to say that he would not dream of intruding on the family's private grief and would stay only for tonight – if that would be convenient?

Gresham waved the limp hand again, in a gesture admirably combining civil hospitality with well bred lack of involvement. 'Naturally.'

Convenient it might be for Gresham, but it was seriously inconvenient for Blake. Cursing Archie Macmillan's insistence on secrecy and wondering, yet again, why he had allowed himself to become involved, he began meditating means of extracting, in the course of a single evening, all the information he needed in order to set a final figure for the mortgage. In Glasgow, he had put enquiries in train to ensure that Archie Macmillan was the true heir under Scots law, and had been satisfied. But if Mr Lucian Gresham were to have charge of the place until Archie chose to declare himself, Blake decided he must err on the conservative side with his valuation.

9

'Have you not finished slicing those apples yet, Mairi?' Rachel demanded. 'We'll never be ready in time, at this rate!'

She should have held her tongue. Predictably, Mairi cut her finger and began bleeding all over the sponge pudding. The splendour of the dinner with which Rachel was so anxious to impress Mr Blake dimmed another few degrees, although it still didn't occur to her that the menu might be overly ambitious.

Three months of family suppers had not, after all, equipped her for a guest as sophisticated as Mr Blake, and she had compounded her difficulties by setting about the preparations with an air of such bustling efficiency that the maids, instead of being merely flustered as usual, gave way to something near panic. As a result, the Hasty Mock Turtle soup was showing more signs of haste than turtle, while one of the girls had tried to hurry the roasts along by moving the main spit – on which a gigot of mutton was slowly revolving – closer to the fire, so that the goose and chickens on the smaller spit below received a prolonged and thorough basting of mutton fat. Worse still, the sauce for the poached salmon curdled and Rachel didn't have enough experience to know how to uncurdle it again.

But worst of all was the knowledge that she was making a terrible hash of things. Even Belinda would notice and say something spiteful. And then Mr Blake would think she was just a nobody and not a very competent one, either. And she couldn't bear that.

She would finish off the preparations and make sure the girls knew what to do about the serving. Then she would go upstairs to change. But she wouldn't come down again. She would pretend she was ill. She would retire to bed, knowing that in the morning he would be gone. It was the only way she could protect herself.

And then she thought, *No!*

10

Without realising it, Blake and Rachel each played the other's game that evening.

Blake's only object was to learn as much as he could about Juran; Rachel's – superficially, at least – to distract the visitor's mind from the deficiencies of the castle cuisine. It meant that the mere fact of Blake's asking questions was enough to force her into answering them – and in sufficient detail to keep his attention engaged, because she didn't dare leave him to the mercies of Belinda and the Greshams. Belinda was so overawed by his cosmopolitan air and strange accent that the chances of her uttering a sensible word were negligible, while Lucian Gresham was habitually a less than perfect host, having no talent for small talk and a rooted dislike of exerting himself beyond it. Aunt Minerva presented a different danger, secure in her belief that social converse – as she called it – was the highest art of civilisation and herself its finest practitioner. Given her head, she would subject their guest to a relentless flow of trivialities that wouldn't end until the ladies left the gentlemen to their port.

Rachel was racking her brains for some means of averting this when Mr Blake did it for her by taking the initiative firmly into his own hands.

From where he sat, it had all looked singularly unpromising at first. 'We do hope,' had said Mrs Gresham, treating him to one of her blinding smiles, 'that you will not object to dining *en famille*? Except when the castle is full during the sporting season, we prefer the intimacy of the breakfast parlour to the dining room, which is somewhat grand for small numbers.'

Having washed and changed in a freezing bedchamber, and with his teeth still showing an independent tendency to chatter, Blake had no interest in the name of the room in which they were to dine, only in its temperature. It was therefore with gratitude that he found himself seated on his hostess's right, with his back to the fire, even though this placed him next to the strapping young woman who was Daniel Macmillan's daughter and had welcomed him with so much gush that he had to make a conscious effort to remind himself that she might not be entirely brainless, merely self-conscious.

It was a nuisance. He had learned to be wary of marriageable maidens who, neither bright nor beautiful, were almost invariably possessed of matchmaking mamas (or aunts) to whom his wealth and unmarried state acted as a magnet. His natural disinclination to reveal either of these facts to his present company was reinforced, and, since the blood that flowed in his veins had only a moderate admixture of the milk of human kindness, he made up his mind not to give Miss Macmillan the slightest encouragement. Which meant he would either have to restrict his conversation to Mrs Gresham, or disobey the social rules by talking across the table to Miss Rachel – whose surname no one had told him – or the Greshams' spotty son, Horace. 'In honour of the poet,' Mrs Gresham had explained. 'My husband is a Classical scholar.'

'Indeed?' Blake said, fervently hoping that talk at the dinner table was not to be restricted to Classical scholarship. By convention, business, religion and politics were ruled out, which didn't leave much, but he had been hoping that someone would oblige by resorting to the weather.

Halfway through the mock turtle soup – whose most pronounced flavours were of pepper and carbonised onions – Mrs Gresham gave him the opening he needed.

'. . . varied, even quite dramatic, if occasionally a little more severe than one might wish. For one's personal comfort, that is to say.'

'Of course. And for cultivating the land, too, I would guess. I should be interested to know something about farming under such adverse conditions.'

11

The ensuing silence surprised Blake a little, since he was unaware that Gresham left everything to do with the estate to Mr McBride, the grieve; that Minerva Gresham, though prepared to recognise a cow when she saw one, took the utmost care to look the other way when passing the field inhabited by Juran's well-endowed Aberdeen Angus bull; that Horace's obsession with Nature's Grand Design led him to

135

condemn farming as an ungodly interference with it; or that it had never occurred to Belinda to concern herself with how Juran earned its living. Only Rachel, her passion growing with the years, was equipped to tell Blake what he wanted to know.

She stumbled at first, misled by the concentration in his grey eyes into thinking that he was assessing every single word she spoke, and her too.

'. . . only a few cattle, because the grazing is poor. All except the house cows have to be sent to the Lowlands for the winter.'

Desperately, she didn't want to sound commonplace. He was probably accustomed to brilliant, witty people, and anyone who didn't measure up to his standards would be of no interest to him. How could she possibly be brilliant or witty about cattle and sheep?

'. . . but you really need thousands of sheep to make them worthwhile, and they have a very destructive effect on the vegetation. If you see land covered with bracken, you can be sure it has been heavily grazed by sheep . . .'

The best she could do was sound fluent and knowledgeable, but it was a poor second best. *Please God, make me sound clever and interesting! Make me sound anything but dull and provincial.*

He said, 'In America we know all about cattle rustlers. I seem to recall hearing that the Highlands had their equivalent in the form of sheep stealers. Are they a problem?'

'Not really. Ours are mainly hill sheep, you see.' Then, hesitantly, because she had no idea whether he had any sense of humour, 'The mountain sheep are sweeter, But the valley sheep are fatter; They therefore deem it meeter, To carry off the latter.'

As if by magic, the austere expression vanished and Blake's cool grey eyes became alive with amusement – an amusement that was entirely for her, an acknowledgement of her existence as a real person, not just an anonymous being sitting on the other side of the supper table. Feeling ridiculously weak at the knees, trying to freeze the smile in her memory, she smiled shyly back and murmured, 'Thomas Love Peacock, slightly adapted.'

Belinda was frowning jealously and Gresham's lips had tightened. Aunt Minerva said, 'Rachel, my dear, it is most improper in a young girl to monopolise the conversation of her elders and betters. I do not know what Mr Blake must be thinking.'

Mr Blake, analysing and docketing every scrap of information with which Miss Rachel provided him, was thinking that, young and gauche though she was, she had a gratifyingly rational mind. It was self-interest rather than sympathy – although Rachel could hardly have been expected to know it – that led him to reply, 'Mr Blake is thinking that Miss Rachel has an admirable grasp of agricultural affairs, and that he is being much enlightened.'

If only – *if only* – Rachel thought, her heart almost bursting, there were some way of inducing him to tell them, perhaps not all about himself, but more than the nothing he had so far revealed. She couldn't bear the thought of him being as much of an enigma when he departed as when he had arrived. She would have given almost anything to know who he was, what he did, where he came from.

'Why don't yer bleedin' well ask, then?' muttered little Ellie Vallette.

So she did.

'Do you own land yourself, Mr Blake?'

The creases bracketing Gresham's cheeks deepened, Belinda tutted audibly, and Aunt Minerva – just as if she, too, wasn't filled with curiosity – exclaimed, 'You must forgive my – er – niece, Mr Blake.'

Tempted, Blake succumbed. 'Forgive her? For what?' – though he knew perfectly well for what. According to Mrs Gresham's rules, asking intrusive questions would be shockingly ill bred, even if he suspected from his experience over the tea tray that the lady considered herself as having a special dispensation from the Almighty. It struck him as unlikely that Miss Rachel didn't know the rules, which meant that she couldn't be quite as artless as she appeared.

Who the devil was she, anyway? Big, bouncy, self-satisfied Belinda treated her openly as an inferior, so she could only be a poor relation, perhaps a cousin of sorts.

Wondering whether mutton-flavoured chicken was some local speciality, he laid down his knife and fork and said, 'No, land is not a direct interest of mine. I am a director of the Clyde River Bank of Glasgow, and since we have many investments in India and China, I spend most of my time in the East.'

With cool amusement, he watched his hosts absorb this information. Gresham, he knew, would consider bankers – Rothschilds, Coutts and Barings notwithstanding – as on a social par with moneylenders, and it wouldn't be long before he began wondering why such a low class of person should have turned up, unheralded, at Juran. His code of conduct, however, would forbid him to enquire outright if Mr Blake were a creditor of the late Daniel Macmillan, just as it had already forbidden him to question Blake's letter of introduction from a thrice-removed acquaintance of Daniel's of whom Gresham had never heard. Which wasn't unreasonable, since the acquaintance was entirely mythical and the letter had been written and signed by one of Blake's clerks at his own dictation.

Blake would have left it at that, had he not noted a gleam in Miss Rachel's eye which made him think it might be politic to put a damper on any further questioning. In the tone of finality, therefore, that normally deterred all but the most resolute, he added, 'Being American by birth, I am not myself well informed about the North British countryside, but the business and banking communities of the East are, of course, littered with Scots – all of them homesick for the Highlands. Which is why I have imposed myself on you. It does not do for a banker to be ignorant of matters that interest the people with whom he does business.'

The implication that it was a banker's natural habit to analyse every new experience was one he always found useful when he wanted to gloss over his more purposeful enquiries, and it ought to suffice on this occasion, he reflected, to set any inconvenient doubts at rest.

It didn't. With obvious sincerity, Miss Rachel exclaimed, 'How exciting! You must be the very first Yankee who has ever visited Juran!'

'Am I?' Blake hesitated. 'Well, yes, I guess, but I would advise you not to be too free with the word "Yankee". During these last several years, when there has been civil war in my country, it has taken on a meaning it didn't have before. Now the war is over, I believe that we would be well advised to stop being Yankees and Confederates and start being Americans again.'

Bored, Gresham drawled, 'Settled your differences, have you?'

Blake almost laughed aloud. There was no one on earth more sublimely insular than an English country gentleman – except, perhaps, a Chinese country gentleman.

'Twelve months ago, almost to the day.'

Miss Rachel, the only one, it seemed, to sense Gresham's *faux pas*, hastened to change the subject. 'Do you travel a great deal?'

It was clumsily done, but Blake appreciated the thought. 'I reckon to spend almost half my life on shipboard.'

'Goodness me. Do you visit Scotland often?'

'Every three years or so.'

It was what Rachel had been desperate to discover. Some day, perhaps, he might come back . . .

And then she heard Belinda say, her colour high and her tones almost as gracious as Aunt Minerva's, 'What a pity that circumstances prevent us from inviting you to remain with us on this occasion. But, as mistress of Juran, let me say that when next you travel in this part of the world you will be a welcome guest for as long as you wish to stay.'

'Indeed, yes,' agreed Aunt Minerva, the smile at full power.

Gresham, less enthusiastically, echoed, 'Umm – ah – yes. A pleasure, of course.'

Rachel waited, scarcely daring to breathe. Inviting a guest to return was automatic in the Highlands, a largely meaningless courtesy, but perhaps Mr Blake didn't know that.

Mr Blake didn't, but he guessed; hospitality was a fetish with many isolated societies across the world. It could be useful. 'I may be tempted to take you up on that,' he said, and it wasn't just a form of words. 'I look forward to it very much. Thank you.'

12

He left the following morning – to everyone except Rachel just another stranger in the long rollcall of those who, over the years, appeared at Juran, stayed for a day or two, and were never seen again. And even she, who spent the whole night, and many of the nights that followed, dreaming about him – dreams of a new and unnerving kind – never suspected what an influence he was to have on Juran's fate, and on her own.

As it was, even praying God to see him again was like asking to be given the moon in her hands. When the chill twilight fell on the day of his leaving, she told herself she was too sensible for that and crossed to the window of her room to stare out over the empty land and the emptier sea.

Only gradually did she become aware, in the distance, of the wild exultant music that haunted Juran's sunsets and dawns all through the long months of winter, the sound of the wild geese calling.

There were thousands upon thousands of them, barnacle geese who came every October from their breeding grounds in Greenland and stayed until April. Soon, they, too, would be gone again. During the day, they fed where they could, stripping the crops, but at night they came home in yapping, barking packs to roost on the salt marshes of Corran.

No matter how often Rachel heard their raucous chorus, saw the powerful formations spill the wind from their wings and tumble in to land, she felt a thrill run through her. There was an elemental majesty about them that had nothing to do with humanity, nothing to do with civilisation. When Mr Allan, in church, preached about the Creation of the world, the picture that always sprang to her mind was of great skeins of geese flying low over the empty western sea, outlined against a grey-gold sky.

Long, long ago – before the Macmillan ancestors had hunted them away – they had roosted at Juran, and it was from *giùran*, the Gaelic for barnacle goose, that the estate took its name.

Juran. Rachel had been only eight years old when she set her sights on it, and no doubt she *had* been too young to guess what the cost might be. She had learned now, and it made no difference.

Watching the wild geese, she knew she would do it all again.

What she had not foreseen was that, some day, she might find her love divided.

13

The Writer to the Signet arrived two weeks later, and he wasn't dry, dusty and finical as Rachel had expected, but a large, merry young man with curly red hair, gooseberry-green eyes, and hands of Herculean proportions.

'I'm David Napier,' he said, 'of Napier, Napier, Nelson and Napier. Confusing, ain't it? I'm the one at the end.'

In other circumstances, Rachel would have smiled back at him. As it was, even her breath had deserted her, and what little remained – in a bubble trapped somewhere at the base of her throat – sufficed for no more than a polite, 'How do you do?' as she retrieved her small lace-mittened hand from his huge paw.

Since Lucian Gresham had appropriated the library for his private sanctum and was not prepared to have his books and papers disturbed to suit the convenience of a mere lawyer, Mr Napier was forced to set up shop – as he put it – on the table in the breakfast room. By the time he had unpacked everything he needed, the white damask cloth – which Belinda had not thought to have removed – was as ruched as the skin on a milk pudding and lavishly sprinkled with cinnamon flakes from the disintegrating leather bindings of *Session Notes* and the *Scottish Jurist*. The young lawyer also appropriated the area of Turkey carpet to the left of his chair, piling on it enough bundles of papers to stock a stationery supply shop. At least it explained the huge amount of baggage he had brought with him. He had looked as if he was proposing to stay for a month.

With everyone seated round the table – Gresham at the foot, Aunt Minerva and Horace on one side and Belinda and Rachel on the other – Mr Napier cleared his throat with a vigorous 'Harrumph!' as if to indicate that he was a brisk and efficient young fellow who didn't propose to waste either his time or theirs on irrelevant legal fustian.

The fire crackled faintly; the Argand lamps on the sideboard, lit because of the greyness of the day, hissed quietly; and a leaf dropped, rustling, from one of the sprays of wild cherry blossom in the Venetian glass vase on the side table.

Which of them? Belinda – or Rachel?

Determined not to stare at Mr Napier, Rachel fixed her gaze on the space between Aunt Minerva and Horace. Whoever had dusted the mantelshelf that morning had replaced the ruby glass goblets and rummers in the wrong order, and the little oil painting of a Spanish courtyard, in its disproportionately wide gilt frame, had slipped and was hanging lopsidedly. She had to fight off a terrible compulsion to get up and straighten it.

'You must all be aware,' said Mr Napier, having found the papers he was looking for, 'of the complications that have ensued from the almost simultaneous demise of the late Mr and Mrs Daniel Macmillan and Master William Macmillan. Having received statements from those who witnessed these tragic events, we believe we would be in a position to convince the courts that Master William predeceased his father. Thus, the fact of Master William's intestacy ceases to be germane to the issue.'

Retying the bundle, he dropped it on the floor to his right, and picked up another from the pile on his left.

'The situation might, however, be otherwise in the case of the late Mistress Macmillan, since matters of *terce*, *courtesy*, *jus relictae*, and *legitim* all enter into consideration . . .

'Our enquiries suggest the extreme likelihood, however, that Mistress Macmillan also predeceased Mr Daniel Macmillan and the aforementioned difficulties may, in any case, be independently resolved by the contents of a separate document signed by the testator immediately prior to his second marriage, the contents of which I will explain in due course.'

The second bundle joined the first on the floor, and the young man addressed himself to a third.

'First I should explain to you the matter of succession in heritage . . .'
Why didn't he say what was in the Will? Or what wasn't in it.

Gresham sat drumming his rather thick fingers idly on the table. Belinda's rosebud mouth was thin with impatience. Minerva wore her warm and interested look. Only Horace and Rachel seemed to be making any real effort to follow what the lawyer was saying.

Sasine . . . search for encumbrances . . . descendants . . . collaterals . . . ascendants . . . lack of destinations-over . . . disponement . . . heirs *in mobilibus* . . . Intestate Moveable Succession (Scotland) Act 1855 . . . heirs-at-law . . .

If he didn't come to the point soon, Rachel thought, she was going to *have* to get up and straighten the picture.

'In the case of males, the heir is always one individual, but in female succession the estate is divided equally between all of the same degree, which is why they are known as heirs-portioners. However,' Mr Napier glanced significantly round the table, 'the eldest is entitled to certain subjects which are known as her *praecipuum*, to which she has sole entitlement. The most important of these subjects, in the present case, is the principal mansion house or family seat of Juran, with its necessary adjuncts.'

Rachel thought, *He's talking about what the law says, not what the Will says. And that must mean the Will didn't say anything about the things that mattered.*

'Surely all this is supererogatory,' Gresham interrupted, his sneer more pronounced than usual. 'There *is* only one possible heir and the matter of the *praecipuum* is therefore irrelevant.' It seemed he had been listening after all.

Although he pronounced the word with perfect sangfroid – one of the benefits of a Classical education – Mr Napier was not impressed. His senior partners might have entered the legal profession when lawyers were expected to be obsequious to their clients, but in his own view the time for that sort of thing had long passed. He was prepared to be courteous, of course, but not to stand any nonsense from supercilious fellows – English, to boot – who thought the law of the land had been formulated expressly to suit *their* convenience. He had met and been patronised by Mr Gresham twice before, and it was going to give him a great deal of private and shockingly unprofessional pleasure to wipe the sneer off his face.

There were only three or four sheets of paper in the pile that now lay before him.

'I will come in due course,' he said calmly, 'to those of the testator's dispositions which were not invalidated by his being predeceased by his heir-at-law, Master William Macmillan. First, however, I am instructed to acquaint you with the contents of the separate deed – to which I have already referred – that was signed by the deceased prior to his second marriage. It is dated at the fourth day of December in the year eighteen hundred and fifty-six, is legally witnessed and in correct order. I have had a copy made for each of the interested parties, that is to say the two heirs-portioners . . .'

He paused expectantly, but no one reacted. Nor did they when he repeated, 'the *two* heirs-portioners and their guardian. As you will see, the document is self-explanatory.'

Rising, Mr Napier handed one copy to Rachel, one to Belinda, and a third to Gresham.

The silence lasted only for as long as it took Belinda to read the few sentences the paper contained.

Then, 'No!' she shrieked. 'No, no, *no*! I don't believe it! It isn't true. It *can't* be true! No, no, *no*!'

14

Rachel thought she would faint with excitement.

Her father's Will hadn't specified which of his two daughters should inherit. But the law decreed that in the case of two daughters the elder should inherit. And the paper proved that she, Rachel, was the true and elder daughter!

Juran was hers.

15

The suspense was too much for Horace. His spectacles halfway down his nose and his eyes blinking furiously, he demanded, 'What's the matter? What is it? *What* can't be true?'

No one else seemed disposed to answer, so Rachel, every nerve, bone and muscle in her body independently aglow, smiled and said, 'The document states that Daniel Macmillan, having had a relationship with Mlle Ondine Vallette in the year 1847, when they were both free to marry, hereby declares that Mlle Vallette's child, known as Rachel Vallette, is flesh of his flesh, blood of his blood, and that he is

Rachel Vallette's true father. Your Uncle Daniel was my real father, not my stepfather. I am Belinda's elder sister.'

Horace's slack mouth dropped open and he uttered an incredulous, high-pitched 'mmmm' that seemed to come half from his throat and half through his nose. Then he turned to Mr Napier. 'Does that mean she's the heir-proportioner who gets the pry-kippy thing?'

'Heir-*portioner*. And *praecipuum*. Yes.'

'So she inherits Juran? Not Belinda?'

'Yes.'

Horace, mouth still exaggeratedly agape, stared at Rachel as if he were having difficulty in adjusting to the thought and she returned his stare, trying – though not very hard – to look embarrassed, even a little helpless.

But her eyes gave her away.

After almost ten years of being treated as an inferior, she would have been less than human if, in the splendour of this moment, she had not allowed some hint of her triumph to show.

16

She was totally unprepared when Belinda turned on her and, fists flailing, screamed, 'She shan't have it! It's mine. It's mine, mine, mine!'

The savagery of the attack was as unexpected as the attack itself, delivered with the full force of a rage more hysterical and potentially far more dangerous than on the day, almost six years before, when she had blackened Rachel's eye and helped to change her whole perception of Juran.

The first blow caught Rachel hard on the point of the shoulder, hurling her sideways in her chair so that the second blow landed an inch or two below the first, paralysing her whole arm and leaving her unable even to raise it to protect herself. Thrown completely off balance, she instinctively used her left hand to grip the seat of her chair so that it didn't topple over, and this awkward position, combined with the bulk of her skirts and her closeness to the table, stopped her from rising or even trying to twist out of reach while blow after blow rained down on her, blows with all the power of her sister's sturdy ten stones behind them.

Lucian Gresham could have stopped Belinda just by stretching out an arm. But he didn't.

It was David Napier who, after a disbelieving moment, jumped to Rachel's rescue, but he wasn't quick enough, stumbling over the pile of papers on the floor and then having to circumnavigate Rachel herself in order to reach Belinda.

Even as he moved, Rachel saw the expression on Belinda's face change, the malevolence come into focus and the mouth stretch into a rictus of a smile. Her hands turned from fists to claws and Rachel instinctively closed her eyes and jerked her head violently away, releasing her grip on the chair and trying, now, to force it to tip over and send her falling out of range of the raking hands.

But Belinda had a long reach and sharp nails and in the fraction of a second before Mr Napier seized her, Rachel felt the skin of her face rip from cheekbone to jaw.

17

Horace said, 'Oh, dear. You shouldn't have done that, Belinda. Would you like my handkerchief, Rachel?'

'I have one, thank you.' Her hand was shaking as she raised the scrap of white lawn to her cheek, which felt as if it was on fire. But there didn't seem to be much blood. It probably wasn't much worse than if the kitchen cat had scratched her.

Clenching her teeth tightly, she regained enough control to say, after a moment, 'It might have been my eye.'

Belinda shook off Mr Napier's grip, her face scarlet, her breathing heavy, her expression devoid of any hint of shame. 'Even if it had been, you'd have deserved it! I don't believe this paper is real. I don't believe what Mr Thing says. You're sly and scheming – and you always have been. I never knew what you were up to, but now I do. You've always wanted to take Juran away from me and William.' Her voice rose again. 'I don't know how you managed it, but it's *you* who's responsible for all this, and you needn't think you're going to get away with it, because . . .'

She was interrupted by the cold voice of Lucian Gresham. 'That will do, Belinda. You have no need to upset yourself.'

He gave no visible sign of emotion as his heavy-lidded gaze passed from Belinda directly to Mr Napier, as if Rachel, sitting between them, was invisible, but his voice was vibrant with distaste. 'My niece is naturally upset. And I, having been deeply attached to her mother, who was my sister, am equally naturally revolted by the very fact of –

145

ah – the girl's existence. Had Daniel Macmillan taken a mistress after my sister's death, one might have understood, although not condoned it. But that he should have dared to marry her when he was already tainted by intercourse with this girl's slut of a mother is quite intolerable.'

The shock, for Rachel, was physical; nauseating. She was conscious of a shiver of heat prickling down her spine and the perspiration springing to her forehead. She felt a whirling dizziness and her limbs became as pithless as plucked dandelion stalks, her stomach like a butter churn. It had always been clear that, for Gresham, the discovery of Ondine's having been a professional cook had placed her quite beyond the pale, and Rachel could appreciate that he must be shocked to learn that she herself had been Daniel's illegitimate daughter. But it didn't entitle him to say what he had said.

Through quivering lips, she gasped, 'How dare you!'

She might as well not have spoken. His voice didn't even falter as he went on to David Napier, 'That, however, is not relevant to the issue. What is relevant is that I find you seriously at fault for having caused my niece unnecessary distress. For that I may well report you to the Law Society or whatever the North British equivalent may be.

'The sequence of your exposition was ill judged. You should have preceded your distribution of this rubbish' – he gestured towards the deed of paternity – 'by explaining that the fact of the girl Rachel being Daniel Macmillan's natural daughter is of no importance in the present situation. I myself may not be acquainted with the minutiae of the law, but I am certainly aware that there is no question of Juran passing to her. An illegitimate child is legally barred from inheriting.'

Mr Napier, leaning over to select one of his law books, lowered his sandy lashes to disguise the satisfaction in his gooseberry-green eyes. He had been looking forward to this.

'In England,' he said, 'you would be correct. According to *English* law, a child who is born illegitimate remains illegitimate until he or she dies. But in Scotland,' he raised his eyes again, 'the law is more humane. It permits legitimation *per subsequens matrimonium*. That is to say . . .'

He couldn't resist spinning it out, prolonging the pleasure.

'That is to say, an illegitimate child is legitimated, rendered legitimate, by the subsequent marriage of its parents, always provided they were free to marry at the time when the child was conceived. As were the late Mr Daniel Macmillan and Mlle Ondine Vallette.'

There was a pregnant silence, then, 'I do not believe it,' Gresham said. Rising, he went to stand by the fire, one elbow on the mantelshelf, one elegantly shod foot on the fender.

It was an overworked trick. Mr Napier, who didn't in the least mind being looked down on in such circumstances, smiled cheerfully. 'That is your privilege. But I assure you that the case has been tested, and in exactly the present application, when another marriage intervened.' He opened his law book at one of its numerous marking tags. 'In Kerr v. Martin (1840), the court held that the fact of an illegitimate child's father having contracted another marriage between the date of the child's conception and his marriage to its mother did not exclude the legitimation of the child.'

He couldn't grin at Miss Rachel, though he would have liked to. She deserved a bit of sympathy, amazing young woman that she was, sitting there with her handkerchief to her cheek and looking really quite calm except for her eyes, which were like melting circles against a cold blue sky, translucently clear but distinctly chilly. Most other young ladies of Mr Napier's acquaintance would have been having the vapours by now.

The sneering lines round Mr Gresham's mouth deepened and his voice thickened. '*The girl is a bastard, however it may be dressed up.* And since she was conceived in England, when her father was temporarily resident there, you will find that English, not Scots law will apply.'

Clever Mr Gresham. David Napier selected another of his law books. 'On the contrary. There was another *per subsequens matrimonium* case in 1840, the father, Sir Hugh Munro, being resident in England but having his paternal home and property in Scotland. The case went to the House of Lords, where it was ruled that Scots law applied.'

18

A log subsided in the grate and there was a flurry of rain outside. The net curtains billowed in the draught that swept from ill-fitting windows to ill-fitting door, caressing everyone's feet on the way. David Napier wondered whether Gresham would like the name of a good carpenter.

After a time, he said, 'Satisfied, Mr Gresham? As guardian to Miss Rachel and Miss Belinda . . .'

'*No.*' Gresham's shallow eyes narrowed. 'To Miss Belinda only.'

'But I have an unequivocal statement that you agreed to act as guardian to the late Mr Macmillan's daughters.'

Gresham said slowly, 'Ah. Yes, I see. I agreed, verbally, to be his daughters' guardian. The position of the apostrophe was not apparent in speech.'

Then, domineering brown eyes clashing with David Napier's wary green, he went on, 'But let us disregard that for the moment. In answer to your question, no, I am not satisfied.'

Rachel remembered, as a child, imagining Gresham's face beginning to melt, and now for the first time she saw it happen. The supercilious detachment vanished and the waxen features began to dislimn, to slacken round the edges into something that was no longer controlled and aristocratic but almost primeval. He looked venomous, dangerous and, she recognised in a flash of startled insight, ineffably vulgar.

His voice, however, was much the same as always when he said, 'Juran must and will go to my niece Belinda. If I am compelled to employ every snivelling little lawyer in your contemptible profession, I will make sure that it never – *never* goes to that guttersnipe child of a backstreet whore.

'Be assured, Mr Napier, that I will fight my niece's case, if need be, all the way to the highest court in the land.'

19

It wasn't David Napier who replied. It was Rachel.

Fighting down the physical revulsion that threatened to overcome her, she spoke with an anger she had never experienced before and would never have dared to express – except that the arrival and departure of a stranger, two weeks earlier, had severed the last bonds of her childhood and, with them, all compulsion to be silent and submit.

Rising to her feet, the bloodmarked handkerchief clutched forgotten in her fist, 'What gives you the right,' she said, 'to speak of any other human being like that? What gives you the right to think of any other human being like that? You have no idea what you are talking about – or *who* you are talking about. You rarely spoke more than a few words to my mother in all the time you knew her and you behave, most of the time, as if I did not exist. You know *nothing* about us; you have no right to judge us. And even if you had, your judgement would be worthless because all you know about real people and real life could be written on the head of a pin.

'You couldn't imagine – even if you were to condescend to try – what it's like to scrimp and struggle and slave, and still remain a decent human being through it all. Yet from the magnificent heights of your ignorance and idleness, and because some ancestor laid his thieving hands on a few acres of the countryside and called himself its lord, you presume yourself superior.

'Well, you are not, Mr Lucian Gresham. And while you are contesting my right to Juran, I shall be contesting your right to be my guardian. I may be wrong, but I cannot believe that the courts would uphold your guardianship of a ward for whom *you* have nothing but contempt – and who has nothing but contempt for *you*.'

CHAPTER EIGHT

❧✿❧

I

'Well, the pirate lorcha had seven guns on her broadside and a 32-pounder in the bows, while there were we in the *Prideful* with only a 12-pounder brass howitzer and a crew of fourteen! It was quite exciting, I can tell you! The pirates began by . . .'

Sophie sat on the grass, gently twirling her parasol and trying to count the number of times she had heard the tale before, with only the most minor variations. Lieutenant Grover's dedication to duty was admirable, she knew, and she was really quite fond of him, but what she really wanted to do was open her mouth and scream.

'. . . and then they loosed a shower of grapeshot on us . . .'

It might have been different if she had been able to view him as a potential husband, but she couldn't, and not only because of her natural reluctance to marry a young man who spent half his life at sea chasing pirates and the other half on land, talking about it. The sad truth was that naval and military officers, besides leading dangerous lives, were seldom based in Hong Kong for very long, so that, although they were lovely to flirt with, they were completely unsuitable as husbands for a young lady who, not being prepared to desert her father, refused to consider taking up residence elsewhere. The younger clerks in the merchant houses were no more suitable, because their terms of employment forbade them to marry until they had been five years in the colony. And the older ones were awfully dull.

Sophie didn't know what she was going to do. In another two weeks she would be eighteen and it was high time she married *some*body. She had found herself behaving quite pettishly the previous evening when Dolly Evans, a nice enough girl but decidedly plain, had confided to her that she was about to become engaged to Mr Berry – Mr Turner Berry, who had tried to force his attentions on Sophie not so very many months ago and, being rebuffed, had never so much as looked her way again. Although he was much too full of himself, he was also one of the few truly eligible young men in the colony and Sophie wondered whether perhaps she had made a mistake.

Ah Foon was no help. All she would say when Sophie bemoaned her situation was, 'Maskee!' which was the pidgin equivalent of a shrug of the shoulders. Herself pledged to celibacy, she saw no reason for Sophie to marry anybody if she didn't want to. But although Sophie prided herself on being unconventional, she wasn't as unconventional as all that.

She was resigned to not marrying for love. Her various crushes had been both uncomfortable and mercifully short-lived and, in any case, everyone said that love was an unsatisfactory foundation for matrimony. But, as she had noted wistfully in her diary only a few days before, it would be nice to marry someone who wouldn't be too tiresome to live with.

'I'm not boring you, Miss Macmillan, am I?'

'Goodness, no, Mr Grover! How could you think so?' Sophie closed her parasol, rearranged her flowered skirts, retied the long velvet strings of her wide-brimmed chip straw *chapeau*, and smiled encouragingly into the lieutenant's anxious eyes.

2

The saga of the pirate lorcha was brought to an unpremeditated end soon afterwards by the approach of a vociferous little procession laden with napkins, serving platters, plates, and glasses with tartan ribbons round their stems. It was St Andrew's Day and the new governor, Sir Richard Macdonnell, was giving a breakfast party in the wooded valley known as Little Hong Kong, a favourite picnic spot on the south side of the island. Although Sir Richard was an Irishman himself, there were so many Scots in the colony that he wouldn't have dared allow their patron saint's day to pass unmarked.

'You must be ravenous, Miss Macmillan!' cried Mr Duff, juggling bottles and glasses with the insouciance that was second nature to a young gentleman who had spent his formative years as a midshipman in stormy seas. 'Off with you, Grover! I hereby claim your place by right of service!'

'Nothing of the sort!' came the spirited reply. 'You can dashed well serve breakfast to me, too, you young cub. Rank takes precedence.'

Another of the newcomers, scarlet of coat and white of breeches, intervened. 'Excellent. Then you can make way for me, the pair of you. The military outranks the Navy, any day.'

Sophie, restored to life by this delightful badinage, was in the act of accepting a glass of cool lemonade from Mr Duff when a voice spoke beside her that very nearly caused her to drop it.

'But a banker outranks all,' it said. 'Good morning, Sophie. Good morning, gentlemen.'

Within minutes, Rainer Blake had put Sophie's admirers to rout, remarking when he had done so, 'And don't ask whether I am saving you from them, or them from you, because I am not at all sure of the answer.'

Sophie raised her eyebrows at him. 'Thank you, Mr Blake. Though you have no need to make a career of saving me when I have no desire to be saved!' She didn't know whether he remembered Canton, but she did.

He grinned. 'Not even from your young pirate chaser? What was it this time, a lorcha or a junk?'

Blake had been back in the colony for only three months after an absence of a year, the year during which Sophie had ceased to be an immature miss and become a grownup young lady. And although previously he had made it abundantly clear that she was of no more interest to him than any other spoilt brat, he now seemed to have changed his tune. She didn't make the mistake of being flattered, because he certainly wasn't interested in her in *that* way. He behaved, in fact, just like a cynical elder brother. Sophie wasn't used to gentlemen seeing her as a source of private amusement – except Gino Venturi, who seemed to find the entire world a source of private amusement – and she didn't like it one bit.

'A lorcha,' she said.

'Bad luck.' He smiled affably, which caused her to regard him with renewed suspicion, and went on, 'But never mind. I sent your swains about their business because I want to present to you the three young gentlemen standing over there pretending to admire the hibiscus. They landed just last evening, so I figure they don't even know what a lorcha is, yet. And if that isn't sufficient recommendation, it might help if I tell you that it will add greatly to your consequence to be the first unattached female in the colony to make their acquaintance.'

Austerely, Sophie said, 'One is always happy to make newcomers welcome.'

'There is that, of course,' Blake agreed. 'But you aren't listening, are you? I said that knowing them would add to your consequence.'

She couldn't see anything special about the young men. None of them was particularly handsome, and their clothes were dark and quite stuffily respectable. There was nothing to suggest that what Blake called her 'consequence' couldn't manage perfectly well without them.

'Why?' she said.

'I'll tell you their names.'

3

Vanderbilt, Rothschild, and Morgan. The names of the most famous financiers in the world. Even Sophie had heard of them.

'Goodness!' she exclaimed, hastily despatching her most radiant smile to where the three young men were standing.

Although a steady stream of visitors had landed on the rocky soil of Hong Kong since the days of its infancy, it was not usually on the itinerary when sprigs of the world's great banking houses set out on their somewhat specialised Grand Tours. The previous few months, however, had seen a widespread economic recession that had led, among other things, to the collapse of the great London bill brokers, Overend Gurney, and of Hong Kong's own Agra and Masterman's Bank. It was rumoured on the island that even Dent's was in danger.

'It is when times are bad,' young Mr Vanderbilt told her sententiously, 'that it becomes appropriate to look in new directions. And although you British have arrogated India and Burma to yourselves, China remains open and appears to offer considerable scope for investment. In China, of course, both my country and yours have treaty provisions guaranteeing most-favoured-nation status.'

'Goodness!' Sophie said. 'How nice.'

And then young Mr Morgan beamed at her. 'Jay is a very serious fellow, Miss Macmillan, and I strongly advise you to pay no heed to him. Gussy and I, on the other hand, know what is due to a charming lady. Allow me to say what a very real pleasure it is to make your acquaintance. I trust you will not think it presumptuous of me if I ask you to call me Spence?'

In the nick of time, Sophie swallowed another, 'Goodness!' and sparkled prettily at them all.

She hoped they didn't always talk like that.

Not to have flaunted her new conquests would have taken more self-denial than Sophie possessed, but she was saved from making a complete fool of herself by the three young gentlemen concerned. As worldly as they were wealthy, they were quick to recognise that, although she was the loveliest and liveliest girl in the colony, she was as innocent as the plainest of her friends.

They treated her, therefore, as a pet, squiring her around, flirting a little ponderously with her, and taking the greatest care not to put her reputation in jeopardy. Or their own. Because while their families certainly expected them to have amorous adventures when they were let off the leash, woe betide any of them who were foolish enough, for reasons of *noblesse oblige* or anything else, to return home with a wife. Sophie was their mutual insurance policy.

She, her lightest wish treated by the Three Musketeers as if it were a royal command, scarcely stopped to wonder what others might be thinking. To do her justice, she was in fact much less interested in enslaving her cosmopolitan new friends than in persuading them what a wonderful place her beloved Hong Kong was. Quite as exciting and sophisticated as London or New York! she assured them, and they were too tenderhearted to disabuse her.

During their four months' stay – an unusually long one, since they were treating Hong Kong as a centre from which to visit not only the coasts of China and Indo-China, but even Japan, far away to the north – there wasn't a ball, supper, picnic, military review, band concert or race meeting that Sophie allowed them to miss.

They went walking, riding and yachting. She showed them the Central Bank of Western India, where the infamous 'drain gang' had recently tunnelled into the vaults and stolen more than 100,000 dollars in notes and gold bullion. She dragged them to Aberdeen, on the south side of the island, to show them where the police had been involved in a pitched battle with pirates. She pointed out to them the shop of the Chinese baker who had put arsenic in the bread in an attempt to poison all the colony's British residents, giving four hundred of them severe indigestion. She told them all about the most fearsome and ruthless pirate of the last decade, a young and wonderfully handsome American named Eli Boggs.

She even took them, though not intentionally, to see Rainer Blake falling off his horse.

5

It was a queer little episode.

The Navy had got up a regatta, followed by a dinner on the flagship for two hundred guests, which was followed in turn by dancing on the quarterdeck, splendidly decorated for the occasion with the flags of all nations, intricate arrangements of bayonets, coloured lanterns, and flowers.

Not until two o'clock in the morning did the party end with the guests being taken ashore in the ships' cutters.

The crowd on the Praya was just beginning to disperse, on foot, on horseback and in sedans, when one of the horses whickered, then neighed, and then began to buck furiously, its rider fighting to stay in the saddle. He failed, and hit the ground hard, rolling over and over.

It was Rainer Blake. Sophie, standing nearby with Joanna Bagford and the Three Musketeers while Lieutenant Bagford tried to find their bearers, clapped delightedly.

'What fun!' she exclaimed. 'Do it again, Mr Blake!'

Twice during the evening she had caught him watching her flirt with her dancing partners and the mockery on his face had annoyed her, as it always did. It made a pleasant change to be able to retaliate.

Beside her, Joanna Bagford giggled. 'Aren't you wicked! But how satisfying to know that there's *some*thing in which he isn't infallible.' Then she, too, began clapping.

Sardonically, Mr Blake rose, bowed, and brushed himself down. He didn't seem to be hurt.

Sophie couldn't see any sign of Mrs Lieutenant Beton, with whom he had spent rather more of the evening than she, Sophie, would have thought respectable.

A few moments later, as her bearers left the Praya to start up the hill for home, she caught a glimpse of him talking with unusual intensity to a clerk from one of the merchant houses. The clerk was scarlet in the face and seemed to be denying something.

6

Whatever people chose to think, the idea of marrying one of her Three Musketeers scarcely even entered Sophie's head. She didn't in the least want to be swept off to England or America, especially as her new friends' conversation turned out, if the truth were told, to be little more enlivening than that of Lieutenant Grover or Mr Duff. Indeed, Jay Vanderbilt and Gussy Rothschild went on and on about commerce on the China coast as if they expected her not only to understand but be interested. Compradores and concessions and godowns, likins and sycees and taels . . .

Fortunately, Spence Morgan could always be relied on to lighten the atmosphere just when Sophie was about to threaten to leave them if they didn't stop talking shop. Spence was sweet, not very tall but distinguished looking, with fair hair, grey eyes and lovely manners. She suspected he would have liked to be left alone with her sometimes but, since the motto of the Three Musketeers was 'All for one and one for all', he never was.

It came as a surprise, therefore, that it was Gussy Rothschild who, as they were strolling along the Queen's Road a few days before the young men were due to leave, burst out with, 'A memento. I must have a memento of this visit.' His eyes, gazing at Sophie in the March sun, were as brown as Indian tea, and there was a tremor in his voice.

Sophie's own eyes lit up. If there was one thing she enjoyed more than flirting, it was shopping. 'The Chinese quarter!' she suggested hopefully. 'Silk, ivory, jade, porcelain . . .'

Ah Foon, convinced that Europeans lost face by visiting the native quarter, rarely agreed to take Sophie there, which was perhaps why she liked it so much. It was smelly, dirty, dangerous and furiously alive, its streets loud with the clatter of weavers and copper beaters, the rattle of Cantonese and Hakka; pungent with garlic and incense and ordure; cluttered with congee stalls and bird's nest soup shops, baskets of leaf mustard and bamboo shoots, racks of salted fish and seaweed, piles of lacquered boxes full of dried sea horses and ground tiger bones, brilliant displays of peacocks' feathers. Vermilion signboards dangled over every doorway and most of the so-called buildings were of the kind known as mat sheds – palm leaf walls hung on bamboo frames under thatched roofs.

Unfortunately, the Musketeers' single foray into the bazaar had convinced them that the place was highly insanitary. And in any case, Gussy's idea of a memento turned out to be not silk, ivory, jade or porcelain, but a picture of Sophie.

'A photograph,' he said.

Sophie's eyes dilated. 'No! Oh no!'

'Please.' He pointed ahead to where, hanging from the balconies, sign after sign proclaimed in bold European lettering, 'Nam Ting,

Photographer', 'Hing Cheong, Photographer & Painter', 'Lai Sung, Photographic Artist'.

Sophie said, 'But . . .'

'*Please*, Miss Sophie!'

At this sensitive moment, Gino Venturi emerged from a building nearby to have an overwrought Sophie very nearly fall on his neck. 'Oh, Mr Venturi! They want me to be photographised and I *really* don't think I should.'

Taken aback by the fervour of her welcome, Gino surveyed the puzzled countenances of the three young bankers for a moment and then said, 'My dear girl, you're making them think the studios are dens of vice. Don't worry, gentlemen. It's Miss Sophie's vanity that's at stake, not her virtue.'

'That's not true!'

'No?' He grinned. 'The Chinese believe in symmetry. A good likeness for them, therefore, means being seen to have two eyes, two ears and a face as round as a full moon. The results, by Western standards, are not flattering – more like taxidermy than portraiture – which doesn't suit Miss Sophie's style at all. I would not recommend it.'

'Thank you,' said Sophie with a touch of asperity.

Noting Gussy Rothschild's crestfallen look, however, Gino went on, 'In any case, lacking colour, a mere photograph could not possibly do her justice. Why not a portrait? Chinese artists are not at all bad and they're quick, too, especially if you choose gouache rather than oils. And, of course,' he added provocatively, 'if Miss Sophie were to take the Juran bowl along for the artist to copy, you could have a portrait of her set against the background of her ancestral home in the Highlands. It would be something – umm – quite out of the ordinary.'

Now that money and mortgages had entered into the equation, Gino was beginning to take an almost proprietorial interest in Juran.

'What a lovely idea!' Sophie exclaimed delightedly. 'Could we do that, Gussy? Please say yes!'

If the portrait did her justice, she thought, she could have a copy as a present for her father.

7

On Gino Venturi's recommendation, they went to Yeu Qua's studio, up two flights of stairs at 93 Queen's Road.

Mr Yeu Qua, a plump, good-natured soul, greeted them with, 'You missee gempum, how you dooa?' his hands clasped over his breast, head nodding towards the specimens of his art which, slightly obscured by a forest of dangling, scarlet-tasselled lanterns, hung on the walls above the handsome camphorwood and bamboo furniture. Automatically pricing the fittings, Spence Morgan reckoned that Mr Yeu must be a shrewd cookie.

The top tier of paintings on one side of the room was of Chinese landscapes; below were portraits of Chinese ladies; and below those a row of Treaty Port scenes. On the other side were flower paintings, bird studies, and two long rows of ship paintings which caused Jay Vanderbilt's eyes to light up.

'Say, this fellow is good! Don't you just love that one of the *Rasselas*?'

'Well, he's good at *ships*,' giggled Sophie, who was beginning to have second thoughts.

Fortunately, since the Musketeers were having trouble with Mr Yeu's pidgin, it turned out that he employed a Portuguese assistant to wait upon Europeans and Americans.

One sitting, Mr Porteira assured them, would suffice. 'Castle background will be task of Mr Yeu's number three brother, Mr Lam. Trees, if required, will be five hundred cash extra.'

'Half a dollar,' murmured Spence Morgan. 'Gee!'

Sophie said, 'Oh, *do* let's have trees!'

'Mr Yeu's number four brother,' continued Mr Porteira, 'will then paint lady's – uh – form seated on chair in foreground. I tell him young female, middling tall, slender. Blue dress, maybe? We do very nice blue. Then only need one hour's sitting for number two brother, Mr Sun, to paint likeness of lady's face.'

'Sounds great,' said Gussy Rothschild dubiously.

8

The day before the Musketeers were due to sail, they went to collect the portrait and the copy Sophie had rashly ordered, sight unseen, for her father.

By the time they reached the street again, tears were rolling down the gentlemen's cheeks and Sophie was sobbing.

'The poor sweetheart looks as if she's been starched and then run over by a logging truck!' wailed Spence Morgan.

'Yeah, and look at the *castle*!' Jay Vanderbilt had actually seen a Scottish castle – Balmoral, to be precise – and it hadn't been blue and white with a pagoda roof.

Gussy Rothschild whimpered, 'Oh, Miss Sophie, it's not fair to laugh but you look like Mr Disraeli got up as a Mary Ann.'

It was a most improper thing to say, but Sophie fortunately didn't know who or what a Mary Ann was. 'No, I don't,' she squealed. 'I'm prettier than he is and I haven't got a beard!' Whereupon the three gentlemen hugged her with great enthusiasm and they all laughed until their sides ached.

It was unfortunate that Euphemia Moore happened to be passing at the time.

9

Next morning, Sophie waved a charmingly tearful goodbye to the ship bearing her Three Musketeers off to India and points west. They had been such darlings and it had all been such fun, like having three big brothers to look after her. She was going to miss them very much. They had promised to write, of course, and she had made Gussy swear to keep her portrait hidden away and only to take it out when he was downcast and needed something to make him laugh.

The bright freshness of winter was over and it was a horrid, grey, humid day that didn't invite outdoor activity, so Sophie was sitting flicking over the pages of *Godey's Lady's Book* and sniffling disconsolately from time to time, when Mrs Moore swept in without giving the houseboy time to announce her.

'Leave us, woman,' she told Ah Foon. Mrs Moore was the kind of person who never condescended to remember the name of any servant other than her own. Ah Foon hesitated, but Sophie nodded at her and, a stiff small figure in her black trousers and blue tunic, she bowed and went.

She had brought up her charge too well for Sophie to say to Mrs Moore, as she would have liked to, 'How dare you walk into my father's house and order his servants about!' so, instead, she invited her to sit down and asked politely whether she would like tea.

'Don't try and fob me off with tea,' Mrs Moore said, seating herself bolt upright on the shiny, buttoned leather of the chaise longue and depositing her steel-beaded black velvet reticule on the seat beside her. Then, smoothing out her skirts with a sharp, brushing movement and plucking off a stray thread, she went on, 'I will come straight to the point. I said to Mr Moore last night, "Mr Moore," I said, "*Someone* is going to have to talk to that girl, and although I am the last person to interfere in what is no concern of mine, that someone will have to be I." Mr Moore was in complete agreement.'

Sophie was not in the mood for being criticised by Euphemia Moore but, unaware of having sinned beyond the ordinary, thought she might as well let the old tabby get whatever it was off her chest as soon as possible so that she would go away again.

'I'm sorry,' she said. 'Have I done something to upset you?'

'To *upset* me? After that disgusting exhibition, you ask me that?'

As a young woman in England, Euphemia Moore had been notable neither for beauty nor accomplishment, and although having a provincial peer for a father and one of England's lesser bishops for a cousin had given her a very good opinion of her own worth, it was not an opinion shared by many in a society which did not rate minor peers or parsons very high. Euphemia had been on the shelf for quite some time when Isaac Moore had entered her life, a rough diamond home on leave from the East and on the lookout for the right kind of wife – one whose birth and upbringing would give him social standing in a colony where the civilising influence of the ladies was being much touted as a remedy for the crass criminality that had predominated during the three years since its founding.

Hong Kong in the 1840s might have been made for Euphemia. When she arrived there, she had found no more than a handful of European women, none of them with a Sir for a father or a bishop for a cousin. In no time at all, she had established herself as the arbiter of gentility, the colony's only connoisseur of what was right, polite and decent, becoming so well entrenched at such an early date that no newcomer had ever been able to contest her rule. Governors' wives might come and go, but Euphemia Moore went on for ever. No one liked her, not even her husband or son, but this had the effect of reinforcing her position. What Euphemia Moore said was law, and that was an end of it.

Today, she was wearing an ochre wool dress with black floss trimmings that emphasised the faintly yellow cast so often seen in the complexions of women long resident in the East, however conscientiously they shielded themselves from the sun. Her hair, or what was visible of it under her tight black velvet bonnet, was an indeterminate pepper-and-salt. The small mouth in her flat-cheeked, pointed face had no colour at all.

It opened and closed like a rat trap. 'Seldom have I been so shocked and disgusted. To see an English girl making an exhibition of herself in the public street! Embracing a *man*! And in front of the natives, too!'

Sophie was silent, fighting down the temptation to point out that it had been not one man but three, and to promise that, in future, she would embrace gentlemen only indoors and only in front of Europeans.

'You have no answer to that, have you?' went on Mrs Moore. 'No! You were a hoyden when your father brought you to Hong Kong as a child, and nothing has changed. But I warn you, Sophie Macmillan, people use another word than hoyden when a girl reaches your age, and that word is "fast"! Much though it grieves me to say so, I begin to fear that you are no better than you should be.'

This time, Sophie couldn't hold her tongue. '*Grieves* you? From your tone, I wouldn't have thought grief had much to do with it.'

'Don't be impertinent. And be so good as to sit down. I dislike having to look up and I have by no means finished what I wish to say.'

If Sophie's knees hadn't been trembling, she would have remained standing but, after a moment, she gave in and sat down on one of the upright chairs beside the table where she and her father sometimes had an informal meal. She wouldn't have thought that being hugged by the Musketeers would have been enough to provoke such an onslaught – though they had been laughing and Mrs Moore didn't approve of unseemly mirth, either. Whatever it was, something seemed to have crystallised all Sophie's past sins in the other woman's mind, her childish escapades, her love of fun, the pleasure she took in harmless flirting, her refusal to pay attention to Mrs Moore's dictates. She hadn't been very tactful about that, she supposed, but she didn't see why she should abide by rules laid down by a disagreeable woman who had not the slightest entitlement to tell her or, indeed, anyone else, what to do.

Mrs Moore's tone had changed when she resumed, almost as if she were making an effort to sound reasonable and persuade Sophie to see the error of her ways. 'There are some people,' she said, 'who excuse you on the ground that your faults are to be put down to high spirits. I cannot myself condone this. In my views, "high spirits" is simply another way of saying wilfulness and lack of decent self-discipline. Even if it were not so, nothing could possibly justify the fact that your flirtatiousness – and there is no other word for it – does not stop at irresponsible young officers and ill bred clerks.'

For an insane moment, Sophie wondered if she was about to be accused of flirting with the governor, or the general, or even – incredible thought – Mr Moore himself.

'Did I, or did I not,' demanded Mrs Moore accusingly, 'see you on the Praya last month, pouting and fluttering your eyelashes at one of the Bombay Sassoons?'

Sophie's mouth opened on a mystified exclamation, but Mrs Moore's voice overrode hers.

'An *Indian*!' she said throbbingly, exactly as she might have said, 'Belial, Zamiel and Beelzebub!'

'He's not an Indian,' Sophie corrected her with hard-held politeness. 'I think the family comes from Persia or somewhere. They're Jewish.'

'Persian or Indian, it makes no difference! I am well aware that you have never known a mother's care, and that there are some things which delicacy forbids a father to discuss with his daughter. For that reason I feel it my duty to warn you that intimacy of *that* sort can have only one end.' A bright colour suddenly stained the pallid cheeks, and her voice sank to the merest whisper. 'Babies. *Chee-chee* babies! That is what will happen if you go on the way you are doing, mark my words.'

Sophie sat with her head spinning, not knowing whether to laugh or be sick.

Mrs Moore smoothed her skirts down again, finding another stray thread. 'Well, I hope I have said enough on that score. And at least, this morning, we saw the last of the other one.'

'The other one?'

Mrs Moore glared as if Sophie were being wilfully stupid. 'Rothschild! The other Jew, girl! The other Jew who has been dangling around you. Though at least a white one rather than a brown.'

Then, as briskly as she had sat down, she picked up the beaded reticule and rose again. 'I have said what I came to say, and I have said it entirely for your own good. I hope you will pay attention to it, though I do not expect that you will. But believe me, if you go on behaving like a – yes, I will say it – like a *trollop* for very much longer, you will find that no self-respecting gentleman will be prepared to marry you. And what will happen to you then? Think about it, girl. Just think about it!'

And with that Parthian shot, she stalked out.

Just in time.

Sophie didn't understand her own temper or why, rare though her outbursts were, they should be so explosive. Other people lost their tempers progressively, so that there was a semblance of reason and logic about it, but with her everything came together in a single, sudden and quite unpredictable surge. One minute, she might be no more than mildly annoyed about something; the next, she was in an unreasoning, flaming rage. It disconcerted her just as much as those who witnessed it and although, afterwards, she could usually work out what had caused it, by then it was too late. In the meantime she had said unforgivable things.

It happened very seldom, because she had been spoilt and pampered all her life. Discounting juvenile spite and Mrs Moore's nagging, neither of which had ever really worried her, she could remember no more than a handful of times when anyone had said so much as an unkind word to her, far less tried deliberately to wound or bully her.

Now, her revulsion at Mrs Moore's rancour and bigotry was consumed in an anger so fierce that there was no space in her for any other feeling at all.

It passed in the end, but she was still shaking as she rose to her feet and went to ring the bell for tea, and there was only one thought in her mind.

'So! No self-respecting gentleman will be prepared to marry me? We will see about that, Mrs Moore. *We will see about that*!

'I say! What's going on over there?' exclaimed the normally imperturbable Mr Turner Berry. 'Looks like one of John Chinaman's revenue cruisers. And a brace of gunboats, by jove!'

With one accord, the little group of picnickers hurried to the edge of the bluff for a better view over the waters beyond Little Green Island and the western limit of the harbour that ruled Hong Kong as opium ruled its addicts, with the weapons of love, need and distrust. Without its harbour Hong Kong would have been nothing. Without opium, equally, it would have been nothing.

There were few places on the island where it was possible to get away from either harbour or drug, though the latter was decently hidden in sturdy chests transferred from ship to warehouse, warehouse to ship, without the wives or daughters of those whose fortunes were based on it even being consciously aware of what it was that paid for their dresses and bonnets, their houses and servants, or any of the other comforts they demanded to compensate them for a life of heat and humidity, torrents and typhoons. They had heard of opium, of course, knew it was useful as a medicine, and recognised it – even defended it – as an item of trade. But in the increasingly genteel decades that had followed the Opium Wars, they had learned to behave as if it were no more than a minor factor in the colony's prosperity.

In which they were wrong. Because, despite its façade of commercial respectability and Christian piety, the island of Hong Kong was little more than an immense opium smuggling depot.

It was not surprising, therefore, that harbour and opium should both have been involved in many of the significant events affecting the colony, though it was the purest chance that among the eyewitnesses on this occasion were the members of a riding party got up by Mrs Commander Bagford for two dozen of what she called 'the young people', by whom she meant the unmarried ones. She herself, though not a day over twenty-two and something of a featherbrain, was acceptable as a chaperone by reason of her marital status.

'Nothing strenuous,' she had written in her chit of invitation to Sophie. The ladies of Hong Kong were inveterate writers of chits, none of them trusting their servants to convey a message in any other form. 'Just a gentle trot to Mount Davis and back. I will have Kang Yi prepare a little tea party for us.'

She could not have chosen a more propitious day or place. The late October weather was delightful, sunny but with a soft breeze from the east, and the exercise itself a joy after the long, hot, humid months of summer when exercise of any kind was unthinkable except in the hours just after dawn. The rains had laid the dust and the paths were resilient, the foliage lush, and the sea as green as emerald. Even the snakes and insects were feeling goodhumoured enough to leave Mrs Bagford's party alone as it wended its cheerful way to the grassy slope overlooking Little Green Island.

Pleasantly revived by the tea, sandwiches, scones and cakes that had been waiting for them, the party was standing chatting in a desultory way prior to remounting when Mr Berry caught sight of the gunboats.

'What the deuce do they think they're doing right on the edge of our harbour!' demanded Frank Moore. 'Dashed cheek!'

Tucking her hand into the crook of his arm, Sophie helpfully stated the obvious. 'It looks as if they're trying to force that junk to come about.'

No one was prepared to believe it at first, despite all the shouting going on between the small, trim steam cruiser and the big trading junk with its high bow and even higher stern. The junk, like all such, had an eye sketched on either side of the bow to enable the vessel to see her way, and the stern was gorgeously painted with scarlet, green and gold dragons and peonies. The huge sails, shaped like butterfly wings, had their fabric gathered over horizontal ribs of bamboo in the way that always made Sophie think they should have been smocked by a sempstress rather than rigged by a sailmaker.

'They're going to try and board!' squeaked Joanna Bagford, her cheeks pink with excitement and her nose even more tip-tilted than usual. 'Oh, how I wish Johnnie were here!'

'They can't be,' said a quiet voice. It was Dolly Evans, who always said everything quietly, as if she wasn't sure that anyone else would be interested in hearing. Her soon-to-be husband, Mr Berry, claimed to find it very restful.

Then suddenly, there was a loud crack and a fountain of water sprang up just ahead of the junk.

Frank, who tended to be boyishly excitable, clapped his hand over Sophie's with such a smack that she said, 'Ooh!'

'They've put a shot across her bows!' He was so busy being outraged that he forgot to close his mouth again and Sophie couldn't help giggling, though it pleased her that, even with his mouth ajar, he was still quite handsome in his own curly-headed way. Considering his parentage, she couldn't think where he had got his looks from, or his amiability.

12

It was six months since his mother had paid her fateful visit to the Macmillan house in Caine Road, and just one day less than six months since Sophie had embarked on her campaign of retaliation.

Frank had been innocently pleased to meet her, apparently by accident, wandering alone in the Botanic Gardens. 'Isn't this cosy! Do you think we might walk together for a bit? You always have so many of the fellows chasing you that I never get a chance to have you all to myself.'

'Flatterer!' Sophie had chuckled. 'And you've no need to ask in that polite way. Doesn't it strike you that I might like to be *comfortable* sometimes? Dashing young officers are all very well, but I can never be at ease with them as I can with you. We've known each other for so long.'

'You looked comfortable enough with Vanderbilt and company.' He said it in a friendly way, not critically, but she thought it would be sensible to lay that particular ghost immediately.

'Yes, but that's because Americans are so easy to talk to.' Except when they happened to be Rainer Blake, of course. 'They say it's because the young ladies there are much more independent than we are and don't expect to be treated as if they're made of porcelain. They even said they knew several who were quite *clever*.'

Frank laughed. 'They were teasing you. I expect they know as well as anybody that ladies, even American ladies, don't have brains the way men have.'

'No. Anyway, I don't think I should like being clever.' It wasn't something she had ever considered before, but to say a girl was clever was the same as calling her a bluestocking, and nothing could have been more *fatal* to her marriage prospects. 'Why don't we just stroll around and look at the plants. Won't it be lovely when they've all grown up to a proper size?'

The Botanical Gardens had been opened only two years before, and although the seeds and plants brought from Australia were doing very well, they still didn't look altogether settled.

'Mmmm. I hope Donaldson knows what he's doing,' Frank said judiciously, as if he were perfectly competent to tell one end of a plant from another and wasn't merely repeating what he had heard from a fellow in the Club. 'If they grow too big they'll blot out the view of Government House and the harbour.'

There were a few strollers around, including a number of acquaintances who had to be nodded to and smiled at, and several respectable young Chinese men wearing white tunics and carrying fans. The band of the 33rd was playing in the little pavilion in the gardens, a jolly 'Oompah, oompah' kind of music, and Frank, just in case Sophie hadn't believed him the first time, said again, 'Isn't this cosy?'

He was glad she felt comfortable with him, because she was the only girl he knew with whom *he* was comfortable.

Despite his two years in Europe, Frank's social accomplishments were not great. He was still not a ladies' man, still prone to stammer slightly in female company. It was his mother's influence, he sometimes thought. It was hard for a fellow to develop assurance when he was always expecting to be told to do this, or not do that, and please not to argue because his mama knew what was best for him. Just at the moment, he was perfectly happy as an eligible bachelor on whose every word young females hung admiringly, but it couldn't last. The trouble was that one never knew how young females were likely to develop as they grew older. Once, when his father was well lubricated, he'd asked him what his mama had been like when she was a young woman. 'Don't know as I recollect,' Moore senior had replied, giving the matter deep thought. 'Much like now, I reckon. Reet governessy.'

'You know, Sophie,' he said wistfully, 'it's a pity you and my mama don't hit it off better.'

Sophie had already guessed that Mrs Moore hadn't chosen to regale her son with the details of her own latest misdemeanours; probably hadn't wanted to put ideas into his head. Silly woman.

Dropping her eyes demurely, she said, 'It's my fault. I know I should be prim and proper like all the other girls, but then I wouldn't be *me*, would I?'

It was a point that hadn't previously occurred to Frank, even when, as so often in the last couple of years, he had found himself defending his childhood friend against his mother's strictures. If Sophie lost her gaiety and her carefree sparkle, she would be just like all the other girls in the colony. Prettier, of course.

'Dash it, no, you wouldn't. And we can't have that!' He grinned at her.

He had a rather engaging grin. Sophie wondered why on earth she had never thought of him before as a potential husband, and supposed that knowing him as a boy must have had something to do with it. He still seemed awfully young, and if the truth were told he wasn't the most exciting person to be with, but there was no denying that he was one of the few young men in the colony who were thoroughly eligible. And she did like him, in a lukewarm kind of way.

'Did you really mean it,' he went on, being one of those people who always needed to be reassured not once, but two or three times, 'about feeling more comfortable with me than with the other chaps?'

'Oh, *yes!*' She gave him the benefit of her most fetching smile.

It was something she had never troubled to do before, and it had the most extraordinary effect on Frank. The brilliant sapphire gaze seemed to be telling him everything he had ever wanted to hear. Suddenly, he knew himself to be all sorts of a fine fellow.

With a decisiveness hitherto quite foreign to him, he said, 'I think I ought to start taking you about a bit.'

Snap!

'Oh, Frank, that would be lovely. I feel so safe with you. If you're sure your mama won't object?'

'Let her try!' he said stoutly.

By the time Mrs Moore had begun to suspect what was going on, it was too late. Frank had been smitten, even if, being fearful of responsibility, he was not yet ready to admit it. He did say, however, with the stubbornness that his mother knew only too well, that he would be obliged if she would refrain from criticising Miss Macmillan, otherwise they would be likely to fall out. Mrs Moore had enough sense not to say another word against Sophie in his hearing, even if she said a great deal out of it.

13

'They *are* boarding her, dash it! What cheek!' said Mr Berry, shading his eyes against the sun-sparkling waters.

'Perhaps the junk's done something it shouldn't,' Sophie suggested, and blinked as every young man in the party turned and glared at her.

'Hush,' Frank said. 'It's a junk operating out of *Hong Kong* and that's a *Chinese* cruiser. That's all there is to it. They've absolutely no right to interfere with our shipping, whatever the cargo. It's an outrage.'

'Cargo?'

'Never you mind.' In hard fact, Frank didn't actually know what the cargo was, but it wasn't difficult to guess.

A century before, opium smoking had become a serious national problem in China and by 1800 all imports of the drug had been banned. But the poppy grew in India and for India's British rulers the trade with China had been much too profitable to be abandoned just because Peking had taken the notion of making it illegal. In the war that had ensued in 1840, the outcome had been defeat for China – though not a sufficiently crushing defeat to persuade the emperor to revoke the ban – and a gain for Britain of the territorial foothold of Hong Kong, ideally located as a smuggling entrepôt.

In the end, of course, the Chinese had been forced to legalise the trade, attempting to control it by means of Customs duties levied at the 'Treaty Ports', the small handful of places on Chinese soil where foreign merchants were officially permitted to do business.

The attempt had proved vain, since it was ludicrously easy for Chinese residents of Hong Kong, whether on their own account or that of the British merchants, to ignore the Treaty Ports and smuggle duty free opium in at all the places where the blue-eyed, fair-haired, instantly recognisable barbarians were forbidden to venture. Those who were knowledgeable about such things estimated that thirty per cent of opium imports entered China legally at the Treaty Ports; the other seventy per cent was smuggled.

Everyone was happy except the Chinese government, which was losing a million dollars a year in revenue. It was widely known that Jui Lin, viceroy of Hong Kong's neighbouring Chinese province of Liang Kwang, felt particularly strongly on the subject.

And now Mr Jui had apparently decided to do something about it – and, insultingly, within sight of Hong Kong itself.

Sophie, the sun hot on her back and the warm wind catching at the skirts of her riding habit and fluttering the veil round her top hat, became aware that her eyes were hurting and she was not comfortable. They had been standing staring for the better part of an hour, during which time a rapidly growing number of onlookers had appeared. The sea being all around, very little that happened on it escaped the notice of interested parties.

'Scandalous . . .'

'Damned Celestials! Think they own the world!'

'Disgusting . . .'

'Macdonnell will have to do something about this . . .'

'Formal protest from the Chamber of Commerce . . .'

'It's Hart who's behind this, you mark my words!'

Mr Hart, Sophie remembered, was an Irishman who, she had never understood why, was working for the Chinese government, trying to reform their Customs service.

'Shameful . . .'

'Blatant contravention of treaty obligations . . .'

'Infamous . . .'

Glancing round, Sophie noticed Gino Venturi standing far over to the left, a telescope to his eye; he had the most amazing knack of being prepared for anything. Mr Isaac Moore, she saw, was also among the newcomers.

Just as she was tactfully removing her hand from his son's arm, she discovered with a start that Rainer Blake was right behind her, looking enigmatic. Mrs Commander Keyber was with him. Mrs Commander Keyber was with him quite often these days.

It was clear that he had been watching her. Nothing ever seemed to miss those amused, penetrating grey eyes of his. But when he spoke, at least he was gentleman enough to lean forward and speak in such a low voice that only she could hear.

'It would undoubtedly be a good match,' he murmured. 'I am about to leave on an extended trip to – er – foreign parts. Knowing what a persuasive young lady you are, I am sure that when I return I will be able to felicitate you.'

And then he compounded his perfidy by glancing at Frank's oblivious back and shaking his head slightly, as if Frank were more deserving of sympathy than felicitations.

She was *not* going to rise to the bait. 'Thank you, Mr Blake,' she said with what she considered a very creditable attempt at puzzlement, 'but I cannot imagine what you mean.'

The infuriating man laughed outright.

CHAPTER NINE

I

An icy rain was sheeting down from the masses of cloud piling into the glen, closing the horizons, smothering the hills in mist. The landscape was a wilderness of grey stone and brown soil, of boulders and rocks and water-worn shingle, of heather the colour of wet cinnamon, of squelching peat and pools full of black water. A more desolate scene it would have been hard to imagine.

'Deuce take it!' said Philip Roy. 'This is getting beyond a joke. We'd better shelter under the overhang and have something to eat. What have you brought?'

One day, Rachel thought, she would bring a slice of dry bread and see what he said to that. The trouble was that he would miss the point entirely and – when she had explained – would launch into a huffy rebuke about a bit of decent picnic food not, surely, being too much to ask in return for his generosity in allowing her to come stalking with him. It was an argument that might have carried weight once, before she discovered how useful he found her for fetching and carrying.

When they had finished the last of her oatcakes and cold roast grouse, Philip refreshed himself from his whisky flask and lit a cigar. 'That's better,' he said. 'Ah! The sky's lightening over there. And listen!'

A ring ousel had begun to whistle on the hillside, and somewhere over in the bracken to their right a cock grouse was crowing.

'We'll get some sport yet,' Philip said with satisfaction.

Rachel raised a sardonic eyebrow. When Philip said 'we', he meant himself and his rifle; otherwise, he used the first person singular. He had always been self-centred; now, with every young female for a hundred miles around wilting at the mere sight of his ruggedly handsome person and hanging on his every authoritative word, he had become appallingly vain.

'What's this about a Hallowe'en party, then?' he asked. 'I don't remember Lucian Gresham ever inviting a soul to Juran in the – how long is it? three years? – since he's been in residence.'

It was a moment before Rachel replied, 'No, he doesn't much care for entertaining.'

'Then why the party? I'll send Fraser over with my formal acceptance tomorrow, by the way. Can't afford to turn down an opportunity of dancing with my favourite female.'

He placed a possessive hand on her knee.

She plucked it off and returned it to him. 'It was Belinda's idea.'

'That sounds more like it. Wants practice at being a gracious hostess, does she? Well, I should be grateful, I suppose. Or my mother should. She's the one who's going to have to educate the girl when we make a match of it. Ah, if only it could be you!' He looked as if he were about to chuck Rachel under the chin and, pointedly, she recoiled.

'A pity,' he went on, oblivious. 'But there it is. She has more to offer than you do.'

2

Gresham had won. Which meant that Belinda had won.

For three idyllic weeks, Rachel had believed herself mistress of Juran, although it couldn't be made public because David Napier and Lucian Gresham had agreed that no one other than the people directly involved should know what was going on until everything had been irrevocably settled, one way or the other.

And then she had received a letter from Mr Napier, who had something to say that he preferred not to put in writing. Would she meet him privately on the Friday of the following week at Inveraray? He understood that the inn was a respectable place.

It would be the first time she had left Juran for almost ten years but, although she should have been exhilarated by the prospect, she had thought about the twenty-mile ride not at all, only about its ending at the inn – which Hogg, encountered on the hill, had told her was big and white and had nine bay windows overlooking the loch.

Afterwards, Hogg had waited, eyeing her speculatively, hoping she was going to tell him why she wanted to know. But she couldn't, of course – and, in any case, wouldn't. Despite his helpfulness on the day of her parents' death, she was still suspicious of him. Politely, therefore, she had bent to discourage his new puppy from trying to clamber up her skirts, handing him back to his owner with a smile and saying, 'This one looks as if he might develop into a fine mountaineer some day.'

Hogg's gaze didn't shift. 'He likes you. D'ye want him? He'd be company.'

She wasn't used to being offered gifts. At Juran, gifts had never been more than tokens – a silver shilling from her father, ribbons from her mother, knitted mittens from Aunt Minerva, slippers carelessly stitched by Belinda and presented in her and William's names, a card nominally from Uncle Gresham but inscribed in Aunt Minerva's handwriting. It was hard to summon up even a perfunctory 'thank you'.

She knew the puppy wasn't going to cost Hogg anything, but it didn't stop her being touched by the offer.

There was no means of guessing how many strains there were in the little animal's antecedents; he was the most mongrelish of mongrels and scarcely less disreputable than his master. He would offend seriously against Lucian Gresham's views about ancestry and purity of breeding.

'Yes,' she said. 'I would like him very much.'

3

David Napier had been waiting for her in the inn parlour, and even as the landlord's wife fussed around her, seeing her settled in a hard, uncomfortable chair and ascertaining what kind of refreshment she would like, she knew something had gone badly wrong.

The terms of his letter had been perfectly commonplace but she had spent most of the intervening days and nights racking her brains for some acceptable reason why the mistress of Juran should be asked to meet her lawyer in what was undoubtedly a clandestine fashion. Now, she realised that her search for an acceptable reason had been a defence against facing up to the one reason that was completely and utterly unacceptable.

She made a pretence of sipping her tea when it came, and even managed to swallow a bite of scone, but in the end she had to say, 'Mr Napier, I wish you wouldn't put off any longer. Tell me what has happened, please?'

And then she realised that he was almost in tears. 'It was my fault. My clerk missed one of the references. He found what we were looking for and went no further. The legitimation judgement in Kerr v. Martin was so exactly what we needed.'

She didn't ask what was his fault, because she had known it was all too good to be true. But her voice wasn't as reliable as she would have liked when she said, 'I thought the case was cut and dried.'

'Oh, it was.' His restless fingers had already reduced one scone to a pile of crumbs, and now he embarked on another. 'It was the right precedent, so far as it went. You *are* legitimate, with all the rights and title of legitimacy . . .'

There was a long silence broken only by the distant sounds of altercation in the kitchen.

In the end, Rachel said, 'But?'

The gooseberry-green eyes lifted miserably to hers. 'But, later in the same case, the court ruled that the legitimation of a child whose parents' marital history was the same as yours should not – should not be allowed to prejudice the rights of the children of the father's intervening marriage.'

She detached her eyes from his and allowed them to stray out of the window to where a fishing boat was unloading. The crew looked cheerful. Nice, normal people landing a satisfactory catch. The loch was mirror calm, a long sea inlet nestling among the soft green hills. Trim, cared for, uncomplicated.

'So although I am the elder, and the legitimate daughter of my father, I can't have Juran after all?'

'No.'

He picked a few raisins out from among the debris and put them in his mouth. 'I thought I should tell you before you heard it from Mr Gresham. He is bound to find out, because that's what his lawyers will be looking for. You could contest it in the courts, perhaps.'

She laughed, since the only other options were to burst into tears or start smashing the crockery. Detaching the purse from her waist, she emptied its few jingling contents among the crumbs. 'Could I? My dear Mr Napier, that – except for a few trinkets of my mother's – is all I possess in the world. I hope you are not expecting me to reimburse you for the cost of your journey here today?'

He shook his red head violently. 'Can you forgive me?'

After some thought, but without visible trace of emotion, she said, 'No, I don't think I can.'

4

There had been a bitter pleasure in not being caught out when, a few

174

days later, Gresham tossed a letter across his desk to her, saying, 'You will see from that that I was, of course, correct. Juran belongs to Belinda.'

She read the letter twice, with quiet care, Gresham not even troubling to watch her but absorbing himself in his Juvenal, a poet whom Rachel had come to detest. For months, she had been copying and recopying him, verse after acrid verse, every time Gresham changed so much as a comma.

'What now?' she said when she had finished.

He didn't look up. 'Your meaning escapes me.'

She had steeled herself. She expected to be told to leave, to find a post somewhere as governess or companion – or whore – to be given, perhaps, a sovereign or two to see her on her way. David Napier had told her that the estate had no assets beyond castle and land, so that being an heir-portioner, which she still was, would be of no benefit to her. There was nothing to be apportioned.

'You wish me to leave, I presume?'

The small eyes glanced up expressionlessly. 'To leave? Scarcely. I was appointed your guardian until you reached the age of twenty-one. I should be in dereliction of my legal duty if I were to send you packing.'

She hadn't thought of that.

'In any case,' he added dismissively, 'Belinda wishes you to remain.'

To crow over her. To repay her for being who she was. Rachel could understand it very well.

Unexpectedly, Gresham rose to his feet and strolled round the desk, magnanimous in victory. He was six or seven inches taller than she and he halted very close to her, so that she had to look up to him as he said, 'You would not, in any case, wish to leave Juran. It is the only home you have. There is, of course, one thing on which I insist. You will continue to be Belinda's "stepsister". The sorry tale of your parentage is hardly something one would wish to become public property.'

There was nothing in his voice that she hadn't heard before, nor any change in the meaningless smirk that always resided on his features. But, shockingly, he raised his hands, placed them on her shoulders and gave them a deep, slow squeeze.

'You are by no means unintelligent, despite your origins. My niece claims that you are sly, but I have observed no sign of it. Rather the reverse. All in all, when you have overcome your disappointment and learned to know your place, you will find life quite tolerable again.'

Her shudder of revulsion was uncontrollable, but Gresham mistook it. 'Yes, there is a chill in the air. Oblige me by sending one of the footmen in to light the fire.'

Back in her own room, Rachel had wanted to weep but couldn't, and in the months that followed – dead, emotionless months – had found herself thinking that perhaps her tear ducts had dried up for ever.

She became expert, however, at avoiding being alone with Gresham, even if she was unable to evade the seemingly careless clasp on her arm in which he publicly indulged himself. He never attempted more, although she knew, uneasily, that he could have taken any advantage of her that he chose.

Cat and mouse, she thought, guessing that his object was to make her fear him physically, as she already feared him – however hard she tried to fight it – emotionally.

5

'When you know your place . . .'

Her place now was little better than that of an upper servant, in some ways worse. Servants at least received wages. But, as Aunt Minerva had explained, the death of 'Belinda's dear papa' had brought to light the sad fact that the estate was living beyond its means, which meant that economies would have to be made. It came as no surprise to Rachel that the economies affected herself a great deal, Belinda, Minerva and Gresham scarcely at all.

For the last two years she had been relegated to supervising not only the cooking and the kitchen, but stocking the storerooms with jams and preserves, smoked sheeps' and deer tongues; to chivvying the maids down to the river to do the laundry; watching over them while they did the spinning and weaving; overseeing the poultry run and the dairy; haggling with the local fishermen; bullying the gardeners; arguing with the crofters.

She was so tired at nights that she scarcely had the energy to dream, and when she did she dreamed mainly of a dark, formidable stranger riding away – away – away – from Juran to a place where the sun always shone and the skies were always blue. She was resigned to never seeing him again, but that didn't lessen the hurt.

There was nothing for her to look forward to. Curiously, it made her stronger rather than weaker. She had been so anxious, once, to belong to the world inhabited by her new family that, throughout her childhood and adolescence, she had tried constantly to behave as she was expected to behave, to turn herself into a neat social fit, a round peg in a round hole. Some of it, she supposed, had been worthwhile; and some of the effects would no doubt linger. But there was no longer any reason to fudge the person she really was, deep inside.

6

Astringently, she told Philip, 'You're so critical of Belinda that I don't understand why you should be thinking of marrying her.'

He shrugged, his eyes on where the sun had begun to break through the clouds. The downpour was changing from shards of ice into large, lazy, scattered drops of rain.

'My parents and hers hatched the notion when we were children. I don't say she would be my choice, but marriage is a business arrangement, after all.'

'Is it? Does love have nothing to do with it?'

He gave a snort of laughter. 'A fellow can get "love", as you call it, anywhere. He doesn't have to marry for it.'

'But surely you want to *like* your wife? You have to live with her.'

From under his strong, straight brows, he gave her what he thought of as his quizzical look, as if wondering whether she was making a bid on her own account. 'Well,' he said, 'I don't have to see much of her. I can put up with Belinda in exchange for Juran.'

Everything a wife possessed at marriage became the property of her husband, to dispose of as he wished. Once Philip and Belinda were married, Rachel's claim to Juran would cease to exist. In all likelihood, she would be expected to leave and she would want to, because she wouldn't be able to bear watching Philip running things as he chose, perhaps even putting the land down to sheep.

Juran was *hers*. In spite of everything, she continued to nourish a small, inexplicable hope that destiny would wave its magic wand and give her, after all, what she so passionately desired. There were so many things she would do to make Juran what it ought to be.

'I've always had my eye on it,' Philip remarked. 'It'll complement Altsigh very nicely.'

His simple, unblushing imperialism was far harder to combat than love would have been, and Rachel had no weapons. The only course open to her was to continue fostering his vague dislike of Belinda, although it was a feeble resort. Belinda was bound to marry some day, if not Philip Roy then someone else. But something might happen. Any postponement seemed preferable to an early and irrevocable end.

She was racking her brains for the right words – the words that wouldn't make her sound like a jealous stepsister, but an ordinarily critical bystander – when the clouds suddenly lifted from the hills and the whole scene was transformed, as if by witchcraft, into something beautiful and magnificent. Nothing remained of the rain except the drops on the heather, sparkling like diamonds in the early evening sun. The rocks, touched with every gradation of light and shade, shed their uniform grey and took on all the colours of the spectrum, from white to darkest purple, while the swollen rills and springs danced out from the slopes, leaping like streams of quicksilver from crag to crag, rock to rock.

'That's more like it,' Philip exclaimed, jumping up and beginning to strip the cover from his gun. 'The beasts should be starting to move downhill any time now, see if they don't.'

Rising and picking up his shot pouch for him, handing him the case of lucifers he had dropped, stamping out the smouldering, discarded stub of his cigar, she said with quiet desperation, 'Philip, Uncle Gresham's tired of Juran and Belinda. He wants them off his hands. That's the reason for the party – to bring you up to scratch, whether you like it or not. He's trying to manipulate you. Everyone in the neighbourhood is coming and every acquaintance for a hundred miles. He wants the whole world to know that you and Belinda are as good as betrothed.'

'What?' But his mind was immediately diverted. 'Get down!' he said, his marmalade eyes gleaming. 'See? Didn't I tell you?'

There were about sixty deer, all hinds, wending their way in single file down towards the floor of the glen.

'Now, what I'm going to do is this,' he told her. 'Pay attention, because I may need you to confuse the scent if I can't get fully downwind . . .'

7

Never in her life had Rachel been so exhausted as when the guests began arriving for Hallowe'en.

The last day of October was a Saturday and travelling on the Sabbath a Presbyterian sin, so the party had developed into a Friday until Monday affair. This would have presented no problem in Daniel Macmillan's day, when house parties were a regular affair, but in Daniel Macmillan's day there had been a horde of servants to cater for the guests. Now, under Gresham's miserly and unsocial rule, there were only Daniel's not very experienced elder daughter and a handful of maids and temporary footmen from the village.

Daniel Macmillan's guests had never brought their children, either, dear little things who enjoyed Hallowe'en so much and would be no trouble at all. Was there space for their nannies, or could someone in the castle look after them and their needs?

A horrified Rachel, watching the infants being lifted down from their ponies or led up from parental yachts moored in the unseasonably sparkling waters of the bay, suddenly realised that she had made no provision for entertaining them. She didn't even know how. Juran had never been the kind of place where children bobbed for apples, or planted rape seed in the garden after dark, or roamed the neighbourhood in fancy dress singing songs and hoping for a few coins as reward.

She picked up her skirts and, with Horace – playing truant from Oxford – in conscientious pursuit, raced down to the village to ask for advice from Tom Tanner.

'Well,' he said thoughtfully. 'There iss cutting an apple before the glass.'

'There's what?'

'You cut it in half before a looking glass, do you see, in a room illuminated only by a single candle.'

'Yes? And?'

'Well, I do not chust recall what happens then,' he admitted ruefully. 'It iss something to do with seeing the image of your future love in the glass. Or there iss eating salted herring, of course.'

'Yes?'

'It makes you thirsty in the middle of the night, and you dream that someone brings you a drink of water, and the someone iss the man or girl you are destined to marry.'

'Really, Tom, it doesn't sound very appropriate for small children!'

'No.' He thought for a moment. 'I know. Fortune telling! Now that would be chust the thing. Ask old Rebecca. She iss a real dab with the white of egg. The hens will need to be laying well, mind, because she needs an egg for every fortune.'

Fortunes told with white of egg? Rachel shook her head in disbelief and turned to Horace. 'Do you think you could arrange things with Rebecca for me? I don't know whether I'm on my head or my heels, so I depend on you.'

'Of course.' Horace was undismayed, no problem too large or too small for his distinguished intellect. He didn't even query the Christian morality of what was obviously a pagan custom.

She smiled at him gratefully and then regretted it as he steered her out through the door. It was a narrow door, certainly, but not narrow enough to excuse the limp weight of his hand coming to rest on her hip.

She tended to forget that Horace qualified as an adult nowadays. Although he was eighteen years old he still contrived to look like an overgrown schoolboy dressed up in his father's clothes, the high-buttoned black serge jacket hanging loose on his narrow shoulders and the smart checked trousers appearing to encase more of empty air than solid flesh. He was still mouse-haired and spotty, but had developed a diffidence about his height that led him to affect a perpetual forward kink at the waist as if someone had just landed him a blow in the solar plexus. Since he was the only member of the family who had ever treated Rachel as a human being, however, she was prepared to forgive him a good deal.

8

She was feeling so harassed as they came within sight of the castle again and saw a new group of guests dismounting before the front door and another half dozen riding up the drive that all she was conscious of, at first, was figures without faces. And then one face leapt out at her.

It wasn't, she told herself. It couldn't be.

Instead of a singing joy, she felt an abject desperation. All she could say was, 'What is *he* doing here?'

'Who?'

'Mr Blake. The American. He was here before, do you remember, in the spring of '66.'

'Oh, that fellow? Yes, the pater's a bit sour about him. He wrote last week, something about Belinda dishing out an invitation last time he was here. The pater didn't remember a thing about it but couldn't very well deny it. So he thought he might as well tell him to come this weekend and get it over with.'

The tears that had forsaken her eyes for two long years sprang to them now. 'And it didn't occur to your father to tell *me*, of course! Where am I to put him? There isn't an empty room in the castle. Horace, you'll have to keep him talking until I think of something.'

And then their paths converged and she had to make an attempt at the right note of reserved cordiality. 'Good evening, Mr Blake. How delightful to see you again. I wonder if you remember Mr Horace Gresham?'

'Of course. A pleasure.'

Horace had disliked Blake on sight, two years before, as he always disliked men who looked as if they had never suffered from spots in their life, but having been cast in the rôle of Sir Lancelot he dutifully rode to Rachel's rescue. 'A chilly day, Mr Blake. Why not come indoors and warm yourself before you go upstairs? You're just the fellow I want to see. I've an idea for making Juran into a Nature Park and it would be a tremendous help if you could tell me all about this Yoze Might place of yours!'

Blake, trying to interpret the anxious expression on Miss Rachel's face, hesitated. Although he had retained no very precise picture of her – neat figure, unusual face, rational mind, unformed personality – he thought she had begun to grow up in the last couple of years. There was more character in her face now. There was also a wariness that he didn't understand.

It was a moment before what Horace had said caught up with him. Yoze Might?

'Yosemmitty,' he corrected him without thinking. Horace glowered.

And then a commanding female voice spoke behind them, the kind of voice that never apologised for interrupting or cared that everyone within a hundred yards could hear what it was saying.

'Miss Rachel – is it? – I wonder if I might trouble you? My woman desires to iron out the creases in my dinner gown but your maids seem unable to understand English. I believe Sir James's man is in the same difficulty over his master's shirt. Perhaps you could . . .'

'Of course, Lady Margaret. I'll come at once.'

9

It was another twenty-four hours before Blake succeeded in waylaying an elusive Rachel on the stairs. Without preamble, he said, 'It seems I am occupying a room belonging to a member of the family and I guess someone must have been ejected to make space for me. I'm embarrassed.'

Two small children, rushing down the stairs, pushed rudely between them and went scampering on.

Rachel, expecting guests to complain not about what they did have, but what they didn't, said a little distractedly, 'Please don't worry about it.'

The children's nanny, with no more ceremony that her charges, shouldered her way between them.

'I am the one,' Rachel went on, 'who should apologise.' She had cleared her own belongings out in such a hurry that it would have been surprising if he had failed to notice. 'A last-minute rearrangement for which the fault was mine.'

'The room is yours, too, I suspect.' His tone was curt, and she had no way of knowing that he had observed, and been irrationally displeased by the fact that she appeared to be at the beck and call of everyone in the castle. She was probably having to sleep in a truckle bed in the attic, he thought.

She was, but nothing would have induced her to say so. All she wanted to say, and did, as she stepped back again to allow a large gentleman to surge past, was, 'If you will excuse me? We are having a bonfire later, and since it's amazingly mild outdoors we may also have impromptu dancing on the lawn. In the meantime, the children are about to have their fortunes told, and I must go and see that everything's all right.'

10

Everything was not all right.

Horace, left to himself, had converted what had once been the butler's pantry into something like a fortune teller's booth at a fairground. Having filched the two burgundy-coloured chenille cloths that were normally used to insulate the thirty-foot length of the dining table, he had tented them from the centre of the ceiling, and pinned to them an assortment of cutout paper moons and stars, a few lengths of swansdown that Rachel last remembered having seen trimming a pardessus of Belinda's, and something that looked suspiciously like Aunt Minerva's best Chantilly lace fichu. At the back of the room he had set up one of the occasional tables from the Blue

Drawing Room, bearing – in default of a crystal ball – the frosted glass globe from one of the library oil lamps. Arrayed round it, in perfect symmetry, was a ring of glass tumblers full of water and on the floor at the side stood a basket of eggs and a large, empty tin bucket.

Rachel waited until the fortune teller paused for breath, and said, 'But, Becca . . .'

Mistress Rebecca MacAlister was seriously displeased. 'Tinkers! Romanies! That iss all the place iss fit for! Och, I haff never been so insulted.'

She was old, Rachel had no idea how old, with a face deeply wrinkled, cheeks that had become concave as saucers owing to the loss of her teeth, and eyes narrowed to permanent slits after a lifetime of being screwed up against the elements. Her complexion was brown as a nut, her hair, falling in wings from a centre parting, the colour of tarnished silver, and she was dressed in her best, a heavy blue serge skirt covered by a huge, spotless white cotton apron; a flowered bodice with a checked shawl-cum-fichu over the shoulders; and the knitted white cap favoured by old ladies in the Highlands, which resembled nothing so much as a baby's bonnet complete with lace trim and long ribbon ties.

Beauty Mistress Becca did not possess, but she had dignity and self-respect and Horace had offended them both.

'He hass filled the place with heathen symbols, chust as if I wass an old witch come to sumon up the Evil One. Blasphemy, Miss Rachel, that iss what it iss. Commerce with the deffil! You will be telling me to wear a pointed hat, next. Well, if it iss heathen superstition you iss wanting . . .'

'Becca!' Rachel said again, more strongly, casting an embittered glance at the unrepentant Horace. 'It's for the children. They expect moons and stars and things. They're outside now, waiting. They'll be so disappointed if you won't do it. And we'll explain that you have the gift of prophecy and that this is *proper* fortune telling, not all that superstitious nonsense about . . . Horace, will you take that stupid crystal ball away!'

She won in the end, though it was a near thing when Belinda came bouncing in, demanding to know what was causing the delay and saying, 'Shouldn't you be wearing a pointed hat, Rebecca?'

The children, of whom there were eight, were lined up noisily outside the door, with four-year-old the Honourable Billy Barrett at their head. When Rachel tried to usher the Hon. Billy into the candlelit presence of the fortune teller, however, he let out a squawk of terror and bolted straight out again into Belinda's arms.

Belinda, having condescended to supervise this part of the children's entertainment largely because three of the eight were Honourables, had no intention of allowing them to report to their mamas that it been nothing but a swindle. So when the children clamoured to watch from the doorway while she went first, she agreed, pretending reluctance.

When she was seated, Becca said, 'In a minute, when I am telling you, you will be putting your hand over the top of the glass, do you see?'

'All right.'

The silence was total as Becca carefully selected an egg from the basket and, with a tap, cracked it against the rim of a tumbler, raising and lowering her hands three times as she allowed the white to go gliding into the water.

'Now,' she said, tossing the shell and yolk into the bucket with a clang that made everyone jump.

Belinda closed the top of the glass with her palm.

The white of egg sank to the bottom and stayed there. They waited for an inordinate length of time, but still it stayed. Rachel wasn't sure whether that was supposed to be a good or a bad omen, but Becca, staring at it intently, finally said, 'Och, it iss the egg. It iss too fresh.'

Belinda, a brassily fashionable figure in her low-necked evening dress with its cream lace underskirt and overskirt of Mexico blue satin caught up at the back into a bustle, cleared her throat slightly as Becca selected another egg and another glass.

This time the water was too cold.

Horace, hovering in the corridor, was despatched to the kitchen for warm water to top up the glasses, while the children chattered and Belinda sighed impatiently.

The third time, it was all right. Under Belinda's hand, wide veils of egg white swirled up, sluggishly at first, into a chaos of fantastic shapes in which were divulged, murmured Becca, the entire Book of Fate.

Drily, Rachel thought they also divulged that the egg was a long way from fresh; it certainly wouldn't have poached well.

Becca began talking in fits and starts, her hissing mumble, product of toothlessness and Gaelic sibilance, hard to make out from a distance. Rachel, at the door, caught mention of flowers and bridal veils and was amused that even Becca should feel compelled to offer her clients romance and bouquets and happiness ever after. This was followed by a spell when nothing was audible, although Belinda's expression ran the full gamut from scorn to reluctant pleasure. Then Becca stopped abruptly. 'There iss nothing more I can tell you.'

Belinda jumped to her feet. 'Just when it was becoming interesting! Oh, well! Now, children, come along!'

But the children were still reluctant and, since Horace would not be persuaded, it was Rachel who went next.

She didn't want to. She didn't believe all this nonsense, of course. She had learned, long ago in her Soho childhood, that whatever apparent aids fortune tellers employed, what they really read were the minds reflected in people's faces. Since there were times when Rachel could barely read her own mind, she thought it unlikely that an old Highland woman who had never travelled further than a dozen miles from home in the whole of her life would do better. So she sat at the table in her practical, figured green gown with its modest train and muslin fichu *à la Vallière*, and, mocking herself, willed the egg white to take up shapes to match her emotions, wild and convoluted and contradictory. Becca ought to have a fine time!

But, as she sat and waited, a chill breath began to caress the back of her neck, spreading its contagion over the whole surface of her skin so that she was already shivering when she saw the hand holding the egg rise and fall, rise and fall, rise and fall, and the white glide into the water and float downwards, soft and swaying, like a jellyfish, to the bottom of the glass.

She covered the glass with her palm, and they waited.

Slowly, slowly, the white began forming itself not into wide veils but threads as fine as gossamer, threads that wove and interwove, gradually, languorously, rising and rising until after five long minutes, clear to see in the very heart of the glass, there stood a tall, slender mountain, a cobweb of white silk, its precipitous faces and needle-like spurs starred here and there with tiny beads of air, silver as mercury.

After a while, Becca picked the glass up and turned it, but the mountain did no more than waver slightly and settle again as before.

Rachel, hypnotised, heard nothing of the children's bored shiftings and rustlings or any of the other noises of the castle. All she heard, and only faintly, was the murmur of the ignorant old woman who sat across the table from her, the woman who, knowing no long words or subtle phrases, knew Rachel better than Rachel yet knew herself.

185

'Sharp,' she began, 'sharp iss what you are. And a lover of secrets. You hide your soul from others. You haff no respect for those who iss closest to you, and you haff no care that the getting of what you want will be hurting them. I see a death in your future, soon, and one – no, two – no, three more that might haff been but will not be. You think you iss sharper than others, but I see two men who iss sharper than you. You will neffer be having all you want. In the end you will haff to choose.'

Rachel hadn't expected a full character study. It was just Becca's limited knowledge of English, she assured herself, that made it sound so unflattering. There was nothing wrong with being clever and critical and knowing what you wanted. Or with fighting for it. And when those who were close to you didn't respect you, why should you respect them?

When the old woman's voice ceased at last, she rose carefully to her feet and, hoping fortune tellers were sworn to professional secrecy like priests and doctors, said, 'Thank you, Becca. I *will* have to mend my ways, won't I!'

But the old woman was too busy moving a new glass into position even to look up.

Rachel said, 'Come along, then, Master Billy. You're not frightened any more, are you?'

11

You will never have all you want . . . you will have to choose . . .

The words echoed over and over in Rachel's mind, like a melody whose notes followed each other so neatly, so inevitably, that it was impossible to drive it from one's head.

They haunted her as she led the children in and out of Becca's sanctum; as she ushered them through to their special nursery tea; as she thanked Becca and saw her off to her cottage, where there was a splendid hamper of food waiting, and a sovereign wrapped in a napkin. They haunted her as she agreed with Jamie McLeod on the tunes he was to play for the dancing on the lawn; as she and Jeannie arranged the furniture in the windows of the Red Drawing Room for those who preferred watching to dancing; as she scanned the card tables set up in the morning room, and the supper tables laid out in the breakfast room; as she surveyed the bonfire Tom Tanner and Jimsy had built outside on the rise, and saw that they were well supplied with lucifers and bog fir roots to light it; as she made sure that Angus had set out the pitch-soaked torches to illuminate the dancing; as she inspected the dishes laid out ready for serving in the kitchen; as she failed to find a moment to swallow a mouthful herself.

She took a glass of wine in her hand, however, so that she would look as if she was one of the company, and was surprised after a while to find that she had drunk it. Horace gave her another.

You will never have all you want . . . you will have to choose . . .

It would be a fine thing, indeed, to be granted the opportunity. But there was irony even in the thought of choice. Never had she seen more clearly than on this day that she was doomed to have *nothing* of what she wanted. Juran would soon slip away from her, beyond possibility of recapture. And Mr Blake even sooner. On him, despite her dreams, she had no claim at all.

12

There had been a lovely, gentle sunset in golds and purple greys, and the sea was flat calm. Even at nine in the evening it was still as mild outdoors as if it were June. A slip of a moon hung on the horizon and the stars were out in force, although the dancers couldn't see them, blinded by the glare of the torches that cut off the circle of their living, lively world from the darkness beyond. The shouting, yelling and hooching that accompanied Highland dancing were like an incantation against the elf folk and kelpies and other unchancy beings that haunted the black immensity of sea, mountain and sky.

Belinda had been hanging on Philip Roy's arm for most of the evening, and he seemed to be resigned to it. Only when the dancing began did he relinquish her, without any great show of regret, to the succession of guests who felt duty bound to stand up with their hostess. Twice, glancing outdoors on her way from card room to supper room, Rachel saw him dancing with one of the Fraser girls, Miss Minnie, who was pretty in a blushing way and seemed to admire him greatly.

He was a fine figure as he went through the reels and strathspeys, kilts flying; a tall, sturdily handsome young man with exuberantly curly red-brown hair and sideburns, peremptory eyebrows, and a deceptive air of openness and affability.

'Give us a sword dance,' someone cried, and other voices were raised in encouragement. Nothing loath, Philip glanced round and

Rachel, catching his eye, nodded and turned indoors to take a pair of blades down from the display above the fireplace in the Great Hall.

As she reached up towards them, a voice at her elbow said, 'Allow me. And let's hope he doesn't cut himself. Blood poisoning can be fatal.'

It was astonishing how the wine had relaxed her. Brightly, she replied, 'If *you* had been hanging on a West Highland wall for two hundred years, Mr Blake, you would be rusty, too.'

She should have held her tongue, because he looked down at her with a companionable grin, and her heart did a double somersault and her false ease vanished. She felt her breath lodge somewhere in her throat, and thought feverishly that it didn't matter because she didn't know what to say, anyway. It was one thing to take part in a rational conversation with him when there were other people present, quite another to be alone with him, her bones limp as a daisy chain, nerves zinging like plucked harp strings, brain as empty as an illicit whisky still on New Year's Day.

Disbelievingly, she heard herself prattling on, 'Don't you dance yourself, Mr Blake?'

The long, firm mouth twitched again at the corners. 'Divinely,' he said, and laid down the swords. 'May I have the pleasure?'

As he took her right hand in his and settled the other low at the back of her waist, a pang of unfamiliar, almost paralysing agony shot up the length of her spine, so that she gave an uncontrolled shudder. But he didn't seem to notice as, softly whistling 'The Blue Danube', he swung her lightly into a waltz.

She was terrified at first of tripping over his feet, missing his rhythm, but after the first, tentative moments that fear, at least, vanished. He was so perfectly in command that she followed him as easily as if she were guiding the steps herself; the tune was lovely; and the flagstones, worn to smoothness by many generations of feet, offered no hindrance to the flow of their movements. It was perfect, dreamlike, and ineffably romantic.

Rachel, who had spent two long years trying to overcome her fascination with this man, and who had almost succeeded because all she had known of love was what her untutored heart had guessed at, discovered that love was more – much more – than just something of the imagination.

And then it was over. When their second circle of the floor brought them back again to the table on which Blake had left the swords, he released her, saying, 'What a pity. But I think we should take these out now?'

13

He had already turned away when he felt her hand on his arm, and glanced down at it. It was a small, shapely hand with ruthlessly short nails and it was withdrawn almost at once.

She said, 'Please, would you . . .' and stopped.

He looked up again, hoping that he might have misinterpreted the gesture, but there was a heightened colour in her cheeks and her eyes were enormous, shining and intensely blue. In general, her looks were nothing out of the ordinary, but for a moment she looked almost beautiful.

Blake had schooled his face over the years to show nothing that he did not want it to show. He was therefore perfectly able to disguise his exasperation with himself for having misjudged things.

He had seen that she was nervous of him and put it down to his being a stranger from a world very different from that of the other guests who made up the house party; titled though many of them were, their minds were as cloddish as their acres. Young Rachel, he thought, was the most intelligent person in the place – if rather inclined to take everything *au sérieux* – and it had occurred to him that a frivolous turn or two round the floor might show her that he was really quite human and not someone to be afraid of.

He had thought her too sensible to have schoolgirl crushes. He had thought her too young and innocent to cause him the slightest physical disturbance.

He had been wrong on both counts.

She said again. 'Please, I . . .' And stopped again.

A majestic voice spoke from the doorway. 'Rachel, why are you taking so long with the swords? Mr Roy and the guests are waiting.'

Blake wouldn't have expected, under any circumstances, to welcome the advent of Minerva Gresham, but her entry saved him from a moment of undeniable awkwardness. However he had handled it, he would have been bound to embarrass the girl.

As it was, he was able to say, 'The fault is mine, Mrs Gresham. I was taking a moment to admire the craftsmanship of the old swordsmiths.'

After that, they went outdoors as if nothing whatever had happened.

When the bonfire began to die down, Rachel fled to her room to wash away the smuts that had been flying everywhere and make herself presentable for the late supper that was the last event of one of the most harrowing days she could remember. She was shaking with tears that threatened to overwhelm her as she hurried upstairs praying that she would not meet anyone on the way. But of course she did. She met Horace coming down.

He looked at her curiously and she knew that, myopic though he was, he couldn't fail to notice her distress. 'I slipped and fell on the lawn,' she volunteered before he could ask. It was a stupid thing to say, because he put a sympathetic hand out to her, and she couldn't stop herself from recoiling.

'I'm sorry, Horace,' she said. 'I'm tired, that's all. Just let me go and tidy myself, and then we can have supper. Will you tell Aunt Minerva and Belinda? The servants can begin bringing the guests indoors in about fifteen minutes.'

She didn't wait for an answer. She didn't care what he thought. It didn't matter. Nothing mattered now.

She had never felt so ashamed. She couldn't imagine what had possessed her. And Rainer Blake had known – must have known – what she had been trying to say.

Kiss me. Please take me in your arms and kiss me.

He had known, and the very lack of expression on his face had been a rejection. He probably thought she was a cheap little hussy, because if a woman gave in to a man, or showed that she wanted to, a hussy was what she was.

She stood in her cupboard of an attic with its rock hard bed, solitary chair, and the shelf bearing basin and ewer, and raged at herself. She, who thought she was so clever – how could she have been such a fool? If she had learned nothing else all the days of her life, she should have learned from her mother's experience, who had given herself to Daniel Macmillan in love and false hope. She, Rachel, had been one result; the other had been years of misery and, in the end, tragedy.

If Rachel had succeeded in speaking the words, if Aunt Minerva hadn't interrupted, if Rainer Blake had been a different kind of man . . .

She didn't even know what kind of man he was.

She did know that she had been so singleminded in her desire that she might have ended by doing exactly what her mother had done on that other night, twenty years before.

Dabbing the cold, wet sponge to her aching eyes, she tried to tell herself that she was making far too much of it; but without success. She knew Rainer Blake was not for her, but knowing it with her mind didn't rule out the hope of a miracle that persisted in her heart. Or hadn't done until now, when she had put herself beyond the pale.

She could never look him in the face again.

15

When he came to thank her, one day and two interminable nights later, for all she had done to make his stay so enjoyable, she stood with her eyes downcast and murmured that it had been a pleasure.

And then she stood, half hidden behind the curtains of the Blue Drawing Room, and watched him ride away for a second time. *You will never have all you want . . . you will have to choose . . .*

With a little hiccup of self-mockery, she turned away and went about her business. It was going to take at least a month before the servants had cleared everything up – washed all the china with soda and endless relays of boiling water; cleaned and polished the silver and wrapped it in baize and put it away; scrubbed out the pans with sand from the beach, and rinsed them, and scrubbed them out again; soaked the bed and table linen in the pool for a day, boiled it for four hours in the big cauldron slung between two alders, rinsed it for four more hours in the rushing waters of the river. And then dried it and bleached it and ironed and darned it and, at last, folded it away with mothballs and sachets of lavender until it was needed again.

All the ornaments would have to be washed, too, and the furniture cleaned of children's sticky fingermarks. The dust sheets would have to be replaced in the rooms the family didn't use. And there were the floors to be scrubbed, every lamp in the castle to be refilled, and every candle replaced.

She overheard Belinda, turning back indoors after waving the last visitors goodbye, remark to Aunt Minerva, 'I can't think why it should be so tiring just having a few people to stay. Shall we go into the drawing room, and have some tea? I suppose the servants will be busy, but Rachel can make it. Isn't it lucky the weather stayed fine? If it's still dry tomorrow, I think I might tidy up mama's roses.'

It was surprising how long the roses continued to flower at Juran when there was a mild autumn. The late, lamented Isabella had apparently known what she was doing when she chose the location for their bed at the top of the retaining wall above the terrace.

'Roses like a west-facing position and a good current of air,' said Aunt Minerva. 'Not excessive, of course. I imagine they would not care for being in the direct blast of salt gales from the sea, but the castle itself protects them from those. And being so high above the terrace, they escape most of the ground frost, too, which can be very damaging. Frost drops, you see, and accumulates in pockets at the lowest levels. I would not have expected them to thrive in peaty soil, but a good deal of subsoil appears to have been mixed in when the bed was built, which may account for the clayey texture. Roses like clay.'

Rachel wasn't interested in what roses liked. She didn't even know why it was necessary to keep cutting off all the dead flowerheads and suspected that Belinda's passion for this task was merely an aspect of her wider passion for organisation – just as her insistence on having Rachel standing by while she did it was an aspect of her need to demonstrate, at every opportunity, that she and she alone was mistress of Juran.

'Do not stay out too long, Belinda,' Aunt Minerva said. 'The sky is looking very threatening. I myself am going in now.'

Rachel, trying to think only the kind of thoughts that were bearable, continued to stand on the path, the awkward trug basket over one arm, the other hand balancing it because the prunings at one end were heavily outweighed by the gardening tools at the other – the knives, trowels and sheep shears that Belinda said were so useful for rough work. Not that she was doing much rough work today as, heavy gardening boots incongruous below the flounced ankle-length skirt and braid-trimmed pardessus, she clumped her way round the bed that lay between path and parapet, clipping here and snapping there.

The sky had become very black, and there was a deep roll of thunder rapidly followed by a searing flash of lightning. Belinda gave an impatient exclamation. 'It's getting close,' she said. 'What a nuisance! I'll just finish these at the edge and then we'd better go in before the heavens open. I don't want my nice new bonnet ruined.'

Her nice new bonnet was in the Russian style, a chapeau of bright blue velvet with black feather edging and chinstrap, and it could scarcely have been less suitable for gardening in the Highlands. Belinda, however, argued with some justification that if it were permissible to wear fashionable clothes only in town she would never have the chance to wear fashionable clothes at all.

Bending, she brushed at the coping with her hand. The necks of the Bourbon roses were drooping and some had flopped over, their sad beige petals plastered to the stone.

And then, still half crouching, she swivelled round from the waist like an actor revelling in the climax of some third rate melodrama and said, as if she would burst if she had to keep the news to herself any longer, 'Oh, and by the way! Mr Roy spoke to my uncle yesterday. We are to be married in June.'

Her face within its black feather frame was aglow. 'And that, dear Rachel, will be the end of all your pretensions! You've always gone on hoping, haven't you? Well, it's over now. Over in every way, because I'm tired of you! When you come of age next summer and Uncle Gresham stops being your guardian, it's going to give my husband and me great pleasure to throw you out.'

There were twelve long years of spite in her words, twelve years of wanting to be rid of the stepsister – the sister – who wasn't worthy, who didn't belong. And she couldn't resist the final taunt. 'So you can go home again, back to the slum you came from.'

It was the last, impossible straw.

Rachel had hated Belinda before, childishly at first but then with a self-discipline that had helped to keep things in proportion. Now, she discovered that she hadn't known what hatred was.

Her eyes flaming in a face suddenly bleached of all colour, she took a hasty step forward, quite unaware that her hand was resting on the foot-long sheep shears with their lethal, triangular blades.

Belinda, whose own anger always took a physical form, saw and panicked, tried to straighten up, to turn and run. But she caught a foot in her cloak and tripped and then stumbled off balance, and the stumble drove her other foot hard into the thick, sticky clay soil, so that she had to pull and struggle to free it. And it came free without warning, and she staggered back against the low parapet.

For the briefest of moments she reeled on the edge, arms flailing, and then disappeared from view leaving only a scream behind her.

The hailstorm broke at that moment, muffling the final, fearful sound of her body hitting the flagstones twenty feet below.

CHAPTER TEN

'It was murder,' Gresham drawled.

His eyes were half closed, as always, their fringe of pale lashes casting shadows in the flickering light. Although there were few men in the year 1868 who had not succumbed to the prevailing tendency to hairiness, Lucian Gresham was one of them, preferring, he said, not to invite comparisons with some simian being lurking in an African jungle. His only concession to fashion had been to grow muttonchop whiskers that had the effect of reducing the width of his jaw and emphasising the sneer around his mouth.

The impression he sought, in general successfully, to convey, was of an aristocratic gentleman who, though perhaps something of a bruiser, was also intellectual, tenacious, and sufficiently detached from the sordid affairs of the world to be able to pronounce on them with an assurance that was no less than Olympian.

Such was his tone as he continued, 'Cold-blooded murder. The girl Rachel pushed my niece to her death.'

Then, producing a thin cigar from his case, he lit it and gave the impression of having withdrawn from the proceedings, as if all had been said that needed to be said.

The procurator-fiscal, who was Glasgow by birth and had a rooted objection to being dictated to by the upper classes, especially when they were English and had much too good a conceit of themselves, glowered at him over his spectacles. 'Ye wud do well, Mr Gresham,' he said repressively, 'to hold your tongue. Your opinion carries no weight wi' me. If ye have anything worthy o' the name of evidence, it will be heard in due course. In the meantime, it is the business of this court to decide the facts of Miss Belinda Macmillan's unhappy end, and I wud be obleeged if ye wud cease obstructing us and let us get on wi' it.'

Having thus dealt with the interrupter to his own satisfaction, the procurator turned back to the slight figure seated across the desk from him, and said kindly, 'Now, lassie . . .'

She was exactly the kind of young woman he would have liked as a daughter, quiet, modestly dressed and not too pretty for her own good. She had been pale enough in her unrelieved black dress and bonnet before the Gresham fellow came out with his accusation, but now every last vestige of colour had fled from her cheeks, leaving her white as death.

Which was not to be wondered at. Her guardian had just said, in effect, that she ought to be hanged.

Mr Briscoe didn't know who would stand to gain if that happened, but he had presided over enough enquiries into unexplained fatalities to recognise that the folk who were quickest to cry murder weren't always the ones whose main desire was to see justice done.

'Now, lassie,' he said again, 'we'll go through everything in your own words. I'll maybe prompt ye now and then, if there's something I need to know that ye haven't told me. We're not here to play guessing games. We just want to get at the facts of what happened. D'ye understand?'

Mutely, Rachel nodded.

The procurator-fiscal's office was panelled in some dark, oppressive wood under a ceiling yellow-black with years of smoke from peat fires like the one now smouldering in the iron grate. There was a hallstand in the corner, laden with damp overcoats and bowlers and top hats and tweed caps, and round the walls was a line of scuffed wooden chairs for the witnesses. A steady hiss came from the gas mantles, their greenish light harsh against the grey filtering in from the outdoors, and the atmosphere was a thick, eye-stinging fug of peat-reek and cigars. There were bars on the windows.

Mr Briscoe leaned his forearms on the big, scarred desk and said, 'Begin from where Mistress Gresham went indoors and left ye wi' the deceased.'

Rachel swallowed. 'Well, the sky was looking very threatening, but Belinda – the d-d-deceased – was anxious to finish pruning the roses. So I stood on the path holding the basket for the clippings and gardening tools.'

'Wud she be in a wee bit of a hurry?'

'I suppose so.'

'Aye, well, it stands to reason if it was looking like rain. Now, just describe to me where the rose bed is. I know about it from the constable, but I wud like to hear it from you, too.'

'Yes. Well, you see, a wedge of the hillside was cut away when the castle was extended centuries ago, and there's a retaining wall rising from the terrace, holding the earth back. The rose bed is at the top of the wall. There's a shallow coping, and then about ten feet of rose bed, and then the path. And the hill rises straight up behind the path.'

'Good. That's a fine clear picture I've got now. Go on.'

Rachel swallowed again, and didn't try to prevent her voice from trembling. Her emotions were in turmoil, guilt over her undoubted part in Belinda's death and fear of the consequences warring with an appalled sense of deliverance. Because Belinda had made no Will and, unless everything went horribly wrong, Juran would be hers, this time without possibility of doubt.

She had no idea why the procurator-fiscal was being so sympathetic towards her, but didn't dare rely on him continuing to be so. She *had* to lie.

'We weren't really talking. There had been a large weekend house party and we were both tired. The sky had got very dark, and there was a roll of thunder and a violent flash of lightning. I said, "The storm's getting close, we ought to go in", but Belinda wanted to finish. There were only the bushes by the parapet left to do.'

Mr Briscoe took his spectacles off, rubbed the bridge of his nose with forefinger and thumb, and put them on again. There wasn't any identifiable expression in his eyes, but Rachel felt marginally more comfortable. It wasn't easy talking to someone whose face was an unreadable montage of moustache, beard, whiskers, and lenses.

He said, 'Was the deceased not feared of thunder and lightning?'

'No.' With the Greshams listening, she couldn't say anything else.

'Are *you* feared of them?'

'A bit.'

'Go on.'

The blood pounding in her head like a raging sea on the rocks of Juran, Rachel said, 'The d-d-deceased, Miss Macmillan, was at the parapet, leaning over.'

'Leaning over the parapet?'

'No, I mean she was bending over some petals that had fallen on the coping. She wasn't leaning over the wall. And then – I don't know what happened.' Her voice broke a little, pathetically, and not from intent. However she distorted the truth, what had happened *had* happened, and it had been horrible.

'It was all so quick. I could hear the thunder rolling again, and I knew there was going to be more lightning and it made me nervous, and I called out to her.'

'What tone did ye use? Did ye maybe shout at her?'

She was taken aback. 'No. Yes. I don't know.'

'What did ye say?'

'Something like, "Well, *I'm* going in, Belinda, even if you're not!" '

'And what did she reply?'

Rachel dropped her eyes for a moment and then raised them again to meet Mr Briscoe's spectacles squarely. 'She didn't reply, but I think she was going to. She swung round sharply.' Fractionally, Rachel hesitated. 'She was impatient with me sometimes, you see, and I think she was going to snap at me. But, swinging round, she seemed to lose her balance. I think her foot got entangled with her cloak, and the ground was muddy and slippery . . .'

'And then she fell?'

'Yes. It was *dreadful*.'

Mr Briscoe could see from her face that the lassie was reliving what had been a very nasty experience. He helped her over the awkward moment. 'What did ye do then?'

'I just stood frozen, and then there was a crash from the sky right above and the hail started. I've never seen hailstones like it. And I dropped my basket and ran across to the parapet and looked over.'

'Aye, well, I think that's all we need to know from ye at the minute.' Mr Briscoe was not entirely convinced about one minor point, where he thought the lassie was being economical with the truth, but he could understand why.

The fair-haired gentleman raised his contemptuous voice again. 'Lies. Lies, every last word.'

2

'Ye were there, were you?' snapped the procurator-fiscal, who had been doing fine without him. 'I don't see your name down on my list as a witness of the occurrence.'

'Not when my niece fell,' Gresham replied, as if the point were irrelevant. 'But I was on the scene within a minute or two, and the girl was standing by the parapet, staring down at my niece's body. Were I an *aficionado* of cheap fiction, I would describe her expression as gloating.'

Rachel exclaimed, 'That's not . . .'

Mr Briscoe flapped a square, competent hand at her. 'All right, lassie, all right. It's facts I'm after, Mr Gresham, not opinions.'

'The expression on her face was a fact.'

The procurator-fiscal snorted. 'Not admissible as evidence. I've yet to see any human expression that isn't open to a dozen interpretations by a dozen folk wi' different axes to grind.'

'Are you accusing me of prejudice?' Gresham's nostrils flared, the first time he had shown any sign of human feeling.

'I am,' the procurator-fiscal told him with deep satisfaction. 'And if ye don't hold your tongue so's I can get on wi' my enquiry, I'll have ye put out.'

The gentleman was silent while Mr Briscoe questioned his plain-looking wife, who confirmed that she had gone indoors before the deceased's fall. Then it was the turn of the earnest and weedy youth who was their son. He, hearing a scream, had rushed out and, simultaneously with the servant Jeannie McLeod, had discovered the body.

Jeannie McLeod proved to be a true Highland connoisseur of doom and disaster. 'Och, I knew in my bones, sir – it iss God's truth I did – that something terrible wass going to happen. Neffer haff I seen a sky so black or lightning so bright. Like Satan's fork, it wass. And then there wass this terrible, terrible scream, and chust at the ferry minute it ended there wass a great crash and the hail came down. Like God's own thunderbolt, your honour. Chust like that, it wass.'

'Yes, yes. So the hail started after the scream? Ye're sure about that, are you?'

'Och, yess, sir. There iss no doubt about it. The one followed the other, chust like the night follows the day.'

'And ye ran out from the kitchen? There is a door from the kitchen to the terrace?'

'Well, not chust from the kitchen, your honour. You haff to go out of the kitchen, and into the corridor, and along to the end. And then you haff to turn to your right and go through the storeroom where the cham and preserves iss kept, and then there iss another corridor where . . .'

'Yes, well that'll do, thank ye. It explains why Mr Horace Gresham, starting from the Great Hall, reached the terrace the same time as you did. Mr Horace Gresham, wud ye confirm that the hailstorm began after the scream?'

Horace, frowning intently, confirmed it.

'And ye found the unfortunate young lady already dead?'

'Yes.'

'Thank ye.'

For the third time, Gresham raised his voice. 'My good man, this is hardly germane to the issue. My niece stood in the way of the girl Rachel's inheriting Juran. The two of them were alone. My niece fell to her death. The girl Rachel was observed seconds later leaning out over the parapet staring down at my niece's body. There is only one possible interpretation in the light of these facts.'

My good man, indeed! An empurpling Mr Briscoe heard little more of Gresham's speech, his mind occupied with the unaccountable omission from Inveraray's nice, modern – well, fairly modern – jail of a nasty, old-fashioned *oubliette* that Gresham could have been clapped into and forgotten.

'If I hear another word from you,' he said, 'I'll jail ye for contempt of court. Hold your tongue!'

Then Rachel spoke without being spoken to. 'Please, Mr Briscoe,' she said quietly, 'my stepsister was five foot nine, and I'm only five foot two. And she weighed more than ten stone where I weigh less than eight. Even if I'd wanted to, I don't think I *could* have pushed her over.'

'Aye, well, it's a good point,' said the law officer approvingly. 'But we'll just have a wee word from Constable Campbell. Where are ye, man? Oh, there ye are. Now, tell us what happened from when the servant from Juran arrived to summon you, and don't take all day about it.'

The constable was a middle-aged man with a face that might have been deliberately designed to neutralise any fears aroused by his stalwart figure. Every line of his body might be upright and decisive, but every line of his bright red face was droopy as a basset hound's. Even his sandy moustache and whiskers looked disconsolate.

'Well, sir,' he said mournfully, clutching his helmet to his breast, 'it wass young Angus – Alec Cameron's boy from Knipoch – and it wass about an hour since it had happened, though he said he had run all the way. Well, I got on my pony but they had lifted the poor young lady up by the time I got there. They had taken her inside and I said to them it wass against the law to move a body but the chentleman – that chentleman there – said it wass nonsense I wass talking, and it would not haff been decent to leave her. And then the chentleman was saying that the young lady here, Miss Rachel Macmillan, had pushed her, so I thought I should see if there wass any kind of effidence.'

'I should hope so. That's what the police are for. Get on wi' it, man.'

'Aye, sir. Well, sir, as you know, sir, most offences in the area iss to do with poaching, though there iss always a mutton-fancier or two . . .'

'Tch! This is an official enquiry, man!'

'Sorry, sir. Sheep-stealer, sir. So I haff made a study of tracking. Well, you know that. Do I haff to explain how I do it, I mean for the record, sir?'

'No.'

'Well, sir, the effidence of the footprints wass that the deceased swivelled round chust where she wass standing, behind the parapet. There wass a big smear with a streak or two across it, as if she had trodden on a fold of her cloak. Right-footed, I wass thinking. And there wass a deep left footprint, as if that foot had got stuck, and another ferry deep heel impression behind, as if she wass off her balance when she freed her foot from the first one. Am I explaining it all right, Mr Briscoe, sir?'

'No, ye're not. Ye'd better just give us your conclusions. I've never known ye wrong, yet.'

'Thank you, sir. Well, sir, I concluded that Miss Belinda Macmillan lost her balance and fell over the wall. And Miss Rachel Macmillan then ran to the wall and looked over.' He didn't pause. 'After having made my investigation of the effidence, I summoned the witnesses and took their statements . . .'

Everyone present shifted and muttered. An overwrought giggle welled up in Rachel's throat. The procurator-fiscal's eyebrows, moustache, sidewhiskers and beard bristled in unison.

In a controlled voice, he said, 'Aye, well, I suppose I deserved that.' Then, wagging a finger at the constable, he went on, 'But don't you play games wi' me, Donny Campbell, or I'll have a word to say to you later. Tell the court *officially* why you concluded that the deceased fell first, and Miss Rachel Macmillan ran to the wall after.'

As if butter wouldn't have melted in his mouth, the constable said, 'The hailstones, Mr Briscoe, sir. There wass no traces in Miss Belinda's footprints. But Miss Rachel Macmillan's footprints wass full of wee pitted marks, where she'd trodden them into the ground as she ran. The hail had melted by the time I arrived, but there iss a lot of clay in the soil so the marks wass still there. They're maybe there yet, if ye want to see for yourself. It would be taking a real long downpour to wash them away.'

Rachel, filled with an almost disbelieving thankfulness, heard scarcely another word. Instead, she sat with gloved hands neatly folded and eyes modestly downcast, wishing she could hug Constable Campbell, or shower a king's ransom upon him, or import a whole Noah's ark of exotic foreign animals whose spoor would keep him absorbed for all the rest of his days. Dear Constable Campbell! Perhaps he would like a Nature Park.

The procurator-fiscal brought her back, in the end, to reality. Gravely fixing his spectacles on her, he gave his judgement in words addressed to everyone present but delivered as if he were speaking to her alone.

'There's no doubt in my mind, and my judgement will be so delivered in writing, that the death of Miss Belinda Macmillan was an accident. Misadventure, it's called. Despite the intemperate accusations made by a certain gentleman here present, and although murder for gain is a common enough crime, I have never in my experience of the law known a well bred woman resort to physical violence in pursuit of it. It's too unreliable. Poison wud be a woman's weapon, more like.

'No one, therefore, can be held criminally responsible for the death of Miss Belinda Macmillan. The deceased was perilously close to a dangerous edge and paid for her folly wi' her life. A plain, ordinary start of surprise, whatever its cause, was all that was needed to precipitate her to her end. Had she exercised more caution, she wud be alive today. I therefore repeat that I find for death by misadventure.

'There is one charge, however, on which I cannot altogether acquit Miss Rachel Macmillan.'

All the tiny, fluttering noises in the office stopped. Rachel couldn't even feel herself breathing.

'Miss Rachel Macmillan says she "called out" to her stepsister, and it sounds harmless enough. But in my considered opinion she did more than call.'

He couldn't know. He couldn't know that she had frightened Belinda to her death. Or that she might – just possibly – have steadied her, even pulled her back from the brink, if she had moved quickly enough.

'It is my belief,' Mr Briscoe went on, 'that Miss Rachel Macmillan called out more sharply than she has admitted, startling the deceased.

Perhaps she even went so far as to shout. Well, it is no crime. In other circumstances no harm wud have resulted. But I feel bound to recommend Miss Rachel to remember, in future, that even a momentary lapse from the low-voiced, well bred calm which denotes the true gentlewoman may bring tragedy in its wake.

'That, then, is the end of this sad business and I thank ye all for your attendance. I wud be obleeged, Mr Gresham, if ye wud wait for a moment, so that my assistant can furnish you wi' the documents giving permission to bury the body of your late, lamented niece and ward.'

4

And so Rachel came into possession of Juran at last, a little over six months before her twenty-first birthday; a little over six months, also, before Lucian Gresham ceased to be her legal guardian. Until that day, she knew no way of getting rid of him.

They all rode back together to Juran without speaking. Rachel was not going to waste her breath on recriminations and the Greshams certainly were not going to waste theirs on apologies.

Horace was first to break the silence, at supper that evening. Singlemindedly as ever, blithely ignoring what seemed to him better forgotten, he swallowed his last mouthful of game soup and said, 'Now that we've got all that nonsense out of the way, we ought to get started on the plans for the Nature Park. Belinda wasn't keen, and Philip Roy just laughed when I talked to him about it, so I'm really quite pleased that Juran is going to be yours. I think what I should do first is write to the people at Yoze – Yosemmitty – and ask them how they run things, don't you? It would give us something to go on.'

Rachel, who had put in an appearance at supper only because she had no intention of giving Gresham the satisfaction of knowing what a strain it had all been, was far too weary to be dragged into the argument that would undoubtedly ensue if she told Horace that nature parks figured not at all in her plans for Juran. So she said what she always said when Horace was riding this particular hobbyhorse. 'It's an interesting idea.'

Another four days passed before Aunt Minerva, also, deigned to address her. Rachel was vaguely relieved. It would have been the wildest exaggeration to say that she had become fond of Minerva, but she no longer resented her – indeed, felt very slightly sorry for her, having come to see that her inquisitiveness about the lives of others was a compensation for the barrenness of her own. From a number of tiny hints over the years, she had also come to suspect that, far from loving her husband, Minerva loathed him. Rachel could understand it very well.

Like her son, Minerva made no reference to what she probably thought of as the 'recent, unhappy events' but asked whether Rachel would like her to go through Belinda's personal possessions with a view to clearing them out, an unpleasant necessity but a necessity nevertheless. The villagers might be grateful for a few things. 'I suppose so,' Rachel said, not knowing whether to laugh or shudder at the thought of Mistress Rebecca sporting one of Belinda's spectacular chapeaux.

It was a month before Gresham said so much as a 'good evening' to her and there was pleasure in not granting him the courtesy of a reply, just as there was pleasure, for the first time in all her experience, in doing whatever she wanted to do, taking account of no one's convenience but her own.

Gresham might continue to control her possessions, Rachel thought grimly, but he was not going to control her life. Her inheritance, this time, was no mirage. Until she was able to tell him to leave, she would spend her days tramping round the estate studying every detail of it, and her evenings with pen and paper, planning. With luck, she would go to bed too tired to dream of roses.

5

There was gossip, of course, in the glens. Although the inevitable rumours about Belinda's death had been scotched – more or less – by the procurator-fiscal's ruling, that was not the end of the affair.

She learned about it from Philip Roy, whom she had neither seen nor heard from since the funeral. She had told herself that his father's death, soon after, probably accounted for it, but she was wary as she waited for him to launch into what he had to say. In the formality of mourning dress and mourning manners, they must look, she thought, like a pair of crows as they sat on opposite sides of the fireplace in the Green Drawing Room.

There were no sympathetic, or even congratulatory, preliminaries. Like the Greshams, or so it seemed at first, Philip had decided to ignore what had happened.

'Now that I'm laird of Altsigh,' he began, 'I'm thinking it's time to establish a few points of reference with everyone round about. We've all been a bit too easy-osy about where our boundaries lie, for example, and it won't do, you know. I mean, I can't afford to have people from Juran shooting my deer.'

'Oh, I do agree. At Juran, we can't afford to have people from Altsigh shooting ours, either.'

That wasn't right. Not 'we', she thought exultantly, but 'I'. Not 'ours', but 'mine'.

Philip glowered at her, as well aware as she that the prevailing wind more commonly caused deer to drift from Juran to Altsigh than vice versa.

'Mphmmm, yes,' he conceded. 'Now, in the interests of local harmony and since we're going to have to get together about these things, I've decided to overlook the scandal of Belinda's death and your part in it.'

It took her a moment to master her feelings, but her 'Thank you, Philip!' – when she succeeded in voicing it – was nicely modulated and really quite convincing. 'I know how much you dislike scandal.'

'Well, it reflects badly on everybody, you know, and with all these parliamentary reform fellows screaming for univeral suffrage the upper classes can't afford to be associated with discreditable episodes like that.' Belatedly, he remembered something. 'And, after all, it was my wife-to-be who died, so you wouldn't expect me just to shrug my shoulders, now would you?'

'No, of course not. But it was really not my fault, Philip.'

'I didn't say it was, did I?'

Rachel didn't waste time trying to follow his reasoning. 'No, Philip.'

'And, while I'm about it, that's not all there is to complain about. It's shocking that Juran should have come to you. Everyone's talking. A stepsister, I mean? And one who spends most of her time in the kitchen, come to that. It's Daniel Macmillan's fault, of course. He never had any real sense of duty to the estate. Or the family. That's what's wrong with the country these days, no proper sense of continuity. It's what I'm always saying about blood lines . . .'

Rachel, her face stiff with anger, nevertheless succeeded in controlling her tongue. Once Philip embarked on one of his diatribes, there was no stopping him except by outright rudeness. And she was going to need his help and advice about Juran; she couldn't afford to alienate him.

'It's queer,' he was saying, 'the more you think about it. Your stepfather's Will must have been dashed carelessly drafted. No foresight. He must just have thought, "William and then Belinda and beyond that it doesn't matter".'

His marmalade eyes were looking at Rachel as if he expected an answer, so she said, 'I suppose so.'

'And you see what happened! It did matter. No, take my word for it, any Last Will and Testament worth its salt should take every possibility into account. Even if your stepfather thought he didn't have any blood relatives beyond William and Belinda, he should have made an effort to find out. I mean, did he even *try* to discover whether that brother of his was still alive?'

For a moment the world went spinning round her head, then she remembered. 'You mean Archie? But he died years ago.'

Philip said, 'We-e-e-ll. He was a bit too fond of the girls, and his father sent him to India. But the fact that he's never been heard of again doesn't necessarily mean he's dead.'

'Oh, stop it, Philip! You're just trying to worry me. My stepfather said Archie was dead and he wouldn't have said so if he hadn't been sure. Give me credit for knowing more about the Macmillans than you do.'

He had lost interest. 'Yes, well. But it's right you should know everyone's talking. Heredity matters in these parts. You needn't expect to find them all dishing out invitations to you just because you've become mistress of Juran. At least there's one blessing, though. Thanks to me, you do know something about running an estate, which is more than can be said for your Uncle Gresham. Can't think why he dismissed McBride. You'll be employing a new grieve, will you?'

'No,' she said. 'No, and *no*. I'm going to run Juran myself.'

6

She couldn't make any useful plans until she knew the state of Juran's finances, and no one would tell her.

There was no point in asking Gresham, so she went first to John McBride, who had been forcibly retired when Gresham decided to mismanage the estate himself. He was a gloomy old man now and resistant to strongminded young ladies, and it took her several visits before she could persuade him to explain why they had never raised barley on the flat ground by the river, never planted trees on the hills, never sent fish to the markets. The answers were simple enough. Fencing and forestry and barrels all cost money. But she couldn't persuade him to put it in terms of pounds, shillings and pence.

So she summoned Mr Mattheson, the estate's local man of business, but Mr Mattheson wouldn't tell her anything at all until she came formally of age. He would visit her again, he promised, on the day after her twenty-first birthday. Raging inside, she made up her mind that, when that day came, Mr Mattheson would find himself dismissed without a character – or whatever the professional equivalent might be.

Her only remaining resort seemed to be a pilgrimage to the city of Edinburgh, which should have been a pleasure except that she was so wrapped up in her thoughts that she scarcely even saw the glories of Princes Street, or the canyons of the Old Town, or the Georgian splendours of the New.

When she walked into the offices of Napier, Napier, Nelson and Napier WS, David Napier couldn't get over it.

'I didn't think you'd ever speak to me again!'

'Well, neither did I,' she admitted candidly, 'but I don't know what else to do. Besides, you have all the papers and things. I just hope that you've learned your lesson from last time.'

His eyes were, if possible, greener than ever and his hands larger as he devotedly clasped the one she extended to him. 'Come in and sit down. I swear on my oath I'll never make a mistake again in *anything* to do with you.'

'Or with anyone else, I hope. You're not sounding like a very good advertisement for the legal profession, Mr Napier.'

He blushed fierily and then gave a sheepish grin. 'My problem is that I'm human.'

Unfortunately, he wasn't much more of a help than Mr Mattheson. If she had stopped to think about it, she would have known that Gresham must have taken Juran's business away from Napier, Napier immediately after the confrontation over her father's Will.

'All I can tell you is that, in the six or seven months before that, Gresham didn't contribute a penny towards anything, not even his and his wife's board and lodging. There's no reason why he should put his own money into the estate, of course, but the danger is that he may have been taking money out. Not illegally, mind you. But he's the kind of fellow who likes his comforts, and he may have used Juran's money for those.'

'The new curtains for his study!' she exclaimed. 'And Aunt Minerva's bedroom carpet. And Horace's nature library! I don't *believe* it.'

David Napier grimaced. 'The books might be debatable, but curtains and carpets would be legitimate expenditure. Can I give you a word of advice?'

'That,' she said with some acerbity, 'is what I am here for.'

'Mr Gresham has been filling the rôle of caretaker. Has he done anything, do you know, to improve the working of the estate?'

'Not a thing.'

'Then I would guess that Juran, as it was towards the end of your father's lifetime, is existing from day to day on the rents from its tenants. If I were you, I'd prepare myself for the worst.'

'*Thank* you.' Rising to her feet, she went to look out of the window, seeing nothing. After a moment, 'I don't understand!' she exclaimed with barely repressed fury. 'Juran must have been well off, once. And not so very long ago. Where has the money gone?'

David Napier couldn't tell her. It was to be left to Hogg to do that.

7

She knew him quite well by now, thanks to the puppy he had given her. Gresham had taken one look at the animal and forbidden him both the house and grounds; as a result, the pup had remained in residence – if Hogg's peripatetic existence could be so described – with the foxhunter.

In the three years of his life, the little mongrel had developed into a ridiculous-looking hound with an ordinarily dog-sized body but ears, paws and tail that would have done credit to a St Bernard. He also had boundless energy, a frolicsome nature, and an ungraceful gait that had suggested his name of Lolloper.

Hogg said, with a twinkle in his yellow eyes, 'Now Juran's yours, you'll be able to take him home with you. It'll fairly rile yon uncle of yours.'

Reeling under her pet's exuberant assault, Rachel stared at him. 'It would, wouldn't it? I hadn't thought of that. Is he house trained?'

'Aye, well, there might be a wee problem there. He's no' very good at houses.'

'He'd prefer a nice tumbledown ruin, would he? Well, that can probably be arranged.'

Hogg was not only far too well-informed for comfort but had a knack of understanding exactly what she wasn't saying. 'Bad as that, is it? Well, ye had to find out some time.'

'Find out what?' She began tying Lolloper's ears in a knot on top of his head and the dog whined in ecstasy.

Hogg didn't answer directly; he rarely did. 'Aye, a spendthrift lot, the Macmillans,' he said ruminatively, puffing on his horrible old clay pipe and peaceably surveying the landscape.

It was a lovely April day, the sun merrily shining, the plump white clouds – the kind that, in children's picture books, always had rather burly Cupids perched upon them – chasing one another across the blue sky, the sea gently lapping on the white shell sand of the beach, the mountains still wearing their caps of snow and the trees leafless but quiveringly ready to burst their buds. The air was like a distilled essence of freshness.

'Ye just need to look at Daniel and old Hector, his father,' Hogg went on. 'I don't know about Archie. He was before my time.'

'Archie?' It was the second time Archie had been mentioned in a few weeks. Before that, Rachel had heard the name only once in a dozen years. It was coincidence, that was all. 'He didn't have much time to be spendthrift, did he?' she hazarded after a moment. 'He died quite young.'

'Maybe aye, maybe no. He was declared "presumed dead" just before old Hector snuffed it in '53 or whenever it was.'

'*Presumed* dead?'

'Aye, it's a bit like a "not proven" verdict in court. Ye know – "not guilty, but don't do it again". Only in this case, it's "you're dead, and don't try and pretend you're not".' Then, seeing the horror in her face, he gave her his gap-toothed grin. 'There, there, lassie! Don't look so worried. It was just a wee joke.'

'Well, I wish you wouldn't joke about that kind of thing. What happened? Do you know?'

'The old man never approved of Archie, so when he was dying he justified leaving Juran to his younger son by saying that, since he hadn't heard of the elder one for twenty years, he "presumed" him dead. It's a lawyers' phrase. Hector was a real old hypocrite, but it was a fair presumption, mind you. Twenty years without a word, and in the place they call the graveyard of the British? Don't you worry your head, lassie. Even if Archie wasn't really dead in '53, there's been the Indian Mutiny since then. That would put paid to him if nothing else did.'

'How can you say that kind of thing?' But Archie, in truth, seemed as unreal to Rachel as the massacre of Cawnpore or the siege of Lucknow. She might have been concerned if she had been no more than Daniel Macmillan's stepdaughter but, as it was, Juran had been left legally to Daniel and she had inherited it legally from him, via Belinda. She had more important things to worry about.

'Sit, Lolloper,' she said. 'Anyway, what did you mean "spend-thrift"?'

'Gamblers. Everyone knows. Old Hector once tried to stake the castle in a card game but no one thought it was worth the wager. And your stepfather squandered everything the old man left him *and* Mistress Isabella's dowry on top of it. We all thought he'd go looking for another well-endowed kitty when she died, so your ma came as a wee bit of a surprise.'

There wasn't anything Rachel could say to that. It was up to her, now, whether she revealed, or continued to hide, the fact that she was Daniel Macmillan's natural daughter. Little Ellie Vallette, who had given Rachel up as a bad job during the last three depressed years, would have taken pleasure in flinging the truth in everyone's face, but Rachel knew that the result would be complete social ostracism instead of the equivocal acceptance she had now. And although she didn't much care if she never saw any of her neighbours again, if there was any cutting off to be done, pride required that she be the one to do it.

She sighed. 'I wish I knew how to make the estate more productive.'

'It takes money.'

'I know. I thought there might be enough to allow me to make a start, even if I had to go slowly at first, but I'm beginning to wonder.'

Hogg tipped his disgraceful stovepipe hat to the back of his head and removed the pipe from his mouth. 'Mind you,' he said, 'there's many would envy you the deer forest. Stalking's a fine recreation for gentlemen.'

She knew him well enough by now to know that he meant something. But she didn't know what, and the weaselly face told her nothing.

'Perhaps,' she said. 'But it's hardly a source of income.'

Rainer Blake had been in Glasgow during the week following Hallowe'en, and his attention, like everyone else's, had been caught by the breakfast headline, 'Beautiful young heiress dies tragically on eve of wedding. Fiancé stunned with grief.'

It didn't sound like anyone he knew and he would have turned the page, had his eye not been attracted by the name Macmillan in the first paragraph.

'Damn,' he said, and Colin Campbell, immersed in the more sedate pages of the London *Times*, looked up enquiringly.

Like Blake, Colin Campbell was in his middle thirties, but otherwise very different in style – a brown-haired, humorous man of middle height whose quiet appearance gave no clue to the fact that he was a very powerful and influential gentleman indeed. Based in Scotland, he had moulded himself, on the surface at least, on what the British expected their bankers to be. Blake, on the other hand, his route to success having been very different, still looked like a pirate even though he seemed these days to be making an attempt to appear more conventional. Colin didn't ask, but he did wonder why; Blake always had a reason for everything. The two men had known each other since they were boys and had the very healthiest respect for each other's abilities.

'Damn,' Blake said again. 'Now, that *has* put the cat among the pigeons.'

Colin returned to *The Times*. If Blake wanted to tell him, he would, though Colin hoped he wouldn't. Blake's ploys tended to be a wee bit intricate for an orthodox banker's taste; a result of all that devious haggling in oriental bazaars, no doubt.

Blake grinned faintly and – reflecting that one benefit of a misspent youth was that it inured you to sauntering into places to which you hadn't been invited and where you weren't wanted – resigned himself to the fact that a return saunter was called for. Because, after Belinda, who? Not, presumably, the poor relation, Rachel, which was a pity for Juran's sake. With mild irritation, he reflected that he still wasn't sure what her relationship actually was; a cousin on the distaff side was what he had deduced originally, but he had never been sure of it.

Lucian Gresham had been virtually running the place for the last three years and the deterioration had been marked, so if Belinda's heir happened to be someone on Gresham's side of the family . . . Horace, perhaps?

This time, Blake decided, he was not going to be rushed. This time he was going to go over the estate with a fine-tooth comb. If he had had the faintest inkling of what a troublesome mortgage this was going to be, Archie Macmillan could have whistled for his loan.

It was not until June, however, after a long and tiring winter and spring of consultations in London, that he was able to spare the two weeks he estimated he needed.

9

In his thirty-five eventful years of life, Blake had learned to take most things in his stride. Even so, he found his brows rising of their own accord when it was revealed to him that the new legatee of Juran was, after all, the competent and much put-upon poor relation, Miss Rachel Macmillan.

Gresham – *mirabile dictu* – greeted his unheralded arrival with a, 'Stay as long as you like, dear boy', but Miss Rachel, glancing at her uncle as if he were being wilfully provocative, said, 'We were obviously mistaken in our belief that you were about to depart for the East when you left us last November, Mr Blake.'

'Yes. I have been no further than London. But I leave for Boston in three weeks to visit with my father, and then come back to sail for China at the end of October.'

'Really? Can't you sail straight from America?'

She asked in a way that reminded Blake forcibly of an autocratic dowager of his acquaintance, and he succumbed to temptation. 'Sure could, but that li'l old Suez Canal opens on November seventeen, and I sho nuff ain't gonna miss being one of the first ones through it.'

Miss Rachel's blue eyes widened.

Mrs Gresham said, 'I beg your pardon?'

Lucian Gresham said nothing.

After a moment the corners of Miss Rachel's lips began to twitch. 'Is that how Americans talk?'

'Some of them.'

'Why don't you?'

'My pa walloped it out of me when I was in short pants. We Bostonians consider it vulgar.'

She didn't know whether or not to believe him. 'Are you really going through the Suez Canal?'

'Honest and true. It'll cut the journey time from five months to only seven weeks and I cannot tell you what a revolution *that* will bring about. Everything – goods, letters, people – will move three times as fast as before.'

'And you yourself will no longer have to spend half your life on shipboard.'

He smiled. 'What an excellent memory you have, Miss Macmillan.'

Later that evening, as they sat over an excellent fricassée of duck, he remarked, 'I remember on my first visit being served a dish of chicken with a most – er – unusual flavour. Mutton, I think it was. Was that some local speciality?'

Miss Rachel's face froze and then she blushed. 'No, it was the result of a slight contretemps in the kitchen.' Then, ignoring his look of amused enquiry, she hurried on, 'I remember also that, when you first visited us, you were interested in Juran as a specimen of a Highland estate. There was something about familiarising yourself with a landscape that obsessed homesick Scotsmen in the East. Is that why we are again being afforded the pleasure of your company?'

Still waters, he thought – and with a touch of acid in their deeps. It was as well that she didn't ask whether he had any particular homesick Scotsman in mind.

'You may recall,' he replied blandly, 'that neither of my previous visits was well timed. My ignorance remains profound and I was hoping I might rely on someone at Juran to rectify it.'

10

There were still a few days of limbo before Rachel's birthday and, her mind and all her senses in need of occupation, she decided to teach the enigmatic, formidable Mr Blake more than he had bargained for.

She didn't understand why he had come back. She would have thought his homesick Scots would have been homesick mainly for the grandeur of the scenery and the freshness of the air, of which Mr Blake had had ample personal experience in the two or three days of his visit at Hallowe'en. But perhaps she was wrong. Perhaps those faraway exiles really did spend their time sentimentalising about tumbledown croft houses and peat fires and kail brose; about illicit whisky stills, and bracken beds for the cows, and the pleasures of redding flax. It seemed unlikely, but she couldn't think of any other reason why he should have come. Certainly not to see her again.

She wished he didn't look so dangerous and disturbing even in the conventional formality of tailcoat and drainpipe trousers. It disturbed her terribly as she set about trying to obliterate every trace of the shameful impression she had made on him the previous year. She was *not* a cheap little hussy. She was an intelligent, sensible young woman and would prove it to him, her manner impeccably controlled even if her heartbeat was not.

As a result, Rainer Blake found himself taken on one of the most gruelling conducted tours in his experience. On the two wet days he was made free of every nook and cranny in the castle, from attics to cellar, as well as the outbuildings and the cottages in the village. Fine days saw them striding up and down mountains, rowing up and down lochs, sailing up and down the coast, and all to the accompaniment of a detailed commentary on wildlife, sport and land management that would have tested the stamina and intellect of a lesser man than he.

'Do you do this often?' he enquired politely on the last day, as they sat on the slopes of Carn Beg recovering their breath.

'Not quite so intensively. I don't know many people who could have kept up. Congratulations.'

She was patronising him and Blake's sense of satire, never really asleep, was immediately aroused. He couldn't recall ever being patronised before by a provincial little miss scarcely out of her teens; though this young woman might still have done it, he suspected, even if she had known who he was and what he was. He was beginning to learn that she took a realistic view of her own abilities. It wasn't something that offended him. People who underestimated their own talents rarely fulfilled their potential in life. Little Miss Rachel had grown up quite a bit in these last months and he was relieved that, in the process, she seemed to have grown out of her schoolgirl crush.

Since she was feeling so superior, he thought, she would be unaware of any need to look to her defences, which gave him an excellent opportunity to discover what he still wanted to know – how it had come about that a despised poor relation had fallen heir to Juran. It seemed unlikely that Belinda had voluntarily bequeathed it to her, while if there had been an intestacy he would have expected it to go to Belinda's cousin, Horace.

Lazily, he wondered what it was about Juran that intrigued him, not only the place itself – though that was developing a stronger, stranger magic for him with each visit – but the family, too; an interest that went beyond a banker's normally cold and clinical concern with the state of his investments.

Even his first visit, years ago, had been enough to make him, on his return to Hong Kong, look at Archie Macmillan and his daughter with new eyes and a sense of something that was more than mere inquisitiveness, though less than personal involvement. Macmillan himself hadn't noticed, of course; he rarely noticed anything less obvious than a blunt instrument. But young Sophie had – and hadn't liked it. Sophie, who was enchanting for about half the time and infuriating for the other half. He tried to imagine her at Juran, deprived of parties and admirers and pretty dresses, and failed miserably.

Her cousin Rachel, he thought, would probably be contemptuous of such vanities, self-contained as she appeared to be and admirably adjusted to the wild, unpeopled splendour of the world around her.

As if conscious of his scrutiny and feeling a need to make diversionary conversation, she smiled suddenly and said, 'Do you see how the islands of Meall and Corran look just like a green question mark painted on the water? You only get the effect on a flat calm day.'

Blake couldn't think for a moment why the names were familiar, and then he remembered Macmillan and Venturi's two Chinese-captained steam traders and had to smother a smile.

Without any particular expression, Rachel went on, 'The channel between them can be a death trap, though. That's where my parents were drowned.'

He was startled. 'I'm sorry. I didn't know.'

'Why should you? When you visited us first, I don't imagine anyone told you more than the bare fact of my father being dead.'

The gears of his brain didn't seem to be meshing properly. Her *parents*? Her *father*? But if Belinda and – what was his name? – William had been the children of Daniel Macmillan's first marriage, Rachel could scarcely be the daughter of a second marriage . . .

'I take it that your mother had been married before?'

The blue eyes turned towards him, interpreting the apparent non sequitur. Then, as if the words were being dragged out of her, she said, 'No. When I said "my parents" I meant precisely that. Daniel Macmillan was my real father. It was just that the wedding ceremony was somewhat postponed.'

'Ah. Yes, I see.'

'My mother was not thought to be a suitable bride. She was a cook in her parents' restaurant when they first met. My father, even when they later married, always refused to advertise the truth of the affair – understandably enough, though as a child I resented it deeply. Even Belinda and the Greshams didn't know I was his real daughter until three years ago.'

Everything was making a kind of sense now, except for one thing. 'Why are you telling me this?'

11

She had thought about it, and thought about it. She didn't want to tell him but, unless she did, she knew with certainty that he was going to find out in a way that would show her in the worst possible light and ruin for ever the ease, the tentative friendliness, that had been growing between them in these last few days.

Tomorrow, she was going to give Gresham his *congé* and he was not going to accept it gracefully.

Although Rachel had few acquaintances, had seen few new faces since the days when Juran had welcomed sporting guests, she believed Lucian Gresham to be one of the most pitiless men on earth. He wasn't evil in the religious sense; it was simply that he was incapable of seeing anyone or anything from any point of view other than his own.

She feared him more deeply than ever, now, though not for every moment of the time and no longer in a physical way. Since Belinda's death he hadn't even laid his not-quite-lascivious hand on her arm. Touching her, she supposed, would seem too much of a contamination to him.

In everyday life, he behaved as if he were impervious to her, had no feelings about her at all, and this helped her to contain her own feelings about him, even to persuade herself that her antipathy was of no great importance, a matter, merely, of disliking his arrogance and being repelled by his looks.

It worked, most of the time.

But she knew that he had the instincts of a cobra, and would strike again tomorrow as he had struck on the day her father's Will had been read and, again, in the procurator-fiscal's office at Inveraray. On both occasions, she had been sick for days afterwards, not understanding why he should hate her so much. Her only sin, she had thought in self-justification and self-pity, lay in being the bastard child of an irresponsible father and a mother who wasn't a lady. She hadn't at first seen what she had since come to suspect, that his malevolence was stimulated not so much by that, or by any real feeling for Belinda, but by an unswerving obsession with the complex web of rights he believed to be owing to his idolised sister, Daniel Macmillan's first wife. It was as if, for him, Isabella was still alive and he her protector.

Tomorrow, she, Rachel, was going to revoke those rights for ever and there was going to be a loathsome scene, all the worse for being superficially civilised – a war of words. A war *only* of words, but how she feared them.

And Rainer Blake would be there to hear.

12

She said carefully, 'Being candid is an infrequent pleasure. Are you shocked?'

'Why should I be? You're hardly the first child to be born out of wedlock.'

He was so matter-of-fact about it that the rush of warmth and gratitude almost overwhelmed her and it was difficult to match his prosaic tone. 'Yes. That's what I think, too, but people can be very stuffy about it. No one outside the family knows, even yet, nor will they if I have anything to do with it. They're at liberty to gossip and speculate to their hearts' content. I was legitimated by my parents' marriage, of course – Scots law permits that – but it doesn't remove the slur. And legitimation wasn't enough to let me inherit Juran while Belinda lived. Uncle Gresham thinks I murdered her.'

'A likely tale!'

Sighing, she rose to her feet and turned away as if to scan the amethyst hills. It meant she didn't have to look at him as she said, 'Gresham hates me – rather excessively, as it happens – and I'm afraid that, unless you choose to leave in a hurry, you will be forced to witness some unpleasantness tomorrow. I propose telling him that his tenure here is over, and he will undoubtedly respond with a less than flattering sketch of my character and antecedents.

'So, in answer to your question, that is why I have told you all this. I shouldn't like you to receive too distorted a version of the truth.'

Gresham was not in the habit of saying, 'I beg your pardon?' or even 'What?' like anyone else. Instead, he drawled, 'Your meaning escapes me.'

Smiling despite the clamminess of her palms and the fluttering in her chest, Rachel repeated, 'Juran is mine now, and you and your family are no longer welcome. I expect you to leave within the week.'

She didn't stop there, because his malice was not going to be averted by any reticence on her part and she found it perilously exhilarating to be forthright for once. 'In all our dealings, you have diminished and denigrated me, but that is over now. I should add that I have no sense of gratitude for anything you have ever done, and no wish to see you ever again. If you should think of returning, you will find that the servants have been forbidden to allow you to cross the threshold.'

Predictably, Aunt Minerva exclaimed, 'Really, Rachel!' but it was no more than a formality. For almost four years, Minerva had been hinting, ever less subtly, that she could scarcely wait to return home to the comforts of Priors Mead in Somersetshire, and there was a glow in her eyes now as she fixed them on her husband – a glow in which there was no sympathy at all, but only pleasure sharpened with a trace of something very like spite.

Blake extracted a slim black cigar from his case and lit it thoughtfully as Horace demanded, 'You don't mean me, too? I mean, I *have* to be here!'

Rachel, all her attention concentrated on Lucian Gresham, the only one of the family who interested her, shook her head.

Gresham raised a soft white hand, its slight puffiness contrasting oddly with the carved candlewax of his features, and caressed one of the neatly trimmed sidewhiskers. 'Nonsense. Juran is our home.'

Rachel laughed in sheer astonishment. '*Your* home?'

'Certainly not yours,' he told her. 'You have no right to it. Horace was Belinda's closest blood relative.'

'Despite what the law says?'

'The law is an ass.'

Thoughtfully, Rachel sat threading the long fringe of her shawl through her fingers. It was a new shawl, the most beautiful thing she had ever possessed, and Rainer Blake had presented it to her as a coming-of-age gift.

'But you couldn't possibly have known about my birthday before you came here!' She had said it because she couldn't think of anything else to say, having so little practice in the art of receiving gracefully and suspecting that the gift was far too splendid to accept from a stranger, whatever status that stranger might possess in the other, private world of her dreams.

Blake could have told her that, as Cantonese workmanship went, the crêpe silk shawl was not much above the ordinary, but to Rachel every inch of it was perfection. There were so many delicate gradations of colour and tone in the sprays of plum and lotus blossoms scattered over its centre that she despaired of ever being able to count them, while the corners were vivid with pheasants and peacocks so exquisitely stitched that in their plumage she could see not only every feather but, so clever was the texturing, the very layers in which the feathers lay. Even the crimson lacquer box in which it was presented was a thing of beauty.

Drily, Blake had said, 'Don't rate my powers of insight too high. In the East one becomes accustomed to carrying a few small offerings wherever one goes. I am happy that the shawl should please you.'

'*Small* offerings?'

She should still have been wearing black, indeed had almost forgotten the pleasures of colour, having spent so much of the preceding four years either in mourning or half mourning. But even as she had gone to look out, from among the few dresses that had escaped Bessie Laundry's dye vat, the plain rose-pink one that would make an admirable foil for the embroidery, she had recognised that, shawl or no shawl, she would still have rebelled at the hypocrisy of continuing to wear mourning for Belinda on this, the most momentous day of her life.

Frowning, she stared into Gresham's expressionless eyes. 'But if you believe Horace to be entitled to Juran, why have you done nothing to put the castle or estate to rights?' And then, when he didn't reply, 'Very well, what about the bills I find are outstanding? Why have you done nothing to settle those?' She wished she had some idea of their total.

'I have my reasons.'

Blake, who had no right to intervene, was irritated into saying smoothly, 'Might I suggest that a guardian who wilfully permits debt to accumulate on his ward's estate might find himself liable? And should the guardian prove to be short of funds on his own account, it would undoubtedly raise questions in a court of law.'

There was no perceptible movement of muscle or vein, no change in colour, but it was impossible to mistake that Gresham had moved straight from condescension to cold rage.

'I will settle the bills when it suits me.'

'And when is that likely to be?' Rachel enquired.

'In a few months, I would imagine.'

'I don't understand.' Could Blake be right? Rachel wondered. Could Gresham possibly be in financial difficulties?

But it wasn't that.

'By that time,' Gresham went on, 'you will find all the estate's creditors baying at your heels, and you will have no means of satisfying them. That is the point at which I will come to your rescue.'

Rachel still didn't understand.

He said, 'Then, and only then, will I pay them off for you – in exchange for legal title to Juran.'

14

'Not if you were the last man on earth!' she exclaimed, the worn old cliché slipping out before she could stop it. 'How can you possibly think I would come to you – you of all people – if I needed rescuing!'

'I know of no one else to whom you *could* go.'

Shock and incredulity warring in her mind, she took a deep, controlling breath and, because she had to say something, said, 'If I should ever be reduced to such straits as to need rescuing, I believe marriage would be a preferable solution. Let me make it quite clear, here and now, that I will do *anything* to keep Juran. *Anything* to prevent you from having it. I mean that with all my heart.'

Lazily, his sneer very pronounced, Gresham rose to his feet. 'Anything? If I knew of anything you *could* do, I might be concerned. As it is, did I not have more important matters to occupy my mind, I might derive some entertainment from following your attempts to find a man prepared to take on responsibility for' – each phrase, each word, was enunciated with intense and separate venom – 'a misbegotten slut of a wife, a decaying castle, a large number of unproductive acres and a mountain of debt.'

And that was all.

He strolled towards the door. 'I have no more to say. Goodnight to you.'

Pointedly, Rachel said, 'Goodnight, Aunt Minerva,' and even more pointedly, 'Goodnight, Horace.'

15

Blake continued drawing quietly on his cigar, and after a time remarked, 'Perhaps I might suggest a stroll down to the beach? A little light exercise tends to be more rewarding than sitting brooding on one's injuries.'

She came to with a slight start and said, perfectly rationally, 'Yes, of course. But I had better leave this behind.' Removing her shawl, she laid it carefully over a chair. 'Lolloper ought to be let out.'

Lolloper, released from the palace of a kennel with which Tom Tanner and Jamie McDougall had chosen to mark Rachel's birthday, greeted her with all the panting, tongue-lolling enthusiasm of a dog who had not seen his mistress for the better part of two hours and then, duty done, abandoned her and rushed off in pursuit of some intriguing scent.

Without speaking, the two of them, Blake and Rachel, strolled down to the beach, picking their way carefully through the great sheet of blossoming sea pinks that edged the sand – sand of white shell and sparkling quartz that was beginning to absorb tones of rose and peach from the soft glow of the approaching sunset. The heads of a small school of grey seals gleamed in the water, there was a ringed plover scavenging along the shore, and a pair of oystercatchers winged low over the surface, black-and-white plumage and long orange-red bills silhouetted against the smoky satin of the sea. The stars were beginning to show, although they were no more than diamond pinpricks against a sky of palest turquoise, translucent as a veil.

The calm was pure delight, refreshment for the spirit, ravishment for the soul.

Pausing to pick up a stray pebble, Rachel studied it for an abstracted moment before showing it to Blake, a wafer of sea-green serpentine smoothed by the waves of centuries.

When he had admired it, she bent slightly and sent it skimming over the surface of the water. It touched once, twice, three times.

It was on the way to a fourth when Lolloper, realising that he was missing something, came thundering along the beach, ears and tail horizontal in the wind of his passing and his intention of joining in the game writ large upon his eager countenance.

Rachel let out an unladylike yelp of 'Stop, you nitwitted animal!' which went entirely unheeded, but Blake, with admirable presence of mind, took off in a flying tackle that halted the offended Lolloper dead in his tracks before he so much as got his feet wet.

'Goodness,' Rachel said, 'I've never seen such a fast reaction in my life! Well, at least it's uncovered another strand in his ancestry that I didn't know about. There's a bit of retriever there, somewhere. Are you wet?'

She was laughing, a vivid, unconstrained laugh that transformed her. She looked pretty – and much more than pretty. Desirable.

Blake rose and brushed himself down, grinning back at her. 'No more than sandy.'

It was then he discovered that she hadn't been contemplating her injuries after all, but had been effervescing inside like a Chinese firecracker. Her whole being was almost luminous as the words came tumbling out. 'I've done it! I've done it! And it wasn't too dreadful after all. I may only be a misbegotten slut with a decaying castle and a mountain of debts, but I've told Gresham to go, and I'm still alive to tell the tale. I've done it!' Her eyes were brilliant. 'And I couldn't have done it without you.'

There was a trace of roughness in his voice, because he hadn't seen quite how much of an ordeal it must have been for her. 'Of course you could. You didn't need me. Anything you want to do, you are entirely capable of doing on your own.'

And perhaps that was true, and perhaps it wasn't.

But the air between them was crackling and, without conscious volition on the part of either of them, she was in his arms, and his eyes were resting on her mouth for a suspended instant, and then he was kissing her.

It wasn't what she had dreamed of because she hadn't known how to dream, or not beyond the dreams of ignorance. The warm pressure of his lips seemed the answer to all her desires, and even when the feeling of his tall body against hers ceased to mean simple closeness and began to mean something else, something thrilling that she didn't understand, she had no knowledge of the magic that was missing, felt no sense of deprivation, only of a lovely, dissolving instability.

She wanted no more than what she had, but she wanted it for ever – wanted them to go on standing as they were, lips meeting, arms embracing, feet firm on the sands of her beloved Juran, the scents of salt and sea pinks, tobacco and maleness in her nostrils and the ecstasy of fulfilment in her heart.

There was nothing to tell her that Blake had no sooner settled her in his embrace than he had heard warning bells ringing.

Most unmarried girls of Rachel's age were so sensitive to a man's touch and shy of his kiss that a civilised lover had little difficulty in keeping his passion in check. It was the product – the unhealthy product, in Blake's view – of a moral code that placed such a premium on women's purity that it would, if it could, have enforced immaculate conception as the only acceptable means of propagating the species.

But the way Rachel accepted his kiss, the rising and falling of her breath, the almost imperceptible vibrations of sensuality that radiated from her, reminded him instantly of what he had so briefly sensed the year before, that, innocent though she undoubtedly was – and although she probably didn't even know it herself yet – she was blessed, or cursed, with a powerful gift for loving. And that was a Pandora's box that, for her sake, no man other than her husband should take it upon himself to unlock.

Certainly not a stranger whose life lay half a world away. Blake believed that for every man there was a time, a place and a woman; and he did not think that, for him, the magical combination was here.

But it was not as easy as it should have been to prevent his lips from opening, his hands from wandering, or his body from betraying him, as they stood like statues in the soft, roseate, seductive light of the afterglow.

16

Never in her life had Rachel been so happy.

She was still lost in rapture when Lolloper, resenting the competition, put an end to the brief idyll by embarking on a tug-o'-war with Blake's trouser leg.

He released her, then, and stepped back, saying unsmilingly, 'I apologise. That was unforgivable of me.'

It was, of course, the correct thing for a gentleman to say in the circumstances, although Rachel had no idea what a lady should say in reply. 'Not at all,' hardly seemed appropriate, and his cool grey eyes, suddenly expressionless, discouraged her from flouting the conventions and telling him the truth.

She must have done something wrong, she thought, because it seemed that kissing her had given him no pleasure. After a moment of speechlessness, she managed, 'I – er – I don't – I . . .'

He helped her out by ignoring the whole thing, picking up their conversation again as if nothing had happened. 'I was saying, as I recall, that I believe you to be perfectly capable of handling your own affairs, and that is true. But perhaps I might give you a word of warning?'

'Please.'

'When you find out the full extent of Juran's debts tomorrow, from Mr . . .'

'Mattheson.'

'Yes. They may turn out to be perfectly manageable. But, if not, you should face up to the possibility, indeed the likelihood, that creditors who have refrained from suing the supercilious, aristocratic Mr Gresham will have no hesitation at all about descending on a solitary, inexperienced, twenty-one-year-old girl.'

'I know.'

They were crossing the lawn now, and soon they would be back in the castle, and everything would be over.

Each word a separate mountain to be climbed, she went on, 'I've no notion how I'm going to deal with them. I've no notion how I'm going to deal with *anything* at the moment. I have all sorts of ideas for improving Juran milling about in my head, but I'm incapable of concentrating on them until I know the truth about the estate's finances, and above all until I get Lucian Gresham off the premises. I'll summon the police to throw him out, if I have to!'

At least she could hear herself sounding sensible and composed, like the kind of person she had, during these last soul-searing days, tried to persuade him that she was.

They picked up their separate candles in the Great Hall. And said their detached goodnights. And went their separate ways.

17

Blake slept badly and Rachel not at all, and in the morning it was raining. When Mr Mattheson arrived, he did nothing to improve the day.

Blake found Rachel in the Green Drawing Room after the lawyer had gone.

She was seated at the piano and greeted him with a sprightly rendering of the first bars of the Wedding March, ending in a nasty clash of chords. 'Are you acquainted with any rich bachelors prepared to take on a misbegotten slut of a wife, a decaying castle and a mountain of debts?'

'You forgot the unproductive acres,' he said. 'As bad as that, was it?'

'Yes. I either have to marry money, or sell Juran – if anyone will buy it.'

He propped his shoulders against the mantelpiece, put his hands in his trousers pockets, and said easily, 'I might be able to help you.'

The silence lasted for a long time, and then she said, 'Why?'

He was interested that she didn't ask, 'How?' But since it would have reintroduced an undesirably personal note even to say that there was nothing personal in his offer, he merely shrugged. 'I have always found it good business practice to have people beholden to me, even if there seems no immediate purpose for it.'

'Oh.' Her wild, disbelieving lift of the spirits subsided and she told herself it was just what she would have expected. His motives would never be predictable, never emotional, always intelligently calculated. The more she saw of him, the more convinced she became that he was the cleverest man she was ever likely to meet.

But although he was fluent and knowledgeable on almost any subject that happened to arise – Highland agriculture excepted – he was as communicative as a clam about what really mattered. About his work and his private life he never spoke. Where facts were at issue, she still knew little more than he had revealed on his first visit to Juran three years before. With a faint trace of hysteria, she wondered if perhaps he already had a wife, two wives, three wives. One in Glasgow, one in Boston, another in Hong Kong . . .

But at least he had answered her 'why' with an answer that she understood.

'I see,' she said. 'And can I ask how?'

'With money.'

Considering how much he now knew about Juran, he couldn't – could he? – be offering a loan on terms that would be impossible for her to meet. Trying to match his lightly sardonic tone, she said, 'Charity, Mr Blake?'

'Do I strike you as a philanthropist?'

'No. What did you have in mind?'

He gave himself a last moment to review the idea that had been crystallising in his head over the last few hours. 'Not a loan. Nothing that would involve you in having to worry about interest or collateral or anything of the sort. Something that is not really to do with banking at all, merely a straightforward business arrangement.'

The rain was easing, as it usually did with the turn of the evening tide, and the light was changing from grey to an indeterminate pallor, milky and opalescent. A baby thrush sat on the outside windowsill, its back to the glass, shouting plaintively and persistently for its supper.

Blake went on, 'You need funds to clear your debts, repair the castle and improve the estate. Right?'

'Yes.'

'Good. Now, as it happens, my partner in the Clyde River Bank would find it convenient to rent a sporting estate.'

Her heart leapt to her throat, but all she did was nod and utter another noncommittal 'Yes?'

'Renting one, you understand, would be less trouble for him than owning one. He is not a sportsman himself, but he has clients to entertain, people like manufacturers, brewers and shipbuilders who would be happy to have a taste of what they think of as aristocratic pursuits. The late Prince Consort and his Balmoralism have a deal to answer for, there.' He shrugged. 'You see how my mind is working? However, before I go on, I guess I'd like to be reassured that I'm not wasting my breath.'

Moving to the small sewing chair by the side of the fire, Rachel sat down – just as if little Ellie Vallette wasn't egging her on to break into a song and dance – and shook her head calmly.

'Great. Now, as I figure it, if my partner – his name, by the way, is Colin Campbell – were to pay you a ten years' rental in advance, it would be a bargain for him because, obviously, he would pay a lower overall rent than in the case of an annual arrangement. And you, of course, would receive an injection of capital that would enable you to settle your present difficulties and embark on future improvements without having to sacrifice anything in return except, occasionally, some of your privacy.'

She cleared her throat. 'What kind of sum did you have in mind?'

'We would have to go into that, but I'd guess we could arrive at a mutually agreeable figure.' He grinned unexpectedly. 'And unless I misjudge you, by the end of ten years you will have improved the place so much that you will be in a highly advantageous commercial position. From all I hear, deer forests are set to become a seller's market which means that the bidding, whether for buying or renting, will go up by leaps and bounds.'

The whole thing was too perfect. Rachel scarcely dared believe it. Idiotically, she said, 'But where would I live?'

'At Juran, of course. Campbell wouldn't be bringing parties very often, and I'd guess for a week at most. You would simply cater for their needs as Juran has always catered for house parties, in consultation with Campbell, of course. He's a widower, so he would need you to act as hostess.'

She fought a rearguard action, but only because her self-respect required it. She wasn't going to spoil this precarious new business relationship by falling on Blake's neck and weeping tears of gratitude all over his starched white shirtfront.

'But everything is so run down,' she said. 'Won't Mr Campbell mind?'

'Not if it suits him in other ways. Anyway, you can embark on some basic improvements the minute you have cash in hand. Might I suggest you make a start with some good thick carpeting and a few roaring fires?'

'We don't have a billiard room.'

'Dear God! How tragic!'

'But gentlemen like to have something to do when it rains. And I could never guarantee that there would be deer to stalk – not shootable beasts, anyway. So much depends on the wind and the weather. Sometimes they drift over the hills to Altsigh and we don't see any for weeks on end.'

'In that case, the gentlemen will just have to shoot birds instead, or catch fish, or play ring o' roses. Really, Miss Rachel, I thought you were a decisive young woman, but I guess I was mistaken. Let us just forget the whole thing.'

It had the desired effect. 'No!' she said at once. 'I agree.' And then, with belated caution, 'But the terms must be right.'

18

By the end of the week, Blake was back in Glasgow amid the shouting and the bustle, the clangour of iron wheels on cobbled streets, the beating of the fire drums, the hammering of construction work and all the other ear-rending noises of a thriving city. He had always been fond of Glasgow in a masochistic kind of way.

Even so, the noise from the building works next door seemed excessive as he dropped into a chair in the bank's splendid new offices on the corner of George Square and said affably to his partner, 'You'll be deaf before you're forty. Which makes it highly opportune that I should have found a nice, quiet, peaceful Highland estate for you to rent. Did you know you had been looking for one?'

'The builders expect it to be another five years before the job's done, so that should work out about right. And no, I do not want to rent a Highland estate, thank you. What are you up to this time?'

'Let's get away from this goddamned racket.'

They went to the new coffee room in Buchanan Street, where there were no handsome Italianate influences, no segmental pediments and no Otis elevator, but where at least there was no sound other than the clatter of china and the murmur of conversation.

Blake said, 'I think I've mentioned Archie Macmillan to you before. One of my lesser Hong Kong customers, small fry trader, always short of capital. Macmillan himself is a poor risk but his partner, Venturi, has his head screwed on very well indeed. They needed another infusion four or five years ago but I didn't feel the business justified it. Then Macmillan came up with the idea of taking out a mortgage on Juran, his family home in Argyllshire.'

'Uh-huh.'

'I visited it when I was over here in '66 and decided to let Macmillan have his loan, but there were a few things I wasn't happy about, so I've had another look. There's been deterioration. The place needs money spent on it.'

Colin Campbell, a patient man, waited to hear what made this particular case different from a hundred others, his curiosity mildly stirred by the very fact that Blake was telling him about it. Blake never volunteered information unless he had good reason for it. There were times when his partner thought he carried the habit of secrecy too far.

'There's a difficulty, however,' Blake went on. 'No one at Juran knows that friend Archie is still alive and I can scarcely enlighten them. It's not only banking confidentiality, but an old family feud.'

Colin shook his head in amused disbelief.

For Blake, embarrassment was a new experience, but he gave no sign of it. 'A Miss Rachel Macmillan has just inherited the place – or thinks she has. And the estate is badly in debt.'

'You'll notice I'm not asking,' Colin Campbell remarked, 'how or why you got yourself into this godforsaken mess.'

'More coffee?' Blake asked. Colin was the only man in the world who could put him through the hoop.

'What you're saying is that we have a wee problem about protecting our interest?'

'Well . . .' Briefly, Blake explained the arrangement he had suggested to Rachel. 'So, with your cooperation, we wouldn't need to worry about maintenance and repairs. It's the legalities I'm not one hundred per cent happy about.'

'Why not? Unless your brains have gone begging, I'd assume the mortgage entitles the bank to expend any sums necessary to keep the place up to scratch and charge them to the mortgagee?'

'Sure, but the rental idea goes beyond that. To be on the safe side, I'd rather make it a private arrangement. If I give you my personal draft, Macmillan will be indebted to me rather than the bank. I can sort things out with him when I get back to Hong Kong.'

'You'll not mind if I ask the obvious. You're quite sure Macmillan does have title?'

Blake shrugged. 'I went into it in '66, and the lawyers told me that, when he chooses to reveal himself, the courts will recognise him as the owner.'

Unlike most hardheaded businessmen, Colin Campbell had a smile that touched his eyes and left his lips alone. He shook his head admiringly. 'It's a fine tale,' he said. 'You're sure you didn't get it out of Mrs Radcliffe? Missing heirs, orphaned maidens, crumbling castles on sea-girt shores . . . Juran *is* sea-girt, I take it? And haunted?'

Blake didn't reply, and Campbell went on thoughtfully, 'If it had been me, now, I'd just have gone back to Hong Kong and told Macmillan his collateral was showing signs of wear and tear. I'd have warned him that, if he didn't do something about it, we'd have to. He can't shuffle off responsibility just for the sake of some damnfool, missing-heir rubbish.'

Just then, a stout man with a beard like a gravedigger's spade stopped to pass the time of day and have Blake introduced to him. He turned out to be from the Bank of Scotland, which occupied most of the building in which the Clyde River Bank also had its offices, and was so interested in Blake's operations in the East that he almost had to be pried loose before the two men were able to get back to the question of Juran.

'Yes, well,' Colin Campbell said. 'After that nice wee reprieve, perhaps you'll feel better able to tell me *why*, as distinct from how, you've committed yourself to subsidising Miss Macmillan, and me to taking part in the charade?'

It was easy to be deceived by Colin Campbell's quiet manner and quizzical brown eyes into thinking his tolerance boundless, but it was not. And among the things he was not prepared to tolerate was being made use of. It was something Blake, seeing him only for a few weeks every two or three years, was inclined to forget.

He didn't apologise. Apologies never cut any ice with Colin. He said, 'Because, if anyone's able to put Juran to rights, she is. On the surface she's a perfectly ordinary young woman, small, not pretty except when she smiles, but underneath she's . . . ' Underneath she was a lot of things that weren't relevant to the present discussion. '. . . she's extremely knowledgeable, intelligent and, I suspect, competitive. Show her a challenge, and she'll respond to it.'

'Maybe so, but leaving aside my personal objections to being involved in this ill-managed bit of joukery-paukery, I'd have thought that was all the more reason to watch your step. You're not being fair to the girl. What happens when Archie Macmillan turns up and takes the place away from her? What would happen if *she* tried to mortgage it? Do you not have a conscience about misleading her? Because that's what you're doing.'

Blake half smiled. 'Okay, so everything isn't perfect. But come on, Colin. Here in Glasgow you can afford to have a conscience. In Hong Kong, it's something you only become aware of when you know someone's looking over your shoulder. The point is that, if Rachel Macmillan knew that Juran didn't belong to her, she would lose interest, and the bank can't afford that. And as for when Archie shows himself – well, it's a family matter and they can sort it out between them.'

'Mphmmm.'

'I'll be intrigued,' Blake remarked carelessly, as if the matter was all settled, 'to know what you think of the girl when you take your first party to Juran.'

Sourly, Colin Campbell said, 'More to the point, what will she think of me? The last time I tried fishing was with a bent pin off the end of the pier at Dunoon.'

You will never have all you want. You will have to choose . . .

She had Juran now, without having to choose, and in one way
Rainer Blake had given it to her. Rachel had no idea how that fitted
into old Becca's prophecy as she wandered her new domain in
delirious, dreamlike solitude.

She had given the living-in servants a few days off because, her
brain told her, it was desirable to take a little time, completely
undisturbed, to survey every nook and cranny of the castle and
identify what needed to be done and in what order. Which roof leaks
most urgently needed to be seen to, which rotting window frames and
wormy timbers should be replaced, which furniture recovered, which
rooms reorganised, which pictures rehung.

On the top floor there were several small, unused rooms Rachel had
never entered before, rooms cluttered with old clothes chests, broken
toys and discarded furniture from a hundred years ago, some of it still
in fair condition and of the simple design Rachel had come to prefer to
the ornateness of the modern. With unexpected pleasure, she found a
kneehole library desk that would do admirably for the Green Drawing
Room, which she intended to convert into a living and working room
for herself.

But as she moved downstairs, floor by floor, her meticulous
notepad and busy pencil became a deceit, an occupation only for her
hands and the lesser part of her mind.

It was the queerest feeling to be entirely alone in the castle, which
suddenly began to seem huge and secretive and very slightly inimical.
Her spine tingling, Rachel thought that, if it had not been mid-
summer, when darkness never came, she might have summoned the
servants back.

Because there were ghosts here after all, though not the ghosts of
the ancestors whose dark portraits lined the walls of the Great
Staircase – stern William, in leather armour and long woollen surcoat;
rakish John, his Cavalier hat plumed and all else lavished with lace;
impeccable James, his hair powdered above the linen stock, his wide-
cuffed coat tailored from snuff-brown velvet, his expression as prim
as if thieving architectural fancies from the Duke of Argyll had never
entered his mind.

The ghosts that thronged the castle, that pushed at Rachel's heels,
yammered in her ears, were quite other. Her mother and father were

there, and William, and Belinda. Even the living, though departed, had left something of themselves behind. In every corridor, on every stair, some trace of Gresham or Minerva or Horace remained. There was only one shade missing, though Rachel tried hard to conjure it up.

Rainer Blake had gone, but because of what he had given her, she knew he must come back.

More than once, as the knowledge of all that had happened surged through her veins, she had to stop and steady herself, to reassure herself that the years of hollow dreaming were over and this was reality. Juran was hers, really hers, at last, and no one now could take it from her.

PART THREE

1869—
1879

CHAPTER ELEVEN

I

'This is getting beyond a joke, Sophie,' Frank said. 'I mean, I know you must be nervous about the intimate side of things. All young ladies are. But you've been keeping me dangling for over a year now and people are beginning to talk. It doesn't reflect well on me, you know.'

Sophie did know. It didn't reflect well on her, either, as Joanna Bagford was always pointing out. When young ladies accepted a proposal of marriage, they were expected to overcome their maidenly shrinkings in a year at most – unless they were of the lower classes and had to wait until they could afford to marry. Sophie had no excuse.

'I don't understand you,' Joanna said. 'Frank is a nice boy, and there's plenty of money in the family. Marriage is roses and thorns, of course, but some of the roses are awfully enjoyable.'

Such as?

Well, having a married lady's freedom certainly counted among them and so, Joanna went on with a faint blush, did b-e-d. The only serious thorns for Sophie would be Frank's parents, 'and even Mr Moore isn't fearfully awful if you catch him on his own.'

What Joanna didn't know was that it wasn't only maidenly shrinking that Sophie was struggling with, but conscience. Because in accepting Frank she had killed two birds with one stone and was now wishing guiltily that she hadn't.

2

Despite everything, she had been unprepared when he had proposed to her on a wonderful December evening eighteen months before.

They had taken chairs to the top of the Peak, up the vertiginous path cut in the early days of Sir Hercules Robinson's governorship to give access to the healthy air of the heights. And the air was, indeed, healthily fresh and fragrant even if the undergrowth of eucalyptus, jasmine, wild indigo and rhododendron was attractive not only to humans but geckos, monkeys, snakes and Hong Kong's huge and varied population of disagreeable insects.

On such a night, however, those who made the ascent were repaid by having a whole magical world spread out before them. Ahead lay a thousand miles of unknown China, and all around were the vast, island-studded South China seas. The sheer scale and emptiness were awe-inspiring, the lake-pooled land behind Kowloon glimmering like a patchwork of satins, the sky a dome of indigo velvet sparked with a million jewels, and the surface of the sea like the patina on a rubbed old shilling piece, shading off to east and west from the wide path of molten silver that lay at the feet of the moon.

Sophie breathed, 'Isn't it beautiful? Like being alone in the universe.'

'Except for the coolies and your amah,' said Frank with a nervous chuckle. 'I'll get Hsu to open the champagne and then we'll get rid of them.' Ah Foon was reluctant to go, muttering about 'plopa missees', but she compromised in the end by settling down in sight but out of earshot.

They sat for a while in silence, Sophie still in her sedan, Frank on the grass beside her, dreamily sipping champagne. Sophie wasn't thinking about anything in particular when Frank startled her by uttering her name in a voice that set her heart pounding.

She nearly panicked. She wasn't ready. She didn't want him to propose to her. She didn't want to change her life. She liked things the way they were.

If, in such a setting, he had thrown himself at her feet, or embraced her ardently, proposing to her in the tones of throbbing passion favoured by heroes in sentimental novels, she would have said, 'No!' instantly and without thinking. Romance was supposed to be fun; emotion alarmed her.

But that was not Frank's style and, besides, any but the most distant wooing was pretty well ruled out not only by the presence of the servants but by the canoe-like poles of Sophie's chair which, projecting five feet behind and in front and curving inwards to within eighteen inches of each other, presented an almost insuperable barrier to anything beyond a polite handshake.

Frank said, 'Sophie, we do get on awfully well, don't we?'

'Yes.'

'And it's not as if we've only just met.'

'No.'

'I was wondering . . . I know I'm not very dashing or handsome . . .'

'Yes, you are!' she said dutifully.

'No, I'm just an ordinary, plodding sort of chap, but I'm very fond of you. And I wondered . . . Well, I've already talked to your father about money, and things like that, and he said to go ahead and ask you, so I'm asking you.'

She swallowed a reprehensible desire to giggle. 'Yes, Frank? What are you asking me?'

'Dash it! I'm asking you to marry me.' He looked up then, his lips quivering slightly. In the brilliance of the moon, his face had the chaste and innocent look of one of the younger and more soulful angels on a Christmas card.

Sophie hesitated. At nineteen and two days she was almost on the shelf. Most of her contemporaries had left the colony for 'Home', or had remained here and married, or were at least engaged. They weren't as tied to Hong Kong as she was, so they hadn't needed to be so choosy.

She said, 'Er . . .'

'I wouldn't expect you to do anything you – didn't want to do!'

She thought he meant he wouldn't stop her having fun at parties and balls, which was sweet of him. It was a point in his favour, too, that his father was wealthy and Sophie knew she was expensive. Once or twice, lavishing her papa's money on some extravagant new bonnet, she had even felt a twinge of guilt. If she were to marry Frank, it would make her father's life easier.

She said, 'But Frank, I was born in the Year of the Monkey, and you're a Sheep. It's not a very good marriage combination. For you, I mean. Because you're quiet and I'm not. What if I started leading you a dance? It wouldn't be fair.'

He gave it serious thought. 'No, it should be all right. I'm a *Fire* Sheep, after all, and I was born during the Hours of the Dragon.'

'Oh, were you?' That meant determination, courage and conviction, which surprised Sophie, because they weren't qualities she would immediately have thought of in connection with Frank. Perhaps they'd show up when he was older.

Only then did she remember his mother.

She said, 'Your mother . . .'

237

He chewed his lip nervously. 'Well, I can't pretend she's going to like it. But, you know, she really has the best of motives even if her manner can be a bit – ummm – unfortunate at times.'

He was looking very earnest, trying very hard, unaware that what lay between his mother and Sophie could not be remedied by any apologia of his. 'When she first came to the colony, you see, it was an absolute sink of iniquity, so she feels very strongly about moral standards. I know she overdoes it sometimes, but . . .' Hopefully, he went on, 'I'm sure everything would be all right if you could just make a few allowances, and perhaps – for a little while – er – well – er – try to behave more sedately?'

Concentrating hard, he poured them both some more champagne.

Sophie inhaled deeply. She had set out to captivate Frank for one reason only, to repay his mama. She had meant to lead him on to the point of proposing – and then to refuse him. And that, she had thought, would teach Euphemia Moore to say that no self-respecting gentleman would be prepared to marry her. But just recently she had been feeling rather bad about it all, because Frank was really smitten, and he was very nice and it didn't seem fair. She *couldn't* marry him just to spite his mother. But she didn't know how to turn him down without hurting him.

And now Frank himself had tipped the balance. Asking Sophie to change her ways just to suit his horrid old tabby of a mother was too much. Much too much.

Exhaling slowly, she accepted the glass from him and, holding it up so that the flying bubbles showed silver against the face of the moon, said, 'We should drink a toast, shouldn't we? Because yes, I *will* marry you. I think we shall suit very well.'

Frank had looked quite dewy-eyed, and she knew that she had done the right thing.

3

She had gone on thinking so for several months, because even being an engaged lady had undoubted benefits. It liberated her from a good many restrictions. Since her husband-to-be seemed to have no objections – indeed, took her popularity as a compliment – Sophie was able to continue going to parties and flirting to her heart's content without any fear that her admirers might try to take advantage of her. Nor did Frank mind when she became involved in the Amateur

Dramatic Corps, something she had always yearned to do and for which she proved to have a natural talent. Indeed, he applauded more enthusiastically than anybody when she appeared, classically and seductively draped in dyed bed sheets, as the blind girl Nydia in *The Last Days of Pompeii* at the Royal Theatre – a grandiose name for one of the mat sheds that were Hong Kong's temporary answer to every accommodation problem. And, week after week during the cool season, he squired her to picnics and regattas given by visiting naval officers and escorted her to balls where, himself an indifferent dancer, he stood and gossiped with the other merchants about the prices of tea and silk, the difficulty of insuring junkborne cargoes, and China's invidious likin or inland Customs dues, while Sophie waltzed and polkaed with every handsome young blade in the room.

Unfortunately, as the weeks and the months passed, Sophie discovered that Frank had a remarkable talent for pessimism, and that he would always, and repetitively, predict the worst. He even became quite irritable when she refused to pander to him because he didn't like being miserable alone. They were soon squabbling like a pair of children.

'But you're not taking it seriously!' he would exclaim. 'Can't you see that if . . .'

'Yes, I am! Is there anything in the whole wide world you can do about it?'

'No.'

'Well, there you are, then. It doesn't seem very sensible to worry yourself sick about something you can't do anything about.'

'You can't expect me not to worry if it's going to affect the company's profits and our whole future!'

'Yes, I can. Worrying only makes things worse. Oh, I *wish* you would stop prosing on and on about it!'

'That's all very well for you to say. I never deny you anything – now, do I? – and it means I've been overspending my allowance. My father gave me a shocking dressing down about it just today. He says it's high time I learned the meaning of economy. He says I was never a spendthrift before we became engaged. He says it's because I'm always giving you presents, and you'll have to stop being so extravagant when we're married, because he holds the purse strings and he's not going to fork out for all your grand new gowns and bonnets. He'd have a fit if he saw all the ribbons and flounces and lace on that thing you're wearing, and it's not even *local* silk, is it? It's

Indian. He says I've to stop letting you walk all over me. When we're married, he says I've to make you an allowance for your clothes and for the housekeeping and not just pay every bill you choose to incur. He says . . .'

'He says you're the sweetest person in the world!' She put her arms around his neck and hugged him. 'I'm a dreadful trial to you, I know. But I'll try to be good. I promise.'

In general, a few minutes and a little wheedling were all it took to restore harmony between them. Frank needed to be made to feel important, and Sophie knew it even if, all too frequently, she ignored it.

She also knew, unfortunately, that not only did she have no positive desire to marry him; she had a positive desire not to. However frequently she reminded herself that he was an excellent match, she was still ashamed, deep down, of the reasons that led her to accept him. But she was committed. She couldn't possibly jilt him. All she could do was go on finding excuses for postponing the wedding day.

4

There was one excuse that she would have given anything not to have. Her father's health.

Although he seldom complained, he had not been well for months, tiring easily and increasingly prone to dyspepsia. After a while he had begun losing weight, and she had thought at first that it was because he wasn't eating enough. She was out a great deal and he had never enjoyed dining alone, so he had fallen into the habit of going to the Club and having a few drinks instead.

But when she interrogated the cook, Fan Shu, he said, 'Missee no likee chow-chow no moa.'

'No likee? How fashion?'

'My no savvy.'

Archie, confronted, admitted that, yes, he was a bit off his food. 'But don't fuss. It's only a stomach upset. It'll sort itself out.'

'You mean it'll go away if you ignore it? Oh, papa! And you're a bad colour, too. You're worrying me.'

Her father licked his lips for the third time in as many minutes. 'Silly puss! All right, I'll have a few days in bed. That'll do the trick.'

In the end, Sophie summoned Dr Dods, blaming herself bitterly for not having done so sooner. But, 'It wouldn't have helped,' he told her with the brutality of long acquaintance. 'He's a stubborn old fool. He's known for months what's wrong with him, but he hasn't wanted to admit it.'

Sophie felt the blood drain from her face. She had been as bad as her father, pretending everything was fine, going off gaily to parties and balls and picnics as if she hadn't a care in the world. If he was really ill, it was her fault.

'He hasn't wanted to admit what?'

Dr Dods studied her for a moment, frowning. She had always been one of his favourite patients, not only because she was so pretty that it was a pleasure to look at her, but because she was indecently healthy and had a vitality that was refreshing in an era when most young ladies cultivated a lassitude of mind and body that made him wonder, sometimes, what the good Lord's purpose had been in creating them.

'I'm not sure that I ought to tell you. It's going to hurt.'

She looked at him doubtfully. 'If it's going to hurt me, then it must be going to hurt him, too. I must know or I can't help.'

There were many people in the colony who would have been surprised to hear the notoriously crusty physician, who didn't suffer fools or wilting lilies gladly and held to a morality of Old Testament rigidity, exclaim, 'You're a *good* girl, whatever people say! Most of your friends would be having the vapours by now. But you'd better sit down, just in case. I hope you mean it about helping, because your father is going to need you in these coming weeks, and he and I would both be obliged if you did not spend them emulating a watering pot.'

She sat on the very edge of the chair, hands so tightly clasped that the bones shone white, every word he said plunging her deeper into despair. She told herself that he was just trying to frighten her. Her father was indestructible. The doctor couldn't possibly mean what the gravity of his expression was already telling her.

'Please, what's wrong?'

'He is suffering from acute cirrhosis and ascitic accumulation. In plain English, that means drunkard's liver and associated dropsy.'

'*No!*'

'Yes. We all drink too much out here, and we're so used to it that it barely shows. Except in the mortality figures. I'll do my best for him. I'll give him iodide of potassium and copaiba and all the usual things, and I'll probably try tapping off the fluid to ease his discomfort. But don't raise your hopes.'

They had left Archie Macmillan upstairs under his single sheet and mosquito net, Sophie's big, handsome, adored father whose flesh had dropped away until he was as thin as an underfed coolie, except for the grotesquely distended abdomen. The room was hot, clammy and airless, and already it smelled of disease and . . .

Flatly, Sophie said, 'He's going to die.'

'Yes.'

'Will he be in pain?'

'Yes.'

Her eyes rose pleadingly to his as the tears began to spill over. 'You'll be able to give him something though, won't you? He's never been very good at – at – at being in pain.'

'Yes. I'll give him something when it gets past bearing.'

By 'something', he knew, Sophie meant just something – anything. But the only something Dr Dods could prescribe to help Archie Macmillan through his last days was opium. The tainted flower. He suspected the man had been resorting to it for weeks past, which meant that the dosage now needed to kill the pain might also be enough to kill the patient. Dr Dods was a Christian, and he wasn't going to have a murder on his conscience. He sighed. Archie Macmillan had never been a devout man but it seemed that he was fated to come, in the end, through suffering to the Lord.

5

'I'll be away for about ten days, perhaps more,' Frank said. 'Macao first, and then Canton.' It was the first time he had been entrusted with any serious trading negotiations and he was very full of himself. 'My father wants me to have discussions with Mr Robertson – our Consul at Canton, you know?'

'Oh. Yes. All right. Do you have everything you need? Don't forget your pith helmet. Look after yourself.'

He made to kiss her on the mouth, but she gave him only her cheek, and he said, 'Yes, goodbye,' and turned away.

Sophie, all too familiar with the slight, injured quiver of his lips, felt like an exasperated mother seeing a sulky child off to school. 'Frank,' she called resignedly, and he turned back to her, his boyish face lightening, to receive a hug of reassurance. It was all he needed.

Then, with weary footsteps, she went back to her father's room. There was a nurse, an Irishwoman who had been with Miss Nightingale in the Crimea, to do all the physical things for him that needed to be done, but it was Sophie who spent the days sitting by his bedside, fanning him, applying damp cloths to his forehead, holding his hand while he tossed and turned and moaned in pain, discomfort and delirium.

The best times for him were the worst for her, the times when he talked on and on, the warm, full-chested, genial Scots voice now no more than a thread, rambling through the confused and misty landscape of the past, forgetting the harsh present and nonexistent future.

Sophie had always known, because he had confided in her since she was very small, the story of how his own father had banished him, a mere stripling, to exile on the other side of the world for sinning a sin that was repellent to the old man's Calvinist conscience. When Euphemia Moore had once told him to his face that he should be ashamed of himself for allowing his daughter to flirt the way she did, Archie had grinned, and winked at Sophie, and said, 'It runs in the family.'

Because she was so close to him, she shared instinctively in the way he felt about his banishment, no more able to look at it in terms of sense or logic than he was. His resentment, his determination to justify himself, were the only things on which she had ever known him obdurate. How often she had heard him say, 'You know I never bear a grudge, but . . .' And it was true. On everything but Juran he was flexible, persuadable, anxious only for harmony.

Sophie did not find it curious, as other people might have done, that it was always Juran he talked about – not about his father, or his brother, or any of the other relatives that Sophie supposed must exist somewhere. It was as if all that remained in his mind was Juran itself, a microcosm of everything he had loved, and also of everything that had driven him away from the life into which he had been born. She had never had any satisfactory image of it, suspicious of the painting on the Chinese porcelain bowl even before Jay Vanderbilt had assured her that no Scots castle had ever looked like that. Even her father, when pushed, had admitted that, well, perhaps, yes, it ought to be a bit squarer, and they didn't have pagoda roofs in Scotland, and the blue was artistic licence. Juran was white when the sun shone and grey when it rained, which was most of the time.

But however Juran looked in reality, Sophie was perfectly able to comprehend, even to share her father's dream of going back there, rich and successful, the prodigal son returning with his own fatted calf on a leash behind him. As she rose and went to stand by the window, looking out over the serried ranks of roofs that tumbled down the hillside from mid-levels to harbour, she knew a terrible sadness that, the day of his death having come, his ambitions should remain unfulfilled. It was something she would have to see to on his behalf, a kind of sacred trust.

But for the moment it could wait. She didn't want to – couldn't bear to – look forward to life without him.

6

Archie Macmillan was still holding on to life when Frank returned from Canton two weeks later, full of his commercial successes but even fuller of the adventure that had befallen him on the way.

'Pirates!' he exclaimed, as if, Sophie thought exhaustedly, pirates were some phenomenon new and strange to the China seas.

'Are you all right? You're not hurt?' It was all she needed to know, but Frank was too elated even to hear the questions.

'Well, we weren't expecting them, you see. They just shot out from behind a spit of land and were on us before we knew. They were on sweeps, so they were faster than us. I can tell you, I thought we were done for when they started throwing fireballs on board. It's not just the fire danger, you know, it's the smell. It's like a mixture of rotten eggs and . . .'

'I know. I said, are you all right? Your colour's awfully high.'

'Yes. Anyway, the idea is to create confusion, so that they can grapple, but we were too clever for them, because we decided to shoot first and take care of the fires later. So we let them have a broadside, and . . .'

'Frank, I must go back to papa.'

'Oh, I forgot. How is he?'

'He doesn't have long now.'

'I'm sorry. Anyway, just to finish, we must have hit their magazine because there was a great red flash and a tremendous report and a huge cloud of smoke, and . . .'

'It must have been very satisfactory for you.'

She said it in a tone of such finality that even Frank noticed. 'Well, it was quite exciting,' he said sullenly. 'I thought you'd be interested. As a matter of fact, I'm not all right. I'm feeling tired and a bit dizzy.'

She put her hand on his forehead, which was dry and hot. 'It's

244

probably the sun. You know it's always worse at sea. Did you keep your pith helmet on all the time?'

'No. I lost it in the pirate attack.'

'And I don't suppose you thought to try and find another. Oh, Frank, you're so silly. You'd better go home and lie down. I would come with you but I daren't leave papa, not now. The end is so near.' The words were no more than a placebo. Soothing Frank's fevered brow came well below her father's deathbed in her list of priorities.

'Thank you,' Frank said. 'I can see I'm being a nuisance to you. I'd better take myself off. Goodbye.'

This time she didn't call him back.

7

The chit from Euphemia Moore was delivered late next morning, and Sophie stood, numbly staring at the small, spiky handwriting, understanding the words but unresponsive to their meaning. Where feeling should have been, there was only a blank.

Her father's voice, weak but more lucid than it had been for many days, spoke from the bed. 'What is it?'

She couldn't lie. He would know it. He had always had an instinct for when she wasn't being honest with him. 'It's Frank,' she said. 'Last night he nearly died. His mother says it was my fault.'

'What happened?'

Reaching home and finding his mother out, Frank had gone straight to bed, and not until a servant went to summon him to supper did it emerge that he was not asleep but in a coma. Sunstroke. Luckily, the Moores' doctor had arrived in time and administered the new Indian treatment of cold douches and cold compresses, otherwise he would certainly have died. As it was, he was recovering, though he was still very weak, his heart still feeble and his breathing oppressed.

If he had died, Mrs Moore went on, Sophie would have been as responsible as if she had plunged a knife in his heart. It had been her duty, knowing he was ill, to go home with him and watch over him while he slept. Her failure in this was, of course, precisely what Mrs Moore would have expected. She should add that Frank would not be in a fit state to receive visitors for some days.

'What happened?' her father asked again.

'Sunstroke.'

The feeble voice mumbled, 'Forty per cent.'

'What?'

'Fatality rate. Not as high as cirrhosis.'

He took a shallow breath, which was all he could manage. Dods had told him that all his internal organs were compressed, flattened by the dropsical fluid that couldn't be drained off. Today, for the first time since he could remember, he didn't feel anything at all. No pain, no sensation. He didn't know whether it was because Dods had got the last dose exactly right, or whether it was the beginning of the end of everything. He hoped so.

'Good way to go,' he whispered. 'Quick. You can be too long dying.'

Sophie dropped to her knees beside his bed, and raised his hand to her lips. Never once, during these long, dragging weeks, had she allowed herself to flinch from the smell of decay that hung around him. Never once, except when he was drowsing or unconscious, had she stood back from him. But every evening, when she left him to the nurse, she had gone to the privy and been sick.

She said, 'Are you weary of it?'

'Damn fool question.' He managed another breath. 'Poor pet. Stupid father. Stupid Frank. Both of us – doing our best – kill ourselves. Frank would have been – no loss.'

'What . . .'

'Weakling. Listen. Everything's left to you. Don't let the Moores have it. Marry someone else.'

Suffocated by the shadows that had so suddenly descended on a life that had always been so happy, so carefree, she couldn't bear to think of the future, wasn't capable of imagining that the day might come again when she would know other feelings than love and loss. 'Don't try to talk,' she said.

'Must. Now or never. You're too young to be alone. Need a husband – to look after you – run, share in firm.'

He had to stop, then, and she said again, 'Don't talk. Don't worry.'

'*Must* worry,' he fretted. 'You need someone. Not Frank. Older. More experienced.'

'Yes, all right. Shhhh.'

'Blake.'

'What?'

His mind was wandering again, which always upset her dreadfully. 'What about Mr Blake? Is something worrying you about the bank?' She knew nothing about money and had difficulty even with simple arithmetic.

'No. Marry him.'

Marry *Rainer Blake*? Who never did anything but deride her and make her feel about two inches tall. He was the most irritating man.

'Oh, papa. He doesn't even like me.'

'Does. Got a soft spot for you. I've seen. And he's clever. He'll know how to set things right. Promise me.' His voice strengthened suddenly. *'Promise me!'*

She couldn't say anything but, 'Yes. Yes, I promise.'

'Better than Frank.'

'I didn't know you disapproved of Frank. Why did you let me agree to marry him?'

Archie Macmillan was very near the end of his resources, but there was a frail echo of the old whimsicality in his voice. 'You wanted to. Always let you do what you wanted.'

And then the tears were pouring down her cheeks and she was sobbing, 'What am I going to do without you? I love you so much. We've always been together, just the two of us. Don't go. *Don't go!* I can't bear it if you go.' Then, sinking her head on the coverlet she gave way, for the first time, to the full flood of her grief.

She had tried so hard to keep it in check. Dr Dods had told her not to be a watering pot because it would upset her father. So she had been stronger than she would ever have thought possible, never letting her father see her other than pretty and smiling and controlled.

It hadn't occurred to her that Archie, fuddled with pain and drugs and fatigue, desperately needed reassurance of how much he would be missed. He had always known that she loved him, as he did her, but knowing wasn't enough.

Her tears were what he craved, and the distress began to fade from his thin face and be replaced by an exhausted peace. The journey he still had to make ceased to seem harrowing, and the last, cold threshold held no more terrors because when he crossed it there would be warmth in his heart.

Summoning what strength remained to him, he raised his hand and rested it on the long, dark silken hair that was so like her mother's – the mother he had almost forgotten. Tina Malory. A lovely girl, but without spice.

Responding instantly to his touch, Sophie looked up and saw, drowningly, something she didn't understand, a look in her father's eyes that sent pictures running fast, like a flick book, through her mind, pictures from Sunday School texts showing little children, their faces transfigured, holding out their hands to the radiance that was Jesus.

Even as she stared in doubt and disbelief, he whispered, 'Thank you', and she understood, and fresh tears sprang to her eyes and she thought her heart would break.

Chokingly, she said, 'Weep for *me*, a little, before you leave me.'

But it was too late. Trying to whisper her name one last time, he gave a sudden harsh gasp, and was gone.

8

Gino Venturi did everything that needed to be done.

In Hong Kong in summer, funerals were not delayed. Twenty-four hours after her father's death, Sophie stood under the hot, low, black sky and saw him laid to rest in the Colonial Cemetery. Even as the mourners – and there were many of them, because Archie had been a sociable fellow – turned away from the graveside, the wind came in with a dragon's roar and the rain began falling as if all the lock gates of heaven had been opened.

Sophie went home in a daze and for almost two weeks knew nothing of the world at all.

9

After that came the time of ultimate loneliness, of trying to face the fact that her father was really gone, not just for a day or a week but for ever. He had been the only anchor she had ever had, or needed, and without him she was adrift. She didn't know where she was going, or even where she wanted to go.

There was nothing for her to do except sit and mope. Not until three months of her mourning had passed would it be permissible to venture into a public place, and it would be a year before she could stop wearing black – which she knew, forlornly, didn't suit her at all. She shouldn't have been thinking about things like that, but her father wouldn't have minded. He had always liked her to look her best.

After a while, in desperation, she set herself to sorting through his personal belongings, the scanty remnants of fifty-three years of life. He had always said he didn't believe in cluttering the place up with useless bits of paper and mementoes, but Sophie was moved to find that he had kept a small watercolour sketch of her mother done by Mr

Chinnery. It was signed and dated Macao 1846, when Tina Malory had been about Sophie's age, and had a liveliness that Sophie didn't remember. Something else she hadn't remembered was how beautiful her mother had been. Indeed, she had so few memories of her that the tears began to flow all over again, for her father and mother, and for the four little brothers and sisters who had died without Sophie ever knowing them.

She was reaching the end of her task and feeling vaguely surprised, and yet not surprised, that she had found nothing whatsoever relating to Juran when a photograph slipped out from among the papers still in her hand. Bending to pick it up from the floor, she saw with mystification that it was a studio portrait of a Chinese woman. There was a chopmark showing that it had been taken by a photographer in Canton, while on the back, in her father's sprawling handwriting, were the words, 'My dearest Mei, October 1856.'

Riffling through the remaining oddments, Sophie found nothing but a few old betting tickets and some receipted IOUs from the Club, so she forced herself to walk to the window and, with shaking hands, to throw back the shutters and flood the room with light.

It didn't change anything.

The woman was not quite young but, by European standards, pretty for a Chinese, with a rosebud mouth and a sweet, shy look that had survived even an exposure that couldn't have been less than thirty seconds; her hair was completely confined within a band embroidered with pearls, and the cloth of her tunic was one of the more expensive patterns.

It wouldn't have been possible for a young lady growing up in Hong Kong in the 1860s to struggle past the age of puberty – the age of dreams and yearnings – without wondering at some stage what English gentlemen had done in the colony before there were any English ladies for them to be spoony with. And it had taken no great powers of deduction – and only a little eavesdropping – to discover that until well into the 1840s most young men had kept native mistresses. It had only been with the arrival of Englishwomen like Mrs Moore that society's attitude to Chinese concubines and halfcaste children had undergone a radical change.

Sophie had always known that her father had lady friends, but had never envisaged them doing more than hold hands. It wasn't something she had really thought about. One didn't, with fathers.

Putting it all together – and hard though she tried to persuade herself that there must be some other explanation – she knew what the photograph meant. This woman, this Chinese woman, had been her father's mistress. It was so shocking that it took Sophie quite a while to begin making allowances because, of course, her father could do no wrong . . .

She worried for days about what Euphemia Moore would say if she ever found out.

10

And then, a month after her father's funeral, the time came when she could no longer postpone going to see the Moores, to sit with the convalescent Frank, and ask his forgiveness, and promise to set the wedding date for as soon as she was out of mourning.

There didn't seem to be anything else she could do. Her father's dying wish that she should marry Rainer Blake had been no more than a sick man's fancy, impossible of achievement, and although her doubts about Frank still lingered, she was able to persuade herself that her decision was sensible and mature. She was really quite fond of him, and in the misery of her father's death, in her loss and loneliness, had grown up enough – or so she thought – to learn a kind of resignation. She couldn't imagine ever being frivolous again.

Even if Frank were still cross with her, she didn't think it would take long to bring him round. And now she had a substantial dowry that would please his father. Mr Moore, a merchant himself, wouldn't be able to resist acquiring the major share in Macmillan and Venturi. He might even put some capital into the firm; her father had often bemoaned the fact that they didn't have enough capital.

But it didn't work out like that.

'It 'ull be a bloody pest,' said Isaac Moore with a sniff. Within the frame of heavy whiskers, he had a deeply lined but curiously immobile face that always made Sophie feel uncomfortable. His expression never changed, whether he was looking at her, his wife, his son, a wallet full of banknotes or – she would have guessed – a python curled up in his bed.

She couldn't believe he was saying what he was saying.

They were sitting in the overfurnished drawing room of the Moores' house in Hollywood Road, which felt less like a drawing room than a place where someone had just taken a long, hot, steamy bath.

It was August and the air indoors was humid to saturation point. Outdoors it was pouring, the lawn a network of straggling pools and foot-shaped puddles where Sophie's coolies had trodden. The coolies, she knew, would be drier than she who had travelled in a covered chair, thanks to their huge, conical, wet-weather hats and the cloaks of overlapping leaves that made them look like pantomime actors dressed up as jackdaws. If she had been at home, she would have been changing her undershift and petticoat for the fourth or fifth time that day. As it was, she could only sit in her mourning blacks and pretend, as everyone else was pretending, to be impervious to bodily discomfort.

But the heat and the humidity, as they always did, made what was happening even worse than it would otherwise have been. Frank's father didn't utter a word of sympathy over Archie Macmillan's death, didn't appear to recognise that sympathy was even required. All that concerned him was that the dead man might have left some loose ends that might incommode him, Isaac Moore, when he came to settle the future of the firm of Macmillan and Venturi. Assuming, of course, that the situation arose.

'I want to have it clear,' Mr Moore said. 'You will inherit your da's two-thirds share in the business, Sophia, is that reet?'

'Yes. I mean, I suppose so.'

'Is two thirds of the business his?'

'Yes.'

'And you are his sole heir?'

'Yes.'

'Reet, then. You will inherit two thirds of the business. That means it becomes Frank's when he weds you. Which means it's up to me what we do about it. By gum, as if I didn't have enough problems on my plate a'ready. I tell you flat, Macmillan and Venturi is not a desirable acquisition. If I can find a buyer, I'll sell. If not, I'll close it down. I just hope your da made sure the paper work was a' reet and proper before he went to his Maker.'

Automatically, Sophie said, 'It's Mr Venturi who looks after the paper work,' but she knew that the shock must be showing on her face and that Mrs Moore must be revelling in it. The only thing she could think of was how much the business had meant to her father. All the Chinese beliefs she had absorbed from Ah Foon during the years of her upbringing, the astrological wisdom, the exaggerated respect for ancestral spirits, came suddenly together so that for a moment she forgot her misery in a deep and superstitious horror. If Macmillan and Venturi were to be casually destroyed, her father's ghost would never rest.

Perspiration sheening every inch of her skin, she said distractedly, 'But you can't do that. You can't close it down. I won't let you. You shan't *have* it if all you mean to do is ruin it.'

Mrs Moore, as genteel as her husband was coarse, smiled with prim satisfaction and said, 'There is nothing you can do to prevent Mr Moore from disposing of it as he wishes.'

But Sophie didn't hear her. All she heard was Frank apologising for her to his father, telling him Sophie was upset and that he wasn't to pay any attention to what she said.

All trace of resignation vanished. With a sudden, violent anger, she exclaimed, 'Frank, how *dare* you apologise for me? You must know how I feel about this. You should be giving me your support, not kowtowing to your father like some mandarin before the Celestial Emperor. It's *unforgivable* of you!'

He didn't reply immediately. But Sophie caught the glance he exchanged with his mother and it gave her a moment's warning of what was to come.

Frank had lost a good deal of weight during his illness and his boyish face was austere when he spoke, even though his words were pettish. 'It's fine for you, but not for me, is that it? I mean, I can remember you paying more attention to *your* father than you did to *me*, the day I had sunstroke . . .'

'That was different!'

'No, it wasn't, and I could have *died*.'

This time, Sophie held her tongue.

With unnatural formality, he went on, 'I have had plenty of time to think while I've been ill, and I have come to the conclusion that we are not suited. My mama has always said so, and I see now that she is right. When I marry, it will be a young lady of whom she approves. Please consider our engagement at an end.' He stopped and then remembered something. 'You may, however, keep the ring I gave you.'

With a titanic effort, Sophie resisted the temptation to scratch his eyes out, although if she had been wearing the ring, she would certainly have thrown it in his face. But diamond rings, even small and economical ones, were not normally worn with deep mourning. When she got home, she would grind it under her heel instead.

There were a great many things she could have said, but she had enough sense to know that recriminations would be pointless and degrading. So, although being dignified didn't come naturally to her, she rose to her feet with quite a good imitation of it, saying in the most patronising tone she could muster, 'Well, I confess to being relieved. Goodbye, Frank. Goodbye, Mrs Moore. Goodbye, Mr Moore.' And stalked out.

She was proud of herself. But although she spent the next twenty-four hours recapitulating in her mind, over and over again, what she could have said, would have said and should have said, it didn't give her nearly as much consolation as actually saying it would have done.

11

Joanna Bagford fanned herself languidly. 'Euphemia Moore is spreading the most terrible gossip about you, of course.'

'Of course,' Sophie agreed. 'Would you like some more tea?'

'Yes, please. Really quite slanderous. About how you didn't care if Frank died. And what an unprincipled flirt you are. How you kept Frank dangling for all those months for reasons she would not care to hint at – though I can't imagine what they might be. Well, I keep reminding people what an old tabby she is, and so does Dolly, but there's no denying that you did let poor Frank down.'

Sophie didn't contest it. She had already told Joanna what had happened. Even if she had gone with Frank, instead of staying with her father, all she would have done was ensure that he went to lie down and rest, and the result would have been the same. As an unmarried girl, she most certainly couldn't have sat and watched over his bedside and Euphemia Moore knew that perfectly well. Sophie's own feelings of guilt were entirely irrational.

Joanna said, 'I do wish you'd defend yourself, because being jilted – especially for what *sounds* like a good reason – does nothing for a girl's reputation.'

'How can I defend myself, when mourning doesn't allow me to step outdoors or see anyone except my closest friends? Besides, what's the point of a vendetta? It will all fade away if I ignore it.'

'Perhaps, but slanders have a horrid habit of persisting. People always remember there was *something* unpleasant, even if they don't remember what.'

Sophie said, 'I'm sorry, Joanna, but I just don't care.'

Sorrow, scandal and seclusion. As the weeks went by and Sophie's natural vitality began to reassert itself, it was the seclusion that became hardest to bear. Surprisingly, she didn't much mind being deprived of parties, or not at first. Looking back over almost four years of them she was able to see how much alike they had all been – the same people, the same places, the same dances, the same music, the same conversation.

But there was one occasion on which she felt horribly left out, and that was when, on the last day of October, the frigate HMS *Galatea* anchored in the harbour and Queen Victoria's son, HRH Prince Alfred, Duke of Edinburgh, landed on the first royal visit ever paid to the colony. It was the most exciting thing that had ever happened, and the ships were covered in bunting and Hong Kong a blaze of illuminations and fireworks and dragon processions.

Sophie stood on the Praya watching, with tears pouring down her cheeks under the heavy veil, and thought of all the gorgeous banquets and receptions and balls she was missing. For a moment, it seemed to her that being in mourning was almost as bad as being dead oneself.

In December she was twenty-one, and she wept then, too, after the quiet tea party for Joanna Bagford and Dolly Evans and one or two others that was all that was permissible by way of celebration.

Afterwards she had to pull herself together all over again.

There were months still to go before she could resume anything like a normal life and she had no idea how she was going to fill them until Gino Venturi unintentionally exasperated her into an idea that she hoped would exasperate him right back.

Not until five months after the funeral did he intrude on her mourning, saying he needed to discuss the firm's future with her. She didn't know whether to be flattered, or annoyed that he had taken so long about it, and replied rather snappishly, 'Well, at least we're not going to be taken over by Moore and Company!'

'I had heard.'

She surveyed him suspiciously, but couldn't fault his politely noncommittal expression. It made her even more suspicious. 'Do you know what Isaac Moore dared to say he was going to do?'

She poured out the whole story to him, but all he did was survey her blandly, saying nothing, like the large, benevolent pussycat he so much resembled.

'Aren't you disgusted?' she concluded.

'Not particularly.'

'But it's outrageous. It's immoral.'

The dimple at one corner of his lips deepened. 'It's business. How little you know, my child.'

That was what did it, because she hated being talked down to. It was hardly her fault, she thought seethingly, that she didn't know anything about business; young ladies weren't supposed to. She said, 'Oh, all right, then. How do you think we should proceed?'

'You mean, assuming that your,' he paused delicately, 'matrimonial plans remain in abeyance?'

'*Yes!*'

'Well, I would suggest we go on as before, although we will, of course, sadly miss your father's talent for maintaining good relations with our customers.'

'*Can* we go on as before?'

'I see no reason why not.'

'Well, I do! Macmillan and Venturi without a Macmillan is . . .' In vain she sought for the word she wanted, and finished rather weakly, 'unthinkable.'

Gino Venturi's fair, mobile brows rose. 'Ye-e-es?'

'So, since I now own two thirds of the firm, I think I should take an interest, don't you? You can teach me what I need to know.'

There was silence except for the whirr of insects, the tweetering of birds, the rustle of lizards on the paving.

'Well, why not?' Sophie demanded, a touch defensively.

Gino Venturi grinned. 'If *you* don't know . . .'

13

It would have been untrue to say that Gino did not regret his partner's death. Archie Macmillan had been a likeable old boy, and good to Gino, even if that goodness had been repaid many times over. There was, however, no denying that Macmillan and Venturi was running very much more smoothly now that it had been freed from the interference of a senior partner whose grasp of the principles of buying and selling had always been rudimentary. Whatever young Sophie had inherited from her father, Gino knew that it couldn't include business acumen.

The notion of Archie Macmillan's featherbrained, if ravishingly lovely, daughter 'taking an interest' in the firm filled him with no pleasure at all, which meant that he would have to devote time to quashing her pretensions. Fortunately, he estimated that this could be achieved fairly rapidly by the time-honoured means of first blinding her with science and then wearing her out with recondite detail.

They settled a few days later in long chairs in the garden beside the goldfish pond, where the striped, spotted, many-tailed gold and silver fish very soon lost interest and retired under the duckweed, taking with them Sophie's excuse for diversionary chatter and forcing her to open her notebook and assume a small frown of concentration.

Smothering a grin, Gino said, 'We'll begin with the general picture. The materials of trade. What we buy and sell. By "we" I mean Hong Kong merchants in general rather than Macmillan and Venturi in particular, because you can't understand our dealings unless you know the context.'

Sophie wrote down 'context', not as a heading but because she wasn't sure what it meant and was going to have to look it up in the dictionary. It was a depressing start, but she didn't let it show.

'Very well, then,' Gino Venturi resumed. 'In China we buy large quantities of things like tea, silk, hemp, indigo, ginger, shellac and lacquer dye. Then we either sell on to merchants here in Hong Kong who specialise in transshipping them to Europe or America, or we ship them ourselves to other Asian markets – India, for example – and sell them ourselves. Clear so far?'

'I think so. But please, could you tell me first – where do we make our profit?'

'We buy at a low price and sell at a higher one.'

'Oh.' She was anxious to try and sound intelligent. 'Don't our customers know that? I mean, they could save money if they just bought from the same people as we do.'

Gino, who had forgotten that such naïvety could exist, found himself briefly at a loss. 'Quite. But experience has shown the present system to be the more satisfactory.'

'Oh. Well, why don't *we* ship things to Europe or America, instead of just India? I mean, wouldn't we make a bigger profit? The prices we'd get would be even higher, so far away.' She knew about that. When she bought English instead of Indian cotton for a new dress, it cost a lot more, and her father had always said it was because of the distance involved.

'Those of us who can afford to ship to Europe – like Jardine Matheson

– do. Those of us who can't – like Macmillan and Venturi – don't. Merchant shipping is a high risk venture. If a ship goes down, the loss is huge.'

'Isn't that what insurance is for?'

'Only in the short term. If you make a habit of losing ships, the premiums soar.'

She was silent. She had only the vaguest idea what insurance was, and no idea at all of what he meant by premiums.

'Satisfied? Very well. So much for exports. With imports the system is the reverse. Some of us buy in goods direct from India, and sell them in China. Others . . .'

'What kind of goods?'

There were only two Indian imports that mattered, and one of them was opium, which wasn't something ladies needed to know about. 'From India, mainly cotton yarns. From Europe and America, factory goods like hardware, nails, handspikes, tin, zinc, painted oilcloth . . .'

Sophie laughed suddenly. 'Knives and forks!'

It was a standing joke in the colony. In the early days of trade, a Sheffield firm, carried away by the thought of three hundred million customers all panting to buy European goods, had declared themselves ready to supply the whole of China – and had forthwith sent out a huge shipment of knives and forks. For years afterwards, Hong Kong's shops had used them as decorations, like spears or guns over a mantelpiece.

Gino smiled cooperatively. 'Not any more. To proceed . . .'

14

And so it went on.

The following week Sophie found herself being lectured about shipping and why Macmillan and Venturi's small fleet of ships wasn't always full of Macmillan and Venturi's goods.

'We don't always have full shiploads ready, so sometimes we hire them out. Native Chinese merchants like to send their goods in British ships, because insurance companies won't insure cargoes carried in junks, partly because of the fire risk. The British flag gets them through the harbour blockade, too. Or they'll organise a convoy of junks and hire British ships to protect them against pirates. That's the more economical method. And then, of course . . .'

The week after that it was Customs duties.

Gino, becoming impatient, now began to put the pressure on and soon things were slipping from Sophie's grasp. She knew it was her fault, because Mr Venturi was very patient with her and never even hinted that she wasn't clever enough to understand. The trouble was that, although she was now finding the principles reasonably comprehensible – she thought – as soon as he started talking facts and figures she was lost. There were such a lot of them, and she had never had a head for such things.

'. . . raised Imperial duties of 7½ million HK taels last year on a total of imports and exports in the region of 125 million . . . bolt of grey shirtings retailing at 2.20 taels in Tientsin rises to 2.50 taels by the time it gets to Shansi . . . we merchants have to pay the likin, that's 2½% tax on goods in transit within China, on top of the port Customs dues . . . unlike Jardine's most of us can't make profits by offering huge loans to the Imperial government guaranteed against the Customs revenue, and at 15% interest, no less . . . last year the Chinese even had the impertinence to open up Customs offices in Hong Kong itself, though Macdonnell closed them down again pretty smartly . . .'

Sophie said, 'You keep talking about the Chinese, but I thought it was the British who run their Customs service. Mr Hart, isn't it? I've never understood why.'

'China owes a large war indemnity to Britain and France, and a few years ago couldn't raise enough revenue to pay the instalments. Their best source of revenue should have been Customs duties, but the Imperial Maritime Customs Service was riddled with bribery. In the end, the service was handed over to a foreign inspectorate to run, to see if they could make it pay. Hart's the man in charge.'

'Oh, I see!' Sophie exclaimed, genuinely interested for the first and only time. 'Has it worked?'

'Depends how you look at it. They've reduced smuggling and increased Customs collections, and the Imperial revenues have risen handsomely, which pleases the British and the French governments very much. But Mr Hart's representatives are not at all popular with us merchants, because most of the increased revenues have come directly out of our profits.'

She had to think about that for a minute. 'You mean our profits used to come from *evading* Customs dues? Smuggling?'

It was exactly what he did mean, but he could scarcely admit it.

He gave her his creamiest smile and said, 'Not quite. Let me put it a different way . . .'

258

He won, as he was bound to do, being a clever man with a code of ethics – though not of a kind St Thomas Aquinas would have approved – that enabled him to manipulate others mercilessly and with a clear conscience, whenever it was to his own advantage.

It took only four one-hour sessions of his ingenious tuition before Sophie said, 'I don't think I'm ever going to master all this.' It cost her a good deal to admit it, but she knew the moment was rapidly approaching when she would scream if he said another word about tariffs or trade figures.

'No?'

She sighed. 'I'm sorry. And I know I shouldn't be taking up your time.'

He gave her his rumpled smile and she thought, not for the first time during these last weeks, how charming he could be when he wanted to. He hadn't ridiculed her at all, or only a little; indeed, he had been both kind and understanding. If she was being stupid, it certainly wasn't his fault.

'Well, if you're sure . . .' he said.

With deceptive leisureliness, he went through the motions of preparing to rise. In the course of the last hour, as it happened, he had been inspired by an excellent idea for circumventing some new legislation that threatened one of Macmillan and Venturi's most profitable sidelines, and he was anxious to discuss it with the Chang brothers before they sailed for Macao, so that they could put out feelers while they were there.

He said, 'I confess that there are some manifests I should like to check before tomorrow, so . . . I'm sorry I haven't been a very adequate teacher.'

'Nothing of the sort. I've been a shockingly slow pupil.' Then, with a surge of sincere gratitude, she added, 'I don't know what Macmillan and Venturi would do without you.'

Neither did Gino. Or, rather, he knew only too well. And then it occurred to him, as he smiled back into the enchantingly lovely blue eyes, that he was tired of being only one third partner in a firm that, without him, would have been forced into liquidation years before. An alliance between one third and two thirds, however . . .

Sophie, turning away to lead him to the gate, heard his voice say softly, 'Such a waste of a lovely lady's time, facts and figures.'

Then his hand on her arm stopped her and before she knew what was happening, he was murmuring '*Bella, bellezza*' and gathering her into a large, warm embrace, brushing her face with lips that were velvety and caressing, then raising her chin gently so that he could drop his mouth on hers.

It was a soft kiss, not at all demanding, and she didn't recoil from it as she had recoiled from Frank's clumsy caresses. It was most improper, of course, even shocking, but in the nicest possible way. Indeed, she thought how comfortable it was, soothing, protective and – in a very quiet way – exciting.

The illusion of safety lasted for a minute at most, until he dropped his hands and drew the full length of her body against his and she became sharply aware that it wasn't a platonic embrace after all. Eighteen months of being engaged had taught her the danger signs, even if she hadn't learned what they actually meant.

'Mr Venturi!' she exclaimed, and began to struggle.

'Come now!' he murmured. 'There are much more enjoyable ways of passing the time than learning about Macmillan and Venturi, unless in the personal sense.'

'This is most improper!'

Ignoring her resistance, he settled his arms around her, and they didn't feel warm and comforting any more, but heavy and menacing. His lips still hovering over hers, he breathed, 'Improper? When we are a partnership . . .'

Really! Sophie thought in exasperation. She didn't in the least want to scream or make a fuss or slap his face, because it would make future relations between them exceedingly difficult, but she would have to do *something* if he didn't stop. Like pushing him into the goldfish pond.

Unfortunately, she wasn't strong enough. But he had made the mistake of cradling her sideways in his arms and she discovered that, with her left hand, she could just reach the bell that always sat on the table. She swung it three times, with vigour, before he even realised where the sound was coming from.

Beating a strategic retreat behind her chair, she said breathlessly, 'That was the tea bell. Ah Foon will bring out the tray in a minute. Would you like some?'

His eyes, in the sun, were like pale blue ice, but only for a moment. Then he laughed and said, 'How thoughtful of you. That would be very refreshing.'

By February, Sophie had left off her heavy mourning and was almost herself again, though an exceedingly frustrated self, her first tentative steps back into society having shown her just how much damage the Moores had done during her enforced absence.

She was greeted with little warmth by her seniors, though that did not worry her unduly. Elderly gentlemen had always been prone to turn skittish when she sparkled at them, so that their wives had never approved of her. Much more troubling was that the younger gentlemen, who would have flocked around her a few months before, now conspicuously failed to do so. It wasn't, she knew, only because she was still wearing black and unable to accept any invitations to dance; it was because she had been jilted. And worst of all was that several of her girl friends went out of their way to commiserate with her on the news of Frank's engagement to Hetty Elstob, the plainest girl in Hong Kong, as if pleased that Sophie, who had always outshone everyone else, was at last being put in her place.

It was a quite unacceptable place. After two receptions and a genteel soirée throughout which she was forced to sit – outwardly subdued and inwardly fuming – on a horrid gilt chair amidst the dowagers, she was ripe for any michief.

She would show them! Conveniently, she forgot that most of her present troubles stemmed directly from an earlier resolve to show somebody – to wit, Euphemia Moore.

More and more, she found herself remembering her last promise to her father; less and less did she consider what an idiotic promise it had been, even at the time. Indeed, meditating on it with increasing frequency, she could see a good deal to recommend it.

Blake was a good deal older than she was, certainly, but so was Gino Venturi and *he* found her attractive, or she wouldn't have had to fight off his kisses. And although Blake had always behaved rather cynically towards her, at least he didn't ignore her as he did all the other girls. Finally, she thought he must surely, at his age – somewhere in the mid thirties – be on the lookout for a wife, because there was no question of him being averse to female company. And she was still easily the prettiest girl in the colony.

She was sure she wouldn't find him nearly so intimidating if she was married to him.

The result of these reflections was that, when she heard of Blake's return to Hong Kong, she donned her most fetching bonnet and most winning expression and set off to inform him that she was prepared to be his wife.

17

Blake had been pleased by the swiftness of the voyage through the Suez Canal, not only because it had justified him in sparing a few days in Bombay for talks with the native bankers there, but because his fellow passengers were not such as he would have chosen to spend any great length of time with.

On his previous voyage, in 1866, things had been very different. Among the passengers, then, had been Robert Hart, and Blake's meeting with him had changed the direction of his life for a second time.

Before that, everything had always come too easily to him; whatever he had set his hand to had flourished. He had made an early fortune, but found it unfulfilling; had taken up banking, and been stimulated by it for a while. But after ten years, although he still found it interesting and sometimes even absorbing, it wasn't enough for him. In danger of being bored, he had needed another challenge.

Hart had offered it, and Blake had never been bored since, his banking now only a secondary interest, a public cover for the secret work that occupied and fascinated him.

Leaning on the steamer rail one day when they were about a month out, Hart had said, with careful casualness, 'Ye've an interesting reputation, Mr Blake – the fellow who succeeds at everything he sets his hand to. It's a rare talent.'

Blake had been amused. 'Talent? You mean confidence trick. All I do is take damned good care never to set my hand to anything I know I'm unlikely to succeed at.'

'Like knitting or lion taming?'

'Like knitting or lion taming,' Blake agreed, wondering what Hart was getting at.

'Ye've never fancied walking the high wire?'

'You'd have to show me the point of it. If I'm going to break my neck, I prefer to do it for a sound reason.'

'Sure, an' we could manage that.'

'Pardon me? The broken neck or the sound reason?'

It had taken a while for Hart to stop beating around the bush, and

Blake had to listen to a good deal he already knew before the other man got to the point.

The Commissioners of China's Foreign Inspectorate of Customs, Hart said, all functioned on Chinese territory where their jurisdiction was formally recognised. But Hong Kong, the contraband capital of the South China seas, was a British possession and neither its governors nor its merchants were prepared to have some damned Customs johnnie poking his nose in where he wasn't wanted and trying to ruin everyone's perfectly legitimate smuggling activities.

'Well, ye know all that already,' Hart had said. 'But it's like this. The work of the Commissioners in the Treaty Ports would be eased a good deal if they had information about who was doing what, and who was handling what in Hong Kong. Some rather more active cooperation at source wouldn't come amiss, either. Well, ye can see that, can ye not?'

And Blake had grinned and said, 'Yes. What you need is a secret agent.'

'Sure, an' I couldn't have put it better meself.'

The upshot had been that Hart had created for Blake the assiduously unpublicised post of Special Commissioner of China's Foreign Inspectorate of Customs (Hong Kong).

In his first eighteen months, before taking time off for this last, extended trip to Europe, Blake had drawn the fangs of more than one respected merchant, taking the most meticulous care that no one knew of his involvement, even, with reluctance, reconciling himself to dressing and behaving more conventionally than had been his custom in the past.

But someone had been suspicious, or possessed of some inside knowledge, right from the start. Blake had never known who or how. The curious thing was that the knowledge had not found its way into general circulation, which argued a particular kind of person.

Blake had, however, begun to attract danger. Hong Kong was a place where violence abounded, so that he could never be entirely sure, when he was attacked, whether the attack was directed at him personally, whether it was even an attack at all, sometimes. He had been thrown from his horse on the Praya once, in the early hours of the morning after a ball, because someone had planted some thorns under his saddle. At the time, he had held a young clerk, of whom he knew nothing good, responsible, but had wondered afterwards whether it might have been a prank by some drunken midshipman. Even so, there had been three assaults that, spur-of-the-moment though they appeared to be, had been unequivocally lethal in intent.

18

As it happened, a fourth had occurred on the very morning of the day when Sophie elected to visit him.

Cutting downhill from Breezy Path on his way back to Pedder Street, he had been murderously set upon, not by the usual gang of Chinese robbers but by a pair of highly professional European thugs, armed with equally professional knives, who had shown no immediate inclination to flee when he fired a warning shot from his Colt. There had been a few exceedingly hectic moments, but Blake was familiar with a couple of tricks new to his opponents and it was, besides, an undeniable fact that knowing one's life to be at stake stimulated the mind wonderfully.

In the end, one of his assailants had made a forced exit from the fray with the aid of a well-placed kick that sent him staggering and rolling down the precipitous steps of Ladder Street, while the second, resorting to an ill advised game of hide-and-seek in a coffin shop, found himself briskly incarcerated in a sample of the merchandise with the lid slammed down upon him.

The outcome might have been satisfactory, but Blake was still mystified, aching in every limb, and heavily bandaged over a stab wound in one shoulder when his clerk announced that Miss Macmillan was here to see him. 'What the devil. . . ?' he thought.

As a result, when Sophie appeared upon the threshold, her smile entrancing and her nerves jangling like temple bells in a typhoon, she was confronted by Blake at his most forbidding. The mocking smile that at once replaced the arrogant stare did nothing to make her feel better, although, had she known it, it was himself he was mocking, not her. She was such a refreshing sight in the circumstances that for a moment he had felt his heart lifting. Which was ridiculous.

She was still wearing blacks, a silk crêpe dress with full but not exaggerated skirts, sleeves of black gauze, and a plain bodice with a wide square neckline filled in with more black gauze, ruffled at the throat. Blake wondered briefly whether she knew how seductive veiled skin was. If so, it was a lesson she had learned recently; not so very long ago her unblushing displays of bosom had scandalised every ballroom in the colony.

Perched on her silken dark head was a wide-brimmed hat of soft, natural straw garnished with black velvet ribbon round the crown, and the overall effect was one of quiet elegance, which wasn't a word that would previously have occurred to him in connection with Sophie. Not since her come-out had he seen her other than flounced and frilled and furbelowed to within an inch of her life. Interestingly, the faint shadows under her eyes had the effect of enhancing her looks. Clinically assessing her, Blake was forced to the conclusion that she was the most beautiful young woman he had seen in the course of his entire career. It was a pity that she was also one of the most extravagant and ill-disciplined.

He sat by the rolltop desk, swivelling gently in his revolving chair, tapping one forefinger lightly against his lips, while Sophie turned large, blue, helpless eyes on him and launched touchingly into a plea for his advice.

'The thing is, I'm so dreadfully stupid about business, and managing, and all the rest of it, and there's no one I can ask. Or no one whose advice I would trust. I mean, the younger ladies don't know much – do they? – and the older ones tell me to take up Berlin woolwork, or read improving literature, or sit down and be quiet and behave myself. Well, it's not really very helpful, is it?' She permitted herself a small, shyly michievous smile.

To her surprise, he grinned back and she went on, reassured, 'Gentlemen are so much better at practical things, aren't they? Well, everyone knows that!'

'Undoubtedly,' he agreed. 'Although I hope you are not about to ask me to come and do some roof repairs for you?'

'Of course not!'

Her gurgle of laughter was infectious. Blake suddenly thought how pleasant it was to forget life's complications for a while in Sophie's frivolous company. She could be quite engaging. He rang the small silver handbell on his desk and told the servant to bring tea.

'So?' he enquired, entering into the spirit of the thing. 'You are in need of worldly advice of the kind only a gentleman can provide. Are you quite sure you have come to the right gentleman? I would have thought . . .' In the nick of time, he stopped himself from uttering the name of Moore. He had heard about that, of course, but had almost forgotten it again in the press of business that always awaited his return from one of his foreign trips.

'. . . your father's lawyers,' he said. 'Aitken and Dicey. They should be competent to deal with most of your problems.'

'Oh-h-h-h-h, I went to them and they were *frightful*! I know I'm not clever, but I'm not a complete dunderhead. They just said I was to leave everything to them. And that's all very well, but . . . I feel so helpless. I don't have *anyone*.'

She tried to look soulful, hoping she wasn't overdoing it, but Mr Blake seemed to be responding quite satisfactorily. Indeed he rose and moved round the desk to take her hand in his. Only then did she see the bandage under his coat and exclaim, 'Oh, you're hurt! What happened?'

'A small disagreement with some brigands. Nothing important.' With surprise, Blake identified the unfamiliar sensation throbbing within his manly breast. Protectiveness, by God! 'Sophie, my pet,' he went on gently, and then three things happened in rapid succession.

Her hand moved a little in his, he felt an abrupt stirring in his loins, and he caught a look of suspense in her eyes that didn't fit at all.

After a moment, carefully, he returned her hand to her and went back to his chair.

Just then, the tea arrived, and not until the servant had gone did Blake enquire pensively, 'What kind of help did you have in mind?'

19

She told him in the end.

'It was my father's dying wish that you and I should be married.' Oblivious to the cessation of his movements, she lowered her lashes demurely. 'I have come to tell you that I am prepared to be your wife.'

Blake was unable to remember the last time anyone had succeeded in dumbfounding him.

It was a long moment before he said politely, 'And what maggot had got into your father's head that he should have suggested such an idea?'

'He was *perfectly* rational!'

'Was he, indeed? Well, I am not in the market for a wife. And if I were, it wouldn't be for a chit of a girl with nothing but beauty to recommend her.'

'*Oh!*'

It had all been going so well, and for at least thirty seconds she had found herself thinking that she might quite like to be married to Mr Blake after all. He was much more exciting than Frank, and much handsomer. In fact he was much the most attractive man in the colony, except when he was being mocking and cynical. She couldn't think what had gone wrong. Preoccupied with the problem, she fluttered her eyelashes automatically in the way that always reduced her admirers to a jelly, and said, 'You are being *very* ungallant!'

He snapped, 'Don't insult me by trying to flirt with me, Sophie. I'm not a callow boy to be taken in by your tricks.' The fact that he had been very thoroughly taken in by them, to the extent of actually being aroused by the dratted girl, annoyed him intensely. 'In any case, I thought I was paying you a compliment. I was under the impression that most young ladies considered brains to be positively dowdy.'

'That's only because gentlemen consider them dowdy. I shouldn't think it would suit *you* to have a clever wife. She might disagree with you instead of accepting your every word as gospel!'

Blake wasn't accustomed to being answered back. 'A sharp tongue wouldn't suit me too well, either,' he replied crisply. 'What else did your father say?'

'He said you would look after me and you'd make sure everything was all right at Macmillan and Venturi.'

'Did he say why I should wish to?'

Sophie hesitated. Her father's theory that Blake had a soft spot for her had ceased to be tenable. She tossed her head. 'Not really.'

'Let us analyse the matter, then,' he said, and she supposed this must be the way he talked when he was bullying his customers. She was really quite glad he didn't want to marry her and couldn't imagine why, for a moment, she had thought otherwise.

'As things stand, my bank holds a lien – via the various loans extended to your father over the years – on a substantial proportion of the firm's assets, and also on Juran. If the firm found itself in serious difficulties, I would be entitled to liquidate in order to redeem the bank's money. You follow me, do you?'

She didn't. 'Yes, of course I do.'

'If I were to marry you and thus be saddled with your inheritance, the only difference it would make would be that – if the firm found itself in serious difficulties – I would find myself, as the bank's representative, in the invidious position of having to liquidate myself.'

She clutched at the only thing she understood. 'I don't see why you're talking about difficulties. Mr Venturi has explained everything to me and business is thriving. Besides, if you were a partner, I'm sure it would *never* get into difficulties.'

'What an impertinent chit you are!' he said with a sudden renascence of cordiality. 'No, my pet, all that your late papa's scheme does is offer me what I already own, or near as dammit. With your charming self thrown in for good measure, of course.' He paused briefly. 'To which I am compelled to say thanks, but no.'

'As you wish.' She shrugged. 'There are many gentlemen who would feel differently!'

And then he grinned, the dark, satanic grin that sent shocks up and down her spine, now as always. 'After what your almost-mother-in-law has been saying about you? My dear Sophie . . .'

Her face went scarlet. 'How do you know that?' she demanded. 'You've only been back in the colony three days. How do you *always* know what's going on?'

He didn't answer, but rose to his feet and moved round to lean against his desk, facing her. 'My dear girl, face the facts. Your father was a dreamer. If you have a grain of sense, you will solve all your problems by selling your share in Macmillan and Venturi and leaving Hong Kong. You could have a perfectly happy and interesting new life in Scotland. Your father's brother died some years ago, and there's a cousin of yours looking after Juran in your absence.'

It was a pity, he thought, for Rachel Macmillan's sake, that Archie's death should have changed the whole complexion of the Juran affair. But the situation had been bound to arise at some stage, and perhaps sooner was preferable to later.

'Oh, and by the way,' he added, 'I put up an extra £5,000 a few months ago to help with some improvements at Juran. I'll talk to Venturi about it. It's immaterial to me whether it's paid back as a single sum now, or treated as an interest-bearing loan.'

She discovered, with interest, that she must have learned more from Gino Venturi than she had thought. 'A few months ago?' she asked. 'When? After my father died?'

'No. In June.'

'He had been ill for weeks by then. He can't possibly have signed anything. Did he even know about it?'

Blake shook his head.

'Well, then! You'll just have to write it off as a loss, won't you, Mr Blake?'

Blake had no intention of arguing money with a chit of a girl. It was something he would have to sort out with Venturi. It occurred to him also that, for the ungrateful Sophie's sake, he ought to go into the firm's current finances, just to be sure that all was well and that there was no danger, however remote, of the bank having to foreclose. As far as he knew, Macmillan and Venturi had been making reasonable profits over the last few years despite the continuing recession. Once or twice he had found himself wondering how.

'Oh, Sophie,' he said in exasperation and, taking her by the hands, pulled her to her feet. 'Go back to Scotland, you idiot girl.'

Sophie's precarious control snapped, and she tore her hands from his. 'Don't tell *me* what to do!'

They were too close for Blake's comfort and he stepped back. 'I thought that was what you wanted of me!' he said provocatively.

'Well, I don't, not any more. I am twenty-one years old and I have no intention of spending the rest of my life dwindling towards the grave in a wet, godforsaken country pinned to the outer margins of the map. There are a great many things I mean to do, and I can assure you that going tamely back to Juran is not one of them.'

'What a little shrew you are!'

Stung, Sophie exclaimed, 'What do you mean "shrew"? I have never been anything but unnaturally polite to you!'

'Damn it all! You assaulted me the very first time we met. At Canton. In the fire.' He was laughing, which provoked her even more.

'You deserved it.' She gestured towards the bandages under his coat. 'And I imagine you deserved that, too.'

She flounced towards the doorway but, reaching it, suddenly turned back. Her gentian eyes were almost black with temper and sparkling magnificently as, in a trembling voice, she said, 'You are the rudest man I have ever met! You are high-handed, and arrogant, and despicable, and I wouldn't marry you if you went down on bended knees. I only came because it was what my father wanted.'

It gave her some satisfaction to see that she had wiped the autocratic smile right off his face, and it was with even more conviction that she went on, every word sizzling with contempt, 'And I will tell you this, Mr Blake. You may tell me what to do as much as you like, but what I am *going* to do is marry the first personable gentleman who asks me, and he will turn Macmillan and Venturi into the goldmine my father intended it to be. Because when I *do* take your advice and go back to Juran, I propose going in the most extravagant style.

'*Good* afternoon, Mr Blake.'

And then she was gone, to walk off her anger along the Praya.

'And who, my God, is that?' demanded Lieutenant Richard Taverner, jumping lightly ashore from the jolly boat of the HMS *Impudent*. 'What a sight for sore eyes! I say, Duff, if that's a specimen of your Hong Kong beauties, why have I never been here before?'

'That,' said Mr Duff repressively, 'is Miss Macmillan and she is not a specimen. And keep your eyes to yourself. She's in mourning for her father; she was an only child and her mother died years ago, so they were very close.'

'A beautiful orphan,' Richard breathed. 'A beautiful *rich* orphan?'

'Well, she inherited the major share in his trading house, but I don't know if she'd count as rich. Moderately well off, I suppose – by naval standards, anyway. Oh, come along, Taverner. Stop staring, we've got things to do.'

A dazzlingly beautiful, well-off young woman with no inquisitive family and a major stake in a trading house! Richard's eyes gleamed. Just what he had been looking for.

CHAPTER TWELVE

❧❧

I

Colin Campbell did not present himself at Juran until the Easter of 1870, partly because he was busy, partly because he saw no pressing need to struggle through snow, sleet and rain to get there, and partly out of simple kindness. From what Blake had told him, he thought Miss Macmillan would probably be grateful to be given time to put her house in order.

Although he had reconciled himself to making the best of the situation in which Blake had landed him, he was not looking forward to it, especially since Miss Macmillan did not sound like the kind of lady whose acquaintance he would normally have sought. Blake had described her as knowledgeable and competitive inside, small and not especially pretty – though with a nice smile – outside. It conjured up in Colin's mind a picture of something between the grocer's wife and the lady who played the organ in church.

Instead, he was greeted by a dainty young woman whose simple grey gown set off her neat figure to advantage and whose warm, smooth complexion was a perfect foil for very blue eyes. The glossy chestnut coils of her hair framed a face that was exactly the shape of a heart, and illuminated by a smile of welcome that made the question of plainness or prettiness irrelevant. Privately, Colin decided that Blake had a queer idea of 'ordinary'.

When she said, 'Mr Campbell, what a pleasure it is to welcome you to Juran,' it was in a voice that was low-pitched and pleasant.

Hard-headed, unromantic Colin, widowed for four years after ten years of a marriage whose most distinctive feature had been its almost indecent placidity, felt the ground shift under his feet.

2

Since he had arrived late in the afternoon, they did not talk of anything more than trivialities until they sat down to the supper table for a meal that proved to be well-balanced and admirably cooked. Colin couldn't remember having tasted better poached salmon or more delicate mutton, and although he approached the puréed greens with some dubiety, having been informed that they were young nettle tops, his misgivings were soon put at rest. The only thing with which he had fault to find was the claret, which was well past its prime.

'An interesting vintage,' he said. 'Do you have any more like it in the cellar?'

'Oh, yes.' She sounded innocently proud. 'As a young man, my grandfather laid down enough wine for his and his son's lifetime, so everything is of a very respectable age.'

'*Everything*? You mean the cellar hasn't been replenished for seventy years?'

'Not as far as I know. Is that bad?'

'No, no,' he lied. 'But it seems a wee bit wasteful to drink it all up, as an everyday kind of thing, I mean. Don't you worry your head about it, though. Just you leave it to me.'

The conversation was stilted at first, Miss Macmillan being quietly businesslike but at the same time reticent, as if she were no more sure than he was of what the whole silly affair was about. Neither of them knew quite where to start and Colin was reduced at one stage to admiring a vase of wild cherry blossom on the side table.

As the meal progressed, however, he became aware that she was fishing for information, trying to plumb the depths of his ignorance, assuming that since he was not a sportsman he knew very little of country sports and, therefore, little of the society in which they were fashionable.

In which she was wrong. Although he was a citizen of Glasgow to his very bones, Colin had never lacked invitations to the country houses of the great. Bankers had the entrée to many places closed to less influential members of the commercial classes. He was even a regular visitor at Balmoral, having been invited first as a guest of Prince Albert and more recently of his royal widow, with whom he was something of a favourite. The Queen, indeed, had come to regard her dear Mr Campbell as a kind of honest burgher on whom she could rely for truthful – and carefully phrased – answers to any questions she chose to ask on the lives and beliefs of Our Subjects.

The fact was that Colin did not indulge in sporting pursuits because he had better uses for his time than crawling around the countryside in acute discomfort, shooting off guns at inoffensive wildlife. Not that he was so tactless as to say so.

'I don't have good vision over long distances,' he told Miss Macmillan, 'and pride forbids me to take part in an activity where I can be guaranteed to miss every single target I aim at.'

'I see. What about fishing?'

'I catch cold when I get my feet wet,' he said truthlessly, knowing that he was making himself sound more like an Ancient of Days than someone who was perfectly fit and well on the right side of forty. But he had his reasons. He didn't need any help in having his comfortable life disrupted by emotions he had not felt since adolescence.

'Oh, dear.' She smiled sympathetically. 'What a shame that you should have to be a martyr to your guests' enjoyment. Now, you must please tell me whether you would like to be shown round the estate as a whole, or in bits, so to speak. I mean, would you like to be taken on separate tours of the fishing beats, and the bird moors, and the stalking corries? I don't know whether Mr Blake warned you that things have been a little neglected? But I have taken on a new grieve, a local man called Tom Tanner, and we are doing all we can to make improvements.'

She had intended to be her own grieve, until she discovered what an enormous amount there was to be done. So she had talked to Tom, who had been reluctant at first, not because he doubted his ability to handle the practical side of the job but because he remembered the armfuls of papers that had accompanied John McBride wherever he went.

'Well, I can't think why he needed them all,' Rachel had said bluntly, 'except to make himself feel important. He never did very much. You, on the other hand, would be doing a great deal.' After a moment, temptingly, she had added, 'You can leave all the papers and calculations to me, if you like.' She knew Tom Tanner was able to read and write, but that didn't mean he enjoyed it.

His good-looking face had lit up. 'Och, well, that iss different. I would like it chust fine, then.'

On the strength of his new importance, he had even condescended to marry Fiona McDougall at last, after 'walking out' for seven years. The wedding had been the most riotous event in the glen in living memory, and there had arrived – three months later – a fair-haired pet of a baby girl who had been christened Meggie. Rachel had caught herself thinking how nice it would be to have babies of her own.

Colin laid down his knife and fork with a well-fed sigh of satisfaction. 'Let's just take things gently,' he said. 'There's no rush. I'm not likely to be bringing any dedicated sportsmen here for a while yet, and from what I've seen of the place it'll do fine. It's got the look of having been here, unchanged, for a good few hundred years and that's what matters to folk who can't trace their ancestry back more than a few decades. The plain fact is that money, nowadays, is in the hands of men who've made it themselves and have no great admiration for those who haven't. Or none that they admit to. They want to see how the other half lives so that they can congratulate themselves on living, not just as well as the hereditary rich, but better.'

'You mean they'd rather *not* have running water and nice, warm rooms? My goodness, I can arrange that easily enough!'

His eyes smiled at her. 'All things within reason, Miss Macmillan. What I'm saying is that there's a kind of upside-down snobbery that it's a mistake to ignore.'

'No right-way-up snobbery?'

'Oh, aye, that too. Especially with foreigners. They've a terrible weakness for the shades of Royal Deeside.'

She cocked her smooth brown head enquiringly. 'It's interesting,' she said, and Colin could see that she meant it. 'I mean, if you were in London or even Edinburgh I wouldn't be surprised at you having foreign customers. But Glasgow seems such a very Scottish place. Not exactly a hub of international finance.'

'Tut, tut! I can see that, if you're to keep your end up with my guests, I'll have to give you a lecture about its place in joint stock banking. Until just a few years back, there was no one in the world who could touch us or even compete with us. The Glasgow system's been copied all the way from here to Hong Kong.'

3

Mr Campbell was a very nice, normal person and much younger and more human than Rachel had expected. She hadn't really known *what* to expect. As a friend of Rainer Blake, he might have been anything from the Lord Buddha to Genghis Khan.

Preparing for this day, she had barely taken time to sit down during the whole of the ten months since Blake's departure from Juran. A careful review of her financial position had shown her that, once the debts had been paid off, she would be able to undertake all the essential improvements only if she exercised a sensible economy. It could not, however, be the kind of economy obvious to Mr Campbell or his guests, who couldn't be expected to do without their tea and coffee, their sugar and wheaten bread, or their breakfast of kidneys, bacon and kippers, all of which were things that had to be bought in.

She had embarked, therefore, on a furious reorganisation of everything Juran was capable of producing for itself. Never had the castle seen such spinning and weaving and dyeing, such knitting and candle making and churning, such soap boiling and brewing and baking. Inspecting the results, Rachel had felt as if she would fizz over with gratification and pride.

But that had been the easy part. The village and land had become appallingly run down, Highland lethargy aggravating what lairdly neglect had begun, and even ten months had barely enabled her to scratch the surface of what needed to be done. No one who didn't live on a remote Highland estate had the faintest conception of what was entailed.

It had looked simple enough on paper, in its own complex way, except that what the calendar proposed, the weather all too often disposed. Her first step had been to try and make everything happen more efficiently, and that meant taking advantage of every single hour when the weather was favourable.

One of the primary tasks of the year was to see the peats cut and dried, because the villagers depended on peat for warmth and cooking throughout the winter. Replenishing the stocks was a diffuse and time-wasting business, spread out over weeks in fits and starts, and the worst hold-up usually came over transporting the thin, black blocks from peat hags to village. The women moved them in creels on their backs, but were inclined to treat it as work to be done only when they happened to feel like it and had time to spare. There was always panic at the last minute when the nights began drawing in. If everyone made a concerted effort, Rachel knew, and if the peats were moved *en masse* by pony and sledge, it would take no time at all. Her problem was convincing the tenants of the fact.

She didn't see how, short of standing by with a bull whip, she could speed up the June work of haystack building. At Juran, haystacks were as big as cottages, the men tossing up huge forkfuls of grass and the women, eight of them to each stack, bedding it down with a rhythmic shuffle of a dance, to the accompaniment of a soft, continuous mouth music.

In July there was the same problem, because flax-pulling was something that couldn't be hurried except by bullying or a spell of favourable weather; the stalks had to be dried for two weeks in the open air before being retted – soaked until the tissues and woody shreds rotted away – for another two. Then they had to be dried again and stored for dressing, spinning, and weaving into linen for shirts and sheets, which was work for the winter months.

August was when the harvest was scythed and tied and stooked to dry, and after that came the autumn bracken gathering, when every hillside looked like Birnam Wood moving to Dunsinane as the women carried their huge loads of brown-tipped curling green fronds, light in weight but vast in volume, down to the low ground to provide bedding for the animals during the winter.

Rachel had argued that, if some of the women gathered and others carried, everything would be over with much more quickly, and the women hadn't resisted her suggestions, merely spent so long negotiating with one another about who should do which that the whole operation took, not half as long, but twice as long as it should have done.

Even so, she wasn't downcast. Indeed, after all the years of repression and lack of direction, she was in the highest of spirits. Impossible though it seemed, Juran meant more to her with every passing day.

She was so much above herself that she was even able to welcome Horace with amused tolerance when he turned up – as he had done three times since last June – to make sure she wasn't interfering with Nature's grand design. He was pleased with her, because she wasn't.

Not yet.

Odder still, she was able to look back and laugh over old Becca's prophecy and the idea of being forced to choose between the two loves that guided her life.

To begin with she had thought about, worried about her other love at least once a day, but gradually her wild tangle of emotions had resolved itself and now – because, she supposed, he had no predetermined place in the round of Juran's year – she thought about him only when she wanted to.

She was in love with him, now and for ever; that was something she thought of as irrevocable. And he was not impervious to her, however detached he had become after he had kissed her on the beach. At that stage in her reflections, there tended to be a protracted, dreaming interval before she went on to what was always the same conclusion. He had kissed her; he had said he admired her; and he had offered her the help she needed, not because he had to, but because he wanted to. It was enough. He would come back, and then . . .

In the meantime, her days were frenetically full, and her evenings taken up with planning. Tom Tanner was proving his worth in every way, pointing out to her that, if they did this, it would mean they could do that, and if they did that, it would allow them to do the next thing. Yes, yes, she would say, and work it out on paper, and discover he was right.

She had been grateful during the winter to have her evenings fully occupied. It still felt strange having the castle to herself except for the handful of servants who lived in, and when she had found herself thinking that she should really flit around, occupying a different room every evening, she had decided to close most of it down for the winter months. The Blue Drawing Room, relic of the reign of Gresham's sister Isabella, had been locked from the day after the Greshams left; Rachel doubted whether she could ever bring herself to enter it again. It reminded her too much of everything she wanted to forget.

In the end she had made a ground floor suite for herself from the Green Drawing Room and the morning room, and was more comfortable than she had been in her life before.

There was only one disadvantage to it all, and the last she would have expected. She had begun to fall out of the habit of people. It now took a conscious effort for her to calm and quieten herself when she had to face someone with whom she was not in daily contact, whether it was Mr Allan, the minister, or Mr Philip Roy of Altsigh. After an evening's conversation with such people, she found her head buzzing like a hive of hysterical bees and every muscle in her body aching with the release from tension.

4

After the first evening, it wasn't like that with Mr Campbell, whose quizzical, relaxed presence very soon disarmed her as it disarmed so many people more elevated than she.

'I'd rather photograph wildlife than shoot it,' he said on the third day of his visit. 'I had a rare old time last month when they were moving the contents of the Hunterian Museum. They'd got all the stuffed beasts loaded onto open wagons and the horses were in no great rush to climb up from the High Street to Gilmorehill. So I followed them and set up my equipment every time they stopped for a breather. I can tell you, you're never likely to meet another photographer who's got a giraffe, a tiger, a gazelle and a polar bear all on the one negative!'

'I don't imagine I will,' she laughed.

'What's tempting me right now is colour. You won't have heard, but there's a fellow called Clerk-Maxwell who made some experiments with it about eight or nine years ago. That's where the future lies. And Juran's the perfect landscape for colour pictures. I'm thinking of setting up in competition with Mr Landseer. What do you think the chances are of persuading a stag to stand still for the length of three thirty-second exposures?'

He was like a breath of fresh air sweeping through Juran. Rachel had never heard anyone talk intelligent nonsense in her life before or, indeed, any kind of nonsense. Laughter, she discovered, came in different guises. Rainer Blake had wit, which was of the mind. Colin Campbell had humour – and that, she thought, was of the heart. And all the while, even as he made her smile over such unlikely topics as Mr Gladstone's first ministry and the design of the new St Pancras station, he reminded her that there was a world beyond Juran, and an interesting world, and a world that was not impossibly far away.

What she failed to recognise was that Colin, in defiance of his own commonsensical resolutions, was deliberately laying himself out to please her. It was a tactic of which she had no previous experience, because no one, hitherto, had cared enough about her to take the trouble.

Rachel liked him, found him wonderfully stimulating, and regretted it when he left. Here at last, she thought, was a friend she could trust.

5

He would not, he had said, be bringing his first sporting party to Juran until August, adding with a twinkle that the Glorious 12th sounded like a fine, symbolic day on which to start his new career as a sporting man.

Since there had been a disastrous outbreak of grouse disease only two years before, Rachel feared that the birds might also turn out to be symbolic unless she and Tom Tanner took steps to guard the nests from predators.

She had the usual disagreement with Philip Roy about what constituted a predator, although at least he wasn't too hoity-toity about her rental arrangement. 'I can't approve of renting,' he said, 'and certainly not to the middle classes, but I suppose a bank is preferable to a brewery or some damned Midlands manufacturer. And at least it'll force you to stop letting the place deteriorate into a sanctuary for vermin, which is what it's been doing. You've been a dashed sight too busy with your tenants to pay as much attention to the sporting side as you should. At least, now, you'll have to make sure that Tanner starts culling the eagles and buzzards.'

She sacrificed Colin Campbell without a moment's hesitation. 'I can't. Mr Campbell is a naturalist with a particular interest in eagles and buzzards and he says they don't do nearly as much damage as the keepers claim. But Tom has declared war on hoodie crows and wildcats, and Hogg has killed quite a few foxes lately, now that I've been able to start paying him again.'

Foxes could wreak havoc among grouse and partridge chicks. Automatically, Philip said, 'Oh, good.'

Rachel waited, but he didn't follow it up. The queer thing was that Hogg actually *had* killed quite a few foxes recently – not, she thought, so much because she was paying him as because she was keeping an eye on him.

She had always been dubious of his foxhunting prowess. When he went on a tour of the lairds to show them the foxes his dogs had killed on their land, the lairds usually took it as fair proof that he was earning his wages. Rachel, however, had gradually become convinced that he was showing the same foxes to everyone. The only time she had ever known him show any turn of speed was when he was possessed of a corpse and anxious, she suspected, to display it to as many of his employers as possible before it gave the game away by beginning to smell high.

She hadn't said anything to anyone else, of course, but she had dropped an oblique hint or two to the little foxhunter himself and it seemed to have worked wonders.

Everything was going beautifully, and she revelled in it all. This was the life she had been born for.

And then, one June evening, she arrived home from an idyllic day on the hills to find not only Horace waiting for her, but Gresham.

It was an index of her state of mind that her first reaction was to laugh, because they were standing on the doorstep, very obviously locked out and looking as if they had been there for some time. She had almost forgotten telling the servants that Mr Gresham was never to be allowed to cross Juran's threshold again.

'Well, well,' said little Ellie Vallette cheekily. 'Come back to look for a collar stud you lost last year, have you?'

Gresham didn't condescend to answer and Rachel was interested to see that he looked smaller than she remembered, perhaps because he wasn't important to her any more. But he still repelled her.

'Come on, Rachel,' Horace said. 'Let us in. I'm dying for a cup of tea.'

She didn't want to appear mean-minded, so she ushered them into the Great Hall and then, throwing down her shot pouch with its burden of notebooks and pencils, knives and measuring rods, said, 'I take it you didn't drop in just for tea?' She couldn't imagine what they *had* dropped in for.

Turning away, she gave three sharp tugs to the bellpull that was now connected to the kitchen. One meant, 'Come.' Two meant, 'Bring logs for the fire.' Three meant, 'Bring tea.'

Gresham, his cheeks hollowing in brief distaste, surveyed the tweed bloomers she had discovered to be ideal attire for the hills, and announced, 'I have something to say to you.'

She smiled, still unconcerned. 'I believe there to be a perfectly adequate postal service.'

'But I will derive more pleasure from saying it in person.'

There was nothing he could do now to hurt her, but her euphoria began draining away and she replied curtly, 'Then please do not take too long about it or you may have difficulty in finding a place to sleep tonight. You will not sleep here.'

Horace said, injured, 'Dash it all, Rachel!' but Rachel and his father both behaved as if he had not spoken.

Sitting down and settling back with the deliberation that had always marked his movements, Gresham steepled his fingers and said, 'As a matter of principle, I am not prepared to allow you to keep what you gained by Belinda's murder. Since the law saw fit to recognise you as Daniel Macmillan's bastard and, on that basis, declared you entitled to inherit Juran, I decided to make it my business to search for something that would persuade the law to see things differently. And I have found it.'

No. All that is over, must be over. He can't possibly have found a way to open it up again.

It was a moment before she said flatly, 'I don't believe you.'

He raised a languid eyebrow. 'No?'

A clattering and shuffling at the service door heralded the arrival of the tea tray, and Rachel, recognising that the Great Hall was not the place for the kind of discussion that appeared to be developing, said, 'In the Green Drawing Room, please, Jeannie.'

When the tea had been poured and the door was safely closed, Rachel waited, saying nothing, while Horace began tucking in to the scones and Gresham slowly revolved the teaspoon in his cup.

'I have,' he said at last, 'been going through the hitherto neglected residue of my late brother-in-law's personal papers . . .'

'You *what*? You have no possible right to have them in your possession!'

'Perhaps not. However, amongst them I found a most interesting document. A document signed by your mother in – ah – 1853.'

When Rachel had been five years old. The year in which she had met her father for the first time.

Gresham went on, 'The document makes it clear that you have no possible entitlement to Juran. Because you are not Daniel Macmillan's daughter.'

7

Without hesitation, Rachel said, 'Nonsense.'

'That's not very polite,' Horace interjected through a mouthful of scone, but again he was ignored.

From the inside pocket of his coat, Gresham produced a folded sheet of paper and tossed it down on the tea tray.

Rachel took one glance. 'This isn't my mother's handwriting. It's yours.'

'A copy. The original is valuable, not to be risked in hands that might destroy it.'

She was still quite unable to imagine what was written on the paper when she dropped her eyes to it, convinced only that, whatever it was, it was a lie.

She laughed when she read the words. They were utterly ridiculous.

'I, Ondine Marie Vallette, hereby declare that my daughter, known as Rachel Vallette, is not the child of Daniel Macmillan of Juran, Argyllshire, North Britain, and that neither she nor I have any claim upon the said Daniel Macmillan.'

Gresham was expressionless when at last she looked up again, but Horace's diffident, amiable face had turned a breathless pink, as if he was finding the suspense unbearable. Astringently, she said, 'Don't get too excited, Horace. You are not about to be handed Juran on a platter for your Nature Park.'

Then she turned back to Gresham. 'If this is not a product of your own literary invention, then it's a forgery.'

But even as she said it, her mother's voice echoed in her memory, shrieking at her father. It had been something about him forcing her to sign a paper. *'And if that was not blackmail also then I do not know what is.'*

'And why,' Gresham rejoined coolly, 'should anyone go to the trouble of forging it? Aside from myself, of course.'

'Exactly my thought,' she told him, though she would have known her mother's handwriting anywhere. She could see no sense in it. No sense at all.

She tossed the paper back at him. 'My dear man, it isn't even witnessed.' It gave her a brief, vindictive pleasure to note how much he disliked the 'my dear man'.

'Besides which,' she went on, 'if it were genuine you would not have come to me with it. You would have taken it straight to a lawyer.'

'But then I would not have had the pleasure of telling you myself.'

She gave the bell a single tug. 'I cannot imagine why you went to so much trouble. Because, even if the document were genuine, it would be superseded by my father's formal deed acknowledging me as his daughter. That was properly witnessed and came later, at the time of my parents' marriage.'

Gresham studied his fingernails thoughtfully. 'True,' he said, 'but there are certain doubts in my mind. Knowing my brother-in-law, I feel that he might have been tempted to give in to some kind of pressure. I can very easily imagine your mother resorting to vulgar blackmail, for example. But we will find out, never fear. As you remark, the second document was witnessed, and I have employed men to trace the witnesses.'

'You *will* let me know what you discover, won't you?' Rachel said in a voice of honey. 'Ah, Jeannie, there you are. Mr Gresham and Mr

Horace are leaving. Will you tell Jimsy to bring their horses round from the stables?'

8

The only person she could turn to, the only person other than Gresham who knew everything about her, was David Napier, but when she wrote to him suggesting an appointment she received a polite reply from his clerk. There had been a bereavement in Mr Napier's close family, which had required him to leave for the south of England. It was unlikely that he would be back in Edinburgh before the end of July. He would see Miss Macmillan's letter, of course, as soon as he returned.

There was no one she could even talk to, certainly not the people she saw most frequently – Tom Tanner, Philip Roy and Hogg, though Hogg, in any case, had done one of his periodic vanishing acts. As a result, it was Lolloper, the faithful hound, who bore the brunt of his mistress's impassioned soul-searching as she marched him round the estate at a pace that, by any reasonable canine standards, was excessive.

She tried to pretend that nothing had happened, that Gresham wasn't waiting for her to make the next move. That Horace wasn't already snapping up bargain offers of hyenas and hippopotami for his Highland Yosemmitty.

She went back to crawling round Juran's hills, making notes, reminding herself of every small individual detail that had to be knitted into the fabric of what Mr Campbell's novice guests needed to be told if they were to appreciate their first experience of stalking and be suitably grateful to Mr Campbell for the privilege.

Ondine had signed the paper when Rachel was five. Why then – when Daniel Macmillan had just come back into their lives?

She kept an eye on the progress of the grouse chicks and found several nests that were new this year.

Her mother would never have set her hand voluntarily to a lie that could in no way benefit her.

She watched approvingly while the village women waulked the cloth for their outdoor shawls and the men's coats, making it thick and felted by soaking it, and beating it and shrinking it. The beating was a social occasion, the women sitting on the ground in circles with their wooden-headed hammers, arms rising and falling in time to their song.

*Ondine must have been forced to sign it, and no one could have forced her to
do that but Daniel himself.*

She even looked in on the dipping sheds, where the men sat with
clay pipes in their mouths and their laps full of big, fat, reluctant sheep,
parting the fleeces strip by strip and rubbing in the mixture of
archangel tar and butter that helped to keep parasites at bay.

Why, why, why?

9

She was the last to know that Gresham had done more than threaten
her, and it was Philip Roy who told her.

For some weeks, the two of them had been engaged in a systematic
attempt to delineate the boundaries between Juran and Altsigh.
Previously, if any question had arisen, someone had simply waved an
arm towards the top of the nearest hill. But hilltops weren't just sharp
edges. They had corries and plateaus, dips and humps, and Philip,
who liked to have things cut and dried, had declared on his accession
that this easy-osy approach wasn't good enough. As a result, Rachel
was being forced to accompany him up every hill where Juran and
Altsigh met – one of the Altsigh ghillies following with a pot of paint –
in order to mark every rock and outcrop along the boundary line.

Common sense not being Philip's forte, Rachel said resignedly,
'Don't you think the paint should go on the north-east face of the
rocks? Otherwise it'll be washed off before we turn our backs.'

'I suppose so. Did you hear that, Dougal? Put it the other side from
the prevailing wind.'

Leaning on his stick, he watched Dougal carrying out orders. 'You
know, this should have been done long ago,' he said. 'I can't imagine
what your stepfather was thinking of, just letting things slide.'

Rachel looked suitably abashed, as if Philip's own father had had
nothing to say in the matter.

And then Philip, his curly red hair riotous in the wind, the
squareness of his jaw emphasised by the short fringe of beard, cleared
his throat resoundingly and went on, 'I didn't mean your "stepfather", I meant your "father". Haven't got used to the notion, yet.'

Rachel, her stomach cold, said, 'I beg your pardon?'

'I've been meaning to talk to you about it. The whole shire's
buzzing. Well, you could hardly expect anything else. And I'm telling
you myself because I've never been one to shirk my duty. I'd been

thinking we might consider getting married, the two of us. But it's the end of that. I tell you straight, I might want Juran but I'd never go to the length of marrying a bastard for it. I don't know why you didn't tell me before. It would have saved me a lot of trouble.'

It was enough to make the angels weep.

After a moment, Rachel said, 'And where did this information come from?'

'Mmm? Oh, Horace Gresham and his father came to stay with me when you wouldn't give them a bed last week. Clever chaps, aren't they? Real walking encyclopedias. Could listen to them for hours.'

It was deliberate, Rachel knew. Previously, Gresham had chosen not to smirch his sister's memory by exposing her husband's infidelities, but now that it was open war that reservation had vanished. And Philip was the ideal repository for Gresham's confidences, being the biggest gossip for a hundred miles around.

'Anyway,' Philip went on, 'you'll see that it's the end of our personal relationship. But I've given the matter some thought and, on the whole, I'm prepared to go on being neighbourly. Within limits, of course.'

Her back straight and her head held high, Rachel said, 'How very magnanimous of you. Thank you, Philip. I appreciate it. How is the paint lasting, Dougal? Do you still have enough for those next two outcrops?'

10

David Napier was rushed off his feet when he returned to Edinburgh after his extended absence and wondered whether it might be possible for Miss Rachel to give him some idea, by post, of the problem she had mentioned. She was unreasonably annoyed to have to do so.

But within a week she received a reply from him that restored him so thoroughly to her good graces that she immediately forgave all his past errors.

'Having searched through our records without success,' he wrote, 'it occurred to me that advice on a matter of such delicacy might have been rendered personally, rather than in writing. I therefore took the liberty of applying for information to the partner in Napier, Napier, Nelson and Napier WS who advised your late father. Although now retired, he is still hale and hearty and in full possession of his faculties. I am pleased to report that he has been able to clarify the situation.

'It transpires that in 1848 Mr Daniel Macmillan consulted him about the possibility of paying a regular sum to Mlle Ondine Vallette for the upkeep of herself and the child she was carrying. Our partner advised strongly against it, since such payments would naturally have been construed as an admission of paternity, encouraging the lady to institute legal proceedings of a kind that Mr Macmillan was most desirous to avoid.

'After the lapse of some years, however, when Mr Daniel Macmillan had succeeded to his inheritance, he once again approached our partner, being by that time wishful of re-establishing Mlle Vallette as his mistress. I should say in parenthesis that this type of arrangement is by no means unusual among the respectable classes, who prefer it to more transient relationships.

'Our partner still felt unable to recommend regular payments without some assurance that the lady would never take undue advantage of Mr Macmillan's generosity. He suggested, therefore, that if the lady were prepared to sign a paper to the effect that neither she nor her child had any claim upon Mr Macmillan, then Mr Macmillan would be able to give the lady, with impunity, any such sums as he at any time felt inclined.

'The paper in question was not drafted by our partner nor, in his opinion, by any member of the legal profession. It is his belief that, uncorroborated and unwitnessed, it would be valueless in a court of law.

'I have taken a formal statement to the above effect from our partner. Unless you wish personally to confront Mr Gresham with this information, I would suggest you authorise me, as your lawyer, to send an attested copy direct to the gentleman concerned.

'I look forward to receiving your instructions and hope that you find this outcome, as I do, entirely satisfactory.'

11

There were tears in Rachel's eyes when she finished reading, tears not of relief but of sorrow and anger for her mother, who had gone through so much because some unfeeling, faraway lawyer had believed she might take an action for maintenance that it would never have occurred to her to take. It seemed that lawyers didn't know that ordinary people couldn't afford to go to law, and certainly not women.

Reading, queasily, of Mr Macmillan's subsequent 'generosity', Rachel remembered the extent of that generosity when it had finally been dispensed. How desperate for those few coins her mother must have been, she thought, to have signed a declaration that denied the very truth of her past and Rachel's whole existence.

At least it seemed that her father was fractionally less guilty than she had always thought, that his abandonment of Ondine and re-appearance almost six years later, after the death of old Hector, had represented more than just an interregnum during which an irresponsible youth had developed into a dissatisfied husband. He must have been terrified of his own father finding out that his younger son was as much a womaniser as the banished Archie.

Archie. It would be interesting to know what had happened to him. But as for wanting to see Gresham . . .

'Please send a copy of the statement directly to my ex-guardian,' she wrote to Mr Napier. 'I have no desire to see Mr Gresham ever again.'

With a flourish she signed it, and sealed it, and then, a great weight lifted from her heart, went lightly down to the beach to admire a sunset wondrous in silver and gold.

CHAPTER THIRTEEN

༺⁕ꕤ⁕༻

I

Richard Taverner was in his late twenties, long-limbed and athletic, blond of hair and tanned of skin, a man of considerable, easy charm and obvious breeding who had served for some years as a naval officer in eastern seas and thus knew a good deal about the China trade.

Even if he had not set his cap at her, even if Sophie had not been looking for just such a husband, she would have been attracted, because there was something curiously thrilling about him, a suggestion of underlying danger, even decadence, that set him apart from all the other young men she had known.

One of the other young ladies who swooned after him when he first began to appear in Hong Kong society in the summer of 1870 – his advent having been delayed by an extended tour of naval duty – likened him to a Greek god, but Sophie rather questioned whether the Greeks would have given their gods crooked noses or the kind of pale, luminous blue eyes that orientals hated and feared, comparing them to the sky peering through a skull.

Sophie didn't hate or fear them, but they made her exceedingly nervous at first, because when Lieutenant Taverner looked at her, it was like having a spotlight turned on her that penetrated right through to her chemise.

He was quite, quite different from Frank. Different, too, from the high-handed Rainer Blake, who had just left the colony, she had been pleased to hear, on an extended business trip to no one knew where.

2

It was not at all easy for a gentleman to catch a young lady alone in the heavily chaperoned and densely populated town of Hong Kong, but Richard Taverner managed it, taking Sophie suavely by surprise.

'How clever of you to find me!' she exclaimed admiringly, keeping up appearances. She could hardly say outright that he might have saved himself the trouble simply by asking for a private rendezvous.

His long-boned face was smiling and the heavy-lidded eyes warm. 'We naval fellows are experts. Pirates' lairs one day. Beautiful ladies the next.'

'Do you enjoy your duties? The naval ones, I mean.'

He joined her where she was sitting on the rocks, watching the tide come in and the soldier crabs corkscrewing themselves into the sand until it went out again. 'Yes, I suppose so. But they begin to pall when we spend all our time on these policing actions. We could do with another war. Without it, I find myself hankering for a nice job ashore. Something challenging that would stretch my mind.'

'Really?' Sophie wondered whether Macmillan and Venturi would be sufficiently challenging for him.

Just then, his arm came lightly to rest on her shoulder and she had to say in ladylike reproof, 'Please, Lieutenant!'

'Do you mind? There's no one to see.'

She didn't mind at all. In fact, it was exciting to feel so close to him. And then she flicked a small, provocative glance up at him and was lost. Because the look in his eyes was like a caress and her heart was doing a polka and she knew that he was on the verge of kissing her. And it would be a kiss unlike any she had ever experienced from cheerful boys in scented gardens, or even from Gino Venturi. It wouldn't be comforting.

It wasn't. It was dry, intense and yet smiling – like a Chinese massage, she thought unromantically even as, loving it, she gave herself up to the sensation of his closed lips moving against hers and causing every nerve in her body to tingle.

So engrossed was she in pleasure and curiosity that she did no more than jerk slightly when his hand left her shoulder and in one long, slow stroke swept down over her sleeve to reach the loose cuff of her habit shirt. She could feel the heat of his hand through the cotton and then the hand itself pushing cuff and sleeve up, smoothing over the flesh of her arm as it went, until the sleeve was rolled back over her shoulder and her arm bared as if she had been wearing a ball gown.

But then his lips left hers and descended burningly on the point of her shoulder and she was suddenly uneasy. 'No, please.'

His left arm was so compellingly round her that she couldn't struggle without the risk of toppling both of them off their rocky perch, but she said, 'No!' and '*No!*' again as he pulled at the bow of her cravat and began to unbutton her collar.

He paid no attention. The creases round his eyes deepened, and his murmuring voice was full of blandishments. Soon, her protests died. He was in no haste and after the first shock she began to respond with hazy delight to his movements, the gliding of lips and hands on skin, the unhurried breathing, the sensation of being stroked and pampered like a contented cat. She could have purred.

And then his mouth was on her breast and she returned abruptly to sanity.

His timing was impeccable. Before she could exclaim or pull back, he was buttoning up her collar again and smiling at her, his head outlined against the pale blue sky – the sky that seemed to shine through the sockets of his eyes.

It was the most disturbing half hour Sophie could ever remember and, afterwards, she was unable to forget it. Was this what it was to be in love?

3

Although she recognised that she ought not to rush into marriage with someone about whom she knew nothing except what he himself told her, Sophie didn't care. Having decided to marry the first presentable gentleman who asked her, she couldn't get over her good fortune that it should have turned out to be Richard.

If Joanna Bagford's husband had not been posted to Shanghai earlier in the year, Joanna might have talked some sense into her, but, as it was, only Gino Venturi made any attempt to remonstrate. He was quite cross, but Sophie couldn't see that it was any of his business – unless he had been thinking of putting in a bid for her himself! – and preferred to listen to her new American friend Robina Gibbings, who hadn't been in the colony long enough to know its rigid protocol and saw no reason why Sophie shouldn't marry her handsome lieutenant the minute her year and a day of full mourning were over.

Virtuously, Sophie thought perhaps she should leave it just a little longer, so she and Richard announced their engagement in August and set the wedding date for the second Thursday in September.

This, it transpired, was still going too fast for Euphemia Moore and her cohorts, even though Richard had taken considerable pains to charm them. It was Sophie, of course, on whom they heaped the blame. Their husbands, better informed, were more inclined to pity the girl.

Opening yet another chit regretting the writer's inability to attend, 'Really!' exclaimed the bride. 'I cannot imagine what all the old tabbies can possibly have settled to do on the 8th. Unless they've decided to take up cricket!'

Robina giggled. 'I should just love to see Mrs Moore in there pitching!'

But though Sophie was annoyed by the steady stream of refusals, there was one absentee whose sardonic presence she was grateful to be spared. Rainer Blake was not expected back in Hong Kong until November. It gave her enormous pleasure to think how amazed he was going to be when he returned and found her married to a romantic stranger!

When the morning of the 8th dawned, however, it began to look as if the marriage might have to be postponed, because the atmosphere was unnaturally warm and humid and there were deep black clouds hanging low over the mountains. Sophie, peering out through the shutters, could see that the Chinese quarter had become a forest of lanterns on thirty-foot poles; could hear a frantic beating of gongs, firing of crackers, and volleying of bamboo petards. All the small ships in the harbour were scuttling for shelter towards East Point, while the larger vessels had their sails clewed, hatches battened down, and every anchor they possessed thrown out towards the north.

Typhoon.

During the next hour a chit arrived for Sophie from the Rev. Mr Beach, then one from Gino Venturi, who had sourly agreed to give her away, then one from Dolly Berry, her matron of honour, and finally one from Richard. All of them said, if not in precisely the same words, 'You can't get married in a typhoon.'

Sophie, who had lived all her life on the shores of the South China sea, surveyed the wedding dress laid out on her bed – its subtle blue and restrained flounces representing a compromise between past cares and future joys – considered the hour, glanced at the sky, and sent chits back to her four correspondents saying, 'Yes, I can.

4

She had the greatest difficulty in maintaining her gravity during the service, especially since her husband, who was in the most exuberant spirits, seemed bent on teasing her into open laughter.

Like a pair of beautiful but mischievous children, one dark and one fair, they stood before the altar while Mr Beach took them through the ceremony at a spanking pace, punctuating his words with occasional nervous glances towards the roof. Sophie wondered why. The cathedral didn't have a spire – the Bishop was always complaining about it – so there was no danger of it being blown down.

Out of doors, the wind blew and the rain fell, but it eventually became clear that there wasn't going to be a typhoon after all, just a nasty storm. Thinking of all the guests who had stayed away to tie things down, getting wet, windblown and overwrought, and all for nothing, Sophie felt a deep, warm, satisfaction.

She didn't mind that it was turning out not to be a very orthodox wedding. Even the choir hadn't appeared to sing the hymns and the average age of the guests who had braved the elements was well under thirty. Sophie's determination to have a proper ceremony with all the trappings had been only a gesture and, the gesture having been made, she was perfectly content. She was going to enjoy herself.

After the service, chairs and carriages alike having vanished at the first typhoon warnings, everyone draped themselves in boat cloaks and, with four of Richard's fellow officers holding a makeshift canopy over the bridal pair, ran laughing and breathless up the hill to Caine Road.

They had such an entertaining party that, when Richard took her at last to the big, covered shelter on the roof, with its mosquito net curtains and the red lacquer bed with its legs resting in saucers of carbolic powder to repel snakes, she was almost looking forward to it.

5

Richard was very quiet and considerate with her at first, though he insisted she took her nightdress off because he wanted to admire her. He wanted her to look at him, too, but she couldn't bear to until he almost forced her.

'My dear, sweet girl,' he said, 'unless you know what's going to happen, it'll give you a fright. And if you don't enjoy yourself, I won't either. So open your eyes and let me explain.'

It sounded reasonable enough, so she unsqueezed her lids a little. His naked body was, she saw, very handsome, with wide shoulders and narrow waist and hips. Hurriedly, horrified, she closed her eyes again, and he laughed.

'All right. Don't look if you don't want to. Give me your hand.'

She did, and found it full of limp flesh that stiffened instantly at her touch, and she couldn't think what it was at first. Then she was struggling to pull her hand away and Richard was stopping her.

'That's the effect you have on me, you see?' he said breathlessly. 'And after a while, when I've caressed you and made love to you so that you're soft and yielding and *wanting*, you'll feel it inside you and then you'll . . .'

His voice broke off.

And then he hissed, 'Oh, *God!*' and without a moment's warning, the whole weight of his body was on top of her and he was groaning, 'I can't wait, I can't wait!'

So sudden was it that Sophie had no real idea, after all, what was happening as his lips fastened themselves to hers and forced them open while one urgent-fingered hand slipped between her thighs and out again. And then there was a blunt-tipped spear sliding inside her and meeting a barrier, and withdrawing and meeting it again, harder, and breaking it, and hurting her, and Richard was letting out a wild scream of triumph that echoed and re-echoed in Sophie's stunned ears throughout the endless, motionless moment before he drew all the muscles of his loins together and buried the full length of himself inside her. Her eyes sprang open then, as she too cried out, and she saw that on his face was a look of something close to ecstasy.

Everything else was over very quickly. Indeed, Sophie was just beginning to feel a very faint stirring of interest when her husband went into some kind of spasm and then collapsed on top of her, gasping – and fell fast asleep.

'Well, *really!*' Sophie thought.

6

Half an hour later, however, just when, aware of a vague feeling of disappointment, she was herself drifting off to sleep, she discovered that the night was not yet over.

In fact, in the three nights that followed, and since she did not share Richard's talent for catnapping, she had very little sleep at all. But she didn't mind, because she was discovering that Joanna Bagford had been perfectly right about b–e–d being among the roses rather than the thorns of marriage.

On the fourth night, however, Richard was in a strange mood and seemed to be avoiding looking her in the face, his lids drooping over eyes that, to his puzzled wife, seemed to have become entirely blue, with no pupils at all. Sounding almost surly, he said, 'Damn it, first is best. What a shame you're not a virgin any more! Perhaps we could have you reconstructed like they do in the red light districts.'

She didn't know what a red light district was, but laughed – as she was inclined to do when she didn't understand what he was talking about – and held his nightshirt out to him, saying 'Do you want this, or don't you?'

'No. And it's time you stopped having all the fun. My turn now. Come on, my girl, I'll teach you a few tricks to please your husband.'

After the first of them, she tried to say that she didn't like them, but Richard wouldn't listen.

'Nonsense. Now, if I turn like this, and you kneel on the bed like that and bend forward . . .'

Sophie didn't want her exciting new husband to think her unsophisticated, so she did what she was told. She was, after all, in love with him.

7

He wasn't easy to live with, and she had to keep reminding herself that it was bound to be difficult at first, living with somebody she scarcely knew, someone so very different from anyone she had known before. Most of her experience had been of cheerful youths not much older than she was herself and very conscious of their company manners; it was natural that Richard, older and more widely travelled, should be different.

But he had given her no reason to think, while he was courting her, that his moods would be so unpredictable. Sometimes he would be his normal, charming, vital self. Sometimes, even during the day, he would fall asleep at the most unlikely moments. Sometimes he would go out for an evening with friends and come back not tired, or even a little drunk, but filled with a kind of universal benevolence that seemed out of character. And sometimes, when he had been at sea for a day or two, he returned tense and short of temper, not just with her – which she would have accepted, because that was what she believed love was all about – but with everyone, even the servants.

It was a cardinal rule of Sophie's, which her mother, daughter of a missionary in Bombay, had dinned into her as a small child, that one should never lose one's temper with servants, not even those unregenerate sinners whose dark deeds were enshrined in the mythology of every English lady in the East – the cook who used his toes as a toasting fork, and the scullery boy who, since his employers used only one side of a plate, thought it unreasonable of them to cavil at the other side being dirty.

Sophie – tired of having to close her eyes to giant spiders and cockroaches, to the chicken having its neck wrung on the kitchen floor, to the loaf being buttered under the cook's insalubrious armpit – had taken over the housekeeping at Caine Road as soon as she was fourteen and old enough to be listened to. Her father had seen no need for her to bother her pretty head with such mundane things – after all, they hadn't been poisoned yet, had they? – but his conversion had been assured when, next time they had roast duck for dinner, he had not been faced with duck stew for breakfast the next morning.

A daily hour with the servants was usually enough to ensure that everything ran smoothly, and Sophie was in the habit of holding her inspection on the dot of ten, after her early ride or stroll along the waterfront in the cool of the day, followed by a bath and a breakfast of buttered eggs, tea and toast.

Her routine was unvarying, because everyone knew that servants were like children and needed to be well governed. First she inspected the fresh food that the cook, Fan Shu, had earlier bought in the bazaar. After that, she doled out the potatoes and flour, the rice and sugar, from the locked storeroom; checked Fan Shu's daily accounts; looked at the copper saucepans to ensure that their tinning was still entire; inspected the pantry, scullery, and kitchen for cleanliness; surveyed the crockery with an eagle eye; and, once every three days on average, reprimanded the scullery boy for using one of the best napkins to rub the soot off the kettle.

It was over the servants that she and Richard had their first row. He came into the kitchen and slipped his arm round her waist just when she was rebuking Fan Shu for extravagance. 'Yes, I know 'Ootnant Taverner likee bird's-nest soup, but *not* when nests catchee three dollars an ounce!' If Fan Shu had been an Indian servant, Sophie would have deducted two cash from his week's wages to remind him to have more sense in future, but a Chinese servant lost so much face by being rebuked that the rebuke itself was punishment enough.

And then Richard leaned forward to look at what else was on the table, and before Sophie realised what he was doing had picked up a leg of mutton and hurled it straight through the window, to the sound of crashing glass.

'I hate fatty mutton,' he shouted at the pitch of his voice. 'Do you hear me?'

His hands were round Fan Shu's throat and he was shaking the man as if he meant to shake the life out of him. 'I – hate – fatty – mutton! Do you hear me? Don't ever let me see it in this house again!'

Fan Shu's face was contorted with the pressure, and the other servants were standing by, frozen with terror, and Sophie was tugging with all her strength at Richard's arm, crying, 'Stop it, Richard! Stop it this minute!' but none of it made any impression.

'I won't have it!' Richard shouted. 'I won't have it! *Do you hear me?*'

Since there seemed to be no other solution, Sophie picked up the rolling pin and brought it down hard on her husband's wrist.

With a yell of pain and astonishment, he released the cook, who fell back, clawing at his neck and making horrible choking sounds.

For an incredulous moment Sophie thought that Richard was going to turn on her. But he didn't. His injured wrist clasped in the other hand, he turned after a moment and strode out of the kitchen.

A few hours later, Sophie tried to have it out with him, but by then he was himself again. 'Servants need to know what discipline is,' was all he would say, before he began to charm her round, voluptuously, as he knew how to do.

She gave in, of course, because he was her husband, and she loved him, and sharing a life, she told herself sternly, had little to do with being pleasant only when one felt like it. This was marriage, and it was up to her to adapt to it and make concessions and ensure that everything ran so smoothly that Richard never had cause to lose his temper again.

It was her duty to be submissive, too, but she had reservations about that after the episode of the unfortunate Fan Shu. If she had been properly submissive, Fan Shu might well have ended up in the mortuary.

As the days passed, however, she began to feel that she had been exaggerating the whole affair.

8

She missed Richard badly when he went back to sea – which he had to do because he couldn't just leave the Navy at the drop of a hat –

watching eagerly, day after day, for the HMS *Impudent* to come flying back home on the tide, smart and dashing with her white paint and gleaming brass.

She was waiting with particular eagerness one evening in November, when they were going to a ball.

Richard was aflame with excitement as he came running into the house and, picking his wife up, swung her round and round, exclaiming, 'Four hundred pirates the less! And we've just passed through the skirts of a typhoon, a real one this time. Can't you feel it in the air? It's going to bypass the island but, by God, doesn't it raise a thrill in your bones! Upstairs, my wench. Christ, but I've missed you. We've a deal of time to make up.'

She was already half dressed for the ball, and Ah Foon had done her hair to perfection. She wanted Richard to make love to her – of course she did – but not enough to be all mussed up. She knew he wouldn't accept that as an excuse, but fortunately there was another one and it happened to be true. She laughed up at him because his high spirits were so infectious and then, turning her mouth down at the corners, confessed wryly, 'It's the wrong time of the month, Richard. I'm sorry.'

He held her at arm's length, grinning.

'What the devil does the time of the month have to do with making love?' he demanded. 'It doesn't bother me, and plenty of women enjoy it more at the "wrong" time than the "right" time. You'll see. Come on, sweetheart, let's get upstairs before I explode with wanting you.'

'No, Richard! No, *please!*'

But he wouldn't listen.

9

It meant that she was already distressed before she went to the ball, where she was to discover that she needed all her strength. And more.

Protocol in Hong Kong was like protocol everywhere in the British colonies that were spreading so swiftly across the nineteenth-century map, scattering it with spots and splashes as red as the blood that bought and sustained them. With a handful of exceptions, these colonies were inhabited by men who had been born in Britain and reared in Britain, and who proposed to retire to Britain and die there. They were transients, first and last, colonial residents whose brief destiny was to rule, to fight, to administer, to trade, above all to channel their ferocious ambition into making as much money as was humanly possible in the fewest possible number of years.

During those years they measured their success by the respect in which they were held by their peers, their place in the colonial hierarchy. In Hong Kong, as elsewhere, the British came and went, and every newcomer was scrutinised to discover where he fitted into the social pattern. Everyone from the taipan of Jardine Matheson down to the most youthful griffin had his appointed place, and on that place depended whether he was invited to receptions at Government House or forbidden, save as a messenger, even to cross the threshold of the Hong Kong Club. Taipans despised clerks; merchants despised shopkeepers; shopkeepers despised sailors; and sailors despised soldiers. Even military and naval wives had to be addressed by their husband's rank in case, by some dreadful error, protocol and the rules of precedence should be breached.

As Mrs Lieutenant Taverner, Sophie would have had relatively little formal social life, but since Richard was also, if still only nominally, the senior partner in a trading house that was somewhere around the middle of the merchant league, they qualified – though not quite automatically – for invitations to some select occasions.

On this night they were going to a full dress reception and ball at Government House. The secretary there, accustomed to assessing The Gup, or gossip of the colony, and having unhesitatingly attributed Sophie's recent unpopularity to the vicious backbiting of that b--- Euphemia Moore, had issued the invitation as much to spite the latter as reinstate the former.

It was fully eighteen months since Sophie had been to such an affair and her toes had scarcely stopped tapping between the arrival of the invitation and the evening itself. She knew she shouldn't have spent so much on a new gown, but she had absolutely nothing that could have been altered to suit the latest fashion. The short, bunchy, puffed bustle had become positively antiquated, and a tablier and double train were essential.

'And what the devil is a tablier?' enquired Richard, listening to her overwrought chatter as Ah Foon began doing her hair all over again.

'You'll see when I put it on. It's a kind of apron affair at the front. And there are lots of lace and fluted trimmings, quite lavish, you know. Trimmings are going to be *very* fashionable in the next two or three years.'

'I'll wager they are.' Richard pretended not to know anything about ladies' fashions, but he did, and Sophie sometimes wondered where he had learned. 'The more elaborate the trimmings, the more work needed to apply them and the higher the price.'

She pouted, her mind elsewhere. 'Don't you want me to look my best?'

10

The silk was paler than her eyes, the gentian trimmings an exact match for them. Above the full, graceful skirts and tiny waist, the small bodice fitted perfectly, finished with a wide, ruched band that continued, like a garland, to skim her shoulders in place of sleeves, displaying her beautiful shoulders to their best advantage. Her hair was arranged in wings at the front, with a thick plait at the back wound into a figure of eight and topped, on the crown, with a large blue silk rose. Her only jewellery was her mother's gold locket. She looked ravishing and she knew it.

She intended to forget the worries of the last few weeks and the last few hours. She wasn't going to think at all. She was going to enjoy herself as she hadn't enjoyed herself since she was seventeen, five long years ago.

Government House was a blaze of light and gaiety when they arrived and Sophie felt a ridiculous, childish excitement at the colour and movement and music, the diamond sparkle of the chandeliers, the feeling of being in a lovely, swaying, revolving flower garden, of being drawn into the welcoming embrace of gold braid and flushed faces and laughing people. Even the old tabbies looked benevolent in their dreary mauves and browns, their dated jet jewellery and artificially puffed hair. It was as pleasant, Sophie thought, to see the end of the monochrome era as it had been the garish one that had gone before. The refined two-tone combinations of 1870 might have been specially chosen to set off the bright dress uniforms and medals of the officers and the plain, distinguished black coats of the civilians.

'A polka,' said her husband with the warm, intimate smile that still – almost – disarmed her. 'May I?'

After Richard, who was unquestionably the most dashing-looking man in the room, she danced with a number of old acquaintances who, seeing her present at Government House, deduced that she must be socially acceptable again and reverted to normality. She danced with a number of gentlemen new to Hong Kong since her last appearance, who professed themselves quite bowled over. She danced with Gino Venturi, whom she hadn't seen since her wedding more than two months before, when he had been unaccountably short of temper, but who seemed to have been restored to his large and reassuring self, his manner as easy, his smile as benign, his voice as creamy as ever. And she danced, very sedately, with some of the older civilians and military officers who enjoyed nothing more than kicking up their heels with the prettiest young woman in the room.

And then, just as she was about to stand up with Mr Turner Berry, who was now married to Dolly Evans, someone materialised unexpectedly beside them – a tall, impeccably clad figure with arctic grey eyes and the kind of authority few people were inclined to argue with.

'You don't mind if I take your place, Berry, do you?' said Rainer Blake, and without waiting for an answer swept her on to the floor.

I I

She couldn't believe it at first, because it didn't show, but he was in a furious rage.

He didn't say good evening, or ask how she was, or compliment her on her looks. 'Why?' he ground out. 'Just tell me why. Last time we met, when you proposed to me – God help us! – you left me wondering what the devil you would get up to next. It never occurred to me you would do something as lunatic as *this*. What in hell did you think you were playing at? Have you no brains at all?'

It was so unexpected, so public, the anger so intense that she felt the blood rush to her cheeks and then drain away completely as she stammered, 'Playing at? What do you mean?'

She had heard that he was back, and had prepared her most bewitching and sweetly triumphant smile for him. Far from retreating to Juran as he had advised, she had made her own arrangements. She had married a wonderfully romantic stranger who was going to fulfil for her all the ambitions she could not fulfil for herself. She had won, she thought, but although it gave her the greatest satisfaction, she had known that Blake wouldn't concede defeat. She had been prepared for cynicism, perhaps even for scorn.

But not for this. It *couldn't* be her marriage to Richard that had brought it on. There must be something else. 'What have I done wrong? What are you talking about?'

300

'Don't be more of a fool than you can help. Marrying a man like Taverner is what I'm talking about.'

She shook her head, trying to clear it. 'I don't understand.'

'Don't you? He's been careful so far, has he? Still playing lovebirds?'

His voice bit like acid and Sophie shuddered violently. She couldn't breathe. She was going to faint; she was going to be sick. She had to get away. She had to escape this man who, in a few harsh words, had already begun to turn her inchoate little fears into huge black monsters.

'Don't speak to me like that!' she gasped. 'I won't listen. Stop it, stop it! People are watching!'

'People be damned.' He tightened his grip. 'If it bothers you, smile. Pretend to be enjoying yourself.'

'I can't. Let me go.'

'You *can*.'

'Why are you talking to me like this?'

'Someone has to.'

The dance was a waltz and he had whirled her through a full half dozen turns before he spoke again, half under his breath but with a ferocious intensity, 'Oh, *God*! I'm as big a fool as you are. You don't know anything. You really don't know anything.'

Somehow, she managed to say, 'I know that I love my husband and that you are insulting him. I won't listen to another word.'

'*Oh, yes. You will, my girl!*' The music was coming to an end. 'Damnation! We can't talk here. Ride towards Jardine's Garden tomorrow morning at about seven.'

'No.'

There was something not unlike desperation in his voice. He said, 'It's your life I'm talking about.'

12

The open air was safer than indoors for private conversation.

Blake and Sophie met by apparent accident and walked their horses, chatting casually, like dozens of other early riders. No one saw anything remarkable in it.

They were both more like themselves this morning, confronting their dread of the meeting in their own different ways. Sophie, who hadn't slept at all, told herself over and over again that it was probably a great piece of work about nothing, while Blake, who hadn't slept either, was shocked to discover that, fearless though he had always thought himself, he was a coward at heart.

How *could* he say to an innocent girl what he had to say to Sophie?

'You're not to be trusted, are you?' he began. 'I take it you just went romping into marriage without making even the most superficial enquiries?'

'I'm not a green girl. I can judge people for myself.' Then, in response to his raised brows, 'And I could hardly go around asking people if they happened to know whether my future husband was respectable or not!'

'Dammit, you have a lawyer, haven't you? A few enquiries in Shanghai would have told you all you needed to know. I had no trouble at all in finding out.'

Impatiently, she demanded, 'Finding out what? That Richard had been a naughty boy and stayed out late? Spent a few nights in the lockup? Kissed the consul's daughter in the moonlight?'

'Are those the worst sins you can think of?' His voice was flat, almost without expression.

She shrugged petulantly. 'Well, if he'd done anything dramatically awful, it would have been in the *China Mail*, wouldn't it?'

They had to stop then and exchange a few words with James Whittall who, as taipan of Jardine Matheson, was not to be passed by with a smile and a nod, like other people. Sophie stood without fidgeting, immaculate in her dark blue riding habit and black bowler, listening politely and with just the right level of female incomprehension while Blake and Whittall discussed a small problem of insurance.

'Good girl,' Blake said as they resumed their stroll, and she replied tartly, 'Thank you.'

'Sophie, will you stop resisting me! One reason why your husband contrived to have himself transferred here, from his previous ship to the *Impudent*, was that he'd made Shanghai too hot to hold him.'

'I don't believe you.'

A public garden was the stupidest place for a conversation like this, but there was no help for it. 'Listen to me,' Blake said, 'and brace yourself. I pray I'm not wrong in thinking you have character under that frivolous exterior, because you're going to need it. The first thing I have to tell you is that, in Shanghai, Lieutenant Richard Taverner was a regular patron of the brothels. Do you know what a brothel is?'

She gulped. 'Yes.'

One day, during her engagement to Frank, he had begged her to

302

stop staring at the sampans of the flower girls, because they were just floating brothels. She had teased him into explaining, in an exceedingly roundabout way, what a brothel was. And no, *of course* he had never been in one!

Trying to be fair, however much it hurt, she said, 'I don't like to think of Richard in such a place, of course, but gentlemen are perfectly entitled to do what they want, however their wives feel about it. Anyway, you're talking about before we were married.'

In general, Blake was as ready as any other man to swallow the doctrine of male superiority, but he found himself saying, 'And that's a damnfool remark if I ever heard one! Brothels are hotbeds of infection. Every time your husband makes love to you, *you* are in danger from him.'

She didn't understand, of course.

Wearily, he went on, 'I'm not talking about colds in the head. Have you heard of the Contagious Diseases Acts?'

'They're something to do with cattle, aren't they?'

'Many people think so. But in fact they're the government's means of trying to control prostitution. There are some diseases transmitted by physical intercourse between men and women that are disgusting and dangerous, and can be fatal. Bodily disintegration, softening of the brain. Madness.'

He had to say it, so he went on in a level, passionless tone that he hoped would carry its own conviction. 'Those are the risks you run every time your husband makes love to you. Those are also the risks for any child you may conceive.'

13

Blake thought she was going to faint, and he wouldn't have blamed her. He could imagine the chill spreading through her veins; her nerves being stripped raw. He knew her brain would refuse to accept it at first.

'No. Richard is perfectly healthy, and so am I.'

'Perhaps. Perhaps he took a cure before you were married.'

She looked straight into Blake's eyes, something close to hatred in her own. 'And perhaps he didn't need to! I'm sorry, but I don't want to hear any more. I don't believe any of this. Even if Richard *had* caught something infectious, he would take the greatest care not to pass it on to me.'

Turning, she began to fiddle with her horse's girth preparatory to remounting, her hands shaking and tears very near the surface. She had put her veil up when they began talking, but now she dropped it again.

Blake said softly, 'Don't run away, Sophie. I haven't finished yet. And believe me, I'm not telling you this for my own pleasure.'

There was a bench nearby, and they sat down on it with a respectable distance between them. Their horses, released, began to graze peacefully.

He said carefully, 'A man doesn't necessarily know when he is first infected, and neither does a woman. And, even assuming that Taverner has taken a cure, you are safe only for as long as he remains faithful to you. Do you understand me?'

'I'm his wife. He loves me.'

'The brothels are full of men who love their wives. They go there to spare them from having to close their eyes and think of England more than once a week.'

'I never refuse Richard!'

It wasn't good news. Blake found that he couldn't look at her but sat with his eyes fixed on his whip, drawing the point of it rhythmically, repeatedly, through his fingers. 'That might be enough for another man, but there is a special difficulty in the case of your husband.'

'No! No, please. *Please*. I don't want to hear any more.'

He couldn't take her in his arms to comfort her, nor even stretch out a hand. Not in Jardine's Garden.

Inclining his head to one of the Butterfield and Swire partners who was riding by, Blake murmured, 'You must. You must know the worst, otherwise what I've already told you will have been useless.'

She gave a little choke that was almost of laughter. 'You mean that wasn't the worst? I can hardly wait.'

'Taverner is an opium smoker. You must have seen signs of it.'

After a long silence, she said, 'I don't know what the signs are.'

She hadn't even known opium was more than a medicine until Frank, trying to discourage her from going shopping in the bazaar, had mentioned opium smoking as one of the evils practised by the most degraded of Chinese in dark and sinister dens of vice off Tai Ping Shan Street.

'The signs? Unpredictable moods. Awake one moment, falling asleep the next. Vastly benevolent one moment, tense and short-tempered the next. Finical about food. Awake half the night. Eyes with pinpoint pupils.'

If they had not been in a public place Sophie would have screamed out her fear and misery and horror. As it was, she stared into Blake's taut, watchful face and said with laborious care, 'Yes, I have seen the signs.'

14

She told him everything, then, or almost everything. Even under his most delicate probing, she couldn't put into words everything that Richard made her do in bed. She didn't even know whether it mightn't all be quite ordinary, the kind of thing every married couple did; whether her distaste arose out of ignorance or prudishness.

But she held back nothing else. She hadn't known how badly she needed to talk about what only yesterday had appeared to be no more than a random assortment of minor worries, disconcerting though they had been. By the end, although she was still trembling, she was sufficiently herself to exclaim, 'I shouldn't be talking to a gentleman about such things at all!'

'You'd get a damned silly answer if you tried talking to a lady about them.'

They rose to their feet, and Blake said, 'You do see what I'm getting at? Why I've told you all this? The opium addict is not to be trusted in any way. He has no sense of responsibility. He will never stick to his promises. And that means you can never be sure that he isn't a threat to you, in bed or out of it. You *have* to protect yourself.'

Even the veil couldn't hide what was in her eyes. 'What can I do?'

'The danger is in your own home and your salvation in your own hands. I can't help you. No one can. But if there is anything that worries or mystifies you, let me know at once. Send that amah of yours – Ah Foon, is it? – to me. I presume she's trustworthy? In the meantime, I'll speak to your husband and if there's any doubt about his present state of health, I'll see that he takes a cure.'

She smiled with an unexpected and unfamiliar sweetness. 'You are being so kind, and I don't deserve it.'

'Well, at least that's one thing we're agreed on.' He half smiled back at her. 'Sophie, I've hated telling you this, but I couldn't leave you in ignorance. We'll talk again, soon. And just remember, don't let him touch you.'

'But how. . . ?'

Brusquely, he said, 'How the devil should I know? I would suggest you try using the brains God presumably gave you. And always remember, it could be your life that's at risk.'

15

When Lieutenant Taverner, the debonair personification of every maiden's dream, sauntered into Blake's office a few days later in response to a politely worded though uninformative request, Blake greeted him with an air of superannuated solemnity that would have scared the wits out of an Old Testament prophet. Just because there was no very great difference in their ages, he didn't want Taverner to make the mistake of thinking that they were going to be talking on equal terms.

It took him no time at all to wipe the smirk off the conceited bastard's face. Having cast himself, with a distaste he didn't stop to analyse, in the rôle of old family friend and honorary uncle to Sophie, he began by regretting that he had been absent from Hong Kong during the lieutenant's courtship of her. He then proceeded to make clear, though not quite in so many words, that he believed the lieutenant to have been more interested in Sophie's assets than in Sophie herself and that, on the presumption that she had no one to protect her, he had taken deliberate advantage of her.

His pale eyes hostile, Taverner said, 'All that is quite untrue. I happen to love my wife. You were not here to stop our marriage, and you would have had no damned right to do so, anyway. Equally, there's nothing you can do about it now. If you have brought me here to enquire, somewhat belatedly, into my background and prospects, I tell you bluntly that they are no business of yours.' He began to rise. 'I will take my leave now.'

Blake studied him with acute distaste. The anger was superficial, a formal response to insults that should deeply have offended his self-respect – if he had had any. But all he had was vanity. And self-indulgence, of course. It occurred to Blake that he was the kind of man who, if things became too uncomfortable, would be less likely to fight than simply to pack his bags and leave. Which might be a solution. He must bear it in mind.

In the meantime, he looked up at the fellow and said, with a cold glitter in his eye, 'Leaving? When I have not begun saying what I wish to say?'

306

'I am not prepared to stay here and trade insults.'

'Oh, I wasn't thinking of doing any trading. Though I guess that an insult from a man one holds in contempt is more flattering than a compliment from a friend.'

'And what is that intended to mean?'

'Sit down again and you will find out.'

By the time Blake had finished – attributing his encyclopedic knowledge of the lieutenant's evil ways to gossip picked up in Shanghai – Taverner had smoked his way through two of the Javanese cheroots he affected and his tan lay like a coat of amber paint on a face from which all other colour had fled. The creases round his eyes and mouth looked as if they had been drawn in with white chalk.

Sophie had said that danger seemed to excite him, and perhaps physical danger did. But Blake's icily assured promise of social ostracism had a different effect. Taverner's ability to charm was his stock in trade and he already knew enough about who was who in Hong Kong to recognise that Blake could ruin him with a word.

'Without money and without reputation,' Blake said, 'someone like you is better dead. And now, please, we will have the truth.'

It was much what he had expected. Taverner had suffered from and been cured of three bouts of clap. 'Well, damn it all, everyone catches it some time. At any given moment, forty per cent of the armed forces of the Crown are taking the cure.' He had been clean when he married Sophie, and faithful to her since. So she was in no danger, 'no danger at all.' And as for opium, it was no different from tobacco, a pleasant relaxant after a hard day.

Could Taverner really be so naïve, Blake wondered, as to think it possible, once opium had him in its grip, that he would ever escape?

There was nothing that could be done about Taverner's weakness for the tainted flower – and opium, in any case, directly endangered the lives only of those who smoked it, unless they needed money to fund their addiction.

What Blake feared, deeply, was the irresponsibility that went with it. He didn't doubt that, sooner or later, Taverner would catch another dose of clap, and whether gonorrhoea and syphilis were two stages of the same disease or, as some doctors argued, two separate diseases, he would be bound to infect Sophie and, through her, their children, if they had any. Blake had seen syphilitic children and knew what it meant.

Taverner was chastened when he left, but Blake didn't believe for a moment that it would last.

He stood at the window gazing out at the busy life of the Praya – the merchants, the clerks, the bearers, the coolies, the ships, the cargoes – and seeing nothing of it. Sophie's salvation was in her own hands. Only she could protect herself.

But how in hell, he wondered, did he go about telling a gently bred girl that she had to inspect her husband's private parts every time she went to bed with him, in case there was a dusky red ulcer, or a crusty grey scab, or a new pit in the flesh . . .

16

Sophie waited for Richard to tell her what he and Blake had talked about, and he did. Within limits.

'Fellow had the dashed impertinence to want to quiz me about my past history and future prospects. I didn't tell him, especially about my most immediate future prospects, because those' – he laid vibrant, possessive hands around Sophie's waist – 'are much too private. Upstairs, my beauty! Right this minute, or I'll take you here and now on the drawing room floor!'

17

During the next weeks and months, Sophie had freedom when Richard was at sea, which was quite often, but when he was at home there was no escape. If she had locked her door against him, he would simply have broken it down.

To begin with, every time he took her to bed, she tried to be grateful for it. She made herself as attractive as she could for him; had some outrageously seductive nightdresses made up, of the thinnest of lawn, almost transparent; gave in to all the demands he made of her, wondering the while whether they were as perverted as she was now convinced they must be – brothel tricks.

But she had no choice. To keep him away from brothels, she had to behave as if she belonged in one. It was the only way to be safe.

And then the *Impudent* came flying into harbour one day and she discovered that it had been in Shanghai for the last week. It was Chefoo the next time. And then Tientsin.

She gave up trying to believe the impossible, that he was celibate when he was away from her.

She feared for herself, but even more she feared conceiving a child who would be born in the certainty of decay and death. There was only one way she knew of preventing it.

Being kept waiting by Dr Dods one day when she had gone to consult him about a strained wrist, she had guiltily taken down the least enormous of his medical dictionaries and discovered that conception only occurred 'if both parties experience exhaustive satisfaction at the same moment'. It meant that if she willed herself to lie still, not to feel any excitement as Richard lashed himself to his climax, it would be all right.

It *would* be all right, because satisfaction and excitement were the last things she felt. All she felt was revulsion.

But what with that, with hating every minute of Richard's lovemaking, and having to look for what Rainer Blake had told her to look for – without Richard noticing – before they even started, she became so overwrought that she was less and less able to pretend what Richard wanted her to pretend, that being in bed with him was the pleasure above all pleasures in her life.

Things reached the stage when, even in the daytime, at meals, at parties, she was unable to feel even remotely at ease with the dashing and charming man who still existed, the man who had first attracted her, who would still have attracted her if it hadn't been for – almost everything.

Her gaiety and laughter became false through and through. She couldn't think why no one noticed.

18

More than anything in the world, she wanted to be free of Richard, but it was impossible.

She even went to see her lawyer.

Mr Dicey was not helpful, a square, solid, humourless man who, like Dr Dods, still thought of Sophie as a child. When she asked him about divorce, he stiffened and looked so shocked that it showed even through the bootbrush jungle of his beard and whiskers.

'Aitken and Dicey,' he said repressively, 'do not handle such matters.'

'I see,' she said. 'For practical or ethical reasons?'

'Ethical reasons.'

Sophie was too ignorant about business to appreciate the full beauty of a system of ethics that considered the opium trade as morally acceptable and divorce as morally unacceptable, so all she said was, 'Do other law firms feel the same way?'

'The reputable ones, certainly. Decent society in Hong Kong has no need for divorce lawyers.'

It was a setback, but she persevered. 'I think you may have misunderstood me. I wasn't asking you to handle a divorce. All I wanted to know was the grounds on which a divorce might be sought.'

'Mmmm. I see. Well, provided you refrain from revealing to me the motive behind the enquiry, I see no great harm in answering. Broadly, a husband may divorce his wife for virtually any sin of omission or commission. Desertion, unfaithfulness, refusal to grant him his – ummm – marital rights. A wife, on the other hand, cannot divorce her husband.'

'*What?*'

'I speak in terms of effect rather than law. The law concedes that such an eventuality should not be ruled out, but prefers not to encourage it. Multiple grounds are therefore required in a lady's case. Infidelity alone would not suffice, for example. Infidelity combined with physical cruelty might be acceptable, although such a thing would be difficult to prove. I cannot, in fact, recall any lady in the colony every having instituted such proceedings, nor would I expect to. Such things may be all very well in London, but not in a highly principled society such as ours.'

This struck Sophie, who for weeks had been incapable of honest laughter, as so comical that she was nearly betrayed into reeling off a list of Richard's iniquities and asking innocently whether such high principles might perhaps add up to grounds enough.

But she didn't. She had asked her question and been answered with a truth more cruel than she had expected. It didn't really surprise her.

She thanked Mr Dicey politely, and bade him farewell – for, she decided privately, the last time. There must surely, she thought, be a lawyer somewhere in the colony who was sufficiently civilised to recognise that women were human beings, too.

She couldn't divorce Richard, it seemed, and she certainly couldn't just walk out. She remembered reading somewhere of a case where a wife had fled to friends for refuge from a brutal husband and he had kidnapped her back and had his action endorsed by the courts. Furthermore, if she left Richard she would be homeless and penniless. All that she possessed was his – or almost all. There had been a new law passed recently which entitled her to keep any personal possessions up to the value of £200 sterling, as well as anything she earned in future, but, triumph though it had been for the suffrage movement, in Sophie's situation it was meaningless.

19

In her diary, she wrote, 'How I yearn for the kind of freedom men have. Even the colony itself is beginning to suffocate me. I remember Mr Blake saying once that it is like one of those isolated villages in southern France, so turned in on itself, so incestuous behind its shutters that it makes your flesh creep. He's probably right – I'm beginning to think he always is – but how can I know? I've never been to France. I've never been *anywhere* except Canton and Hong Kong, and I'm twenty-two years old and if I don't go soon I never will. There must be other kinds of people in the world, people whose lives aren't entirely given up to business and backbiting.'

Or brothels and opium.

It was with overwhelming relief that she grasped an opportunity to be free of her shackles, if only for a day.

Macmillan and Venturi's steam traders, the *Meall* and *Corran*, were captained by two Chinese brothers, Lao and Li Chang, whom Sophie had met once or twice down at the wharves when she had been with her father.

She remembered them particularly, because except for their dress neither of them looked the least bit like a sailor. Lao, the taller and elder, wore round, steel-rimmed spectacles that, in conjunction with brows angling downwards from two deep vertical creases above the bridge of his nose, made him look more like a worried professor. But her father had told her that his looks were misleading, that, far from being serious and responsible, he was more likely to be found diving head first into some mad enterprise or picking a quarrel just for the pleasure of it. The younger brother, Li, short, plump and vulnerable-looking, was the careful one, especially when it came to his own comfort. 'Delightful chap,' Archie had said, 'and diabolically cunning. They make a good pair.'

And now, said Gino Venturi, Li was to be married and would consider his unhumble self and bride deeply honoured by the presence of his employers.

'Richard's away,' Sophie said.

'I know.'

'Me? I *couldn't*! An Englishwoman going to a native wedding! What would people think?'

'Scotswoman. Anyway, do you care?'

With astonishment, she heard herself saying, 'No.' And then, after a moment, 'No! I *damned* well don't!'

Gino Venturi threw back his head and laughed.

20

Predictably, Ah Foon nearly had a fit, disapproving heartily of the whole idea and pointing out that if anyone recognised Sophie as a European it would be a case of *hong dong yi shi*. There was no way of putting this into pidgin and no need to; it had been a familiar phrase since Sophie's childhood, meaning that, if she didn't behave herself, the fat would be in the fire. If Sophie went at all, Ah Foon insisted, she would go in Chinese clothes and then perhaps the 'plopa missees' wouldn't find out.

All the more fun, Sophie thought.

Scolding endlessly, Ah Foon saw her properly dressed in an embroidered Chinese tunic and trousers of dark plum brown that helped to smother the blue of her eyes, and Sophie herself drew thin kohl lines round her lids to alter their shape. She had been going around for days practising keeping them half closed. Her hair was in a bun at the back of her neck and she was wearing very blunt, round-toed slippers that, except on close inspection, hinted at bound feet. Since she had sat out, hatless, in the garden for a week, her complexion had taken on a golden tone that was reasonably convincing, even if she didn't think she liked it much. She didn't propose to open her mouth all day.

She wouldn't have to, because Ah Foon was going with her, clad in her best off-duty dress of flowered turquoise green tunic over black satin trousers. Sophie hoped that the liberated Ah Foon wasn't going to be too superior towards Li's poor little bride, who was so lacking in independence that she was content, like the great majority of ordinary Chinese women, to marry the young man her parents and the marriage diviner had chosen for her.

It would have been hard to live in Hong Kong without running the whole gamut of Chinese processions – the procession being something to which the Chinese were notoriously addicted – and Sophie had often thought what fun it would be to take part in one. The shouting and gong beating, the wailing of horns and clanging of cymbals, although designed to frighten off evil spirits, managed to sound unremittingly cheerful, and the scarlet banners and tasselled lanterns that were supposed to be equally alarming were redolent only of gaiety and good humour.

The covered sedan chair that went, under riotous escort and in a storm of rice and firecrackers, to collect Li's bride from her parents' home was the most blinding thing Sophie had ever seen, all scarlet lacquer and silver, with a fringed scarlet cover over the arched roof and a second cover that looked like nothing so much as a dyed fishing net. Perched on top was a fat, flower-decorated finial, and the doors and panels that filled the window frames were marvels of ivory, painted flowers and peacocks. The bride shared the sedan only with some burning joss sticks. She had to be completely closed in during her journey to the groom's house, in case she came within sight of anyone or anything that might harm her – which meant almost anything from cats and dogs to a wedding procession going in the opposite direction. Sophie hoped the bride would be all right. There had been a sad case recently where the journey had been long and the poor bride had been found dead of suffocation at the end of it.

The groom's home was in an area where Westerners seldom ventured, and as the procession began to wend its way through the narrow, densely packed, steeply pitched streets, Ah Foon hissed at Sophie, 'Eyes front' – just like some drill sergeant on the parade ground. Once, Sophie might have wondered why. Now, she knew that many of the leaf-walled mat sheds were not just homes where respectable Chinese laid down their heads at night, but brothels and gambling houses and opium dens.

She was aware, suddenly, of an intense curiosity about them, a desire to march inside and see what it could possibly be that drew her husband to them in his dedicated progress towards destruction. In which of these noisy, dirty, smelly, rat-infested haunts might he have been today, had he not been safely and healthily at sea? Sophie had no idea whether his fellow officers knew of his vices; it was hard to believe that they didn't, but he was very good at covering up.

It wasn't far to Tai Ping Shan Street, which was draped throughout with scarlet banners instead of the washing which usually hung from the houses like strings of blue bunting. Elder brother Lao Chang was standing worriedly on the threshold in his rôle as head of the family, and Gino Venturi was lounging amiably against a nearby pillar. Sophie felt inordinately pleased with herself when his eyes passed over her without recognition.

Then the bride descended alive and safe from her chair, a vision in embroidered black silk tunic, scarlet skirt and phoenix coronet, and stepped formally over the charcoal stove on the threshold, whereupon Li, his plump features solemn, hit her lightly over the head three times with a closed fan and raised her veil.

Sophie, with a gasp of laughter, revised her preconceptions about placid Chinese brides, because the girl's pretty, powdered face showed clearly that Li had hit her a good deal harder than he should have done, and that he was going to hear about it later.

The rituals that followed ended with the bride and groom being ceremonially escorted into their bedchamber, after which the guests broke up into groups to partake of tea and sugary confections. It was time, Sophie decided, to make her presence known. Sidling up to Gino Venturi, she said childishly, 'Boo!' though it didn't quite come out like that, because the confections were so excruciatingly sweet that she felt as if her teeth had been glued together with honey.

'*Madonna mia!*' It was a moment before his eyes lit up.

She couldn't read anything in his face other than the usual faint derision, and it annoyed her. He was just like Rainer Blake, never showing anything other than what he wanted to show. Though perhaps she was being unfair to Blake, who had become much more approachable lately.

'I make an excellent Chinese lady, don't I?' she demanded.

'Mmmm. A little too tall, perhaps, but otherwise – er – remarkable as long as you keep your eyes downcast.'

She said, 'I feel I ought to thank Mr Li for inviting me.'

'My dear girl, not *quite* the best moment! Why don't you make do with Lao.'

To Sophie's surprise, Mr Lao was deep in conversation with Ah Foon. They were talking low-voiced Cantonese, their voices rattling back and forth in what sounded like question and answer, command and acknowledgement, argument and counterargument. Infuriatingly, Gino Venturi joined in after a moment or two. It had never occurred to Sophie that he spoke anything beyond pidgin.

'And what,' she asked when they had finished, 'was that all about?'

Gino said indulgently, 'Ah Foon and the Changs have an acquaintance in common.'

'You, too?'

'Me, too. But let me introduce you. Lao doesn't appear to have recognised you yet.'

Lao declared himself, his roof, his brother, and his ancestors deeply honoured, etcetera, etcetera.

Surveying the guilty trio doubtfully, Sophie concluded that her suspiciousness was unjustified. Nothing could have been more innocent than the looks they returned to her. So she smiled and asked some intelligent questions about the rôle of the official matchmaker, and the diviner, and what remained of the ceremonial.

And then it was time to go home.

21

A few days later, Dr Dods confirmed her private fears. She was pregnant.

'Don't,' he said, 'allow your husband to impose his desires on you until you're delivered of the child, do you understand? It is not to be recommended for either mother or baby.'

She told Richard she was going to have a baby, and his pale blue eyes went blank for a moment and then brightened until they were almost luminescent. She could still see how striking he was, with his magnificent body and blond hair, his tanned long-boned face with the high brow and strong, crooked nose, the mouth that was always twisted a little as if in wry self-congratulation.

Before he could speak she hurried on because, whatever fatherly delight he was going to express, she didn't think she could bear to hear it. 'And Dr Dods says we mustn't – make love again until the baby is born, because it's dangerous.'

He did speak, then. 'Old wives' tales!' he said with a contemptuous laugh.

It was too much. After all the weeks of keeping silence, she burst out at him at last, screamed at him like a harridan, threw at him every ornament, every piece of china, every piece of glass she could lay her hands on, her voice almost incoherent through the wild tears that racked her. If she had had a knife, she would have killed him.

'. . . evil, depraved, vicious, corrupt . . .'

She had never let him suspect that she knew his secrets, because when speech could do nothing to mend things it seemed more civilised to keep silent. But now it all poured out in an hysterical torrent that Richard barely understood at first, because the words she used were the genteel euphemisms that were all she knew for the realities that threatened her and the baby she so much feared for.

'. . . filthy . . . disgusting . . . disease . . . decay . . . hate you . . . loathe you . . .'

He stood, at first, and laughed. But after a while he became impatient and went to her and slammed the back of his hand across her face with a calculated violence that she thought at first had broken her jaw.

'Bitch!' he said.

Then he walked out of the room.

22

She retired into herself after that, and let the future look after itself.

Soon, she became preoccupied with the changes in herself; with watching her body soften and break and stretch; with surviving the sleepless nights, when she had to remember to lie on each side in turn, and the aching days constricted by the foot-wide belt Ah Foon insisted she wear to support the child.

As she mindlessly swallowed the chicken, pigeon and duck broths that Fan Shu made for her, she became dazed and obsessed. She dreaded people, but needed them and couldn't reach them because they kept receding from her. When Dolly Berry proudly brought her own new baby on a visit, it was as if they were on the other side of a wide river. Ah Foon seemed miles away, Richard hundreds of miles, and Rainer Blake, the one person to whom she so desperately wanted to stretch out her arms for safety and shelter, thousands.

Ah Foon brought her messages from him once or twice, but she could find no meaning in their careful phrasing.

Sophie knew it was wrong to feel as she did, that she should be sleek with contentment, that it was a natural process for women to bear children. But all that happened was that she remembered her own four dead little brothers and sisters, and her mother laid out lifeless with the last of them in her arms. Her mother, whom she had barely known, and her adored father who had taken his pleasure where he found it in his own big, warm, genial, unthinking way.

The world went past like a shadow play while she leafed through every memory she had of her parents, trying to understand them.

After a while, friends like Dolly Berry and Robina Gibbings began talking about decorating the nursery, somewhere pretty for the child when it came. Had she settled on a month nurse? Mrs Fox was very reliable, Dolly said. And a wet nurse? Mrs Irvin should be available at about the right time.

Every superstitious instinct Sophie had was against preparing for her child's birth, and she resisted for as long as she could, but in the end people began wondering why, and she had to give in.

In the meantime, she was not aware – although Rainer Blake, or indeed, Gino Venturi, or even the Chang brothers could have told her – that Richard was indulging himself in a comprehensive tour of Hong Kong's multitude of opium dens and brothels, including the ones in China town, where the colony's rulers had long ago given up even trying to enforce medical inspection and control.

CHAPTER FOURTEEN

❦

I

'Macdonalds, Macleans, Macdougalls, yes – oh, and a Macnaughten! No Macmillans, though. Not in India. I did come across one in China, during the *Arrow* war. What was his first name, now?'

Captain Kennedy cudgelled his brains while Colin Campbell's other guests, mainly youthful, jollied him along.

'Come on, Kennedy! You'll be forgetting your signalling code, next. How about John?'

'Or William.'

'Alastair.'

'Hamish.'

'Zebediah.'

'Angus.'

Rachel sat and smiled as if it were no more than the game the young men thought it was.

Captain Kennedy had been bemoaning his imminent return to duty. 'The West Indies station this time. Well, it'll make a change from the Channel Squadron. Join the Navy and see the world!' They had already heard about his experiences in the Crimea, and at Canton at the beginning of the *Arrow* war, in India during the Mutiny and China during the siege of Peking.

Rachel had stopped listening when the story had moved away from India, but afterwards she had said casually, 'I remember hearing that the East is littered with homesick Highlanders. Did you come across many from this part of the world?' She couldn't, now, think why she had asked, because she didn't want to know the answer.

The captain snapped his fingers impatiently. 'I'm sure it began with a J.'

'James.'

'John.'

'Joseph.'

'Jacob.'

'Jarvey.'

'Jonathan.'

'I've got it,' he said. 'It was Archie.'

He beamed at his friends and then, turning to Rachel, went on, 'A fellow of about forty, he was, as I remember. He had hair much the colour of yours – what I could see of it through the smoke and soot! It was when the Chinese set fire to the factories at Canton, you see. We took him off from the shore in our pinnace, him and his little girl. A real pet, she was, the most adorable child. She must have been about seven or eight, I suppose. Her name was Sophie. D'you think they might be relations of yours?'

Decisively, without even stopping to think, Rachel said, 'No. No relation,' and was grateful when the conversation took another turn with the irrepressible Mr Parkes exclaiming, 'Oh, trust you, Kennedy! Can't remember a *fellow's* name for love or money, but when it comes to a *lady* . . .'

2

'No,' Rachel told herself. Archie Macmillan – Juran's Archie Macmillan – couldn't possibly still have been alive in 1856, when he had been 'presumed dead' in 1853. It wasn't the same man. It would be stretching coincidence too far. There must be dozens, hundreds of Archibald Macmillans scattered across the world. The Scots were inveterate travellers.

But the age was right.

She tried again. Even if it *was* her father's brother, what did it matter? She herself had inherited Juran perfectly legally. Uncle Archie simply didn't enter into it.

Except that the claims of a legitimated child were always open to challenge by those favoured souls who had been legitimate since the day of their birth.

Every night for almost a week she found herself waking in darkness, tossing and turning, arguing with herself, knowing she couldn't leave it dangling. She had to find out. She had to find out, without giving the game away. She had to find out, without – dear heaven! – Gresham also finding out. What a godsend Archie would be to him! And Sophie, too, the 'real pet', the 'adorable child' who must be twenty-two or twenty-three now, the same age as Rachel herself.

When Colin Campbell's house party finally left, she travelled with them in the yacht as far as Glasgow and then took a train to Edinburgh. All the way, over and over until her head was splitting, the wheels beat out their rhythm in her ears – Archie and *Soph*ie, Archie and *Soph*ie, Archie and *Soph*ie. Why couldn't the girl just be a plain Jane, or Mary or Margaret?

As she made her way to David Napier's office, the wind howled mournfully, So-oh-oh-oh-phie, So-oh-oh-oh-phie.

Blind as on her previous visit to the architectural splendours of Princes Street, the handsome gardens, the looming castle on its rock, Rachel clutched the sealskin shoulder cape tightly round her throat and wondered why the wind should have so much more of a cutting edge here than it did in the west.

'You're frozen, Miss Rachel!' exclaimed David Napier, taking her hand between his two huge paws. 'What you need is a glass of sherry.'

She looked round his office and promptly sneezed, though she thought afterwards that it was a reaction more to the sight of the dust than the dust itself, which layered everything from the hundreds of books, many of them on the edge of disintegration, to the piled-up bundles of papers that took up two thirds of the remaining space. The windows looked as if they hadn't been cleaned since she had been here last, more than two years before.

She said, 'I take it you don't have many small children among your visitors?'

'The last one was about three years ago. When he left, the panes were so covered with finger drawings of apples and houses that we had to get a cleaner in. After that I made a rule, no infants. It's the coal smoke from the Old Town up there that does it; it tends to drop into the valley and you just have to resign yourself to it. You can tell why the place is called Auld Reekie.'

She explained why she had come, and he said, 'Oh, dearie me! Dearie, dearie me!'

'What I *do not* understand is why you've never mentioned Archie before. You must have known about him. Everyone else seems to.'

'Well, he hadn't been heard of since the early 30s, and I didn't see any need to worry you.'

Her lips tightened. 'Really? I would be grateful in future if you would leave it to me to decide what I should and shouldn't worry about.'

With regret, David Napier noted that Miss Rachel had learned to give orders. But he too had learned something, which was not to look abashed even when he felt it. He met her eyes squarely. 'As you wish. I take it, by the way, that you have heard no more from Gresham?'

'Nothing.'

'Mmmm. I wonder what he's hatching now.'

'Nothing,' she said again. 'There's nothing he *can* hatch. But I'd feel safer knowing where I am in the case of Uncle Archie.'

'Yes, well, as I see it, and assuming that the fellow in Canton is or was the right man, the question is not just whether he's alive or dead but, if he's dead, *when* he died.'

'Why?'

David Napier developed an intense interest in his laced fingers. Napier No. 1 in the partnership of Napier, Napier, Nelson and Napier had been regrettably prone to take his clients' instructions very much more literally than he himself, Napier No. 3, thought wise. His grandfather's view, in fact, had been that, if he kept everybody happy, the situation would probably never arise where debatable points of law actually had to be put to the test. As a result, when old Hector Macmillan had insisted on having his Will phrased as he wanted it phrased, Grandfather Napier had let him get away with it.

Napier No. 3 took a deep breath and raised his gooseberry-green eyes. 'Old Hector Macmillan,' he said, 'left a Will in which he said he presumed Mr Archie to be dead and was therefore bequeathing Juran to Mr Daniel.'

'Yes.'

'Unfortunately, there was a clear implication in this that the estate would have gone to Archie if he had been alive. Archie first, Daniel second. If Archie had turned up again during your father's lifetime, the courts would almost certainly have given him possession of the estate. You follow me?'

'Just about,' she said with more than a trace of sarcasm.

'Now, then . . . The two normal routes of bequest are through eldest sons of eldest sons of eldest sons. Failing sons, or daughters if the worst comes to the worst . . .'

'Thank you.'

'. . . an estate would go to the collaterals, in other words full brothers of the deceased. If Archie had died before your father, leaving only a daughter, the courts would probably have upheld the Will and confirmed Daniel in possession. Besides being the surviving brother, he had a son himself to follow on. Yes?'

'Yes.'

Mr Napier, having sounded quite decisive up to that point, began floundering. 'But if it turns out that Archie outlived Daniel . . . ummm . . . If he were still alive today we might find ourselves in serious difficulties. He'd have a good claim, when you take Miss Belinda's intestacy into account and you being only legitimated, rather than legitimate. In that situation I wouldn't be very sanguine, really.'

'You're not being very helpful, either,' Rachel told him roundly. 'And there's one thing clear to me. If old Hector's lawyers had been doing their job properly, we would have had none of these problems.'

'Yes, well, there is that. But old gentlemen can be very stubborn, you know.'

'You surprise me. What about the third possibility? That Archie did survive my father but has died since?'

'I think – only think, mind you – that the estate would be regarded as having reverted to Archie, rather as if Daniel had never existed. So Archie's heirs would have entitlement.'

The chill of the outdoors was still in her bones. That, she told herself, was the only reason why she was shivering. Rising, she went over to the black grate with its struggling fire and wiggled her fingers in front of it.

'What you're saying is that, if Archie died before my father, I *might* be entitled to inherit. But if he died after my father, I might *not*.'

'Well – er – I – it's complicated.'

'So I gather.'

'I would have to do some case research.'

'Then please do!' She sighed. 'Though I must say, I see no point whatever in having somebody "presumed dead" if they can come strolling back after goodness knows how many years and have all their legal rights restored to them!'

'It's not quite like that. I mean, it's different if the courts do the presuming, rather than just some old gentleman. The courts always err on the generous side – there was one case when they insisted on presuming someone still alive eighty years after he disappeared. Scots law does overdo things a bit, there. It needs reviewing. The English have more sensible limitations.'

With asperity, Rachel said, 'Sense does not appear to me to be something with which the law has any acquaintance at all.'

4

She snatched an hour to look at the shops on Princes Street but the prices were shocking. Three guineas for a dress length of Japanese silk, a shilling for a pair of stockings. She hadn't seen so many shops since she was a child in Soho, when a penny had been as unaffordable as three guineas now. But at least, now, she could walk inside and look, instead of being chased away by large men in braided coats.

There was the loveliest design for a ball dress in myrtle green foulard, with a low square neck, bows on the shoulders and an unusual skirt with the fabric swept up at the back into something that was more like a pile of folds than a bustle. Rachel gazed at it for a long time, but there was no sense in coveting it. Quite apart from the fact that it needed someone tall to wear it, she couldn't imagine ever putting it on at Juran, where bare shoulders were an invitation to pneumonia. It took two months of heatwave before the eight-foot-thick walls soaked in enough warmth to raise the temperature indoors to anything even approaching tolerable. Rachel's evening gowns, such as they were, all had high necks and long sleeves. It would have been nice, she thought, just occasionally to burst out of her cocoon and wear something really gorgeous and extravagant, but there was no sense in wishing.

She found a genteel boarding house for the night, and reached home again late the following evening, feeling as if she had been all the way to the source of the Amazon by public transport, and grateful for the silence after all the noise and bustle.

But it was a silence filled with voices.

'The first thing to find out is whether it was the right Archie in Canton . . . hair much the colour of yours . . . the most adorable child . . . if he'd dead, the courts might feel they had to make a choice between you and Miss Sophie . . . fire . . . the Chinese . . . no, a law firm like Napier, Napier isn't equipped to search for people on the other side of the world . . .'

How queer, she thought, to be the unknown Sophie, to be born and grow up as a foreigner in an alien land among people who worshipped heathen gods and burned everything down about your ears if you annoyed them.

Before Rainer Blake had entered Rachel's life, all she had known about China was what she had read in *Peter Parley's Annual*, but afterwards she had scoured the shelves of Juran's book room in search of something more. There had been nothing except a picture book entitled *Manners and Customs of the Chinese*, which hadn't had much useful to say. Since then, although in preparation for Blake's return she had read and reread every book on every topic that seemed likely to interest a man with his kind of mind, she had never gone back to *Manners and Customs of the Chinese*. She did so now.

5

'I have never been more mystified,' she told Hogg next day. 'Nothing but funny little men with pigtails, blue frocks and quaint habits. They eat birds' nests and spend half their time lying on couches with singsong girls, smoking opium. The book doesn't say what singsong girls are, but they don't sound very respectable to me. Frankly, even if the people in the pictures looked less like dolls and more like humans, I still don't think I would like them!'

Hogg said ruminatively, 'I saw a Chinaman once.'

'Really?'

'In '51, when the queen opened the Great Exhibition. He was in among the foreign diplomats queueing up to shake her hand and everyone thought he was an emissary from the Emperor of China. The queen was fair bowled over. Then it turned out he was a common sailor off an East Indiaman, all dressed up in his Sunday best. Got in the queue by mistake. True!'

She smiled, not really listening. At least, now that Gresham had spread the truth about her background all over the countryside, she was able to talk more freely to Hogg, who had constituted himself her unofficial confessor and adviser. His advice wasn't always good, but it was nearly always stimulating. It had been he who, in his own indirect way, had suggested the ultimate goal for her endeavours. Her mind was now made up that, when the contract with Mr Campbell ran out, she was going to transform Juran into a commercial stalking estate – open as a hotel might be, and at exorbitant prices, to any seasonal sporting party that was prepared to pay. Bankers, brewers and Philip Roy's 'damned Midland manufacturers' included.

'I keep wondering what she's like. Sophie, I mean. Thin, fat, tall, short? Soft-voiced or loud? Dark or fair? Well dressed or a frump? A bluestocking? A flirt?'

'Och, that's the least of your worries. Me, I'd be wondering why she and her pa are lying low. Have they not given ye even a hint of their existence?'

'None. I don't understand it.'

He shrugged his skinny shoulders. 'Maybe they like China. Maybe they're not interested in Juran.'

'I wish I could think so, but it wouldn't really solve anything. I'm tired of the uncertainty. I have to find out about them without giving the game away, and I don't know how.'

Hogg took the pipe out of his mouth and peered into its disgusting bowl. 'D'ye not think there'd be some kind of list – official, I mean – of folk who make their bawbees in the China trade?'

'Well, there could be, but how on earth would I get hold of it? Or even find out what it's called?'

'Maybe Mr Campbell could help.'

She was sure Mr Campbell could, but her mind went blank when she tried to think how to approach him. It wasn't only that she had so firmly denied, in his hearing, the possibility of a relationship with Captain Kennedy's friend of Canton. She was terrified that he might cancel their rental agreement if she gave him reason to suspect that she hadn't been entitled to make it; he was a banker, after all. And losing the rental would be an unmitigated disaster.

For a moment, it all seemed beyond her. 'I just don't *believe* this!' she exploded. 'You would have thought all that fuss about legitimation and inheritance would have been enough to use up my entire allotment of trouble and strife for a lifetime. And now I find myself saddled with a completely different set of complications to worry about!'

6

In the end, she resigned herself to writing to Colin Campbell, phrasing her letter with the greatest care, grateful not to have his quizzical eyes upon her as she wove her evasions into an apparently frank and logical whole.

To her astonishment, she wrote, after Captain Kennedy's mention of an Archibald Macmillan in Canton, she had discovered – by pure chance – that there had been an Archibald in her own family, who had gone to India many years ago and had never been heard of again. No doubt the name was coincidence, but her sense of family duty prevented her from letting the matter lie. Her lawyer being unable to assist with enquiries, it had occurred to her to turn to Mr Campbell, knowing that he had business associations in the East. Would it put him to too great an inconvenience to ask Mr Blake (for example) whether he knew of an Archibald Macmillan? Rachel realised that 'the East' was a very large area, but perhaps the British community was quite small. . . ?

Mr Campbell wrote back promptly, professing himself delighted to help Miss Macmillan in any way possible, but warning her not to be too optimistic.

There was no hint in the letter of the acute unease of Mr Campbell's conscience. Week after week, month after month, the conviction had been growing in him that Rachel Macmillan was the one woman in the world he wanted for his wife, and to have to lie to her was intolerable. But because of Blake's involvement, he had no option other than to withhold from her even the scanty information he possessed. Colin couldn't remember being deeply angry more than once or twice in his life, but every time he thought of the deal Blake had so carelessly set up, he could feel his blood beginning to rise.

7

A few weeks later, Rachel was sitting patiently on a wooden stool outside Willie Thompson's cottage at the end of the village, her stockinged foot extended while he measured her for a new pair of boots. Since the ground was nearly always wet in the glens, footwear didn't last long, but although the villagers usually went sensibly barefoot the gentry were expected to keep up appearances.

Insofar as it was possible, Willie's foot measuring department had been designed to satisfy the requirements of propriety as well as practicality and was therefore situated on a flagged area outside his door and partially embowered by whin bushes that, while ensuring that shoemaker and customer had no unseemly privacy, effectively guarded against any inadvertent public display of leg or ankle.

Willie said, 'The other foot, now. I hear Mr Horace has come to stay?'

Rachel wriggled her shoulders slightly, brushing off a beetle that had dropped on the back of her neck from the heather thatch above. 'No. I'm not expecting any more guests until next month.'

She hadn't seen Horace for quite a while and supposed he must still be at Oxford, driving his tutors demented with his God-given certainty that he knew better than they did.

'Maybe,' said the shoemaker. 'Maybe.'

A shadow fell across her extended foot. 'Oh, there you are, Rachel!' said Horace. 'They told me at the castle you were down here somewhere.'

Rachel glared at Willie Thompson. Talk about jungle drums! One day she was going to find out, if it was the last thing she did, how the villagers always knew what was going on at the castle before she did.

Without perceptible cordiality, she said, 'Goodness gracious! Horace! And when did *you* arrive?'

'Half an hour ago. I say! You've been changing things since I was here last. We'll have to talk about that. There's a lot of things I want to talk to you about. That's why I've come.'

8

'I mean, what's that fencing I saw down by the river?'

It was always distracting to be in company with Horace when he was trying to walk and talk at the same time, since all his attention was occupied by what he was saying and he had none left over to direct the disposition of his limbs. Instead of putting one foot in front of the other in a normal, civilised fashion, he progressed sideways, his lanky figure twisted towards his hearer, in a series of hops and skips interspersed with long, awkward strides. He was like a pair of scissors whose blades didn't quite meet. Rachel could never concentrate on what he was saying because she was always expecting him to trip over something and fall flat on his face. Unfortunately, he never did.

'The ground's all dug up,' he complained, 'as if you were going to plant something!'

'How clever of you to notice. And not only *going* to plant, but *have planted*. Oats and barley. Food. It's awfully useful. You can eat it. Horace, do look where you're going!'

'I know what oats and barley are. But you don't have to grow them. Why can't you just buy them, like other people? They're not natural.'

Mellifluously, she said, 'Not natural? But Horace, surely food plants must be the most natural things on earth. Don't you remember? God said, "Behold, I have given you every plant yielding seed which is upon the face of all the earth; you shall have them for food".'

'Well, I was actually talking about not being natural to the

327

landscape, but they're not natural in your sense, either, at least not the plants we grow nowadays. I mean, look at Darwin!'

Rachel looked but was not enlightened. 'Who?'

'You can't not know about *The Origin of Species* or his new one on *The Descent of Man*!'

'Yes, I can. Horace, the newspapers take days to get here and I seldom have time to read them anyway. You know that.'

'You mean you haven't heard of Nägeli's researches, either? Or Mendel's?'

'No, and let me tell you here and now that I don't want to.'

Horace pushed the spectacles agitatedly back on his nose. 'But you have to. It's essential.'

'Essential to what?'

'Essential to the Nature Park,' he said, as if she were being wilfully obtuse. 'The seeds you've planted are no good, you see. They're improved strains. They've been tinkered with by man. If you're having a Nature Park you have to leave everything to its own devices, to develop as God intended. I should have thought that was obvious.'

With laudable calm, she said, 'Oh, it is. I would be deeply ashamed of myself if I *were* having a Nature Park. But – I – am – not!'

It was like talking to a brick wall. 'No, but I must tell you about the Doane Washburn expedition to Yellowstone. That's in Montana, in America, you know, and the local people there have suggested a plan to make it a *national* park. Just imagine if . . .'

Rachel had always thought that Horace had simply inherited his father's capacity for ignoring what he didn't wish to know. Now she found herself wondering if he even took it in at all. She considered saying, 'Did you hear me, Horace?' and then decided not to bother, because arguing with Horace was one of the least productive occupations imaginable. The only thing he was consistent about was sticking to his guns; when it came to logic he didn't know the meaning of the word. Indeed, trying to lead him through a reasoned argument was like having a wet eel by the tail.

By the end of the evening, as usual, she had become remarkably tired of his views on Nature and even more tired of his views on field sports, which interfered, he claimed, with the purity and perfection of God's creation.

'Perfection? Well, you may think it perfect for deer in their dozens to waste away from hunger because there are too many of them for the food supply. But if you had ever, as I have, seen a starving hind having

328

her eyes pecked out by hoodie crows, and too weak to fight them, you might feel differently.'

'No, I wouldn't. It's *natural*, you see.'

'Natural, fiddlesticks! I don't see how you can possibly reconcile your high moral views about Christian charity and mercy with support for a Nature that is every bit as red in tooth and claw as Mr Tennyson says.'

'Well, I'm sorry for the deer, of course, but . . .'

'But you're not prepared to help them. You're not prepared to have the numbers culled, quickly and cleanly, to avoid unnecessary suffering?'

Typically, he evaded the point. 'I don't remember my father or any other of Juran's guests being worried by unnecessary suffering. All they were interested in was bagging a ten pointer so that they could hang the head on the wall!'

'I *quite* accept that. But what you're saying is that, just because some people don't have the right motives, the whole system is vitiated.'

It occurred to her suddenly that Horace had no idea what winter could be like in the Highland hills. He had always been away at school or university during the worst of the year.

Conditions weren't really bad yet, but they would be. She said, 'I think you'd better come up with me into the hills tomorrow.'

9

Tom Tanner was taking Jimsy and two of the ponies up to Carn Dearg, with a target of four hinds, so Rachel and Horace went to Carn Beg.

Horace knew so little about the practice, as distinct from the morality of stalking that he didn't question the pony with the deer saddle, or the presence of Angus the ghillie, whom Rachel left to wait for them at what in better mapped territory would have been a convenient crossroads. He even accepted, though not without argument, that a rifle might be necessary in case they found an injured animal that needed to be put out of its agony.

It was the most miserable kind of day, wet, cold and dismal, but Horace minded less than Rachel. Indeed, he was garrulously interested as they trudged uphill along narrow tracks whose muddy and uneven surfaces, studded with projections of rock like jagged cobbles, were swiftly turning into pouring rills. Despite the roaring gusts of wind at the lower levels, it was comparatively still on the high tops to the east, where the clouds were sitting like dirty cotton waste, their edges teasing down into motionless grey veils over the slopes. In no time at all, Rachel and Horace were wet through.

Horace removed the knitted woollen toorie he was wearing, wrung about half a pint of water out of it, and said, 'This is spiffing! It's just what I imagine the world was like at the Creation. Yes, I look forward to the task of keeping it this way.'

'Oh, do you? And what makes you think you'll have the chance?' Her mind was on the deer and where they were most likely to be found in these conditions, and she spoke without thinking.

'Well, I know we haven't talked about it yet, and I'd like to see how we get on in bed first – before we marry, I mean – but I don't see any problem there.'

She knew her mouth must be open because the rain was getting into it.

'*Horace*! I haven't the slightest intention of marrying you, and as for going to bed with you – it's an outrageous suggestion!'

'It wouldn't be the first time, though, would it?' he asked, just as if it was a perfectly normal, respectable subject for conversation. 'I'm dashed sure something happened at that Hallowe'en party a few years ago. I remember meeting you on the stairs, and it wasn't hard to put two and two together about what you'd been up to. You were all flushed and excited. I can't say I liked it – in fact I thought it was dashed immoral, and still do – but I'm prepared to make allowances. I mean, I'm fond of you. You've always reminded me a bit of my mother – it's your smile, I suppose.'

And that, she thought grimly, would teach her to go around borrowing other people's smiles. She couldn't think of a thing to say, except, 'Shhhh. We'll disturb the deer if we go on talking like this. If you must talk, keep your voice right down. I'm not sure how near we may be.'

'All right.' He had always been an obliging young man. 'It's just that, if you married me, Juran would be mine without any more fuss and it would save my father the trouble of going on looking for your mother's old lovers.'

Rachel gave her head a brief shake to clear it of the blank incomprehension that appeared to have seeped into it. 'Going on looking for *what*?'

'Well, if he could find other people who slept with her as well as

330

Uncle Daniel, it would be as good as proof that the document stating you weren't Uncle Daniel's daughter was the true one. I say, was that something moving in the mist there?'

'Get down!'

They were on a slope of peat bog that had been frozen hard a few nights before and now carried a slick of water over thin, crackling, breaking ice. As they lay there, motionless, the discomfort became so acute that it verged on the sublime, like some kind of soul-shriving penance. Rachel could feel the water entering at the neck of her heavy tweed coat and trickling intricately down the whole length of her until it finished up in her boots.

Everything around them was thunderous with sound, furious with the roar of falling water. On the edge of the mist, shapes formed and reformed, nebulous, deceiving, fantastical. After a while, one of them congealed into the reality of an old beldame of a hind, ears pricked and nose twitching inquisitively. But she was up wind of them and couldn't pick out their grey and peat-stained forms from the ground to which they were plastered. After a minute she tossed her head and trotted off back into the mist.

'You cannot possibly mean,' Rachel hissed, 'that your father is hoping to find someone who slept with my mother twenty-five years ago? I've never heard anything so ridiculous.'

'People keep diaries, you know. I say, I feel like a liquefying icicle, don't you?' His chin was buried in the peat and he was staring into the mist.

'Shhhhh.' Instinct told her there were more beasts nearby. Slowly and carefully, she slid her gun into position and took aim at where the old beldame had appeared, shifting partly on to her left side and steadying herself on the point of her elbow.

Her instinct was correct. Soon there appeared another pair of pricked ears, and this time they belonged to a weakly-looking hind, her coat thin, red and harsh, who certainly wouldn't survive the winter.

Rachel's finger was just tightening on the trigger when Horace turned his head and saw what she was about. Instantly, he lunged out to knock the gun from her grasp, and his hand struck the barrel close to the stock.

It swivelled in a ninety-degree arc as it went off.

After a moment, Horace said, 'Uhhhh!' staring disbelievingly at the toorie which had been swept off his head and was lying in the mud a few feet away. The pompom, which had taken the direct hit, remained attached only by a single strand of dirty purple wool.

Rachel, one hand to her shoulder, numb from the swing of the stock, was speechless at first. Afterwards, she swallowed most of what she would have liked to say and confined herself to, 'You fool. You *fool*. Have you no sense at all?'

Horace's eyes were blinking furiously and his face was chalk white under the smears of peat. 'I didn't think.'

'You never do.' An almost forgotten memory came back to her of the day of the eagle's nest, years before, when William might have been killed. 'It's time you learned,' she said. 'Next time might be too late.'

There was another, more immediate thought in her mind. If the gun had swung just another inch, she might have found herself accused of murder.

Again.

10

Despite being entirely the wrong shape for it, Horace was the original bouncing ball. Although he went to some pains to point out that guns were dangerous things, and that if Rachel had not been carrying one his life would not have been put in danger, he was sufficiently recovered after a bath and an admirable dinner to feel able to congratulate her on the excellence of her housekeeping and especially of her cooking.

Since he had consumed a redoubtable quantity of venison à la Rob Roy, she had a severe struggle with herself. But curiosity as to how he would justify guzzling the meat of an animal whose killing he deplored was defeated in the end by simple prudence and the fear of starting him off on the road to vegetarianism – a dead end road in the Highlands, where even eggs and milk were restricted seasonal delights, and all else a culinary nightmare of oats, barley and kail.

'Since I'll be looking after the Nature Park when we're married,' Horace went on, 'you'll be able to spend more time in the kitchen. And, of course, there'll be the children, too.'

Rachel closed her eyes and opened them again. 'Horace . . .'

'Well, I know you haven't said yes, yet . . .'

'You noticed!'

'. . . but it's the only sensible answer. *You* won't have to give up Juran, and *I'll* be able to get on with setting the place right, the way it ought to be.'

She fixed an earnest gaze on him. 'But Horace, you haven't said you love me!'

'Uh . . .'

'Whereas I . . . Oh, Horace, I have been hiding my feelings for you all these years! My admiration for your intellect, your godliness, your dedication to what you believe to be right, your clear-eyed vision, your . . .'

She rose and went to stand close to him, her eyes on a level with his chin, her face a picture of maidenly modesty, her hands raised to give an embarrassed little tweak to his tie. 'My devotion to your *self*,' she whispered.

There was a moment's stupefied silence before Horace closed his mouth again, gulped, looked pleased, and then showed all the signs of being about to engulf her in a less than intellectual embrace.

'Oops!' said Rachel, and skipped smartly back.

She should have remembered that Horace had no sense of humour at all and was awake to every slight, real or imagined; ridiculing him was the worst insult she could have offered him. She should also have remembered that the concept of forgive and forget was entirely foreign to his nature.

But all that happened at the time was that he clamped his rather slack lips together and said, with an austerity that surprised her, 'That was a mistake, Rachel. I am not a man to be taken less than seriously. On my next visit, I will hope to see that you have mended your ways. In the meantime, on consideration, I am prepared to overlook your unbecoming levity.'

'Thank you! But please do *not* overlook the fact that I have not the remotest intention of marrying you!'

11

And, of course, there'll be the children, too.

Rachel, waving Horace goodbye two days later, pictured a string of miniature replicas cantering off behind him and was compelled to retire to her bedroom where she could laugh until she cried without the servants thinking she had gone mad.

But her thoughts slipped off at an unexpected tangent and her mirth soon faded.

She was twenty-three years old and knew nothing of love or marriage except dreams. So much of her energy in these last years had been concentrated on Juran, which was no more than earth, stone and mortar, however cherished and desired. Suddenly, passionately, she knew that she wanted more, much more. Until now, she had thought of Juran as belonging to her and, in time, to the man who was the other half of herself. Now, with newly opened eyes, she saw children there, too, children who would know none of the restrictions of her own early years but be free to laugh and play and run about as children should. Children who were hers. Children who were loved.

She would *not* let life pass her by.

But if everything was to be perfect some day, as she willed it, what she dared not do in the meantime was relax her efforts.

12

It was late in October when Colin Campbell presented himself at Juran with the information Rachel desired and dreaded.

'It appears,' he said, trying to sound cheerful and as if it was a matter of no great import, 'that our two Archibald Macmillans are one and the same, though I fear I'm not bringing you much in the way of detail. Blake was sending me some urgent documents, and no doubt he was in haste to catch the mailboat, so he didn't do more than tack a kind of codicil on the end. He says the Archibald Macmillan of Canton moved to Hong Kong some years ago. The place of his birth was Juran, in Argyllshire. And he died in – let me see – the summer of '69, leaving one daughter, Sophie, now Mrs Taverner, who is in the family way. And that's the sum of it.'

They were sitting on opposite sides of the fire in the Green Drawing Room, with the oil lamps glimmering softly. Colin couldn't see Rachel's face very clearly, but he thought she had lost colour and her pallor had the effect of emphasising the faint blue rings under her eyes, rings that hadn't been there when last they met. It angered him, whose only desire was to protect her, that she should have been worrying so. She was sitting, apparently relaxed, in one of the big chairs, her arms resting on the buttoned and padded hide, but there was a tiny monotonous sound which, when he identified it, proved to be the sound of a fingernail scratching back and forward, back and forward, on the leather.

He said, 'Is that what you wanted to know?' hoping she might confide in him. If she didn't, their conversation in the future was going to be as full as pitfalls as a honeycomb was full of holes. It was bad enough already, because she had no idea that he knew anything about herself or her family beyond what she had told him. Which wasn't much.

After a moment, she said, 'I'm surprised Mr Blake didn't mention them when he was here. Does he say whether he knows – knew – Mr Macmillan personally?'

And that was a nice wee pair of pitfalls for a start. 'He doesn't say, but it's likely, I'd guess, Hong Kong not being a large place. In business, though, you can be acquainted with a lot of folk without having any notion where they were born.'

'I suppose so. Macmillan's a common name, too. There would be no reason for him to make the connection.' Unless Archie had been one of the homesick Scots who littered the East. But no. Blake's turning up at Juran had been pure coincidence.

Prudently, Colin remained silent.

'Did he say whether Mrs Taverner had any other children?'

'No.'

Mrs Taverner. Sophie. Who in recent weeks had taken up residence in all Rachel's nightmares, a hateful spectre with changing features that melted into and out of the surrounding dark. Sometimes she bore a family resemblance to Belinda, a Belinda screaming, falling, rising again with blood and bones reassembled into an articulated skeleton under a crown of beech-leaf hair. Sometimes she was yellow skinned, slant eyed, inscrutable and malevolent, the personification of everything unpleasant Rachel had ever read about the heathen Chinese.

It – did – not – matter! David Napier had suggested that the courts might, if the circumstances arose, make a straight choice between Rachel and Sophie. *Well*, Rachel thought, *if the circumstances ever do arise, just let them try!*

Annoyingly, tears began rising to her eyes. She was weary of standing on her own feet and Colin Campbell was a very sympathetic person. She ought not to keep things to herself any longer.

'I'm sorry,' she said with a sniff. 'I'd better tell you all about it.'

It took the better part of an hour, because it seemed to her that, if she were confessing, she might as well confess everything, not just about Daniel and Archie, but about her own birth and ambivalent legal position, about her mother, and Belinda, and Lucian Gresham and all.

'And I don't know what to do about anything,' she said finally. 'When I was still guessing about Archie and Sophie – Mrs Taverner – I tried to think of all the possible ways of clarifying things. I even wondered whether it mightn't be sensible to write to Sophie. But I wouldn't know what to say, and even just by the act of writing I'd be forcing the issue, wouldn't I?'

'I'm afraid so.' Colin was relieved to have it out in the open. He had been finding it very trying, having to review every word he said before he said it.

She took a deep breath. 'It would be a bit like writing to you without actually *asking* whether you felt you had to withdraw from our contract.'

'What?' He was astounded. 'Why in the name of the wee man should I want to do that?'

'I might not be entitled to have entered into it.'

Colin Campbell's humorous face, with its slightly beaky nose and soft brown moustache, lightened. 'Guid sakes! It's well seen you didn't fight your way through all the whereases and whereuntos. I could back out if you were to leave Juran for ever or, God forbid, meet your death, but not otherwise. You've no need to worry your head about that.'

The firelight caught the slight moisture still on her cheeks as she smiled back at him. He was a *very* nice man. She said, 'Well, that's a relief.'

'Do you want my advice? Well, maybe not my advice, but my assessment of the situation! Bankers know more about the law than they sometimes wish they did.'

'Yes, please.' She meant it sincerely. 'I can't think of anyone else whose advice I'd trust as I would yours.'

He grimaced slightly. 'Aye, well, if that's true it sounds to me as if you could do with expanding your acquaintance. Anyway – whatever your Mr Napier says, I have no real doubt that Juran should have gone to Archie, and from him to Mrs Taverner.'

Her heart sinking again, she said, 'But it didn't. And I've always understood that possession was nine points of the law?'

'That's true enough. And, of course, the courts are entitled to take more than the letter of the law into account, otherwise there would be times when they might never reach a decision. But if it did come down to a direct choice between you and Mrs Taverner, she has the advantages of a husband and at least one child. The law, I fear, is always happier when there's a man to take charge of things and the possibility, to put it at its lowest, of sons to follow on. You have neither. Who, the courts would ask, would inherit after you?'

She exclaimed, 'That's more or less what Mr Napier said, but I didn't believe him. It's positively feudal!' She couldn't utter another word for a moment, filled with rage at the injustice of it all, rage at the knowledge that, to be sure of Juran, she might find herself forced to marry and have children just to satisfy some purse-lipped, dry-as-dust Writer to the Signet, or the College of Justice, or whoever's business it happened to be.

Colin Campbell said, 'You could always marry *me*, of course.'

13

He regretted the words as soon as they were out, because they made it sound as if what he had said just before had been dishonest, his proposal of marriage an attempt to buy her. Whereas it wasn't like that at all.

Granted that he wasn't an ardent and dashing young man, and never had been. Granted that it had taken a while for him to be sure of his own mind. Granted that he still thought the fifteen years difference in their ages too much, although he was still a couple of years under forty.

But despite all that he had intended, when he asked her to marry him, to make it an occasion of wine and roses.

Instead, seeing her so unexpectedly helpless, he had found the words come tumbling out without will or thought. He hadn't even had the foresight to put his arms around her.

She had soft, shapely lips, firm at the corners. Seeing them part slightly, he hurried on, 'Before you say no, my offer is from the heart. It's got nothing to do with the law, or whether Juran is or isn't yours.' His mouth was dry. 'I love you, you see?'

The only time he had ever spoken those words before had been to his first wife, and only when she was dying. She had appreciated them, because they were spoken out of kindness, but she had known as well as he that there had never been more than affection between them.

Rachel was visibly taken aback but, in the pause that followed, Colin would have needed to be a much vainer and less perceptive man not to see that she was wondering how best to say no without hurting him. He would have expected it, if he'd given himself time to think, but to his surprise, he found that he wasn't unduly discouraged.

Her voice creaked a little. 'You are so kind, and you're the best friend I could ever have.'

'But only a friend.'

'I don't know. At this moment, I'm so wrapped up in Juran that I can't think of anything else.'

In Colin's view, she was obsessive about the place, and he didn't think it was healthy.

She said, 'Can you forgive me?'

'Of course. You never know, I might ask you again some day.'

She smiled at him, the clear blue eyes dark in the firelight and their expression unfathomable.

It never occurred to him that she might be thinking about another man.

About his partner, Rainer Blake.

It was well over two years since she had seen him and she knew that he usually visited Europe at two or three-year intervals. It couldn't be long now.

'Come soon. Soon,' said the whisper in her heart.

CHAPTER FIFTEEN

I

'I've measured out the doses for you,' Dr Dods said. 'He's to take one tenth of a gram by mouth three times a day. I'm giving him corrosive sublimate of mercury to begin with. If it doesn't work, we'll try red iodide. In the meantime, see that he takes it.'

'Thank you,' Sophie said.

The doctor didn't look at her. 'When I say "see that he takes it", I mean it. Because if he's left to himself, he won't.'

'But . . .'

'He's had it before and he knows it's not pleasant.' Dr Dods looked up from packing his instruments back in his bag, his grey, ageing face neutral. 'He'll have trouble in walking. He won't be able to raise a glass. He'll lose his appetite, and have stomach pains and nausea. He'll have a permanent headache and he'll be delirious sometimes. The smell of his breath will make you want to vomit. In the end, you'll both be thinking the cure is worse than the disease. Well, just you remember – it isn't.'

She said, 'Don't you think it might help if you told me what the disease was and whether there are any precautions I should take myself?'

'No, I don't.'

Somehow, she managed to keep a grip on her temper. 'Why not? I behaved perfectly sensibly when my father was dying. Why should things be any different now?'

There was silence while he looked at her. Then his eyes shifted and he clicked his bag closed, saying, 'It is not something I am prepared to discuss.'

'No? When my father was ill, you were ready enough to tell me what was wrong. You implied that drinking oneself to death was a perfectly respectable thing to do! But this isn't. "It is not",' she mimicked savagely, ' "something I am prepared to discuss." What you mean is that you're too squeamish to warn me that my husband is a danger not just to himself but to me and my baby. You would rather have our deaths on your conscience than sully a lady's ears with the disgusting truth. Well, fortunately, not everyone is like you. I *know* what's the matter with him.'

She was breathless and her heart was pounding, but she would not, could not stop. 'And you can't even conquer your prudery enough to remind me to abstain from "marital relations". That's the phrase, isn't it? I suppose you expect my husband to do the abstaining for me, like a fine English gentleman?'

Dr Dods was a good doctor and an honest one, but he was also a man of his time. 'You should be ashamed of yourself!' he spluttered. 'I'll not hear another word from you.'

And he turned and went.

2

It was some weeks now since Richard had been released from the Navy but, despite Sophie's forebodings, things hadn't turned out quite as badly as she had feared.

Since the day when he had struck her, the day she had told him she was pregnant, she had locked her door against him and moved Ah Foon in to share her room. Frail though these defences were, they had made a radical difference to her frame of mind. Feeling safer, she began to feel less despondent, even about the baby.

Richard hadn't remarked on the change in sleeping arrangements. His wife's bed now, it seemed, came very low on the list of his cravings, from which there was no longer anything to hold him back, not even the periods of abstinence that service in the Navy had enforced.

During the course of those weeks – not gradually, but rapidly – his flesh had dropped away and his seaman's tan had begun to fade to an unhealthy yellow. But although the brightness of his eyes seemed to his watchful wife to hold a hint of feverishness, he lost none of his ability to charm.

Or to charm the ladies, at least. Although Sophie's pregnancy barred her from appearing in public, the two of them occasionally received and accepted informal invitations to private houses, and Sophie saw what she had never seen before, that while the ladies were charmed the gentlemen were not. They conversed with him, certainly, but not for long. She began to wonder whether she was just imagining a hint of reserve in their manner towards him – and towards her. It was horrible to think that they might know, or guess.

But she smiled in public and, in private, prayed.

Until the day came when Richard, declaring that Dr Dods' treatment had worked a cure, went out for the evening and didn't return for two days.

When he did, he was full of vigour and opium, and he found Sophie in the drawing room.

She fought him all the way while he raped her, but without hope and without success.

3

Afterwards, a silent Ah Foon helped her to bathe and put her to bed and stayed with her, as she tossed and turned, weeping, moaning, 'Oh, God! I hate him so much. I wish he would *die*. What can I do? The baby. I'm so afraid for the baby.'

4

That same evening, they were committed to attending a small supper party at the Berrys' cool, airy house on the Peak, and since the social niceties still, somehow, had to be observed, Sophie dragged herself up and dressed and sat while Ah Foon did her hair for her, and then went downstairs.

Richard was waiting in the hall. 'Christ, I'm aching all over,' he said.

She wasn't going to give him the satisfaction of saying that so was she, but he must have read it in her face, because his own face went rigid and he screamed at her, 'Not because of that, you silly bitch!'

And then he glanced at the palms of his hands and swore violently in words that, this time, Sophie didn't understand but didn't need to. There was a mirror in the hall with the eight sides that meant good luck, and he almost ran to it and stared at himself, and swore again, mindlessly and continuously for what seemed an eternity.

In the end, Sophie said, 'What is it?'

'The rash! The rash! Can't you see it?'

She looked, and saw some copper coloured spots on his forehead and, because she couldn't think of anything else to say, said aloofly, 'Oh, dear! Are they hot? Do they itch?'

'You stupid cow! You *stupid* cow! Go to your fucking party and leave me alone. Leave me alone!'

She left him in a chair, cursing still, crying and sobbing with great long-drawn moaning, whining sobs whose terror was an almost tangible thing.

5

He had gone when Sophie returned home. She asked the houseboy if the lieutenant had said when he would be back, but the answer was as she would have expected. 'My no savvy.'

She told Ah Foon, who had also been out – at her amahs' club, she said – to go to bed, and Ah Foon was soon snoring like a grampus, whatever a grampus was. Sophie hadn't the heart to wake her up again. She was being so good, and Sophie depended on her so much.

Drained of emotion, she stood at her bedroom window, wide awake, her mind racing, plunging, swooping and soaring like a bat at dusk under the trees. How could she go on like this? How *could* she go on?

She couldn't divorce Richard. She didn't have enough money to run away from him. And even if she did, the law could force her to return, however vile he was, however much she hated him.

As she stood, her eyes unfocussed, the moon slid out from behind a cloud and lit up the roofs on the hill below, sloping down to the harbour. She blinked in the sudden brightness and saw for the first time, perhaps because of the way the light was catching it, that the roof of the house nearest was marked with two spirals pointing directly towards her. Although they were probably due only to some discoloration of the tiles, the effect was of a two-horned monster, which was dreadfully inauspicious, and she wondered suddenly if it might be throwing bad *fung shui* influences towards Caine Road. Certainly, the house had known nothing but bad joss for these last three years.

She would have to ask a geomancer to come and look at it, because it was stupid living in a house that was doomed to trouble. Perhaps things would get better if they moved.

Unbidden, the thought of another house slipped into her mind. A castle. Juran.

342

She had never thought of Juran as a refuge. Rainer Blake had said once that the bank more or less owned it, because of the loans, but that hadn't prevented him from suggesting she should go there. And his suggestion had angered her so much that she had more or less rushed off and married Richard. Oh, God, what a fool she had been.

She wished she were better at understanding money and business, because she didn't know what the situation was about Juran, whether it was legally hers or not.

But it was a long way away. She might be safe there.

6

In the alleys off Tai Ping Shan Street there were many mat sheds whose withered brown walls were decked with signs, once scarlet, covered with black Chinese writing; which were lit, frowstily, by oil lamps that might once, bright and polished, have come from some Aladdin's cave; whose floors were thick with filth and whose air stank of hair grease, rats, urine and something else that was sickly sweet.

In one of these sheds, a tall man in European clothes and a coolie hat was reclining on a long wooden bench, jammed amongst half a dozen Chinese whose eyes, like his own, were glazed, and whose heads, like his, were supported on a communal wooden pillow.

It was his turn for the pipe. He had reached the listless stage, but he still fumbled in a kind of haste as he held the bowl of it in the flame of a lamp and stuffed into it the sticky little ball that smelled like rotting vegetables. Then he lay back and sucked in the vapour, holding it inside him until he could hold it no longer and at last, slowly, slowly, releasing it through his mouth.

He would have taken another pull except that the man next to him, his need beyond bearing, dragged the pipe from his grasp. The European, on the blessed edges of oblivion, murmured, 'Hey!' but no more.

It was just after midnight when two newcomers entered. They were Chinese and they were not there to smoke opium.

Without fuss, they took hold of the European's arms and levered him to unsteady feet, then led him outside to where another man was waiting, a man whose height belied his Chinese dress.

After a murmured consultation, the four of them moved away into the darkness.

7

Sophie had just dropped off into a troubled sleep when the front door gong clanged twice, decisively.

It was four in the morning, and she waited, a chill spreading through her, as Ah Foon turned over, and grunted, and sat up mumbling, 'What that?'

After a moment, the houseboy gave a rat-tat on the bedroom door.

'Missee, missee. Two piecee p'lice gempum wanchee see. Chop chop, missee.'

'How fashion?'

'My no savvy.'

'Yih! My walkee.'

She climbed shakily into a morning dress, her immediate thought that something must have happened to one of the servants. The Hong Kong police took no interest in respectable people.

And then she thought that perhaps Richard had done something to bring them here.

One of the policemen was a sergeant, a big Sikh in a striped turban with brass buttons down the front of his dark green uniform coat, the other a very young Chinese with knee length breeches, white puttees and a cone hat.

What Richard had done to bring them here was be murdered.

8

He had been murdered in China town, in a dark alley – stabbed many times, and robbed, and left where he lay.

The sergeant told her with some pride, in Punjabi English which she found hard to follow, that in earlier years the damned rascals would have hidden the cadaver away so that it was never found, but since Sir Macdonnell had enrolled many more Sikh and Scotch policemen it was hard for rascals not to run into patrols. The unhappy Mr Taverner had not been long dead when he was found.

This was going to cause great weeping and wailing in the colony, was it not? English gentlemen would not lie down under being done to death by damned Chinese.

'No,' Sophie said. 'I mean yes. Thank you.'

Inside her, the baby moved and then was still.

It was impossible to hush up the circumstances of Richard's death, and there was indeed an outcry in the colony. The new governor, Sir Arthur Kennedy, who had arrived a year previously, gave the Captain Superintendent of Police a stiff reprimand, but the captain's discomfiture failed to lead to an arrest. Richard's murderers were never caught.

So chaotic were Sophie's emotions and so ill was she that, afterwards, she remembered no single detail of the days that followed.

The funeral was a blur of naval officers and solid, black clad, bearded gentlemen with top hats and watch chains, all of them offering her their deepest condolences while failing to disguise that they regretted the manner of Richard's death more than the fact of it. What was the colony coming to that an officer and a gentleman could be robbed and murdered with impunity!

The ladies were no less outraged, some of them genuinely upset over the death of the handsome lieutenant even if they could not stop themselves from speculating about what he might have been doing in China town, alone, in the dark of the night. No one, Robina Gibbings assured Sophie, was paying any heed to Euphemia Moore's mutterings about the danger which attended any gentleman who was foolish enough to become attached to Mistress Sophie.

Only when it was all over and she had the house to herself again, only when, sick and exhausted, she went to lie down for an hour and found herself needlessly locking her door, did relief wash over her in a huge wave.

It was finished, the tension, the sense of living on the edge of an abyss. She had nothing more to fear. She was sorry that Richard Taverner had been murdered, the vital, charming man she had agreed to marry and had thought she loved for a few brief weeks. For him she wept a tear, because it had been such a waste of a life, and she could be sad that there had been not a soul truly to mourn him. Perhaps, some day, she would be able to look back on the happy times. But the murder of the other Richard Taverner, the husband who might have been a murderer himself, though with weapons more insidious than a knife, was something she could not regret.

It was coincidence that he had died so soon after he had raped her, after his latest symptoms had appeared. Coincidence that Ah Foon had slipped out for an hour that evening. Coincidence that his body had been found not far from Tai Ping Shan Street, where Sophie had attended a wedding six months before. It was all coincidence. The only influence at work had been luck. Or perhaps *fung shui*.

Superstitiously, she knew she would have to pay for it, and she did.

Ten days later, her baby was born prematurely, a daughter.

Dead.

10

Not for weeks was Sophie well enough to move downstairs and lie on the sofa in the dim, stuffy drawing room, listening to the formal condolences of all the ladies who had always been acquaintances, never friends. Ladies who enjoyed other people's misfortunes, to whom gossip was meat and drink.

'The shock of my husband's death,' she said, over and over again. 'That was what caused it.'

And perhaps it was true. She persuaded herself that Dr Dods, in spite of everything, would have given her some hint if it had been otherwise. But all he had said was, 'It happens, it happens, and no one knows why. It is God's will.'

It made her loss greater, because she couldn't tell herself it was for the best.

The doctor allowed three months to pass before he said, 'I should give you a thorough examination, just to be sure all's well,' and she thought at first that it was still to do with the baby. But afterwards he said gruffly, 'You're all right. I can give you a clean bill of health. In every way.'

She hadn't thought she had any more tears to shed, but she had been wrong.

11

As soon as she had the strength to go outdoors, she found herself beginning to gravitate, in the cool of the morning and the declining heat of the evening, towards the cemetery that, after only three decades of the colony's existence, was already almost full. Richard was buried at the far end, but on Sophie's hysterical insistence, the verger had agreed that baby Tina should be laid to rest under the strip of grass that separated Archie Macmillan's grave from the one next to it and that her name be added to his headstone.

If some people thought it strange that the baby should be interred next to her grandfather, not her father, for once they had the grace not to say so.

Sophie's first pilgrimage to the cemetery was made on a Monday. On the Thursday of the same week, she was sitting, mind empty, eyes resting on folded hands, when she became aware of a figure standing over her and looked up to discover that it was Rainer Blake, from whose company, thanks to her illness and mourning, she had been completely cut off since Richard's funeral.

'Well, that's a relief,' he said cheerfully. 'I was beginning to think you had retired into purdah for life.'

'Rainer!'

'Oh! We're on those terms now, are we?'

'Do you mind?' Embarrassed, she tried to cover up her mistake. 'Are you visiting a grave here?'

'No, you idiot girl, I'm visiting you.'

'But how did you know I'd be here?'

'This is your fourth evening in a row, or so my spies tell me. That makes it almost a ritual.'

He grinned, sat down beside her on the grass, and made it even clearer that he did not propose drowning her, as everyone else had done, in sympathy or sentiment. 'Tell me, apart from coming here, how do you occupy your time when mourning forbids you to do anything but mope for a year? I have always thought purdah a shocking penance to pay for having been so careless as to lose one's nearest and dearest.'

She frowned because it seemed such an insensitive thing for him to say, but he ignored it. He said, 'Thank God I'm male, so that it doesn't apply.'

'Yes. It's unfair discrimination!' She couldn't help smiling.

'That's better. Sophie looking crushed and subdued is a worrying sight, I can tell you. Well, what *do* you do?'

'Nothing.' It was almost a wail.

'*Really* nothing?'

'Well . . .' She looked a little shamefaced. 'In these last few weeks, I've felt the most shocking need to sweep away every trace of my marriage to Richard, everything that reminds me of him.'

'Now that,' he said encouragingly, 'sounds like an admirably healthy reaction. Tell me more.'

'I've sent his clothes to the Mission for Seamen.'

'Good.'

'And I had his personal possessions packed up and shipped to England, to an elderly aunt who's the only relative I know of.'

'Good.'

'And I've had all the furniture cleared out of his bedroom and dressing room and distributed around the rest of the house, and moved other furniture in to take its place.'

'Great.'

'But it still isn't enough.'

His face was serious for a moment, grey eyes narrowed against the sinking sun. Sophie couldn't tell what was in his mind.

If there had not been a good many casual strollers in the cemetery, he might have told her, or shown her. As it was, there was only a slight vibration in his voice as he said, 'My poor Sophie, he did give you a shocking time, didn't he?'

'Well, yes. But Dr Dods says I have nothing to worry about . . .' She hesitated, hoping he would understand without her having to put it into the loathsome words she could scarcely bring herself to enunciate.

Blake, who was not a religious man, thanked God profoundly.

'. . . so I am able to be reasonably philosophical about everything.'

'Except the baby.'

All the time they had been talking, she had been absently twisting the delicate mourning ring on her finger.

'Except the baby.'

He stood up abruptly, brushing the grass clippings from his trousers. 'I can't stay, but if I were Dr Dods I would prescribe a complete redecoration of the house. In which my advice is entirely at your disposal, though I can't guarantee that it will be on offer more than two or three times a week.'

She was so bemused by the thought of him being within reach when she needed him that all she could say was, 'You mean change *everything*?'

'Everything.'

So she did. In the weeks that followed, the heavy velvets went, and the ornate European furniture that had reminded her father of his native land, the land Sophie herself had never seen. Blake arranged for her to be shown a selection of good, plain Chinese mahogany tables and cupboards with a touch of brass on them, and bamboo-framed chairs and sofas on which she was able to strew bright, flowery cushions. She took the patterned Axminister up from the tiled floor

348

and scattered it with rugs. She had wall shelves put up for her books, though there were only a few of them. Books were so expensive in Hong Kong and so liable to be eaten by silverfish that she had never acquired the habit of reading them. Then she resorted to Blake again for advice on watercolours to deck the empty spaces on the walls, and he found her some pretty flower paintings.

She even treated Mr Sweet Song – Mr Happy Song's umpteenth descendant – to a rustling new bamboo cage and bought, from a lady who was about to leave Hong Kong for England, an aspidistra stand like a chopped-off Corinthian column on which to set the Juran bowl.

By the time she had finished, everything looked fresh and charming, and all trace of Richard and their marriage had, indeed, been obliterated.

Or so she thought.

12

By that time, too, except for the gap baby Tina had left in her heart, Sophie was herself again. Looking back over the last three years she thought that perhaps she hadn't done so badly. She would have been a paragon indeed if, considering her sheltered childhood and the blind ignorance of life in which young ladies were so conscientiously reared, she had contrived to take in her stride all the disasters that had befallen her.

So much restored was she that, one morning, when summer had dragged to its end and the fine weather was just beginning, she woke in such seditiously high spirits that she thought she would explode if she couldn't find an outlet. Not for another two months could she put off the most oppressive of her widow's weeds. Not for another two months could she wear a face that was other than sedate and gently mournful. It was intolerable.

There was only one person who would understand, so she sent a chit to Rainer Blake begging him to think of something.

Blake was amused. 'You can hardly expect me to cooperate,' he wrote back an hour later, 'in Mrs Taverner's desire to ruin her reputation. However, in the hope that it will be sufficiently adventurous for you, I would suggest a sail to Lantau, where there are no old tabbies to be scandalised.

'Even so, I feel some chaperonage would be advisable. Would you like to ask Robina Gibbings, who is the only lady I can think of scatterbrained enough to consent? Her husband is in port at present, so perhaps he might accompany us. Would tomorrow be soon enough for you?'

They set sail unobtrusively in a hired junk, just after five the next morning, before there were many people about, Sophie in the Chinese tunic and trousers she had worn to the Chang wedding and Robina, fair hair hidden under a scarf, dressed in what she said was her maid's off duty wear. She did truly sympathise with Sophie's desire for some sea air after the suffocating formality of the last months. And wasn't it fun? Like playing truant from school.

From the moment of setting foot on board, Sophie was filled with an unshadowed happiness. The motion under her feet, the warm breeze in her face, the wide pale green waters and hummocky little islands that looked like solidified haze in the early light, made her feel not so much that she was being reborn as filled with entirely new life and vitality. She didn't want to talk, dance, sing or laugh aloud. All she wanted was to lean on the wooden rail and revel in the freedom of it all.

The others left her alone, Blake because he had a shrewd idea of what was going through her head, and Robert and Robina Gibbings in deference to her supposed mourning. As Robert reminded his wife in a mutter that would have been audible in a Force Nine gale, Taverner had been a sailor, after all, and she probably wanted to say goodbye to him in her own way.

They landed in a small, sandy cove at the northern end of Lantau, by which time everyone was relaxed and ravenous. Blake had taken charge of the provisioning, partly because the surest way for Sophie's escapade to become public knowledge would have been for her to tell her cook to produce picnic food for four, but also because he suspected that Robina's imagination didn't stretch beyond cold Maryland chicken. Blake had nothing against Maryland chicken in its place – i.e. in Maryland – but food was one of his pleasures and in the course of a varied career he had learned always to prefer local dishes. There was little, he felt, to be said for steak-and-kidney pudding in tropical climes.

'Ease up!' he told Robina, who had never tasted Chinese food in all her three years in Hong Kong. 'I absolutely guarantee no red-cooked dog or stir-fried cat.' Instead, there were prawn mooncakes, cold noodles with chicken and sesame sauce, green and silver salad, smoked liver and roast duck.

Afterwards, they sat for a while chatting, and the rest of the day passed delightfully, strolling, sketching, admiring the scenery, enjoying the sensation of being carefree that was, as Blake said, the purpose for which picnics had been invented. Carried away by the ease of their Chinese *pajamas*, Sophie and Robina even paddled at the edge of the sea. Towards dusk, the men climbed into the dinghies that Blake had providently brought for the purpose, and set off to try their luck at some rough shooting.

13

When they returned proudly with their bag – a single jack snipe – it was time for supper before they set sail for home, a warm meal this time, heated in steamers over the charcoal brazier on which the crew cooked their own food.

They ate it in the cabin which took up almost two thirds of the junk's length, its roof standing four feet proud of the deck.

Blake said reprovingly, 'I'm ashamed of you, Mrs Taverner, that you have shown no signs of recognising this splendid conveyance, this butterfly of the sea, this . . .'

'Should I?'

'Damn it all, it's one of yours. I hired it from Macmillan and Venturi. It was the only vessel I could find of the right size at such short notice.' He grinned. 'Don't worry. It would be a chance in a million if any of the crew recognised you, especially in that outfit. The Chinese find it quite as difficult to tell Europeans apart as Europeans do Chinese.'

Robert Gibbings, a gusty gentleman, rattled his fingers on the table and said, 'Come now, Blake. Europeans – among whom I take you to include us Americans – do, at least, have different colour eyes and hair. And a wider variation in height and build, too. I mean, look at us!'

'Yes, but even so . . .'

Just then, there erupted into the surrounding silence a loud scream, followed at once by a succession of sharp explosions and an outburst of many voices shouting and jabbering. Sophie, completely disoriented, thought for a moment that the entire population of Hong Kong's Chinese bazaar was trying to come aboard. But this wasn't Hong Kong.

Then, 'Pirates!' yelled Gibbings, preceding it with something that sounded remarkably like a 'Whoopee!'

The next ten minutes were chaotic, because by the time Blake and Gibbings reached the deck the crew of the junk had made a unilateral decision to abandon ship and the two men found themselves alone facing a dozen times their number of pirates, who were already pouring in over the stern and sides.

Momentarily blinded by the transition from the lightness of the cabin, they didn't waste time trying to assess the situation.

'Fire as your guns bear,' roared Gibbings, who had once been a gunnery lieutenant and tended to revert in moments of crisis, and the two of them let off their shotguns, both barrels, almost as one. It was a shock to see in the flashes from the barrels that the muzzles were almost touching the breasts of men they had scarcely known they were firing at.

'Two down!' yelled Gibbings cheerfully, and then, 'Deck cabin! Gives us a breastwork!' and they ducked behind it while the pirates, entangling themselves in the chaos of ropes and beams, tried to swarm over it to get at them. For what seemed like a lifetime, there was nothing but noise and shouting and muzzle flashes and responding screams and groans, until the pirates began throwing fireballs, deadly grenades that exploded with a fearsome crash and not only set fire to everything around but filled the air with a uniquely noisome, suffocating smell. It was like the breaking of every bad egg that had ever been laid in the whole history of the world.

Blake and Gibbings took turns in firing and reloading, whoever was firing using revolver in one hand and shotgun tucked underarm in the other. The danger was so close that they could scarcely miss, and although they had to take a moment every now and then to slap out smouldering patches on their clothing, each flash was echoed by a groan or shriek.

After a while, their assailants' enthusiasm showed signs of waning.

'Good shooting!' roared Gibbings, and Blake replied breathlessly, 'They're easier than snipe, but we're not going to win.'

It was the girls he feared for, swearing at himself for having brought them into this kind of danger even while he cudgelled his brain over the mystery of why it had arisen. Most pirates in these enlightened times went for richer prey than a quartet of picnickers.

'We need to create a diversion. Give us the chance to get away,' he said. 'Any ideas? We want to take to the punts. *Damn!*'

'Hit?'

'A blade. Nothing serious, I don't think.'

And then Sophie's voice spoke in his ear, hurried, excited, but well under control.

'What a horrible smell. The charcoal stove is still alight. And there are the lamps. There's plenty of oil.'

Discharging his revolver in the face of a big brute with moustaches down to his waist, Blake gave a grunt of laughter. 'Christ! Well, it's *your* insurance, I suppose!'

The charcoal, tossed over the roof of the deckhouse with a scoop, and the oil, swilled out of the lamps, worked magnificently, feeding the flames that the fireballs had started, so that, in no time at all, the deck cabin was ablaze and roaring, the fire driving hard towards the pirates on the evening breeze that flowed from sea to land.

Nothing could have been better.

Behind the deckhouse, however, it soon became overheated. 'Time to go,' Blake yelled and, jumping down into one of the boats, hauled Sophie down after him. Gibbings almost threw his wife into the other.

'Good luck!' Blake shouted, and Gibbings shouted back, 'See you at the Club for breakfast!'

And then they were gliding away on silent oars.

14

Sophie said interestedly after a while, 'Are you sure we're pointing in the right direction?'

'Can't see,' he replied, pulling as smoothly as if he were taking part in a regatta. 'I've got my back to it. Are you all right?'

'Yes, thank you.' She wasn't going to admit that she was shaking like a leaf. 'It made me feel quite sentimental. Reminded me of our very first meeting in the fire at Canton. I didn't like you a bit. What about your arm? Can I help row?'

'No.'

'I do know how.'

'Uh-huh?'

'I learned when I was a child.'

'Sure, rowing up and down a few yards of dead calm river. We're in open sea now, my pet.'

'Well, it was at Macao, actually. But all right. I'll just sit here and twiddle my thumbs.'

'I don't care what you do as long as you stop chattering. I need my breath for rowing. When we're further away and it doesn't matter if you catch a crab I guess you can take one of the oars, but at the moment I prefer them nicely matched, thank you. In the meantime, please don't hesitate to mention it if the wind starts blowing down the back of your neck instead of across your cheek.'

'Why?'

'In the absence of a compass, wind and stars are the best navigation guides.'

'Can you read the stars?'

'Yes. Now be quiet.'

Giving herself up to the almost mystic pleasure of release from fear, of their swooping movement through the darkness of the sea, the darkness that wasn't dark at all but almost phosphorescent, Sophie had no idea whether it was one hour or three before she became aware that Blake was casting frequent glances over his shoulder, as if searching for something.

And then he said, 'Great! Time for a rest. Unless I miss my guess, that island over there is Kau Yi Chau. Halfway home.'

They landed in a bay fringed with silver sand and braceleted with fan palms and hibiscus and pampas grasses and after Sophie had helped Blake pull the dinghy out of reach of the lapping waters, he flung himself down with a groan of relief and, addressing the stars, declared, 'Never again, *never* again will I – ouch! – allow myself to be teased into taking pretty young women on illicit picnics!'

'In the plural? Do you do this kind of thing often?'

She was laughing as she sat down beside him, and he laughed back at her, his teeth flashing white against the tanned skin, his eyes gleaming like washed ice. He had shed coat and waistcoat for rowing, loosening the neck of his shirt and rolling up his sleeves, so that instead of being a figure of authority, assured, ironic and formidable, he suddenly seemed a hundred degrees more human and a thousand degrees more rakish. Despite the physical strain of the last few hours, the impression of vitality was breathtaking.

Without thinking, she said, 'You look like a *proper* pirate. Not one of our vulgar Chinese friends but the romantic kind from the Caribbean that maidens dream about.'

He grinned and stretched luxuriously, then rolled over to plant his hands on either side of her waist and murmured, 'The kind who carry them off to secret lairs to have their exotic way with them? I thought that was desert sheikhs.'

In the shimmering light he saw her face change, the flawless face

354

with its brilliant, longlashed eyes, straight nose, and generous mouth. Her dark, almost black hair, always so exquisitely dressed, was still anchored at the back but had shaken loose at the front and sides. She looked neither flirtatious nor even aware, but almost pensive.

15

The time, the place, and the woman . . .

The sand was their magic carpet, the sky their private heaven. The shackles that prisoned them all their days – business and black bombazine, duty and decorum – fell away magically, as if the fetters had been only a dream, and this was the reality.

He buried his fingers in her hair and stared for a long, long moment into her eyes, murmuring, 'What a witch you are!' before his lips touched hers with a tenderness that deceived her, so that she thought the kiss was an end as well as a beginning, and that this brief, dissolving delight was all that was to be granted to her.

But then he gathered her into his arms and she discovered that he, too, had fallen victim to enchantment. A fierce exhilaration swept through her, filling every vein with liquid fire, as his lips hardened and became more eloquent and demanding, so that she could not have stopped herself from responding, even if she had wanted to.

Her hands on his shoulders, she felt the private warmth of him through the once-crisp fabric of his shirt, limp now and moulded to muscles taut as ropes, and as he turned her in his arms to kiss her throat and the soft quivering skin below, she felt another tautness hard against her. The thrill reverberated throughout her whole body with an intensity that would have told him everything he needed to know – if he had not already known it.

There were no trappings of black bombazine to hinder them, only the Chinese silk of tunic and trousers, swiftly stripped away, and then his mouth was buried between her breasts and one hand was straying over her flesh while the other cast off the garments of his own that still divided them.

They were together then, as they belonged, and there was no part of her that did not melt under his hands and lips, no nerve in him that did not spring and shiver at her touch. And when the suspense was beyond bearing, when he sank himself in her and locked them together, it was as if this had been their destiny since the beginning of time.

When they returned to sanity, the stars were still there, the breeze balmy, the sea still lapping on the shore.

They lay for a while, not speaking, and then Blake propped himself on an elbow and asked softly, 'Do you love me?'

'Love you? Mmmm . . .'

He grinned and, rising, went to his coat to find the flask of good French brandy that he always carried when he went on any kind of expedition.

Handing it to a blissful Sophie, he said, 'Don't drink it all. Having been slashed at with a rusty cutlass, I figure some antiseptic might be a good idea.'

She sat up, exclaiming remorsefully, 'Heavens! I'd forgotten. Has the bleeding stopped? Let me see.'

He laughed, because it was the only thing about him that she couldn't see. All he wore was the handkerchief he had tied round his arm as a bandage hours before.

She laughed back at him, and even that was enough to start his body stirring again so that he had to turn away and begin pulling on his nether garments because, much though he regretted it, they had to get home before the dawn. Then he tossed her clothes at her and said, 'For God's sake, put those on.'

'Why?'

'Dammit, don't you realise how desirable you are?'

'Am I?' she said curiously. 'You know, I never thought you felt anything for me beyond a kind of proprietorial irritation.'

'As bad as that, was I? Well, you were irritating enough, God knows. But if it gives you any satisfaction, I can tell you exactly the day I began to feel differently.'

'Sit down and let me undo that bandage. Oh dear, the knot *has* tightened up. When?'

'The day you proposed to me.'

'Really? But you were *awful* to me.'

'Self-defence, it's called.'

'Oh. Are you ready? Grit your teeth, because I'm going to anoint you. It doesn't look *too* bad.'

She was behaving very well, but soon, he knew, she would be filled with guilt and fear, as any well bred young woman would be after the madness of this last hour.

It had, indeed, been madness, but he didn't regret it for a moment.

His eyes, like hers, on the fresh handkerchief she was binding round his stinging arm, he said, 'Will you marry me, Sophie?'

It was then that he discovered she had hidden depths, because she didn't drop everything and throw herself thankfully into his arms. Instead, she gave a faint gasp and then, raising one exquisite, if ruffled, brow, replied, 'You don't have to do the gentlemanly thing, you know.'

'Don't I, indeed?' He was shocked. 'Do you know why I'm still a bachelor at thirty-eight years old?'

'No.'

'Because I have never before asked any woman to marry me.'

'Not even for gentlemanly reasons?'

'What an outrageous question! No.'

'Goodness, how on earth have you managed?'

He gave a spurt of laughter. 'I haven't had any problems. Someone told me in my youth that the virtuous man can be defined as one who, prior to his marriage, takes care never to go to bed with a virtuous woman. It struck me as an excellent principle to which I have always adhered. And don't you dare look at me like that, my girl! Unlike some people, I do *not* frequent brothels. You would be surprised at the number of respectable married ladies in Hong Kong who are happy to oblige.'

'*Really?*'

'No, I am not going to supply you with a list of names! You should be ashamed of yourself.'

Mischievously, she murmured, 'Well, there's Mrs Commander Keyber, and Mrs Lieutenant Beton, and . . .'

'*Sophie!*'

Then, blushing slightly and tweaking the ends of the bandage into neat rabbit's ears, she said, 'You don't think I could just be your mistress, do you? I'm not sure that I like being married.'

He had no idea whether she was trying to tease him but, just to be on the safe side – and because he very badly wanted to – he took her decisively back into his arms.

Fifteen erotic minutes later, unlocking their bodies with a slow, lithe deliberation calculated to cause her every last ounce of exquisite torture, he murmured, 'You were saying?'

'I was saying, I don't like being married. And if what we've just been doing is what it's like to be a mistress, I'd rather be your mistress any day, please.'

'Well, you can't.'

She had been afraid, in spite of what he had said, that his desire to marry her had been no more than an inescapable sequel to their lovemaking. But now, looking behind the smile in his eyes, she saw with passionate thankfulness that it was not so.

She said, 'Then it seems I have no choice.'

17

Not for another two months – a year after Richard's death – could they announce their engagement, and Sophie, despite Blake's protestations, insisted on waiting four months beyond that before they were married. She remembered very well the colony's disapproval when she had married Richard too soon after coming out of mourning for her father and was determined not to repeat her error.

This time, she vowed, she was going to do everything correctly.

It was comforting to be able to put the blame on what The Gup, or gossip, would have said and, for a short while, Sophie even convinced herself. But the truth was that baby Tina's death was still too close to her, so that the very thought of bearing another child preyed dreadfully on her nerves. She went cold every time she thought of what might have been the sequel to that magical interlude on the way home from Lantau, when past danger and future fear had been so utterly submerged in the present demands of love and need.

Given six months' grace, she told herself, everything would be all right; because she loved Rainer with an intensity she could never have imagined.

In the meantime, to prevent herself from fretting about the things that really mattered, she began fretting about things that didn't.

'But I've just redecorated the whole house, and I like it. Why can't we live at Caine Road?' she wailed.

'Because my house at East Point is healthier, and larger, and *I* like it.'

'But it's full of books and pictures. It's not exactly cosy.'

'Neither am I. Now will you go away and let me get some work done?'

His work took up a great deal of time; all too often, he was busy when Sophie wanted to talk, dismissing her as if she were a pretty but importunate domestic pet who was unlikely to have anything important to say on any subject. She couldn't imagine him ever asking her opinion even about the cut of his coat, or listening if she offered it. But he was a man, and she wouldn't have expected anything else.

She fretted, too – while accepting their congratulations with slightly excessive charm and gratitude – about Mrs Commander Keyber and Mrs Lieutenant Beton, about Phyllis de Vinne and Juliet Thorowgood, although her worries about them were, on the whole, cancelled out by the delightful knowledge that the colony had been completely taken aback by her success in capturing the heart of a gentleman who was not generally believed to have one.

Something else she found to fret about was compatibility. Rainer was an absolutely typical specimen of a Snake person – shrewd, intellectual and materialistic, ruthless in pursuit of his objectives and both possessive and demanding in his private relationships. All the experts said Snake and Monkey were a far from ideal marriage combination, promising an endless battle of wills and wits. In fairness, however, Sophie had to admit that the experts weren't infallible; they had promised excellent auspices for her marriage with Richard.

But Sophie worried about it, just the same.

18

Blake was worrying about something entirely different. Who was trying to murder him?

Less and less was he prepared to believe that the attack on the junk at Lantau had been coincidental. The island wasn't pirate territory and, in any case, the days had gone when the fraternity were prepared to waste time on stray travellers and loot that wouldn't amount to more than pocket money. It seemed to him conclusive that they had persevered with their attack despite the toll he and Gibbings had been exacting. They wouldn't have done that without very good reason indeed.

Someone had paid them, and he couldn't think who.

There were half a dozen businesses in the colony of which he was unprovably suspicious. Leafing through papers and ledgers, he confirmed yet again that, although their profit and loss accounts looked about right, they had nevertheless been paying suppliers well over the odds for their goods. It was as clear an indication as any that smuggling was their business, or part of it. And that would provide them with a very good reason for wanting to get him out of the way.

But who? One of the firms on his list was Macmillan and Venturi, of which he would become two thirds owner when he married Sophie. It was from Gino Venturi that he had hired the junk.

It was a damnable nuisance. He didn't doubt that, if he began taking an active personal interest in the firm, he would be able to get to the root of what was going on, but since he didn't make the mistake of underestimating Venturi's ingenuity he knew that it would take time. Of which he had none to spare. And not even for a few months was he prepared to risk finding himself the innocent partner in a shady business. Venturi was too tough-minded to be frightened onto the straight and narrow path merely by implicit threats.

Better to stay on the outside, Blake thought. There was always the chance, though he considered it remote, that Venturi would dig his own grave.

The happy result of these reflections was that he was able to be unexpectedly cooperative when Sophie, inspired by a magazine article on the suffrage movement and memories of her own difficulties when she had wanted to leave Richard, complained, 'Even you must admit it's unreasonable that everything a woman owns should be taken away from her as soon as she becomes a wife.'

'It's the law of England, my darling, and that means it's the law of Hong Kong.'

'That doesn't make it fair. Look at Macmillan and Venturi. It was my father who founded it and built it up and left it to me. If I had been a son rather than a daughter, no one would insist on taking it away from me.'

Since she was expecting Rainer to explain it all in terms that would pass right over her head, she was astonished when he said obligingly, 'No one's *insisting* on taking it away from you. As your husband, I'm perfectly prepared to repudiate my legal right to your assets.'

'Can you do that?'

'If Mr John Stuart Mill can do it, I see no reason why I can't.'

'Mr who? Do you mean everything could stay mine?'

'Yes.'

'Juran, too?' It was queer to think of Juran, her father's loved and hated family home, as an 'asset'.

'Ah, well, Scots law is tricky there – something to do with medieval feus. It might well remain yours, whatever happens. I don't know.'

'What about this cousin who's looking after it?'

'Rachel? She's . . .

'A *female*? Why didn't you tell me?'

'I don't remember you asking.'

'What's she like, for goodness' sake?'

'Capable, serious, about your age, illegitimate by birth, half French . . .'

'She doesn't sound very respectable!' Sophie frowned. 'Anyway, I didn't mean that. Is she pretty?'

'Only when she smiles. But to get back to the point, you may keep Macmillan and Venturi with my goodwill. I don't imagine Venturi is likely to object at having a sleeping partner.'

She tossed her head at him enchantingly. 'Don't leap to conclusions. You never know. I might start taking an interest.'

'Oh, might you? We'll see about that.' He took her in his arms to kiss her. 'In my view, you will have much better things to do when we're married.'

19

They had such a huge, extravagant wedding that, afterwards, Sophie fell straight into the bridal bed and fast asleep.

She opened dazed and smiling eyes at dawn, to the knowledge of her husband's lips drifting seductively over her face and his hands over the smooth curves of her body, his touch a benison, a promise of gentleness. But the promise was deceptive.

It was six months since they had made love under the indulgent stars, under the sway of the same enchantment, seduced by the same delight, the same wondering thrill of discovery. Now, that lovely languor was consumed in a passion infinitely more powerful and Sophie found herself swept along on a wild, ecstatic tide of torture and rapture, until she thought she was dying and cried out in fear of hell, only to find it flare into unimaginable glory.

She wept afterwards, lying exhausted in Rainer's arms, frightened and confused, her emotions ravaged by the severity of the storm. Gentle once more, he kissed the tears away and after a while made love to her again, this time giving her the warm, slow, sensual pleasure that was what she desired.

She did not tell him, nor did he guess at first, how much the intensity of his desire had disturbed her – or that, as the days and nights passed, she found her nerves crawling as she waited for him to progress, as Richard had done, to the demands that had so revolted her. That he did not only prolonged the misery of expectation. When she was with him, she couldn't believe that he would ever ask such things of her, but she didn't dare question, because he might say yes. Or he might be repelled, and stop loving her.

Because she loved him so much, she pretended it was otherwise – and thought he was deceived. And because he loved her so much, he did not at first disabuse her.

20

In public, they soon acquired the reputation of being the happiest and handsomest couple in Hong Kong and Sophie was delighted to live up to it, revelling in being invited everywhere and treated as a person of importance. Soon, she was spending such enormous sums of her husband's money on pretty clothes that even he was moved to remark on it.

Surveying, one evening, the delectable picture she made in a ball dress of sea green satin, whose matching gauze overskirt was heavily ruched and bunched and caught up with nosegays of artificial roses, he said, 'Christ! How many yards are there in that?'

'Forty,' she admitted.

'Well may you blush!'

'But it *is* beautiful, isn't it?'

'Yes, my darling, and so memorable that you won't be able to wear it more than a couple of times. My banker's instincts are revolted. Do, please, try to be more sensible.'

She was wildly extravagant over the house at East Point, too, having in the end agreed to Blake's suggestion that, since she was set against selling her father's house at Caine Road, she should rent it furnished to some of the temporary residents who were forever coming and going in Hong Kong.

Unfortunately, her redecorations there had been so successful that she couldn't resist trying her hand on East Point, too, which seriously provoked her husband, who disliked having the almost monkish austerity of his domain ruined with flowered cushions and knick-knacks suitable only, he claimed, for a lady's boudoir. Especially when they came at exorbitant prices.

Sophie made the best of her limited retaliatory powers by complaining constantly about his secretiveness and his absences. 'I never know whether you're off to Macao or Timbuktu! You never tell me anything except, "I have to be away for a few days on business". You'd think I wasn't interested!'

'Well, all I ever hear from you is about gowns and gossip,' he said unkindly, 'so I didn't think you *would* be interested. However, since you ask, I am off to Europe very soon on a trip I postponed because of our marriage.'

Her face lit up. 'You'll take me with you, won't you? Oh, *please* say you will. Please, please, *please!*'

It was hard to refuse her when her eyes were shining as if all the stars in the universe were sparkling behind them.

He took her in his arms and kissed her, though not too ardently, because he was learning the boundaries of her ease. 'It wouldn't be sensible, my darling. I'm going straight to Scotland to spend a couple of weeks talking business, and then coming straight back. I've too much to do here to take any extra time off. You'd be bored stiff. When the economy starts looking up again, I promise I'll take you on a proper honeymoon, when we can enjoy ourselves.'

She tore herself from his arms, disappointment making her foolish. 'You don't love me!' Her tears came in a torrent. 'You'll be away for months. If you loved me, you couldn't bear to be separated from me. What am I to do without you? What am I to do?'

And although, every night until he sailed, he made love to her in the way she responded to, in the way that brought them most closely together, he didn't succeed in soothing away the resentment in her heart.

CHAPTER SIXTEEN

I

The envelope was addressed to 'The Occupier, Castle of Juran, Argyllshire, North Britain', but Rachel recognised the handwriting and was struck by a revulsion so acute that the muscles of her stomach went into spasm and the breath lurched out of her lungs to lodge at the base of her throat, so that she had to swallow, and swallow again, before she was even able to think.

Gresham. Again. She had thought all that was over.

In the four years since she had been free to do what she wanted at Juran, she had transformed both castle and estate. Never had things run so smoothly. Never had so much been achieved. From being a scene of all too typical Highland lethargy, the village had become a thriving little community, its activity ceaseless between April and October. The farming side of things was Tom Tanner's responsibility and Rachel wasn't directly involved, but sometimes she found that she couldn't stay away, forgot her dignity and clambered up on top of the haystacks to join the women in the treading, or passed a few enchanted hours at harvest's end helping the smallest children with the gleaning.

Where the castle was concerned, not a leak dared to show itself, not a fragment of mortar to crumble. There were carpets in the main rooms, now, and regular fires had almost conquered the old, all-pervading smell of damp. Every stick of furniture in the place had been moved a dozen times until Rachel was satisfied that everything was where it fitted best. Outside, the walls had been freshly harled so that they showed white as snow in the sun of a long, dry summer. The lawn had been levelled and the grassy ride that led to the front door bordered with shrubs, some of them quite exotic. There was a Mr Osgood Mackenzie up north at Inverewe who had succeeded in growing even semi-tropical plants and when Rachel had written to him for advice he had been most helpful.

Sometimes, when she came walking or riding home of an evening, she would stop for a moment before turning the last bend, because the joy and the pride were almost too much. And then she would move on and see Juran laid out before her – the cherished land and the shimmering sea, the impeccable white block of the castle in its bower of green and amethyst, its windows shining rose and gold in the light of the setting sun.

It was hers, and more hers than it had ever been because, as it now was, she had created it.

Would she ever be sure of it, while Gresham lived, while Sophie lived?

2

She didn't have to open the letter to know that every word would reek of malice and contempt. Whatever Gresham had to say would be material for her lawyer to deal with, but he had written to her directly and would always write to her directly, because he didn't want his hatred filtered through an intermediary.

Briefly, she thought of sending the letter, unopened, to David Napier, but there was no sense in postponing the evil day. She ripped it open and discovered that there had, after all, been substance in Horace's warning of two years before.

There were two papers inside, the first a brief note from Gresham.

Without preamble, he wrote, 'You will be interested to know that, having put enquiries in train some time ago, I have now traced one of your mother's former lovers. That it should be only one is, of course, a disappointment to me, but to have expected more after such a lapse of time would perhaps have been over-sanguine. I enclose a copy of the man's sworn testimony. In view of the contents, no court would doubt that your mother was a whore and you a bastard fathered on her by any one of a succession of nameless customers.'

The words danced before Rachel's eyes, although she knew that the testimony, sworn or not, must be a lie. If she was certain of one thing, it was that her mother had not been a whore.

It took a considerable effort of will to turn to the other sheet, to read it coldly and logically, as if it had nothing to do with her.

'I, Benjamin Rebecque, of the restaurant La Corbeille in Wardour Street, London, hereby swear that . . . in the months of August, September and October in the year 1847 . . . frequent carnal intercourse with the woman known as Ondine Marie Vallette . . . I at that time being employed in the kitchens of a restaurant near to Chez Vallette . . . shared her favours with others . . . remember the year particularly because the overrated chef Soyer gained an inflated reputation from his soup kitchens for the poor . . . potato famine in Ireland . . . Jenny Lind sang in London and I saw Her Majesty arrive for the first performance . . . great murder case in my native France when the Duc de Praslin murdered his Duchesse . . . remember the months particularly because it had been a long, hot summer and the relief was great in the kitchens when it came to an end . . . keep no diary because I have no time to write in it but have an excellent memory . . .'

The English was too good, by far, for a French kitchen hand, but there had probably been a lawyer to take it down. Rachel didn't doubt that the liar who called himself Benjamin Rebecque really existed.

If he was prepared to swear to his lies in court, she would have to disprove what he said.

How?

Round and round her mind went, darting off, speculating. It was madness! Twenty-six years! How was it possible to discover anything at all about a time so long ago – about this man Rebecque, even about her mother? She had no idea whether any of the Vallettes were still alive, the family Rachel had never seen, although her mother had once or twice walked her past the restaurant when she was a child. What would they be likely to remember of the year when Daniel Macmillan came into Ondine's life? Would such witnesses even be acceptable in court?

When Horace had warned Rachel of what Gresham was up to this time, she had laughed the whole idea off as ludicrous. She had been wrong.

What could she do? *What could she do?*

Before she could even take time to think properly, or do anything at all, she had one of Colin Campbell's stalking parties to contend with. Five gentlemen in addition to himself, he had said. No wives. He doubted whether they would wish to do much stalking. Their concern was to discuss important business in surroundings where they would be assured of privacy.

She was sad that Colin Campbell had become a little distant since he had proposed to her and been refused, although he was as kind and considerate as ever.

It was the end of September, and the equinoctial gales had blown themselves out. The clouds had retreated from the mountains leaving them crowned with the first snow, and the sound of the stags roaring echoed back and forth across the water. Warmed by the declining sun, the hillsides to starboard of Colin Campbell's little steam yacht *Matilda* ran the full gamut of golds from acidulated green to gamboge and burnt umber, while the islands to port were plunged in shadows of indigo, Prussian blue, purple and violet-grey.

Rainer Blake, on his previous visits, seven years and four years earlier, had arrived on horseback and seen much to criticise. Now, as the islands fell away to the south and the yacht approached Juran's small anchorage, he was afforded a very different vista of what looked a very different place – a castle whose disrepair had been not only halted but reversed, surrounded by grounds that were trim and well cared for and a landscape that, while far from manicured, no longer suggested the last wilderness on earth.

Blake felt a stirring of satisfaction. Rachel Macmillan had done him proud. He had asked Colin about her, casually, and been surprised to hear that she was not married, nor seemed likely to be.

She was waiting for them in the hall, wearing a detached smile and a dress Sophie would have died rather than be seen in. Not that there was anything wrong with it except its restraint; there wasn't a ruche or a puff in sight. Blake had forgotten what an admirable figure she had.

He had remembered her as rather plain, except when she smiled, but now she had acquired a grace of manner, an elegance, above all an assurance that had transformed her. She still wasn't a beauty, she still wasn't pretty, but she had style. If this had been France she would have been idolised.

Even so, she looked absurdly young to be the mistress of a castle and ten thousand acres of increasingly desirable land as she stood aside to allow Colin Campbell to welcome his guests over the threshold, which mystified Blake because he didn't remember her as being of a retiring disposition. And then, as her eyes smiled surprise at him, he realised with a surge of amusement that she had cast herself in the role not of hostess but high-class housekeeper.

It was logical enough and she did it very well indeed. As she told the servants where to take the gentlemen's baggage, he could see that she was unobtrusively assessing each guest and allocating his bedroom accordingly. The high colour, age and spreading waistline of Mr Junius Spencer Morgan rated a room only one flight of stairs up, while the aspiring young Radical politician, Joseph Chamberlain, was despatched to the third floor in the central tower.

4

She presided beautifully over supper, her manner slightly formal, and took little part in the conversation after the beginning, when the older gentlemen felt that courtesy required them to put the little lady at her ease by talking down to her. She endured it very well, and displayed commendable patience with Lionel Rothschild's catechism on gardening in the Highlands, a subject in which, Blake seemed to remember, she had formerly shown little interest.

'The short summer is the difficulty,' she explained. 'We find that any hardy plant that, in the south, would flower in or before June does well – though in August rather than June. But anything that flowers later is not worth planting at all.'

'By jove, then, I know what you want here, Miss Macmillan!'

Baron Lionel wore his hair in a style not unlike his friend Disraeli's, waving down from a side parting and turning under in a bob which, every so often, he patted carefully, as if to be sure it was still in place. He did so now, his pouched eyes beaming. 'I have precisely such a garden at my place at Gunnersbury, y'know, no flowers at all. All green, patterned with wet stones and pebbles.'

'It sounds ideal. Certainly, we have no shortage of the raw materials.' Miss Rachel's eyes didn't even flicker.

The baron went on, 'I'm talking about the Japanese style, you know? It's very new to us in this country, but I think I have caught the effect to perfection. In fact, when the Japanese ambassador visited me he was most impressed.'

Blake seemed to remember hearing that what the thunderstruck ambassador had actually said was, 'We have nothing like it in Japan.'

Testily, Morgan broke in, 'You and your gardens, Rothschild! I guess Miss Macmillan has better things to occupy her time. It sure must take some organisational skills to avoid running out of salt and pepper when you're this far from a town, eh, Miss Macmillan?'

'It has been known to happen,' she smiled. 'We produce a good deal of our own food, however, and the rest I bring in from Glasgow.'

'Say, do you buy from young Tommy Lipton? I've been hearing

about him. Now, there's a guy who's learned all about American marketing methods!'

'Yes,' Colin Campbell intervened quizzically, 'and Glasgow's going to take a while getting over having a herd of pigs dressed in kilts paraded through its streets to advertise his Scotch bacon.'

Blake's attention began to wander. The dining room was a considerable improvement on what it had been. Rachel had moved it from the ground to the first floor, to a room that looked as if it had been newly panelled and had a pleasant stone grate with a log fire burning in it. The windows commanded magnificent views over the bay and the islands. The long, warm evening light was flooding serenely through the windows and there was the promise of a superb sunset.

Rachel's voice broke into his reverie. 'I hope you approve?'

'A mind reader, are you? Yes, very much.'

'For some reason we always seemed to be at table when the sun went down so that Mr Campbell's guests were beginning to feel badly frustrated. They either had to miss the sunset altogether, or rush out and see it while the food grew cold. It's much better now. On wild nights we draw the curtains and scarcely notice the out-of-doors at all.'

But Blake's responding smile was abstracted. He wasn't here to talk about sunsets and Scotch bacon and Japanese gardens, but about business that was of the gravest importance. Because, however prosperous and tranquil the world appeared to be on the surface, there were rumours of imminent bank failures in the USA and stock exchange crises in Berlin and Frankfurt, while the bank rate in Britain had been fluctuating violently between three and eight per cent. There was no doubt at all in Blake's mind that there was a new recession ahead. Plans had to be laid, strategies agreed, and his own time for discussion was strictly limited.

He would have been happier to forego supper, excellent though it was, and get down to work.

5

Rachel had thought she was going to faint when she saw him disembarking from the *Matilda*.

Her first reaction was horror – as it always seemed to be – because she wasn't ready, and she didn't know what to say to him, or what he would say to her. This was reality, not a dream, and there were other people present, important people, so that he couldn't just walk up to her, and take her in his arms, and tell her everything in a single kiss.

There had been times when she had tried to convince herself that she was mad to be so in love with someone she had seen three times in her life and might never see again, who was a mystery and a challenge to her, who might have been the Grand Turk in person for all she knew about him.

But it made no difference.

So she sent up a prayer of thanks to God, a real prayer that had nothing to do with the 'Thank you, God, for everything' that punctuated Mr Allan's services as regularly as the passing round of the velvet offerings bag; Mr Allan hadn't yet caught up with the fashion for open plates designed to shame people into giving. Then she put a guard on her expression and her heart, and stood waiting to read a message in Rainer Blake's eyes as they met hers.

It didn't come, but the circumstances were hardly propitious. And anyway, she told herself, even declared lovers, after years of separation, didn't take up exactly where they had left off, but walked warily at first, until they were sure that what had been between them was still there.

He was to be at Juran for a week, and in the country for much longer; on the last occasion when he had been home on a visit from Hong Kong he had stayed for more than a year. There was time.

She turned her attention back to what Mr Lawson was saying in the bored drawl that seemed to belie his words.

'. . . the Franco-Prussian war. As you know, that little affair boiled down to a direct duel between Chassepôt and Krupp, guns versus guns. It must not be allowed to happen again. With our modern technical advances, war in the future should be the province of government, industry and banking . . .'

6

There were to be no more concessions to charming little ladies. When it wasn't Mr Lionel Lawson – head tilted backwards to ensure that his stiff collar should displace not a hair of his luxuriant sidewhiskers – holding forth on the future of war, it was silver-haired Mr Junius Spencer Morgan, with his over-sized Roman nose and American twang, talking about the consortium he had lately organised to float a loan of $50m to the Parisian government. When it wasn't Mr Morgan, it was Baron Rothschild, being opaque and not quite English about an idea for increasing the British shareholding in the Suez Canal. And when it wasn't Baron Rothschild, it was the slender, monocled and rather affected Mr Joseph Chamberlain propounding his ideas for taxation readjustment and tariff reform.

Colin Campbell and Rainer Blake listened intently and said little.

Messengers came, bearing messages from the telegraph office in Glasgow, and went, bearing other messages in reply. Colin Campbell's guests seemed to be in communication with half the world. On the second day, a quiet, grey man arrived to keep a confidential record of the proceedings. None of the gentlemen so much as ventured out of doors for four days. Instead, from first thing in the morning until an hour before dinner in the evening, they sat round the big table in the Red Drawing Room, talking, arguing, making notes, as intent as if the whole future of the Western world rested on their deliberations. It didn't occur to Rachel that this might be the literal truth.

At first she told herself it was no more than vexing that she couldn't find an opportunity to be private with Rainer Blake, blocking out the knowledge that it would have been easy if he had wanted it. But by the time four days had passed – each day, each hour, each minute a denial of all she had dreamed – she was almost in despair.

Having met him 'accidentally' on the stairs three times, she had found her pleasant remarks courteously but ruthlessly cut off as he excused himself either to return to the conference or change for dinner. She tried to talk to him at meals, too, but with no better results, and it was hard, in any case, to behave naturally with Colin Campbell's perceptive eye on her. Even after dinner, when the conversation briefly became general, turning to science, art, and music before Colin summoned his guests to the whist tables, Blake gave no indication of any desire for her company.

The signs were unequivocal but she would not believe them. All she needed, she told herself, was a little time with him to re-establish the relationship there had once been between them, the relationship she believed had sprung from a sense of recognition, a knowledge that they were two of a kind. After that, the attraction would reawaken. She knew it. She *had* to know it. He had kissed her once and, however he had behaved afterwards, it had meant something to him at the time. It would happen again, given the opportunity.

But there was no opportunity.

Her heart like lead, she volunteered to show him the new billiard room, into which, she told him, she had moved every single stag's head that had previously adorned the walls of the castle, but although he smiled at the conceit he had no desire to see how striking it looked. She even said forthrightly that she would be grateful for a private word with him.

'About what?'

'Well, you were so kind as to arrange the rental agreement with Mr Campbell, and . . .'

'I believe it's working out well?'

'Oh, yes!'

'Then if all you want to do is thank me, you may take it that your thanks are acknowledged, and you have no need to feel yourself in my debt.'

Despite his friendly smile, it sounded dismissive, but she didn't think it was intended to be. This particular 'stalking party' was turning out to be quite unlike any of the others she had played hostess to. None of the guests was here to be entertained, and their concentration was absolute. She herself was supererogatory and, indeed, felt overawed by the power and authority she sensed around her.

Although she had known, in an unrelated corner of her mind, that both Colin Campbell and Rainer Blake were men of influence, she had never suspected the extent of it. That Rainer Blake's word should help to mould the destiny of nations was something she found infinitely thrilling.

There was time, she went on telling herself. There was time. When all the business discussions were over, there would be a day or two when everyone would take the opportunity to relax and perhaps take a gun out or do some sea fishing.

And then Rainer Blake, meeting her on the stairs, stopped her to say, 'Forgive me, Rachel . . .'

Her heart soared.

'I guess I should have told you before, but I have been so engrossed that I forgot. I had an urgent message from Hong Kong on Wednesday, and if I leave tomorrow at first light I should just catch the next sailing for China. I hope it won't inconvenience the servants to let me have an early breakfast? At about six, perhaps?' He smiled. 'I'm sorry we haven't had the opportunity to talk, but I am impressed by the improvements you have made to Juran. And please accept my gratitude for your hospitality.'

The smile broadened. 'You have a remarkable talent for it!'

7

She wasn't the first woman in the world to have been confronted with such a predicament, the first woman to be in love with a man who appeared indifferent to her, the first woman determined to change things.

The trouble was that she didn't know how to go about it. And there was to be no time, after all. No time even to think.

When Blake retired to his room just after midnight, Rachel was waiting for him, out of his line of vision so that he wouldn't notice her at first. She didn't want him to stand with the door embarrassingly open, waiting for her to leave.

But she had no idea how finely honed his instincts were. Even as he took his first step across the threshold he sensed the human presence. Here at Juran, the chances of it being someone after his hide were nil, but he stopped dead, just the same.

Then, recognising the scent of lace, he sighed. 'My dear Rachel,' he said, 'think of your reputation. What can I do for you?'

'I wanted to see you.'

'Yes, I figured that. You haven't exactly made a secret of it.'

Leaving the door wide open, he crossed to the bed, tugging at his four-in-hand necktie and unbuttoning his jacket. 'I'm flattered, but I have an early start and, besides, if you want to talk about Juran, and rental contracts and the like, you should be talking to Colin. I was only the instrument of that arrangement and, frankly, at this moment there isn't a thought in my head other than sleep.'

He was offering her a way out, but she didn't accept it.

'It's not Juran I want to talk about. I want to talk about us.'

He sat down and began unlacing one shoe. 'Us?'

He glanced up at her and then away again, so that all she received was a glimpse of wintry eyes and a faint smile curving the long, hard mouth.

She had risen to her feet when he entered, meaning to go to him, and stand close to him, and let him read in her face what she wanted to say. But he had wrecked that plan by leaving the door open and sitting down, and behaving as unconcernedly as if she were his sister or someone else with whom he didn't have to stand on ceremony.

Most of what she had thought of saying had flown from her mind, but she tried to collect it together again. He was the kind of man who would be resistant to feminine wiles, and Rachel didn't know any, anyway, though she could *make* him love her, given time. But that wasn't something for words. She had to remind him that he found her attractive – didn't he? – and that they would be ideally suited, because she was not a silly little romantic miss, and she was quite clever and businesslike and knew how to handle distinguished people, so that she would be an excellent wife and hostess for him, and she would be able to . . .

Baldly, she said, 'I love you.'

Further along the corridor, Baron Rothschild called after his valet, 'The checked waistcoat tomorrow, remember!'

'Yes, sir. Goodnight, sir.'

Downstairs a door slammed.

In Blake's room there was silence as he devoted his attention to unlacing the second shoe. Then he said, 'You don't even know me.'

'I know everything I need to know.'

He dropped the shoe on the floor, with deliberation, and the thud of leather on carpeted stone was like the last chord of a funeral march. Then he rose to his feet and moved to stand before her, his hands resting loosely on his hips, his shirt carelessly open at the throat where he had undone his front collar stud.

'No, my dear, you don't,' he said.

8

Although in matters of business Blake's brain was functioning as efficiently as ever, in the matter of human relationships he had no spare capacity at all.

The urgent message from Hong Kong had been from Sophie, who had discovered within days of his sailing that she was pregnant and had written a panic-stricken letter to him, care of the Clyde River Bank, Broomielaw, Glasgow.

He hadn't even needed to read between the lines to recognise that she was cold and terrified, that the memory of her previous pregnancy had taken possession of her mind – the fear in the begetting, the illness during its course, and the tragedy of its end. The letter showed every sign of having been written in a highly emotional state, and he kept telling himself that the mere act of pouring it all out on paper must have been sufficient to calm her down.

But she had written, 'I won't have it. I won't!' and he had nightmare visions of her resorting to some abortionist in China town. She was half the world away and he didn't know how to stop her, his beautiful Sophie, who had been so badly hurt, who was still so innocent about so many things, who needed all the love and protection he could give her. He shouldn't have left her, and he cursed himself bitterly for it. It was nine weeks since the letter had been written and she had been alone all that time, without a word from him.

If she had telegraphed, she could have caught him at Bombay and he would have gone straight back. But he doubted if she knew what the telegraph was, and it hadn't occurred to him to explain it to her. He wasn't used to having a wife, and the telegraph was an adjunct of business, not private life.

But though he had used it to reply to her, two days before, he hadn't dared to be specific in it. The system linking the Far East to Europe had been in operation for only three years and was still neither reliable nor private. In business everyone resorted to code, but there was no code he could use to Sophie, and he could scarcely even tell her not to worry without it being a ninety per cent certainty that everyone in the colony would immediately begin speculating about what she was not to worry about.

It was only Sophie he could think about, only Sophie who mattered to him.

9

Rachel said again, 'I love you.'

'You may think you do . . .'

'*I do*! And you must know it. Don't you remember, on the beach last time you were here, you kissed me? It meant something to you, as well as to me, I know it did!'

'A kiss in the sunset? That's the stuff of romance, my dear, not reality.'

But she wouldn't allow him to brush it aside. 'I knew then that we belonged to each other, and we still do, if only you would give it a chance.'

So vibrant were her feelings that they were like a current of sparks flowing between them as she moved closer to him. The shoulders revealed by the wide black lace neckline were soft as satin. She wore a pretty little gold brooch on a black velvet ribbon round her throat, and the skirt of her dress below the handspan waist was swept backwards and up in a huge black velvet bow. The glossy chestnut hair was piled high and the wide blue eyes shadowed beneath.

He remembered it all too clearly from last time, that subdued sexuality that had set warning bells ringing, as it did now, telling him to stop before anything started. Because failing to stop would mean never to stop.

His body stirred, as any man's would have done, and he exerted every ounce of willpower to control it, detesting himself for this betrayal of Sophie, whom he loved with an intensity greater than he would have believed possible. Once he had been a cat who walked by himself, but now no more.

He didn't know what the devil Rachel was aiming at, other than his bed, and since treating her gently appeared to pay no dividends he said bluntly, 'I think you misunderstand the situation. I am not in the market for a mistress. And I already have a wife.'

Her clear skin was suddenly flooded with pink, and her eyes opened wide, the eyes that were handsome enough but in no way comparable with Sophie's. And then all the colour drained away, and she stepped back from him and said with an almost successful attempt at dignity, 'I'm sorry. I didn't know.'

He smiled then. 'We've never had occasion to discuss it, have we?'

'No. I'm sorry to have troubled you. Goodnight. Sleep well.'

She closed the door quietly behind her, and he had no way of knowing that his words had destroyed seven years of dreaming, made a hell of her fool's paradise, brought to ruin all her lovely, stupid, substanceless castles in the air.

10

Next morning, lips tight and death in her heart, Rachel watched Blake ride away. Four days later, the *Matilda* sailed with her reduced passenger list. Colin Campbell's guests thanked Miss Macmillan with sincerity for her hospitality and she heard them remarking to Mr Campbell on what a successful idea it had been to hold their conference here.

And then she was left to herself and the sights and sounds that signalled the beginning of Juran's long winter, the wild, haunting, primeval roar of the stags, and the noisy flurry of the migrating fieldfares that, year after year, with uncanny timing, arrived to strip the rowan trees at the very moment when the berries were at the perfect stage for jelly making. This year she could scarcely even summon up a pretence of the annoyance they expected of her in the kitchen.

She had failed. And she had no more time to waste, no more years to spare in the hope that, some day, she would be given the opportunity to try again. She scourged herself for everything she had said and hadn't said, for having lost herself in the maze of her passion for this one, desperately desired man.

She had been so obsessed that she hadn't even asked him if he knew anything of Mrs Taverner, her unknown, hated cousin Sophie.

11

She had to stop thinking about Rainer Blake, and the only other thing there was to think about was the threat from Gresham.

Needing physical activity to divert her mind, she decided to go to London herself and see what she could discover about the mysterious M. Rebecque.

Well aware that the journey was unlikely to be productive, she almost gave up when she began trying to arrange it, it was so complicated finding out even about timetables. Only once had she been on a long train journey before, when she and her mother had travelled from London to Glasgow for her parents' wedding. Child though she had been, excited though she had been, she could still remember the appalling discomforts, with no corridors, no food, no lavatories, no sleeping accommodation, hard seats, poor lighting and no heating except for a shared footwarmer. The journey had taken about twelve hours, as far as she remembered, not counting the changes and waiting on platforms, and she didn't think she could face anything like that again, though she supposed that things must have improved in the seventeen years since then.

In the end she sent a note to Colin Campbell asking if he could possibly advise her. He did better. By return of post, she received all the information she needed, and more. His clerk, he said, had ascertained that, starting from Glasgow, she would only have to change once if she took the Caledonian to Carlisle and then transferred to the London and North Western, which by a fortunate coincidence, had introduced its first sleeping car service on October 1st. It was expensive, and first class only, and she might have to share with someone else – unless there were no other ladies travelling alone, in which case she would have the double compartment to herself. It even had a wash basin, by the way, and how was that for progress?

Rachel would have paid her last penny to travel in something that wasn't a torture wagon and calculated that, if she spent only two nights in London, staying somewhere cheap but respectable, she could justify the cost of the sleeping compartment. She could even manage with a single valise if she took no change of clothes beyond two French blouses and two chemises, petticoats, sets of drawers, and corset covers. She would take some cold venison with her for the journey, and some bread and butter, and perhaps she would be able to get a cup of tea on the platform when the train stopped somewhere, even though she couldn't drink much; sleeping compartments there might now be, but no lavatories.

The rhythm of wheels on rails was an insistent lullaby and, to her own surprise, she slept. She felt amazingly fresh when she descended at Euston and made her way through the bustling, grandiose hall that was so like the cathedral she had mistaken it for in her childhood, and then passed under the enormous portico that didn't seem to do anything except stand and look splendid. The earsplitting noise of wooden wheels on stone, of horses neighing, porters shouting and boxes clattering, was just as she remembered. Familiar, too, were the smells of smoke and ordure, flowers and sweat, the roughness of grit and dust on the wind. Looking up, she saw a slice of sky, yellow-grey as marzipan on a cake.

She had loved it all once, before she had given her heart to Juran.

12

After she had found a respectable boarding house in Bloomsbury Square, she set out for Wardour Street and the restaurant La Corbeille, to look for the questionable M. Benjamin Rebecque. She hadn't decided whether or not she was going to speak to him, try to make him see sense, admit that after the lapse of a quarter of a century there might be confusion in his mind between Mlle Ondine Vallette and some other lady. Everything depended on what kind of man he was; whether he was the kind to give an honest answer to an honest question. Rachel doubted it.

She had forgotten how much warmer and drier it was in London than in Scotland. October notwithstanding, the sun was shining in the grand thoroughfare of Oxford Street, with its big ornate buildings, their ground floors mostly occupied by shops with sun blinds out to protect the merchandise and, coincidentally, the passersby. The roadway was full of horse drawn buses travelling west to Regent Circus or east to the Bank; of hansom cabs and brewers' drays and delivery carts; of respectable and well-dressed people who all looked supercilious and rather bad tempered. That was something else she had forgotten, that people in the smarter parts of London weren't nearly as obliging and kindhearted as they were in Scotland.

Turning into Wardour Street, she began to search for La Corbeille, finding with a wry pleasure that Soho was still as she remembered it. In Oxford Street there had been none but English voices; in Wardour Street, just round the corner, there were none but French. It was like changing countries, moving into the narrow canyon with its tall, flat-faced buildings, where people lived above the wooden-fronted shops and hung their washing out of windows from which stout, peasant-looking women chattered volubly to friends in the windows across the street.

There were French butchers and bakers, French wine shops and French schools, and it didn't take Rachel long to find the restaurant she wanted. La Corbeille turned out to be a wretched-looking place, with filthy windows and a door no more than two feet wide. She stood for a moment, hesitating, inhaling the cooking smells. Her mother had always said that the way to choose a restaurant was to stand in the doorway and sniff. This was not one in which she would have consented to eat. But Rachel braced herself and went inside.

The room was about thirty feet long by twelve wide, with a low, dirty ceiling and half a dozen dining booths along either side, so dark that the likelihood of customers being able to see what they were eating was infinitesimal. Rachel thought it was probably just as well. There were only a few people eating at this hour, most of the customers being busy smoking, playing cards, and arguing. It answered one question at least. La Corbeille was not the kind of place where a genteel female could sit over a cup of coffee, ears pricked, hoping to identify a waiter or kitchen hand. Rachel went over to the marble-topped bar.

'Monsieur Rebecque?' she enquired decisively. 'Benjamin Rebecque?' The name Benjamin wasn't easy to pronounce in French and her tongue tripped over it. '*Il est ici*?'

The answer was unmistakably surly. '*Pas ici. Salaud*!' The patron spat resoundingly into the spittoon.

He wasn't here, and he was a swine. Rachel took a deep breath, immediately regretting it, and embarked on trying to find out where he was. She might have saved herself the effort. The *salaud* had been a useless kitchen hand, a worse waiter, and the *patron* had not felt compelled to shed a tear when he had chosen to walk out some weeks ago, never to be seen again. Where did he lodge? The *patron* had no idea and the waiters whom he deigned to consult had none, either.

It was a relief to emerge from the place into the marginally sweeter air of the street. Rachel stood for a moment, hesitating, and then began to walk again because it was a mistake for a woman to stand idly on a street corner in Soho. Her thoughts had been so fixed on M. Rebecque that she was not yet prepared for Chez Vallette.

She walked on to Old Compton Street, and up Dean Street, then down Frith Street, and up Greek Street to find herself back in Oxford Street again looking in shop windows, postponing the moment of decision when she would confront the only family she possessed. Her grandfather, she estimated, must be in his late seventies if he were still alive, and her uncles probably in their forties or early fifties. One of them, at least, must survive, because the clean looking restaurant in Dean Street with the pink-and-white checked curtains, the glass door and polished brass holder for the day's menu still had the name Vallette painted in curly gold lettering on its fumed oak fascia.

13

The menu was adequate, though not ambitious, and the cooking smells appetising. Rachel could not have eaten there if it had been an English restaurant – a strictly male preserve – but the French were more civilised. She walked in and sat down at one of the small, round marble tables in a corner.

Her entry was barely acknowledged, but the place was half empty and a thin woman took her order for an omelette and a glass of wine without any sign of shock or disapproval. The omelette was excellent, and the *vin de table* of an acceptable standard. Under Colin Campbell's occasional tutelage, Rachel had become a much better judge.

The man behind the zinc counter must be one of her uncles, she concluded after a time, watching and listening carefully as he greeted his regular customers. Was there a resemblance to Ondine? She couldn't decide. His hair was somewhere between brown and fair, his eyes blue, but he was big and burly where Ondine had been plump and dainty. The very old man sitting, with an air of belonging, at the table in the far corner by the kitchen door was a different matter. In the line of his nose and the set of his brows, she thought she could see something of her mother.

It took an immense effort of will for her to approach the man behind the counter and say, 'Monsieur Vallette?'

'Yeh?' She had forgotten that English would be natural to him. Like her mother, he must have lived in London since he was a child.

'May I introduce myself?' He looked wary but nodded, and she went on, 'You had a sister named Ondine.'

His eyes narrowed, but then he had to turn away and greet a customer and fill a carafe of wine for him, and pass the time of day. He looked disappointed to find that Rachel was still there when he had finished.

'I had a sister,' he agreed.

'I am her daughter, your niece.'

'Yeh?'

It wasn't very encouraging. She said tartly, 'Don't let excitement get the better of you, will you?'

'Why should I? My sister was a flighty woman who brought disgrace on the family. She could have mothered a dozen daughters, for all I care.'

'I was her only child.' Rachel hadn't really expected to be hugged to an avuncular bosom, kissed on both cheeks, and plied with wine and questions, but she had thought there might at least have been forbearance after all these years. 'Don't you want to know what happened to her?'

He shrugged. 'I know already.'

'You *know*?'

'Yeh. There was a man here a few months ago, asking about her. He said she had married the Scotch fellow after all, and they were both dead now.'

Why hadn't she thought? It would have been natural for Gresham to send someone here in the course of his so-called researches into the past. 'What did you tell him?'

Her uncle shrugged again. 'Nothing. He wanted to know about her other men friends twenty-six years ago. How should I remember?'

'Quite right!' she said approvingly. 'How should *anyone* remember what happened twenty-six years ago! My name is Rachel, by the way. Rachel Vallette Macmillan.'

'I am Charles. It was a good omelette, yeh?'

'Excellent.'

'Since you are my niece, I will not charge you for it.'

'Thank you. But I need you to help me. Would you testify that my mother was a good and respectable girl when she was young?'

Again he turned away to exchange a word with a customer, and then turned back and, with visible malice, hoisted her with her own petard. 'How should I remember that, either?'

He wasn't interested. For him, the past was past. She glared at him. 'Is that my grandfather over there? Can I speak to him?'

'You can try.'

She went and sat down beside him, and gazed into his pale, watery eyes, and smiled like a dutiful, loving granddaughter, and talked and talked and talked. He wasn't deaf, because she had seen him exchange a few words with one of the waiters, but he might as well have been. She thought perhaps his only relationship with the world, now, was through the routines that had been familiar all his life.

But she persevered, punctuating almost every sentence with the words, 'your daughter, Ondine.' And in the end, the rheumy eyes flickered and the slack mouth opened and her patience was rewarded.

'I have no daughter,' the old man said.

14

She jumped to her feet and, with no more than a nod to her Uncle Charles, stalked out of the restaurant.

'Told yer so!' said little Ellie Vallette with morbid relish.

And it was, of course, just what she had expected, though that didn't make it any better.

She had reached Bedford Square, hurrying along at a pace that caused heads to turn, before she admitted to herself that what she had really been looking for wasn't evidence about her mother's past. What she had hoped to find was that she wasn't alone in the world after all, that she had a family, a real family, someone to call her own.

But her family had rejected her. Rainer Blake had rejected her. And she had rejected Colin Campbell.

Self-pity was not one of her habitual vices and that, perhaps, was why it now hit her so hard.

She travelled back to Glasgow that same night, though she had to pay for her unslept-in bed at the boarding house and then share her sleeping compartment with a hoity-toity governess who snored.

Descending from the train at Bridge Street Station, she felt as if she had been put through a wringer so, instead of walking all the way, she took a horsedrawn tram to Renfield Street and walked from there to Colin Campbell's offices on the corner of George Square.

She hesitated when she saw them. They were very large and splendid and didn't look as if they were used to having travel-stained ladies plod wearily up their front steps. But although the first gentleman to whom she gave her name was quite as hoity-toity as her late travelling companion, another soon appeared who couldn't have been kinder. It was he, it transpired, who had made her travel arrangements and he was most anxious to reassure himself that everything had been all right. When, having thanked him sincerely, she said that she would like to tidy up, he hurried to find one of the bank's lofty lady typewriters, who told Rachel that she operated a machine so advanced that few people had yet heard of it but wasn't too lofty to take her down to a well hidden corner of the basement, where there were a mirror and other more urgent necessities.

And then she explained to Colin Campbell, as succinctly as she could, what she had been doing and why.

'So, you see,' she concluded, 'I was wasting my time and I have no idea what to do next. Mr Napier told me once that lawyers weren't equipped to search for people, and I can't think who else but you to turn to for advice. Do you mind? Is it improper of me to ask you? It's at times like this that I realise how inexperienced I am.'

Colin surveyed her quizzically. 'My, my! Now, that's a confession I would never have expected to hear from Miss Rachel Macmillan.'

She had the grace to blush.

Colin was aware of a powerful desire to take her in his arms – a desire that, he told himself, was positively indecent at this hour of the day – but he had stymied himself once by showing his feelings at the wrong time and he was not a man who made the same mistake twice.

Despite her refusal to marry him – and admonishing himself for a fool – he had recently bought a house in the new Great Western Terrace, a far grander house than, as a childless widower, he could possibly have been said to need. He rationalised it to his friends, and to himself, by its comparative proximity to the Botanic Gardens, which was a great place for photography. And, of course, there was plenty of space for a studio and a darkroom. He hadn't mentioned a wife.

Before he proposed to her again, he thought it wouldn't do any harm to remind her that men were useful things to have around.

'You should have told me all this before. You've let it get out of proportion. Gresham's playing a damnfool game and he'd be laughed out of court, if ever it came to that.'

'Would he?' She cheered up a little.

'Just ignore him,' Colin said.

'I can't.'

'All right, then. I'll put out some feelers for you.'

'Feelers?'

'Those waving things lobsters have on their front ends.'

She chuckled. 'No! I meant, *are* there feelers you can put out?'

'Bankers can find out anything about anybody, if they want to.'

Colin didn't think he was going to have much trouble over M. Rebecque. When folk disappeared without warning from their homes and jobs, their reasons almost always boiled down to love or money. In the present case, it was clear enough which, and it shouldn't be hard to make the link with Gresham.

What troubled him more was his own continuing problem of divided loyalties. He had suggested to Blake that he ought to tell Rachel about the Archie Macmillan mortgage, but it had been a bad moment because Blake had just heard that his wife was ill and was preparing to hurry back to Hong Kong. Colin hadn't even known he was married. Keeping his own counsel was such a fetish of Blake's that Colin sometimes wondered whether his right hand knew whose balance sheet his left hand was adding up.

But his marriage was an uncovenanted blessing. Colin had been uneasy at the way Rachel's eyes had followed him around.

Since there wasn't a place nearby to which he could decently take a lady, he sent out to a good local chophouse for some lunch and he and Rachel shared it in his office, talking neutrally of Juran and future plans and occasionally of photography. He even produced some house party photographs he'd taken three weeks before, and she admired them dutifully, remarking on how well Mr Chamberlain had come out but singling out no one else at all. Then she left for Juran.

A week later, Colin had all the information he needed. He hesitated about seeing Gresham himself, but since he had, as yet, no right to interfere in Rachel's affairs, decided he'd better leave it to her to deal with.

17

It gave Rachel a weary pleasure to write to Gresham inviting him to visit her, in terms designed to make him think he had won.

It was a grey, wet, cold, windy November day when, with Horace in tow, he rode up to Juran for the last time – she hoped – wearing a heavy brown tweed ulster with a shoulder cape and a wideawake hat pulled well down and attached by a cord to one of his coat buttons. Even so, he looked chilled to the bone. Horace, on the other hand, never worried about getting wet, as if he were naturally aquatic. He wasn't, Rachel reflected with private amusement, a frog who had turned into a prince, but he did look rather like a fish sometimes.

Sympathising more with the horses than their riders, she resigned herself to putting the two men up for the night, and sent one of the girls to their rooms with tin baths, hot water and towels. Then they dined coldly and with extreme formality, Rachel and Gresham saying nothing, Horace indulging in his usual extended monologue on Yosemite and Yellowstone.

But afterwards, with the servants dismissed, Rachel prepared to enjoy herself. This was an evening Gresham was never going to forget, because she meant to shock him out of his pretensions for good and all. She intended to begin by lulling him into a false sense of security, so that the shock would be all the greater when it came. She would have to handle it carefully, she knew; his vanity might be so sublime that he was scarcely more aware of other people's words than of their feelings, but even he must sense that she hated him as much as he did her.

Doing her best to sound feminine and helpless, she said, 'Why are you so intent on blackening my poor mother's name? I used to think, when you were harsh about her, that it was only the heat of the moment, but it's more than that, isn't it? I don't understand how you can be so unkind.'

It sounded hideously false in her own ears, but Gresham lapped it up in the most satisfactory way.

385

His arrogant brows rose the merest fraction. 'Kindness and unkindness do not enter into it. Neither does your mother. Justice is the issue, and it is my object to prove that you have no right to the possession of Juran.'

'Well, we've been into that before. But this "proof" of my mother's moral laxity . . .' She frowned. 'Twenty-six years is a long time. There can't be many people who remember exactly what they were doing in a particular week or month so long ago.'

'Perhaps, but the memory may easily be stimulated by events which are on public record, as in this fellow Rebecque's case. His sworn testimony exists, and there is no way in which you can disprove it.'

Which might have been true, had it not been for dear, kind Colin Campbell. 'You are saying that it's Mr Rebecque's word against everyone else's?'

'What I am saying is that there is *no* "everyone else." '

'But you must have gone to my grandfather's restaurant, didn't you? And they *must* have told you that my mother was a perfectly respectable young woman before my father appeared on the scene.' She paused, looking wistful. 'I wish you would tell me what they said. What they were like.'

Under her eyelashes, she glanced at Horace. But he didn't appear to have any suspicions, either.

'What they were like?' Gresham repeated. 'You cannot possibly imagine that I would set foot in such a place. Indeed, I do not believe that I am entirely sure where Soho is.'

'How did you find Mr Rebecque, then?'

'I had a man make enquiries, one more familiar with London's seedier parts than I. A retired police constable, as it happens.'

From choice, she did now what during the years of his residence at Juran she had done under instruction, and rose to pour brandy for him.

'Horace? What will you have?' He looked more like a fish than ever – a cod, to be precise – and little Ellie Vallette chirped inside her head, 'Water, with a large dash of salt, please.'

'I'll have brandy, too.'

Her back still turned, she asked, 'Is Mr Rebecque a – a respectable man?'

The sneer on Gresham's face migrated into his voice. 'Yes, it *would* be of interest to you, I suppose, to know what type of man your father – or one of the candidates for the position – is or was. I have no idea whether the fellow is "respectable".'

Handing one glass to him and the other to Horace, who at least had the grace to thank her, she sat down again. Gresham looked quite relaxed in the big, padded leather chair with the earpieces that kept out draughts.

'I don't need to wonder about my father,' she said calmly. 'My father was Daniel Macmillan.'

He wagged a soft white finger at her and shook his head reproachfully on the thick neck. 'No. And you have admitted as much by inviting me here. I have incontrovertible evidence to the contrary.'

She laughed, ready to begin turning the tables. 'My dear man, the word you want is not "incontrovertible" but "circumstantial", and frail enough at that.'

The 'my dear man' pricked him as she remembered it doing once before. The slashes framing the waxen cheeks deepened as his upper lip lifted disparagingly but he said nothing, twirling the brandy gently in his glass, his eyes intent on the rich amber glow of its contents against the firelight.

Reflectively, she went on, 'The truth was that my father was unable to marry my mother while his own father was still alive, but that he went back to her as soon as the old man died.'

Neither by look nor intonation did she give him any warning at all. 'And really, one could hardly blame him, a red-blooded man married, not by his own choice, to a frigid apology for a woman like dearest Isabella . . .'

Horace exclaimed, '*Rachel!*' but Gresham sat still as a graven image, only his eyes like black beads showing a semblance of life.

Rachel went on '. . . and what a wilting lily she must have been. Quite as self-centred as you, Gresham, and too lethargic even to raise a hand if she didn't have to. I cannot imagine how she bestirred herself sufficiently to conceive and give birth to two children . . .'

And that struck home.

'You slut! *How dare you!*' He could scarcely force the words out, the heavy muscles of face and neck standing out like cords, and the thick, white, pore-less skin flushed red as rubies.

Now she was getting somewhere. But she managed to control her excitement, to continue sitting back at apparent ease as, judiciously, she replied, 'It's not a question of daring. For years you have been spreading slanders against my mother. Now it's time for me to strike back.'

He opened his mouth again but this time she overrode him, and her voice was savage with contempt. 'As for the famous Mr Rebecque, what a *fool* you are, Gresham! I have irrefutable proof that you paid him £100, a fortune to such a man, for his so-called testimony. It's known as bribery, my friend, and you didn't even have the sense to pay him in cash.

'You're a fraud and a liar, and it is going to give me the greatest possible pleasure to expose you. I wonder, have you any idea what the penalties are for trying to pervert the course of justice?'

'You have no such proof.'

'Oh, yes. I have.' Her voice carried complete conviction. 'You can't imagine yourself behind bars, can you? But you will when the doors clang closed behind you. I will enjoy coming to visit you.'

She had no intention of carrying things as far as that. All she wanted was to see the last of Gresham; for his defeat this time to be so unequivocal that, even if he wasn't totally silenced, any threat from him in the future would be no more troublesome than the whining of a wasp round her head, irritating, inconvenient, but never in danger of being fatal.

His eyes were dilated and not entirely in focus, the sneer sitting uneasily on a face that was no longer the face she knew, as he said thickly, 'Even if what you say were true, which it is not . . .'

Rachel's heart began to turn cartwheels inside her and she could have shouted aloud in exultation. Because she had achieved the impossible; she had *really* penetrated his armour. The autocratic, arrogant, patronising aesthete, Mr Lucian Gresham, had succumbed to the most vulgar of all human weaknesses. He had lost his temper.

'. . . any legal action you chose to take,' he was mouthing, 'would result in your mother's sins being spread over the front page of every newspaper in the land. You would not like that.'

With a smile as sparkling, as overflowing with stars as Aunt Minerva's had ever been, she met his eyes and was satisfied, the soul-warming delight flowing through her veins like some divine current. 'No, I would not. But I assure you, I could survive it if, as a result, you got what you deserved. It would be some small recompense, at last, for all you have inflicted on me over the years. And, you know . . .' She paused for a long, carefully calculated moment. 'I have the feeling that you would enjoy, even less, having your sister's frigidity spread over those same pages. As it would be. I would make sure of it.'

Never had she seen such an expression on any man's face.

And then, in a searing flash, she understood what it was all about.

What it had always been about. It made sense of so many things.

The sainted Isabella. The sister to whom he had always been so close.

Without conscious volition, she spoke her thoughts aloud, almost wonderingly. 'Do you have nightmares, still, about her being in bed with her husband, doing all the things husbands and wives do to beget children? Do you . . .'

18

His glass hit the floor with a tinkling crash, and a splash of brandy set one of the logs flaring.

Gresham was on his feet, one hand clawing at the stiff wing collar and the other tearing at the breast of his coat. His sulky mouth was open and he was trying to draw in breath in huge, tearing gulps. But the air wasn't getting to his lungs because the muscles of his neck were as taut as steel hawsers and the movements of his chest no more than useless flutterings. There was sweat standing on his forehead, and his body was swaying as if he were about to fall.

Horace was on his feet, crying, 'Father! Father! What's wrong?' but it was several seconds before Rachel's disbelieving eyes communicated with her brain and she jumped to her feet and pushed Horace out of the way so that she could steady Gresham and push him back into his chair before he fell in the fire. He was so unbalanced by then that he landed half over the arm with his head trailing and his hands still futilely pawing the air round collar and coat.

'Help me, Horace!' Rachel snapped as, with fingers that were all thumbs, she struggled with Gresham's tie and collar and stud, pushing his hand aside and feeling it ice-cold and nerveless. Even his jacket buttons wouldn't open to her frantic touch.

Fuming at her own uselessness, she left him to Horace and ran to the bellpull and tugged and tugged until one of the servants appeared at a run, still trying to fasten his coat. 'The doctor,' she said. 'Ride for the doctor.'

When she turned back, Horace was standing between her and his father, arms spread wide as if to protect him, tears pouring down his cheeks and his slack mouth quivering. 'Don't come near him,' he cried hysterically. 'I won't let you come near him. It's all your fault.

'If he dies, you will have killed him.'

CHAPTER SEVENTEEN

❦

I

When Blake's ship steamed into Hong Kong harbour, Sophie was waiting on the Praya, visibly pregnant, her eyes brilliant and her hand pressed to her throat as if excitement threatened to overwhelm her.

Such was the wave of emotion that swept over Blake that it took a harsh effort of will for him to unclamp his white-knuckled hands from the rail and wave to her as if he had never doubted for a moment. All he wanted to do was hold her to him for ever, to love her and protect her, never to leave her again.

In the hour before he was able to land, they scarcely took their eyes from each other.

2

Public displays of affection, beyond a peck on the cheek, were not permissible, so it was not until they were back at East Point that he could even kiss her properly. Her response was highly satisfactory, even if she displayed a regrettable tendency to withdraw her mouth from his in order to chatter.

At least it was chatter with which he had little fault to find.

'I love you so much . . . I've missed you so much . . . I've been so miserable without you . . .'

'Stop talking. Kiss me.'

'Yes, but . . .'

'Kiss me.'

It was all they would be able to do in the months until the baby was born, because making love was forbidden and Blake would not ask her to do for him the things that would have eased his own desire. Although Sophie absolutely refused to speak of the physical side of her first marriage, he had guessed – such was her tension when he relaxed his own careful restraint – that Taverner must have been inconsiderate, selfish, probably brutal with her. It was hard to counter, and something that couldn't be countered with words. Often, during the six months before he had sailed for Europe, he had told her that he would do nothing, *nothing* that she didn't like, and she had seemed to believe him. But he knew that her fears still lingered. She needed time as well as love.

When the delight of having him back began to assume sensible proportions, he was concerned to discover that, although her initial despair had passed and she was suffering none of the frightening symptoms of her previous pregnancy, she was still incoherently terrified of what lay ahead.

'I know I shouldn't have written to you as I did, but I needed you so much. Please let's talk about something else. There's three months still to go, and I shall go mad if I haven't anything else to think about. Oh, darling, it *will* be all right this time, won't it?'

'Of course it'll be all right. Don't worry.'

Her voice rose. 'Don't worry? It's all very well for you. *You* don't have to go through it. Don't worry! Every man's answer to every woman's problems! I know it's well meant, but it's not startlingly helpful when you come to think about it.'

He grinned. '*Touché.* All right, what shall we talk about?'

'Anything! How did you feel when my letter arrived?'

'Horrified. I was in the middle of a conference, and forced to depart not only in unseemly haste but at the crack of dawn, to the inconvenience of all and sundry, fellow bankers and castle staff included. Not even for you was I prepared to ride fifty miles through trackless wastes on a pitch dark night.'

She giggled. 'What are you talking about? I shouldn't have thought there were many trackless wastes around Glasgow. I saw somewhere that the population was about half a million.'

'There's still space around it. But, anyway, we were at Juran.'

'You were *where*?'

'We borrowed it,' he said with something less than truth. 'It's a great place for private and confidential gatherings.'

'Well, I hope they're *respectable* private and confidential gatherings! I don't think I like that. You mean my cousin sort of – sort of – lets the place out?'

'Mmmm.'

'Well, perhaps you can tell me more about her now!'

Blake grinned. It was like teasing a kitten with a piece of string.

Sophie seemed to find it deeply frustrating not to be able to put a face or personality to her cousin.

'We didn't see much of her. Juran's in good shape, though, thanks to her ministrations, and she's an excellent hostess. A very competent young woman, in fact.'

'She sounds boring. What does she look like?'

'I've told you before. Small. Neat. Rather stylish, though not where clothes are concerned. I can't remember her wearing a single dress you would have looked at even once. Or, no, there was quite a handsome evening dress, but it was black so you wouldn't have looked at it twice.'

'Is she pretty?'

'No. But it's a face you wouldn't forget. And she has an attractive smile that lights up her eyes.'

Sophie had heard enough. 'She sounds a paragon. But you're not asking what *I* did while you were away.'

'Besides writing letters calculated to scare the pants off me?'

3

'I wanted to take my mind off things, and I thought, if I really concentrated, I might learn enough from Gino Venturi to dazzle you when you came back, so that you couldn't complain that all I thought about was gowns and gossip. So I presented myself at the offices one day . . .'

She had worn a serious expression, a dark Madras cotton dress, and a bottle green *marin anglais* bonnet with the trimmings removed.

Everyone had seemed duly impressed, and Gino Venturi had ushered her into the office that had been her father's and, later, Richard's, with something that was very nearly a bow.

He had been wearing his most emollient smile and, rather crisply, she had asked, 'And what is that intended to mean?'

'Admiration, dear lady,' he replied promptly.

She had been 'young Sophie' to him when she was a child, and then 'Miss Sophie', 'Mrs Taverner', and finally 'Mrs Blake', and with each change of title their relationship had become cooler and more distant. She didn't know why 'dear lady' should sound like a calculated insult, but it did.

'As senior partner,' she retaliated, 'I thought it was time for me to take a more positive interest in the business. There is, of course, a

392

good deal of which I am ignorant, despite the instruction you gave me a few years ago. Perhaps we might take up our lessons again?'

And that, she thought, hadn't been too bad at all.

His mobile brows rose, and he puffed out his lips soundlessly in what might have been an 'Oh, ho!' Then he said, 'I am at your command,' and grinned, and sauntered out of the room again, hands in pockets.

Overcoming a powerful desire to summon him back so that she could slap his face, she glanced round the office and felt slightly lost. It didn't look as if it had ever been used much. Her father had done most of his business at the Club, and she supposed Richard hadn't spent more than a few stray hours here during the whole course of their married life. She had no idea what they had actually *done*. She didn't know what she was going to do, either.

If it hadn't been for Gino Venturi, she would probably have abandoned the whole idea.

As it was, observing the grubbiness of the walls and the layer of dust on everything, she realised that there was a least one thing she could do this very minute. Picking up the tarnished brass bell from the big square desk, she rang it vigorously and, when a nervous-looking Chinese clerk came running, said with a sweeping gesture, 'My wanchee ollo washee, chop chop! Can do?'

He stared at her and, after a moment, said, 'Washee?' as if he had never heard of soap and water before. 'Maskee.'

Which meant – 'Um, er, well, maybe.'

'There's no "maskee" about it! I want the whole office washed down now, today, at once. See to it!'

4

Blake laughed. 'And what happened after that?'

'I had a very clean office.'

'And?'

'I can't decide whether Gino Venturi was trying to help me learn, or to stop me from learning. It was just like last time. He told me so much in such a short time that my mind closed down. I know a lot of phrases, but I've no idea what they mean. What, for example, is the coolie trade?'

They were sitting in the garden under a star-spangled December sky, and she didn't see the careful look that came over her husband's face.

'Not "is",' he said. 'Was. There are new mines, plantations and goldfields in places like Australia and America where they're desperate for a supply of cheap labour. Until we banned the trade, shipowners loaded their vessels to the gunwales with Chinese from Macao and transported them, under contract, to where they were needed. It was as bad as the old trade in African slaves.'

'You mean it's illegal now?'

'Yes, though only for vessels registered in Hong Kong. The trade from Macao still goes on in foreign bottoms. And there's no law against collecting coolies along the Chinese coast and taking them *to* Macao. The theory is that where they go after that is their own concern.'

'I see.'

Blake would have preferred not to hear the relief in her voice.

'And what are "protecting tigers"? They sound very picturesque.'

'They're not. It's a name for the kind of armed escort vessel merchants sometimes hire to protect their junks against pirates.'

'How dull.'

'Possibly. But by a curious coincidence, merchants who choose not to hire them usually find themselves wishing, later, that they had. Why?'

'I only wondered.'

The last thing Blake had wanted, even before this, was for Sophie to involve herself in Macmillan and Venturi, but he had dug the pit for himself by making it legitimate for her to take an interest. She was too naïve to be entrusted with his suspicions about Gino Venturi, so he set about trying to coax her out of it, laughingly enumerating all the things it would not be permissible for her to do, even if they proved to be within her competence.

Convention, he said, would forbid her to have any direct relationship with customers or suppliers. European customers wouldn't take her seriously, and Chinese suppliers would simply look through her, as if she didn't exist at all. Accounting was Gino Venturi's province and, however irritating he might be, he was amazingly good at it. The hiring out of Macmillan and Venturi's small fleet of ships was efficiently handled by one of the senior clerks, an Indian called Dadabhai Naoroji, who spoke Cantonese with a Bombay accent you could cut with a knife, and he had a Welshman for an assistant, one Evan Ellis, a shifty young man who was, however, perfectly good at his job.

Since it didn't occur to Sophie that her husband was one of the few men in the colony to whom Macmillan and Venturi's shadier endeavours were of professional interest, she thought he was trying to discourage her only because he didn't like the idea of her spreading her wings.

She tucked her arm in his and said soothingly, 'Never mind, my interest didn't last long. I had to stop going in to the office as soon as the baby began to show. I don't promise never, ever, to go back, mind you . . .'

And with that he had to be content. When the baby came, he thought, she would forget the whole idea.

5

Sophie's labour lasted three days, the long agony of the birth merging insensibly with her tortured memories of baby Tina's death into something she was never to be able to put into words. Her brain recoiled from it, rejected it, so that no detail remained, only chaos.

When, with infinite patience, Blake tried to persuade her to talk about it, all she could say, to herself as to him, was, 'It was awful'.

But at least, blessedly, the infant son who had been put in her arms for a moment before she fell into a long, exhausted sleep, deep as a coma, was unharmed by his hard passage into the world, and from the moment Sophie woke again, she could scarcely bear to be parted from him.

She couldn't remember ever knowing such bliss as sitting with him in her arms, suckling him. Nothing on earth would have induced her to employ a wet nurse, and she felt quite sorry for Rainer, excluded from heaven by being only a father, though he was almost as besotted as she was by the pink and chuckling little mite whose official name was Archibald Macmillan Blake.

The only thing was, 'I don't want another child,' she wept pitifully, whenever her husband began to make love to her.

He knew it wasn't uncommon for women who had recently given birth to be hesitant about resuming sexual relations, but as the weeks passed, and then the months, the knowledge didn't help. She was so inarticulate that, although he wanted to understand – would have given almost anything to understand – he had no frame of reference, no faintest hint of where he should begin to try and break down the barrier. And there was another thing. His own cast of mind was such

395

that, however often she told him she couldn't talk about it, he still believed in the depths of his heart that what she meant was – wouldn't.

'Damn it to hell! I'm human, too!' he exclaimed one night when, as so often, she had welcomed his arms around her and then begun shivering like a frightened animal the moment he was aroused. There was pleasure in it for neither of them and, for him, a dreary distaste as he withdrew from her, as he always now did, at the moment of climax.

'I love you,' he said with all the force at his command. 'I want to *make* love to you. We cannot go on like this.'

'Just a little longer,' she pleaded, as she always did, and because he loved her he gave in, as he always did.

But the strain was acute and, because she was more beautiful than she had ever been, he began to make increasingly frequent trips away, to the China that occupied so many of his thoughts. He might have reached his varied destinations more rapidly by sea, if there had not been considerations of secrecy to be taken into account, but speed was relative and the journey as instructive as its goal. In any case, it suited him.

Rich fields, graceful hills, rocks sculpted by wind and rain, mountains towering and majestic; gilded temples and bright pagodas; noble rivers and rare plants; all sorts and conditions of men. And space. Only America could match it, but America was familiar, China still and forever strange.

6

When Archie was six months old, Sophie decided to pay a visit to Macmillan and Venturi again, just to look in, she told herself, in case there was anything interesting happening. Rainer was away, and she was bored and restless. It was the typhoon season, which always had that effect on her.

Ah Foon tried to prevent her from going out. 'No good day. Big wind come.' The Chinese claimed that, prior to the arrival of the 'big wind', a particular sound became audible in the air, a sound they described as a small noise whirling round at intervals. No one other than the Chinese seemed able to hear it, but Sophie didn't think it should be dismissed just because of that. Gino Venturi did.

Indeed, his exasperation over her demands to know whether he had taken precautions was such that the cream in his voice turned sour.

'For God's sake, girl, we've had four typhoon warnings in the last three weeks and nothing has come of them except a bit of a breeze. We can't afford to send the junks scuttling for cover again. It not only wastes time, it demoralises the crews. And as far as the steam vessels are concerned, both the *Wildgoose* and the *Mamma Mia* are at the wharves in the midst of loading. If we stop, we'll still have to pay charges and wages. And the profit margin is low enough already, without that.'

'And what if there *is* a typhoon?'

'There won't be.'

'I see! If you say it often enough, the *tai fung* will hear you and just go away?'

'*Dio santo*! It's a question of calculating the odds. Can't you see that?'

'Yes, I can. And since nothing has come of the last four warnings, the odds are in favour of this one being real. I'm the senior partner and I think we shouldn't be loading the *Wildgoose* and the *Mamma Mia*, we should be unloading them. Then at least if we lose the ships we won't lose the cargoes, too.' Gino Venturi looked out at the sky, puffing his lips as he always did when he was thinking.

'It looks fine enough, but it's sultry,' he said reluctantly. 'All right, I'll keep an eye on the barometer. It's been falling for the last few hours.'

It was the first victory Sophie had ever had over Gino Venturi and it pleased her inordinately.

She smiled at him so vividly that he couldn't help but respond. His eyes, crinkling disarmingly back at her, were of the same blue as Richard's had been – the light blue that the Chinese and Japanese called the badge of the barbarians – but whatever Gino Venturi was, he wasn't a barbarian. She couldn't think why she had ever suspected him of being involved in Richard's murder. It had been the Li wedding, she supposed, and seeing him in that conspiratorial huddle with Ah Foon and the Changs. She suddenly found herself wondering what his birth sign was.

'The same as yours,' he said.

'Really?'

It meant he must be just twelve years older than she was. She had always thought him more.

'Monkey plus Monkey!' she exclaimed. 'We ought to make a good team.'

'Provided,' he replied promptly, 'that we don't make the mistake of blaming each other in the face of adversity. Am I right?'

She said, 'Let's hope the question doesn't arise.'

7

By midday the sky had clouded over and the barometer was still falling, but more steeply. The waters of the harbour were running a long, heavy swell and sampans and junks had begun to appear from all points of the compass, though they didn't seem to be making for shelter.

By mid-afternoon the first poles had gone up in China town – the poles with the lanterns on them – and the gongs were beating and the firecrackers snapping. By that time, too, Gino Venturi had been down to the wharves and stopped the loading of the cargo boats. He had also, without compunction, stolen extra anchors for them from the chandlery store of a neighbouring trader who hadn't yet seen fit to start worrying, and had told the Chang brothers to get the *Meall* and *Corran* off to one of the typhoon shelters at once, if not sooner.

By early evening no one could doubt that a typhoon was coming. The horizon in every direction was like a vast, congealing bruise, a purple that wasn't purple, a black that wasn't black, and above it the whole sky boiled with clouds, thick and filthy, moving not like ordinary clouds, all in the same direction, but rolling round, and back, and sideways so that it seemed as if the thunder that reverberated from peak to peak of the Nine Dragon hills of Kowloon was the sound of the clouds themselves colliding, and colliding, and colliding again, like celestial cannonballs run deafeningly amok.

While most of Macmillan and Venturi's staff had spent the afternoon sealing up every door and window in the offices and hammering battens over every crack and aperture in the warehouses, Sophie had virtuously devoted herself to packing files and papers into stout wooden chests that would withstand disaster if the roof or the building itself were to collapse. It was the first test of her dedication. Fighting off a desperate desire to hurry home to her son, she gritted her teeth and refused to stop until Gino Venturi finally said, 'Enough!'

She would have had to go sooner if she had left Archie at East Point, but the tenants of the house at Caine Road had recently left and she had decided to move herself and Archie in for a few days while she made up her mind what was needed in the way of repairs and redecoration.

Caine Road wasn't far so, escorted by an impossibly jovial Dadabhai Naoroji, who claimed to enjoy 'a good blow', she set off at a brisk walk that soon developed into a run. The sea had built up a huge surf and the sky was midnight dark, lit only by occasional flares from ships already in distress. Even as Sophie ran, the lights of Hong Kong itself began to go out because it was too dangerous to leave them on when winds of up to 130 miles per hour could be expected, winds searching and hungry enough to start fires that the sporadic rains might not last long enough to put out.

The typhoon wind was among the most savage forces in Nature, evil, wanton and destructive, inconceivably powerful.

Had it not been blowing from the north and still gathering its breath, Sophie might never have reached home. As it was, the muggy, arbitrary thrust of it swept her up the hill, stumbling and tripping, sweat starting from every pore, until she reached the house and found that the servants had already taken all the right precautions. The jalousies were up, the wooden shutters that resembled thick-slatted Venetian blinds and could be made fast with vertical bars. Everything outdoors that was movable had been moved to where the wind could not get at it.

The front door alone had not been barred, though it was bolted and she had to beat hard on it before the houseboy opened it for her. To Dadabhai Naoroji she shouted, 'Come in, you must come in! There isn't time for you to get home yourself before the wind strikes.' But he beamed at her and shouted back, 'No, no. I am jolly fine, memsahib. See, I have gone. *Namasti!*'

Even as she slipped through the door, the big wind struck, and she and the houseboy had to lean hard on it in order to close it again. The roaring was so loud that he didn't even hear her screams of 'Push! Push!' but stared at her blankly as if he were having to read her lips. They had a last glimpse of the rain coming down in swirling, spiralling sheets and the harbour whipped up into a foam as white as soap suds, and then it was done.

Sodden, breathless, exhausted, Sophie leaned against the door and saw in the light of the single candle that the mercury in the barometer was standing at just twenty-seven inches.

8

It didn't seem worth changing into dry clothes because the warmth was so oppressive and the humidity so high that Sophie thought she would probably be wet through again in no time at all.

So she put a shawl over her shoulders, and took little Archie from his baby amah and sat with him in her arms, and waited.

She had been through major typhoons before – the one in '67; another in '70, soon after she had married Richard; and a third a year later. They had been in daylight and they had been bad. But this was in darkness, and it was the worst.

There was nothing to do other than sit and try, unavailingly, to keep the fear and dread at bay.

After a while, she found that she was weeping all over the baby, who was whimpering and restless, tossing in her arms, struggling occasionally and letting out little wails that stabbed her all the way through to the heart. She knew he must be miserably uncomfortable and terrified, though with a different – simpler – terror than her own, and she became obsessed by not being able to explain it to him, not being able to convey to him that it would all be over in a few hours or a day, or two days. That it would end, somehow, some time. That, however it might seem, he hadn't *really* been torn from his happy, gurgling little life and flung into some torment that would go on for ever and ever, amen. But even if he had understood the words, she thought, he probably wouldn't have understood the concepts. Did babies have any appreciation of beginnings and continuances and inevitable ends?

She held him tight, and talked to him, and chuckled at him, and prayed that he couldn't feel the blind panic that possessed her.

She prayed for Rainer, too, wherever he might be.

With all the doors and windows tight, the air was suffocating, claustrophobic, the heat and humidity lying like a weight on every limb. All the candles and lamps had been put out so that the darkness became a menacing, malevolent thing, full of noises that made no sense, of crashings and tearings, howlings and groanings that might have been right outside the door or a mile away, that might represent only a shrub being whipped by the wind or all the soil on the Peak disintegrating into an avalanche of mud that would sweep down and smother the entire colony, burying everyone in it until the time came to rise again for the Judgement Day.

There were other sounds, too, low and intimate, that came to Sophie on a different level of hearing – the rain being squeezed through the walls and forming into beads that gathered together and dripped from the arches of the doors; dry, rustling whispers that might have been the lampshade fringes moving or a lizard scuttling down the wall; an eerie slithering that she told herself must be a cloth sliding from table to floor because it could not, *must not* be a snake that had wriggled its way indoors for refuge.

She couldn't see. She couldn't see.

And always the counterpoint of little Archie's whimpering and the keening of the servants in the kitchen.

The house was of brick on granite foundations, and as the typhoon became ever more violent and the wind slammed against its outer walls everything began to shake and there was a sharp crack and a ripping sound, and then another, and another. For minutes on end it seemed that the very foundations were moving, while the jalousies shuddered as if the tempest were about to blast them free from their anchorage and send them crashing inwards through the window frames.

Sophie jumped to her feet, then, with Archie still clutched tight in her arms, and backed into the centre of the room to wait for the end – for the next gust to force its way in and shatter her cocoon, whirling herself and Archie out into the maelstrom, carrying them away on the wings of the gale to dash them to death on the rocks or in the sea.

Rainer, Rainer, a voice moaned in her head.

Midnight came, and it still hadn't happened. Instead, the wind moved round so that instead of striking flat against the walls it was glissading along them with an unearthly whine that cut through Sophie's nerves so that she thought, if it didn't stop, her brain would fall apart.

She wondered if she were indeed losing her reason when, against every law of human and divine probability, she found her ears able to distinguish human screams and shrieks that were far away but not too far, and splintering noises, and the solid smashing sound of something huge and heavy being thrown and thrown again, relentlessly, against something no less huge and heavy. It was like the sound, monstrously magnified, of the laundry girls slapping dirt out of the washing against the rocks.

When she forced herself to be logical about it, she realised that the wind, if not the waves, must briefly have quietened as the eye of the hurricane reached the island, and that what she was hearing was coming from the harbour; was the noise of junks and sampans being smashed to matchwood by the tide; of steamers being hurled against the Praya wall; of people screaming as disaster took them, too, in its grip. To their Tanka owners, the sampans were home as well as transport and there might be five generations crammed inside each fragile hull. Even when the roaring of the tempest began again, Sophie could still hear, inside her head, the sound of all the lost souls crying.

By the time dawn came, six hours after it had all begun, everything was over and, though the wind still blew, the rain had begun falling in the solid torrent that always signalled the last buckets of heaven being baled out.

With a white-faced baby asleep at last in her arms, Sophie dragged herself up and went to look at the barometer. It was rising.

More than anything, she needed to breathe. So she opened the door.

9

The first thing she saw on the street in front of her was the wreckage of the upstairs balcony, but she thought dully that it didn't matter. The house was still standing, still had its roof where the roof ought to be, and that was all that counted.

The second thing she saw was the body of Dadabhai Naoroji.

He was no more than half a dozen yards away, lying face down, spreadeagled under a length of stone coping. Even as Sophie took a hesitant step towards him she saw that it was no use. His neck had been broken by the falling pediment of the house next door, which must have been one of the first things to go.

She didn't want to look at him; didn't want to feel that she should have *ordered* him to come in with her; tried to tell herself he had been an adult, and the choice had been his.

And so, wanting only to tear her eyes from his body, she looked upwards and outwards – and saw what the typhoon had done to Hong Kong.

She had often heard people use the phrase 'a scene of devastation' and had thought she knew what it meant. She had seen the work of typhoons before. But her imagination had never encompassed havoc like this.

The gusts that had swept the colony had left hundreds of houses in ruins, thousands roofless; windows smashed and signboards torn adrift; had turned the streets into canyons so packed with wreckage that it was hard even to pick out the pattern of them. The remnants of a sedan chair were impaled on the pinnacle of the Clock Tower, and Sophie could see sampans marooned on dry ground far inland. Every single tree had been combed of its leaves and most of them uprooted.

It took several long, dazed minutes before she realised that one reason why everything looked so strange was that so many landmarks had gone. The Civil Hospital and St Joseph's Church had been reduced to rubble. On the Peak, the governor's Mountain Lodge was stripped and gaunt as a skeleton.

Impossibly, the harbour was a more dreadful sight than the land, because there was nothing to confuse the eye, nothing to blur the reality. Miles of the Praya wall had gone and it looked as if the sea with its detritus of what had once been junks and sampans must have surged in as far as the Queen's Road. There were ships still careering drunkenly around the brown, yeasty waters, others of which nothing could be seen but a web of masts and rigging rising out of the shallows. The hospital ship *Meanee*, which seemed to be the only vessel in the harbour that had held to her moorings, had all four of her anchor chains twisted into a single mass of tangled iron, and the superstructure of HMS *Tamar* was reduced to a bare herringbone of struts and braces. There was ruin and destruction everywhere.

Trying to close her mind to the thought of how many people must have died, Sophie turned her eyes at last to her own house. The balcony had gone, of course, and great segments of stucco had been ripped from the walls, leaving the brick exposed. Shattered roof tiles were everywhere. The jalousies, she saw with a churning of the stomach, wouldn't have stood much more of the wind's battering and searching. If even one window had given way, the channelling of the gale's power onto the facing wall could have been enough to bring the house down.

10

She had fed the baby and was sitting limply on the side of her bed, raising a cup of tea shakily to her lips and wondering what to do first, when there was a flurry of movement behind her and the teacup went flying, and Rainer swept her into his arms.

Neither of them could speak at first. Neither of them wanted to. All the barriers were down, and although Sophie was neither very clean nor very fresh and Rainer seemed to be grazed and bleeding all over and covered with mud and dust, their lovemaking among the ruins was more beautiful by far than when they had first come together on their romantic starlit island.

Afterwards, Sophie wept all over him from happiness.

'Take care,' he said. 'That mud's only just dried. Do you have any idea how delectable you look with your hair falling all over the place and that little pout on your lips? Very kissable.' He kissed her again.

And again, many times.

I I

He had arrived back just before the typhoon broke and had gone to East Point, 'where I expected to find my wife and son. I have made three forays during the course of this night, trying to reach you, with the results you see.'

Ostentatiously, he replaced the sling on his damaged arm.

She smiled damply. 'You're never here when I need you. Oh, Rainer, I was so afraid. I needed you so much.'

'I'm not much of a protector, am I?' His one good arm was round her, and she couldn't see the expression on his face.

'No. Why was it so bad?'

'We were dead in the path. There was an exceptionally high tide. And there was an earthquake when the gales were at their height.'

'Was that what it was? I felt the whole house shudder and thought it was the wind.'

'I imagine you did. Anyway, the damage to property alone must amount to five or six million dollars. Thank God the Clyde River Bank doesn't deal in buildings insurance.'

'How *very* fortunate,' she agreed valiantly. 'And how lovely it must be to think of all the people who are underinsured and will be trying to borrow from you to make up the difference. Have you decided on your interest rate yet?'

He laughed. 'We *are* learning, aren't we?'

'The death toll must be terrible.'

'They estimate two thousand in the harbour alone. God knows, there won't be enough long bamboo in the colony for the Chinese funerals. A notice has gone up already warning people not to go to the Praya unless they're prepared to see some tragic sights.'

'Oh, dear,' she said. 'And I have to go down and see what's happened at the offices.'

It hadn't occurred to her until that moment, but she knew it would be the right thing for a senior partner to do.

'You will do no such thing.'

'I beg your pardon?'

'The waterfront is no place for a woman, and won't be for some time. Take my word for it.'

'Why should I?'

'Because I say so, dammit! What do you expect after the worst typhoon in the colony's history? There will be looters, I have no doubt, and robbers by the hundred, ready to kill for a few pennies. Most of the buildings will be unstable. And the drains have burst, so there will be disease . . . My darling, please! Tell me how many men you need to help with the repairs here and I'll see what can be arranged, then you must go home to East Point. The damage isn't too bad there.

'In the meantime, I must go. The governor needs every able-bodied man there is and I must check first what the damage is at the bank. Pedder Street took the full brunt of the tidal waves.'

She couldn't resist it. 'I see! It's all right for you to go to your bank, but not for me to go to my offices!'

He thought she was being provocative, so he laughed, and kissed her, and then went in to chuck their son under the chin and receive a huge, sleepy smile in reply. And then he left.

Sophie, dizzy, ecstatic, deflated, looked around her at the wreck of her childhood home, and sighed, and set to work.

CHAPTER EIGHTEEN

❧❧❧

I

Rachel insisted on a church wedding in Glasgow when she married Colin Campbell. She wore white satin and a veil and orange blossom, and was attended by Tom Tanner's four-year-old Meggie, who was really too young but good as gold.

Horace had written, forgivingly, to say that in spite of her having reduced his father to a bedridden wreck, his mama would consent to act as her matron of honour, and that he himself would give her away, but Rachel, her hand shaking so much from nervous hilarity that the words were barely legible, had declined politely. She had made other arrangements, she said.

Even the guests from Juran failed to recognise the small, thin man who did give her away, because no one had ever seen Hogg clean before, or respectably dressed. All they noted was that he was a retiring old fellow who didn't have a word to say for himself but appeared to have a great partiality for *petits cornets de saumon fumé* and *tartelettes à la marjolaine*.

Keeping an eye on him in case he started pocketing them, Rachel explained, 'A friend of my family. He's not very talkative, I'm afraid, and rather deaf.'

There were three hundred fashionable guests, stained glass windows, an organist, a choir, and a lavish reception afterwards, but it still brought back to Rachel's mind that other wedding eighteen years before, with its thirty overbred members of the landed classes in the borrowed house with the smell of boiled potatoes in the hall. She had thought it very splendid at the time.

Now, catching sight of herself in one of the gilt-framed mirrors, her slim princess-line dress elegantly draped into a train at the back, she remembered the vast lavender expanses of her mother's crinoline and sighed faintly. Poor mother. What a disaster it had all been.

Once, she had wondered where the echoes of that marriage would end. And she had learned that, despite the deaths of Daniel and Ondine, William and Belinda, despite even Gresham ceasing to be a threat, still they murmured on. Even so, now that she herself was married and hoped to become the mother of a thriving brood – six would be nice, she and Colin thought – she was able to feel quite philosophical about far-off Sophie and her family.

Colin was watching her, the smile in his eyes matching hers as she looked back at him. He wasn't the romantic foreign prince she had once dreamed of, or the other romantic foreigner she was doing her best to forget, but she loved him, not disturbingly, but warmly and with gratitude. She was going to make him a perfect wife, she had resolved, pampering him in every way, troubling him with none of her own concerns. And they would be happy and contented, and for their children Juran would be home, where they could laugh and be free and be loved.

2

Until not so many years before, nightdresses had been garments of awesome severity, but things had changed recently and Rachel climbed into her bridal bed in a pretty foulard with tucks and ruches and even some lace trim. It was still buttoned up tight at neck and wrists, of course, because Glasgow was a chilly place in the early months of the year, especially in the gap between midnight and six in the morning, before the servants slipped in to relight the bedroom fires.

She had to wait half an hour before there came a knock on the door and Colin entered, nightshirted and dressing-gowned and looking a trifle sheepish. But there was a twinkle in his eye as he said, 'I thought I'd better give you time.'

It would have been impossible for Rachel to live at Juran for eighteen years without seeing bulls and rams at work but, preparing herself for this night, she had found it inordinately difficult to imagine the peaceable Colin so engaged. And with her, too! She had no idea how she was going to like it, but she was determined not to behave like a shrinking violet. She was, after all, twenty-six years old even if completely inexperienced.

With a nervous smile, she threw back a corner of the heaped blankets and said, 'Quickly!'

He made a pretence of shivering, and it eased the first physical contact. Until now, he had never done more than kiss her, not passionately and virtually at arm's length. Which had been very proper of him, if a little disappointing.

They lay side by side for what seemed a considerable time, Rachel beginning to think, a touch impatiently and not at all romantically, 'Well?' Colin had been married before, so he couldn't possibly be nervous, too.

Then he turned towards her and, in the light of the dying fire, she saw a deep solemnity in his face. 'I'm going to tell you something I've never told a living soul.'

A dreadful premonition swept over her, and it was hard to make her 'Yes?' sound interested and untroubled. Perhaps he didn't want to – or couldn't – do what a husband was supposed to!

'You know I've talked to you about my first wife, Marian, and what a sweet and gentle person she was?'

'Yes.'

'Well . . .'

Go on, she willed him. *Go on.*

'Well, she'd been brought up by a maiden aunt and no one had told her anything about – er – anything. So our wedding night came as a wee bit of a shock. When I tried making love to her she went off into floods of tears and – well, I couldn't very well force her, now, could I?'

The relief was enormous, though Rachel couldn't think why he was telling her. 'No, of course not,' she said understandingly.

'That's not all. Because, you see, she just couldn't get over her shrinking. And in a queer way, it became less and less possible to force her as time passed. She was such a dear, sweet soul.'

He stopped as if that was that.

Astounded, disbelieving, Rachel said, 'You mean. . . ?'

'I mean I was married for ten years and I never once made love to my wife.'

'Heavens!'

'And I just wanted to get things straight. Because, if you're going to feel the same way, I'd rather you'd tell me now before I get over-excited.'

For all of ten seconds, Rachel struggled to contain herself – and then she was laughing, and Colin was laughing, too, and then he was kissing her and undoing buttons and, all things considered, they had a thoroughly satisfactory and enjoyable wedding night.

Marriage to someone as important as Colin opened up a whole new world to Rachel, a world that she found immensely stimulating; she couldn't understand her husband being so blasé about it. Clever people, the theatre, books, music, shops . . .

She had every excuse to go shopping, because Colin, having done little to his recently purchased home other than put essential furniture in it, had given her a free hand.

Once she had accustomed herself to the modernity and splendour of it, she saw what a very handsome house it was, set towards one end of a massive and stately terrace whose Classical façade was broken only by ashlar banding and pillared porches. Theirs was not one of the larger houses, which were full scale mansions, but consisted of two main storeys over a deep basement almost hidden by elegant railings, with rooms that were spacious and finely proportioned. In front was a steep, grassy bank, heavily planted with shrubs, that dropped down to the wide main road and helped to cut off the worst of the traffic noise.

Rachel spent most of the first weeks engrossed in books and magazines, trying to discover – with no personal experience to build on other than a Soho attic and a Highland castle that made its own rules – what her taste actually was. In the end, despite a slight hankering after the new Aesthetic style, she decided that what was called Free Renaissance would suit the house best.

Gilded cornices and Louis Seize knick-knacks, Classical busts and curtain swags, blinds painted with floral motifs, panelled dadoes, deep-buttoned green velvet chairs, jardinières for the aspidistras, flower vases like funeral urns, and a multiplicity of occasional tables so fragile and spindly that Colin swore their only purpose was to be sent flying by folks' coat tails. He had reservations about the wallpaper, too, which had a small, pretty, widely spaced pattern on an off-white ground.

'One winter of coal fires,' he said, 'and you'll need a whole bakery's-worth of bread to get that clean again. You've been spoilt, living in the country, that's your trouble!'

It was the strangest feeling not to be at Juran during the long, lonely winters, but Colin said from the start that, as long as Rachel spent the busiest and most socially active part of the year in Glasgow with him, he wouldn't object if she wanted to be at Juran from Easter until October. He could join her at weekends, either alone or with guests.

Juran had become his when they married, and he'd said, 'I've a good mind to keep it. It's daft for you to be so possessive about stone and mortar.'

'Well, if *you'd* had everyone busily trying to take it away from you, you'd be possessive, too. You needn't make it sound as if I'm unbalanced about it.'

'I'm not so sure about that.'

But he had given it back to her as a wedding present, saying, 'Another ten years, I'd guess, and they'll have repealed these antiquated laws about married women's property. It's going to put a terrible crimp in a husband's sense of generosity.'

4

Before they were married, Rachel had always welcomed Colin's visits not only for the pleasure of his company, but because – love Juran though she did – there was no denying that it lacked intellectual stimulus. There had been times when she had felt as if her brain was atrophying.

Now, she found herself returning there to give her brain a rest, because she had never dreamed how active a banker's life could be or how necessary it was for him to know something about every single thing that was happening in the world – from the threat of Colorado beetle in Europe to the first gold in the Transvaal, from the establishment of a central parliament in New Zealand, to the discovery of how to extract phosphorus from iron, from the imminence of a Franco-German war to the Sale of Food and Drugs Act. He even took Rachel to a Moody and Sankey revivalist meeting because he wanted to see how many of the labouring classes had turned up to have their souls saved.

'Why on earth. . . ?' she had demanded, amused.

'Well, think about it. If they swear off strong liquor, their work'll improve and production will increase.'

'Unless,' she pointed out, 'they're so sanctimonious about it that their fellow workers finish up by murdering them.'

He laughed and ushered her into the brougham. 'I'm glad I married you,' he said.

Somewhat to her annoyance, Rachel found her stock in the glens rising after her marriage – not because she had managed to marry someone respectable despite her origins, but because that 'someone respectable' was recognised as such by no less a personage than Her Majesty, Queen Victoria.

When she and Colin were invited to Balmoral, everyone knew about it as soon as they did, and she was scarcely back at Juran when she was surprised – if not for long – to meet Hogg on the hill, trying unavailingly to whistle his terriers to heel.

'It's a while since we've seen you hereabouts,' she said, eyeing him with mock suspicion and hanging on to Lolloper's collar for all she was worth. 'How's the foxhunting trade these days?'

'Just like me. Easy-osy. Had a nice time at Balmoral, did ye? I hear the old battleaxe was blithe to see "my dear Mr Campbell".'

Rachel glanced at her fob watch. 'It's a whole two hours since I arrived home. You're slipping, Hogg!'

He grinned, a grin that had become yellower and more gappy during the years of their acquaintance but had changed in no other way at all. She worried about him sometimes, because he was nothing but skin and bone. Highland winters were hard on an old man, and she was always expecting to hear that he'd been found frozen to death in a ditch, but she'd never been able to think of any way of helping him. He was sensitive about charity.

'Aye, aye,' he said. 'Did ye ever think when ye were a wee lassie playing in the gutters that one day ye'd find yerself supping your tea with the Queen?'

'I'll have less of the gutters, thank you.'

He laid a forefinger along one side of his nose and winked. 'It's all right, lassie. That's our private secret. C'mon now, tell us about the old wifey. Did she have her crown on?'

6

Having spent the preceding three weeks trying to persuade herself that queens were only human, Rachel had been disappointed to discover that she was right.

Balmoral had smelled of wood smoke, leather, trophies of the chase, coldness and damp. Indeed, Colin had told her that one government minister had treasonably refused to come unless someone guaranteed that his bedroom would be heated to at least 60°F. It was just like being back at Juran in her childhood, Rachel had thought unenthusiastically as she huddled up close to Colin in the high feather bed.

She wasn't to be presented to the Queen until lunchtime on the following day, because the royal morning was filled with business and guests were expected to amuse themselves by admiring the tartan indoors and the roses out.

'Yes, I know you hate roses,' Colin said, 'but I'd be obliged if you'd keep it to yourself. Repeat after me – Gloire de Dijon. That's the pinky-apricot climber; remember to admire the scent. And that's Madame Falcot over there, and this is Maréchal Niel. As long as you can get your tongue round those, you can be as ignorant as you like about the rest. Then Her Majesty can feel superior to you.'

He warned her about the scenery, too. 'It's not a patch on Juran, but it's royal, and that makes it special. I'm feared she'll insist on taking you to her "little bothy" at Glassalt Shiel. Make sure you cover up, because the midges there are without exception the most voracious I have ever come across.'

He was right.

The only known midge repellents were paraffin oil and tobacco smoke, and Rachel was more than happy to follow her gracious sovereign's stout, black-bonneted example and puff and choke away at one cigarette after another. Once she realised that Her Majesty's midges were a source of pride, she was able to guarantee herself a place in the royal favour by assuring the Queen that Juran's midges were *very* much inferior to Balmoral's. Quite mealy-mouthed, in fact.

Since the Queen had a tenacious cast of mind and knew little of the West Highlands, the company at dinner – which consisted of four princesses; the queen's oldest friend, Lady Churchill; her permanent Lord-in-Waiting, Lord Bridport; and a government Minister in Attendance, whose name Rachel never quite caught – had to listen to a great deal about midges (from Her Majesty) and Juran (from Rachel and Colin) as they waded through their haggis, venison and potatoes, followed by an unusually whisky-full Atholl Brose. The gentlemen were able to escape to the billiard room afterwards, but the ladies were less fortunate. Not until they were settled in the late Prince Consort's sanctum did Her Majesty consent to stop talking and allow one of the princesses to read aloud from Mr Hardy's *Far from the Madding Crowd*.

Rachel was worn out by the time they went to bed, but Colin said she had done very well.

The Queen seemed to think so, too, because she presented Rachel, on parting, with a photograph of the royal family in one of its informal moments, and said graciously, 'Goodbye, Mrs Campbell. We will look forward to seeing you again.'

7

'And you won't believe it,' Rachel concluded, 'but she wears a portrait of the Prince Consort round her neck, and whenever she sees something that interests her, she holds the portrait up so that Albert can see it, too.'

'Well, well, well,' said a fascinated Hogg. 'What it is to have friends in high places! It seems to me that marrying Mr Campbell is the best thing ye ever did. I can see ye're enjoying life fine.'

And she was.

The only trouble was that the months passed, and then the years, and despite two false alarms she and Colin remained childless.

CHAPTER NINETEEN

❦

I

'But I must have *something* to occupy me when you're away!' Sophie shrieked. 'You can't imagine what it's like. I've grown out of gossiping and tea parties and picnics, and you're not here to take me anywhere, anyway. What am I supposed to do with my time? And *don't* tell me to stay at home and look after Archie. I worship him, but twenty-four hours a day is too much.'

Blake said tightly, 'I have forbidden you to involve yourself in Macmillan and Venturi.'

'You can forbid me as much as you like! Why should I pay attention to what you say? You never pay attention to what *I* say. You pay no attention to me at all.'

'You exaggerate.'

But it was true that he had distanced himself from her. He had no choice. The love and desire, anxiety and relief, that had brought them together after the typhoon had been disastrously fruitful, and Sophie had conceived, and had lost the child within weeks. After that her fear of childbearing had become, if possible, even greater than before.

Willingly, Blake could have throttled Dr Dods, who had told Sophie that the only acceptable method of family limitation was abstention; that the whole idea of 'voluntary motherhood' and artificial contraception was directly contrary to the will of God, indecent, depraved and obscene. And although Sophie had replied spiritedly that 'sensible' seemed to her a better word, she was unable to rid herself of the idea that it was wrong. Even without that, she would have hated, as much as Blake, did the new vulcanised rubber condoms he had begun using for her sake. They were thick, clumsy things, but they were the only reliable method there was.

The tensions were becoming too great. Blake thought that if they had been different, cooler people and less in love, they might have been able to handle the problem, keep it in some kind of perspective.

But, given who they were, it was impossible. He couldn't even touch her without having to think first, had to control himself every moment of the time he was with her.

'You're being utterly unreasonable!' Sophie went on. 'You seem to think my cousin Rachel is wonderful because she *does* things, and she's competent and capable and whatever else it was – but not me! All you want me to do is stay at home and have babies. You don't think I have a brain in my head. Well, I don't know whether I have, but I want to find out!'

Suddenly, her face crumpled and the gentian eyes filled with tears. 'Oh, my darling! Listen to me, screaming at you like a fishwife! What's the matter with me? What's the matter with us? Why has everything gone so wrong?'

He took her in his arms and dropped a kiss on her shining hair, but said nothing. Everything had been said too often before, and there was no healing in words.

2

Somehow, Sophie knew, she *had* to find a way of disentangling the rope that was strangling all her loving impulses, the rope whose triple strands were birth, death and memories. Why, why, why, should everything have been all right – perfect, beautiful – on the island and after the typhoon? It was as if the marriage bed itself was some kind of malign reminder of what for five years she had been trying to forget.

Rainer had said, 'I have made all the concessions I am capable of making. It depends on you, now.' She knew it, and raged at herself, hiding it for the sake of her pride as she hid the uncertainties that beset her, the knowledge that all her confidence had flown.

Everything she touched seemed to go wrong. Frank had jilted her, Richard had become a drug addict, baby Tina had died and the other baby, too, who had gone from her before she could give it a name. And now her marriage to Rainer was in ruins because of something she knew to be her fault – her utter inability to deal with terrors that he couldn't understand and she didn't know how to overcome.

The more she sat at home, the more she worried and the worse things became. She had to do something. Even if she could prove to herself that she needn't be a failure in everything, it would help, and the only way she could see open to her was through Macmillan and Venturi. If she failed there, she didn't know what she would do.

Gino Venturi had never seen her so subdued as when she went to him and, all desire to play the grandiose rôle of senior partner forgotten, asked him to sit down and talk sensibly to her without trying to blind her with science, or laughing at her, or simply ignoring her.

Something of her determination or, she thought afterwards, of her desperation, must have communicated itself to him.

'I've tried to be too ambitious before,' she said, 'starting at the top instead of the bottom. Is there, do you think, something not too difficult I could take over and look after by myself, without needing to know everything about how the business works? And without treading on your toes, of course?'

'I like the sound of that,' he said, 'the not-treading-on-my-toes bit. I would not want you poking your elegant nose into my more nefarious activities.'

She laughed. His warm, light, humorous voice denied the very possibility of knavery. Entering into the spirit of the thing, she enquired, 'And what might those be?'

Gino was adept at telling the truth in a manner that led people to think he was joking, just as he was adept at lying with an appearance of perfect truth. 'Oh, merely a few minor things like dealing in hard money rather than bills . . .'

'*That* sounds as if you're fiddling the books.' She had learned something, if not very much, from her earlier forays.

'Certainly not! The Mexican, Japanese and American trade dollars we use in the colony assay at slightly different silver contents and therefore have slightly different values in relation to the Chinese tael. If one is selective in one's dealing – and I am *very* selective – there's a nice little marginal profit to be made.'

'I don't understand.'

'I didn't think you would,' he said cheerfully. 'Broken dollars are handy, too. Although they're used as common currency they have no specified currency value. The smaller silver chips mount up quite handily.'

'They do?'

He grinned his most engaging grin. 'No, I don't go around with a dustpan and brush. It's more subtle than that.'

'I'm sure it is. Anything else?'

'Only Customs dues.'

'Oh, *don't* say we evade them? What happens if we get caught? Think of poor Isaac Moore.'

Unfortunately, she spoiled it by giggling. Five of Isaac Moore's ships had recently been arrested and were being held by Customs at Canton. Their owner – of course – claimed they had done nothing wrong, but the general opinion in the colony was that formal complaints would be flying back and forth for at least two years before Isaac Moore got his ships back. Sophie, who had by no means forgiven the Moores, hoped he never got them back.

'Evade them?' Gino exclaimed, shocked. 'Of course not. We merely evade the places where we would be asked to pay them.'

Having thus taken the sting out of the trickier questions it might later have occurred to Sophie to ask, Gino felt sufficiently beneficent to agree to giving her some work to play with. He himself would continue to manage everything as before, of course, except that he would relinquish to her the buying and management of such cargoes as a mere female might be expected to understand. Which boiled down to tea *from* China, and cotton shirtings *to* China.

Sophie was pleased. Her father had always said tea and cotton were very important.

Gino did not, unfortunately, see fit to mention that things had changed since Archie Macmillan's day. Britain had halved its import duty on tea in 1874, which had brought an influx of new dealers interested only in a quick profit. They had soon flooded the market with teas so adulterated with blackthorn leaves and twigs and dust that they had given all China teas a bad name.

Nor did he explain that the Chinese hated Manchester cotton goods, which they said were 'all gum and sticky stuff'. The shortage of American staple during the Civil War had led British manufacturers to use poor quality fibres that needed to be heavily dressed with flour and tallow; afterwards, when the price of tallow rocketed, they had begun using china clay instead. This had not only increased the weight of the fabric but had other effects that could only be counteracted by the use of deliquescent salts – which became nastily mildewed on the voyage from England to Hong Kong. All of which meant that the final purchaser had to wash his new shirting before he could use it – and one wash was enough to turn it into a dishcloth.

With business in tea and cotton already so bad, Gino reckoned that even an amateur like Sophie couldn't make it worse.

There were times without number, in the months that followed, when all Sophie wanted to do was fling herself on Blake's chest and say, 'I don't know the answer. Help me. Make things right for me.' But she couldn't.

They became more and more shut out of each other's lives. He never mentioned Macmillan and Venturi, and neither did she. He continued to be away a great deal, too, and although he now satisfied her complaints to the extent of telling her where he was going and how long he expected to be away, he never explained what the business was that took him to such places as Nanking, Tientsin, Peking, even to as far north as Mukden in Manchuria.

'Arabella Berling,' she said, when he mentioned that he would be leaving for Ningpo in a few days, 'tells me that her husband heard from Mr Chatsworth, who heard from Mr Koch, who heard from Cornelia Trafton, who heard it from Mr Pentland, that there is a rumour that you are investigating the financing of foreign railroad concessions in northern China. Are you? I feel such a fool being told, by someone I scarcely know, what my own husband is up to! I had to stand there looking as if it were all something frantically secret that I, of course, knew all about but couldn't possibly divulge!'

The Berlings were new to the colony, and Sophie hadn't thought Arabella at all attractive – she was a rather wishy-washy blonde and thirty-five if she was a day – until Rainer had begun singling her out to talk to, and sometimes to dance with, though not often enough for anyone other than a wife to notice. He seldom stayed at Sophie's side nowadays, and stood up with her only for dances that involved little physical contact.

He laughed aloud. It was the first time for months that she had seen his grey eyes light up, felt the surge of animal vitality in him, and she thought her heart would break. 'What's funny?' she asked a little wistfully.

'My poor darling! I'm sorry, but I cannot divulge it either. Though if the colony thinks I am chasing railroads, so much the better.'

'What *are* you chasing then? I don't see why you have to be so secretive.'

He laughed again. 'It's the nature of the beast. Are you ready? We don't want to be late for the ceremony.'

It was the end of Sir Arthur Kennedy's governorship and he was to be presented by the Chinese community with a ceremonial umbrella, which seemed, Rainer remarked cheerfully, unlikely to be of any great practical use to him where he was going, which was Queensland, Australia, a place remarkable for its low rainfall. Afterwards, there was to be a laudatory address from the Protestant Missionaries and another from the Members of Council. Then Sir Arthur was to retaliate – Blake's word – with an address to the community and a kindly message for the Police Force.

Blake and Sophie, with a fidgeting Archie between them, sat through it all, the perfect model of a perfect family.

In the evening, there was a public dinner at the City Hall, which Blake and Sophie also attended. They were still the handsomest couple in the colony.

Sir Arthur having departed in an aura of universal benevolence after a reign during which he had done nothing whatsoever apart from be polite to everybody – even, for a while at the beginning, the Chinese – he was replaced a few weeks later by Mr John Pope Hennessy, the fourth Irishman in a row, who was greeted with perceptibly less benevolence. Even so, no one quite foresaw that it was to be a case of downhill all the way for the whole of his five years in office.

Blake and Sophie sat through all the welcoming ceremonies, with Archie between them, and attended the ball afterwards.

They attended Choral Festivals, too, and the opening of the new Temperance Hall, and when the Horticultural Society held its annual flower and vegetable show Sophie won first prize for her tea roses, which gave her much satisfaction because it was a prize that Euphemia Moore had won every year since the show began.

Archie had his fourth birthday. He was a dark, slender child with blue-grey eyes, and both of his parents loved and spoiled him unmercifully. Had not Ah Foon kept her stern, disciplinarian's eye on his baby amah, he would have been impossible. As it was, he was utterly disarming, not a little mischievous, and knew exactly how far he dared go before Sophie or Blake said, 'Enough!'

5

In all honesty, Sophie had not expected to find much interest in what she was doing at Macmillan and Venturi, but as time passed her attitude changed. Her first few small successes had given her enormous satisfaction, even if it would have been greater still if anyone had congratulated her. If Rainer had even asked how things were going.

She had floundered at first, of course. But then Gino had said, 'No Chinese merchant would lose face by negotiating with a woman, so I'll let you have Tan as your assistant. He's Chinese-born, and as negotiators go he is good.'

Tan turned out to have the most amazing talent for tracking down, and buying at favourable prices, all the most desirable teas – Hysoa and Twankay, Gunpowder and Imperial, Soochong and Bohea. If it hadn't been for him, the bad name ordinary China tea had acquired in Europe might have forced Sophie into abandoning tea dealing entirely. As it was, she brought her housewife's experience of shopping to bear and made the decision to buy and sell only the best. It had presented her with some intricate problems of marketing that proved to be thoroughly absorbing.

In the case of cotton shirtings, it took her two years to decide to start importing from India instead of England and she then became so carried away by the thought of the profits she could make by using the firm's own ships that Gino Venturi discovered her one day, lost in a dream, blissfully admiring the money signs dancing before her eyes. He was almost sorry to have to explain about the costings she had left out of her calculations.

Sophie was ready enough to admit that she still wasn't very good at figures and hopeless at understanding a balance sheet. It always mystified her how both sides managed to add up to the same answer. That, she thought, was probably why she found the firm's annual accounts so puzzling. She knew very well that business was thriving, but the accounts never seemed to show more than a derisory profit.

She asked Gino about it, and he laughed at her. 'Don't trouble your beautiful head about it. I am the accountancy wizard, remember?'

Talking down to her in that tongue-in-cheek way was one of his most irritating habits. 'Oh, very well,' she said airily. 'I shall ask Rainer, then!'

She wouldn't have done, of course, even if he hadn't been away in Chinese Tonkin. He was always away when she needed him. This time, the house at East Point had been broken into. Nothing very much seemed to have been taken, and Sophie was puzzled.

Blake, returning a few days later, said succinctly, 'Papers, I'd guess. There are a number of people in the colony who would be happy to have a sight of some of my more confidential records.'

'How delightful! Well, I wish you would tell your criminal friends to direct their curiosity towards your office, not our home!'

'I don't like this any more than you do. But breaking into the bank is virtually impossible. I figure they were taking a chance that I might have brought some papers home.'

'They should have asked me,' said Sophie, in no way mollified. 'I could have told them that, since you live at the bank – when you're in Hong Kong at all, that is – bringing papers home would be quite superfluous.'

He didn't rise to the provocation. 'I'll see what I can do about finding a watchman.'

'You don't fancy the job yourself, I suppose?'

7

Two nights later, true to form, Rainer deposited her at East Point after a reception at Government House and said, 'I'm going back to the office for a while. I'm expecting a telegraph from Europe and it ought to be dealt with immediately. There are some queer emanations coming from Scotland at the moment.'

'From my cousin Rachel?' she enquired in a voice that was sugar sweet. 'Perhaps you haven't told her recently how much you admire her.'

'Christ! How did this bee find its way into your bonnet? All I ever recall having said is that she's a capable young woman. I scarcely even know her! The emanations – if you must know – are coming from my partner, Colin Campbell. Now, will you take yourself indoors and let me go and do some work?'

It was an oppressive night and the reception had been one of the most gruelling affairs Sophie could remember, during which Mr Pope Hennessy had offended more people in a shorter space of time than she would have thought humanly possible. She was tired, and her feet hurt, but her mind refused to settle.

She lay awake for a long time, and when she fell asleep at last she fell straight into a nightmare. She was surrounded by flames, but it wasn't one of her familiar nightmares of the junk at Lantau or the blaze at Canton. There were other people in those dreams, but in this one she was alone.

She managed to struggle up to a sitting position, but then the terror paralysed her and she couldn't do anything but scream and scream, aimlessly, hopelessly, until hands came to her at last out of the scarlet haze and tried first to lead her, and then to lift her. But she fought against them in a frenzy, still screaming without cease, until whoever it was hit her hard enough to knock her unconscious. It made no difference. She still knew what was happening. Knew that it was Rainer and that he was throwing her from the crackling, flaming balcony into a blanket below. Knew that, even as he threw her, the balcony on which he stood was collapsing in a shower of blazing timbers.

There was a sound somewhere inside her head that wasn't a cry or a shriek or even a moan, but a faint, thin, substanceless whine. The sound of a soul passing.

8

She woke with a violent, terrified start to discover that she was, indeed, sitting up in bed and that the flames were real, leaping upwards through the still air in the corner by the window. Leaping up through the floorboards from the room below, where Archie slept with his amah.

She tore the mosquito net aside and, her heart raw with dread, fled to the door and flung it open, not even thinking of what she would see there, knowing only that, even if the whole hall and staircase were an inferno, she had to reach her baby somehow. The sense of nightmare still clung to her, fogging her brain so that she felt alone and helpless, moving heavy-limbed through a void, through a silence that belonged to dreams, not life. She didn't wonder why the fire gong hadn't sounded, why there was no shouting and screaming, why there was no sign of the servants.

No conscious thought told her that opening the door would feed the flames. No whisper of reason sent her running instead to the balcony to shout for help, or climb down to the terrace and hammer on the gong for somebody, anybody, to come and do what she herself could not do – put out the flames.

It was Archie alone who possessed her mind.

The draught from the door sucked the flames up the staircase towards her, pretty flames still, rimming the balusters and handrail like ceremonial illuminations on a ship's rigging. There was a roaring somewhere but she could make no sense of it until a great sheet of fire shot out from the corridor below, flashing across the hall in a dragon's tongue of yellow and purple and thick black smoke, and vanishing again as suddenly as it had appeared.

She had enough wits, then, to recognise that the fire must have taken a grip on the first floor, so that the servants, who slept on the ground floor at the back, probably didn't even know there was anything wrong.

My baby, my baby!

Her own voice keened in her head as she drew the frail lawn skirts of her night shift about her and began to run barefoot down the stairs to where he was, oblivious of smouldering carpet and burning wood and the fragments of smoking plaster already beginning to shower down from the ceiling.

She was three steps from the foot of the flight, blind to everything but the space from which the dragon's tongue had leapt, when something touched her, and she tripped, and fell headlong on to the landing.

The tongue of flame shot out again, and she could feel the searing, raging hunger of it inches above her head before it vanished again and she lay for a moment, sobbing inside herself, 'Archie! Oh, my baby!'

He had gone from her, she knew, and the insubstantial whisper of his fear and his going were beating madly now inside her brain. She had to find him and hold him. She had to go with him.

Hastily, heavily, she began to drag herself to her feet, feeling no pain even when she gripped the burning baluster to steady herself before she walked into the corridor, and the flames.

And then a small voice said, 'Mummy, are you all right? I didn't mean to make you fall.'

9

Never in her life before had she felt anything with such intensity.

After a while, Archie sniffed back his tears and said, 'Mummy, you're squashing me.'

The feel of his slight body in her arms and his head against her breast was all she wanted in the world, but somehow she succeeded in unlocking her suffocating grip and scooping him up in a rational, adult way, and running down a few more steps towards the hall before the dragon's tongue shot out again. It was no more than an ordinary fire now.

Together, they banged on the big gong outside the door that served as a general alarm and made enough hullabaloo to wake the dead. It was only then that Sophie remembered the amah.

'She was awfully sleepy. I couldn't make her wake up,' Archie said. Already, his fright was beginning to fade. He'd never been allowed to bang on the gong before. It made a spiffing noise.

The servants were as terrified of fire as Sophie was, but she had to count them all to make sure the house was cleared before she dared tell the houseboy to prop a ladder against the window of Archie's room, just in case it was possible, from the outside, to save his amah. Access from the inside was unthinkable except for those bent, as Sophie had been, on self-destruction.

Sophie had been brought up never to order a servant to do something she was not prepared to do herself. It meant that, still in her night shift – though with a shawl tied round her hips for decency – she was halfway up the ladder when Rainer arrived, his face taut, and took over.

It annoyed her a little. She had really been managing quite well. Apart from the amah, not even the lowliest of the servants had been so much as scorched.

The volunteer fire brigade also turned up eventually, in ones and twos, urging on their chair bearers with merry shouts of 'Chop, chop!' Gino Venturi was among them, his splendidly polished gladiatorial helmet making him look more like an ancient Roman than ever, though Sophie was gratified to see that he wore a frown and hadn't taken time, as the others had done, to change from evening dress into uniform.

No one could make any suggestion as to to how the fire might have started. But the seat of it appeared to have been just inside the window, near the amah's bed. She had been suffocated by the fumes from her mattress. Perhaps, someone suggested without any apparent ironic intent, she had been burning a joss stick for luck.

Whatever the truth, there was not a great deal of the house left by the time the fire and the fire brigade had finished with it.

Rainer was much more concerned about Archie than about Sophie. Which was, of course, perfectly right and proper. It didn't occur to her, receiving no more than a peck on the cheek, that he might have his own good reasons.

In a low voice, she said, 'I love you.'

It was true. It had always been true. The fire had taught her many things.

But not enough, it seemed. She might as well have said, 'What lovely weather we're having.'

'Yes. Now, listen. Robina Gibbings can give you and Archie a bed for the night, or what remains of it . . .'

Archie, riding piggyback, bounced wildly up and down. 'Daddy, daddy! Mummy let me beat the gong! It made a spiffing noise. I bet you heard it, didn't you?'

'The whole of Hong Kong heard it. Settle down, you young monkey!'

'He's over-excited,' Sophie said automatically.

'Yes. And tomorrow you can move into Caine Road. Lucky it's empty at the moment. I'll get a room at the Club.'

'No!'

'Well, we'll see.'

11

Turner and Dolly Berry held their annual, open air, end-of-summer ball at their house on the Peak a week later. Three years before, returning from furlough, they had converted part of their grounds into a court for the lawn tennis that had become all the rage in Europe, and now turned the court into a dance floor by the simple expedient of laying a drugget carpet over it.

Since they were always careful to set the date for one of the nights of the full moon, and since the Chinese lanterns were festive, the catering excellent, and the view beautiful, invitations were much sought after.

Sophie was exhausted, although she didn't show it, having spent the preceding days sorting out what could be saved from East Point and supervising its removal either to Caine Road or into temporary storage. Rainer, after instituting enquiries into the cause of the fire, had made a swift decision not to rebuild on the old site but to lease some land on the Peak for a new mansion in the American Colonial style, and had been closeted for most of the time since then with a Chinese builder and the French architect, M. Hermite, who had been responsible for designing the City Hall ten years before. Sophie thought such a mixture of influences would have been insanity in anyone else, but Rainer always got what he wanted from people.

Even, soon, from her.

As their coolies carried them up to the Peak, she went over and over in her mind what lay ahead. Nothing could have been more romantic than the setting of the Peak by moonlight, and she prayed that it would help her say to him what she was determined to say, tonight or never.

The ball began well. Dancing in the open air was delightful, and the moon shone and the sea shimmered in the approved fashion. Everyone was in a good humour, knowing that the typhoon season was over and the most enjoyable part of the year to come. Trade was unstable, but that was easy to forget for a few brief hours.

Sophie danced with Rainer, and then with her host, and then with Mr Berling, and Mr Koch and Mr Trafton. Rainer danced with Dolly, and Robina, and Frank Moore's wife, and Arabella Berling, whose blonde hair looked almost white in the moonlight.

It was very ageing, Sophie thought.

Halfway through the evening, her husband came to murmur in her ear, 'One of my clerks has just come up with a message. An urgent telegraph has arrived for me and I'm afraid I must go down to the bank. Don't let me spoil your enjoyment. With luck I'll be back but, in case I'm not, I'll leave you the guards.'

The hours passed, but he didn't come back. Sophie wasn't worried that anything might have happened to him. Although he had a knack of attracting danger, she knew he was eminently capable of looking after himself.

What worried her was that he was ruining her plans.

She danced. She nibbled delicate little mouthfuls of this and that. She sparkled relentlessly. She looked divinely slim in the new, hurriedly made, low-necked pink faille ball gown with its princess seaming and hip sash of wide velvet ribbon embroidered with flowers. She drank champagne punch. She thought how dared her husband abandon her for the sake of his boring business. She drank more champagne punch.

In the end, with the other guests, she took her leave of Dolly – who had blossomed amazingly in the years of her marriage – and ordered her coolies to carry her home.

As they pattered along Caine Road, the hired guards loping alongside, she saw that practically every lamp in the house was lit and there were two bearers loading a handcart outside the front door.

Rainer came striding into the hall to greet her with a crisp, 'I'm sorry to have to let you down but I have to board ship almost at once and I have no time to spare. My packing is done, except for the waistcoats you salvaged from East Point. Where the devil have you put them?'

She stared at him for a speechless moment. '*Board ship*? But you can't! Where can you possibly be rushing off to at two hours' notice?'

'The telegraph was from Colin Campbell in Glasgow. The City of Glasgow Bank has collapsed and it has thrown the whole Scottish banking community into disarray. I am needed for urgent consultations.'

'*Urgent*? In Glasgow? When it'll take you seven or eight weeks to get there!'

'If I don't catch tonight's sailing, it will take me a good deal longer than that.'

'But what about everything here? What about me?'

'What about you?'

'Well, you can't just go like this!'

'Why not?' he asked with iron politeness. 'Will you miss me?'

Carefully, she sat down. Carefully, she smoothed out her skirts. Carefully, she looked up at him, only to discover that he was consulting his watch.

'I have very little time, Sophie. If you have something to say, please get it over with.'

She had screwed herself up to it and couldn't even contemplate postponing it for another six months. But if he was in this mood, she was going to say it without abasing herself.

Her back poker straight and her eyes sapphire bright, she said, 'I used to think that if you really loved me, you wouldn't – *couldn't* – leave me for months at a time. I still think that, if you really loved me, you wouldn't shame me by' – she fluttered a hand, not knowing quite what words to use – 'paying intimate attentions to other ladies.'

He made no attempt to deny it, but his lean features tightened, and a slight frown appeared.

She went on, 'I may be wrong about your feelings. I don't know. I *do* know that much of the fault is mine.' Her voice began to break. 'I know you think I haven't really tried to set things right, to get over my fears, but I have, I *swear* I have. And what I wanted to say was, can't we start again? I can't bear to go on as we are. *I love you.*'

There was an odd, searching look in his eyes. 'Do you?'

She nodded, because she knew that what came next was the difficult bit.

'How much?'

She had to make two attempts at it. 'What do you mean?'

'You know what I mean.'

The colour went from her face, but she held her eyes staunchly on his, and tried to be honest, which was a mistake. 'In the fire, before I woke, I dreamed you were dying trying to save me. It taught me something. And I think . . . I think everything would be all right now.'

He turned away then, with a half laugh that had no humour in it. 'You think? Such passion, my dear! You mustn't overdo it.'

13

There was so much pain and desperation in her cry of, 'Rainer!' that it stopped him.

'You *can't* go,' she exclaimed, 'I need you so much! Oh God! We've been married for more than five years, and you're *never* here when I need you!'

Slowly, he turned and for a moment she saw his profile outlined, hard as a cameo, against the light coming from the room behind. Then he was facing her again.

It was the face she had always known, striking, tanned, ascetic, the lines deeper than they had once been and the slender wing of silver in the black hair giving distinction to looks that had always been dramatic. But there was something chillingly unfamiliar in voice and eyes when he answered her, even though the words themselves seemed harmless enough

'You're saying that I am a bad father?'

It was so unexpected that she stumbled over the words. 'No, of course not! Archie worships you. Most children never see much of their fathers, anyway.'

428

He sighed. 'I wasn't talking of Archie.'

'Then I don't understand . . .'

'I was talking of you.'

She still had no conception of what he meant.

He said, 'I think this is what has always been wrong between us. You came to me for help when your father died, as someone to look after you. You came to me again when you were married to Taverner. And when the worst was over, you came to me not from passion but to be comforted and protected from past memories and the possibility of future pain. I let you down, I'm afraid, because I'm not a monk and perhaps too much of my love for you has been of the body.'

It was too unexpected, too improbable a concept for her to grapple with at a moment's notice. All she could do was cry, 'But it's not like that at all! It's never been like that! I didn't want just to be comforted and protected after Lantau, or after the typhoon!'

He nodded. 'If it hadn't been for those two occasions, I doubt if I would still be here now. But, my dear, we can't have pirate attacks or typhoons every day, to persuade you to come to me naturally. Think about what I've said, and you will see that I'm right. I must go now.'

She jumped to her feet and ran after him in a flurry of pink faille, grasping his shoulders, holding to him with all her strength as she cried again, 'No! It's not like that at all! It's too stupid for words! Can't you see that you're trying to make sense out of something that sense doesn't enter into? Trying to make both sides add up to the same on some idiotic balance sheet. Human beings aren't like that!'

He shook his head. 'There must be sense in everything, somewhere, or life isn't worth living. It's no use, Sophie. I'm not a father, I'm a lover. And if I'm not a lover, I am nothing.'

And then, because in spite of everything she was a part of him, he took her hands in his and kissed them.

This time he did not turn back, though still in his nostrils as he went was the scent of the hibiscus in her hair.

CHAPTER TWENTY

✦❦✦

I

Economic depressions had come and gone, the Eastern Crisis had come and gone, the Russo-Turkish war had come and gone. But the British didn't believe it and went on singing, with cheerful bellicosity, 'We don't want to fight, but, by jingo, if we do, We've got the ships, we've got the men, we've got the money too.'

Colin Campbell said sourly, 'It's a pity the "we" doesn't include the City of Glasgow Bank.'

On October 2, without warning, the bank had stopped payments, and by the time the month was halfway through, Colin, who was one of the investigators appointed to look into the affair, knew more about the bank's finances than its own directors, who had falsified the accounts – not very competently – in the hope of covering up bad debts of over £7 million against securities of less than £2 million.

It wasn't the kind of thing banks were supposed to do.

Colin didn't normally inflict his business problems on Rachel, or not in detail, but when she arrived back in Glasgow after having closed up Juran for the winter, it was as if two weeks of rigidly suppressed rage had at last found an outlet.

'For sixteen years it's been open to them to trade as a limited liability company, but oh no! And look what happens. All the individual shareholders are going to lose everything they've invested, and more. Because every last one of them's going to be called on to pay out another five times the value of their investment to make good the bank's debts.'

She hadn't even taken her hat off yet. Soothingly, she said, 'But if they own shares, they can't be exactly poor.'

'Don't talk daft. When savings are hard won, folk buy bank shares with them because they think they're the safest investment there is. They'll be ruined, you mark my words! Six out of seven of them will be bankrupt by the time they're finished. It's a public scandal, that's what it is!'

Rachel kissed him on the cheek. 'I'm back,' she said.

'Yes, dear. It's thrown the whole banking system into chaos. From now on, every bank is going to have to carry out an independent annual audit, whether they like it or not.'

Absently, she said, '£5 million can't be easy to lose. What on earth did they spend it on?'

'Oh, land in New Zealand and Australia, property at Karachi and Rangoon, buildings here and in the colonies, shipping, life policies, every dratted thing that a bank should *not* get itself involved in.'

'Hold your hand out,' she told him, and placed the stem of a brandy balloon between his fingers. 'Colin, why are you so upset? You're usually so calm.'

'Och, I've no patience with stupidity. Thank you, my dear. And now there's a panic. Trade is shaky, credit's impaired, the public's so suspicious that it's rushing to take its cash out of all the other banks, which is going to cramp everybody's style even more. I hope you're not expecting me to escort you anywhere for the next few months, because life is going to be just one damned thing after another.

'Oh, and by the way, Blake's coming over from Hong Kong. He should be here towards the end of next month. I thought we could put him up, since we've plenty of room and it would give us more chance to talk. You don't mind, do you?'

2

Her heart lurched, though only a little; no more than it always did when she heard his name mentioned.

After seven years of dreaming and five years of forgetting, she flattered herself that nothing remained but a strange, sweet sentimentality. She was a contentedly married woman, with a husband who loved her, and the only thing she still wanted of life was children.

'I don't mind in the least,' she said. 'I'll have the blue bedroom got ready for him.'

Colin, despite his apparent preoccupation, had noted her brief hesitancy. It was a queer thing, he sometimes thought, that he knew her so well in so many ways – but not in all. Mostly, it was because she was a good wife who knew better than to burden a busy husband with her own small worries, but there were some things she might have talked about and didn't.

She seldom mentioned her disappointment over their continued childlessness – though he was as disappointed as she about it – and now she had even given up speculating about her dratted cousin Sophie and her family, who had been creeping more and more into the conversation in the last couple of years.

Colin himself had put a stop to that. He had always held that her obsession with Juran – and any threat to it, however hypothetical – bordered on the unhealthy. It was a fine place, of course, and he was fond of it himself, but Rachel had no sense of proportion about it. 'You're my wife now,' he had said one evening. 'Juran doesn't matter any more. If your cousin should come back and want it, we will let her have it. *It is not important.*'

She had stopped talking about it after that, though if he'd been a betting man, he wouldn't have given odds that she'd stopped thinking about it.

Where Blake was concerned, he hoped – no, he was sure – that she'd forgotten the mild infatuation he'd seen in her eyes that time when Morgan and Rothschild and the rest of them had been at Juran. As conferences went, it had been thoroughly productive. Baron Lionel still talked about it.

He took a sip of brandy and said, 'If, as I suspect, you're already thinking that you might ask Blake about Mrs Taverner, I'd be obliged if you'd do it when I'm not present. You know my views.'

He was a considerate man, but not to excess, so he kept his eyes on his wife's face and saw the flicker of guilt in her eyes before she laughed and said, 'On your head be it!'

3

After a fast voyage, Blake reached Glasgow on November 23 and found it almost unrecognisable except for the weather.

'What the devil's happened to the place?' he demanded of Colin Campbell as his cab set him down at Great Western Terrace.

Colin smiled, his brown eyes as quizzical as ever. 'The City Improvement Act is what's happened. In these last half dozen years there've been so many old buildings knocked down that even we natives are hard put to it to find our way around. Come in before you drown. You'll remember my wife?'

Rachel smiled, the smile with the gleam of humour that was like a statement of partnership in some pleasant, private conspiracy. She looked the perfect hostess and reassuringly at ease, Blake thought, remembering the circumstances of their last meeting. He presumed she had got him out of her system by now.

He bowed formally. 'Your servant, Mrs Campbell, though since you have been Miss Rachel to me for something like a dozen years, you must forgive me if my tongue slips occasionally.'

'Rachel will do very nicely,' she said. 'Now, I imagine you would like a bath after your night in the train. If we have breakfast in an hour, would that suit you?'

'Admirably, thank you.'

4

Everything ran on experienced and beautifully oiled wheels. At whatever hour the gentlemen returned from their conclaves at the bank, they could always be sure that, precisely forty-five minutes later, an excellent meal would be set on the table before them. At whatever hour of the morning they chose to breakfast, breakfast would be ready.

There was nothing Blake had to ask for. There were fresh towels and fresh soap in his room every day, fresh sheets on his bed every night. His discarded linen was laundered between his going out in the morning and returning in the evening. His coats and trousers were steamed and brushed daily, his shoes cleaned nightly. His room was supplied with letterheads, notebooks and writing implements, in variety. There was a decanter of brandy, always topped up, on the table in the alcove, and a carafe of fresh water and tin of shortbread by his bedside. His own Chinese servants, he thought – though he did not, of course, say so – could scarcely have done better.

5

And then the day came when Colin had to take an early train through to Edinburgh while Blake remained in Glasgow for a noon meeting with someone from the Clydesdale Bank.

It was a wet and windy morning, and pitch dark when Colin left at 7 a.m. waved off by a wife who was by no means wholly awake. The popular belief that country people were always up with the lark was true enough, as far as it went. It was just that, in the depths of winter at Juran, neither people nor lark bothered to rise before nine, because there was nothing that could be done until night began to fade from the sky. Rachel still had difficulty in adjusting herself to the city habit of working by the clock rather than the light. It reminded her too much of the days of her childhood when, under the auspices of the city-reared Miss Irving, she had been made to practise the harp in the cold and the darkness, to eat breakfast and start lessons, all before what she now regarded as a civilised hour for rising.

She returned to the breakfast room, shivering a little in the grass green morning gown that, though respectably buttoned from chin to toe, lacked all the tiresome underpinnings and tight lacing that would be required later in the day. Breakfast was the only meal a lady could enjoy with an unconstricted digestion, and Rachel sometimes found herself wondering how the wives of Colin's fellow bankers ever succeeded in swallowing enough food to become as stout as they were.

Blake was still sitting glancing through the *Glasgow Herald*, a Chinese robe thrown over shirt and trousers, a cup of coffee in his hand. The curtains were drawn against the weather and the dark, there was a fire burning merrily in the hearth, and the gas lights flickered companionably. It was a pleasant, intimate scene, more like the day's end than its beginning.

Rachel was annoyed that Blake hadn't developed wrinkles, or turned grey, or started running to fat. The thin wing of silver in his hair made him look more striking, and in a strange way younger, than ever.

She poured herself another cup of coffee, served herself some crisp bacon from the silver warmer on the sideboard, and, sitting down, began to butter a slice of toast. It always took her brain an hour or so to wake up, and the same was true of her appetite, but since this might be her only opportunity to be alone with Blake she braced herself, alert or not, to launch into what she wanted to ask him. Colin, having said he didn't want to be present when she talked to Blake about Sophie, had been taking a perverse pleasure in never being other than present when Blake was in the house.

'I wonder,' she said, biting unromantically into her toast, 'if you remember Colin writing to you once, to ask you about a Mr Archie Macmillan in Hong Kong, and his daughter Sophie?'

All these years, and her cousin was still no more than a name, a mystery, almost a mirage, except that a mirage wasn't real and Sophie Taverner was.

It was a moment before he looked up. 'Yes.'

'You wrote back to say that he had died and that Sophie was now Mrs Taverner.'

'Yes.'

'I wondered . . . She's a cousin of mine. A kind of cousin. Can I ask – are you personally acquainted with her?'

'I am.' His eyes dropped again to the newspaper.

It was like talking to a Trappist monk.

Rachel said, 'I know nothing at all about her, you see, and I thought you might tell me.'

He turned the page with something of a rustle. 'She is about your age, an unusually beautiful woman, with one son.'

There was a tap on the door, and Ethel's face appeared. 'Can I clear away, Mistress Campbell?'

'Yes. But leave the coffee, in case Mr Blake should want another cup. I'll ring for you when we've finished.'

Knowing that there was a strong likelihood that she would have to tell Blake the story of Sophie's debatable right to Juran, Rachel had no desire to be interrupted. Because although she hadn't, in truth, even known of Sophie's existence nine years earlier when Blake had first suggested the rental proposal – hadn't known that there was the slightest doubt about the legitimacy of her own claim – he might not believe her. And if he chose to think that she had tried to manipulate him, it was going to be a very uncomfortable interview.

6

'Tell me more, please,' she said. 'I imagine you must know more about her than that.'

One corner of his long mouth curled, and Rachel saw that there was a half smile in his eyes, a smile she couldn't interpret. She could have wept, then, because in that look she saw again the stranger who had ridden up to Juran when she was barely out of the schoolroom, and caused havoc in her heart. Who had kissed her once on a sunset shore. On whose dreamed-of love she had built so many naïve and stupid hopes.

She was thirty years old now, and had thought she knew better. But if he had opened his arms to her at that moment, she would have walked straight into them.

It seemed that he wasn't going to answer, so she said, 'I had better explain why I am interested.'

'No.'

Blake's work for Customs had led him to become more rather than less laconic with the passage of time, so that he never volunteered information unless he was persuaded that there was a cast-iron case for it. The other side of the coin was that it was almost unheard of for him to refuse information when it happened to be on offer.

But he had not the slightest desire, he reflected sardonically, for Rachel to begin explaining to him the saga of Juran and its ownership; it was much more convenient that he should continue to appear ignorant. More comfortable, too. He had set up the rental arrangement purely in the bank's interest, and had very soon begun to feel uneasy about it; even more uneasy about leaving Rachel in ignorance of Archie Macmillan's legal right to the place. The trouble was that, the longer the deception had gone on, the less possible it had become to admit to the truth, because Rachel had seen him as a knight in shining armour, riding to Juran's rescue, and to hers. That, he supposed, was why she had thought herself in love with him.

He wished she had not developed into quite such an attractive woman. She had always seemed oddly young to him before and socially ingenuous, but marriage had given her a mature charm that had previously been lacking.

'You have no need,' he went on, 'to explain anything to me. Your personal affairs are no concern of mine.'

'I suppose not.' She rose to her feet and went to stand gazing into the fire, the coal fire that gave out so much more heat and burned for so much longer than the big, swiftly consumed logs of Juran. She felt her cheeks becoming hot as she said, 'Then, do you perhaps know whether there is any likelihood of my cousin coming back to Scotland?'

After a long moment, he repeated, 'Likelihood? I – I have no idea.'

The hesitation was so unlike him that she turned, to see that his eyes had gone curiously blank.

7

The possibility of Sophie returning to Juran simply hadn't occurred to him.

He could not go on living with her as his wife, but to divorce her was not to be thought of. The cruelty of it apart, the only grounds would be her recent refusal of conjugal rights, and he was damned if he

436

was going to stand up in court, in Hong Kong of all places, and tell the world that his wife refused to go to bed with him. She had equally inadequate grounds for divorcing him; his despairing resort to a mistress wouldn't suffice. In any case, there was Archie.

Many of his spare moments on the voyage had been spent planning the rearrangement of the house he was having built on the Peak, so that it would be possible for them to live together and yet apart, without anyone other than themselves being the wiser.

Rachel said, 'It's just that – well, Juran is mine, but I suspect that she might think she has a claim to it.'

He, too, had risen. Now, he took a few restless paces to stand on the other side of the hearth from her.

He could not answer with outright lies. And the deception had gone on too long.

There was sympathy in his voice when he said, 'She does have a claim. Juran is her birthright.'

'It is *not*.'

'My dear girl, her father was still alive when you inherited. It should have been his. And if his, then his daughter's when he died.'

'No!'

She stared into his eyes, briefly mesmerised by the fire's reflection in them, two little dancing flames against the clear, lucent grey. There was a curl to his lips and the slanting brows were drawn slightly together, as if he were frowning and smiling at the same time.

Only then did her brain catch up with the implications of what he had said. 'How do you know all that?'

He raised a hand to her cheek to brush back a stray lock of soft brown hair.

'Sophie is my wife,' he said gently.

8

'But . . . She's married to someone called Taverner!'

He shook his head. 'He died. She and I have been married for more than five years. We have a son called Archie.'

'No. No! *No!*' Her face was frozen, but her eyes were enormous and there was disbelief in them and horror and anger. She was so white that the mole on her cheekbone stood out harsh as a beauty patch on the face of some Georgian dandy.

'Yes, yes, yes,' he said, and pulled her into his arms.

The taste of her lips was salt with the suddenly pouring tears, and although every barrier in the world should have lain between them, from the moment of their touching all thought was suspended. There was only an urgency of need, a desperation that admitted neither asking nor answering, a union that would not be denied.

Rachel had never known, and Blake had tried hard to forget, the full driving force of a desire that carried them along on a torrent too wild for sanity, too furious for tenderness. Not for a second did his lips leave hers as with hasty hands they undid what had to be undone, untied what had to be untied.

And then they were on the floor before the fire, and its light was glimmering on their skins and his lips were still on hers and his hands clamping her to him as he plunged himself deep, deep, deep into the warm, cushioned cavity waiting so avidly to receive him. For a long, infinitely sensual moment they lay in illusory stillness, he throbbing powerfully inside her while her muscles teased and tantalised him, pulled and plucked, until they were locked together so tightly, so indivisibly, that it seemed they could never be parted again.

After a year, a few seconds, a lifetime, he gave a low groan and began moving inside her, not gently, but driving hard and fast and deep, which was what she wanted and had always wanted, without knowing it, so that she began to feel sensations she had never felt before, to think she would die, drowning and delirious, in the wonder of them.

But it did not last, could not last, because the intensity for both of them was too great to bear and had to have an end.

Dazedly, Rachel saw from the gilt and marble clock on the mantelpiece that it had taken less than ten minutes for the years of love and longing to be fulfilled at last.

9

Colin arrived home again at half past nine, not having gone to Edinburgh after all. Waiting for the train to leave, he had checked through his papers and discovered that a crucial balance sheet was missing. Since it wasn't worth going without it, he had returned to the bank where an intensive search by his senior clerk had failed to discover it.

'So,' he told his wife, 'I've set one of the juniors to copying the office duplicate. But it'll be a long business and it occurred to me that Blake might possibly have the original. Is he still here, or has he gone?'

'How tiresome for you!' Rachel exclaimed sympathetically. 'But I'm afraid he left a while ago.'

'He did, did he? I thought I saw him walking off along the terrace as I arrived and nearly drove after him. It's an infernal nuisance. If there's one thing I can not abide, it's wasted time. You're looking a bit peaky, my dear. Are you all right?'

'Yes. Yes! It's just that getting up early doesn't agree with me. You know that. Why don't you sit down for a few minutes, and I'll tell Ethel to make you a cup of tea? It'll revive you.'

And it might have done, if he had not been so sure that it *was* Blake he had seen. And if, under his wife's neat and controlled exterior, he had not sensed a glow – a heart's ease – that pained him as cruelly, as intimately, as a knife twisting in his guts.

CHAPTER TWENTY-ONE

I

Sophie said, 'Do you have the figures for the Madras cottons, or do I?'

'You have them.' Gino Venturi stretched his legs, put his hands in his trousers pockets, and sat back in his chair looking bored. Sophie had been fired by the notion of sitting down and analysing the business in the hope of identifying their most, and least, profitable fields of operation, and Gino regarded it as a waste of time. He already knew the answers, he said. What he didn't say was that he preferred Sophie shouldn't know them too. She was becoming too inquisitive for comfort.

But whether or not he approved, Sophie's mind was made up. She was tired of Gino playing his cards so close to his chest. There was an economic depression, and it wasn't just local. There had been wild speculation in the share market. Freights were falling so steeply that everyone's vessels would soon have to be either laid up or run at a loss. Profits had diminished almost to vanishing point and trade in general had seldom been more unstable. Three firms in the colony had sunk without trace – Elstob's, Turner and Aubry, and Bell and Dodgson.

Sophie had learned a good deal in the last three years, but she still didn't know by what magical means Macmillan and Venturi managed to stay afloat, and Gino wouldn't tell her.

A curtain had come down between them recently. Before then, she had been able to turn to him for help and he had responded with the derisive tolerance that marked all his dealings with the human race. But now, although the derision was still there, the tolerance was less apparent. It was as if he had pruned his attitudes as he had pruned his body; the rumpled look persisted, and the smile was no less disarming, but the overlay of comfortable flesh had dropped away, and he had begun to look not only younger but harder, a man to be reckoned with. Sophie trusted him less but respected him more.

Shuffling the Madras figures into their proper place in the pile, she remarked, 'Isn't it nice to be cool! I have a theory that the European brain wasn't designed to function at temperatures above 70° Fahrenheit. What the colony needs is somewhere cool for everyone to retire to in the hot weather. The way Anglo-Indians retire to Simla.'

Lazily, Gino smiled. 'The Abode of the Little Tin Gods. It's an idea. Who, after all, could be tinnier, or indeed closer to the Almighty, than our own dear governor, the Pope?'

Sophie chuckled. Mr John Pope Hennessy's nickname had been inevitable from the moment it became clear that he thought himself infallible. 'If that isn't blasphemy,' she said, 'it's certainly *lèse-majesté*. Talking of little tin gods, however . . .'

Rising, graceful in her simple office dress of Black Watch tartan with its narrow white frill round the high neck and cuffs, she went to the window and looked out.

Gino Venturi watched and waited, a goodly number of emotions warring behind the deceptive blandness of his eyes.

She said, 'My husband, to be precise.'

If she had been looking at him, she would have seen Gino's eyelids drop and the merest hint of a smile touch his lips. Had he still been carrying the flesh of years past he would have served admirably as a model for the Buddha.

'I've never pretended,' she went on, 'to be good at figures, but that five thousand pounds – that debt of my father's that Rainer said was an extension of the Juran collateral – is still showing in the books . . .'

'Plus interest.'

'. . . and I can't see why we haven't paid it off. When I ask him about it, all he says is ask *you*!'

She turned. She had become increasingly suspicious of Gino's accounting, though the worst she thought was that he might be using the debt to make both sides of his horrid balance sheet agree.

Gino, fixed with a penetrating stare, buried his hands deeper in his pockets. 'Your husband didn't want it paid off.'

'Why?'

'Mysterious are the ways of the little tin gods. Perhaps he thinks we need it more than he does.'

'Perhaps! Do we have any records of how the money was spent? I know Rainer said it was necessary to keep the place in repair, but shouldn't we have had receipts or something of the sort?'

'*Madonna mia*! Are you doubting your husband's word?'

'No, of course not.'

Though it was exactly what she was doing.

2

He arrived back from Scotland a few days later, having had, he said, a fast trip both ways. He had spent only ten days in Glasgow, and no, he had not been to Juran. And since Caine Road must be rather crowded, he had booked himself in at the Club until the new house on the Peak was ready.

Sophie said, of course, if he would be more comfortable there, and would he mind if she finished her morning inspection before they talked?

Afterwards, he gave her a light kiss on the cheek and a Shetland shawl knitted from wool so fine that it could be drawn through a finger ring. She said she would put it away carefully until she reached the age of needing a woolly shawl.

For Archie, he had brought a tam o' shanter bonnet, a kilt, a tartan-clad toy soldier and a bag of some fudge-like stuff called 'tablet' that Sophie said would ruin the child's teeth.

He played with Archie for half an hour, which enabled him to avoid meeting his wife's eyes during a conversation that might, for all of intimacy there was in it, have been between strangers.

Then he left, his conscience in no way eased, because although he had not known what he would do if she came running to his arms, he had not expected her to be so distant, so calm and controlled with him. It was as if, in a mere four months, she had grown up and grown away from him. He had hurt her, he supposed, more than he had intended.

He had deliberately chosen the worst time of day to see her, a time when everything was bustle, because it had seemed preferable to launching straight into a privacy full of dangers. Though the moment must necessarily come.

Sophie watched him go, her false calm vanishing even as the door closed, the tears of heartbreak springing to her eyes. All she had wanted was a sign and she would have met him halfway, more than halfway. But she had resolved that she would not make the first move, because during these last months, in a quest for the truth about her love, and his, she had confronted too much that was painful.

What had hurt most in the scene between them before he had sailed was his saying that his love for her had been too much of the body. She couldn't forget that or explain it away to herself, as she had explained

442

away his theory that she had turned to him as a substitute for her father. There had been truth in that, she supposed, though only at the very beginning and only because there was fifteen years difference in age between them. It had seemed a great deal when she was younger, though it was nothing now. The reason she loved him was – because she loved him.

But love meant sharing, and that, she knew, was where everything had gone so dreadfully wrong. They had shut each other out from half of themselves. She hadn't been capable of making him understand her irrational physical fears; though she would have tried, if she could have understood them herself. And he had kept her in ignorance about the part of his life in which she wasn't directly involved – his work, about which she knew nothing.

Her mind scanning the years, she had begun putting together his unexplained absences, the guard he always kept on his tongue, his knowledge of everything that went on in the colony, his occasional brushes with danger and the way he always went armed. The answer had been horribly unsettling. He couldn't, she told herself, be on the wrong side of the law. But his life was so unorthodox that it was hard to believe that he was on the right side.

Tell me, she thought, as through her tears she watched the tall, limber figure striding off down the hill. *You must tell me.*

3

It was the time for crackers and gongs and lanterns, for banners and peach blossoms, for chicken meals and sticky sweets and scarlet envelopes of good luck money. For red, red, red and noise, noise, noise everywhere, and dragon dances along the Praya.

Where previous governors of the colony had looked on the Chinese celebrations with the air of tolerant adults watching undisciplined children at play, Mr Pope Hennessy took the eccentric view that the Chinese were adults, too. In the opinion of the foreign community, his regard for their customs and usages was not only much exaggerated, but positively dangerous.

Rumour had it that in this, the second New Year of his governorship, he was proposing to take a personal part in the dragon dance. Seeing was believing, and the route had never been more crowded as the hundred-yard-long dragon – the procession of shouting, laughing, dancing Chinese, heads and shoulders lost within the

443

brilliantly painted and decorated bamboo and fabric framework –
waggled its rumbustious way through the thoroughfares of the town.

Before the dragon hove into view, Lao and Li Chang, captains of
the *Meall* and *Corran*, had been standing at the end of Bonham Strand
arguing with a cheerful group of their fellow captains about whether
staying ahead of the procession mightn't offer better entertainment
than following on behind. It seemed quite natural, certainly not
suspicious, when the two of them broke away from the group and
began pushing their way east towards where their ships were berthed,
singing and shouting with the best, greeting everyone from friends
and acquaintances to people they had never seen before with '*Kung hei
fat choi*', the wish for prosperity.

Undoubtedly, it was one of the best New Year festivals anyone
could remember. Everyone in Hong Kong was on holiday.

It was only when the brothers reached their ships that they
discovered that everyone was not, after all, on holiday.

The guards they had left on the gangways had been replaced by
police lieutenants, and the uniforms on deck were not those of Chinese
seamen.

The *Meall* and the *Corran* were under arrest, and so were their
captains.

4

It was Lao who got away, ducking and weaving through the crowds
towards the offices of Macmillan and Venturi, hoping that the
watchman might know where Mr Venturi was to be found.

As things transpired, he didn't even have to ask, because Gino
Venturi was there in person – leaving the offices surrounded by a
brass-buttoned escort and with a heavy official hand on either arm.

5

Not until next day was Sophie able to find out anything useful about
what was going on, and even then she didn't find out much.

She was angry enough, at first, to be stupid, demanding rhetorically
of the Captain Superintendent of Police why he had seen fit to arrest
the junior rather than the senior partner of Macmillan and Venturi. It
was only when she received the chilling reply that Hong Kong's jails
were not designed for ladies that she began to grasp the full seriousness

444

of the situation and descended, though not too rapidly, from her high horse. After that, the captain was more cooperative. Mr Venturi had not, he conceded, been arrested on any specific charge, but was being held 'pending enquiries'. And as for the ships, they had been searched and found to be clean. They would probably be released within a day or two.

It was the younger Chang who subsequently came to her with the gossip.

'Lao is busy,' he reported resignedly. 'I tell him he not able to repair damage, but you know him. Always grateful listener to any word of advice, but then goes and does thing he intended to do in first place.'

'Damage?' Sophie snapped. 'If the police have caused damage to the ships, I will make a very serious complaint!'

'Not that kind damage. Something you better not know about. Hey! My new son really fine boy. You should come see him!'

Despite everything, Sophie laughed. Li, the fragile blossom who could not bear dissent, harassment or bickering and whose primary concern was always with his own comfort, had nevertheless succeeded in fathering four sons and three daughters in the eight years since his wedding day. Sophie sighed sometimes, remembering what a strange day it had been, and what fun.

'Perhaps,' she said. 'But what have you found out?'

'Rumour. Very mysterious. Make no sense. Gentleman concerned very clever, though. Maybe he have reasons we not understand.' He smiled buoyantly.

All too familiar with Li's habit of having a good word to say for everyone except his brother, Sophie told him, 'Perhaps I had better be the judge of that. Who is the gentleman we are talking about?'

'Your husband,' Li replied. 'Lainer Bake.' Chinglish speakers always had trouble with their 'r's and 'l's.

After a very long moment, Sophie found her voice again. 'And the rumour is – what?'

'It is Mister Bake who set police on Macmillan and Venturi.'

'It isn't possible! Why? Why should he?'

Li shrugged cheerfully. 'See? I tell you. Very mysterious, but maybe he know what he doing.'

'Oh, I'm *sure* he does!'

6

She sent a chit to the Club asking him to come and see her, and he wrote back that he would do so as soon as it could be managed. In the meantime, he was exceedingly busy and he was sure she would understand.

In a cold rage, she went to his office.

He wasn't there.

Next day, the Clyde River Bank foreclosed on Macmillan and Venturi.

7

Sophie, her office locked against her, was sitting at home in the drawing room, a fire lit against the chill of the February evening, when Blake arrived. Archie's wooden railway engine, the tartan soldier and a big, bouncy ball were lying at the side of the fire as if she and the child had been playing with them before Ah Foon haled Archie off to bed.

Blake's ice-grey eyes assessed and approved his wife's severely businesslike dress, a tailormade in a blue several shades darker than her eyes, with no train, the hem two inches off the ground, and a black bodice cut like a man's coat over a simulated waistcoat in blue. She looked very beautiful as she stared at him, wordless, puzzled, trying to make sense not of the disaster that had overtaken Macmillan and Venturi, but of Blake himself.

Only when he had poured himself a glass of brandy and sat down opposite her did she speak. 'You've come to explain, I take it? Can you?'

He hesitated briefly. 'If you're willing to understand.'

It was then she discovered that the gulf between them was a thousand miles wide.

'*Don't you dare patronise me!*'

There was such sudden, cold, violent loathing in it that he felt the blood leave his face. 'Sophie . . .'

'Be quick,' she said, 'because I don't know how long I can stay in the same room with you.'

For almost the first time in his life, he had no idea what to say, where to start. He had called in debts from a good many people in his time, but never from someone he loved. And guilt didn't help.

446

Regaining control, she said in a crisply businesslike voice he had never heard from her before, 'Start at the beginning, please. According to rumour, it was you who reported Macmillan and Venturi to the police. I would like to know' – she ticked each question off on her fingers – 'first, if this is true. Second, why. And third, what are the crimes involved?'

Nothing had happened to release him from the bonds of secrecy. 'Why should I have had any part in letting the police loose on Macmillan and Venturi? You know very well that rumour is seldom to be relied on. But I can probably enlighten you on the third matter.'

She knew him better than he thought. 'I see. You *were* involved, but you don't wish to lie. Very well, tell me about the crimes.'

His jaw tightening, he said, 'Gino Venturi is an unusually intelligent man who never fails to spot an opportunity when it offers, and will create one when it doesn't. But he is vain, which sometimes makes him careless. He takes chances. And he is being held now because, this time, he has taken chances with the wrong people.'

'You.'

'As it happens, no. The laws of Hong Kong are not my affair. But I have been suspicious for years, which is why I have always been opposed to your involvement in the business.'

'You didn't think to warn me?'

'No.'

'In fact, you have spent all the six years of our marriage suspecting him, probably laying traps for him, just as if I wasn't involved at all?'

He didn't answer and the silence seemed to last for a long time before she broke it. 'Very well. What chances has Gino been taking?'

Blake's lips twisted into a humourless smile as he swirled the brandy in his glass. 'Take your choice. How about a nice little currency swindle? Stringing Annamese copper cash from the Mint at Tokwawan, which isn't legal tender, in with Hong Kong cash? That way, you can expand fifty honest strings into a hundred dishonest ones and nobody the wiser until the strings come to be broken up.'

'That doesn't sound very terrible to me.'

'It would if you were poor and your only string of cash turned out to be fraudulent. Or what about the coolie trade? When that was made illegal, Venturi at first got round the problem by helping would-be emigrants as far as Macao, no further. What he has been doing recently, however, is taking not men but *girls* to Macao, and not

447

voluntarily. Kidnapping, it's called. Their subsequent fate is to be shipped out to brothels in the Straits Settlement, California and Australia, where there are thousands of Chinese contract labourers and only a handful of women.'

'I don't believe it.' She laughed angrily. 'Can you imagine Lao or Li – or any other of our captains – hopping ashore at some Chinese village and bundling screaming girls down into the hold? Especially Li. He's the most courteous soul alive!'

Blake rose and went to lean his shoulders against the mantelshelf, hands in pockets. Looking down at her, he said reasonably, 'There's no use denying it because you don't *want* to believe. I'll give you one more example. Did you never wonder why Macmillan and Venturi's ships were so rarely attacked by pirates? Well, I'll tell you why. Venturi has been buying them off, not with money but with information about when other merchants' ships are scheduled to sail, in what company, and with what cargoes. And the result, Sophie, is that many ships have been lost and men have died.'

Her eyes were blue and hard as sapphires, and infinitely hostile. 'It isn't true. That's as good as saying that Gino is a murderer!'

8

There were other things he could have told her, but he didn't, because she thought of Venturi as a friend. And it didn't matter now, with Venturi behind bars.

So he said merely, 'The cases aren't yet cast iron, but they will be. And that's why I've called in the loans *now*, before Venturi's sins are made public and affect the value of the company. I figure we still ought to be able to sell for a fair price.'

'*Sell?*'

'My God, what do you think this is all about? Listen, Sophie! Macmillan and Venturi has been doomed for years. The day of the small shipping business has passed, and so has commerce in its old form. If you look at Jardine Matheson, at Lapraik, at Chater, you'll see where the future is. It's not commodities any more, it's economic and shipping services, insurance, industrial investment. If you were to compete, you would need not only substantial capital, but financial wizardry and access to governments. Believe me, I know!'

'I'm sure you do!'

'Don't be sarcastic. It doesn't suit you. Please, forget the emotion and try to understand. If we sell now, we should realise enough to repay the bank's loans on both the business and Juran. If we leave it longer, we might have to sell Juran, too.'

She flung to her feet and moved to confront him where he stood before the fire. 'Yes, I like that! The royal "we"! How dare you stand there and coolly tell me *you* have decided to sell the firm in order to save Juran! You have looks, power, money, authority, and you think they entitle you to get away with anything. Well, let me tell you this. If something has to be sold, then it's Juran that must go in order to save the firm. If I am never going to return to Scotland in style, I am never going to return at all, and *I will not have you* taking the decision out of my hands!'

'Juran is viable,' he said. 'Macmillan and Venturi is not.'

'And what does that mean?'

'It means that where the firm is concerned you have no choice. No choice at all. Face up to it, Sophie. It's over.'

Until now, he hadn't known, hadn't wanted to know, how important it all was to her, but seeing the look in her eyes he was grateful that there were no blunt instruments within reach. Feeling hemmed in, far too aware of her nearness, he put his hands on her shoulders to move her aside, but at his first touch she tore away from him, on her face a searing revulsion.

Grittily, he said, 'I am not going to rape you. It's merely that my coat tails are getting scorched.'

'Please don't touch me again.' She sat down, her spine rigid. 'Why is Juran viable?'

'The prices of Highland sporting estates are soaring, and there are not many of them. Frustrated purchasers are therefore delighted to rent. As from this year, Juran will be producing a very satisfactory income.'

'*For whom*? And why "as from this year"?'

If her temper had not been out of control, she would not have made the elementary mistake of asking him two questions at the same time and so allowing him to choose which to answer.

He ignored the first and, because it was so unimportant in the wider context of their lives and future, answered the second with careless imprecision. 'Until now, any income has been vitiated by the repairs loan.'

He hadn't given her credit for the acumen she had so recently learned.

449

She pounced. 'Ah, yes. The famous £5000. Do I deduce from that strange way of putting it that the loan has now been cleared?'

He had never troubled to explain the special arrangements involved, not even to Venturi. It had never seemed necessary. But now, apparently, it was.

When he had finished, Sophie studied him with a spuriously quiet interest, her elegant head cocked. 'Let me be sure that I have this right. In return for your initial loan, you have had ten years' interest on it, the use of Juran for ten years whenever you cared to visit it, and you still expect to have the £5000 paid back to you?'

'Yes.'

'You don't think such a return a little excessive?'

His face relaxed into a dry smile. 'I'm a banker. Money is my business. If it hadn't been for your father's foolish obsession about no one at Juran knowing he was still alive, none of it would have been necessary.'

'Perhaps it wouldn't have been, if you'd told him how much his obsession was going to cost him! Rainer, will you stop prowling around!'

It was the first time she had addressed him by name since he had arrived, which, he supposed, was a step in the right direction.

'What fun you have been having,' she went on with a brightness as artificial as her earlier calm. 'All that lovely profit, with a Highland estate thrown in for use whenever you happened to be in Scotland. Not to mention my charming, capable cousin Rachel! From what you say of the agreement, I assume she thinks she owns the place?'

'She does. But my visits have been brief. The rental agreement was made in the name of my partner in the Glasgow branch, Colin Campbell. Whose wife your cousin now happens to be.'

'Better still!'

She sounded delighted, and he couldn't understand it until she went on, 'I remember you telling me, before we were married, that you had never needed to go to brothels because all your needs were catered for by other men's wives. Nothing changes, does it!'

9

It had been a bow at a venture, an attempt to hit back, an irrational expression of fury, misery and hurt.

And then Sophie saw that she had drawn blood.

He, who never lost his temper, lost it now. 'You don't know what you're talking about,' he snapped. 'And this argument has gone on quite long enough. I know you're angry and disillusioned, and that you blame me for everything that's happened in the last few days, but you'll see the sense of it, in time. What we have to do, right now, is forget about it and get on with trying to make sense of our lives again.'

She gasped in disbelief. 'You . . . You . . . You turn my whole world upside down and then tell me to forget it! You betray my love and trust, and tell me to forget it! You ruin my business for the sake of your own outrageous profit, and tell me to forget it! You save Juran because you don't want it sold over your mistress's head, and tell me to forget it! You . . .'

'*That's enough!*' His hands were gripping her shoulders, his eyes like icicles and every muscle in face and body like a spring coiled to snapping point, but she felt neither fear nor regret, only a bitter triumph that, at last, she had penetrated his armour and shown him she was capable of fighting him on his own ground, that the tie between them was, after all, more than physical.

The tie that had been, but now was broken.

With a deep, cold savagery, she said, 'Yes, it's enough. And since you have been so busy playing God that you have left me with nothing else to do, I am going to leave you, and take Archie, and go to Juran and disabuse my cousin of the idea that it belongs to her.

'Because she can't have both Juran *and* you.'

10

Nothing Blake could say would move her.

Two months later, just after Archie's fifth birthday, Sophie and her son sailed for Scotland.

PART FOUR

1879–
1880

CHAPTER TWENTY-TWO

I

The world beyond Hong Kong was as much a foreign country to Sophie as it was to Archie, although it didn't begin to feel really strange until Singapore and then Colombo were left far behind.

Sophie, who had worried badly about how Archie would respond to the long weeks at sea, soon discovered that he had less difficulty in filling in the time than she did.

'That's because we P&O chaps are experts,' the purser told her cheerfully. 'Master Archie's is the third generation of infants we've ferried from the East to Europe so that they can grow up in a civilised climate, and frankly, Mrs Blake, they're a dashed sight less troublesome at four or five than they are when we ferry them back again, at seventeen or eighteen!'

It was an enormous relief. Archie missed Ah Foon, of course, though not nearly as badly as Sophie did herself, but she had been able to arrange for him to share the English nurserymaid employed by Henrietta Turner, the wife of a Shanghai shipping merchant, who was taking her two small children home to Cheltenham to grow up in their grandparents' care.

Hetty Turner wasn't someone Sophie would have chosen to make friends with, but there was no denying that having a travelling companion had its uses. There were altogether too many lone gentlemen with roving eyes on board, and Sophie very soon tired of warding off invitations to play quoits, or take a stroll round the ship, or watch deck cricket.

She didn't want to travel. She wanted to *arrive*.

Something else she didn't want to do was sit and think. After a week she threw her stitchery overboard, because it encouraged her to do just that. It seemed that everyone else on the ship had someone to go home to, whereas she was launching herself and Archie into an unknown void. She spent a great deal of time shaking with nerves, telling herself she was mad, missing Rainer dreadfully except when she was too busy blaming him for everything that had happened. If a magic carpet bound for Hong Kong had landed on deck for refuelling, she would have leapt aboard instantly.

Grimly, she tried to take her mind off things by settling down to some of the books she had packed, but found that Mr Hardy, Mr Trollope and Mr Meredith had nothing to say to her. They were too dull, too real. She should have brought Ouida.

Archie behaved like an angel until they reached the Suez Canal, where the heat was intense, and the wind came off the desert like the blast from a furnace, and there was sand everywhere. Even camels and Arab encampments weren't enough to banish his fretfulness. But everything changed when they arrived in the Mediterranean. The East was behind them and before them Europe, heritage of the past and promise of the future.

It was such a delight to see something other than endless ocean that Sophie, at long last, began to feel the thrill of adventure, to think that perhaps she hadn't been mad after all. Everything was pure pleasure, and although she had been told about it often enough, she found herself constantly exclaiming about how like Hong Kong it all was – the ports set on narrow strips of land between mountains and sea, the serried ranks of Classical-looking buildings climbing up the slopes, even the quality of the light. When they reached Malta, Archie danced up and down shrieking, 'Mummy, mummy! Ladder streets! Just like ours!'

And then, after seven weeks, they arrived at Tilbury and romance gave way to reality, the beautiful, unfamiliar historical past to the equally unfamiliar, but quite unbeautiful present.

In Hong Kong there had been no railway trains, no factories, no tenements, no dirty smokestacks, no thick, oily bronze rivers, and although there had been grime and squalor in abundance, it had been loud and vital and Chinese, and no one had seemed to resent it. But here complexions were grey, faces haggard, expressions shifty, and there was a dinginess everywhere that Sophie found repellent. It was as if people spent their lives feeling chilled, hungry and sour.

Sophie had been maided on the voyage by the wife of a Sergeant MacAlister of the 79th, who was returning to his regimental depot in Scotland, and the sergeant declared himself more than happy to escort Mrs Blake and her little boy as far as Glasgow. Sophie didn't know what she would have done without his kindly shepherding as they travelled north through a dirty, seemingly endless succession of industrial towns and her heart sank steadily towards her fashionable new walking boots.

But the die was cast.

So she quartered herself gratefully on some cousins of Dolly Berry's, consulted a lawyer, made all the necessary arrangements for storing the furniture and other possessions that had travelled with her on the ship, and finally – leaving Archie behind – set off for Juran.

2

She had no intention of turning up with a begging bowl in her hand. Juran was hers, and that was all there was to it. She would see 'cousin Rachel' and make the situation clear. After that, she would decide whether to live in the place, or sell it – which would be more sensible, because Sophie couldn't even begin to imagine herself presiding over an estate half the size of Hong Kong island, set in the middle of nowhere. Besides, the lawyer had confirmed what Rainer had told her, that people were falling over themselves to pay huge sums for such places.

Juran could never be other than a second best to her. Despite all that had increasingly irritated Sophie about Hong Kong in these last few years, it had always been her home and would always be the place she loved most.

Or so she thought until she reached the hills of Argyll and discovered their magical peace and quiet and impersonal beauty. No estranged husbands, no criminal partners, no teas and cotton shirtings, no chambers of commerce, no banks, no balance sheets, no trade recessions, no gossips. She reflected on the last one for a moment, and then mentally crossed it out; a place without gossip was altogether too hard to believe in.

She hadn't realised how great the combined weight of her burdens had been until they fell from her shoulders.

She had given up trying to anticipate what the castle would look like, thinking only how odd it was that her father should have left before photography had even been invented; smiling to herself at the thought of him struggling to describe the place, in pidgin, to a Cantonese porcelain painter. It wasn't to be wondered at that the image on The Bowl – given a little exaggeration of the roof line and the removal of the saltire flag of St Andrew from the turret – would have looked perfectly at home on a willow pattern dinner service.

She could still remember Jay Vanderbilt, who had seen Balmoral, laughing uproariously and assuring her that, whatever Juran might look like, it didn't look like that.

And, of course, it didn't. Clean, white, smart and enchantingly picturesque, it lay in the sunset glow like a neatly cut jewel in a velvet case cushioned by shadowed trees and silver sand. It was beautiful.

Despite a lifetime's preconceptions, Sophie knew that – now, at this turning point in her life – this was where she wanted and needed to be.

3

'You had better come in,' Rachel said.

The lingering smile faded from Sophie's face, although she was still able to feel brief amusement at the smoothly spoken but grudging words before there sprang back into her mind, fully armed, the altogether unamusing thing that she had been trying so hard to forget, and so hard not to forget, since the evening in February when her husband had betrayed himself.

Inquisitive, inimical, intent as two alien cats, Rachel and Sophie were both resolved to give no hint of their feelings to the other. A woman wholly confident of her position had no need even to acknowledge – certainly not to fear – enemies. And ladies did not scream at each other on doorsteps, or anywhere else for that matter.

It meant that both were at their most tightly controlled and insolent worst.

Sophie said, 'Perhaps you will arrange to let my two guides have some refreshment and a bed for the night? And then I think we should have some tea and talk things over.'

'Of course.' Rachel's voice betrayed no more than her face. 'But we can do better than that, I hope. It is one of the laws of Highland hospitality that one always makes a special effort for guests who are unlikely to pass one's way again. If you would make yourself at home in the Green Drawing Room,' she gestured with a small but practical-looking hand, 'I will speak to my cook. Then we will have a glass of Madeira before supper – a French habit of mine.'

Sophie raised one elegant and faintly satirical brow. 'Thank you, Mrs Campbell. That will be delightful.'

'Not Mrs Campbell,' Rachel corrected her, 'or not at Juran. In the

Highlands, it is customary for married women still to be addressed by their maiden names. Here, I am Mistress Macmillan.'

'Really?' Sophie said interestedly. 'Then I should be Mistress Macmillan, too. How amusing! That ought to confuse everyone *most* effectively!'

The drawing room proved to be quite pleasant once a servant had lit the lamps, and Sophie reflected that she wouldn't need to make many changes – white paintwork rather than cream, and a cheerful tartan carpet in place of the drab forest green; fresh flowers in preference to castor oil plants and aspidistras, and perhaps a few game trophies on the walls. She had already decided to be generous and allow Rachel to take anything for which she had a particular fondness, though not to excess. The lawyer had told her that the lady's husband had a perfectly good house in Glasgow and was generally believed, in financial circles, to be one of the warmest men in a city which did not lack men of means.

The lawyer had also told her that her own title to Juran was incontrovertible. Mrs Campbell, not having been legitimate at birth but only legitimated, would have a poor case. The one point in her favour – one not to be underestimated, mind you! – was that she had been in possession for some years. But the Campbells were childless, which would make the courts wary. The absence of a natural heir always raised the possibility of further legal problems in the years ahead, which the courts, naturally enough, did their best to preclude. No, Mrs Blake had nothing to worry about, especially since she had a boy of her own.

And then the drawing room door opened again and Rachel walked from the darkness into the light, and Sophie saw, with shock, that she was pregnant, and very pregnant, and revelling in it.

4

They had the most inanely polite conversation over Madeira and supper, progressing from the charm of log fires to the coaling problems of the P&O; from wild goose shoots on Corran to duck farming in Kowloon; from salmon to civet cat, midges to mosquitoes, and clegs to cobras. After that it was extremes of climate, Sophie winning in the matter of high temperatures and Rachel on low. And although Hong Kong scored on severity of rainfall, the Highlands carried the palm for frequency.

All the time they were eyeing each other while pretending they weren't.

Rachel had insensibly come to visualise Sophie as the Hong Kong version of an Indian memsahib, a dislikeable species of which she had met many examples during her marriage to Colin. She had found them, almost without exception, to be conceited, condescending and prone to order everybody about, while their conversation was largely incomprehensible, heavily larded with the esoterics of empire – district officers and zemindars, dirzies and dhobis, forward policies and Afghan alliances, sepoys, suttees and trips up country and, ever and always, 'as dear Lord Lytton – the viceroy, you know? – said to my husband quite recently . . .'

Expecting Sophie to be one of this breed, she had found her expectations instantly confirmed by the other woman's autocratic air and supreme self-assurance. But although Rainer had said she was beautiful, Rachel hadn't expected her to be so utterly ravishing. Even the imperious half smile couldn't diminish the perfection of her features, or the dishevelment of a twenty mile ride obscure the slender grace of the figure under the sapphire-blue riding habit. She looked expensive, too.

Rachel, who, having been up in the attics for most of the day, was wearing an ancient dress that had been let out and let out again as the months passed, was bitterly jealous – and that Sophie was four inches taller than she was did nothing to mollify her.

. This was the woman who laid claim to everything Rachel had fought for, who had already stolen from her the man who was rightfully hers. The knowledge that Rainer had married Sophie while Rachel herself was still free, still building castles in the air, had been the unkindest cut of all, and for the seven months since that discovery, Rachel had nourished for her cousin a deep personal hatred that was of quite a different order from the hatred that had gone before, a mild thing in retrospect, it now seemed, woolly, desultory, almost objective.

Sophie was scarcely less taken aback, though in a different way. Knowing Rachel to be half French and illegitimate, and having convinced herself that she was ruthlessly self-interested and avariciously disposed, she could not relate this image to the respect-able – indeed, perfectly ordinary-looking – young woman who now sat across the table from her. Rachel's chestnut hair was soft and silky, and her complexion flawless, but there was nothing else in the least striking about her and Sophie didn't expect to be given evidence of the smile that, according to Rainer, transformed her. It was impossible to tell whether her figure would be good when she wasn't pregnant, but Sophie decided, to her own satisfaction, that it wouldn't; she had never known a small woman who wasn't dumpy. And as for her dress! Even making allowances – which Sophie thought very charitable of her – for her cousin's impending motherhood and people's tendency to dress plainly in the country, she still couldn't repress a shudder. The woman was, quite simply, bourgeois.

Mystified, Sophie wondered whether she could possibly have been doing Rainer an injustice. Cousin Rachel wasn't his style at all.

But she was about seven months pregnant, and Rainer had been in Glasgow seven months before.

5

It was an excellent supper; an omelette first, lightly flavoured with samphire, then the freshest of brown trout rolled in oatmeal, and finally a tart of preserved peaches and rowanberries. Since French wines had to be fortified with brandy for their journey to the East and, even then, were slow to recover, Rachel's good white Bordeaux was a rare treat for Sophie, though she would have died rather than admit it.

Afterwards, Rachel apologised, with more formality than sincerity, for the briefness of the menu, which gave Sophie her opportunity.

'It was exactly what I would have chosen myself,' she said charmingly, 'and admirable in every sense. Tell me, do you think your cook would agree to stay on when you leave?'

It was so much the kind of *faux pas* a memsahib might have made that Rachel did not at first recognise it as deliberate.

When she did, Sophie sensed a wave of anger so acute that it was almost tangible, the first intimation she had had that there was passion under that controlled exterior. *Well, well*! she thought, startled.

'Tea in the drawing room, I suggest,' Rachel said after a moment. 'Do you have friends in the neighbourhood, or shall I tell my housekeeper to prepare a room for you?'

'If you would.'

Tea having been poured – which Sophie identified, with regret, as a rather coarse black from one of the new plantations in Ceylon – she said easily, 'Let us not, please, have any misunderstanding about this. Juran belongs to me.'

461

Although she would have expected her cousin to be conciliatory, because the woman could scarcely help but know that her claim would never stand up in court, she was not unduly concerned – indeed, found herself relishing the prospect of battle – when Rachel looked back at her and said softly, 'Oh, no, cousin Sophie. You're wrong. You – are – quite – wrong. I have been through far too much for it. Juran belongs to *me*.'

Sophie smiled. 'I can see that you have been a most conscientious caretaker.' Again she felt the vibrations of anger, but she had expected them this time, had set out to provoke them. Cousin Rachel deserved to be insulted. So, calmly, she went on, 'But you have no claim to ownership. My lawyer tells me that your father inherited the property only because my father had been presumed to be dead. In fact, he outlived both your father and your half sister and was therefore, for a second time, the legal heir. His claim was superior to that bestowed on you by your legitimation. And since I was his sole heir, Juran is mine. I am afraid, my dear cousin, that there is no possible doubt about it.' Without thinking, she took a sip of tea.

Rachel, observing the smothered grimace, reminded herself to tell Mairi to make it even stronger at breakfast time.

'We must therefore talk,' Sophie went on, as if everything were settled, 'about a date for you to leave. I have no desire to rush you, but unlike you I have no other home in this country. I expect you will want to spend the last few weeks of your confinement in Glasgow, so that would possibly be as good a time as any.'

It was with difficulty, although she gave no sign of it, that she forced the last words out, the certainty that this woman was carrying Rainer's child bitter on her tongue.

'Perhaps we might agree on the middle of next month?'

6

'I doubt it,' Rachel said, and her eyes were wide, cold and watchful. 'Indeed, I find it hard to imagine us ever agreeing on anything.'

Her back was aching, so she sat down in the chair she had had brought down from the attics. Its style was unrepentantly Great Exhibition, its back and arms wreathed in French-polished mahogany antlers, but it was the only chair she could find in which she was remotely comfortable.

'I, too, have a lawyer,' she said. 'And I have needed one. My ownership of Juran has been challenged several times over the years, without success. You might care to think about that, because the law of inheritance can be a very grey area.'

She paused, choosing her words. 'You are, of course, at liberty to challenge me, if you wish, but I would warn you that you are likely to find it a protracted and expensive business and in the meantime, of course, I will still be here. Possession is nine points of the law.'

There was one more thing she found it necessary to say, and she dropped her eyes while she said it because she was afraid that they would give her away. 'Until these last few months, the courts might – just *might* – have favoured your claim, because you had a son. But things are different now.'

Instinctively, her hands moved to cradle her stomach. For the second time in her life, Rainer Blake had given her the greatest gift he could bestow. The first had been Juran; it had always seemed to her that, in suggesting the rental, he had made a gift to her of the place she loved.

She wondered how much the other woman knew or guessed. Hating her, Rachel *hoped* she knew.

But glancing up again – and unaware that Sophie, having spent a good many years building ramparts against the gossips of Hong Kong, had learned how to disguise even such pain and revulsion as now possessed her – she saw her cousin's lovely dark blue eyes assessing her and the shapely lips pursed in faint calculation, and was disappointed. It annoyed her irrationally that her unwelcome guest should have chosen the most relaxed chair in the room and looked as if she were completely at home, the jacket of her riding dress unbuttoned and the pleated white habit shirt open at the neck to reveal a heavy, handsome gold chain.

It was intolerable that this exquisitely dressed and pampered beauty, who had probably never done a stroke of work in the whole of her life, who had certainly never known struggle or disappointment, misery or tragedy, should come stalking into Juran without so much as a by-your-leave and expect Rachel meekly to pack her bags and depart.

Oh, no, my fine lady!

After a moment, Rachel went on, 'This is the first time you have been to Juran. What do you think of it?'

'In what sense?'

'Its condition.'

Sophie always – or nearly always – gave honour where honour was due. 'The estate appears to be well cared for and what I have seen of the castle is in excellent repair.'

'Quite so. Ten years ago the castle was falling down and the land a wilderness. I have worked from dawn to dusk – and after – for most of those years to restore it to the state in which it is now. I have had no thanks for it other than my own satisfaction. And now, because for some reason it happens to suit your convenience, you appear out of the blue and expect me to hand it over, like the caretaker you called me, and go away, and not bother you again. I repeat, my dear cousin, that the answer is no.'

'When were you born?'

Rachel's eyes narrowed suspiciously. '1848,' she said after a moment.

'So was I. And the month?'

'June.'

'At what hour?'

'Breakfast time. Just after nine.' Suddenly, an explanation dawned on her and she smiled in scorn and disbelief. 'You cannot possibly be talking about horoscopes?'

'Of course. Chinese, though, not Western. The Chinese are much more sophisticated.

Sarcastically, Rachel said, 'You must tell me what future you foresee.'

'That's not what the lunar horoscope is about. It's about character.'

'Really!'

'And we were both born in the Year of the Monkey.'

'Then we should have a lot in common.'

Sophie shook her head, the dark and slightly ruffled hair gleaming in the firelight. 'Something, but not everything. You were born in the Hours of the Snake, whereas I was born in the Hours of the Rat.'

When you were seven months pregnant, it was hard to jump to your feet, but Rachel did her best. 'What an unpleasant assortment of wildlife,' she said disdainfully. 'But I am afraid I have little patience with superstition. Perhaps you would like to be shown to your room, now. I would advise an early start in the morning.'

Absently, Sophie said, 'Yes.'

That Rachel was a Monkey with the Snake in the ascendant meant that she was flexible and full of guile, a jealous and competitive woman who would live by only one sanction, her own. That she would not hesitate to take even an unscrupulous way out of a trap. That the possibility of defeat did not exist for her because, however well she might conceal it, she knew herself to be intellectually superior to everyone with whom she came in contact – with, perhaps, the exception of people born under the one sign that Sophie preferred not to think about.

If Sophie had known beforehand, she would have gone better prepared.

7

'Horace, my friend,' wrote Philip Roy a few days later. 'How are you? It will surprise you to have a note from me but, if you should be coming up this way in August, could you have a look in at Purdey's and pick up my new gun stock for me? It should be ready on the 20th.

'While I'm writing, I have news that will interest you. You'll never guess who turned up at Juran the other day! Someone I wager you didn't even know existed. Well, I didn't, so it stands to reason you didn't, either. It was – The Missing Heir.

'Ho, ho! as Sweeney Todd would say.

'Everyone thought that Daniel Macmillan's elder brother had died years ago in the East. Well, it seems he didn't. And he had a daughter. And the daughter came riding up to Juran last Thursday, cool as you please, to claim her inheritance.

'Rachel, as you may guess, sent her about her business, but I have the feeling that the lady may have a good case. And remembering what you told me when we had that bosky evening a year or two ago, about how you felt Rachel had let you down and wasn't worthy to be owner of Juran, I thought you'd like to know. Because the cream of it is, my friend, that I'm told The Missing Heir is the most beautiful thing ever seen in the glens. She wears a wedding ring *and* a mourning ring, and there's no mention of a husband, so we think she's *a widow*!

'There might be hope for you yet, my boy! In case you want it, I enclose the Glasgow address where she's staying. She left it with Rachel, who obligingly tore it up and threw it in the waste basket.

'Yours &c. Philip Roy.'

8

Rachel's baby was born early in September. The month nurse and the midwife, with ghoulish pleasure, had warned her that since she was small it would be a hard birth. And it was. But Rachel would have gone through the fires of hell without complaining.

It was a boy. It couldn't have been anything else.

Next day, Colin sat by her bedside in the upstairs room at Great Western Terrace and, decent, kindly man that he was, prayed for her to tell him the truth.

She said all the things proud mothers were supposed to say. Wasn't he perfect? Wasn't he beautiful? Wasn't he good? And look how he was waving his little hands in the air!

'He's a bonny wee fellow,' Colin said.

'And a clever wee fellow,' she chuckled, smoothing a finger over the dark downy hair. 'See how he keeps his eyes on me, as if he recognises me already? He even arrived the very day he was supposed to.'

But Colin, with the deepest reluctance, had spoken to the doctor. 'About two weeks overdue,' that gentleman had said, surprised. In his experience, most husbands reacted to the news that they were to become fathers by ignoring everything that happened from that day until the day when they became fathers indeed; the months between were their wives' problem. 'There's nothing to worry about,' the doctor had said reassuringly. 'First babies are often late.'

It wasn't conclusive. But after almost five childless years of marriage . . .

Colin remembered, only too well, the morning during Blake's visit last November, when he had *known* something had happened between them.

'Yes, my dear,' he said, 'but don't build too many hopes on him. Bairns are notorious for growing up to be a disappointment to their folks.'

Rachel laughed. 'What a canny old thing you are. A real banker! No, he'll never be a disappointment to me.' And then, perhaps because of some association of ideas, she chuckled again and, dropping a kiss on her son's sleepy head, cooed at him, 'And isn't cousin Sophie going to be cross!'

It was the one, unforgivable thing.

Although it was hot for Glasgow in September, Colin felt a chill touch him and, because there were some feelings too painful to hide, rose and went to look out of the window.

'And that's the truth of it, isn't it?' he said flatly.

466

'What do you mean?'

'You needed a son to get the better of this cousin of yours, and you were prepared to go to any lengths.'

Little Daniel emitted a howl of astonishing power and Rachel exclaimed, 'Poor pet, did I hug you too hard?' and began rocking and soothing him.

Colin waited and, after a while, she said again, 'What do you mean?'

He shrugged wearily. 'Rachel, Rachel! I've known your obsession too long. I persuaded myself that you married me because you loved me, and maybe you did – a bit. But you wanted children. And somehow we haven't managed to have any . . . I failed you, and so you went to Blake.'

If it hadn't been for the suspicion that had taken possession of his brain in these last long months, he would have recognised the honest shock and horror in her cry, 'No! No, Colin, *it wasn't like that!*'

'I don't think you know *what* it was like any more,' he said.

The silence was a terrible, suffocating blanket, and inside Rachel there was panic. Never, since she had told Colin about the baby, had he given her a hint that he doubted her. She couldn't understand why he should doubt, because he had made love to her twice, in his usual quiet way, in the ten days after Rainer had left. It meant that baby Daniel could be his. But the doctors said that babies were born of mutual passion, and she hadn't even understood what that meant until Rainer had taught her the ecstatic physical reality of it. They said, too, that the days immediately after the menses were the ones most likely to be fruitful, and that also matched.

In a deeply ashamed way, she wanted the baby to be Rainer's. And where Colin was concerned, she knew that it didn't really matter who the baby's father was. Letting Rainer make love to her had been what mattered. That had been the real betrayal of dear, kind Colin, whom she *did* love, though not in the way she loved Rainer Blake.

She couldn't hurt him by admitting that Rainer had even touched her. For every reason in the world, she *had* to persuade Colin that baby Daniel was his son. For his own sake, and for the baby's. For her sake, and for Rainer's. And lastly, because she couldn't bear that her son should suffer, as she had done, from the taint of bastardy.

She committed herself then, so that afterwards she couldn't go back without making everything worse. She said, 'Colin, Daniel is *your* son. Our son. Why should you doubt it?'

But it was almost as if he hadn't heard her. 'I don't think I'd have minded so much if you'd been infatuated with him. I know he's a man who attracts women, and you've never been entirely immune to him. But it wasn't that. And I'm afraid I can't forgive either of you for what you did.'

Helplessly, Rachel shook her head back and forth, back and forth. 'Colin, you're wrong. You're wrong! How can I make you see . . .'

He interrupted her in a voice that was not that of her husband but of the powerful, hardheaded businessman whose word, for many people, was law. 'That will do, Rachel. I don't want any more lies. Try and leave us both a few shreds of dignity.'

And then he swung round to face her. 'I don't understand you. You're a clever, charming woman and most of the time I couldn't have asked for a better wife. But you've this terrible blind spot. I remember we talked once, before we were married, about how much stronger your legal position would be if you had a husband and a son, like your cousin Sophie. But oh, Rachel, can ye not see the difference between abstract speculation and a squalling, red-faced, dependent wee bundle of flesh and blood. All that bairn is to you is a weapon.'

'That's not true! And don't call him "that bairn". He's *yours*, Colin. He's *ours*!'

The old, quizzical smile touched his eyes and he shook his head. 'Leave it, Rachel. I've never been much of a one for fiction.'

9

He was more generous that she deserved. 'I've thought about it, and I'll not divorce you. It would be a fine scandal for a leading banker to name one of his own fellow directors as co-respondent. I'll subscribe to the pretence that we're still married. I'll even acknowledge the bairn, because there's no reason why he should suffer, and it makes no difference to me.'

After a moment, his voice filled with bitterness, he added, 'Anyway, he'd be no good to you as a weapon, would he, if he were known to be a bastard.'

'Colin!'

'But I don't want to see either of you except if I should need you to put in a public appearance as my wife. Since Juran matters more to you than anything else in the world, you can go back to living there all the year round. It should suit you fine, and we can cobble some kind of excuse together. Your health, maybe. The smoke of Glasgow's bad for your lungs.'

She was silent.

He said, 'Have you written to Blake?'

'Of course not. There's no reason. *The baby has nothing to do with him!*'

She looked absurdly young and vulnerable, lying in bed in her plain white nightgown, the long chestnut hair loose on her shoulders and the baby sleeping quietly in her arms.

Colin kissed her on the cheek and left her.

10

Sophie, after her visit to Juran, had found herself in something of a quandary. She had expected resistance from Rachel, but not a resistance quite so absolute, and there had been a menacing confidence about her cousin that was a little worrying. Since Sophie didn't want to become entangled in legal proceedings until every other possible avenue had been explored, she resigned herself to remaining in Glasgow for some time yet.

Rainer had sent her a message before she sailed, telling her he had made arrangements for her to have unlimited credit at the Clyde River Bank, but she had no intention of taking advantage of this except as a last resort. Calculating her costs as carefully as when she had been buying Indian shirtings, she had rented a neat little villa on the south side of Glasgow and moved in with Archie, her various trunks of possessions, one children's nurse, one cook-housekeeper, and a girl of seventeen who claimed to know all about laundry work, hairdressing and lady's-maiding but departed in a huff the first time Sophie criticised her ironing.

Grimly, Sophie embarked on an intensive course of domestic self-improvement. She was perfectly well acquainted with the principles; it was just that in practice her thumbs always seemed to get in the way. All the little things Ah Foon had done, like washing stockings and pressing ribbons, took her hours.

They had been in the house for six weeks when, one day, she was surprised to hear a cab clatter to a halt outside her front door. Glasgow, she had discovered, was not a place where visitors were in the habit of arriving unannounced, and they certainly didn't do so in common cabs – or not the half dozen friends-of-friends who were the total, lawyers excluded, of Sophie's acquaintance in the city.

469

The *carte de visite* meant nothing to her, but so many acquaintances had come and gone during the Hong Kong years that, with a few exceptions, their names were no more than a blur. However, the face of the tall, thin, gangling man with the diffident manner and poor complexion who followed his *carte de visite* into her drawing room proved to be no more familiar than his name.

He smiled at her myopically and said, 'I don't suppose you know about me, but I know all about you.'

It was not the most propitious opening, but since the man was so patently harmless, Sophie merely raised a frosty eyebrow and remarked, 'I find that hard to believe. Perhaps you will tell me to what I owe the pleasure of this visit?'

He pushed his round, metal-framed spectacles back on his nose and exclaimed, 'I say, they're right. You *are* smashing looking! And your grammar's smashing, too. That's unusual, you know?'

'Is it?'

'Well, people often put an extra "do" in, or stick the preposition on the end of the sentence. It's very slovenly.'

Trying to remember what exactly she had said to merit this encomium, Sophie replied, 'Thank you, but what can I do for you?'

'Well, it's not so much that.' Sitting down uninvited, he perched on the edge of his chair, gawky elbows resting on gawky knees. His clothes looked as if they had been tailored with someone quite different in mind. 'It's more a case of an interdependent and beneficial partnership.'

'It is?'

'Actually, the proper word is symbiosis, but it's a new word and I thought you mightn't have come across it.'

In a moment, she was going to laugh. 'You must tell me more.' If, as she half suspected, he was going to try and sell her a new cooking stove or laundry wringer, his approach at least had the merit of being original.

'Yes, well. I've come to talk to you about Juran.'

And that required a moment's readjustment. 'I see. Well, before you begin, Mr Gresham, perhaps you should explain your own position in the matter.'

'Don't let's stand on ceremony. Anyway, no one calls me Mr Gresham. I'm Horace. Sophie's a pretty name.'

'Thank you, but until we establish whether our symby-whatever-it-was justifies a less formal approach I would prefer you to make do with "Mistress Macmillan".'

470

'All right.' He didn't seem to mind being put in his place. 'I'm your Uncle Daniel's nephew by marriage. My father's sister was his first wife.'

'Which makes you . . .' She had to think for a minute. '. . . a kind of half cousin to Rachel Macmillan, though not a blood relative. And no relation to me at all.'

'That's right. Now, I'd better start by telling you all about Rachel, hadn't I? Because I'm sure there's a lot you don't know.'

With extravagant cordiality, Sophie said, 'That *would* be nice.'

11

All she knew about Rachel, apart from what she preferred not to think about, was the barest outline of her career – her illegitimacy and legitimation by her mother's marriage to Daniel Macmillan, the death of her parents and stepbrother and then of her stepsister, her subsequent accession to Juran and her marriage to Colin Campbell. Except for the illegitimacy, most of it had been culled by Sophie's lawyer from newspaper files.

Horace's version left her gasping.

He was still talking at teatime, when the flow had to be interrupted because Archie always had tea with his mother. But after this hiatus, which seemed longer than it actually was – Horace having grasped the opportunity to enlighten them about Nature's grand design – it was back to Rachel again. He stayed for supper, too, his full-lipped and rather loose mouth opening and closing with a relentless regularity that made Sophie think of nothing so much as a carp at feeding time.

It was very clear that Horace had an axe to grind and that the story Sophie was hearing made no concessions to Christian charity. Indeed, she began to suspect that he was more than slightly unbalanced on the twin topics of Rachel and Juran. But his bespectacled earnestness carried conviction and she had little difficulty in identifying where facts ended and prejudice began.

'Mind you, I'm not saying she had anything to do with her parents and William being drowned, but she never said a word about being Daniel's real daughter until the day the Will was read. So that gives you some idea of what a scheming girl she was even then . . .

'She was furious when my father proved she wasn't entitled to inherit after all, and that Juran was to go to Belinda . . .

'And then Belinda and Philip Roy got engaged and two days later –

471

bang! – Belinda had her accident. My father's still convinced Rachel murdered her. Well, I mean, it was too convenient, wasn't it? Once Belinda was married, Rachel hadn't a hope of inheriting. She got off a murder charge because she was all butter-wouldn't-melt-in-her-mouth-ish at the procurator-fiscal's enquiry and there was some so-called evidence about hailstones . . .

'My father found this letter in Rachel's mother's handwriting, stating that Daniel Macmillan wasn't the girl's father, and the only evidence she could produce against it was circumstantial . . .

'Then my father found one of her mother's lovers from just about the right time, and Rachel invited my father to Juran to talk about it. I didn't trust her, so I went too. She said the most terrible things to him, literally goaded him on until he had a rupture of the heart right there before us. He could have died of it. As it is, he's been bedridden ever since. He'd always been perfectly healthy before . . .

'And the trouble is, she's so good at manipulating people. For years and years she even persuaded *me* that she was kindhearted and didn't deserve all the bad things that had happened to her. But then . . . I mean you just need to look at the way she wheedled money out of that banker fellow! My father said the estate was so laden with debt she couldn't have gone on, but this fellow Blake forked out everything she needed. In my own view there was more than money between them! Still is, probably. I wouldn't be the least bit surprised if this baby she's just had turns out to have black hair and grey eyes! After all, her mother was a whore, and "like mother like daughter" . . .'

Sophie, her nails digging so hard into her palms that they felt as if they were drawing blood, had to make a deliberate effort to interrupt. 'Would you like a glass of port or brandy, Mr Gresham?'

She and Rainer had parted. Everything was over between them. It was only injured vanity, she told herself, that aroused this violent anger and jealousy in her when she heard his name coupled with Rachel's. That he should have been at that woman's beck and call all these years!

By the time Horace had finished, any lingering doubts Sophie might have had about taking Juran away from Rachel had been laid permanently to rest. In the face of such a damning indictment, the strong element of personal animosity in her desire to destroy Rachel had been smoothly subsumed into a meritorious wish to see justice done.

Horace sniffed, a habit that was beginning to grate on her nerves. 'If only my father had known of your existence,' he told her owlishly, 'we could have settled the matter long ago! To be frank, I've been floundering, rather, and I'd almost given up. But your arrival changes the whole complexion of things.'

'Perhaps it does, but I'll be equally frank,' Sophie said with a trace of tartness. 'I can't afford to go to law. Whatever the rights or wrongs of the case, I really have no desire to spend the rest of my days waiting for a parcel of lawyers to make up their minds.'

He had been hopping up and down like a restless sparrow, but now he rose to his full, weedy height and told her in a voice resonant with significance, 'My maternal grandfather made me his heir. I have plenty of funds.'

'How nice for you.'

'I meant that I would be very happy to assist you.'

'Yes, that's what I thought you meant, but . . .'

'There would be one condition, though, and a crucial one. As I told you at tea, I'm anxious have Juran turned into a Nature Park, so I'd have to have an absolute guarantee that you wouldn't go on ruining the place the way Rachel has done. I mean, you wouldn't go crawling round the hills shooting things, would you?'

Judiciously, he surveyed the perfect face in its frame of dark hair, and the elegant figure in the indigo blue cotton dress, its bodice neatly tailored and its hips draped with panniers in Madras check. 'You don't look as if you would.'

'Well, not in this dress,' she agreed limpidly. 'Conditions, how-ever, don't enter into it. I couldn't possibly accept financial help from a gentleman who isn't even related to me.'

'Oh, all right.' Despite his many faults, Horace Gresham appeared to be a most obliging man. 'Anyway, I've got another idea. The only thing is that it's not quite ripe for being put into execution. Perhaps it would be better if you didn't know about it just yet.'

'Very well,' she said abstractedly. She was beginning to find him rather tiring; Rachel could have told her that prolonged doses of undiluted Horace always had that effect on people.

Horace was put out, because he would have expected the decorative Mistress Sophie to try and tease him into telling her what his idea was – not that he would have done so, of course, though it was simple enough. If he married her, which he had no objection to doing since she was by far the prettiest girl he had ever seen, it would relieve her of all scruple about making use of his money. Then they could take Rachel to court and win.

Horace being Horace, it didn't occur to him to ask whether she already had a husband. Philip Roy's belief that she was a widow was good enough for him.

'I think, perhaps,' Sophie said, 'that we have discussed as much as we usefully can at this stage . . .'

He shook his head vigorously. 'Not quite. Because there is one thing you, and only you, can do, and – you'll understand why in a moment – it's something that has to be done soon.'

CHAPTER TWENTY-THREE

I

Only once in her life before had Rachel felt so deeply depressed – when Juran had been taken away from her and given to Belinda. She had been resentful then, as she was now, because in the six weeks since baby Daniel had been born she had come to think it more and more unjust that Colin should reject her so obdurately on the basis of unfounded suspicion.

'Not unfounded suspicion,' he had replied when she said so. 'Deductions from a number of indicators. It's what a banker's training and experience are all about.'

On her last day at Great Western Terrace, supervising the packing of what she intended to take into banishment with her, she told herself it was stupid to feel so low. She had, after all, been alone for most of her life in one sense or another, though the last five, almost six, years of marriage had weakened her. And she had baby Daniel now. She would feel better, she told herself, when she got to Juran. Everything would be in its full autumn livery of purple and amber, flame and gold; there would be snow on the hilltops and crispness in the air. There would be majestic, thrilling sunsets, and the gales would blow and the sea roar, and she would draw the curtains and sit by the fire and think about what she should do.

There was a knock on the door and one of the maids stood there with a salver in her hand. 'Please, ma'am, there's a telegraph message for you. The boy's waiting in case there's an answer.'

The telegraph was from Tom Tanner.

It said, 'Mistress Sophie Macmillan has moved into castle. Refuses to leave. What instructions.'

Furiously, Rachel telegraphed back. 'Call the police and tell them to throw the woman out.'

But when she stormed back to Juran in person late the following day, it was to find that the police were not prepared to cooperate.

There had been no question of Sophie breaking and entering, of course. And when the word 'trespass' was mentioned, the lawyer who had accompanied her pointed out that trespass meant 'without permission of the owner'. Blandly, he had produced documentation to prove that Mistress Sophie *was* the owner. Or near enough, in the view of Sergeant Cameron, who remembered, as a wee laddie, forming one of the juvenile delegation that had waved Archie Macmillan off on his travels to the other side of the world.

'My, we fair envied him,' he told Sophie, and Sophie immediately endeared herself to him by asking to have every single detail of that exciting day recounted to her.

Rachel arrived just as the officers were leaving. 'Is that woman still here? I insist that you remove her, by force if necessary! I will not have her in my house.'

The sergeant had been hoping to get away before Mistress Rachel arrived, but he said stoutly, 'Och, now, mistress, I canny do that. It's a family dispute, and we canny go round arresting folk just because they're no' able to see eye to eye. Mistress Sophie here isny breaking any law I can think of. Ye'll just have to sort it out between yourselves. Anyway, we'll be off now, and good day to you.'

Sophie was standing in the Great Hall with a smile on her face.

'Out!' said Rachel.

'No,' said Sophie.

Impasse.

<h1 style="text-align:center">3</h1>

In the weeks that followed, Rachel tried everything.

When Sophie stepped outside for a breath of air, Rachel had all the doors and windows locked against her. But Sophie merely waited until one of the servants emerged and then strolled peaceably in again.

She refused to allow Sophie to sit down at table with her. Sophie therefore took possession of the morning room and had delightful private picnics and rollicking games with Archie. The little boy's laughter seemed, to Rachel, to echo from every stone in the castle.

She instructed the servants to do nothing – *nothing* – for her cousin Sophie, whom she refused to address either as Mistress Macmillan or, which was even less acceptable to her, Mrs Blake. But that proved a failure, too, because Sophie had a way with her no less compelling than Rachel and was soon reducing the kitchen to chaos by personally preparing heathen Chinese dishes that left every pan in the castle in need of washing.

Rachel forbade the servants to speak anything other than Gaelic to cousin Sophie, but that didn't work either, because cousin Sophie merely laughed and replied in a strange tongue that sounded like baby talk with an 'ee' tacked on the end of every other word.

Sophie, in fact, was rather enjoying herself and so was Archie, who thought it all uproariously good fun. Never in his short life had he had so much of his mother's undivided attention.

Rachel, feeling as if everything was slipping away from her, couldn't see it for the farce it was. All she knew was that she couldn't defeat any legal challenge to her ownership of Juran until such a challenge was made. And Sophie gave not the slightest sign of doing anything about it, but spent her time giving Archie his lessons, revelling in the scenery, and flirting with the recently widowed Philip Roy who, like most of the neighbourhood, had been in almost indecent haste to pay a courtesy call on Juran to inspect Archie Macmillan's ravishing daughter.

Some of the visitors were people Rachel hadn't seen for a dozen years, and she felt quite sick at the way they all instantly accepted Sophie as one of them.

4

For months after the police raid and the Clyde River Bank's subsequent foreclosure on Macmillan and Venturi, Rainer Blake remained pinned to his desk in the office on Pedder Street, to all appearances the banker he had always been but engaged, for much of the time, on a tidying-up operation of considerable complexity.

Even as he studied, analysed and evaluated, however, he found his thoughts straying painfully towards Scotland, wondering what Sophie and Rachel were getting up to in their contest over the ownership of Juran, and how young Archie was liking the land of his ancestors. Sophie had very little money of her own, but had drawn nothing from the funds Blake had arranged for her. She had been a spoilt, wilful and undisciplined child, and there were times when he thought she hadn't changed at all.

About Rachel, he tried not to think. He could scarcely count the number of times in his life when the bored wives of neglectful husbands had thrown themselves at his head – which was a damned queer turn of phrase, when you came to think about it. He had never noticed that it was his head they were interested in. But it hadn't been like that with Rachel.

Rarely, before, had his conscience troubled him. Never, before, had he betrayed a husband he admired and respected. Always, he had prided himself on his control over the emotions that caused other people to make such shambles of their lives, but he discovered now what a hollow pride it had been. He discovered, too, that it was harder than he would have anticipated to lay the sombre truths out before him and look at them without evasion and without sophistry.

God Almighty! What a hash he had made of things.

5

When he went back to his analysing, he found no solace there.

For ten years he had been suspicious of Gino Venturi, but had never had the evidence he needed. Now, he had – and more, because there were some things he had not known. From a jigsaw of inoffensive-looking clues, he found himself building up a secondary picture that made dangerously unpleasant sense.

He had always thought that he himself had been the target of Venturi's sporadic attempts at mayhem, but it seemed now that he had not been the only one.

After Archie Macmillan's death, Venturi had set his mind to acquiring, first by fair means and then by foul, the two-thirds share in the business that had gone to Sophie. He had been ready enough to bide his time, trying first merely to discourage her interest in the firm, hoping that she would sell out to him. He hadn't dared – probably couldn't afford – to make her an offer when trade was flourishing, so he had waited for a period of recession when the value of her share would be at rock bottom.

And then Sophie had frustrated him by rushing into marriage with Richard Taverner. Blake, staring abstractedly out of the window,

478

found himself wondering whether Venturi might have had a direct hand in that young man's subsequent downhill progress. Certainly, it had been Venturi, in alliance with the Chang brothers, who had assisted the lieutenant in departing a life that would soon have become as much of a burden to him as it had already become to his wife. For that, at least, Blake was grateful. If Venturi hadn't done it, he would have had to do it himself.

Sophie having been widowed, Venturi's options had been to marry her himself – or murder her, intending to buy her share from her heirs in distant Scotland, who wouldn't know the value.

Hence the attack on the junk at Lantau. Even at the time, Blake had been surprised by the scale of it and the organisation. It had been in a different league from the slash-and-run tactics he was accustomed to. But all he had done at the time was curse himself for being such a fool as to hire the junk from Venturi and thus give him ample warning of where he himself, Blake, was to be found.

And much more recently, there had been the fire at East Point. Venturi must have assumed that Blake would be at home. And by that time, of course, disposing of Sophie wasn't enough; disposing of Sophie and Blake wasn't enough. There was young Archie, too; their heir.

Towards Venturi, Blake felt a fierce, cold anger. It was as well that he couldn't get his hands on the man, but he was going to take the greatest pleasure in seeing him get his comeuppance.

It disturbed him very much, therefore, when Venturi escaped from custody, and from Hong Kong.

6

There had been a blizzard overnight, as there occasionally was in late November, although the snow never lasted. January and February were the bad months in the Highlands.

The sky had cleared magically afterwards, and the whole landscape lay under a veil of purest white, touched in the corries and crevasses with purple and violet and crowned with faintest gold from the sun tracking low over the hills. The trees wore swansdown muffs, and the intricate mahogany lace of the birches sparkled where the snow had begun to melt before freezing again into faceted diamonds. Crystals of ice lay like fur on the grass.

'Will ye stop bouncing around and sit down, lassie!' Hogg said.

'The bairn'll get seasick if ye're not careful. There's a nice comfy rock here out of the wind.'

'I don't want to sit down.'

'Suit yerself.' He put the pipe back in his mouth. It wasn't a clay one these days but a good briar that had belonged to Rachel's father.

She said, 'I'm sorry. I'm a bit restless.'

'Aye, so I'm hearing.'

She snapped, as she always did when she knew she was being gossiped about. 'And what does that mean?'

'It means ye're upsetting every last soul on the estate by ordering them about like the Great Cham instead of talking to them like human beings. You shouldn't let Sophie get under your skin.'

'*Sophie*, is it?'

'Well, two Mistress Macmillans about the place are a wee thing confusing,' he pointed out reasonably.

'Hm! It wouldn't be so bad if she didn't behave as if it was all going to go on like this for ever!'

He shrugged his thin shoulders. 'It could.'

She swung round. 'What do you mean?'

'It's a big place. You could share it, easy enough.'

The circles under her eyes were almost as blue as the eyes themselves. 'And whose idea was that? Have you been discussing it with her?'

'Och, she doesn't confide in me. I doubt she even notices my existence.'

Rachel sat down with Daniel in her arms. He was so well wrapped up that he was almost invisible so she pulled the shawl down a fraction in case he was smothering; then she saw that his little nose was blue with cold and pulled it up again. An irritable howl rewarded her.

She said, 'She could hardly avoid noticing you!'

Hogg's appearance never changed. Rachel knew that his ancient black coat and checked breeks, collarless shirt and mouldy chimney hat couldn't possibly be the same ones she remembered from twenty years before, even though they looked the same. She had wondered, sometimes, if he spent all his spare time scouring old clothes shops for replicas.

'Never you mind the state of my wardrobe,' he said, giving her his yellow, gaptoothed grin. 'It does me fine. And I've no bother deciding what to put on when I get up in the morning. No, the sharing was my notion.'

The pipe, apparently of its own volition, made a squeaking, gurgling noise and Hogg stared into the bowl as if expecting something nasty to pop out and bite him.

After a moment, he went on, 'But ye know, ye haven't put your finger on the real problem yet.'

'Have I not! You're wrong there, my friend.'

'No,' he persisted. 'The problem is Sophie's got nothing to lose. And you've everything to lose.'

It was truer than he knew.

A drop of rain splashed on her hand, and then another, and another. But it wasn't rain, it was tears.

It was the first time she had broken down and she needed comforting so badly that she was grateful even for Hogg's arm round her shoulders, despite the smells of unwashed human and shag tobacco that accompanied it.

'I've lost Colin already,' she sobbed.

And then it all came out, not in indelicate words and certainly not coherently, but although the gist was that Rachel had fallen innocent victim to her husband's false suspicions, there was enough obliqueness in her tale of woe for Hogg, possessor of an oblique mind, to guess at what she wasn't saying.

'There, there, lassie!' he said. 'There, there!'

And a right fankle it was, too, he thought. Colin Campbell had always struck him as a tolerant, civilised man who wouldn't leap to conclusions without good reason, but even had it been otherwise Rachel's self-pitying denials would have struck Hogg as less than a hundred per cent convincing.

He couldn't think what had got into her, letting a fine man like Mr Campbell down for an arrogant-looking foreign bastard like Blake.

'So whose bairn is it?' he asked eventually, and Rachel, abandoning all pretence, all hope, all self-delusion, wailed, '*I don't know!*'

Hogg wasn't an expert. 'Can ye not tell from what he looks like?'

Sniffling, Rachel withdrew the shawl fully from the baby's face. It was the first time Hogg had seen the child properly. Halo of brown hair, red face, button of a nose, squeezed-up eyes.

Disappointed, he admitted, 'Aye, well, that's not much help.'

'*Nothing's* any help.'

It was clear to Hogg that Rachel wasn't doing any thinking. Most of her common sense seemed to have deserted her and she wasn't herself at all.

'We'll have to put our minds to it,' he said. 'In the meanwhile, though, ye'd maybe get on better if ye tried behaving a wee bit more sociably with your cousin instead of living in a state of open war.'

7

Encountering Sophie on the stairs later in the day, Rachel said with elaborate carelessness, 'Supper will be at seven this evening, if you feel you might care to join me?'

'Thank you, I'd like that.' It was one of the most infuriating things about Sophie that her courtesy couldn't be faulted.

They talked politely, like strangers meeting for the first time. Rachel was curious about the kind of life Rainer and Sophie had lived in Hong Kong, more curious still to know why her husband had not accompanied Sophie to Scotland. She couldn't bear to think that he had meant what he said when they parted, about never seeing her again. Surely, *surely*, what had been between them was too strong.

But for all the information she elicited from Sophie, she might as well have directed her probing and artificially innocent questions – sounding just like Aunt Minerva, long ago – at a stone wall. She was not, of course, aware that Sophie had been asked probing questions by inquisitors far more experienced than she; that she came, in fact, a very poor second to Euphemia Moore.

Sophie had no intention of telling Rachel the story of her life, but she didn't mind talking in a general way about Hong Kong and the unexpected resemblances she had found at Juran – the way the mist sat in the hollows of the mountains, just like a Sung painting; how she had at first mistaken Juran's buzzards for kites; the way the rain came down as if it would never stop.

'Do you speak Chinese?' Rachel asked.

Sophie smiled. 'Not allowed. The Chinese are forbidden to teach it to us barbarians.'

'But how do you manage?'

'In pidgin. The vocabulary consists of a few hundred English words with a sprinkling of Hindustani, and the grammar's Chinese. It's quite easy once you get the knack of it. You've heard me use it.'

'Is that what it was? I thought it was – er – Hong-Kongese.'

'Cantonese. It has the same staccato sound, that's all. It's very direct, too. Where a servant here says, "Iss it your supper you would be haffing?" in Hong Kong it would be, "You want eat?" It saves a lot of time.'

'I imagine it does.'

Sophie might be prepared to talk about Hong Kong, but Rachel didn't reciprocate by talking about Juran. Indeed, Sophie soon found that saying something approving about Juran was the quickest way to raise Rachel's hackles, as if she hated the idea of Sophie liking the place.

And Sophie, in fact, loved it, everything from the endlessly changing light as the clouds raced across the sky to the delicate little plants lurking in the undergrowth on the hills, plants that would not have survived for a day amid the tough-minded flora of Hong Kong. There wasn't much about Hong Kong that was either delicate or subtle. Even the Highland cold was something that both Sophie and Archie adjusted themselves to quite quickly and it had been wonderful to wake up that morning to snow, which neither of them had ever seen before, and to find the world transformed into a magical landscape of white mountains shaded with indigo, of trees sparkling with frost, and burns transformed into forests of gleaming, tumbling icicles.

Disparagingly, Rachel said that snow was always tiresome but that, at this time of the year, it would soon melt into a disagreeable yellow-brown slush. When one had an estate to run, the practical disadvantages of snow were more important than its beauty.

'I am sure you're right,' Sophie said amicably. 'Tell me, what do you think about this proposal to build a tunnel under the English Channel to France?'

8

By the time a few more days had passed – yellow-brown slush and all – Rachel had begun to admit, to herself if no one else, that Hogg was right and that she was going to have to curb her emotions and give serious thought to resolving a situation that was at best undignified, at worst intolerable. Sophie's had been the first act of aggression, when she had moved in, but after that it had been Rachel who had instituted all the warlike moves. Fuming, she knew that Sophie was making it look as if she, Rachel, was in the wrong. Fuming even more, she racked her brains as to what Sophie hoped to achieve by her polite campaign of persecution.

It was something Sophie herself didn't know, but she was perfectly

483

content to wait and see what happened – until the subject of Christmas cropped up.

'No,' Rachel said curtly, 'my husband will not be joining us for Christmas. It is not a public holiday in Scotland.'

Sophie wasn't going to have Archie deprived of his Christmas treat. 'Oh? Then I will arrange a little party for the children on the estate.'

All the colour drained from Rachel's face and an expression came into her eyes that made Sophie wonder suddenly whether some of Horace's accusations might, after all, be less farfetched than she had thought.

'No.' The negative was unequivocal.

Sophie felt her own temper rising. It was the first time it had happened since she arrived, because she had been exercising the most rigorous self-control. Pride, after all, required it in the presence of this woman who had been her husband's mistress.

But this was for Archie. 'You are being very small-minded,' she said.

It was after supper, and they were sitting in the no-man's-land of the Great Hall, Sophie with her stitchery, Rachel pretending to concentrate on the day before yesterday's *Glasgow Herald*.

'I repeat, no,' Rachel replied. 'Juran is mine and its people are *my* people. There will be no such party unless I give one. And I do not intend to.'

Sophie, making a sound of impatience, jabbed her needle into the canvas and tossed the whole thing to the floor. 'So, we are at that again, are we?' she said. 'You appear to think that if you say "Juran is mine" often enough, it will be so. Well, I am sorry to hear that Mr Campbell will not be joining us, because there is a question I had been saving until he arrived. However, perhaps we should have it out now.

'Juran, you say, is yours and you have spent a good deal of time and money during these last ten years on restoring it. Perhaps you would care to tell me where the money came from?'

'It's none of your business.' Rachel snapped it out automatically but then, unable to see any good reason why she shouldn't reply, went on, 'As it happens, before Mr Campbell and I were married, he rented Juran from me as a place to bring sporting parties to. He paid me a ten years' rental in advance.'

'Quite,' Sophie said. 'Though, as I understand it, the original arrangement was made through the good offices of my husband.'

With housewifely care, Rachel began to fold up her newspaper. 'Yes.'

'Mr Blake arranged it, and Mr Campbell received the benefit of it. But where do you think the money actually came from?'

Rachel's hands were still. 'From my husband, Mr Campbell.'

Crisply, Sophie said, 'No. It was I, through my late father's business, who footed the bill. Plus interest. You see the implications? Both Mr Blake and Mr Campbell, by acknowledging that the responsibility for the repairs was mine, acknowledged that Juran was mine.'

Rachel's brain froze. Her, 'I don't believe you,' was entirely instinctive.

'I thought you might not. That was why I was hoping Mr Campbell would be here to confirm it.'

Rachel rose to her feet with a laugh that, even to herself, sounded artificial. 'My dear cousin, neither of our husbands is a lawyer. They were wrong. But it gives me very great pleasure to know that it is *your* money I have been spending for the last ten years!'

She stalked out of the room.

9

Hours later, she was still sitting by the dying fire in her bedchamber, recognising with a terrible bitterness that the man who had said he loved her, and the other man whom she had loved for almost fourteen thankless years, had both deceived her. Until now, she had thought that Rainer Blake hadn't known anything of Archie Macmillan's claim to Juran until he married Sophie; which had allowed her to believe that he had arranged the rental advance in good faith and entirely for her, Rachel's, sake. But now, it seemed, he *had* known, and so must Colin. And neither of them had said a word to her all these years.

Both of them had betrayed her, manipulated her, used her.

She didn't know if she could bear it.

10

By the time Juran's cold-hearted Christmas Day was over, she had made up her mind. She would go to Colin. Throughout the years of their marriage, he had kept secret from her the one thing that would radically have affected all her calculations, and she knew him well enough to know that he must have been embarrassed by it. She would use it as moral blackmail if she had to.

Unfortunately, she would have to go in person and hope that the thaw lasted until she got back, otherwise the track that did duty as Juran's road would be impassable. It would have been sensible to wait until winter's end but the very thought of waiting two or three months was anathema. On the day after Boxing Day, therefore, she set off after giving a long list of instructions to Daniel's nurse and telling Sophie with savage amiability that she could consider herself in charge of Juran for the next two or three days.

I I

Rachel and Colin had always spent the weekend after Christmas with his widowed sister in Edinburgh and she thought it unlikely that he would have changed his habits, so she went there directly, rather than to Glasgow, arriving late and finding lodgings for the night in the same house in George Street where once, it seemed a long time ago, she had stayed when she visited Edinburgh to consult David Napier. She wondered vaguely how he was these days.

After morning service in St Andrew's Church, followed by tea, bread and cold beef at the lodging house, she walked in the pleasant if precarious sunshine to George Square. Colin's sister Jane always had 'a wee snooze' after Sunday dinner and Rachel knew she would catch Colin alone.

His face was expressionless and his welcome less than warm. 'I've no time,' he said. 'I'm wanted at Balmoral.'

'But Her Majesty can't be there at this time of year?'

'No, but she's got a bee in her bonnet about some winter photographs and John Brown says the snow's lying. She's determined it's me who should take them, the good Lord knows why. I've got my equipment, but I need to get to Dundee tonight and borrow some plates from Jamie Valentine. Then I can go straight on in the morning.'

'But I want to talk to you.'

'Talk away, if you must. Just don't expect me to pay attention.'

She talked while he sorted out what he wanted to take, and packed up all his equipment, and made notes of this, that and the other. She talked while the sky clouded over and the rain began. She went with him in the cab to the ferry, still talking, and crossed the river Forth with him.

486

It was pouring by then.

'This is daft,' he said when she ran out of breath at last, having repeated every single word that had been exchanged between herself and Sophie since the day of their first meeting in June. 'There's no use coming any further with me. I don't know how to help you, and, even if I did, I'm not sure that I would. I've said it before, many a time, and I'll say it again. Your passion for Juran is unhealthy and destructive, and I don't like it. Anyway, I'm a banker, not a lawyer. How's the wee boy?'

'You're not listening to what I'm saying! All you're doing is thinking about exposures and apertures and wet collodion plates. If you'd only give your mind to it, I know you'd think of something. You're too clever not to.'

He shook his head.

'Oh, Colin, *please!*'

But his resistance was total.

Hurt or not, she wasn't going to give in. She still hadn't used the rental weapon, so when the Dundee mail train arrived with its four smart claret-coloured passenger coaches and the fifth one of varnished teak, she bought a first class ticket and got into one of the compartments in the second coach with her husband. Since it was the Sunday after Christmas, the train wasn't very full, so they had the compartment to themselves.

The rain was already drumming against the windows, and by the time the train had got up speed it had turned to barley sugar streaming down the panes. The wind was high, the engine labouring hard and noisily against it. Cold, damp draughts whipped in round the doors and the edges of the glass. Rachel was used to bad weather at Juran but there, at least, one could shut it out. Here there was nothing but a single small oil lamp to act as the frailest of barriers against the storm and the dark. The sense of bleakness was overpowering.

She broached the subject of the rental at last. 'And I'd never have accepted the money if I'd known.'

'Aye, well, that's why no one told you. But in view of the mortgage . . .'

'The what?'

'Did you not know? Blake gave Archie Macmillan a mortgage on Juran. That's why you were privileged to have Blake visit you. Inspecting the collateral.' The bite in Colin's voice was detectible even through the noise of the engine and the wind and the rain. 'And the mortgage having been given, the collateral had to be kept in repair.'

Rachel felt dizzy for a moment. Because what Colin was saying was that, never once in all the years – not for a day, an hour, a minute – had she truly been mistress of Juran, or of her own destiny. She had been only a puppet.

She scarcely heard his next words. 'I'll grant you, Blake was in an awkward position with Archie Macmillan determined that no one at Juran should know he was still alive, but I thought the whole thing misjudged and I said so. It put me in an awkward position and I still don't know why I let myself become involved.' He stopped and gave a mirthless laugh. 'Yes, I do. I did it out of friendship for Blake.'

Rachel knew that her chin was quivering, and clamped her lips between her teeth to control it. The oil lamp was smoking and she made a vague gesture with her hand as if it was the smoke that had brought the moisture stinging to her eyes.

'Whether you wanted to be involved or not,' she said at last, 'you took very great care to keep me – me, who you said you loved – completely in the dark.'

Colin sighed, his fingers plucking at the needle sharp end of a horsehair curl that had pushed its way out through the moquette upholstery. 'By the time we were married it was too late for knowing about it to do you any good. And you must have learned enough about banking confidentiality to recognise that I couldn't have told you anyway. There's no use looking at me like that. I can – not – help – you.

'We'll be at Leuchars soon, and I suggest you get off the train there. I don't want you coming all the way to Dundee with me, because you'll have to stay the night. And, frankly, I've had enough.'

'No,' she said. 'There's another station before we cross the Tay, isn't there? I can get off there and find a room for the night.'

He sighed.

Back and forth, back and forth went the argument. Colin thought he had never known anyone as single-minded as Rachel could be about Juran.

She was having to shout now, because of the noise of the elements, but it didn't stop her. 'I still,' she told him for the tenth time, 'can't get over you knowing all along.' And then she said something she hadn't said before. 'It makes me ill even to think of you not telling me. It was such a betrayal of our marriage . . .'

He had been staring out of the window, but at that his head came round. She had never seen such an expression on his face before, not even when he had told her he knew about the baby. There was hurt in it, and revulsion, and above all contempt.

'You to talk of betrayal!' he said, and she could hear his rigidly controlled voice with perfect clarity under the raging of the storm. 'You who gave yourself to Blake with the sole intent of getting a son you could use as a weapon against his own wife! You make me sick, the pair of you. It's Mrs Blake I'm sorry for – but maybe I wouldn't be if I knew her. I find the human race increasingly unattractive.'

Rachel wailed, 'Oh, Colin, why won't you believe . . .'

'Here's St Fort, my dear. This is where you get out.'

He dropped the window and leaned out to open the door; then, so strongly ingrained was the habit of courtesy, stepped out onto the platform to help her down.

She had no choice any more, so she said, 'Yes, this is my station. Goodbye, Colin. Look after yourself.'

12

She walked slowly along the platform, only coming to a dazed stop as the train moved out and the rest of the passenger coaches and the brake van slid past her. She didn't look at the train because she didn't want to see Colin turn his face away from her.

She was soaked already and having to brace herself against the wild fury of the wind, but she did it automatically, staggering under the gusts, aware – because twenty-three years at Juran had taught her always to be aware of where the weather was coming from – that the gale was a north-easterly roaring in to funnel itself into the firth of the Tay.

Half blinded by rain and wind and sudden tears, she watched the rear lights of the train vanish into the darkness and, with them, the husband who had been her best friend in the world, good and loving until she had done what he could not forgive. She should have known better than to mistake his tolerance for weakness.

Emotionally exhausted and bitterly despairing, she looked back on the kindly years, marred only by her own obsessive need to have a child. Was it too late to put things right? If she gave up Juran, rejected all that she had fought for so stubbornly all her life, would Colin have her back? At this moment there was nothing in the world she wanted more.

It was so dark that, once the rear lights of the train disappeared on to the bridge over the estuary, she could scarcely tell whether her eyes were open or closed and had to make a conscious effort to flex the lids. Three times she did it and each time it was as if the rear lights still flashed on her retina.

She bestirred herself at last and plodded tiredly towards the ticket office where the ticket collector, ready to lock up, was surprised to see her. He didn't think anyone had got off and, glancing at the clock, which stood at ten past seven, shook his head in disbelief at the silly woman who had been standing out there on the platform for ten torrential, gale force minutes.

There were no more trains that night, he said. She could maybe find a bed at the farm. It was just a wee bit down the road.

It took her twenty minutes to get there, but half an hour later she was warm and dry in a borrowed nightgown and tucked up in bed with some good, sustaining broth. In the end, she fell into the sleep of total exhaustion.

So it wasn't until well into the following morning that she heard that the Tay Bridge had collapsed a few minutes after seven the night before.

The Dundee mail train, with more than seventy people aboard, had just entered the two-mile span and had plunged straight into the raging waters. No one had known anything about the disaster until the train became seriously overdue at Dundee, although there was a rumour that the firebox had sent up three great flashes as it went.

And no, there were no survivors.

13

Not for thirty hours did Rachel learn that Colin was still alive.

No one had known where to find her except the ticket collector – who didn't, in any case, know who she was – and he was too busy with the chaos and the searching, the enquiries and the newspaper men, even to give her a thought.

It meant that she had lived a lifetime of guilt, heartbreak, soul-searching and self-loathing, before she arrived again at Colin's sister's house in Edinburgh and learned that he was safe.

He had continued to stand on the platform as his wife walked away from him, eyes and mind concentrated on the small, lonely figure faintly visible in the weak illumination from the compartments. The train had begun moving before he realised it, and the gale had slammed the compartment door closed; the handle had been so wet that he couldn't get a grip on it to open it again.

So he had waited until Rachel disappeared before he, in turn, went to the ticket office and asked the collector to signal ahead to the station at Dundee that he'd left his cameras and luggage aboard the train, and would be across first thing in the morning to pick them up. He'd spent the troubled night in the waiting room and on the shore.

'He's gone back to Glasgow now,' Jane Campbell said. 'He's got work to do. And you needn't look to me for sympathy. I don't know what's the matter between you, but it must be gey bad.

'I said to him, shouldn't he let you know he was all right, but he didn't seem to think the question of whether he lived or died was especially high on your list of priorities.'

TWENTY-FOUR

❧❧

I

Rachel arrived back at Juran on the afternoon of New Year's Eve, suffering from the worst cold she had ever had.

To Sophie, however, it was immediately apparent that a cold wasn't all that ailed her. Wherever she had been, whatever she had been doing, it had not worked out. Her face was peaked, her eyes empty, her manner withdrawn. She didn't even snap when Sophie said, 'Shouldn't you go to bed?'

'Dho, I can't. It's Hogbhanay – I bean Hogmanay – and we always have a first-footingh party at bidnight. It'll go on till three or four. I have to see that cook's bade the shortbread and the black bun and got everythingh ready for the Atholl Brose and . . .'

'It's all done,' Sophie said.

'Oh. Is it?'

It was a dangerous moment. But then the door opened and Rachel exclaimed, in tones of loathing, 'Oh, God! *Horace!* What are you doingh here?'

2

Horace, offended, said he'd just arrived to see the New Year in, although the truth was that he'd wanted an excuse to come and see how Sophie was getting on and make sure she wasn't weakening. It was pleasing to discover that, after a few months of Highland air, she was looking more beautiful than ever. There were a good many things he still had to find out about her, but the more he saw of her the surer he was that she'd make a fine wife for him.

Rachel was just saying, 'I hope you're not thinkingh of stayingh bore than a day or two,' when the doorbell clanged.

It was another unexpected visitor. A tall, bland, fair, rumpled gentleman who was asking for Mistress Sophie.

'Good heavens!' Sophie exclaimed with genuine pleasure. 'Gino Venturi! How nice. When did they let you out?'

3

For a brief moment, Gino wished he hadn't come when his hostess reeled off to him the barbaric list of what they were having for supper – cock-à-leekie, haggis and neep purry, roastit bubblyjock, and trifle. 'Traditional New Year's Eve fare,' she told him, repressing a sneeze, and retired to her room for an hour's rest.

As things turned out, it was one of the most enjoyable evenings any of them – with the exception of Horace – had spent for many a long month.

Rachel listened enthralled as the engaging Mr Venturi revealed, over the chicken and leek soup, that he had not been precisely 'let out' of jail in Hong Kong, but, overcome by a claustrophobia to which he claimed always to have been subject, had taken independent steps to release himself.

He had subsequently had rather a trying journey to Milan, where he had spent a few weeks recovering from his ordeal at the family home – the prodigal son fêted, in the absence of fatted calves, on a *chiocciole al mascherpone e noce* so exquisite that it was beyond words to describe.

'What's that?' Horace asked.

'Pasta shells in a sauce of cream cheese and walnuts.'

'Oh.' Unimpressed, Horace helped himself to a plateful of oatmeal sausage and puréed turnips.

'Now, however,' Mr Venturi went on, 'I feel it is time to begin taking more positive steps towards the future. In which matter I have encountered a small obstacle in the form of a shortage of funds.'

'Well, it's entirely your own fault,' Sophie told him severely. 'I was never more shocked than when I heard what you had been up to.' The curious thing was that, despite the fact that she now knew him for a charlatan, she had caught herself, several times over the last few months, hoping that he wasn't having too bad a time in prison.

'My dear Sophie, it was only a few minor misdemeanours!'

'Yes, I know, but . . .'

Over the roast turkey, Rachel and Horace learned that the minor misdemeanours amounted to no more than smuggling, slave trading, currency swindles, kidnapping and piracy.

'Coo-er!' muttered little Ellie Vallette, awed.

As it happened, Rachel was also fascinated by the discovery that Sophie had not, after all, spent her entire life being pampered and indulged, but had dirtied her slender, elegant hands in the murky waters of commerce. Which appeared, in Hong Kong, to be very murky indeed.

'If only you'd been more careful,' Sophie complained, 'we'd never have found ourselves in such a pickle. I really don't know why you should come looking for sympathy to me, of all people.'

'Well, it wasn't sympathy I had in mind,' said Mr Venturi, raising his spoon to attack the sherry-soaked sponge and custard pudding. 'But perhaps,' he went on smoothly, 'we can talk about that some other time?' He looked enquiringly at Rachel.

'By all beans!' Rachel said lavishly. 'Stay as longh as you like. Any friend of by cousin's . . .'

4

Although Gino was by no means sure who the pallid, bespectacled Horace was, he seemed very much at home. It was with pleasurable anticipation, therefore, that Gino fell in with Rachel's suggestion that the gentlemen might like to retire to the billiard room after supper, where Mr Venturi could smoke if he wished.

Horace was as anxious for information as Gino, otherwise he wouldn't have contaminated himself by even entering the billiard room, which he disapproved of every bit as much as he disapproved of smoking.

He didn't have anything against billiards, provided there was no betting involved, but the room itself was the ultimate proof that all his strictures to Rachel about interfering with Nature's grand design had gone unheeded. Not only did it contain two stuffed eagles in glass cases; the walls were positively smothered in stags' heads, forty-eight in all, most of them 'royals' or twelve pointers but including a few fourteens and sixteens. Under each was a brass label stating by whom it had been shot, and when.

Gino, glancing along, noted several distinguished names, among them Chamberlain, Delane, Browning, Rothschild, Prince Something-von-Something-und-Something, and an assortment of French and English dukes and earls.

Being a sportsmen's wet weather refuge, the room contained in addition to stags' heads and billiard table a piano, chairs of various shapes and sizes – all snoozable in – and a brace of bookcases accommodating a wide range of reference works; a bound set of parliamentary papers relating to financial legislation; an incomplete set of the Waverley novels; and a run of Bohn's Standard Library, none of whose volumes appeared to be in immediate danger of falling apart from over-use. Which, in Gino's view, wasn't surprising, since most of them had titles like *The Miscellaneous Works and Remains of the Rev. Robert Hall, Schlegel's Lectures on Dramatic Literature,* and *Taylor's Holy Living and Dying.*

Lighting a cheroot, he turned to the gentleman in the badly fitting dinner suit and said amiably, 'What a delightful place this is. I know nothing of the Highlands, or indeed of the Macmillans . . .'

It was all that was needed. Horace was the proverbial fount of all Macmillan lore, and by the time the two of them were summoned to take part in the midnight festivities, there was very little that Gino didn't know. He had come to Juran for a purpose entirely to do with Sophie, but Horace's revelations about Rachel opened up such a promising new field that it left him very thoughtful indeed. He needed time, he decided, to consider.

5

Early on the morning of January the second, Rainer Blake reached Glasgow on an unheralded visit from Hong Kong, and booked himself in at the North British Hotel. Then, bathed and breakfasted, he strolled across the road to the bank's offices, his conscience under iron discipline.

He had heard nothing of Sophie and Archie for nine long months, except for a card picturing the ladder streets of Malta, the address in Sophie's hand, the message, brief and laborious, in his son's. He had never really believed that Sophie would have the tenacity or the independence to carry out her plan, but he had been wrong. Where they were, how they were, he had no idea.

He hoped Colin might know something.

Colin did.

There wasn't a trace of the familiar humour in his eyes, and his voice was as friendly as cold steel when he cut off Blake's preliminary civilities. 'If you have business, get on with it.'

Blake, eyes narrowed, shook his head.

'Then, if it's other things you have on your mind, I can tell you that my wife and yours are both at Juran. With your sons. I'm sure they'll all be blithe to see you. It's more than I am.'

The world rocked slightly under Blake's feet.

'Christ!' he said, and sat down abruptly.

6

While two days in bed had done a good deal to ease Rachel's cold, two days' uninterrupted meditation on her problems had done nothing to lighten her mood. Nor was she ever at her most conciliatory in the mornings.

It was with a thoroughly jaundiced eye, therefore, that, descending to breakfast on the Saturday after New Year, she observed her three uninvited and unwelcome guests seated round the white damask table partaking of porridge, game patties, cold venison, mutton chops, oyster sausages, omelettes, devilled kidneys, grilled bacon, toast, muffins, oatcakes, anchovy paste, marmalade, honey, tea and coffee, and amicably discussing their plans for the day.

Sophie was being offensively proprietorial about the weather, explaining to Mr Venturi that at Juran a cloudless sky was not something to be admired. She waved a hand towards the window. 'It's the moving clouds that make the landscape so magical. You can watch the contours change before your very eyes. The weather here is a source of recurring delight.'

'Though only,' Rachel intervened acidly, 'for those who don't have to go out in it. I myself, Mr Venturi, take a more realistic view than my cousin. Clouds mean rain and have nothing whatever to recommend them.'

'Nonsense!' exclaimed Sophie.

None of them could remember, afterwards, how such a minor disagreement had flared so rapidly into open war, but in no time at all – or so it seemed – the two ladies were bandying accusation and counter accusation across the table in a furious confrontation over the ownership of Juran.

Insofar as it was possible for their slightly bemused hearers to follow the intricacies of the argument, Rachel appeared to be adducing the immorality of her parents and the existence of baby Daniel as justification of her claim, while Sophie's case revolved round young Archie's love of the place and some obscure references to her father's exile and subsequent struggle to make a success of his business.

496

'Struggle!' cried Rachel, her voice rising another few semiquavers. 'When I think what a struggle I have had, all through my life, and always alone. I have lost *everyone!*'

'And very conveniently, too,' mumbled Horace through a mouthful of oatcake and honey.

Rachel ignored him. 'I have lost my father and mother, my brother and sister, I have nearly lost my husband . . .'

Three sets of eyebrows rose, none of her listeners having been let into the tale of Colin's near demise in the Tay Bridge disaster of the Sunday before.

'While you, my *dear* cousin,' Rachel concluded crushingly, 'come sauntering back here after a life of comfort and ease and expect me just to hand Juran over to you for the asking, and . . .'

'Comfort and ease!' shrieked Sophie. 'How dare you? What do you know about my life? If we are to talk of tragedies, my own mother died when I was an infant and my father before I came of age; my first husband was an opium addict, who met a well deserved end by being stabbed to death in a back alley in China town; I had one little daughter who was stillborn and another child who miscarried.'

Briefly, Rachel was silenced, while Horace – a moral man – began urgently revising his views about Sophie's suitability as a wife.

Gino Venturi, to whom none of it was new, murmured unfeelingly, 'I make it Sophie five, Rachel four. Going, going . . . Do I hear any advance on five?'

But Sophie hadn't finished. 'And then, *and then*, I discover that my husband has fathered a child on *you*, my own cousin, who have been manipulating him, playing on his generosity and sympathy all these years . . .'

Rachel, retaining just enough sense not to enter into arguments about her son's paternity, had no trouble in finding something else to contest. Leaping to her feet so violently that her chair tipped over and hit the floor with a crash, she cried, '*Manipulating* Rainer Blake? Ha! When all the manipulating has been done by . . .'

There was a second crash and she stopped in mid flow.

Three pairs of eyes turned towards Horace, who had slammed both fists down on the table with a violence that rocked everything upon it.

Then he, too, rose to his feet.

'I have never,' he said in a shaking voice, 'been more disgusted in all my life. I have known for years that Rachel wasn't to be trusted, but this,' his eyes blinked furiously at Sophie, 'has been a revelation. You lied to me. You told me you were a widow . . .'

'I *didn't*!'

'. . . and now it turns out you're married to that banker fellow. *And* you've been married before – to a drug addict! *And* I clearly heard you condoning his murder! You're both as bad as each other. Neither of you knows what morality is. Neither of you is fit for decent company. And neither of you is fit to be trusted with Juran.'

Then he flounced out of the breakfast room and, half an hour later, out of the castle, ill packed bags slung from the saddle of a surprised mare.

Sophie giggled.

After a moment, reluctantly, so did Rachel. 'I've been trying to get rid of him for years,' she said. 'Thank you, Sophie.'

7

And then the normal daily life of the castle began to flow around them again, and nowhere was safe from marauding servants, anxious to dust or lay fires or make beds or ask for orders.

The cook presented herself to Rachel to have the day's menus confirmed. Baby Daniel's nursemaid set off with her charge in a perambulator for their ritual walk along the shore towards the village. Archie clamoured to go with them as usual on his fat little pony. Philip Roy sent a servant to invite the two ladies to dine at Altsigh the following week. Sophie and Gino set off, at Gino's suggestion, for a walk on the hill.

They were halfway up Carn Beg when Sophie said, 'But Gino, I really have very little money, and certainly none to lend. I simply can't help you. Let's sit in this hollow, out of the wind.'

The hollow was only just large enough to protect the two of them from the chill north-westerly that belied the brightness of the January morning, and Venturi pulled Sophie closer to his side, tipping a conspiratorial wink at a solitary redwing, left behind in the autumn migration, that was standing on a nearby rock glaring at them from under its bad-tempered eyebrows.

Sophie gave a gurgle of laughter. Once, she would have shied away from such close contact but all she did now was admire his effrontery.

Despite the stresses and strains, these last three months at Juran had given her a new perspective on life, shown her that there was no need always to feel like a clockwork toy that was never allowed to run down, that peace of mind was possible even when there was no peace in one's heart.

Gino said, 'I wasn't going to ask you for a loan.'

'That's all right, then.'

'No, a few sovereigns in my pocket would be of no use to me. What I need is capital. Not necessarily cash. A piece of Juran would do.'

'I beg your pardon?'

'You heard, *la mia bella*.'

She entered into the spirit of the thing. 'And which piece do you fancy?'

'I don't mind, as long as it's large. About half, I suggest.'

She frowned, the smile still lingering, as she wondered what on earth he was driving at. 'You're not – you can't be – proposing mariage to me? I already have a husband, you know.'

'Well . . .' His voice was exaggeratedly caressing. 'One can never be sure how long a husband will last in the dangerous climate of today. However, what I was thinking of was more a marriage of interests.'

'You mean symbiosis,' she told him austerely.

'*Davvero?*'

'It's an interdependent and beneficial partnership. I have one already, thank you.'

'Ah, but not one like this, I am sure.'

'Gino, will you stop fencing! What are you talking about?'

8

He was talking about blackmail.

'A foolish habit,' he said, 'this writing things down in diaries. You probably don't remember, but you confided far more to paper than was wise during your marriage to the late and unlamented Lieutenant Taverner. For example . . .'

'Are you trying to pretend that you've read my diary? Don't be silly. You can't have.'

'Not recently, of course, but the one that began in '71 and ended abruptly in '78 was most illuminating.'

Below them, a stylish little steam yacht came dashing into the bay, sails rigged fore and aft of the single funnel, brass gleaming, white paint fresh and new, teakwork glowing. The sails came down with naval precision and the anchor chain rattled out smartly. Sophie could just make out the name *Matilda* on its bows. It didn't mean anything to her.

She said, 'The diary ended abruptly because the house was burned down and it was swallowed up in the flames!'

'Well, no. It wasn't there to be swallowed up. You had been burgled few days before.'

Sophie stared at him. The thief, Rainer had thought, had been looking for papers to do with his banking, and it had never occurred to Sophie to see whether her diaries might be missing; they were of no interest to anyone but herself. After a moment, she said mockingly, 'Yes, I can just picture you with a mask and a jemmy! Really, Gino, not your style at all.'

His dimples deepened. 'How well you know me. It was Evan Ellis, as a matter of fact. Naoroji's successor, whom you sacked for always standing too close to you and making you nervous. He wasn't pleased.'

Her coat had triple shoulder capes, but Sophie suddenly felt the chill of the wind. Ellis had been a spiteful young man, who might well have done such a thing. 'And he passed the diary on to you? I hope you paid him well?'

'After inspection. After I'd seen the entry in which you said you wished Richard would die.'

She didn't remember writing it, but she had certainly thought it.

'I found myself,' Gino went on meditatively, 'wondering whether Mrs Taverner might have had a hand in her husband's sad fate.'

'Don't be a fool!'

'Oh, I don't suggest you wielded the knife. There was probably someone prepared to arrange that for you.'

She didn't understand.

'The lieutenant's successor,' he prompted her gently.

'*Rainer*? I've never heard anything so ridiculous!'

'Don't laugh. Your semi-detached husband is no saint.'

'You hate him, don't you? I've never known why. But if ever I heard the pot calling the kettle black . . .'

9

Smoothly, she removed his arm from her waist and rose to her feet. Then she looked down at him and said, 'It's going to rain. We should go back.'

'What? No answer?'

'What do you expect me to say?'

He, too, rose and they began walking down the hill. The sun had gone in and there were huge, threatening clouds scudding across the sky with a strong, blustery wind at their tails. The wave crests were short and white inshore, but further off the grey-green seas were breaking on Meall and Corran with three thousand miles of Atlantic power behind them.

Sophie found it immensely invigorating. Gino Venturi did not.

In the teeth of the wind, she said, 'You disappoint me, you know. You're forgetting that we are in Scotland, not Hong Kong.'

'*Mamma mia!* Who could forget that?' He pulled his coat collar up round his chin.

'What I meant,' she said, her eyes dancing, 'was that threats that might seem perfectly tenable in Hong Kong don't cut much ice here. You've no evidence and no witnesses. No one would believe you. Perhaps a few lairds might decide they didn't want to know me after all, but that hardly matters.

'Do give me credit for a little sense! Because if you "expose" me for the shocking person you say I am, the only remotely likely result would be that I would lose Juran to Rachel. Which would profit you not at all. Bang would go your hopes of "a piece of it". No, really, Gino, you're clutching at straws!'

By then, they were walking up the drive towards the castle, and suddenly he put out his hand and stopped her, holding her arm in an iron grip as he said, his voice hardening, 'There are other straws. I merely chose the most acceptable. However, if you insist . . . Horace, though he doesn't know it yet, will provide the money for overturning Rachel's claim, which is weak. She was born illegitimate and her son, of course, is a bastard of your husband's.'

Sophie looked up, then, beginning to struggle against him, all amusement gone from her eyes, and saw that his were like chips of ice.

'No,' he said. 'Let me finish. You and your husband have parted, and these are lonely places. I think I could persuade you to make a Will leaving Juran to me rather than to young Archie. In recompense, you understand, for your husband's destruction of the business to which I have given half my life. Strange, isn't it, how everything comes back to Blake in the end?'

The menace was open and unequivocal. Sophie knew, then, for the first time, that Rainer had been right and she had been wrong.

Gino Venturi was dangerous and she was afraid of him.

10

And then everything happened at once.

Blake himself walked round the corner of the castle.

After the space of a single, disbelieving, delirious heartbeat, she cried out and wrenched herself free of Gino's grasp and began running towards him, and he was running towards her, and he had his revolver out, and then Gino was lunging forward, reaching her before Rainer did, and swinging her as a shield before him.

And Rainer was shouting, 'Don't move. For God's sake, my darling, don't move!' and Gino Venturi was hissing in her ear, 'No, don't move, or I'll kill you! I swear I will!'

But she didn't heed either of them because, if Gino had a weapon, he was going to have to get it out and if she struggled hard enough he wouldn't be able to do so without letting her go. So she fought him with all her strength and kicked at him and stamped her heel on his toes and did her best to scratch his eyes out.

He was still swearing and cursing when Rainer reached them and put his revolver to Gino's head and took Sophie in his spare arm and gasped, 'Christ! I damned near had a seizure! What in hell's name is *he* doing here? Oh, my darling, I'll never let you out of my sight again. For God's sake, go and get someone from the castle to help me tie this bastard up, so I can kiss you!'

Fortunately, two of the yacht's crew came strolling up the drive just then, so that Sophie didn't have to leave him, but was able to stay and be kissed with the utmost thoroughness and in full sight of anyone who happened to be looking.

11

Indoors, Colin Campbell was confronting his white-faced wife.

'Why didn't you tell me,' he said, 'instead of me having to trick Blake into it by letting him think you'd confessed? I'd have understood.'

'Would you?'

'I don't say I wouldn't have been hurt. I don't say I'd have forgiven you straight off, but I *can* understand that kind of passion, you know. Especially when it's the culmination of something that's been

502

building up for years. Blake says it was an ending, not a beginning. Was it?'

She sighed. 'Yes. I didn't see it at the time but when I thought you'd been killed last Sunday, I knew who really mattered to me.'

After he had kissed her to his and her complete satisfaction, she sniffed and said, 'I was so ashamed of letting you down. Plain, common, physical desire taking over when I'd spent so much of my life priding myself on being strong-minded, always using my brain . . .' Then she stopped abruptly. 'No! If I'm being honest, my brain never had a chance where Rainer was concerned. He was the absolute personification of all my childish dreams of romance.'

A little wistfully, Colin said, 'Am I not romantic?'

She laughed, and it was a fine free sound. 'My dearest, romance isn't proof against five years of you dropping your collar stud down your back and expecting me to fish it out! Anyway, we've always had something far better than romance. Oh, Colin, I *do* love you so much.'

There was one thing more, and she didn't know whether she dared say it, because men weren't very good at seeing some things. But she risked it. Her eyes firmly fixed on her husband's middle waistcoat button, she said, 'I know it doesn't change the fact that I let you down but, well, the baby's four months old now, and he's got brown eyes and brown hair, and – I think he's beginning to look like you.'

Colin didn't move and after a while she was forced to look up. She said tentatively, 'Hogg thinks so, too.'

And then it was Colin's turn to laugh. 'Oh, well! That settles it!'

The old, quizzical look back in his eyes, he went on, 'You're telling me we've got started at last, are you?'

Speechless, she nodded.

'We'd better follow it up, then,' he said, settling her in his arms for another good, satisfying kiss. 'I seem to remember it was six we were thinking of, wasn't it? We've got some catching up to do.'

12

Because so many things had been so suddenly, so magically resolved, no one was prepared for the appalling crisis that followed.

Rainer and Colin having haled Gino Venturi off in the *Matilda* for Inveraray – which, according to Colin, boasted the finest jail in Argyllshire – Rachel and Sophie were just sitting down to a late and welcome lunch when there was a knock on the door and Tom Tanner entered, dragging Daniel's nursemaid behind him in floods of tears.

Still in a daze of happiness, Rachel diagnosed a broken cradle rocker, or a torn baby dress, or perhaps a touch of colic. And then her euphoria vanished and she was on her feet, her hands gripping the edge of the table to steady herself. 'What's wrong? What is it?'

The girl opened her mouth, but all that emerged was a wail of, 'Oh, ma'am! Oh, ma'am!'

'*Tom?*'

His brown hair and the fringe of beard round his jaw were greying now, but he was still handsome, still had a beautiful smile when there was reason for it, was still one the nicest men Rachel had ever known. But now his hazel eyes were full of anger and distress.

'This stupid lassie,' he said, 'hass lost the wee ones.'

Almost imperceptibly, Rachel's tension began to relax. Her first fear had been of some dreadful accident. But however 'lost' the wee ones, they were too wee to be seriously lost.

And then Tom went on, 'Her feet wass hurting, she says, and Mr Horace came and said he would take the bairns for their walk, so that she could sit down and haff a rest. It wass more than three hours ago. And Mistress Rachel, I haff been down to the shore, and found wee Daniel's perambulator hidden among the rocks and it iss empty. I found Master Archie's pony, too, grazing the machair. But there iss no sign of the boys, and no sign of Mr Horace.'

Sophie said, her voice sharp, 'He's probably taken them for a ride on his horse.'

And Rachel said, 'He's very thoughtless. It won't have occurred to him that we might be worried.'

But they stared at each other and didn't believe a word of it.

Rachel closed her eyes and pinched the bridge of her nose between finger and thumb, trying to think. 'Tom, you'd better get together all the men you can. The rain can't hold off much longer and I don't want the children soaked through. Could you ask if anyone in the village has seen Mr Horace, with or without the children? He left here soon after breakfast. He borrowed Treacle, the mare, from the stables; I assumed he was intending to send her back from Inveraray.'

'Aye, all right. I'll do it straight away. Come along, you daft lassie.' The door closed behind them.

Sophie said carefully, 'Let's not get things out of proportion. It's only Horace. He's harmless.'

'Yes, of course. The trouble is that he never thinks.'

There were two occasions she specially remembered, when Horace hadn't thought. On the first of them, William had nearly tumbled down a cliff face to his death. On the second, the bullet from the gun Horace had struck aside had missed his own head by an inch. He wasn't to be trusted. And this morning he had been angry.

Her voice grating, she said, 'He'll have taken the children up the hill to show them Nature's grand design laid out before them. I have *never* known anyone so *abominably* single-minded and *infuriating*! When I get my hands on him, I will throttle him.'

'And when you have finished with him,' Sophie said, 'I will tear out his liver and lights.'

They tried to smile at each other.

13

A small hand tugged at Horace's jacket and Archie's voice said, 'Uncle Horace, I don't like this dirty old hut and I'm hungry. Can we go home soon?'

'Be quiet, I'm thinking.'

Horace was pleased with the speed at which his mind had worked earlier on in the day, and reflected that it would teach them all a lesson. No one ever gave him credit for his superior intellect. Rachel had always talked down to him, and in the last few days even Sophie had developed a shockingly bad habit of saying, 'Don't be silly, Horace!'

The revelation of Sophie's perfidy had cut him to the quick. She had deliberately misled him into believing she would make a suitable wife for him, and now it turned out that she had not only spent most of her life consorting with criminals but was actually married to that arrogant American fellow who had always treated him as if he were of no account.

Horace no longer doubted that there was bad blood in the Macmillans, every single one of them. Archie Macmillan senior had been banished as a result of his wenching, and his brother Daniel had fathered a child on a whore and then dared to aspire to, and win, Horace's pure and virginal Aunt Isabella. If that wasn't depravity, Horace didn't know what was. As for Rachel, her sins had already been legion – and some of them lethal – even before the revelation that the son she had tried to pass off as her husband's was in reality the child of Rainer Blake. And Sophie was as bad as all the rest.

Archie tugged at his sleeve again. 'Can't we go home, Uncle Horace?' And then the infant in his lap gave an ear-splitting howl and Horace became aware of a creeping sensation in the region of his groin.

Dumping the baby unceremoniously on the floor, he mopped at the dark patch on his trousers while Archie piped solicitously, 'Oh, dear. Did you wet yourself, Uncle Horace?'

Before the scene in the breakfast room had been half over, Horace had known he was going to have to think up a new grand strategy to replace marriage to Sophie, a plan that would encompass winning Juran for himself, showing how clever he was, and revenging himself on the two women who had let him down so callously.

The idea of kidnapping the children had come to him when he was no more than a mile from the castle, and he had simply turned his horse about and ridden back to where he could be sure of waylaying them on their morning outing. Now, six hours later, he was beginning to regret not having done any advance planning. He was hungry himself, and all there was in his saddlebags was a small package of food one of the kitchen maids had given him to sustain him as far as Inveraray. Opening it, he found a bottle of ale, another of milk, some oatcakes and a piece of the strong local cheese. Looking at the unhappy infant on the floor, he wondered vaguely whether babies could eat oatcakes and cheese and whether they were any good at drinking out of bottles.

He had kidnapped the children not, of course, with the idea of asking money in exchange. He was going to insist that Rachel and Sophie each signed a document – a deed of gift, he thought – abjuring their claims to Juran and assigning them to him. As long as there were two separate documents, then it didn't matter which of the women had the better title in law.

It was a good plan.

Since the mothers, by now, would probably be distraught, and since he had no great desire to spend longer than necessary in this damp and chilly old hut in the hills, he decided he might as well get on with the next step. On a page from his notebook, he set out his terms and then went outdoors and pinned the message to Treacle's saddle.

There was a heavy fog, as was to be expected on a January evening, but he knew the mare would soon find her way back to her comfortable stable. Untying the reins from the trunk of a gnarled old Scots pine, he gave her a slap on the rump and said, 'Home!'

Then he turned and went back inside the bothy that had once provided shelter for those who brought the village livestock to the high pastures in summer.

Clever though Horace knew himself to be, he didn't realise quite how clever he had been in his accidental choice of refuge. Because, over the decades, the rivulets and streams that had once watered the pastures had shifted and the old beds had silted up. It meant that, when conditions were bad, even those who knew the hills well, who would know about the bothy, had no landmarks at all to guide them on the tortuous climb up to it.

14

There were ten thousand acres of moor and mountain to be searched, ten thousand acres full of potential hiding places.

Rachel sat with her elbows on the table and her fingers pressed hard against her mouth to keep the terror at bay. Separating them a little, she said, 'He can't have taken them high. The mare isn't good on rough ground, and he'd have to carry Daniel, and Archie's legs aren't very long.'

She had to behave as if she were utterly sure that he had stayed with the children, because otherwise she began to think of Daniel abandoned in the hills, and although she knew – she *knew* – that the prey of golden eagles did not, despite what the gamekeepers said, include even lambs, far less four-month-old babies, there were centuries of Highland lore to deny it. Every time she closed her eyes she could see the eagle's seven-foot wingspan and its talons extended for the kill.

There were wildcats, too, and foxes, and hoodie crows that pecked the eyes out of animals that didn't have the strength to defend themselves.

She shook her head violently, and took a deep breath, and fixed her eyes on the face of Tom Tanner, who had come in at nightfall to report that he and the men had systematically scoured all the lower levels of Carn Beg and Carn Dearg, while the women had worked their way along the shore for five miles in either direction. Even when Mr Campbell and Mr Blake arrived back, he remarked, he couldn't see that they'd be much help, because they didn't know the terrain well enough; it would be suicide for them to go out searching in the fog and the moonless dark.

Rachel said, 'Thank you, Tom.'

She wanted to say, 'We must go on. We must.' She knew that she herself, regardless of sense or reason, *would* go on. No one knew the hills of Juran as well as she did. She could find her way about them blindfold.

Instead, with a faint, drained smile, she acknowledged the common sense of what he had said. 'We can't do any more until first light. The children are well wrapped up, and they're healthy and well fed. They'll be all right. *They will be all right.* But I won't be going to bed tonight, and I don't imagine any of us will. So if you have an idea, any idea at all . . .'

Sophie came into the room just then, skirts splashed and torn, a great streak of peaty mud on one cheek, her eyes red and her face exhausted but her voice under control. She said, 'Is there some kind of map of the estate? You never know, it might suggest something.'

It wouldn't, Rachel knew. Every detail of it was already incised in her mind. But she said, 'Yes, I'll get it.'

15

It was late when the *Matilda* crept back into the dark bay, under sail and to the accompaniment of the leadsman's cry.

Horace's message had arrived hours before. He had been explicit – Rachel's and Sophie's claims to Juran in exchange for their children's lives. 'You will hear from me again,' he had concluded. 'And when you do, I will expect you to have the documents waiting for me, in proper legal form, signed and witnessed.'

Blake, grey eyes hard, tossed a glass of whisky bitters down his throat and said, 'He's a fool. No court would entertain such documents, signed under duress.'

Sophie said, 'No. But even if they did, it's irrelevant. Archie is a million times more important to me than Juran. I can't speak for Rachel, of course.'

Even in these few hours, Rachel had learned things about herself that she had never known.

'Juran doesn't matter,' she said.

Colin, who for years had prayed to hear his wife utter those words, felt neither relief nor gratitude but a surge of the purest and most personal hatred for Horace, who had forced them from her lips.

They spread the estate map out on the dining room table, weighted at its corners with candlesticks, and stared at it for what seemed like an eternity.

'Let's try to be systematic,' Colin said. 'If he took the bairns up on his horse with him, he could have ridden maybe five miles along the road before we even knew they were missing.'

'More, surely?' Sophie exclaimed. She had washed hurriedly, and there was still a smudge of peat at the side of her chin.

'No. A baby and a six-year-old would be a fair handful in 'the circumstances. I've given my own nephews and nieces enough rides in the past to know what I'm talking about.'

Blake asked, 'Would he go north or south? I don't know what the road's like to the south.'

'Neither does Horace. He usually comes from the north-east, so he'd be likely to go that way, through the hills.'

'But not as much as five miles. No more than two or three.' Rainer tapped the map with a long forefinger. 'Probably no further than here.'

Sophie directed a questioning frown at him and he put an arm round her waist. 'Don't let your wits go begging, my darling. Hiding the children's only part of it. He still has to communicate with us, and for that he won't want to be too far away; he has nothing but his two feet now that the mare's back in the stables. Is he a good hill walker, Colin?'

It was a question Colin was destined never to answer, because at that moment Rachel's nerves snapped. Panic had been rising and rising inside her until she couldn't control it any more. Inside her head was a terrible, whirling chaos, and the wings of a thousand birds were beating inside her chest, and the tears were pouring down her cheeks and she was screaming, 'Stop it, *stop it*, all of you! I can't bear it! How can you be so calm? How can you all stand here talking when we should be doing something? What if he's just left them somewhere, alone in the hills? In the dark. In the freezing mist. In winter, when the foxes are hungry, and the wildcats, and the . . .'

Colin had her by the shoulders and was shaking her, his face taut and his eyes boring into hers. '*Control yourself.* Don't let go. It's the worst thing you can do. Rachel, my dear, *my dear*! Steady on, steady on.'

To the others, it seemed a very long time before the hard grip of his hands and the love and sanity in his voice had their effect at last, and she gulped and tried to smile and said, 'I'm sorry.'

For a long moment Colin held her to him. He, too, was shaking. Then he said, 'Why don't you see about getting us all something to eat? Blake and I are ravenous.'

It sounded heartless and it wasn't true, but he knew the cook would have gone to bed and it would give Rachel something to do.

Sophie, white as a sheet, said, 'I'll come and help.' She was sorry for Rachel, because the baby was very young and young babies were fragile, but it was Archie who possessed her mind. Archie, cold and hungry and frightened somewhere, held prisoner by Horace who was – must be – mad. For the third time in the six short years of his life Archie was in a danger that was worse for him because he was a child and didn't really understand. The typhoon, and the fire, and now this. With all the power of her mind and her love, she tried to send a message to him, a message that said, 'Don't worry, my darling. It will be all right. It *will* be all right.'

17

When the women had gone, Blake said, 'You know the fellow better than I do, Colin. Is he insane?'

'Not according to the McNaghten rule, but he's not balanced in any sense you or I would understand. From what I know of him he's oblivious to everyone but himself; and his parents, maybe. Anyone who offends against the law according to Horace had better watch out. And since he fancies himself as a stickler for morality, he'll consider himself justified in doing almost anything he feels like doing.'

'That's a frightening appraisal, if you carry it to a conclusion.'

His brown eyes sombre, Colin said, 'I've no wish to be melo-dramatic, but I'm afraid it may not be an empty threat we're faced with. Rachel and Sophie are worried about the bairns being cold and hungry and frightened, but they don't really believe, deep down, that Horace would harm them. I'm not so sure. I think he might well kill them if he felt it would help him preserve his precious Nature's grand design. But whether I'm right or wrong, he won't let them go until he has these damned documents he wants. It'll take time, and time is something we can't afford. A Highland hillside in winter isn't a place for wee ones.'

Blake was no stranger to violence but he couldn't relate it to the harmless-seeming Horace. He couldn't imagine Horace deliberately laying hands on the children. But he *could* imagine him, out of ignorance if nothing else, letting them freeze or starve to death, and he had to exert every ounce of willpower to force his brain to keep a grip on reason. *My son, my son . . .*

His voice uneven, he said, 'Murder would transgress his moral code.'

'No.'

'No,' Blake repeated after a long moment. 'You're right. There's only the narrowest dividing line between the will of God and the *karma* of the Hindus and Buddhists. If Horace has got it into his head that it's the children's fate to die for what he regards as a greater cause, I agree with you. I wouldn't bank a string of cash on his moral code. Dear Christ, what are we going to do? If the weather doesn't clear, how are we going to find them?'

18

Rachel made sandwiches, which the men ate absently and Rachel and Sophie with difficulty. But the coffee was welcome.

When they had finished, Rachel said, 'I'll take the tray downstairs. No, it's all right, Sophie. I can manage.'

But Sophie, for no good reason, was suspicious and, after a few minutes, withdrew her hand from Rainer's sustaining grasp and said, 'She's probably washing up or something useless like that. I'll go and help.'

There was no sign of Rachel when she reached the kitchen, but the other door was ajar. Tearing it open, Sophie raced along the corridor, through the storerooms and along the second corridor that would bring her to the terrace. The outside door was just closing.

'*Rachel*! Wait! Where are you going? I'm coming with you.'

'No.'

'Yes.'

'It's only a guess and I don't know whether I can get there. But, if Colin and Rainer are right, it's the likeliest place within range.'

'Wait, then, and we'll all come.'

'No. It's too risky. And I may be wrong.'

Sophie snatched an old gardening coat from its peg on the wall and flung it round her. '*My* baby's there, too,' she said tightly. 'I, at least, am coming with you, whether you like it or not.'

And so, together, they went out into the raw, black, fog-shrouded January night.

19

The dawn broke, cold and sodden and grey, and the cloud didn't lift despite the wet wind tearing across the tops.

Horace couldn't see more than half a dozen yards when he left the hut, slamming the door and sliding the outside bolt into its socket. There was a steep drop on his left into a corrie, a crevasse walled and floored with scree and lichened rock, which this morning was full of nothing but swirling mist.

There was silence except for the rain and wind, but he knew he wasn't alone. And, sure enough, his ears soon caught the staccato bark of a dog fox somewhere nearby, and then the vixen's answer, a repeated skirling sound, a wailing that was unearthly, eerie, magnified by the mist so that it seemed to be no more than yards away.

It set his heart hammering, and he stood for a moment before he began to direct his careful steps downhill, bearing slightly to his left. Despite the many dips and rises, as long as he kept descending he knew he was bound to reach the shore in the end, and from there to the castle was easy. Not like searching the other way. Even if you knew exactly which point on which hill you were heading for, you could never find it in the mist.

The wind whipped at him and his soaking clothes clung to him, ice cold, as, unaware that his instinct for the easiest route was taking him almost exactly in the steps of the mare the night before, he struggled on his way, slipping and skidding in his smooth-soled riding boots, tripping over clumps of dead and dripping heather, skirting million-year-old outcrops of soaking grey rocks, searching myopically for the deer paths that would take him safely across black and squelching bogs.

He didn't realise that he was no longer the only human being on the hill until he heard what he thought was another dog fox barking. And another, and another. Which was impossible.

And then, suddenly, a whole pack of mangy terriers, questing noses down, burst out of the mists towards him, terriers with a small, thin old man at their heels and, immediately behind, two other men he hadn't expected to see, and didn't want to.

Of the two, it was Colin Campbell, whom he wouldn't have

512

thought of as a violent man, who reached him first and threw him to the ground, and began choking the life out of him.

20

Blake hauled Colin off, though it was a close thing when Horace, restored to speech, gasped that he couldn't lead them to where he'd left the children because he wouldn't be able to find it again in the fog.

Blake's own hands were itching as he ground out, 'Yet you left them there! Alone!' And Horace, drenched and shivering in body but his nerves at fever pitch, retorted hysterically, 'There's time enough to find them when you've got the documents.'

He was saved by Hogg's voice shouting from somewhere ahead, 'The mare's scent is still good and strong. Are ye coming?'

Colin said, 'Don't let me see you again, Horace. Ever. Or I won't hold myself responsible for my actions.'

Then he and Blake hurried off again into the mist.

21

Rachel and Sophie reached the bothy twenty minutes before them.

It had been five interminable, heart-stopping hours since they set out to follow the banks of the castle burn up to the point near its source where there was a large outcrop of rock splashed with white limewash. It was only just visible, even to eyes adjusted to the dark. Rachel said it marked the boundary between Juran and Altsigh and that there were similarly painted stones at intervals of about fifty yards all along the ridge. She estimated that forty markers, or perhaps forty-one, should bring them to a point almost directly above the bothy that was their goal. They should be able to find it, approaching from above, because it was no more than a hundred yards below the ridge.

It was simply a matter of following the line of the markers in the pitch dark and freezing fog – without, although neither of them mentioned it, losing each other in between, or breaking their legs or their necks by straying into some mist-filled corrie or tumbling over some unseen precipice.

They crawled most of the way, one inching ahead while the other remained as a temporary human marker, calling back and forth to each other to keep in touch, shouting at first but learning after three terrifying misjudgements to drop their voices to a conversational pitch that didn't seem to be distorted by the mist, didn't echo from every point of the compass like the cries of elf folk tempting travellers to their doom.

The sky had lightened by the time they reached the fortieth marker and began casting downhill, but it wasn't until the forty-third that they found the bothy.

The children had been on their own for more than an hour by then, and it was enough.

22

When Colin, Rainer, Hogg and the terriers arrived, the filthy, blanketed bundle that was baby Daniel had been fed and was fast asleep in his mother's even filthier arms, while Sophie was sitting on the earthen floor with a frightened, hungry, tearstained Archie in her lap, holding him as if she would never let him go.

It gave Blake the most piercing joy of his life to find his wife safe – and then to have his son look up and, seeing him for the first time for more than nine long months, smile a smile of grubby but ineffable bliss and say, 'Daddy! Daddy, where have you *been*? We've missed you so much!'

EPILOGUE

January
1880

EPILOGUE

I

'The bank be damned,' Colin remarked a few days later. 'It can manage without me.'

'Colin!' exclaimed Rachel, shocked. 'What if we get snowed in?'

He grinned shamelessly back. 'That's what I'm hoping. We never had a honeymoon the first time, did we? And now that you've recovered from your ordeal and don't feel you have to devote yourself to the wee one for every single hour of the twenty-four . . .'

'*Colin!*' She blushed.

He had forgiven her, it seemed, without reservation, and she loved him very deeply, as she loved Daniel. Knowing it, she was able at last to see Juran in perspective; she still loved it, of course, but it was no longer all-important to her. She could and would give it up, if she had to.

Looking back over the thirty-two years of her life, she would have thought that she had experienced every emotion of which the human heart was capable. But there had always been one missing, and she knew now what it was. Serenity.

She sighed a little, from sentiment more than sadness, over the end of her long-held illusions, her long-dreamed dreams. And, if she were truthful, there was still a trace of hurt – though she knew it would soon go – in seeing Sophie and Rainer together, so perfectly matched, Sophie at the full height of her beauty, slender, dark, blue-eyed and ravishing; and Blake, tall and lithe, coldly and elegantly magnetic, still as exotic to Rachel as when she had first set eyes on him fifteen years before. The thin white wing in his black hair gave him tremendous distinction, but the tanned skin and grey eyes, the hard and handsome features seemed to Rachel scarcely to have changed at all.

Looks apart, the most striking thing about Sophie and Rainer, she thought, was that their minds were so perfectly in tune.

This was not, as it happened, an altogether accurate assessment. Indeed, there had been a nasty clashing of chords when Sophie had recovered sufficiently from the emotional crises of the preceding days to remember her husband's sins. But Rainer had abased himself in the most gratifying way over his lapse with Rachel and had promised never to stray again. He had also promised to stop behaving as if he were God, and to stop keeping secrets from his wife.

As an earnest of good faith, he told her all he knew about Gino Venturi.

She gasped. 'You mean *Gino* was responsible for the pirate attack on Lantau and the fire at East Point? And you didn't think to warn me? Well, isn't that just like you!'

He told her, too, about his rôle as Special Commissioner for Customs.

She gasped again. 'So you *were* responsible for the raid on Macmillan and Venturi! Really! You might at least try to look embarrassed about it.'

He grinned. 'The worst thing about that was that, since I couldn't admit I was involved, I couldn't tell you the truth about why I had to instigate the raid as hurriedly as I did. It was a pity, because you'd have enjoyed it. Shall I tell you now?'

Laughter bubbling over from her eyes, she exclaimed, 'My dearest love, things are going to be *very* different when we get back to Hong Kong, believe me! Well, go on!'

'The reason why speed was of the essence was that your damnably enterprising Chinese brothers . . .' He paused provocatively and was rewarded.

Sophie jumped as if she had been stung. 'My *what?*'

'Your Chinese brothers. Your father had a mistress before – and after – he married . . .'

'Yes, I know.'

'And they had two sons, Lao and Li. *The Changs*, my love. They've been keeping a fraternal eye on you, in their own eccentric way, ever since your father died.'

After a long, awed moment, she said, 'Richard?'

Blake nodded. 'They went to Venturi about him. I wish they'd come to me instead, though the result would have been the same.'

'Heavens! What would Euphemia Moore say if she ever found out?'

'Well, if *that's* your only response to such a shocking revelation . . .' He laughed. 'In the case of the raid, the Changs knew the firm needed capital and were about to embark on a thoroughly criminal enterprise that would have resulted in prison sentences all round. Perhaps even for you. I had to move very fast indeed in order to forestall them.'

'I don't believe it. They're a delightful pair. They're not criminals!'

'Just innocent bystanders at the pageant of life? Well, maybe. Anyway, you may remember that the governor was proposing to take a personal part in the New Year celebrations? Lao and Li had made some ingenious arrangements to kidnap him and hold him to ransom.'

Brightly, Sophie exclaimed, 'That wouldn't have been a crime. That would have been a public service.'

'Possibly. But I do deserve some thanks, don't I, for the fact that they walked off scot free?'

'I owe you so much,' she said.

And then, after a brief, faintly smiling silence, she swept away once and for all the trouble that had for so long divided them, the trouble that Blake had found himself still fearing to mention.

'I tried to show you last night that I'm not afraid of love any more,' she said. 'Juran's a magical place for taking stock and learning what one's priorities are; it's the beauty and quietness and timelessness of it, I suppose. Despite everything, I've felt freer and more at peace here than ever in my life before. And even if I hadn't already reached the conclusion that my fears weighed very lightly in the balance against love, Archie being kidnapped would have settled it. The fear and pain I felt then, for him, eclipsed all the other fear and pain I have ever suffered, or could ever suffer.'

She smiled with great sweetness. 'So there it is. I love you, my dearest dear. With no reservations.'

After that, there was no holding back for either of them when he took her in his arms.

3

The only problem that remained was Juran, and it was easily resolved.

The following afternoon, as the snow, to Colin's intense satisfaction, began gently to fall, enveloping Juran in a soft ermine cloak, the four of them gathered round a blazing fire in the Green Drawing Room to feast on tea and hot buttered toast and scones fresh from the oven.

Sophie said, 'I love Juran, but my life is in Hong Kong. The only thing is, I'm not sure about Archie.'

Rachel and Colin had talked about it; Rachel took a deep breath. 'Would it help,' she said, 'would it help . . .'

Colin took her hand and held it, and she went on, 'Would it help if you left me with Juran for my lifetime, on the understanding that I bequeath it to Archie when I die?'

Rainer and Sophie, too, had talked. Sophie asked, 'But what about Daniel?'

Rachel gave no sign of what it cost her to reply. 'We will bring Daniel up in the knowledge that Juran will never be his. He will not feel deprived.'

And so it was settled.

'There's only one point that still ought to be made,' Rainer said, his eyes alight with amusement. 'Which is that you will – won't you, Colin? – take care to see, when Rachel makes her Will, that it is a hundred per cent legally foolproof?'

Colin's humorous brown eyes crinkled responsively. 'Not a hundred per cent,' he replied. 'A hundred and one.'